Six Smokin' Hot Cowboy Novels by Six of Today's Hottest Cowboy Authors

Cowboy Heat

Hell Yeah! Series, Book 1

Sable Hunter

~~*~*

Cowboy Jackpot: Christmas

Cowboy Jackpot Series, Book 1

Randi Alexander

~~*~*

Her Fated Cowboy

Harland County Series, Book 1

Donna Michaels

~~*~*

Ride of Her Life

The Buckle Bunnies Series, Book 1

Paige Tyler

~~*~*

Sex Ed Cowboy Style

Ugly Stick Saloon Series, Book 1

Myla Jackson

~~*~*

Cowboy Up

The Sweet Shop Series, Book 1

Melissa Schroeder

~~*~*

Cover Artist: Ramona Lockwood (Covers by Ramona)
~~*~*
"COWBOY HEAT"
Hell Yeah! 1
Copyright © Pending Sable Hunter
"COWBOY JACKPOT: CHRISTMAS"
Cowboy Jackpot, Book 1
Copyright © 2012 Randi Alexander
"HER FATED COWBOY"
Harland County Series/Cole
Copyright © 2013 Donna Michaels
"RIDE OF HER LIFE"
The Buckle Bunnies Series
Copyright © 2012 by Paige Tyler
"SEX ED COWBOY STYLE"
Ugly Stick Saloon, Book 1
Copyright © 2011, Myla Jackson
"COWBOY UP:
The Sweet Shoppe Series, Book 1
Copyright © 2013 by Melissa Schroeder
~~*~*

This is a work of fiction. Names, characters, places and incidents are either the product of the author's imagination or used fictitiously, and any resemblance to actual persons, living or dead, business establishments, events or locales is entirely coincidental.

This ebook is licensed for your personal enjoyment only. This ebook may not be re-sold or given away to other people. If you would like to share this book with another person, please purchase an additional copy for each recipient. If you're reading this book and did not purchase it, or it was not purchased for your use only, then please return to place of purchase and purchase your own copy. Thank you for respecting the hard work of this author.

ALL RIGHTS RESERVED. No part of this book may be reproduced or transmitted in any form or by any means, electronic or mechanical, including photocopying, recording, or by an information storage and retrieval system-except by a reviewer who may quote brief passages in a review to be printed in a magazine, newspaper, or on the web -without permission in writing from the author.

TABLE OF CONTENTS

Page	Story
1	Cowboy Heat by Sable Hunter
131	Cowboy Jackpot: Christmas by Randi Alexander
203	Her Fated Cowboy by Donna Michaels
409	Ride of Her Life by Paige Tyler
497	Sex Ed Cowboy Style by Myla Jackson
575	Cowboy Up by Melissa Schroeder

Cowboy Heat

Hell Yeah! 1

By Sable Hunter

Six brothers. One Dynasty—
TEBOW RANCH.
Meet the McCoy brothers and their friends —Texas men who love as hard as they play.
Texas Cowboys and Hot Cajuns – nothing better.
HELL YEAH!

Prologue

Hungrily, she kissed a path down his muscular chest, working her way down to his cock. He was magnificently and wonderfully made.

"I need you, Cher. My whole body is on fire for you. Suck it, suck it hard." Tristan tangled the fingers of one hand in her hair; the other kept the door closed, even as the magistrate tried to break through to arrest him.

Danielle was eager to please him. There was nothing she would not do, nothing she would not try – he only had to ask. Lovingly, she molded his strong thighs, gazing up at him with adoration. Increasing the pressure, she used the tip of her tongue to tease the tiny slit at the end of his cock, mimicking the move she hoped this instrument of delight would soon make into her empty, aching pussy.

Libby licked her lips. Oh, yeah! If only she had a guy like Tristan. Giving a man a blowjob seemed like it would be a total turn-on. She squirmed a bit in the hospital bed. What she wouldn't give to know what it was like to make love. Maybe, she would get a cucumber to practice on – just in case. One day, she promised herself, one day she was going to need this skill.

"Come up here, my dear." Tristan pulled her to her feet. "One sweet kiss before we are taken. It's my turn to please you." She thought he was about to kiss her lips, instead he pulled her bodice down gently, cupped her breast and latched his hot, greedy mouth onto her distended, eager nipple.

"Oh, yes, Tris," Danielle massaged his shoulders, kneading the muscles as she threw her head back and moaned. She loved the excitement, the urgency of his passion. The mix of pain and pleasure as he suckled at her swollen breast, using his teeth to tease the distended tip was exquisite. How would she survive without him?

"How are you feeling, Libby?"

"Cheez-n-Crackers!" Startled, Libby threw her romance novel high into the air. It landed square dab on the top of the doctor's bald head. "Sorry, Doc. You scared me!" Libby held her chest, glad that heart failure didn't run in the family.

"Were you reading porn again, Libby?" Doc Mulligan loved to tease Libby Fontaine. She was as cute as she was sweet.

"It's not porn, Doc. It's erotic romance, there's a big difference, you know." She lay still as the physician checked her vital signs.

He was listening to her heart, but it didn't stop him from continuing his bantering. "Oh my, it must have been some good stuff. Your blood pressure is slightly elevated."

Libby blushed and hid her head in the pillow. "It was pretty hot."

"Explain to me the difference between porn and erotica. I need to be informed. Who knows? I might want to pick up a copy of that 'shades of grey' book everyone is talking about." Doc Mulligan managed to keep a completely straight face.

Libby grinned. She liked when the doctor joked around. Due to the disease she had battled for so long, opportunities to socially interact with people were few and far between. Many days, she had been too ill or fatigued to enjoy anyone's company. Now, her blue eyes sparkled and a dimple came out to play, just past the corner of her top lip.

"Not erotica, erotic romance. Huge difference!"

Doc Mulligan laughed. Libby was such a delight. Never a frown, never a down day – no matter how bad the diagnosis. "Excuse me, O ye hedonist extraordinaire."

"Whadjacallme?" Fits of giggles escaped as the doctor made a funny face at her.

"A hedonist, my dear, is a person whose life is devoted to the pursuit of pleasure." All the while, he was making notes on his clipboard.

"All right, sign me up, I think I'd make an outstanding hedonist. Pleasure seems preferable over pain any old day." Even though she smiled, Doc Mulligan knew she was remembering all of the trauma she had endured through the years. Cancer could be a cruel disease.

"I don't blame you, my dear." Refusing to be negative, he picked back up on their earlier conversation. "So explain it to me. what's the difference between porn and erotic romance?"

"That's easy." She flipped over on her side, so he could listen to her breathing from the back. "Porn is explicit, graphic descriptions of sex. Erotic romance may be a tad explicit, but the girl and boy love each other very much and there's always a happy ending."

"Ah, a happy ending, that's always good." In his profession, he didn't see nearly enough of those.

"Yeah." Libby grew quiet. What she wouldn't give for a happy ending.

"Tell me, Madame Hedonist, do you have any experience being racy?" He knew she didn't, but perhaps he could persuade her to consider it. Not with him, of course. He was a grandpa!

Libby snorted, laughing. "No, of course not. I've just read about it in books, like the one that just accidentally whacked you across the head." Straightening her hospital gown, she scooted around until she presented a prim and proper picture. "You, better than anyone, know that I haven't had the opportunity or the strength for men or sex." She sobered.

Doc Mulligan took her small, soft hand in his. "Let's talk, little one."

"That sounds ominous." Libby stiffened, expecting the worst.

"No, no," he hastened to reassure her. "In fact, I have good news."

Her eyes got big and round with hope. "Good news?"

"Yes, Libby, you're in remission."

A glow of ecstatic happiness flushed her little, heart-shaped face. "Remission? Are you sure?"

"Yes." The old gentleman smiled and patted her hand. "For right now, you're cancer free."

"For right now?" Libby waited for the other shoe to drop.

"Yes." He pulled his spectacles off and met her trusting gaze. "Libby, I won't need to see you again for at least six weeks. We'll do some more tests at that time. We'll be able to tell by your blood count level whether or not the remission is a true one or just a temporary elevation due to the last blood transfusion. For now, I want you to get out of this bed and live life as hard as you can. I want you to travel and date and be as hedonistic and racy as your little heart desires. Doctor's orders."

The possibilities skittering across her mind showed all over her face. "I've been working in the diner, and I have a little money saved. Doc, I could go camping and learn to ride a horse. Maybe, I could even try starting my line of designer handbags. You know if I end up living, I'm going to have to find a way to support myself. I don't want to be a short order cook for the rest of my life. And... and . . ." she blushed sweetly.

"Meet a man and make some of those erotic, romantic fantasies come true, perhaps?" Libby was like a daughter to him. He had been treating her leukemia for a long time.

"I don't know about that," she shyly answered. "I wouldn't even know where to start."

"Sure, you do." He picked up the used, battered book off the floor. "You've been cramming for this exam a long time."

"Reading about something and doing it are two entirely different things." She didn't have much faith in herself. Nevertheless, this was an unexpected reprieve. "It would be fun to try."

"Yes, you need to enjoy yourself, Libby," Doc Mulligan encouraged. "I want you to be happy."

Suddenly, Libby distinctly heard something else in his voice, a wistful tone. "You don't think the remission is a permanent thing do you?" She said the words slowly, dreading to hear his answer.

Determined not to lie to her, he took a deep breath. "With your specific type of cancer, it seldom is. There is only about a twenty percent chance you'll stay in remission longer than a couple of years. However, who knows? Miracles do happen. And we will get a good indication of how it's going when you come back and visit me in a month and a half." Picking up her hand and kissing it, he made her a promise. "We'll pray for a miracle."

Libby squared her shoulders. "Two years is twenty-four months or seven hundred and thirty days. It's not forever." Wiping a happy tear from her eyes, she gave Doc Mulligan a heart-stopping smile. "But, I'll take it."

Chapter One

"You can do this, Libby." Bess assured her as she scurried around and finished packing the well-worn blue suitcase which appeared to pre-date World War I. "I have complete faith in you. You are a wonderful cook, a good housekeeper, but most importantly, you have a kind heart. I wouldn't abandon my boys to just anyone, you know. I've been taking care of them for six years."

"I'm going to do my dead-level best not to disappoint you, Miss Bess," Libby carried the garment bag and followed the harried housekeeper of the Tebow Ranch to her red minivan. "What's Aron's favorite dessert? What did you tell me?" She wanted to do her best by all of the McCoy brothers, but she especially wanted to please Aron.

"He loves chocolate, anything chocolate. Oh, and early in the morning, he goes crazy over homemade cinnamon rolls and strong coffee. It helps him get going. He's the one you need to pamper. After all, Aron stepped in and took on the responsibility for the entire ranch and all of his brothers when Sebastian and Sue were killed." As she settled herself behind the steering wheel, the older woman caught Libby's hand and pulled her close. "If you need anything, talk to Jacob. He's a rock. Remember, he knows about your condition. If things get too much for you, go to Jacob."

Libby pushed the heavy braid off her shoulder and hugged Bess Morrison. "Jacob is my friend. He has been for a long time. He knows that I don't want the rest of the family to know about the cancer. I feel great, and I'm tired of seeing pity in people's eyes." She grinned and winked at her mother's best friend. "I want to be a normal girl on the make."

"Well, you won't have to look very far for prospects. Five of the McCoys are marrying age – and they're all sexy as sin." The older woman blushed at her own comment. "But Aron has taken himself off the market – or so he says." As she pulled the car door closed, she was rolling down the window. "You could change his mind, if you tried. I know you want to, so don't try and tell me any different. Your Mama knew what was going on. She told me about that bronze you bought all those years ago." Bess looked at Libby Fontaine and saw a precious, beautiful girl who'd never really had a chance to spread her wings and fly.

Libby's face flamed. Was she that transparent? Lord, she would have to be careful. Being the brunt of the McCoy boys' amusement would be highly unpleasant. "Aron McCoy is a legend; he would never be interested in a girl like me. Besides, you know I can't marry anyone.

My, my....my future is too uncertain." She looked over her shoulder to see if anyone was around. It would be just her luck to turn around and find her lifetime crush standing right behind her.

"A girl like you?" Bess huffed in reproach. "Any man would be lucky to have a sweetheart like you. Besides, it doesn't have to be about marrying, necessarily. I may be an old fogey, but I'm not that old. Just have a good time." As she backed up, she gave Libby one more directive. "All the boys are special, but take extra special care of my baby, Nathan. You'll probably have to remind him to do his homework every day. Also, watch out for Isaac. He'll pull the wool over your eyes, if you let him. He thinks he's a ladies' man." She put the brakes on, not able to let go of her boys without saying just a few more words. "Jacob is our dreamer, he loves everything about family life and nothing would make him happier than seeing the ranch like it used to be – full of family, fun and tradition. Joseph lives every day like it could be his last. He would walk a high wire, if the circus came to town. Listen to him; sometimes he just needs to talk. Noah tries to come across as all business, but he has feelings just like anyone else." Grabbing Libby's hand, she squeezed it. "And cut Aron some slack if he comes across as unfeeling. He's still recovering from his short, unhappy marriage to that viper Sabrina Jones. He thought he was being 'Mr. Responsibility' by bringing a woman into the house, a surrogate mother for Nathan. Aron was trying to complete the package, do the right thing. But, it backfired on him – big time. Sabrina wasn't wife material, and she certainly wasn't maternal. She sapped all the joy out of Aron, and nearly tore up the family in the process."

Libby hadn't ever heard the whole story, but she couldn't stand the thought of anybody hurting Aron. "Don't worry, Miss Bess. I'll take good care of your boys." She walked beside the van as she waved goodbye to the woman who had given her a great gift. While Bess was off to tend her granddaughter through a difficult pregnancy, Libby would be having the time of her life. Everything she had been dreaming of was at her fingertips: a chance to live on a ranch, an opportunity to learn to ride a horse, acres of beautiful Texas ranchland to explore, and six good-looking men to spoil.

* * *

Aron McCoy rode alongside his brother. "You know this Libby Fontaine?"

"Yeah, I went to high school with her." Jacob was determined to keep Libby's secret. He intended to be deliberately vague. As long as Libby was able to do her job, her medical condition shouldn't be a factor. After all, it was a temporary gig. Bess was only slated to be gone for three months. "She is an excellent cook. Bess said she's worked at the Kerbey Lane Cafe on Guadalupe in Austin off and on for several years. She was even featured on that cooking show with the guy who has the wild, white hair and wears his sunglasses backwards. You know the one that drives all over the country and features local restaurants on his television show."

"I don't know the show, but I know Kerbey." Aron had played linebacker for the Texas Longhorns and knew the dining choices in Austin like the back of his hand. "They make great pumpkin pancakes."

"I'll ask if she'll whip us up a batch for breakfast one day soon. How's that?" Jacob swung off his horse, an Appaloosa mare, and opened the gate to the stable.

"Sounds good to me." Aron dismounted and led his golden Palomino stallion, Sultan, into his stall. "Jacob, is Libby one of your women?" He knew Jacob had been involved with half the eligible females in the county. At one time, Aron had been as popular with the women as his brothers, but his experience with Sabrina had taught him that loving a woman came with too high a price tag - both financially and emotionally.

"No," Jacob hastened to put that idea to rest. "Libby's a pretty girl, but she and I are just friends." As Jacob removed Abigail's saddle, he glanced over the wall to where his brother was cutting the wire off a couple bales of hay. "She might have her eye on a particular guy already." Libby had no idea Jacob knew of her fascination with his older brother. If she did, she probably would've never agreed to help them out. Jacob longed for Aron to find someone to love - and to his notion, the perfect woman for the job was Libby Fontaine.

* * *

"Something smells great!" Nathan yelled as he bounded through the mudroom door. Like the rest of his family, Nathan never met a stranger.

"Hi, I'm Nathan." He slid to a stop right in front of Libby. At thirteen, he was already as tall as she was.

Libby laughed at the state of Nathan's boots. "My name's Libby. I see you've been in the barn with the horses." Wrinkling her nose, she pointed at the dirty, smelly footprints he had tracked across the kitchen floor – her freshly mopped kitchen floor. Libby had wasted no time getting into the job. Right now, she was feeling great. Her energy level was practically as high as her level of excitement.

"Whoops. Sorry, Libby." Nathan laughed with her. "Bess would wale the tar outta me for bringing horse poop in to the house on my shoes." He stopped where he was, pulled his boots off and headed to the back porch with them.

"Clean them off while you're back there, don't just chunk them out in the yard." At his laugh, she knew that leaving them dirty had been the original plan. "I won't wale you, but if you'll clean them up and bring me the mop, I'll give you a surprise." Libby knew how to make friends – with brownies. Libby's brownies were a thing of beauty. She took a couple of plain boxes of brownie mix, substituted cream for water, butter for oil, added extra chocolate syrup, a ton of chocolate chips, and a couple of teaspoons of instant coffee, and voila, she had a masterpiece. She called them her orgasmic brownies, not that she had a whole lot of experiences with orgasms, but she lived in hope.

With a sugary incentive like brownies, it didn't take Nathan long to get the horse manure off his shoes and return with the wet mop. "Bess said you are really nice and that I would love the food you'll fix for us." He hung his backpack on the back of one of the kitchen chairs and plopped himself down to wait for his treat.

"Let me clean this up and I'll cut you a man-size brownie," she promised him. Nathan was already a handsome young man. She could see the family resemblance strong in his features. All of the McCoy boys were incredibly good-looking – Aron especially. She was nervous about seeing him for the first time, not that he would know her from Adam. Libby had existed on the periphery of Aron McCoy's world. She had been in junior high when he finished high school, but she had never missed one of his football games. The leukemia had struck her the next year, but she had still kept up with him when he had played college ball and rode the rodeo circuit. Finishing with the touch-up, Libby returned the mop to the back porch. "There, we've got that spic and span again." Washing her hands in the sink, she proceeded to serve Nathan a huge slab of chocolate confection and a tall glass of milk.

"Thanks, Libby." Nathan's eyes grew big with pleasure. He took a huge bite and sighed blissfully. "This is better than anything Bess ever fixed." High praise, indeed.

"I appreciate you saying that sweetie, but don't tell Bess, you'd hurt her feelings. She loves you very much." Libby sat down beside him and began the makings for a huge green salad.

Nathan studied her while she worked. "You sure are pretty, Libby." Even though he was barely a teenager, the compliment made her blush. She was not used to flattery. In fact, no male had ever told her she was pretty before.

"I don't know if I'm pretty, but it's nice of you to say so." Libby grinned at him. "Kind words will not get you out of your homework, however."

"Aw, Libby." She was relieved that they seemed to be getting off on the right foot. Taking care of Nathan was one part of the job that she had been worried about. Cooking and cleaning would be a breeze. The only other concern she had was acting normal around Aron. It would be awful if he discovered that she fancied him.

"What time's supper?" Nathan asked between bites. Typical boy, he couldn't finish one meal before worrying about the next one.

Libby glanced at the clock on the wall. "It's four o'clock. I'll have it on the table by six. How does that sound?"

He nodded his approval of her timetable.

"Why don't you do your homework in here with me? I'll try and help you, if you need it." She hoped his lessons wouldn't be over her head. Libby had missed a great deal of school between chemotherapy and blood marrow transplants. Still, she had managed to graduate from high school and had even taken a few courses at the Austin Community College, courtesy of The Rockwell Foundation. Libby's earnings at the diner barely covered her rent. Her medical bills were either all government gratis or part of the hospital's teaching program. The Rockwell Foundation specialized in giving a helping hand to people trying to build a life for themselves while they lived with cancer.

Nathan hung his head. All of a sudden he looked extremely uncomfortable. Libby didn't push, if he had something to tell her, he would. "I have trouble with my school work sometimes," he confessed softly.

Sitting down beside him, she got her own brownie to munch on. "That sounds pretty normal. I've had trouble with some of my subjects, too." And that was no lie. Just as soon as she would catch up, another flare-up of leukemia would set her back in her school work.

"Yeah, but I was born with something they call dyslexia. I can read pretty good, if I take my time and concentrate, but its writing papers that eats my lunch. I have a paper to write, and I dread it because I have a hard time spelling and using words." He looked so miserable that she gave him another brownie.

"I tell you what...I met this girl a few years ago that has the same condition you have. She's a junior in college now, and writes papers all the time. I know she uses some type of special program on her computer that's made just for people with dyslexia. I'll call her and check it out. How does that sound?"

"Thanks, Libby." Nathan smiled at her as he drained the last of the milk from his glass with a slurp. "I'll take any help I can get." Libby laughed. The youngest McCoy was going to be easy to love.

* * *

"Are you banned from the pool hall?" Joseph asked Isaac as he stepped up on the wide front porch.

Isaac was the bad-boy of the family. Each of them had dealt with their parent's death in different ways. Joseph had turned into a daredevil and Isaac spent most of his time acting out. It seemed that he thought the more hell he raised, the less pain he would feel. He had spent two nights in jail just during the past three months. "Not yet, Shorty's threatening me, though."

"Why did you see the need to rearrange that stranger's face?" Joseph eased down into the swing. None of them had wanted their mother's outdoor furniture removed, but as the McCoy brothers had matured and filled out, the furniture got smaller and smaller.

"He was full of shit, that's why." Isaac was unrepentant. He lowered his voice, just in case Aron was nearby. Without a doubt, he was still in the doghouse over last night's pool hall incident. "How was I to know that cocky little Yankee would be so sensitive? I didn't really intend to insult the out-of-towner, but I didn't believe for a minute that man had played in the finals at Vegas. I could have let that lie pass, but when the skinny little weasel claimed to have beat Minnesota Fats, I couldn't keep my mouth shut." Isaac laughed, remembering. "I told him the only way he could have won that match would have been if Fats was blind drunk and had one arm tied behind his back. The idiot popped me right upside the mouth. I guess I should have kept my trap shut, or lowered my voice. But hell, I'm a McCoy; I don't have the ability to whisper. One thing led to another, but the end result was the best damn bar fight I've had in at least – well, three weeks."

Isaac was so busy telling his story that he didn't see Aron standing right behind him. "I guess you'll be working off the damages."

Shit! "Where did you come from?"

"I walked up right behind you, Bad-ass." Aron stepped around his brother. "Wash up, supper should be on the table." He stepped into the Tebow ranch house. It would always be his mama's home. Looking around, he appreciated the workmanship on the massive log structure. His daddy had built it with his own two hands, with his and Jacob's help. The interior had been lovingly designed and decorated by the most gracious lady that ever walked the hills of central Texas. Aron would always miss his mother. Sabrina sure hadn't made any effort to put her stamp on the place. All she had wanted to do was spend McCoy money like it was going out of style – and flirt with his brother Jacob. To give the gentle giant credit, Jacob had been oblivious to most of it. And the morning he had caught them in bed together, Jacob had slept through most of the whipping he had tried to give him. Aron had dragged him out of the bed before he realized that Jacob had not even known Sabrina had crawled under his covers. She was just trying to start some shit, and she had succeeded. Aron had moved her off Tebow land that very afternoon.

The divorce had taken three months to finalize. Sabrina still carried a grudge. For some unknown reason she had expected a hefty divorce settlement. After all, the McCoys were well-off. But, Aron's lawyers had seen to it that she walked away with almost nothing. That had been four years ago. Four years without a woman. Four years without sex – unless you counted the times he let himself get overly friendly with his right hand. Yanking his own dick was no substitute for making love. Sometimes he missed pussy so bad he ached, but he certainly didn't miss Sabrina. Now, he was determined not to bed a woman unless it was on his own terms – no rings, no strings, and no promises. It was hard to find a woman who would agree with his terms, especially in this neck of the woods.

Everybody knew the McCoys, and they knew what the family possessed. Women tended to want a secure future, and Aron McCoy had security written all over him. But, he was determined to stay foot-loose and fancy free. Hell, before it was over, he'd probably have to use that damn pocket-pussy Isaac had bought him for a joke. Shit, no! The day he poked his hungry dick inside of that cold, unfeeling plastic was the day he would know it was time to hang up his hoe.

* * *

He would be walking into the dining room at any moment. Steady. Steady. Libby cautioned herself to remain calm. The meal had turned out better than she'd anticipated. She had decided to prepare one of her specialties: rich lasagna made with Italian sausage, flavorful buffalo mozzarella and a homemade marinara sauce that would knock your socks off. It tasted as good as it smelled. She had sampled a little corner of the finished, gargantuan casserole. Libby loved to cook, but feeding six large males would be a challenge. She would have to tweak all of her recipes to make sure she made enough for everybody to have seconds, as well as leftovers for midnight snacks.

As each brother came in, she had met him with a smile and a huge glass of sweet iced tea, the elixir of choice in the south. Of course, she knew Jacob. He had been President of the Junior Service Club as a teenager and he had single-handedly taken on her cause. Several times, he had headed up fundraisers and benefits to raise money for her treatments and untold medical bills. That was Jacob, a gorgeous hunk with a heart of gold. He was always involved in the community. Libby knew he coached a little league team and served on the disaster relief committee at the community center.

The rest of the boys she knew by sight only. None of them had ever been formally introduced to her. Jacob did the honors. They didn't have any memory of her at all. Libby wasn't surprised, for most of her life she had felt invisible. There had been no dates, no proms, no slumber parties or gossip sessions.

Cancer tended to make you an island. The only attention she had been used to receiving was during uncomfortable appearances at the charitable events held in her honor, or while enduring the poking and prodding of a bevy of medical students in a teaching hospital. When you didn't have adequate insurance, the teaching hospital was where they usually sent you. Putting those sad thoughts out of her head, she focused on the rest of the McCoy family.

Joseph was a doll, Libby noticed. He was very comfortable in his own skin, exuding a confidence that is rarely seen in a man under thirty. "Miss Libby, it's a pleasure." She felt her cheeks warm as he kissed her hand. Jacob had told her his brother was an extreme sports nut – a very successful one. He rock-climbed, raced dirt bikes, rode bulls and busted broncs. Libby knew that whatever Joseph did, it suited him well. His body was in tip-top condition.

Isaac had walked in and picked her up, swung her around and then introduced himself. She had dissolved in a bout of giggles at his: "Finally! A woman in the kitchen that I can intimidate." He had set her down and formally shook her hand. "Libby, don't believe half of what you hear about me. I'm not as bad as they say I am."

"He's worse," Noah interjected as he accepted his icy beverage. "Isaac is our resident badass." He had held Libby's hand and turned her around slowly, as if she was standing on a lazy-susan. "Goodness, you are a little doll. If I wasn't already in love with a tall willowy blonde…" he ended wistfully.

"Harper Summers doesn't know you're alive." Isaac quipped. Something that could have been hurt passed over Noah's features. Jacob had told her that Noah was the practical one of the family. He had a good financial head on his shoulders; Tebow Properties had flourished under his care. While Aron managed the trust fund that their parents had left, Noah managed the day-to-day finances for the ranch. He was a heady combination - a Greek God physique, a handsome face and a beautiful mind. Libby decided she was in beefcake heaven.

Nathan had helped her set the table. She was going to fall for Nathan, hard. He was thirteen, and although she was too young to be his mother, he rattled every maternal bone in her body. Libby knew that the likelihood of her ever having children was slim to none. So the chance to spoil this young man was going to be pure pleasure.

The McCoy brothers surrounded her, teasing and playing, making her laugh at their jokes and smile at their antics. They were doing their dead level best to make her feel at home. From out of nowhere, a chill ran up her spine and her toes began to tingle. What in the world?

Then she felt the heat.

Aron. It had to be.

Refusing to look around, lest she betray her fascination, Libby pretended immense interest in what Jacob was saying, even though she wasn't comprehending a word.

* * *

Aron McCoy walked into the dining room and his cock went stiff as a board. When he saw the dainty little doll standing there in the midst of his rambunctious family, he felt like someone had whacked him upside the head with a 2 x 4. As his gaze hungrily moved up and down her exquisite curves, his blood pressure shot up like a rocket and a sudden burst of heat rushed through his body.

Lord Have Mercy!

Aron almost forgot where he was. He had been lured by the incredible smell of Italian food and the warm, enticing scent of garlic bread. His stomach was doing cartwheels, begging to be introduced to the dishes responsible for wafting those delicious aromas. When he stepped into the dining room, however, all thoughts of food went sailing out the window.

Lord Have Mercy!

She was breathtaking.

He didn't know where to look first, or where to look longest. Tight jeans encased a sweet, heart-shaped little butt that made him want to bare his teeth. Her legs were long and all he could think about was what they would feel like clasped around his hips. A form-fitting, red T-shirt proclaimed that she was "Raw Honey – Sweet as Sugar, Twice as Addictive". The implications of those words practically had him bowing at her feet. He bet her cream would taste like raw, wild honey. His fingers itched to see if he could make them meet around that trim little waist. When his eyes roved northward, tears almost came to his eyes. She bounced a little bounce in response to something funny that Jacob had said, and when she did, he wanted to step forward and catch those sweet little tits before she hurt herself. Maybe, he ought to change his job description – he could go from being a simple cowpoke to a full-time, full-service breast support man. By their jiggle and wave, there was no doubt in his mind that those tits were real and in dire need of about an hour of attention from his hands and tongue.

Realizing he was about to embarrass himself, he took off his Stetson and held it below his belt buckle, effectively hiding her unexpected and tremendous impact on his libido. His smooth move did not go unnoticed by Noah, who smirked from across the room. Casually, Aron shot him the finger. Asshole. He couldn't remember the last time a woman had affected him this way, if ever. Watching his brothers surround the tempting little morsel, Aron opted to utilize a tactic which had come in handy when the McCoy's would be out carousing pre-Sabrina. They had tried to avoid stepping on one another's toes, romantically speaking. Whenever one would see a little filly who caught his eye, he would look at her and simply say one word that would alert the others that she had been claimed and was strictly off-limits to the rest of the McCoys. Stepping closer to the table, he loudly proclaimed, "Tag!"

As soon as the word had left Aron's mouth, the younger men looked up at him in surprise. Isaac bit back a snort, and Jacob simply said, "Thank God." Their brother had finally decided to come out of hiding.

Libby wondered at the word Aron shouted. Was this some type of fire drill or a weird game they played? She could feel him looking at her, 'God give me strength', she prayed.

Libby, as of yet, had not turned to face him fully. And he had to see her – now. "Turn around, Baby. Let me see your face." Confused, Libby did as he requested. Slowly. Uncertainty made her hesitate, but when she had made a complete 180, she heard him catch his breath and she raised her eyes.

Aron.

There was no way she was going to hide the joy that she felt, so she didn't try.

Her smile lit up his world. His body began to instantly heat as if it had been graced by the warmth of the rising sun. Aron tried to move forward, but he was frozen, immobilized, entranced. Muscles that he hadn't used in a while began to loosen, and before he knew it, Aron McCoy was smiling. My Lord, the woman had the cutest, sweetest face he had ever laid eyes on. All he could focus on were pink, kissable lips. They were trembling ever so slightly. Aron felt the world tilt just a fraction, he wanted to follow that irresistible pull and enjoy the silky softness of that delectable mouth. He heard her let out a soft, sweet sigh.

Memorizing her features, he let his eyes slide over the smooth curve of her cheek, the endearing turned up nose and cheekbones that begged to be traced with his tongue. When he met her gaze, Aron was surprised by the beautiful color of her eyes. They were huge, a deep dark violet, surrounded by smudgy dark lashes that made them look like amethysts nestled in velvet.

Knowing she expected him to say something, he tried to get his brain to engage with his mouth. All he could manage was "Where did you come from?" As if his words released the brakes on his feet, he found himself walking up to her as bold as could be. There was no way he could hold himself back. He had to be as close to her as possible. She stood her ground, bless her heart.

Time slowed down, and she lost herself in the wonder of his nearness. For years, she had dreamed of the day when she would be this close to Aron. He was a big man. Shoulders as wide as a John Deere tractor were encased in a crisp, white western shirt – the kind with the silver snaps. As she looked at him, she couldn't help but think how it would feel to reach right up, grab that shirt right under the collar, and just jerk it open. Those snaps would come in handy if one wanted to get him naked in a hurry. She bet his chest was magnificent, ripped and sculpted. He would look just the way those heroes were described in the romance novels she loved to read. Would his skin be smooth or would he be sexily furred? Damn, it would be fun to find out. 'Look up, Libby, look up' she thought to herself. She knew her eyes were hung up just north of his belt buckle. Gravity and lust were pulling them south. With a jerk, she looked up and when their eyes clashed, she felt it clear down to her pink parts. God, he was potent.

If she didn't touch him, she would die. She took a deep breath. 'All right,' she thought, 'let's go for casual and friendly.' "Aron, it's good to meet you. Thanks for letting me fill in for Bess. I promise to work hard, and I will take good care of you…I promise." Geez, how lame could you get. Oh, well. She offered him her hand.

*　*　*

'Hell yeah! You'll take care of me, no doubt about that.' He'd lay awake tonight imagining the ways she could take care of him. Aron forgot about the five pairs of eyes which were watching them in rapt attention. He just had to touch. A handshake was much too mundane to satisfy this particular need. His hand met hers. First touching the tips of her fingers with his own, he slid the palm of his hand up hers, before finding the pulse at her wrist with his forefinger. When he could feel the beat of life that flowed through her veins, he caressed that spot, memorizing the rhythm. A sweet little gasp escaped her lips and she shivered. Damn*!* Her whole body trembled, as if in the first throes of orgasm. Aron closed his eyes, realizing this was one woman who would be capable of turning him inside out.

Libby leaned toward him; her breasts almost touched his chest - almost. She could feel her nipples swell in greeting. It was as if there was an irresistible, gravitational pull between her body and his. Shyly, she looked up at him. His eyes were the color of a dark blue lapis. If she were more schooled in the ways of men, she might have thought she read desire in those lazuli eyes. Not possible. This was Aron. And she was just…just Libby.

"Our supper is getting cold. Do you think you two could tear yourself away from each other long enough for us to eat?" Isaac always said just what he thought. At the break in the incredible tension in the room, the boys began taking their chairs.

"Shut-up, Isaac. Mind your manners." Aron didn't turn loose of Libby's hand; instead, he turned it over in his own and led her by it to the dinner table. Waving at Jacob to move out of the way, he held the vacated chair out for Libby to sit in. It was the chair to the right of his. Jacob had to move to the other side of the table. He didn't seem to mind.

"I need to serve the food," Libby began. Aron pointed to the stove and then to Joseph, who stood and proceeded to pass the lasagna and the garlic bread to Noah, who started it down the table for the family to each dish a portion of the delectable food into their plate. The boys were bamboozled, since they had never witnessed their older brother acting this way. He was eating Libby up with his eyes, as if she was a lioness in heat and he was the predatory head of the pride, the only male allowed to mate.

Looking around at the puzzled expressions, he ordered. "Eat." They instantly obeyed.

Turning his attention to Libby, he realized he was still holding her hand. It was his eating hand, so he was eventually going to have to turn it loose. Reluctantly, he did so. Now, it was time to get down to business. "Libby, I'm Aron, the eldest of these useless rascals."

His eyes crinkled at the corners when he smiled. Libby wanted to reach out and soothe the sexy little wrinkles. He had a heavy five o' clock shadow that she would give a thousand dollars to feel rasp across her breasts. Whew! It was a good thing she didn't have a thousand dollars or she would be propositioning him right here at the supper table. Finding her voice, she managed to answer. "I know who you are, Aron. When you played ball for Kerrville, I rarely missed a game," she confessed shyly.

"Why don't I remember you?" He visually caressed every nuance of her face. She was so exquisite that he wanted to have *her* for supper, rather than the lasagna.

Libby racked her brain for a way to answer his question and not give away too much of the sad truth. Leukemia had come calling, and effectively took her out of all social circles. She didn't have to answer. Thankfully, Jacob came to the rescue. "You were the alpha male, Aron. The rest of us mortals merely existed on the outskirts of your orbit. Libby's twenty-five. She would have been in junior high when you were reigning supreme on the football field and behind the lockers."

"I hate I overlooked you, I bet you were as cute as a button." He never even looked over at Jacob. Accepting the passed around dishes from Joseph, who sat at his left, he filled his plate with lasagna, and then he served Libby's plate. "There you go, Sweetie. Eat up." Apparently, it was important to Aron that everybody eat their fill. More than likely, this was his way of ensuring their well-being.

"Thanks, I hope you like the food." Libby's appetite was completely gone, or rather, it had changed its focus. Now, her appetite was for one scrumptious cowboy who was setting her heart to racing a mile a minute and making her sweat in places that didn't bear thinking about. Nathan, who sat to her right, elbowed her. She jumped and faced him. "Hey! What was that for?"

"This is the best food I've ever put in my mouth, Libby. I want you to stay with us forever."

Instead of making her feel complimented, the words served to sober her up. Forever. She didn't have forever. She had two years, at the most. Maybe. Two years to live a lifetime, and Tebow ranch was where she would begin.

"You had better never let Bess hear you say that, Nathan." Noah shook his fork at his younger brother.

"How long will you be with us, Libby?" Joseph reached for the butter, even though the garlic bread already dripped with the creamy condiment.

"I guess it all depends on how Bess's granddaughter gets along. Maybe I'll be here three months, six at the most. That is…if you're pleased with my performance." At her words, Aron groaned audibly.

All eyes turned to him, and he had the good grace to look slightly chastened. The innocent words which had come from her tempting mouth had gone straight to his dick. He definitely wanted to be on the receiving end of one of her performances, and by God, he needed to perform in the worst way. "I'm sure we'll get along just fine." There. That sounded like he was halfway sane.

"Have you ever lived on a ranch before, Libby?" Noah asked between bites.

"No, but it's always been a dream of mine. While I'm here, in my spare time, I would like to experience everything about ranch life. I want to learn to ride a horse, rope a calf. I'd even like to help with the harder work like branding." This confession made the boys all talk at once. All of them were volunteering to teach her their specialty.

"Hey!" Aron quelled the racket. When all was quiet, he simply stated. "Whatever Libby wants to learn, I'll be the one teaching her." At

Libby's confused look, he tapped her on the end of the nose and smiled another one of those ten thousand watt scorchers.

Effectively, he changed the subject. He didn't know how he felt about the other boys spending time with Libby. She might not be Sabrina, but he didn't want another woman coming in between him and his family. Besides, he wanted Libby all to himself. "How do you know Bess?" There, that seemed like a safe enough topic.

"She and my Mom were friends for years. They went to school together. Mom's gone now, my Dad, too."

"So, you're all alone. Sorry, Honey." Aron looked serious for a moment, and then he continued eating.

Libby went back to her food, then something wild started happening under the table. Several times, she felt his knee bump hers, linger, and then rub gently. Once could have been an accident, but three times? It had to be intentional. The implications had Libby's head spinning. This attention from Aron was more than she had ever dreamed possible.

"I'm grateful to Bess for bringing you to me." Aron's softly whispered words flowed straight to her breasts. Instantly, her skin began to tingle and grow warm and her nipples swelled and hardened. Before she realized it, they were eagerly protruding, and the thin little T-shirt was an insufficient barrier from prying eyes.

Seeing the effect his words had on her, Aron instantly excused himself and in a moment returned with one of his shirts from the laundry room. Draping it over her shoulders, he whispered. "Slip this on." He winked at her as she flushed as much from arousal as embarrassment. "I'll take care of you."

It had gotten quiet at the table, "What?" Aron challenged. "Libby was cold."

At last, the meal was over. Everyone was very appreciative of the lasagna, the salad, the garlic bread and the blackberry cobbler she had whipped up from the fresh berries in the crisper. Bess had plenty of food laid back for her to use, she wouldn't have to do much grocery shopping for a while. When Nathan was through, he stopped at her chair and kissed her cheek, "Thanks for everything, Libby. Especially the help with the homework. And the brownie," he grinned.

"Where are the brownies?" Isaac zeroed in on the mention of chocolate.

"That huge cookie jar by the rotisserie is full. Help yourselves."

"Don't eat them all," Aron cautioned.

Before she thought, Libby put her hand on his arm, and whispered, "Don't worry, Aron. I saved half the batch back for you. They're in your office in a plastic tub. Bess told me that chocolate was your weakness."

Chocolate wasn't his only weakness, that fact was quickly becoming apparent. Aron was touched. He didn't know what he enjoyed more, the news of the chocolate treats hidden back just for him or the light touch of her hand on his skin." The touch. Definitely the touch, he decided.

Jacob herded those out who wanted to linger around Libby. He wanted to give his brother room to work. Things were heating up much faster than he had ever hoped they might. Aron had been so hurt by his ex-wife. She had moved into Tebow and proceeded to make them all miserable, especially Aron. Sabrina had spent Aron's money as if she was pouring water through a sieve. Then, there was the 'incident', when he had been a pawn in Sabrina's plot to destroy Aron. And it had almost worked. But, Libby had the power to change everything. Libby could be an answer to his prayers.

This was the first time he had seen Aron show any signs of life around a woman in years. Jacob was fascinated, because Aron's desire for Libby had hit harder and faster than anyone would have ever believed. With a grin on his face, he left them to it.

"You don't have to help me; I'll have this straightened up in a jiffy." Libby worked automatically and quickly, flushed with heightened awareness. God, Aron made her so nervous. It was wise to keep her hands occupied, she had never been so tempted to throw caution to the wind and aggressively touch a man in her life. This side of her was a surprise. Oh, she knew she liked to read about sex, but she didn't know her blood would run so hot. Only the fear of rejection made her keep her hands to herself.

"The quicker we're finished, the quicker I can take you in my arms." Shocked, Libby stopped and simply looked at him. Could he read her mind? Was he serious? Dared she hope? This was exactly what she had yearned for. Doc Mulligan had said this was her chance, the time to do whatever she longed to do, and experiencing love – or sex – was at the top of her list. To be able to love Aron would be the fulfillment of her dearest dream. "You can shut your mouth, Baby. You're gaping." Laughing, he took the dishrag from her hand and proceeded to wipe down the table. Pulling herself together, she washed up the last of the pots and started the dishwasher to do the rest. Aron made her hyper-sensitive, primarily because she was aware of every movement of his body, every accidental touch, every breath he expelled. Finally, they were through. Libby spread the washcloth over the central divider of the sink, and turned to see what Aron was doing.

He was right there. Lord, in heaven. He was right in front of her. Brazenly, he took one half-step forward and they were suddenly touching all the way from chest to hip. A surprised gasp of delight escaped her lips and she felt a little faint.

Before she knew what was happening, Aron had framed her face with his big, warm hands. She looked up at him. God, he was so tall and broad. The thought passed through Libby's mind that she could settle herself against him, and with his arms wrapped around her, nothing would ever hurt her again. Aron could keep all her ghosts at bay. It seemed that he could even keep the specter of leukemia from ever touching her again.

Aron was in lust-shock, pure lust-shock. His big hands cupped her soft, little face. Out of nowhere, she turned her head and kissed his hand, her sweet gesture almost bringing him to his knees. His stiff rod jumped in his drawers. While she had been working around the kitchen, he had been enjoying himself, studying every inch of her delectable body. Aron couldn't believe it. Libby was absolutely perfect. Perfect breasts. Perfect hips. Perfect legs. Perfect for him.

"Libby, may I kiss you?"

He moved his thumbs over the pretty pink blush on her cheeks, sending a ripple of excitement through her.

"Don't say no. I think I'll die if I don't get a taste of you."

Goosebumps rose over every square section of her body. Aron wanted to kiss her! "Please," was all she could manage to say. When he lowered his head to capture her lips, he blocked out all the light. She welcomed the darkness; it was momentous, like the total eclipse of the sun. God in heaven! Aron didn't rush, he relished. Beginning with the softest kiss imaginable, he let their lips introduce themselves, one to the other. Light little caresses, delicate little forays with his tongue that made Libby want to reach out and grab it with her teeth. She made a tiny little grunt of frustration that made Aron laugh with delight. "You are too cute."

She couldn't resist, her hands wouldn't be still. She placed them on his biceps and explored the intriguing bulges. "Hmmm," she groaned as she felt them tighten under her exploration. Aron still hadn't kissed her fully, he nibbled on her top lip and licked at the corners of her mouth, all torture designed to heat her up into a tizzy. Standing on tiptoe, she tried to take over the kiss. Waiting a lifetime for something made one highly impatient.

Without warning, Aron picked her up and sat her bottom down on the kitchen counter. This put their heads on the same level, and he didn't have to bend over. With one hand, he swept her knees apart and stepped in-between them. Reaching behind her, he clasped her hips and pulled her forward. "Wrap your legs around my waist. I need to feel your heat."

Shaking with desire, she complied with his wishes, but she let hers be known also. "Kiss me right, Aron. Full on the lips. I'm so hungry for you." At her frank request, he stepped back to take it all in. She was delightful!

"You little minx." He reached over and bit her where the soft skin of her neck met her collarbone. "I'm getting to it, don't be so impatient. I've waited a lifetime for someone like you, so let me play."

Despite his instructions to be patient, she just couldn't. Feeling brave, she wrapped her arms around his neck and pulled him forward. He grunted with approval. "Hell, yeah." Then, he gave her what she wanted. Finally. Hands sliding to the base of her neck and tightening in her hair, he fitted his mouth over hers; he sucked on her lips, taking in all of her sweetness. Her little tongue darted out and met his full on. They twirled and swirled, tasting and nipping, devouring one another in a blissful kiss. Thank God for her erotic romances, she knew exactly what to do. Hooking her feet behind his knees, she pressed herself to him. He pulled away from her, resting his head on her shoulder, breathing harshly. "My God, Libby. You're like a little stick of dynamite."

Holding him tightly, she kissed his neck, taking little bites, then soothing them with her tongue. "Is that bad?" His heart was racing, but then so was hers. When he wasn't able to answer, she finished her thought. "And to think, this is my very first kiss."

It took a moment, but her words finally sunk in to Aron's thick skull. Fighting reality, denying what he had heard, Aron let his lips brush over her neck, up the smooth line of her jaw, and around to the tender place under her ear. "What did you say?" Surely, he had heard wrong.

Libby hadn't stopped her sensual onslaught. She was about to give her first hickey – ever. He tasted so good. She sucked on his neck like she was auditioning for a vampire movie. She wanted more. Reluctantly, she stopped long enough to answer him. "You're my first kiss. My life so far hasn't been exactly normal. I've been sort of isolated and out of circulation, family problems…" she offered against his skin.

With one last sweet kiss, Aron pushed back from her until only their hands were touching. "Baby, are you telling me that you're a virgin?"

He didn't look happy.

Well, hell.

Libby could sense that everything had changed. She felt guilty. Why should she feel guilty? Somebody had to be her first. "Yes," she slowly answered.

"Damn."

Aron backed off, even more. She reached to pull him back, but he evaded her touch. Embarrassed, Libby let her hands drop.

"I don't do innocents, love. I refuse to be the one to besmirch your virtue."

Besmirch? Besmirch? "What if I want to be besmirched?" she questioned, more disappointed than she ever thought she could be about anything.

"I'm sorry, Baby Girl." Aron put his hat back on and gently picked her up off the counter and sat her down. "You don't know what you're asking." With those last sad words, he turned and walked away.

Chapter Two

What had happened? When she realized Aron was really walking away from her, she immediately felt bereft and cold. He didn't do innocents? Well, hell. Tears welled up in her eyes. She hadn't realized that inexperience could be such a turn-off to a man. It must be like getting a job. You had to have experience to get one, but nobody wanted to be the one to give you the chance at getting the experience. Maybe if she were prettier. Libby didn't really have a handle on her own sex appeal. She didn't have any idea if there was anything about her that would appeal to a man. At first, Aron seemed taken with her, but that might have been an act. Maybe, he was just the kind that liked to tease. Well, the joke was on her. She was left achy and empty, her breasts were swollen and sore and her feelings felt like someone had taken them out and stomped on them.

Mechanically, she went through the motions to ready everything for the next day's meals. She had decided earlier that gumbo and grilladas would be just the thing. They were dishes she could put on early in the day and the longer they cooked, the better they would be. With a heavy heart, she also carried out Bess's directive concerning Aron. She mixed up a batch of sweet roll dough so he could have hot cinnamon rolls with his coffee. Checking everything one last time, she started for bed. She could hear the McCoy brothers while they were watching television, and it sounded like they were having the time of their life.

Turning out the lights, she avoided the voices coming from the den and hastily made her way up the stairs to the haven of Bess's room. Throwing herself on the bed, she let the tears flow. Rats! How was she supposed to face Aron now? He had awakened every cell in her body to untold delights, and then he had just walked away. Looking around, she felt as if the room was trying to close in on her. God, she had to get outside! She couldn't stand to stay in the house one more minute. Where could she go? She needed to cool off and she could think of only one solution – the stock tank she had spied earlier would be just the thing. If Aron didn't want her, she would just wash his touch right off of her body. There wasn't anything wrong with her. Was there? She didn't have a swimsuit, but no one would follow her. Least of all Aron, as he didn't want to have anything to do with her.

* * *

Aron was miserable. Quaking with desire, he tried to walk off the hard-on that was still trying to warp his zipper. He had done the right thing. It didn't feel like it, but he had done the right thing. He wanted to feel Libby in his arms more than he wanted his next breath, but there was no way he was getting involved with someone who would expect something from him, something he wasn't prepared to give.

He fled the house, trying to find someplace where he could get Libby off his mind. Lord, he could still see her face; he could still feel the softness of her skin. Damn, he had hurt her. Needlessly. Why had he come on so strong? He had acted like a randy fool. Who would have thought she would be an innocent? Hell, if he slept with Libby now, she would start picking out china patterns and wallpaper samples. No, it was better to cut it off before the whole mess got out of hand.

Aron retreated to his studio. This was his sanctuary. After he'd graduated college and retired from the rodeo circuit, he had been hungry for something to do besides just running the ranch. Through an odd series of events, sculpture had become his focus. Aron needed an outlet for his energy and he had always enjoyed working with his hands. During one of his trips to Mexico to check breeding stock, he had met Degas Santiago, a rich rancher who was also a sculptor. The man had intrigued him. While attending a party to meet the countries Ambassador to the United States, he had spent the night at Degas's home and he had graciously shown him around his studio, allowing Aron to try his hand at molding a piece of clay. Much to his surprise, he found he had a knack for it. Now, several galleries would buy every piece he could turn out. He could still remember the first sculpture he had ever made; it had been a horse standing on an outcropping of rock. The muscles of the animal were delineated and one could see every hair in its mane. He had called the horse, *Freedom*. What made it even more important was that he had made it for his mother. She had been over the moon about it. Then, he had lost her.

After the accident which had stolen his parents. Aron had immersed himself in work and family, but he had still taken time to sculpt. He'd needed the distraction, especially when escaping Sabrina had been the only way to hold on to his sanity. The first showing he had participated in had been held in tandem with the State Fair Rodeo in Dallas. It had been a simple misunderstanding, but someone had bought that piece right out from under his nose. The director of the exhibit had not distinguished *Freedom* as being a for-exhibit-only piece and the saleslady had sold it in error. The price had been right, but Aron would give his right arm to get it back. At first, he had been angry. But it was an honest mistake. Ever since then, he had been on the lookout for it. Rodeo people were a pretty close knit group, and one day he would cross paths with the person who had bought what he never intended to sell. The buyer had paid cash however, so it was like looking for a needle in a hay stack.

Tonight, he sat in the dark in his studio. For the first time, Aron found it was not a haven...it was damn lonely. The king-size bed over in the corner beckoned to him. How he would love to see Libby Fontaine draped across it, naked as the day she was born. Shit! All he wanted to do was march back over to the main house, find Libby, and hold her soft, little body tight in his embrace. He would kiss her over and over and then; he would allow his steel-hard cock to sink into the rich velvet of her womanhood. But that wasn't meant to be. Libby deserved a husband who loved her and children who adored her. He could offer her neither of those things, so it was better that he offered her nothing at all.

A splash outside the window of his second story studio alerted him that something was messing around the stock tank. Aron couldn't imagine. There was nothing corralled in that lot; all of the horses and cattle were grazing out in the pasture land or they were shut up in the barn. What in the world?

He looked. He saw. He ached.

Libby walked up to the stock tank, trailing her hand in the cool, clear water. The glow from the security light was bright enough that he could see her quite clearly. The night was still enough that he could hear her sigh. She held the towel together over her breasts; her legs were long and sleek and bare. Moonlight gave the pale skin of her arms and legs an iridescent quality. She could have been a wood nymph come out to play. Aron was totally enchanted. How he had walked away from this sweet thing was one of life's great mysteries. Midnight dark hair hung to her waist in thick, spiral curls. For a few tense minutes, Aron forgot to breathe.

The towel dropped.

Aron groaned.

Underneath that towel was nothing but beautiful, smooth, creamy skin. God in heaven, she was nude! Gloriously, magnificently nude! How long had it been since he had seen a naked woman outside of the pages of a magazine? Too long. Way, too damn long. And no woman he had ever been with had looked like this one. The clothes she had encased herself in ought to be taken out back and burned. They were a sacrilege to nature. Nothing should ever hide those luscious hills and valleys from his hungry eyes.

Libby still had her back to him. It appeared she was trying to figure out how to climb into the tank. There was a ladder about twenty feet to the left of her, but if he called out that information he would give himself away and she would vanish from his sight like a frightened fairy. She placed her hands on the rim of the tank and tried to pull her little self up and over. Partially successful, she managed to get her incredible tush elevated so that he could see a sweet little vee and past that – paradise.

Aron couldn't help but smile as he listened to her little grunts as she exerted herself. She wasn't very strong and soon she dropped back to the ground with a disappointed huff. Aron rubbed his palms on his denim-covered knees, aching to rub them over the tempting curve of her bottom.

"Turn around, Baby. Turn around." At that moment, he would have gladly given his share of Tebow to see her breasts. "Turn around, Sweetheart, lest I die," he whispered.

The Lord giveth…blessed be the name of the Lord. Libby turned and bent to pick up the towel. Twin globes of perfection hung down like the most delicious melons. Sweet Jesus! Honey-dews! Aron licked his lips, imagining how it would feel to claim those beauties, massaging them until she arched her back in ecstasy. He opened his mouth, slightly, as if in anticipation of fitting his lips over those incredible swollen tips. He was in lust! Deep, intense, nerve shattering lust! Aron had never been privileged to suckle on nipples as large as hers. Sabrina's nipples had been stingy, just like the rest of her. But Libby had nipples that were pink and puffy, just begging to be tongued and sucked.

Never before had he faced the possibility of erupting like a geyser without a single touch from his own hand or anyone else's. Unzipping his fly, Aron freed his enormous cock, seeking to gain some relief.

There was no way in hell that he was going to be able to stay away from her. She was the most tempting, succulent goddess he had ever been privileged to pay homage to. Walking around the tank, he heard her satisfied little exclamation when she finally found the ladder. In just seconds, she was up and over and the splash made him shiver. How he longed to cover her body like those warm, lucky waters.

Smiling, he watched her frolic in the water. Right by herself, she laughed and played. Aron wondered if she was lonely. Surprisingly, he wanted to know. Seeing her enjoy these few, stolen moments after the difficult day she had endured, tugged at places in his heart that he had thought were out of commission. Unable to resist, he placed one hand on the windowsill and the other on himself and began stroking. Aron rested his chin on his forearm, captivated by her beauty and charm.

Then the game changed. Completely.

Libby began to touch herself.

Hypnotized, his mouth fell open as he gazed at her in rapt admiration. He watched her lean back on the rim and raise her body in a float. Aron had to bite his lip to keep from crying out when she cupped her own breasts and began to caress the tender mounds. Mesmerized, he watched her shape them and coax them into bountiful little mountains of gorgeous female flesh. When she began to pull on her nipples, stretching them out and milking them between her fingers, his hips bucked, begging to be allowed to join in the party. It wasn't just a few half-hearted tugs, Libby seemed to relish the attention she gave her tits. Apparently, she had spent a great deal of time practicing this particular skill, and God, if Aron had been called upon to judge her performance, he would have given her a perfect 10.

Aron was holding himself firmer now, getting more and more excited by the second, pumping his cock in long, smooth strokes. Libby's sensual little performance had him leaking pre-cum and a raging eruption wasn't far off. God, it was good! He imagined joining her in the warm water, slipping up close and covering one of those luscious nipples with his eager lips. God, he would suck and slurp, devouring all of that precious womanly flesh like a starving man presented with a T-bone steak. Damn!

Aron's breath hung in his throat when he watched one hand slip down past her waist to the dark little patch of curls. Her fingers curled and dipped, rhythmically working on her sweet spot. She thrashed in the water, trying to stay afloat, even while her legs and hips pumped in absolute abandon. Aron's hand kept up with her erotic dance, his own level of excitement reaching plateaus that he had rarely ever scaled.

Then, the world stopped turning. Aron knew that if he died at that moment, he would have no regrets. Libby's enjoyment sent him roaring off the cliff, flying apart in ecstasy. Huge plumes of cum sprayed up and over the windowsill, raining down the side of the barn. Never had he climaxed with such a violent explosive force. His eyes never left her, his ears were attuned to every word she screamed. And if he lived to be a hundred, he would never forget the sound of her husky little voice. For as Libby Fontaine brought herself to a glorious completion, it was his name she had shouted. "Aron! Aron! Oh, God, Aron, I want you so much!"

A broad smile overspread his relaxed features, while drops of sweat stood on his brow. At that moment, there was nothing in heaven or on earth that would have prevented him from going to her. All logical thought fled his mind. His body was clamoring with a need that took him completely over. Even though he had just experienced an incredible climax, Aron's thirst to taste her hadn't been quenched. He was already harder than he had ever been in his life. Hastily he made himself decent, putting his still excited rod back in his shorts. With shaking hands, he fastened his jeans and with his belt still hanging open, he went to join her. As he rounded the corner of the barn, he heard the splashing sound of her body emerging from the water.

When Libby pulled herself up the ladder, she found herself face to face with Aron. A hastily indrawn breath was the only sound she could make. Had he seen her? Had he heard her cry his name in the midst of her passion? Mortified, she turned to leap back into the darkness of the water.

"No, no, Baby." Aron reached out and grasped her wrist. "Don't run away from me, Bathsheba. You tempt me beyond what a mortal man could ever hope to resist." He pulled her forward and licked off the droplets of water that hung from the tips of her nipples.

The touch of his lips on her breasts made her pleasure center go molten. This sudden turn of events had Libby's head spinning. Aron was here! But, what did that mean? Leaning back away from his potent tongue, she crossed her hands over her breasts, and hung her head, not knowing what to think. Was this just another game? Would he tease her for a few more minutes, then walk away? Everything within screamed for her to open her arms and fit her wet body to his large, warm frame, but she didn't want to be pushed away for the second time.

"Don't hide from me, Libby." Aron pulled at her arms, revealing the luscious body that he craved more than food or air. "As much as I want to take you right here where we stand, we've got to talk. Will you come upstairs with me, to my studio?" He picked the towel up from where she had left it and gently wrapped it around her body, for the moment covering the precious treasure he coveted with every fiber of his being.

"Talk? You want to talk?" Libby's mind wasn't working very well. Still, there was no way she could ever turn him away. She had wanted him way too long to miss an opportunity to spend time with him.

Before he could answer her question, she appeared to make up her mind and held out her arms to him, and he gratefully picked her up. With one hand under her knees, he clasped her close, and quickly walked to the back stairs of the barn.

Every step he took, he kissed the top of her head, and she gave into instinct and nestled her cheek into the strong muscles of his shoulder. "Have you changed your mind about wanting me?" Libby couldn't help but ask.

"Oh, Babe," he tenderly answered, "there was never any question about my wanting you."

Kicking open the door of his studio with one booted foot, Aron deposited her gently onto his bed, flipping on the bedside lamp so he could see her clearly. His fantasy from earlier had blessedly come to life.

She ran her palm down his cheek, enjoying the coarseness of his whiskers. "Will you make love to me now?"

Everything within him clamored to take her up on what she offered—right damn now. Hell, being chivalrous was torture. "Libby, I have to say something first." Aron hesitated, not knowing how to proceed.

What she said next floored him.

"Is being a woman's first lover more trouble than it's worth? Is it not pleasurable for a man?"

Her innocence humbled him. Before he could reassure her, she continued to speak.

"Would it be better for you if I found someone else to...deflower me?"

With one forceful move, she was flat on her back and he was on top of her. "Hell, no! Your first time is a precious gift, and the man lucky enough to introduce you to the pleasures of love making will be one damn lucky son-of-a-bitch. I can only imagine that sharing your first experience would be heaven on earth for me. After all, I bet you're going to be soft and sweet and tight enough to drive me mad." Aron was kissing down her neck and all across the tops of her breasts. "So if there's any damn deflowering to be done, I'll be the one to take care of it." His ferocious look sent the once serious Libby into a spate of giggles.

Her spunky personality began to emerge. "Well, I hate to put you out. After all, I know how busy you are." She pretended to try to roll away from him and he tightened his grip on her until she could barely breathe.

"Hold on, Libby. Let me be serious for just a minute. Okay?" He rubbed his nose up and down her cheek, inhaling her clean, sweet smell. Surrendering to him completely, she lay back, allowing him to look deep into her eyes. "If we're going to do this, I need for you to understand something."

"Okay." Libby held her breath. What was he talking about?

"I can't offer you anything." As he said the words, somehow they didn't ring true in Aron's mind.

"What do you mean?" Was he talking money? Surely not. Or, maybe – white lace and wedding bells? She didn't have any use for either.

"I mean that I'm not making you any promises. I don't want anything permanent. I don't ever intend to marry again, so what we have will be just..." He groped for the right word. He hated to sound crass; after all she was an innocent.

"Sex." She supplied the word for him.

All right, she understood the score, but that didn't tell the full story. Aron stilled himself, waiting to see what her reaction would be. Would she push him off of her and leave in a huff? Would she start to cry? God, don't let her cry.

For a moment, there was only silence.

Then, she shocked him again, right down to the soles of his feet.

"That sounds just about perfect to me. Just sex. Yes, I believe that will fit right into my plans." Her expression was calm, as smooth and serene as the surface of a Hill Country lake.

Aron narrowed his eyes and tried to decide what species of femininity he was holding. "What did you say?" he growled.

Libby giggled again. Give a man what he asked for and he still wasn't happy. "I said that 'just sex' would work for me. I don't—I can't make any promises either. My future is uncertain at this point and anything of a permanent nature is out of the question." She spoke slowly, carefully weighing each word. She didn't want to ever lie to Aron, but she intended to walk away without him ever knowing about the cancer.

"So, let me get this straight…" He had to make sure.

"Good, Lord." Libby laughed. "I want you, Aron. Will you make love to me already?"

"Hell, yeah!" Who was he to question the beneficent goodness of the Almighty? What a gift this woman was! He moved to her side and turned her to face him. "Let's kiss some more."

Immediately, she draped one leg over his hips and scooted impossibly close. "That sounds wonderful. Your kisses are sweeter than Mounds candy."

"Hey, if we're talking candy bars, I'd rather be an Almond Joy instead of a Mounds." Lord, he enjoyed picking at her. She was more fun than a barrel of monkeys.

"What's the deal?" She played back. "They're both coconut!"

"Yeah," he said as he nipped at her chin. "But Almond Joys has nuts, Mounds don't." She squealed as he pinched her on the butt cheek. "And if you'll slip your little hand between my legs, I'll prove to you which category I fall into."

"Oh, you are too much." Excitement flashed through Libby's body. This time she didn't wait for Aron, she fisted her hand in his hair and pulled his head to hers.

He was hypnotized. Closing his eyes, he welcomed the magic. Libby took the tip of her tongue and teased him. Sweeping from one side of his mouth to the other, she coaxed him into giving her entrance. Aron played hard to get. This didn't put Libby off a bit; she just became more determined.

Opening her lips, she used her teeth to gently scrape and nibble all around his mouth. The feel of his beard stubble was making her quiver. Dipping her hips toward him, she playfully pressed her aching center up against his granite hard ridge.

When she ground against him, Aron's passion exploded. He thrust his tongue into her honeyed warmth and kissed her voraciously. Pushing her onto her back once again, he held her hands up over her head. "There is no way in hell you are unschooled!" he challenged. "You are blowing my mind!"

"I've read hundreds of erotic romances when I couldn't do anything else," she softly confessed, conspiratorially. "And I practiced. With a cucumber."

"You stuck a cucumber up your…?" he feigned horror.

"No." Libby was giggling so hard, she could barely catch her breath. "I sucked on it, so I would know how to…"

And that was as far in her explanation as she got. Aron reached between them and pulled her body free of the towel, then he kissed his way from her lips, past her chin and then to the valley between her breasts. "I'll let you show me what you've learned with the cucumber a little later, but right now I've got to latch my lips onto these sweet little tits. When I saw you getting excited right in front of my eyes at the dining room table, I almost came in my shorts." He plumped both breasts together, pushing the nipples close so he could trail his tongue from one to the other. "You have got the prettiest nipples," he crooned. "Watch." Fascinated, she saw him take a whole nipple and areola in his mouth and suck on it like a child would the top of an ice cream cone. She couldn't keep her eyes open however, for the pleasure was so intense she thought she might pass out.

"Oh, Aron," she gasped. "That feels so good." Libby couldn't contain herself; she undulated in his grasp, but he just latched on harder. Greedily, he lapped and sucked on her as if she were life-giving ambrosia from the gods. He made pleasurable noises in his throat while he ringed the hard nubbins with his tongue, feasting on her like there was no tomorrow. "I fantasized how your beard would feel rubbing against my skin." At her whispered description, Aron demonstrated to her that while the fantasy was good, reality topped it by about a thousand percent. Soon, her hips were bucking upward, seeking any kind of release. Realizing she was in need, Aron slid one hand down to her mons.

"I could suck on your breasts for hours, but it seems to me there are other parts of your body that are demanding attention." Aron was in heaven. He had never had so much fun making love. Sabrina had been a stingy lover, and he had been forced to make do with stingy bouts of sex—few and far between. Never had she lifted her hips, begging him wordlessly for his touch. When he slipped his fingers past the apex of Libby's thighs, he was met with a welcoming heat. She was wet for him. "You do want me, don't you?"

"Yes, please, Aron." She opened her legs wider. He didn't even have to ask. Before she knew what to expect, he had slid down her body, kissing his way to her navel. There he stopped to minister to the tiny well, afraid it would feel left out on his epic journey. With stingless bites, he nibbled his way down her tummy, stopping to blow a raspberry, just to hear the sweetness of her laugh. Then she stopped laughing.

"Oh, my Lord," she prayed. He was kissing her *there*! Never had she felt anything like it; never had she even imagined anything like it.

With his wide hands, he held her open, then he made himself at home. He lapped at her cream like a happy tomcat, smiling to himself as he heard her groan with pleasure.

"Do you like that?" he asked as he settled down to the task in earnest. Lifting her hips with his hands, he kissed from hipbone to hipbone, stopping in the middle to worship her, giving her clit a quick little lick.

"Yes!" she purred. "More!"

"Patience," he teased. Aron drove his tongue as deep into her channel as he could, then he proceeded to tongue-fuck her, "You taste so good, Libby," he praised her as he licked his way back to the pearl that peeked out from its little hood, like a shy child waiting to see if it would be invited to play. "Hold on, Baby. I'm going to make you feel good. You're going to like this." He proceeded to do as he promised and he had to forcibly hold her down.

Hot waves of joy rained down upon her, searing her with bolts of molten white electricity. Oh, she had cum, but always by her own hand, never by the talented tongue of the man she—even in the mindless frenzy of orgasm, she wouldn't let her mind say the words. A scream of rapture burst from her lips, and a shocking thrill of pleasure bloomed like fireworks in her brain. "Aron!"

He licked his way up her body, rejoicing in the tremors of her climax. "Are you protected, Libby?" God, please say yes. Aron couldn't stand the thought of sheathing himself with a synthetic barrier. He wanted to feel every iota of her being.

"I'm on the pill," she panted. "Boy scout."

Again, she made him laugh. "Don't you mean, girl scout?"

"No, I took the pill because I was scouting for boys."

"You'd better not be scouting anymore, Sweetheart." He tickled her up and down her ribs, while she wiggled and squiggled with joy.

Finally, face to face, they quieted. "I've found what I was looking for." She brushed a soft strand of hair from his forehead. "At least, until it's time for me to go," she reassured him with a reverent kiss over each eyelid.

Aron hugged her close, then once more parted her thighs and caressed her silky folds with a soft touch. "I'm going to stretch you just a little bit. I don't want to hurt you. I want it to feel good." Trusting him, she laid back, allowing him to do as he wished. But, then, she eyed that white shirt with the snaps and grinned. No better time than the present to make that particular day dream come true. She placed her hands on the lapels of his shirt and pulled hard. It parted as easily as if she had said, 'Open Sesame'. To give him credit, he didn't look very surprised. Maybe he was used to being ravished.

"My Word," she marveled. "Look at this chest!" He was utterly magnificent. Crisp dark hair covered flesh that just begged to be petted. Little brown nipples looked in dire need of being kissed and miles of muscles seemed to scream for her to map them with eager fingers.

At the determined look in her eye, he paused in what he was doing – just to wonder at her fascination with his beat-up old body. "Make yourself at home. What is mine is yours." He thought about just laying back and letting her enjoy herself. Finally, the call of his desperate cock won out, and he started back to working at her pussy in earnest, readying her softness for his possession. All the while, she entertained herself by stroking his chest and tonguing his nipples, nipping and kissing every inch of him she could reach. Had he ever experienced anything like her before? He didn't think so. Libby was a wonder. She seemed to crave him. Him. Aron wasn't used to reciprocal attention. The sex he had participated in had mostly been one-sided, vaguely satisfying, but nothing to write home about. This...this was a whole different ball game. Libby wasn't just participating; she was recruiting, coaching and leading the cheers.

What Aron was doing south of her equator finally captured her attention, causing her worship of his chest to slow down a bit. As his fingers pushed up inside of her, she drew in a breath and held it. Oh, his fingers felt so much better than her own ever could have. For one thing, they were longer and fatter...and then they were his, which made all the difference.

He began a rhythmic invasion of her femininity with one finger, until she was squirming with pleasure. Two fingers and she sought his lips, needing to connect with the one who was bringing her such joy. His question came out of the blue. "Have you ever put a toy of any kind inside you, Libby?"

"No," she answered between kisses. "I've worn tampons, I'm okay."

"I'm slightly bigger than a tampon, Sugar." He continued to press into her, adding a third finger to the mix. Hurting her was not an option. But if the heat she was producing and the little whimpers and purrs coming from her sweet lips were any indication of her excitement, she was ready for him. Still, he pushed her toward another climax. It was best to be sure.

Virginal, she might be, but she still caught on to what he was doing. "Aron, no. Stop! I don't want to come, yet. I want to wait until you're inside me. I want to wait for you." She tried, in vain, to hold off the impending climax. "I'm going to use up all of my orgasms." She truly seemed dismayed.

Chuckling he kissed her, even as he deepened the sensual assault. "God loves girls more than he does boys, Libby. He made you so that you could come over and over again. It's just us poor unfortunate males who have to wait and recuperate." Aron punctuated his words with kisses to her face and neck. "So, don't fret. Let me hear you. Purr for me, Kitten. Come for me. Don't hold back." Latching on to one nipple, he gloried in her response as she rode his hand to nirvana.

Libby was literally gulping for air. Never had she envisioned pleasure like she was receiving from Aron. Then a thought occurred, "Roll over," she demanded. How could she have forgotten this? It would be like going to Florida and missing Disneyworld.

"What?" he asked in a daze. He was past ready to claim her. His penis was strutted with passion and anxious to enter the Promised Land.

"I've got to get a look at you." She pushed at his shoulder, trying to get him to lie flat.

"What?" he asked again. There wasn't enough blood in his brain to allow him to comprehend her request.

. "I want to see you, all of you. Especially your joystick." Libby was serious.

"You're killing me, Libby." Aron didn't know whether to laugh or cry. She maneuvered herself from underneath him and he moaned with frustration.

"You've still got most of your clothes on. How did that happen?" In the blink of an eye, she set to work undressing him. His shirt was hanging open, his belt was unbuckled, but other than that, he was fully dressed. "We've got to get your boots off, first." Helpless, he lay back and watched her work. Here he was, as hard as a rock, and she was gallivanting around like a butterfly. She did have a point about the clothes, though. Finding a reserve of strength, he began to help her undress him. Aron was easily distracted, however, by the sway of her breasts and the cute little dimples on her bottom. When she had him down to his shorts, she sat up beside him like it was Christmas morning and she was waiting to open a gift under the tree.

With wide eyes, she gently traced the outline of his stiff cock. Aron swore he had never swelled to such proportions before. A lot of things were different with Libby—the laughter, the passion, the sheer joy one could find in another's body. Glancing at him, as if in permission, she began the unveiling.

Getting up on her knees, she straddled his legs, so that she was sitting over his calves. Grasping the waistband of his boxer briefs, she tugged down—and out he sprang in all of his glory. "Look at him!" she exclaimed with joy. "Aron, he's so beautiful!"

He didn't know whether to laugh or moan when she leaned over and grabbed him with both hands. She began kissing him from tip to root, all up one side and down the other. Any other time he would have been gung-ho for her enthusiasm, but right now he was about to go all Mount St. Helens on her. He put a hand down to pull her up, when she placed one more soft, sweet kiss right on the weeping tip end. "You are remarkably, wonderfully made." She kissed him again, quoting from one of her favorite novels.

That was it. He couldn't take anymore. Grasping her by the waist, he flipped her up and over. She squealed in surprise, as he got her into position. "No more teasing, love, or the game is going to be over before the quarterback even gets on the field." Spreading her thighs, he maneuvered himself over her.

"Are you heading into the end zone?" she queried with a straight face as he settled his body down onto her, pushing the blunt end of his cock into the gate of her tender opening.

He was so thick; she didn't know how in the world her body would ever accommodate him.

"Going for a touchdown." He grinned as he pressed forward a half-inch. Suddenly, the sensation overwhelmed him. He hadn't ridden bareback since way before Sabrina. She hadn't wanted to feel his naked cock inside of her. She'd said she couldn't stand the way it felt when he came inside her body. He couldn't imagine Libby ever saying anything such a thing. His eyes rolled to the back of his head. Sweet Jesus! Ecstasy! She was warm, wet, silky, tight, and as soft as the inside of a cream puff. "I'll never last," he moaned.

"Aron, give me your hands." He looked down and she was holding her hands up, wanting to weave their fingers together. He sat up and pulled her hips up and over his thighs. Pressing forward he managed to push another inch inside of her. Giving her what she wanted, he held her hands, and then he began to pump. Libby was incredibly snug, squeezing his organ like a tight little vice. Watching her face, he looked for any sign of discomfort, but all he could see was happiness, pleasure and a hunger he had never seen on a woman's face before. "More, Aron. Give me more," she urged him on.

He didn't have to be asked twice; he pushed steadily into her until he was buried to the hilt. Then, he had to stop for a second. The pleasure was just too intense. Miraculously, she was making these tiny little movements deep down inside, massaging and clasping him with her sheathe. "Are you ready?" he asked, hoping to high heaven she would say 'yes'.

"Please, please," better than yes. Way better. Still holding her hands, he pushed them over her head and began driving into her with an unrelenting linear motion. Soon, they were both grunting and moaning with delight. "Oh, that's good, Aron, so good." She pushed her breasts into the air, begging him to suck her nipples.

He was a talented guy; he could do two things at once, so he granted her mute request. Teasing, he nipped her and she bucked upward with delight. "Oh, I like that!" she moaned.

"Oh, you Doll." he praised her as he prepared to adore her other breast. "You like everything."

"I like you, Aron McCoy," she exhaled in a rush, another orgasm barreling down on her like a freight train.

"I like you, too, Libby." Too much, maybe. As she reached her peak, the tiny flutters of her pussy around his cock almost sent Aron into orbit. The sexy little sounds she made as the ecstasy rolled through her body nearly did him in. He had to hold on, just a little more, it was just too good to stop. "Come on, Baby, that's the touchdown...let's go for the extra point." He urged her on, gyrating his hips, nudging her cervix, searching to give her all the pleasure he could. The sound of his balls slapping her bottom in a jungle beat only spurred him to increase his driving speed. Never in his life had he experienced sex like this. Where had she been all of his life?

Libby was incoherent with pleasure as he kept pushing her to accept more, and she was only too glad to take what he dished out. "Sweet Lord," she whispered as she arched her back, pushing as much of her breast as she could into his mouth. The harder he sucked, the more she wanted. She knew she liked to read about sex, but she had no idea she would be such a glutton when it came to the real thing. It was Aron. He was the reason. No other man could possibly affect her this way.

His body stiffened as he neared his climax, the pleasure so intense he thought the top of his head might blow off. He mindlessly thrust into her creamy depths, her little body a welcome port to his marauding demands. Flashing, crashing bombardments of ecstasy pummeled into him with a fiery culmination. He abandoned himself to bliss, letting all of the tension of four years of discontent and celibacy flow out of him. He cried out his deliverance as he released great jets of cum deep within her.

His eyes never left her face, she was so beautiful. Closing her eyes in ecstasy, her body kept moving, milking him, clasping him, begging for more. At last, in absolute contentment, he stretched out over her, covering her, claiming her. She might not realize it, but Libby Fontaine had come to his rescue.

She held him close, stroking his back, just listening to him breathe. "Thank you Aron, that was unbelievable." Libby planted a small kiss on his shoulder. He was heavy as he lay on her, pressing her down, but she welcomed his weight. It made her feel precious and wanted—for a little while, at least.

Her words of appreciation roused him from his lethargy. "Thank you, Sweetheart. You don't know it, but you broke a drought for me. It's been four long years since I've had sex."

Four years? Libby didn't know what to think. Sheesh! Any port in a storm—all horses are grey in the dark—anybody would appeal after four years. "Four years? I can't believe an exciting man like you would ever do without sex for that long," she spoke carefully.

What the hell, Aron decided to get in touch with his feelings and open up. "My ex-wife, she did a real number on me; she burned me, spurned me and hung me up to dry. It's taken me this long to trust a woman enough to get this close." He realized what he had said. "I guess that means I trust you, Libby."

"I'm glad, Aron. I won't abuse your trust. We'll keep what happened within these walls our secret. The other boys will never know it even occurred." She brushed her lips once more over his shoulder and pushed lightly so he would let her up. "I guess I need to go to my room, the alarm clock will go off pretty early. I'm going to try and beat all of you up by at least an hour."

"Hold on." Aron stopped her from moving. "I don't intend to flaunt our relationship in front of Nathan, he's too young. But I don't care if he knows there's something going on between us...that we're seeing one another, sort of. As far as the rest of those yahoos go, I want them to know that I've roped you, hog-tied you, branded you and fenced you in my spring-fed pasture. From now on, as far as they're concerned, you belong to me."

"Tag?" she asked with a smile.

"Exactly, I don't want them getting any ideas. They know I don't ever intend to remarry, but they can't expect me to be a monk for the rest of my life, either. They'll understand. And, what we did tonight...well, I intend to do it twice a day and four times on Sunday." As he said those words, he punctuated them with kisses until she was writhing beneath him in a fit of giggles. "Sweetheart, you just gave me the best ride I could ever imagine, and I have no intention of it being a once-in-a-lifetime event." He finished off by blowing on her stomach like he would a toddler.

She flung her arms around his neck and hung on. "Thank you. That's what I wanted, too. I wasn't going to ask for it, though. I didn't want you to think I was making any demands."

Climbing from the bed, Aron pulled on his jeans. He held his shirt up for her to wear, since all she had worn to the stock tank had been a towel. That hit him sort of funny. "I can't believe you snuck out of the house in only a towel!"

"You had me all hot and bothered, all I could think about was cooling off," she admitted.

"Cover up more next time, Baby Doll. I'm the only man I want looking at your body." Before she could answer, he picked her up and stalked off.

"I can walk."

"Yes, you can, but you don't have to. You've got a big, strong man to carry you. Besides, you're barefoot; there might be grass burrs or snakes crawling around." At the word snake, she catapulted upward in his arms, almost draping herself around his neck. "Hey! Now I know what to say to make you snuggle closer. Afraid of snakes, are you?"

"Horribly, I can guess one could say—phobic." She was still shaking, just thinking about the horrible, slimy creatures.

"Good thing I'm tall then, they'd have to be on stilts to reach you up here or..." he snorted, "fall out of a tree on you." That elicited another movement in his arms, this time she burrowed into his chest and he just laughed some more. "You are so cute."

He propped her up on one knee while he opened the door, then locked it behind him. Carrying her up the stairs, he stole a few kisses on the way, just for good measure. When they passed Bess's room, she grunted and made a little motion with one foot. He just kept on going until he was behind closed doors. His bedroom door. Laying her on the bed, he set the alarm clock and went to the bathroom. Returning with a wet washcloth he wiped her off gently between the legs, then kissed her right dab on the clitoris, then moved up to kiss her right over her heart. She sighed sleepily, giving him a sweet smile. "Are you sure you want me to sleep in here with you?"

"This is where you will sleep from now on." He didn't even realize the implications of what he was saying.

"Until it's time for me to go," she added and he grunted noncommittally. That didn't sound right. Where in the hell did she think she was going?

Aron didn't even realize his mind was slowly changing.

Chapter Three

Aron knew he needed to sleep, but he couldn't resist just taking the time to look at her. She lay on her side and he was cuddled up against her back, nestled together like two sugar spoons. He had to grin though, because every once in a while she would push her little bottom back into his groin and wiggle it just a little. The first two times she did it, he thought she was awake and trying to start something sexy, but the little angel was asleep—fast asleep. That tempting little move was just her body's natural reaction to him. To him! She didn't want to sleep away from him—not touching during the night—like Sabrina. Libby was like a warm, soft kitten. She didn't mind being held and stroked. Occasionally, he would run the palm of his hand from her shoulder down her arm or from her waist over her hips, just acquainting himself with her body and its response to him. Slipping his arm under her head, he pulled her back so he could kiss her on the temple. When he did, she let out the softest, sweet, little breathy sigh. It made his heart turn over. God, was she real? Was she as sweet as she seemed to be? Could she be happy on Tebow away from the city lights and the malls? Could she be happy with one man, instead of a troupe like Sabrina required? All of these questions rolled through his head, until exhaustion allowed him to rest.

Much later, Libby pulled herself from Aron's arms. It was only four-thirty. When he pulled her back again, she rolled over and kissed him gently on the lips. "I'm getting up, you rest for another hour." With an incoherent little grunt, Aron snuggled down under the covers. Libby made her way back to Bess's room and into a warm, welcoming shower. She was sore in places that made her excited just thinking about them. Aron had loved her long and hard and she wouldn't have traded one second of it for the whole world. She knew there would come a day when this memory would get her through some dark, lonely hours.

It was so tempting to go back in and swipe a few more kisses; something told her she could probably interest him in even more if she tried. That was a heady feeling, sort of like a power trip. Sickly, little Libby Fontaine could make the great Aron McCoy sit up and beg. Well, maybe. He needed his rest, however, and she had a job to do.

The kitchen was a welcoming place. All of Tebow was warm and inviting, a huge log house with acres of exposed beams, golden oak flooring and huge stone fireplaces. It would take a lot of hours and hard work to keep this place spic and span. But, Libby would do it—gladly. But first, the cinnamon rolls. She popped them in the oven, made a strong pot of coffee and some sticky, ooey-gooey white icing for the rolls. Soon, a heavenly smell would rise to the rafters. While they were cooking, she prepared three gigantic frittatas with potatoes, eggs and sausage, and after, a pan of homemade biscuits. A noise from the pipes alerted her that someone was up—probably Aron. Quickly, she filled a tray with the rolls and the coffee and sat it at his place at the table. That way, if he wanted to take it to his office, it would be ready for him. She also ran outside, retrieved his newspaper, and placed it on the tray.

Although it was late summer, the air conditioner was turned down low. Inspiration struck and she hurried to the laundry room and found a thick fluffy navy blue towel. The oven was warm, so she rolled it up and laid it within the toasty confines for about ninety seconds. Testing it with her fingers, it was perfect. Hurrying up the stairs, she darted in his room and crept into his bathroom —prepared to lay it on his sink and then slip back out. Like a flash, without looking, she opened the door and stuck her hand in to deposit the warm offering. A hand gripped her hard, stopping any further movement. With one smooth swing, Aron pulled her in and right up against his naked, damp body. Covering her mouth, he began to feast. "What are you doing sneaking in on me, Angel? Were you warm for my form? " he joked.

'Yes, always,' she thought.

Reaching behind her, she pulled the towel and unfurled it, wrapping him in its soothing warmth. "Damn, that's nice." He enfolded her in his arms again; he would never tell her that the towel was in his way. Her body was much more welcome, but the thought of the toasty towel was one of the nicest things anybody had ever done for him. "Are you trying to spoil me?"

"I'm trying to pamper you," she said against his throat. Then, she pulled back. "My frittatas!" She yelped. "Hurry down, Aron. I have a surprise for you."

He watched her go with a smile. Suddenly the world was a much brighter place.

* * *

Aron closed his eyes in ecstasy. "These are the best damn things I have ever had in my mouth." A broad grin spread across his face. "Except for these..." He lunged for Libby, picking her up in his arms and fitting his mouth over one breast—bra, shirt and all.

"Aron, that's going to show," Libby gave a token protest. But, God it felt good. He applied suction and she felt her vagina contract in jealousy. Walking to the laundry room, with Libby wrapped around his waist, he continued to suckle at her breasts with vigor. When he sat her up on the dryer, there were big wet circles on her black T-shirt. "I don't have any more clothes down here," she whispered loudly.

Ignoring her anxiety, he fished out one of Nathan's shirts from the dryer. Turning to her, he started to divest her of the marked garment. When his eyes settled on the two wet circles, he felt his staff rise to the occasion. "Man, I've done myself in." Aron groaned as he stripped the soiled garment off, peeling her bra cups down and feasting in earnest. Libby cradled his head to her breast, thinking this had to be one of the sexiest things she could ever imagine. Laughter interrupted the romantic interlude. Not their laughter, it was coming down the stairs, and soon would come around the corner. Gently pulling the cups back up, he slipped Nathan's shirt over her head.

"What if they find us in here? What are you going to tell them?" she inquired, but he just smiled. Picking her up, he walked back into the kitchen.

When he stepped into the dining room, he planted another proprietary kiss on her lips, right in front of the whole family. The laughter stopped, the talking stopped, and you could have heard a pin drop, until Jacob sighed and said, "Well, hallelujah."

* * *

Libby made herself at home. She mopped floors; she polished banisters and washed windows, always checking the horizon for one particular wide-shouldered cowboy. Having gotten up at four-thirty, she had moved several mountains by ten-thirty, so she allowed herself to venture outside and explore. The gumbo and grilladas were on simmer, so lunch and supper were practically done. She had asked Jacob if it would be all right to make a phone call to Bonnie Drake, the friend she had told Nathan about. Bonnie wasn't home, but she had left a message explaining what she needed to know. Bonnie would call back when she had time.

Hearing a horse whinny in the barn, she took off toward the beloved structure on winged feet. Forever she would treasure the sight of big old red barns, because one had been the sight of her most precious hours—becoming Aron's lover for the first time. Peeking inside the barn, she discovered that the occupant wasn't Aron, it was Joseph.

"Hey," he greeted her. "Want to get down and dirty with me?"

"Oh, yeah," Libby answered. Excited. Not sexual excitement, just plain old 'glad to be alive' excitement.

Aron, standing two stalls over, stilled in concern. Was history repeating itself? Walking softly, he slipped up on the two—one whom he loved, the other whom he was fast beginning to worship. Instead of a risqué scene of two cheating people, he found his brother shoveling horse manure and his doll-face pushing the wheelbarrow. "Hey, Joseph, don't make the munchkin do the heavy work."

Seeing Aron, Libby launched herself at him, and he caught her easily. "I want to help. It's fun to muck around."

"What did you say?" He laughed, knowing what she said, but wanting to fluster her anyway. "It's fun to...what?"

Playfully, she punched him, then squeezed him tight. "I missed you."

Aron's heart tightened. He refused to analyze the situation; he just enjoyed it.

* * *

Libby worked with Joseph until a quarter to twelve, when she took off to make a pot of rice and pour up the iced tea. All five of the older brothers worked the ranch. Jacob had told her that Tebow ran thousands of head of prime Beefmaster and Longhorn cattle. Right now, it was time to move the weaned calves and vaccinate them for Brucellosis. It was hard work, but at least they were close enough to all come in for lunch. The gumbo was chicken, sausage and shrimp, thickened with filet and rich with Creole spices. Libby had even made some pecan pralines for dessert. The Fontaines were all from New Orleans originally, so Libby had a whole plethora of Louisiana specialties.

"My God, it smells good in this house!" Isaac shouted. He bounded in, grabbed Libby and threw her in the air. Before he could catch her, she was gone. Aron had easily stepped up and delivered her from his brother's clutches. It wasn't that he didn't trust Isaac, but Libby belonged to him. "Watch it. Be gentle with my girl." He sat her down and fixed her a bowl of gumbo himself. This was the second time he had served up her meal.

"Isaac, could you teach me how to drink and shoot pool?" Libby asked as Isaac and Aron both choked on their tea.

"What did you say?" Isaac asked her for clarification, his eyes locked with Aron's.

"Would you take me to a bar and teach me to shoot pool and maybe do tequila shots?" Innocence laced her voice, as she took small, delicate bites of the warm stew.

"Uh," was all Isaac managed to get out of his mouth, before Aron asked the obvious.

"Why in the world would you want to do something like that?" By God, if anyone was going to take her to a bar, it wouldn't be Isaac, it would be him.

"I have a lot to learn, and I only have a few months," she reminded him, knowing that they thought she meant here at Tebow—while she meant healthy.

"What do you mean?" Aron asked. "Why are you trying to cram a whole life time of living into just a few months?" Libby looked up and saw that Jacob was watching her closely. Crap! Finesse, Libby. Finesse.

"Well, my dream has always been to live on a ranch, and I'm here. I want to take advantage of the situation." She was careful at this point. "I'm also getting to do…other fun stuff." She bugged her eyes out at Aron, who grinned. "But I also want to walk on the wild side, just for a night or two. Who better to show me those things than Isaac?" It made perfect sense to Libby.

"If you want to go, I'll take you." Aron settled the matter. No argument.

Libby thought, 'we'll see'. "Are you sure you want to be seen in public with me? After all, I'm only a passing fanny." She was whispering, but every McCoy heard her.

Aron looked slightly uncomfortable. Libby was not a passing fancy or a passing fanny. "It's fancy, Libby…not fanny."

"Oh, the other made more sense, actually." She was serious. Cute, but serious.

"What do you mean, Libby?" Noah looked at his brother with censure in his eyes.

Shit! Aron hadn't wanted to deal with this in front of his brothers. "Just leave it, Noah," he ordered his brother.

Libby instantly realized she had spoken out of turn. "I'm sorry," she whispered to Aron. "I just assumed they understood what's going on."

"Understood what?" Joseph asked.

"It's okay, Aron. Joseph, I don't want you to argue." Libby tried to repair the damages.

Aron looked at his bowl, not knowing whether to feel guilty or angry. He opted for angry. "It's just none of their business, Libby," he spoke softly, but sternly.

"Sorry," she murmured. Picking up her bowl, with only a few bites missing, she placed it on the counter and turned to run up the stairs.

"What have you done?" Jacob asked his brother, point-blank.

"Libby knows the score." Aron wouldn't meet his brother's eyes.

"You told her she was just a short, sleazy affair?" Jacob had stood up and walked over to his brother's chair.

"I didn't use the word sleazy." Aron bit off every word. "I just leveled with her. I explained that I wasn't interested in anything permanent, that I had no intention of remarrying and that I couldn't make her any promises."

"Classy, Aron, classy." Disappointment dripped off every word that Jacob spoke. "Don't you know that Libby is a keeper?"

"She said that a casual affair fit right in with her plans, that she couldn't make any promises, either." Even to Aron's own ears, his words sounded pitiful.

Jacob stood there for a moment, like he wanted to say something else. After a while, he just shook his head, sat back down and ate in silence.

"Go to her, Aron." Noah implored, all of their eyes cut to their big brother, hoping he would do the right thing. "She's such a sweet, little thing. You don't want to leave her crying up there all alone. She didn't do anything wrong."

Aron didn't argue with his brothers. They were right. Throwing down his napkin, he hurried to the stairs. Trust Libby to force the truth out in the open, even when he didn't want it there. He went to his room first, after all that's where he told her she belonged. She wasn't there. Next, he checked Bess's room. It was empty, also. A tingle of panic crawled down Aron's spine.

Heading out the back door, he started searching for her. He found her in the barn, brushing down Kismet, Jacob's Appaloosa. As she groomed the big horse, she talked to him. "You are so good-looking. Did you know that?" Moving behind the big horse, Aron held his breath. Kismet was a good animal, he never kicked, but you had to be careful when you put yourself in the reach of hard, deadly hooves. "I like to brush you. It makes me feel better." Aron started to go to her, but she continued to talk, so he listened. "I made Aron angry. I didn't mean to. I would rather cut off my finger." She moved on around the big horse, until all Aron could see of her was just the top of her head. "He's a good man. If things were different…" then her voice faded to a whisper. Aron couldn't stand anymore. He walked up to Kismet, leaned over and picked her up.

Libby was startled. "Cheez-n-Crackers!" she yelped. The odd little saying almost made Aron cry. What was wrong with him? This one little woman was turning his world upside down. When she realized what was happening, she melted into him. "Don't be mad at me, I'm sorry. I'm so sorry. Aron, I was just trying to keep things light. I didn't know they would misunderstand."

When he felt dampness on his neck, he almost lost it. "I'm not mad, Libby. It's okay; it was all my fault, not yours. I can't expect you to know what's going on in my mind unless I tell you. All you knew was what I told you. Don't cry, Sweetheart. I can't stand it. Don't cry."

Trying to please him, she steeled herself and wiped her eyes. "From now on, I'll keep my mouth shut, I won't say anything. I promise. Coming between you and your brothers is the last thing I would ever want to do."

At once, Aron thought of Sabrina and the delight she took in causing trouble. She would be laughing right now, instead of tearfully begging his pardon. "Don't hold your tongue on my account. If I'm not man enough to stand by what I say, I don't need to say anything at all." He kissed the trail of tears from her cheeks.

"Can you tell me what I did wrong, so I can make sure and not do it again?" she hiccupped the question.

Blowing out a breath, Aron bit the bullet. He didn't want to hurt her any more than he already had. "They wanted what you and I have to be real. My brothers worry about me. It's their hope that I won't grow old all alone."

Leaning her head against his chest, she rubbed the material that covered his steel-hard pecs. "Tell them that it is real."

He grew very still.

She continued to speak. "For whatever time it lasts, it is real. That's no lie, not on my part anyway. I'm not pretending. I think you're the most wonderful man in the world, and I'm the luckiest woman to get to spend even one hour in your arms." He tightened his grip. "So tell them not to worry, while I'm here, I'll treasure you. And after I'm gone, you'll be so used to being loved, that you'll turn every cactus and rock upside down looking for someone to replace me."

Her words made his heart ache. He didn't really understand it, but the feeling was sharp enough to make him close his eyes in pain.

Replace her? Not a chance in hell

* * *

Everywhere he looked, Libby was there. He watched her running in the pasture with the horses and the dogs. She held her hands over her head, as if she was trying to catch the wind. That afternoon at supper, there was a jar of wildflowers sitting in the middle of the table. Libby had reheated the gumbo and at three o'clock she had carried each brother a steaming bowl. It had been her fault their lunch was disrupted and she didn't want them going hungry on her account.

Nathan had come bounding off the school bus at four o'clock and Libby met him at the bus stop. She helped him carry his books, as he munched on some warm chocolate chip cookies she had brought with her.

Aron watched from a distance. Libby was great with Nathan. She had gotten the name of a spell check program that would make Nathan's school work much easier for him. Noah had immediately ordered one and installed it on Nathan's laptop. The only problem that Aron could see was that Nathan was getting too attached to Libby too fast. He knew he could control his emotions—after all, he was a grown man, but Nathan was going to get hurt. He hated to do it, but he was going to have to speak to Libby about it.

* * *

"What are grilladas, Libby?" Nathan asked, even as he shoveled them in.

"What do they taste like?" she challenged him to analyze the flavors.

"Beef and tomatoes." She nodded that he was right. "Onions and peppers and rice."

"That's most of it, but there's also broth, raisins, spices and Worcestershire sauce."

"Wortawhat?" Nathan laughed.

"It's a sauce made from lots of spices and also anchovies."

Six sets of cutlery clattered on the plates. "Anchovies?" Joseph looked dismayed. "I don't like anchovies."

"You can't taste them, can you?"

"No."

"Eat." Aron ordered. If they ate every time Aron ordered them to do so, they would be as big as horses.

Jacob wondered if he was the only one noticing that Libby was fast becoming an essential part of the family.

* * *

"Where are you going?" Aron watched Libby head toward the back door. He was about ready to go to bed. First, he wanted to warn her about Nathan, then he wanted to make love.

"I'm going to go milk the cow."

Hell, she was serious. "At ten o'clock? She'll be asleep." Aron almost whined. He was horny.

"I promised Jacob that I would do it at three, but I took everybody a bowl of gumbo, instead." Aron walked behind her as she purposefully strode to the barn. Libby acted like she lived here. Funny, Aron didn't mind at all.

Harrumph! He thought he had been the only recipient of the afternoon gumbo treat. He wanted to be special in Libby's eyes.

"Jacob said that the cow's tits hurt if she isn't milked regularly." Libby's words hit him right between the legs. Aron knew he was probably crazy, but Libby was turning him on with her udder talk.

"It's teats on a cow, Baby, not tits."

"Same thing."

Aron groaned.

"Why are you making funny rackets?"

"Because all your talk about teats and tits is stoking a fire inside of me, that's why. My dick is all awake and excited."

"Oh," Libby's voice went soft with excitement. "I'll milk fast, okay?" She got her stool and her bucket and she settled down to do as Jacob had instructed. Grasping the teats, she began to pull, rhythmically. Bossy swished her tail and Libby ducked. But she kept pulling on those cow teats, and the milk was filling the bottom of the bucket. The more she pulled, the more Aron remembered the night that he watched her milk and knead her own puffy little nipples. He watched for a few seconds more, then he growled. "Get up, Libby. My hands are stronger, I can do it faster."

She complied, but she fussed. "It was a learning experience, Aron. I wanted to do it."

"You're killing me, Sugar. I'll teach you everything you need to know—upstairs, in my bed. All I can think about is you pulling on your own nipples in that stock tank, and how I'm going to do the same thing to you in just a minute." His words effectively cooled her anger and heated her everything else. Soon, she found that her hips were moving in concert with the sound of the streams of milk hitting the side of the bucket. As Aron finished up, Libby walked over and locked every barn door. She pulled every shutter tight and secured every entrance. Then, she walked back to where Aron was rising and behind his back, she stripped down to her altogether.

Little hands crept around his waist and began to unfasten his buckle. "What are you doing?" Aron asked hoarsely.

"Giving us both what we want," she whispered in his ear as she nipped the lobe and licked him on the neck. Soon, he was as naked as she was, and God Almighty, he was fine. Perspiration glittered on every surface, delineating every bulge and ripple. Stepping up to him, she ran her fingers up his chest, through the crisp hair and around his nipples. Then, boldly, she bent down and cupped his sac. "Is tonight cucumber night?" she asked hopefully.

"No, too excited." Aron was honest. "I have something else in mind." Showing her what he meant, he put both hands at her waist and lifted. "Wrap your legs around me, Libby-sweet." The endearment warmed her heart.

All thoughts of Nathan and his request slipped Aron's mind for the moment. Taking her hips in his hand, he lifted her until her breasts were mouth level. "I wish you had milk, I'd suck you dry."

His words rushed right to her womb. To have milk, she would have to be pregnant. With his child. Glory be! What she wouldn't give for that to be true! He swirled his tongue around each nipple. Next, he scraped his teeth over them, nipping ever so slightly. It might be wrong, but Libby liked a bit of pain with her pleasure. It made her feel so alive.

Traveling outward, he gave her little love bites all around each breast, stopping to mark her in a place that no eye but his would ever see. The deep suction made her hips move against him. "Suck my nipples. Please Aron, suck them hard." She almost smiled when she said that. How many times had she read that phrase in one of her erotic novels? And to think, now it was her turn to say it. Glory be! And when he did as she asked…the earth moved. She could swear it did. Nothing could beat the incredible sensation of a man's mouth at your breast. Womb-clinchers. That's what Aron's breast kisses were—womb-clinchers. She could feel every sharp pull all the way to her always-meant-to-be-empty womb. Despite the bite of sadness, she fell apart in his arms, quaking from one of the hardest orgasms she had ever experienced.

"Did you like that, Libby? You must have, you came so good. No woman has ever exploded for me like that, not just from my kisses on her breasts." Aron rewarded her with a few more. "You are so sweet. Now, let's get down to the business at hand."

He held her with one strong arm and guided his cock into her with the other. She was more than ready to receive him and gasped with awe as he impaled her on his thick rod. "Oh, yeah," she sighed in relief. "There is nothing in the world that feels better than you inside me." She kissed him on the neck. He was so strong. He didn't bother to back her up to the wall or anything, he just manually moved her up and down on his manhood, huffing his satisfaction with each pump. With admiration, Libby smoothed her hands over his shoulders, down his back and then watched in rapture as his beautiful butt clenched and unclenched with each thrust. He had magnificent legs and thighs. They were perfectly muscled and as thick and strong as tree trunks. There was no way she was going to be able to last very long at this rate. Why should she try? After all, God loves girls best, that's what Aron told her. As she swan-dived off the cliff of rapture, Libby wondered how in God's name would she ever live a day without him.

In. Out. In. Out. God, she tightened on the down stroke, causing the sides of her channel to provide enough friction to drive him bonkers. "Libby, I could make love to you forever. Sweetheart, you are so good." Her full faith and trust was in him. She didn't resist, or fear a fall. Never had a woman been as free with herself as Libby. She was a wonderful gift, an undeserved wonderful gift. Out of the blue, she had walked into his life and proved to him that not all women were selfish bitches; some were sweet angels with broken wings. As he pumped into her relentlessly, letting his climax overtake him, Aron decided that he wanted to know just why Libby thought a future between them wasn't possible. Not that he wanted a future with her, mind you. But, he wanted to know.

"You are an incredible lover, Aron." Libby lay on his shoulder, back in their bed.

"You speak from such vast experience," he teased.

"I speak from the standpoint of four orgasms a day, minimum." She playfully bit him on the shoulder.

"Only four?" He eyed her pointedly. "You have had at least five or six a day. I've been counting."

"I said at the minimum."

"Libby, don't let Nathan fall in love with you," he breathed, knowing his words were going to cause her pain.

He felt her little body draw up into a knot.

"What? What do you mean?" she asked so carefully.

"I can see he's getting really attached to you. It's going to hurt him when you leave." Aron didn't analyze his own feelings on the topic. He couldn't afford to.

"What do you want me to do? Be unfriendly?" Emotion was choking her words as they tried to come out of her mouth.

"Well, no." That wasn't what he meant.

"Not cook his favorite foods? I cook all of your favorite foods." Libby was trying desperately to understand. How could she please Aron, if she didn't understand?

"No, that's not what I mean, either." This wasn't easy.

"Do you not want me to help him with his homework?"

"I need you to help him. The rest of us don't always have time to." This wasn't going very well.

"What do you want me to do then, Aron?" Libby was at a loss. Did he want her to leave?

"I don't know, Libby. I just don't want him to get hurt. You're just so easy to love."

She heard his words; she wondered if he realized what he had just said. He was easy to love, also. Libby could have left him in the bed, and returned to Bess's room. His words had hurt her. Badly. She already loved Nathan, and if the truth be known, she was already deeply in love with Aron. Still, lying stiffly, she weighed her options. Leave or stay? Time was so precious and fleeing fast. She decided to stay. Brushing off the hurt from her shoulders like water off a duck's back, she let her muscles relax and fitted her body into his. "I'll remind him often that I'm only temporary. I'll mention my leaving every day. And I'll talk about Bess, and how much he misses her. Does that sound good?"

There was no resentfulness in her voice. He let out an elongated sigh of relief. Libby was so reasonable. "Yeah, Baby. That'll work just fine."

Snuggling down into his body, Libby decided there would be plenty of time to hurt later. For right now, she just wanted to love.

The next day brought trouble. Jacob had promised Libby he would teach her how to ride a horse. Aron had wanted to do it, but he got called away to a meeting with the family lawyers about the management of their parent's trust fund. The economy was hitting everything hard, so it became more of a challenge each year to invest in ventures that provided a decent return. It was also his responsibility to review all the allocations that were meted out to worthy teenagers and sick children. They also had a program to loan out money to cancer patients who wanted to further their education. Necessary business, but Jacob knew Aron hated to be away from Libby and that he would get through the day as quickly as humanly possible.

After listening to Libby plead, Jacob had relented and chosen Molly. She was the most gentle of their horses and he knew Aron would kill him if he let anything happen to Libby. Oh, Aron talked big and pretended that his time with Libby didn't matter to him, but Jacob knew they were falling in love with each other. He also knew that Libby felt like her time was limited, but Jacob was a big believer in positive thinking, faith and miracles.

From his work with the various fund raisers for cancer victims, he knew Doc Mulligan personally and when the Doc had learned that Libby was coming to work on Tebow, he had given Jacob a call himself. The Doc had cautioned Jacob about Libby taking any unnecessary risks. Doctors and science didn't really understand what threw someone who had cancer into remission, or out of it, but there were some studies which suggested that trauma to the body could shorten a remission period. Anyway, there was no use taking chances—that's why he had chosen Molly.

Jacob also knew about the test she had to return for in less than a month. Hopefully, by that time there would be good news and Aron would start coming to his senses. Libby belonged on Tebow. Libby belonged to Aron. Jacob had never been surer of anything.

"Hold the reins like this, Libs. Not too tight." He led the old horse around, adjusting Libby's feet in the stirrups. "That's right. You don't have to be afraid. Molly is as gentle as a lamb."

Libby wasn't afraid; it was just a long way to the ground. Her balance wasn't the best in the world, but this was one thing she had promised herself she would do while she still felt good. "You're doing great, Libby. I'm going to walk you over to the corral and you can just go round and round in a circle until you feel secure enough to take a real jaunt." Jacob's words were reassuring. He wouldn't let anything happen to her, not if he could help it. Smiling, she knew Jacob was fond of her, but he was also scared of Aron.

Aron cared about her. Libby knew that he did. But even if Aron changed his mind about the nature of their relationship, it still wouldn't change the reality of her disease. No, she was in remission, she reminded herself. Remission. She knew the statistics, there was no use playing like she didn't.

"Okay, take off." He set Molly and Libby into a safe little circular path. Or it would have been safe if a big ole chicken snake hadn't decided to crawl across the enclosure. Those old chicken snakes knew no fear. Aron wouldn't let any of them be killed because a) they didn't have any chickens or eggs and b) chicken snakes ate their weight in rats, regularly. Molly didn't know they were harmless, however, and Libby was deathly afraid of even a rubber snake. So when Molly shied from the snake, Jacob hollered, causing Libby to jerk. Molly bucked and Libby trying to hold on - saw the snake, and all hell broke loose. Libby came crashing down. Jacob thought that everything was all right. It was just a little fall. The snake hadn't looked back and Molly didn't step on Libby. But, Libby didn't move. He ran to her and found blood all over the back of her head. She had hit the top railing of the fence on her way down to the ground.

Chapter Four

Aron was homesick. He hadn't even been gone a whole day, but he was nearly aching with longing. And it wasn't Tebow he was homesick for, or his brothers. Aron was homesick for Libby. She had slept in his arms all night, but right now he felt as if a piece of him had been cut off. Never would he have believed that a little slip of a girl could get under his skin the way she had. He thought about her all the time.

Libby had surprised him. She fit into their life like she belonged. Nothing was too much trouble; she pitched in and helped in every project they took on. That is—she tried—Aron had a hard time trying to keep her safe. Other than her overblown fear of snakes, she was absolutely fearless. Just the other day, he had caught her trying to coax one of their biggest Beefmaster bulls into a stall so she could give him a bath. The dignified, registered, blue-blood Warpaint was not amused. Neither was Aron.

Again and again it hit him how different from Sabrina that Libby was. He had received a call from their neighbor, Clyde Cummings, an elderly widower. He had requested one of the boys to come over and help him pull a tractor loose that had got stuck in the mud. In the process of trying to free it himself, the old man had hurt his back. Libby had taken Clyde casseroles and soups for a week, until he was feeling up to par. Nothing like that would have ever even occurred to Sabrina. The nice things Libby wanted to do for others reminded Aron of his mother.

The day before yesterday, one of Aron's prize heifers had begun to calve. It was her first, and Aron was worried about her. The bull he had bred her to was big and he didn't want to risk any birth complications. Nothing would do Libby, but she get to attend the blessed event. When Aron had been forced to put his arm up the cow's birth canal and turn the calf, Libby had been right there with hot water and towels. (Not that he needed hot water and towels, but he humored her.) When they finally pulled the little bull free of his mother, Libby had thrown her arms around Aron and almost knocked him down. She had named the little bull Muffin. Now how was that going to look on the official Beefmaster Association Breeder's forms? Actually, Aron didn't care. He was so enamored of Libby that he was almost giddy.

And the sex. Lord Have Mercy, as he always said. The sex was utterly incredible. She was so sweetly responsive, eager and uninhibited—yet, at the same time, enchantingly innocent. It was a heady combination and one that kept him in a state of constant arousal.

Libby had made herself at home at Tebow and, most especially in his heart.

Although the trip had been a necessary one, Aron was glad it was almost over. Never had the road seemed so long from Austin to Kerrville. Never had he been so tempted to floor it. When he got to the last leg of the journey, the dirt road that led from the blacktop to the Tebow ranch gate had never looked so welcoming. He noticed the wildflowers that grew along the way. Had they always been so bright and colorful? Everything seemed better somehow. The air was sweeter, the food tasted better...hell, he even liked his worthless brothers more.

Mostly, he couldn't wait to hold her in his arms again. Last night's loving had only left him hungry for more. That was the way it always was. He just couldn't get enough of Libby Fontaine. Lately, he had been rethinking his future. He had made a decision. A huge decision. He wanted Libby in his life; there was no way he could face a lifetime without her. Marriage wasn't the word he would use just yet, but he was definitely thinking long-term. The only problem was convincing her of that. Something was holding her back. He knew she cared about him. There was no doubt in his mind, since she showed him every day in more ways than he could count.

Why was she so adamant that their time together was short? Yeah, he knew it had been his idea to start with. Hell, he was ready to admit he was wrong. Yet every time he put limits on the relationship, she had been only too happy to agree. Aron didn't like for her to agree so damn readily. He wanted her to fight for him. So, when he got home, the mission had changed. Win Libby Fontaine was his new goal.

When he started up the drive, he knew instantly something was wrong. It was only three o'clock and all of the brother's trucks were there. They were pulled haphazardly around the front, as if they had all been in a hurry to get out and get into the house. His heart clutched in his chest and a wave of anguished concern ripped down his back. The air left his throat, seized in his lungs like wet concrete, and the blood pulsed into his head. He didn't want anything to happen to any of his brothers, but all he could think about was—Oh God—don't let anything have happened to his precious Libby.

He drove faster as he got closer and ended up skidding his King Ranch dangerously close to the wide front verandah steps. Leaping from the cab, he took the steps three at a time. Charging through the front door, he yelled, "What the hell is wrong? Libby! Libby, answer me right now!"

"We need to call Doc Mulligan." This was Jacob's voice. A doctor? Who was Mulligan? By, God he'd find out. He followed the voices.

"Shit, Aron's here." That was Isaac.

"Like he's not going to find us?" Joseph stage whispered. "We're in the den, Aron!"

Aron barreled into the 'man-cave' as Nathan called it and saw four of his brothers kneeling by the leather sofa. And in front of them was—aw hell, it was his Libby.

In a few short moves, he had displaced brothers both left and right. Kneeling at her side, he whispered, "Libby? Sweetheart?" She was so small and pale and her eyes were closed.

"What the hell happened?" He looked directly at Jacob, pinning him with his menacing gaze.

"Aron, oh Aron." Libby opened her eyes, held out her arms, and as he took her, she began scooting over into his lap. "I am so glad you're here, Aron. So glad. I missed you so."

As Aron cuddled her close, he demanded again. "What happened to her?"

"She fell off of Molly." Jacob's voice was level and quiet.

Aron's hands at once began moving over her body.

Isaac snorted. "It's her head, Aron." Laughing, he said, "I thought I'd tell you before you felt her up in front of us."

"Hush up, Isaac. There's nothing funny about this." Aron's voice was direct and succinct. He held her with one arm, while he began parting her hair, looking for a wound.

"She hit her head on the fence when Molly threw her." Jacob sounded as guilty as he felt.

At Aron's indrawn breath, Libby feared for Molly and Jacob's safety. "It wasn't Jacob's fault, I begged him to teach me. And it wasn't Molly's fault. It was that humongous, horrible deadly snake that scared us!"

Aron fought with everything he had not to smile. This was too serious.

"It was a chicken snake." Jacob muttered dryly.

"A huge, ugly, vicious chicken snake!" Libby was very anti-serpent.

"Why aren't you in the hospital?" He looked at Libby, then at the brothers.

"No, no, no, no." She clung to his neck. "No hospital! Some of the worst days of my life have been spent in hospitals." Aron pulled her closer still, if that was even possible.

Jacob knelt by her and took her hand. Aron's eyes widened. "Libby, see the doctor, please." Jacob's voice was low, but he spoke from his heart.

"I'm fine, Jacob. I don't need to see him." Her eyes pled with him to let it drop. Knowing that Aron would take up Jacob's mantra, Libby changed her tactic. "Aron, please take me to our room. I want to lie down and I need you to hold me."

That's all it took. Aron rose and started off with her. Before he left the room, he turned and faced his brothers. "If I ever come home again and find her with so much as a paper cut, there will be hell to pay. I go off and leave the most precious thing I have in the world in your care and you let a horse throw her," he paused and a small smile escaped his lips, "and a Godzilla-sized snake nearly swallowed her whole. It will not happen again!" With that he stalked off, Libby held close to his heart.

"Yeah, this is a temporary thing. You can tell. He don't care a thing in the world about her." Isaac observed dryly.

* * *

Throwing back the covers, he carefully laid her down. "Where's your little jammies, baby?" She hadn't worn many sleeping things since the night they became lovers, but he had seen her in sleeping shorts and a tank.

"They're in my suitcase under Bess's bed."

"Baby, why are you still living out of your suitcase?" He put his hands on his hips and looked down at her pointedly.

"I don't stay in that room very much, and this is your room, so the suitcase is more mobile." He looked at her for a moment, and then walked out. Where was he going? Then, it occurred to her – he had gone to Bess's room to hunt her clothes. She held her breath, afraid he would look in the closet and find the pasteboard box that held her most precious treasure. She had purchased Aron's very first sculpture. It was a mustang stallion, head thrown back and mane blowing in the breeze. It was so good that one would think that horse would leap right off of its stand. She didn't know why she was afraid for him to find it – it's not like it would make him angry or anything. Still, a girl had to have some secrets. He didn't need to have his ego grow any bigger than it already was.

In a few seconds, he was back. Relieved he didn't find the box, she saw that he had confiscated her other belongings. He set the suitcase on the bed and took out all of her meager wardrobe. She was embarrassed for him to see how very little she had.

As Aron unpacked for Libby, his throat closed up a little bit when he counted five pairs of panties, two bras, four pairs of jeans and ten tops. This was all she had? Well, he would have to do something about that. He could see a shopping trip in their future. Turning, he emptied two of his drawers, rearranging his things to make room for hers.

"You don't have to do that Aron."

He ignored her argument. Instead, he set about undressing her. Pulling off her top and jeans, he studied her curvy little body. Kneeling by the bed, he unhooked her bra. He kissed each breast, just one time.

Next, he pulled her lacy pair of pink panties down her legs and leaned down, kissing the apex of her thighs, right above her small patch of curls. "You scared ten years off my life, Baby. Hold up your arms." Slipping the tank top over her head and the shorts up her legs, he then quickly shucked his clothes, throwing them left and right. "Scoot over." Immediately, he wrapped himself around her, holding her so tight she could barely breathe. "I can't stand the thought of anything happening to you."

"I'm fine. I promise."

"Why was Jacob so insistent that you see a doctor?" Aron carefully enunciated every word, indicating that he expected an answer.

She had no intention of ever lying to him; she would just water down her answer so it was harmless. "I used to have a slight medical condition."

"What kind of medical condition?" Aron rose up, capturing her hands and holding them over her head, effectively immobilizing her. "And I expect a straight answer, Libby."

"It was a blood disorder, but I am perfectly healthy, right now." God, let me be telling him the truth, she prayed.

"A blood disorder...Baby, what does that mean?" Aron began kissing her face, murmuring little endearments against her skin.

"It means I'm fine, I promise." God help her if she was lying. "Aron?" It was time to pull out the big guns. "Aron, can I kiss your winkie?"

A man could swell from an insult, he was proving it. "ELIZABETH, I DO NOT HAVE A WINKIE!"

Libby giggled so hard she snorted. Before she could catch her breath, he was laughing along with her. "Okay, okay. Let me try again. Aron McCoy, sir. May I kiss your Gargantuan Purple Helmeted Warrior?"

"That's more like it, and yes you may." He grinned at her mischievous smile. Then, his blood pressure started to rise. The sexiest woman he had ever been lucky enough to touch had just asked permission to give him a blowjob. "Are you sure you feel like it? You don't have to. I'd be happy just holding you close all night."

"Lose the shorts." She sat up, anxious to get his mind off blood disorders. "Now, you realize I've never actually done this before." All of a sudden she was unsure.

"Anything you do to me will feel incredible. The excitement comes not from the act, but more from who is touching me." He pulled down his shorts, his Johnson was already eight inches long and five inches around, and it wanted whatever Libby wanted to give him. "Where do you want me?" Aron was giving her control.

"I want to sit on the bed and you stand between my legs." He got up off the bed, and turned to face her. She sat in front of him, her luscious hair falling in waves around her shoulders. Spreading her legs, she held out her hand. "Come to me, Baby."

Excitement was making his toes curl. "You know I won't last long this way."

"You won't have to, Aron. This is going to excite me as much as it will you." He stood still, fully at her mercy. Taking a deep breath, she eyed her prey. "My mouth is watering just looking at you, Aron. My lands, you are beautiful." Her first move surprised him. Instead of going right for his dick, she cradled his balls. Gently massaging them, she tested their weight.

"Ohhh, Little One, you have talented hands." Closing his eyes, he pushed his hips toward her, begging for more. She didn't let him down. Libby took his penis in her hands, as if she were about to say a prayer, her palms flat, fingers meeting at the base. Pulling him close, she kissed it gently, putting her mouth over the head. Aron jerked in her hands. Using the tips of her fingers, she began to massage him, putting one fist over the other she twisted up and over Aron's cock, touching the tip of her tongue to the little open slit every time it was exposed. Soon Aron was shaking, just waiting for the gentle, wet touch. His hips began to buck, so she gave in to what she wanted. Slipping her lips over the top, she opened her throat and accepted as much of him into her mouth as she could. "God, Libby. I thought you said you've never done this before." It was difficult for Libby to be still, so she just matched the movement of her hips with her mouth. "Suck me, suck me, Libby." Tightening her lips, she provided as much suction and heat as she could. "Oh, yeah, that's it. You're so good," he praised her.

Letting go with her hands, she accepted another half inch down her throat and drew him closer. She kneaded his tight butt, loving the feel of all that incredible muscle. Emotion welled up in her heart and she groaned her pleasure. The vibration of her throat caused Aron to buck forward. Removing her hands from his hips, she grabbed his fingers and moved them to the back of her head. Slipping her mouth off for the slightest second, she requested, "You take control."

It was music to his ears. She was wet, tight, hot and exciting as all get out. Twisting her hair around one hand, he held her at his mercy. Aron was so excited that it was hard to be careful, but he refused to hurt her. Still, her mouth was absolute heaven and getting to pump into her at will was beyond compare. His dick swelled to almost bursting, his blood ringing in his ears. Her mouth was so sweet. Her little tongue was never still; it put as much pressure on him as her lips did. A frantic frenzy took over. He held her face still and pumped deep. Angling her head, he nudged his length down her throat. Bless her heart, she didn't gag even once. She opened herself up to him and provided him a place to play. Swallowing, she heightened his pleasure ten-fold. He would bet his life this was pure instinct on her part. But God, she had no idea how it made him feel. "Swallow again, Precious. That was wild." She did as he asked. Suddenly, she made her lips impossibly tight, sending him over the edge. "Damn! Baby! Do you want me to pull out or can you take it?" He was asking if she would swallow. He waited for a sign from her. Gritting his teeth, he held back until she clasped his hips again, holding him in place, letting him know she intended to accept his release into her mouth. "Lord Have Mercy," he mumbled. She was relentless, bearing down with the sweetest tension. Bellowing aloud, he shot his essence down her throat and she accepted it like she was born to it.

Afterward, she was reluctant to let him go, moving her tongue against him even in his spent state. Bending over, he took her face in his hands and as he pulled out of her mouth, he placed his lips over hers, showing her how grateful he was for the gift she had given him.

Pushing her back, he followed her over. "You are perfection, did you know that?" Rolling to her side, she snuggled up to him.

"I did pretty well for my first time, huh?" She nudged her face against him, petting him like a contented cat.

"There is no one like you, Libby. No one even comes close."

Moving against him again, he realized she was in need. "What do you want, Doll? I'll do anything, all you have to do is ask."

"Will you put your knee up against me, between my legs, and let me ride? I've fantasized about doing that." Just hearing the words come out of her mouth made his cock twitch back to life.

"Gladly, Doll. Pleasing you is the greatest pleasure I could ever have." He positioned himself to accommodate her request, pressing his knee between her thighs.

"Wait, Aron. I'm already wet. Let me change and put on something clean. You don't want to get my stuff all over your leg." She got up off the bed and went to dig in the drawer where he put her underwear. His mouth dropped. Was she serious?

"Come back here, Libby." She stopped to see what was wrong. "Pull off your panties, Baby. I want to feel all of you—wet and wild— right against my skin. Feeling how excited you are is like a badge of honor for me; it's my way of knowing I'm doing something right." He held his hand out to her.

"Are you sure?" She was serious.

"Honey, if you leave your sweet cream on my thigh, all it'll do is please the hell out of me." Flashing him a little smile, she hung her thumbs in the waist band of her sleep shorts and pulled down, revealing his private treasure. Already he was swelling, but first he would give her what she asked for and then he'd give her what she needed. Taking her by the waist he lifted her, and as she came over him, he set her down on his thick thigh, fitting the hard muscle right against her swollen center.

"Aron, that feels so good." He bent his leg and let her mold her body to his. Wrapping both her legs around one of his, she held on for dear life and began to pull her clitoris back and forth over his hair-roughened thigh. Laying her head on his shoulder, she let herself go.

Aron was absolutely enchanted. He'd never seen anything so erotic in his life. Her mouth-watering, heart-shaped bottom was bobbing up and down and her incredible breasts were scrubbing up and down on his chest revving his engines to the highest gear. Unable to stop himself, he plucked at her nipples, causing her to moan. She humped his leg and honest to God he thought he would die. "Libby, you are fuckin' miracle."

With glazed eyes, she looked at him – she was in a frenzy. "This is wonderful, Aron – but please tell me you're hard. I need you so badly I could cry."

With a triumphant shout, he picked her up and moved her down to his cock which was standing up straight – ready, willing and able. "Take me, Libby. Rise up and let me in."

Heated and aroused, she reached between her legs and closed her fist around his fully engorged cock. Holding steady, she eased down, taking him inside of her. "Oh, God, Aron. You are so big. You fill me up so good." Libby shivered with absolute delight as she lowered herself fully until she was completely impaled.

Aron sighed. There was no greater pleasure in the world than working his way into her warm welcoming pussy, savoring the feel of her taut inner muscles parting just for him. "You've been wanting to take a ride—now's your chance. Give me your hands, Sweetheart." She did, her eyes wide with excitement, their radiant flames warming him deep inside.

"I don't know how to move, you've got to help me." Before when they made love, Aron was always in control. Now that she had the reins, she wanted to do it right.

"My pleasure, Doll, my pleasure." Aron was so ready to rock and roll, that it took every ounce of control he had to take his time with her. This was about Libby, damn it. "You don't have to bounce up and down. It feels better for both of us if you rock gently back and forth to begin with." He felt her move, Holy Mother of God, she was sweet, like pure warm liquid velvet. "Yeah, just like that. See Baby, you wanted to ride something, now you are. You're too precious to risk on a real horse, so I'll just let you ride my rocking horse."

If it hadn't felt so good, she would've laughed at him, but her clit was having a party on his pelvic bone as she rode herself to heaven and back. Before long, she sped up, her intimate strokes settling into a perfectly delicious pace.

Her breasts were bouncing sweetly and his hands couldn't stay away. Aron decided to offer his support, so he cupped her tits, massaging her sensitive rosy nipples as she gyrated and undulated on his stiff cock. Libby dug her nails into his thigh in reaction.

For a while, he let her have her fun. If he wasn't about to explode – he could have watched her rapturous expression all day. Soon, however, it began to get serious for him. He was going to cum, regardless. Wanting Libby to finish first, he decided to help out a little. She made it easy. All he had to do was swirl his fingers around her clit and tell her what he wanted. She was so in tune to him, it was scary. "I need you to come, Doll. You've driven me mad with desire and I can't hold out much longer. And I refuse to come before my Libby finds your pleasure." That he was able to have a semi-coherent conversation was a miracle. Before he could get his explanation finished, the tiny contractions began. "That's my girl! Ah, Libby, you are a goddess." She put her hands on his rippled stomach and ground down on him. Her pussy gripped his cock, gripped it and squeezed like a fist. Letting go, he clutched her by the hips and lifted her whole body a couple of inches in the air. Aron drove into her with thrusting, staccato like strokes. "Yes! Yes!" he shouted, his own climax overtaking him. Every neuron in his spinal column sizzled with satisfaction.

Libby watched him come, the pleasure manifesting itself on his face. He was a beautiful sight, arching his back, forcing that mile-wide chest up so she could caress and knead it as he convulsed beneath her. His cock was shooting ropes of cum deep within her. She wanted to memorize every sensation, every feeling, every thought. His muscles strained, his neck bowed, his eyes shut, God, he even began to whisper her name in a prayer like litany. It was just too much. "Aron! It's starting again, I just came and now – oh Lord – I'm coming again."

In his mindless euphoria, he was aware she held her own breasts, pulling at the nipples, doubling her pleasure, prolonging the joy. Overwhelmed, he sat up and pulled her close, shaking with the sweetest release he had ever experienced.

Libby held his head, wiped the sweat from his brow, pushed his hair back and kissed him right between the eyes. "There is no one like you.

What did I ever do to deserve the gift of these precious days with you? Until my dying day, I will treasure every second I've spent in your arms." Hugging him close, she caressed him until he calmed.

"Libby, you've taken me by surprise. I never expected to find anyone like you." Reverently, he framed her face and touched their lips together in a tender kiss. He lay back, pulling her down with him. Still intimately joined, she lay on his chest, mindlessly rubbing her fingers over his upper arm. Aron wanted to say more, but when he looked down – his baby was fast asleep.

The next morning Libby said she felt as good as new. She was still getting up at least an hour before everybody else and they were all becoming fat and happy from her exquisite cooking. Aron had woken up with a whole host of things he wanted to do. Primarily, he intended to learn as much about Miss Fontaine as possible. He was going to escort her out on the town and take her camping. In Aron's own cowboy way, he planned on wooing Libby.

* * *

Libby was worried to death. Something was wrong...Aron had changed. As she put together Nathan's brown bag lunch, she weighed her options. What she wanted, she couldn't have. She wanted Aron. She wanted a future. Libby wanted to live on Tebow and get pregnant with Aron's babies. Libby wanted to live.

Okay, so she hadn't been given a death sentence. After all, she was in remission. In three weeks she would have a check-up, and if all still looked good, well then—who was to say that she wouldn't live to be eighty? Holding on to the cabinet door, she pinched the wood so tightly she wouldn't have been surprised to find marks left from her fingers.

"Libby?" It was Nathan. "Do you have some lunch for me?"

Behind Nathan came Aron and Jacob. They were headed to a cattle auction. Aron had asked her to go along, but she had promised herself that today would be the day she made a detailed grocery list. The pantry and freezer were beginning to need refilling. Next, she would have to find out the logistics of how she would get there and how to pay for the food. It hurt Libby to have to ask those questions; she wished more than anything that these men were her family, and that taking care of them was more than just her job.

Seeing Aron reminded Libby that she needed to talk to Nathan at the first opportunity and remind him of her temporary status. Handing Nathan his lunch, she answered, "I sure do, Big Man. Ham and cheese sandwiches, apple chips and lemon bars. Does that sound like something you'd like?" Nathan stepped forward and clasped her around the waist.

"Thanks Libs." He had heard Aron call her that. "And thanks for helping me with the paper last night. You are really smart. I didn't know there were so many different Indian tribes living in Texas so long ago. And that program saved my life, it made everything a lot easier. I don't know what we ever did before you came along."

Returning his hug, she looked guiltily at the men watching her. Why did she feel like she was doing something wrong? Trying to do as Aron asked, she cleared her throat and began. "You did just fine before I came. Miss Bess took great care of you and when I'm gone, she'll be right here taking good care of you again. You know I don't want to leave, but I have to. This is your home and Bess's. I'm just merely passing through." Patting Nathan on the back, she looked up at Aron with a small smile and an expectant look, seeking his approval. She was trying to do as he asked.

Aron excused himself from his brother and whacked Nathan on the shoulder as he left to catch the bus. His baby was looking at him with the saddest eyes. He knew she was just doing as he had asked; she was trying to remind Nathan that her time on Tebow would soon draw to a close.

Well, to hell with that!

He should never have asked her to distance herself from any of them. He was a fool, and it was time this fool set things straight. She had turned away from him and was watching Nathan walk toward the road. He slipped up behind her and caught her back against him. She melted into him like butter on toast.

"Did I please you?"

Turning her in his arms, he pushed her back and back until he had her cornered in the butler's pantry. "You have pleased me in countless ways, Libby: the heat of your kisses pleases me, the feel of your pebbled nipple on my tongue pleases me, and the grip of your pussy around my aching cock pleases me. I'd say everything about you pleases the hell out of me." He held her flat against the wall, both of her hands captive in one of his. Touching his forehead to hers, he pinned her down. "But, I find that what you did this morning, telling Nathan we would get along just fine without you – that pleased me not at all." Aron growled out the last words.

Straining to read his expression, Libby was confused. "I did as you asked, Aron. I reminded Nathan I was leaving, and that Bess would be back where she belonged."

"I know you did as I asked, but you didn't take one thing into consideration." He began to rain peppery little kisses all over her face, attempting to convey to her how much he cherished her.

"What's that?" He had magical kisses. Libby arched her neck, giving him full access to her neck, and when he dipped down to the open vee of her T-shirt, she shamelessly thrust her breasts against him, begging for him to take his petting to the next level.

Aron laid his head on her shoulder, allowing her to lower her hands, and she immediately settled them around his waist. He said nothing for a few moments, and then he spoke softly, "You didn't take into consideration that I am a fool, I can't stand the thought of you leaving. Sweetheart, I don't ever want you to leave." Dropping to his knees, he nudged her shirt up with his nose and he kissed her soft, flat belly.

Libby was shaking. Cradling his head in her hands, she turned his face up to look at her. "Aron, it's okay. I know Bess is coming back, and I know there's no legitimate place for me here."

"You're wrong. There is a place for you here. In my home, in my room, in my bed, but most importantly...in my heart." Damn! He was about to make a declaration in the crappin pantry. Without asking, he picked her up and headed for the stairs.

"Aron, it's not even eight o'clock. We just got up, and you have to leave for an auction in less than an hour." Not that she was complaining, she would never, ever turn down a chance to love on Aron.

"I realize that, but I forgot to do something last night." Thank goodness his door was open, so he didn't want to slow down long enough to open it, but he did kick it closed. "I can work wonders in an hour."

"Yes, you can," she agreed with him. "You are a master of the erotic experience, a connoisseur of caresses, an oracle of orgasms..." Aron tackled her and for a few wonderful moments, they wrestled around on the bed. "It's not fair..." Libby gasped.

Aron straddled her, holding her immobile. "What's not fair?" he queried, smiling like the devil he was.

"You're so much bigger than me, I don't have a chance." Her mouth puckered into a pout, which he kissed away.

"You like me bigger," he teased, his eyes alight with mischief, rubbing his groin against her privates.

"Well, true." He had her full attention. Lord, he was an irresistible force.

Aron sobered, climbing off and stretching out beside her. "You like me bigger, because I can take care of you."

She stared into his eyes; they were the color of a summer storm. "I've enjoyed that sensation, yes." She couldn't bring herself to say the words which would lay claim to him. She didn't have any right to expect his care. She was temporary.

"Let me take care of you now, Libby." Slowly he undressed her, kissing each exposed area tenderly before moving on. Next, he shed his own clothing. No words were necessary. He knew she wanted the same thing he did.

Sitting up on the edge of the bed, he pulled her into his lap. He placed her smooth back to his front. Libby nestled into his lap snuggly, with a wiggle. His organ was distended to such a degree, that when she opened her legs, he slid right in between them, not entering her, but cradled securely within the folds of her labia so that her clitoris was riding high on the head of his cock. She could look between her legs and see the weeping tip. "This feels good."

She reached down and caressed him and he groaned. "Hold on, don't get ahead of me here. You know how you affect me." Opening the drawer of his nightstand he took out a little vial of oil.

"What's that?" Curiosity got the best of her.

"Massage oil," his voice was husky with desire.

"What are you going to massage?"

"You."

"Oh." Her breath hitched in response.

He rubbed the oil on his hands. A little earthquake of excitement shivered up her spine. He felt the tremble, and he chuckled, knowing she was dying of anticipation.

"I smell chocolate."

"Mmmmmmm, love chocolate, it's my favorite flavor." He licked the side of her neck and she quivered. "No, I take that back—it used to be my favorite flavor. Now it's number two." Nipping her shoulder blade, he clarified, "You're my number one flavor. But to be specific, the scent I'm about to massage into your soft skin is Chocolate Crème Brule."

"Sounds yummy." Actually, it did. Several places on her body were calling for a taste.

He rubbed the oil into his hands and she practically shouted hallelujah when he cupped her breasts. From this angle all she could do was lay back and enjoy. Dang! There were so many things to enjoy; she decided to count the ways. One, his chest felt glorious against her back as she slowly moved from left to right and back again. Two, those talented hands were shaping and kneading her breasts as if they were molding clay and he was creating a masterpiece. Third, her vagina was opening like a night blooming flower, aching to be claimed and filled. "Aron, it's too much."

"No, it's not." He proceeded to love her from head to toe. Sinking his teeth into her neck, he held her still like a stallion would a mare. With his forefingers, he traced circles around her nipples – wide, concentric circles that shrunk with each lap.

"Please, please." she begged. If he didn't touch her nipples, she thought she just might scream. The warmth of his hands and her body combined to heat the fragrance so that the chocolate smelled like hot fudge. "Nipples, Aron, please pinch my nipples,"

"My Libby's a little Wild-woman," he growled approvingly. He rewarded her boldness. Taking both nipples between his fingers, he rolled them, arousing her to frantic heights. Twisting her head back, she blindly sought his lips. Aron feasted at her mouth, sucking on her tongue, as he manipulated her breasts into trembling mounds of passion. Her cream was anointing his cock, proclaiming a desperate need for his brand of possession.

In a fever-pitch, she was totally uninhibited, abandoning all pretense of propriety. "I've got to have you, Aron. Please, come inside me – I'm so empty." She raised her hips in supplication. "Take me, Sweetheart, don't make me wait. I need you so." Libby was pleading, begging for his love.

Aron lifted her, his hardness seeking her heat like a moth to a flame. She opened to him, her vulva swollen and flushed a deep rose. With a moan of relief, her body stretched to receive the full length and breadth of his pulsating staff. Almost immediately she flew apart, he literally had to hold on tight to keep her from catapulting out of his arms. She shook, her body shuddering with intense spasms. Aron was amazed at her ability to give herself over to him, taking whatever he offered and giving him more than he ever dreamed he could demand. "That's my good girl. That's my baby."

Her unmitigated enthusiasm was a powerful aphrodisiac. Aron became a mad man, his hips pistoning in and out of her like an out of control jack-hammer. Laying back, flat on the bed, he pulled Libby back with him. "Stay with me, Cowgirl," he encouraged as he bent his knees to give her body something to push down against. Using her breasts as the world's most glorious hand-holds, he moved her up and down on his shaft, her whole body sliding up and down the full length of his torso. Wrapping a leg over each of his, she moved in tandem with him until he bellowed his fulfillment. Shivers and jerks of pure pleasure made her whole body quiver in response to his powerful climax. They lay quietly for a time, until he coaxed her to turn over on top of him. There was something he had to say, and there was no better time than the present. "Libby, look at me."

She was wonderfully sated, but lifted her eyes to meet his. Unable to resist, she shifted upward to place her lips softly on his. One sweet heartbeat later, she whispered, "You have made me so happy, Aron."

"Libby," he began, but she interrupted him.
"Aron, I want to have a few adventures. Would it make you mad if Joseph taught me how to sky dive?"

Chapter Five

"What?" he yelled so loud, he almost knocked her out of bed. He had been about to proclaim his undying love and she was thinking of ways to kill herself.

"He assures me it will be perfectly safe." She was biting that lower lip with those little pearly white teeth and looking like she was anticipating an ice cream cone.

"Libby..."

"And, I know you nixed the idea at first, but tonight—I'd really like to ride Isaac's motorcycle with him to the pool hall. He's going to teach me how to play snooker." She was lying right on top of him, her chin held up in her hands, her eyes wide open and twinkling. If she had asked him for the deed to Tebow right then, he would have signed it over. God, what he wouldn't do for her.

"Why are you so determined to live like there's no tomorrow?"

His innocent question ripped a hole in Libby's heart.

"None of us are promised tomorrow, Aron. I want to live today, just in case there is no tomorrow. But, rest assured. All of this other stuff is just fluff. I want to do it, don't get me wrong. I have a battle to fight and an enemy to face, so I want to enjoy my life now—today." Taking his face in her hands, she held him still, so there was no chance he could miss what she had to say. "But, what you have given me—the gift of you—puts the rest of it to shame." With one last smacking kiss, she jumped up and started to hurriedly redress. He lay there, sort of numb struck. What had happened? He had been about to declare his unending devotion and now the love of his life was off to bar-hop and throw herself out of an airplane.

"Libby, I nearly had an apoplectic fit when you took a baby spill off a fourteen year old nag."

She didn't do it often, so she didn't do it well, but what the hay! Libby proceeded to pout. Her bottom lip snuck out from her top lip, just a tiny fraction, and she made her eyes round and sad.

It didn't take much...he couldn't stand it. "Come here." He held out his arms. The fact that he was still outstandingly naked, just added to the hug appeal. She bounded across the room to him. Catching her, he held her close.

"I'll be careful, I promise."

"I have conditions." He rubbed her back, wishing he could tie her to the bed and keep her there. That flash of fantasy almost made him forget what he was about to say. Libby...tied to a bed...

"What conditions?" She didn't sound resentful at all. In fact, she sounded pleased that he cared enough to demand them. She spoke from the comfort of his lap, her head resting on his wide shoulder.

"You jump attached to Joseph." He was serious about that part. "And I wait at the landing spot with a truck load of mattresses."

He felt her body vibrate with giggles against his chest. "What else?"

"You can ride Isaac's motorcycle if you wear a helmet, and if he doesn't drive any faster than thirty-five miles an hour." Her little fist tapped him lightly on the chest.

"Okay, forty-five." Hey, he was being generous here.

"Any more?"

"Yes, he can teach you to play snooker. But no tequila shots and I will come and check on you at some point in the evening."

Big sigh. "All right, Mother." Frankly, it felt fabulous to be cherished. God, how she would enjoy a lifetime of his brand of loving.

Something large and hard poked her in the thigh. "I am not your mother."

"No kidding."

* * *

Aron tried to put the pieces together. He had a Herculean task on his hands. Winning the hand of the exquisite Libby Fontaine was going to require dedication and concentration.

Something was not right. Aron decided he would corner her and make her talk about herself. No, he had to be more subtle than that.

"Do you like that bull?" Jacob pointed to the spotted longhorn standing on the auction block, ready to be bought by the highest bidder.

Shit! He had lost track of where he was, much less what was for sale. "What do you think?" Aron put the monkey back on his brother's back.

"You're not paying a bit of attention are you?" Jacob knew Aron.

"No, I'm worrying about Libby." He really was. She was hiding something monumental from him, and he didn't know why.

"What about Libby?" He forgot to hide the concern in his voice. Aron picked up on it right away.

"You know something, don't you, you scoundrel?" Why was it that Jacob was closer in some ways to his lover than he was?

"What I know, I can't tell." At least Jacob was honest. And hard-headed.

"If you keep information from me, and I end up losing her—I'll never forgive you." Aron laid his cards on the table.

Jacob let out a tortured breath. "Let me think about it."

"Don't wait too long." Aron admonished him.

"You're a smart guy," Jacob encouraged him. "See if you can figure it out."

While Jacob bought and sold cattle, Aron tried to put two and two together. It bothered him how little he knew about Libby. To know her body so intimately, he knew very little about her life. One thing was for certain, he intended to rectify the situation.

Going back to the day she fell off the horse, he remembered Jacob saying the name of a doctor. What was it? Montgomery? No. Monroe? No. Mulligan, yeah. Mulligan. He took a pen out of his pocket and wrote the name on the back of his auction program. He saw Jacob take note of his remembrance.

What else? Oh, her innocence—Libby had said that she hadn't had a normal life up to this point. Something about a family problem. Whatever it was, it had kept her from interacting with men to any degree. He hated to think about her having problems, but he couldn't regret that he had been the sole recipient of all the incredible passion Libby had stored up.

Third, she'd said she was going to have to fight a battle and face an enemy. Damn! That didn't sound good. Aron wondered if she was in some type of trouble. Didn't she know that he'd move heaven and earth to help her? Not that he had told her in so many words, but right now, she didn't act like she wanted to hear any talk of forever. And forever was exactly what Aron wanted to nail down.

"Are you ready to go?" Aron looked up and the auction was over. Crap! He had missed it all.

"Yeah, I guess so. Did we do good?" Actually, he didn't really care a whole hell of a lot—one way or the other.

"Excellent. How about you, got a handle on Libby, yet?"

"Hell, no." But, he was working on it.

"Keep plugging at it, you'll figure it out."

* * *

It was hard to stand by and watch Libby ride off on the back of Isaac's hog. He had insisted she wear a helmet and reminded her that he would be dropping into Shorty's at some point during the evening. Standing until he couldn't see the dust from the motorcycle, he slowly turned to walk back to the now empty feeling house. With a heavy heart, he realized this was just a small taste of how it would be if Libby were really gone. Not going to happen—he promised himself that. A step or two later, his cell phone rang. It was Trahan, the PI he called upon from time to time about various things.

"McCoy."

"Aron, I have a small lead on the buyer of that bronze you've been trying to track down."

"Tell me." He still wanted to know, but oddly, it wasn't as high of a priority as it used to be.

"The other artist who was exhibiting with you at the time was a woman. I think her name was Martinez. Anyway, I found her and I questioned her about that day, and she recalled the woman who bought 'Freedom'."

"A woman? That's not much to go on."

"The reason it sticks out in Martinez' mind was that she had seen the buyer before. She didn't recall a name, but she does remember a story on the news about the woman having had cancer and there was a benefit of some kind for her medical bills."

"So, this woman spent hard earned money that people donated to her on a bronze when she didn't have enough to pay her doctor and hospital bills?"

"Doesn't sound right, does it?"

"No, it doesn't. I guess it's a start, but I don't know how I can use the information."

"Thought you'd want to know."

"Thanks."

* * *

Libby was fascinated by the pool hall. She hadn't dressed up, since she didn't have anything to dress up in. But, she was definitely having a good time. The music was loud and very country. Several cowboys had asked her to dance, and she had taken two up on it. Both times, either Isaac or Jacob had cut in when they felt the man was taking liberties. She hadn't felt threatened at any time, but she appreciated the McCoy brothers' concern. It wasn't like they were cramping her style. Libby wasn't there to find a man—she had one. At least, she was claiming him. Not that they were dating or anything. He had never said anything about taking her anywhere. Still, she would rather be with him—anywhere— than with anyone else in the world.

Still and all, like her mom used to say, this place was far better than she had expected. She was here for the experience, and so far, she wasn't disappointed.

Aron could have brought her, but she knew he would have positioned her at his side and under his arm all night and she wouldn't have gotten a taste for the true atmosphere of the place. With the other two McCoys along, Libby could go out on a limb and not fear falling off.

The billiards game was a blast. Isaac taught her how to hold a cue stick and how to rack up the balls. He had even held her close while she learned the proper way to make a shot. There had been no flirting; all the brothers treated her with great care and the utmost respect. They knew who she belonged to – at least for now.

Aron had put his foot down about the tequila shots, so Libby had opted for wine coolers instead. They were really, really, really good. This was her first venture into the world of adult beverages. Every time Jacob and Isaac walked off, Libby ordered another. She hoped they brought enough money to pay her bar tab. She should have felt bad, but right now—actually—she was feeling pretty good.

There were about a dozen men in the place who couldn't keep their eyes off of her. They watched her sway and twirl, right by herself. She had no idea how sexy she was, or that Isaac and Jacob had walked around and informed all of the drooling men she was off limits. They made it clear she was Tebow property, belonging to the big man himself, Aron McCoy. No, Libby didn't have a clue. She was in her own little world. Dancing right by herself, minding her own business. With her wine coolers.

Isaac who was on Libby-patrol, had to take a bathroom break. And while he was gone a group of new men came in. When Jacob noticed, there were several wranglers circling her like Mako sharks. He swooped in and gathered her close. "How many of those drinks have you had, Cutie?"

"Eight." Libby answered with an absolutely straight face.

"Eight!" Jacob exclaimed. "Shorty, why in the hell did you let her have eight wine coolers?" He shouted across the bar.

Shorty grinned, but yelled back. "There's not much alcohol in a wine cooler."

"There is when you've had eight of 'em," he grumbled under his breath. Hell! Aron was going to kill them all.

"Hello, Lover." A sultry voice purred next to Jacob's ear. "Care to introduce me to your tipsy little friend?" Venom dripped off every word.

Jacob's stomach turned over as he recognized Aron's ex-wife's voice—Sabrina. If he hated anybody in the world, it was this woman. "I was never your lover, Bitch." Jacob bit the words out at her. He hadn't forgiven her, nor would he—ever.

His attitude sobered Libby to a degree. "Jacob?" she called his name in confusion.

"It's okay, Libby. This is nobody you need to be concerned with." He held her protectively to his side, as if Sabrina was a disease that would rub off on her.

"She'd best be concerned." Sabrina draped a skinny arm around Jacob's neck. She was over-made up, under dressed, and her perfume had been applied with a heavy hand. "I didn't have my fill of you. She just might have reason to be jealous."

Sabrina's tongue might be dripping sugar, but her eyes were like poisonous darts. These McCoy men owed her—big time. She had been cheated out of a fortune.

"I'm not with Jacob," Libby informed her. "I'm with Aron." Jacob was surprised Libby would publicly claim Aron. He glared at her, pleasantly surprised.

"Interesting!" the woman exclaimed. "Jacob, does she know who I am?"

"Who are you?" Libby asked, just drunk enough to care.

"I'm Sabrina McCoy, Aron's wife."

The smooth answer made Libby's skin crawl. Her eyes narrowed. "No, you're not. You're divorced. You weren't a good wife." Libby repeated things well.

"Aron wasn't much of a husband. And being his wife wasn't much of a life."

Her flip answer made Libby's blood boil. "Anyone lucky enough to be married to Aron McCoy should get down on their hands and knees and thank the Lord for their blessings." This was a long speech for an inebriated woman.

"The only blessing about living at Tebow was the smorgasbord of gorgeous McCoy men to sample. Jacob here, was one tasty morsel." She leered at Jacob. About that time Isaac walked up. "And here's the tastiest one of them all." Isaac looked grim, and his mouth was twisted as if he had bit into something bitter.

"You didn't sleep with Aron's brothers." Libby was furious, her beautiful features filled with anger.

"I didn't?" Sabrina teased Libby. "And how would you know?"

"I know them. And they wouldn't betray their brother that way." She was emphatic in her support of the McCoy brothers.

"Where is your lover, if that is what he is? And why are you here with Jacob and Isaac if you belong to Aron? Are you following in my footsteps, Sweetie?"

The woman was beautiful. Libby could see why Aron would have been attracted to her. And she was dressed to kill. Libby felt plain and out of place next to her. "That's none of your business," Libby flared. "But I can promise you that Aron's brothers treat me with the greatest respect."

"How about the younger one? Nathan, was it? Is he still as much of a stupid retard as he used to be? Wasn't he born that way? Was it a birth complication or something?" Sabrina stood there looking smug while she lambasted every member of the family that Libby loved so well.

"He has dyslexia, you baboon. I've heard enough from you! That's it." Libby handed her wine cooler to Isaac. "You're going down, you loud-mouthed Jezebel!" Without warning, Libby propelled herself right on top of Sabrina Jones—ex-McCoy. Before Sabrina could get her bearings, Libby had knocked her into a table filled with glasses and beer. Then into another table. Crashes of glass and gasps of amusement echoed through the bar. And it wasn't over.

"Catfight!"

Libby would not give up. Every time Sabrina would try and get away, Libby would get right in her face again. Isaac held Jacob back, both of them fascinated at the little thing's determination. When she picked up a chair to bash over Sabrina's head, Jacob's common sense finally won out and he intervened. Shorty was not happy. He was on the phone and naming names. Jacob held Libby off the ground while she kicked and wiggled to get down and back into the fight. "If I ever see you anywhere near a member of the McCoy family again, I'll take you apart with my bare hands. I'll rip your hair to smithereens. I'll break both your knee caps and stomp your toes…" The threats trailed off as Libby was carted out of the bar to ensure the safety of the clientele. Isaac followed at a safe distance.

Isaac was troubled to see that Sabrina had landed a blow or two. There were bruises and scrapes on Libby's arms and a dark, fist-shaped mark was starting to show on her left jaw.

"You have got to come and get them, Deputy; I'm tired of these McCoys tearing up my place." Shorty called on his cell phone.

"Shit, Jacob. We're about to get arrested," Isaac whispered. He couldn't afford to spend any more time in jail.

"Actually, I think Libby is the one in trouble," Jacob observed—which was worse, much worse.

"With the law. That's nothing. We're the ones up shit creek without a paddle. We have to face Aron."

Isaac was right—and that was a scary proposition.

* * *

Libby had never seen the inside of a jail. It was as fascinating as the bar had been. This was a new experience she hadn't counted on. She had question after question and soon all the deputies all had pained looks on their faces. Jacob and Isaac sat to one side, their hats in their hands, and waited for one very large Texas tornado to blow in.

"Isaac, I thought I told you that if you got into another bar fight I'd take the cost of the damages out of your hide." Aron stormed into the sheriff's office, growling like an angry bear.

"It wasn't Isaac, Mr. McCoy." A friendly little Barney Fife type approached Aron with a clip board in his hand.

"Jacob? Well, hell this is his first offense; you ought to let him off."

"The problem wasn't just the damage, Mr. McCoy. It was the terroristic-type threats," the deputy cheerfully explained.

"Jacob was making terroristic threats? Against who?" Aron couldn't believe this. He was probably defending Libby's honor. If anybody had touched his baby, they wouldn't live to see another day.

"It wasn't Jacob making the terroristic threats, Mr. McCoy, nor Isaac."

"Well, then you have the wrong people in custody. There were no other members of my family there to cause trouble," Aron roared.

"It was Libby," Isaac muttered low enough that he thought maybe Aron wouldn't hear.

He heard.

"What did you say?" Aron was pole-axed.

"Libby was the one in the fight. She was the one making threats." Isaac lowered his head and winced as if anticipating a blow.

"My Libby isn't capable of doing those things." Aron had no doubt about the truth of his statement.

"It's true, Mr. McCoy." About that time Sheriff Foster joined them.

"Who in the hell did she fight with or threaten?" Aron still didn't believe a word they were saying. And just where in the hell was she? He looked around. She wasn't anywhere in sight.

"She attacked and made threats against one, Sabrina McCoy." The Sheriff looked perplexed, as if he had just made the connection. "Does that name ring a bell with you, Sir?"

"Shit. Yes." It was all beginning to make sense now.

"Where is Libby?" He looked around at all the people who had failed him.

"She's back in the holding cell."

"THE HOLDING CELL? YOU PUT THAT SWEET LIITLE GIRL IN A CELL?" The walls of the jail began to vibrate.

When he bellowed, Libby heard him.

"Aron! Aron! Sweetie, I'm back here! Come meet these nice criminals."

* * *

There was a whole herd of Texas longhorns stampeding through Libby's head. "I'm never taking another sip of alcohol as long as I live." It was Saturday and the boys had decided to take a rare day off from any and all duties. Mainly, because Aron insisted. Libby needed him. He was in the man cave, on the middle cushion of the big leather couch and she was literally draped across his lap. Her head lay on the left cushion, her feet were on the right and her middle was cradled across Aron's thighs so he could rub her back.

"A sip wouldn't have hurt anything, Baby. It was the ninety-six ounces that brought you down." He would never tell her, but her soused was the cutest thing he had ever seen.

"I'm so sorry, Aron. I've caused tongues to wag." Her voice was muffled in the material of the couch.

"Don't you worry about it; you're my champion." She bounced a little, and then groaned. He smiled. And he wasn't kidding—he would have given anything to see her lay in on Sabrina. Libby cared. There was no doubt about that…this was proof positive.

"Don't make me laugh, it causes me great pain."

He pushed her shirt up so he could enjoy the silk of her skin as he continued his petting. "I want you to think about something while you're recuperating. A pattern is beginning to emerge in your escapades." He waited for her to grunt before he continued. "On your first adventure you fell off Molly."

Her garbled response made him smile.

"I know it was the snake's fault, but still you got hurt." He began to draw pictures on her back, and then they turned into words. "Second, you wanted to learn to shoot pool and you got involved in a bar-fight, which I appreciate, by the way. Like I said, you're my champion. Sabrina needed to be brought down a notch, and we couldn't do it. The thing I hate is that you got hurt once more. Cuts, scrapes and a big ole' bruise that hurts my heart."

"I'm okay. I just can't believe I've spent time in jail. How am I ever going to live down my unfortunate incarceration?" Was she crazy? Aron was writing on her back, and if she kept real still—maybe she could tell what he was writing.

"Libby, I had you out of that cell ten minutes after I arrived. Your total time-served was only an hour and a half." He kept writing and she kept trying to make it out.

"But, I'll never be able to answer the question— 'Have you ever been arrested?' —with a NO again."

"Would you like me to try and get your record expunged?"

"No, I don't think so." She let out a heavy sigh. "I think I'll eventually learn to live with it."

I love you. I love you. I love you.

That time, she got it.

Oh God, he was declaring himself by touch. No surprise, there. Touch was Aron's specialty. She didn't move. The sensation of him tracing those sweet words on her skin was infinitely wonderful. Should she react? Should she let him know she could tell what he was doing? He began speaking before she could decide.

"Can't you be satisfied with sexual adventures?" Aron sounded hopeful.

"My sexual adventures with you are always very satisfying." Honesty is the best policy. Usually.

He was still tracing that momentous phrase on her back.

I love you. I love you. I love you.

Every part of her body wanted to turn over and plaster herself against him, claiming the declaration and making one of her own. But, she couldn't. Not until she knew more about her remission. Maybe the tests that Doc Mulligan would perform in a couple of weeks would tell her if the remission was going to hold. If he said yes, she didn't know what she would do. "Libby?"

"Yes, sir?"

"Tell me what your dreams are?"

What could she say? Her walking-dream was asking her what her dreams were. "Let me sit up." Easily, he turned her and when she got her bearings, he had her cradled in his arms. "Honestly, I haven't spent much time dreaming."

"How can that be possible?" He traced that same little litany on the exposed skin of her chest, then rubbed her neck, sliding his hand on up to cup her chin. "A beautiful woman like you should have her dreams fulfilled as a matter of course."

"Thank you for saying I'm beautiful. Last night when I saw your ex-wife, I didn't feel beautiful at all. She's absolutely gorgeous." She buried her face in his hand.

"Sabrina can't hold a candle for you to run by. You are so far out of her league." Aron was emphatic. "She's passable…you are gorgeous."

"You're absolutely scrumdidlyumptious yourself." She held her face up for his kiss.

"Quit that." He laughed. "You're being cute because you're trying to evade the topic. Dreams, Libby–Lou, talk to me."

Start with something safe, she cautioned herself. "I've always wanted to make handmade designer handbags. I can sew and I have a knack for putting odds and ends together." She sat up straighter, getting a little excited in her description. "I like to take scrap material that I find in the sale bins at the fabric store, cut it out and sew it up and decorate it with buttons or beads or tassels—whatever. It's so much fun and each one is an original. A Libby-Lou Creation!" She smiled at him so sweetly, his heart rose in his throat.

"A Libby-Lou Creation?"

"Oh, I just made that up, because the words sound cute coming out of your mouth." He leaned over and kissed her.

"I like it. Okay, purses are dream number one. What else?"

"Well…" She ran one finger over the fine dusting of hair at the open vee of his black tight-fitting western shirt. Then, in a daring move, she began doing exactly as he had done before.

I love you. I love you. I love you.

He tensed at the feel of her finger, quickly looking down as if he could catch her at it. Their gazes fused and she picked her finger up and traced his lips. Aron trembled at her touch. "Tell me your dreams, Libby."

"I would love to go—" She stopped and turned in his lap, straddling him. He wrapped his arms around her and pulled her up until her breasts were pressed luxuriously against the hard muscles of his chest. Repeating, she began to whisper in his ear.

Aron was expecting to hear something totally outrageous. Instead, his throat muscles tensed as emotions battled for the upper hand. Adoration won—hands down. This is what she whispered, "I would love to go on a picnic—with you."

"A picnic? Libby, I'll take you on a picnic anytime you say. How about we do that and go out on the town to boot?"

As soon as he finished the sentence, she hopped a little in his lap, which caused those stupendous breasts to bounce against him. Under her splayed femininity, his cock began to grow, seeking attention.

"Really? You would like to go out with me—in public?" He was stunned at her inference. Did she think he was ashamed of her? He didn't get a chance to defend himself; she started chattering like a magpie. "You'll have to take me to the bank so I can cash a check. I didn't bring any of my dresses with me." She didn't say that her dresses had all been old and too small. There was no use sounding totally pitiful.

"Sweetheart, when was the last time a man took you to dinner or out on a date?" He wanted to know, he just didn't want to know.

Libby thought for a second, and then answered. "Kevin Tucker took me out for pizza and to the video arcade when I was 15."

"That was ten years ago, Libby. What have you been doing for the last ten years?"

Heck! How was she supposed to answer that? Not truthfully, that's for sure. Unless…ah, the romantic approach. Truth, nonetheless. "Waiting for you."

"Libby…"

"If you don't have time to take me to the bank, maybe I can borrow the truck. I need to go grocery shopping, anyway."

"Why do you need to go to the bank?"

"To get money to buy something pretty to wear." Men were so dense.

"Why don't you have any money?"

His question was put out there and then he was silent. She didn't say anything, either. What could she say?

"Hellfire and damnation, Libby!" he yelled, almost dumping her from his lap. "Why haven't you said anything?" When she said nothing, he threw his hat clear across the room. "I haven't given you one red cent for what you've done at Tebow."

"I don't want anything." She announced quickly.

"What?"

"It wouldn't feel right."

"Why?

"Because..."

"Why?"

"Because it makes me happy to take care of you."

"Hell, Libby." Aron squeezed her tight. "I never expected you to come here and work yourself to death for nothing. You will accept the money, and I won't take no for an answer."

Libby grew still in his embrace.

"Okay?"

"I have an address you can send it to…"

"What address?"

"I have a debt I have to pay off."

Immediately, it crossed his mind that she might have debts like Sabrina ran up on him. "Credit card bills?" The tone in his voice sharpened.

"No, it's a student loan, sort of." She didn't mind him asking. Leaving his lap, she went and got her purse from the kitchen. Returning, she held up her bag. It was an attractive purse decorated with beads and leather. "See, I made this." Not waiting for a comment, she pulled out her wallet and handed him a slip of paper. "Just send whatever you were going to give me to this address."

Aron felt like a heel. He took the paper and jammed it into his front pocket without reading it. "Libby, I'm sorry about all of it."

"It's all right, Aron. I don't blame you. After what Sabrina did, you've got every right to be cautious."

"You've never given me any reason to doubt you in any capacity." Aron was eating humble pie. "Do you feel like going to town now?"

"Don't I need to stay and fix lunch for everyone?" This was the first morning that she hadn't prepared breakfast for them in weeks. The boys hadn't known how to act when Aron had set out assorted cereals and

milk. You'd have thought they hadn't eaten in a week.
"They can eat sandwiches."
"They won't be very happy."
"Who cares?"

* * *

Libby packed a knapsack Aron had given her with a few belongings. She was going camping! Today had been tremendously exciting. He had taken her to town and escorted her from place to place. They never made it to the bank, he said it wasn't necessary and they had started their round of shopping at a little boutique. Aron had gone crazy and much to Libby's chagrin he had bought her three complete outfits. She grumbled all the way down the street as he carried her packages.

"Get used to it. I intend to spoil you rotten."

The grocery store had been an adventure. Libby learned a valuable lesson; never take a hungry man to the supermarket. They ended up with four over-loaded, piled-high carts. One would have thought that on a ranch as big as Tebow they would butcher their own beef, but all of the cattle on the ranch were registered purebreds, and you don't eat show cows. So two of the carts were meat, almost exclusively. Libby loved to cook and Aron loved her cooking so he made sure she had every spice, herb and oil her little heart desired.

The longer the day wore on, the more Libby realized what she would be missing if she walked away from Aron McCoy. He made everything fun and every moment a joy. Being with him on an ordinary day was better than an adventure any day.

Chapter Six

"You wanted to ride a horse, so come on Love, climb on." Aron held out his hand.

"Sultan is a really tall horse." Libby marveled. The golden Palomino stood sixteen hands high and weighed almost twelve hundred pounds. She placed her foot in the stirrup and he picked her up easily. "We're riding double?"

"Oh, yeah. We've got about an hour ride to the camp-site and I intend to have a helluva time with you." He sat her in front of him in the saddle. Aron was a big man, so the space between the saddle horn and his groin was snug.

"I like this." Her honesty warmed his heart. She had put her hair into a loose braid and he pushed it to one side so he could kiss her neck.

"So do I, so do I."

"We are going to be all alone, aren't we?" She didn't want anyone interfering in their time together.

"This is Tebow land, Libby. There'll be no one but us. I have a satellite phone in my saddlebag, if we need help. We won't see another living soul for the next two days."

"Maybe that's a good thing, considering the way I'm dressed." Libby didn't understand, but Aron had asked her not to wear pants—or underwear. He had spread a finely woven blanket over the front of the saddle, thereby making her a nice soft nest to sit on.

"You're dressed perfectly." She wore a red sundress that was now pulled up so high her bare bottom was nestled in the cradle of his thighs. The trail that Aron headed Sultan down was dappled in shade. "Look over there." Through a break in the copse of trees she could see a beautiful lake, and standing on the shores of the lake were hundreds of heads of longhorns.

"Wow, they're magnificent animals."

"Yes, they are. Big John, our oldest bull has an eighty inch spread to his horns, tip to tip. We raise them for breeding only and recently I sold a cow to a rancher in New Mexico for one hundred and seventy thousand dollars."

"Good Gracious!" She had no idea.

"I'm not a poor man, Libby." Aron didn't brag about his means, but he wanted Libby to understand he could take care of her.

"I know you're not, Aron." Raising both arms to touch his neck, she shifted in his arms for a kiss. "But I'm more interested in your non-financial assets."

"Good answer." How non-Sabrina could you get? "Time to get this show on the road." Without any warning, he pushed her elasticized sun dress down to her waist. Libby gasped in surprise and instant arousal. "Sultan knows the way." He doubled the reins and laid them across the horse's neck. "Lean back so I can have unhindered access to those beauties."

Gladly, Libby did as he asked. "I love the way your hands feel on my breasts. The little rough spots on your fingers make me want to wiggle. "

"Good to know my calluses are worth something to somebody." Aron let his hands slide up until he had picked both of Libby's tits up and lifted them until it would be possible to bring to life one of his sinful daydreams. "Lick them, Libby. Lick your pretty little nipples."

"Me? That's your job?" Libby was perplexed. This, she had never even read about.

"They're right there, honey. You are bountifully blessed. Pleasure yourself for me."

With only a moment's hesitation, Libby bent her head and darted out her tongue to taste the tip end of her own breast. "Huh!" The sensation was not an unpleasant one.

"Now, the other one." She continued to follow his instructions. "Now, suck them for me." Aron's arousal went from atomic to nuclear at the sight of Libby's lips tugging on her own feminine flesh.

"Ummmmm," Libby mumbled as she sucked at the pebbled peak. It was the oddest sensation. Zing! This felt absolutely incredible. Tingles of pleasure were racing the two feet or so that separated her nipples from her clit. Without being told, she abandoned one nipple and latched on to the other one. Behind her, Aron chuckled.

Libby turned loose long enough to mumble. "Wow. If I'd known how good this felt, I would have been doing it all the time." At that revelation, Aron abruptly lowered her hands from her breasts.

"Oh, no. Forget, I introduced you to that wicked little pleasure. I refuse to be replaced," Aron laughed.

Still slightly dazed, Libby didn't realize what was happening until she felt herself being lifted and turned in the air. The next second, she found herself belly to belly with her man. "Now, it's my turn!" She began to unbutton his shirt. She was eager for more tactile delights. His hands fumbled with his belt buckle and zipper. When his actions registered with her, she looked up at him quizzically. "Is this even possible? Or safe?"

"I've never fallen off a horse in my life, Libby. And I'm not about to start now. Trust me, Sultan and I will keep you safe." He pulled his cock from his pants and then proceeded to delve between her thighs with eager fingers. "Mmmmm, feels like you're already as slick and satiny as can be. Come here, love. Pull your legs up and put them around my waist."

With a minimum amount of contortion, Libby found herself maneuvered until she could gratefully slide down on his turgid cock.

Aron was already grunting with pleasure. "Now, this is an adventure, Libby-mine." She couldn't answer, all she could do was cling to his shoulders and coo with delight. In her position, and not wanting to spook the horse, the only movements she dared make were internal, but her efforts did not go unnoticed. "Damn, that feels unbelievable!" He buried his face in her neck and just wallowed in the wondrous rush of love that washed over him.

"Aron, open your eyes and watch where we're going. I can only see where we've been."

At her bossy little directive, Aron wiggled deep inside her. "You're not supposed to be able to process thoughts. Why aren't you mindless with rapture?" Who would have ever thought that sex could be so joyous? What used to be a necessary bodily function was now a celebratory event.

"I am mindless with rapture," she assured him as she rubbed her chest against his. "God, that feels good."

Aron was already leaking pre-cum and the tight fit of Libby's little pussy made him grunt with pleasure. "Now, this is an adventure, Libby-mine." She couldn't answer, all she could do was cling to his shoulders and coo with delight. In her position, and not wanting to spook the horse, the only movement that she dared make was internal, but her efforts did not go unnoticed. "Damn, that feels unbelievable!" He buried his face in her neck and just wallowed in the wondrous rush of love that washed over him.

"Aron, open your eyes and watch where we're going. I can only see where we've been."

At her bossy little directive, Aron wiggled his cock deep inside her. "You're not supposed to be able to process thoughts. Why aren't you mindless with rapture?" Who would have ever thought that sex could be so joyous? What used to be a necessary bodily function was now a celebratory event.

"I am mindless with rapture," she assured him as she rubbed her nipples deep into his crisp chest hair. "God, that feels good."

At her audible euphoria, Aron's level of arousal sky-rocketed. "Not going to last," he vocalized through clenched teeth. Standing up in the stirrups, and holding her upright, he rammed into her with tremendous force. Her ultra-sensitive pubis was grinding against his pelvic ridge, eliciting spurts of tremendous sensation. As she peaked, Libby reached out and bit Aron right at the point where his neck met his shoulder.

That was all it took, Aron roared with release. Bucking upward, he emptied himself within her, forever claiming her as conquered territory. Sultan pranced and sidestepped, but Aron did not falter or relinquish his hold on his beloved.

Libby felt no fear, only an absolute and utter elation.

Sinking back down, they cuddled and murmured little nonsensical phrases of praise and worship. The word love might not have been verbalized, but its presence was undeniable.

Teasing, Libby observed, "Sultan is so well behaved. This wasn't the first time you performed this equestrian feat, was it?"

"Actually, it was. Although, I will admit I have fantasized about it a time or two." Planting a smacking kiss on her forehead, Aron deftly reversed her position.

Sighing, she settled herself against him while he adjusted her clothes. "That was the most fun I've ever had on horseback, Libtastic." His manipulation of her name was becoming a precious oddity. She couldn't wait to see what else he would come up with.

"What is this, a Hilton resort?" Libby was shocked; she had expected a clearing and a campfire. Instead, there was a quaint, rustic cabin with mammoth rocking chairs on the front porch and a stone fireplace. There was even running water and a shower the size of a grotto. "Aron, this is tremendous!"

"It's the McCoy hunting cabin. Mom would go hunting with Dad and she didn't like to rough it. Dad wanted her company so he spruced it up for her."

"Your dad must have loved your mother very much." Libby didn't realize she sounded wistful.

Aron wanted to reassure her she was equally loved, but he also knew she wasn't ready to hear it. Something was holding her back. He suspected she had interpreted his skin-calligraphy the day before – and if he weren't certifiably insane, she had reciprocated. He fully intended to push the issue – sooner rather than later.

There was a complete kitchen and three bedrooms. The bathroom was downright luxurious, but the piece de' resistance was a king-size hammock which had been professionally engineered and securely hung between four strategically placed trees. Libby suspected the trees had been planted for this specific purpose. Walking up to the hammock, she began to have sensual visions. "Aron, after while . . . .could we. . . "

"Make love in the hammock?"

"Oh, yeah." A nip on her butt caused Libby to levitate about eighteen inches. "Aron," she squealed. He had squatted down behind her, totally captivated by the way she was pulling on the thin cotton sundress she wore. Unconsciously, she had been fiddling with her dress, pulling it forward, leaving her bottom lovingly molded in thin see-through cotton. "Fooling around in this hammock is definitely on the agenda."

Aron had it all planned out. The fridge was stocked and he had changed the sheets on the bed. But, right now he had a couple of surprises up his sleeve. "Let's go, Precious."

"Where are we going?"

"Fishing."

"Do we have to use real live bait?" Libby pushed her bottom lip out in what was becoming his favorite expression – except for that dazed, rapturous look she got when she came apart in his arms, shivering in orgasmic ecstasy.

"What did you expect to use?" There was no chance he would lose his patience with her, she totally beguiled him.

"A piece of wienie?" she looked hopeful.

"Lucky for you I brought some." He loped back to the cabin and came back with a wiener for her. The picturesque little lake was no more than a hundred yards behind the cabin and there was a dock built out over the watery expanse. He loved the way she looked with her legs dangling in the water.

He grinned, watching her push a piece of the meat-stick down over the hook. "You don't mind if I use a minnow do you?"

"No, but let me turn my head. I don't want to see you skewer it on the hook." She dutifully turned away while he baited his hook. Soon both of their lines were in the water, their bobbers floating on the surface.

Secure in his superior fishing capability, Aron announced. "The last one to catch a fish cooks supper."

"You're on, Buster." Libby accepted his challenge. They sat for a few minutes; enjoying the profound peace of the idyllic setting, taking joy in one another's company. Aron was leaning back on one arm, one leg propped up with one foot in the water. But, soon he felt a little hand nudging on his. "Can we hold hands?"

"Sure." He sat up, so she could reach him easier. She twined her fingers with his, then brought his hand over into her own lap and clutched it close. It was such a tender moment; Aron found himself swallowing back emotions he had never felt before.

"FUDGESICKLE!" Libby screamed, as she threw herself right on top of Aron. He had to scramble to catch her and still manage to keep both of their fishing poles from falling into the water.

"What happened, Baby?" He asked from underneath her.

"Something bit me!" she squealed.

"Where? Did a wasp sting you?" Aron held her and everything else secure as his eyes searched her body for welts.

"No, it was a snake!"

"Libby, a snake did not bite you."

"Look!" she flounced to one side and held her lovely little leg right up in his face. He almost called a halt to their fishing to carry her up to the hammock and prematurely begin the sexual phase of their outing.

A light red mark did mar the creamy smoothness of her skin, but it was not a snake-bite. "Oh, Puddin', that's a perch-kiss."

"A what?" She pulled her leg into her lap to inspect the grievous injury.

"This lake is full of little white perch. They've always enjoyed nibbling on the legs and toes of unsuspecting humans who invade their domicile." Watching her study the little red mark was captivating, but when she bent down and kissed her own leg, he lost it. "Hey, you're treading on my territory, Precious."

Giggling, she looked up at him. "Well, you've got me kissing other parts of my body – I thought this wouldn't be out of line."

He leaned over and grazed his lips over the fast-fading mark. "There, now. Forget what I taught you earlier. I'll do all the Libby-kissing around here; I have no intention of being phased out as obsolete. Next thing I know you'll be using a dildo." He was just about to kiss his way to parts north, when Libby exploded.

"Look! Aron, look! I've got a bite!" Sure enough, Libby's bobber was going crazy. She grabbed her pole again and began a tug-of-war with whatever was playing with the hook.

"Wait. Wait. Let him get a hold of it real good, you want the hook to set before you pull your line out of the water." She followed his instructions, barely able to contain her excitement. When the bobber completely disappeared, she jumped up and began backing up to allow her catch to emerge from the murky depths.

"Help me, Aron. I think I've caught a whale!" Aron laid his pole down, amused as all get-out. Standing up, he helped her pull in her catch. It wasn't a whale, but she had got a real good-sized bass. "Look at him!" Obviously, Libby was happy. And when Libby was happy, Aron was happy.

"Looks like I'm cooking supper." He pulled the fish up in a net, removed the hook and was about to slip the fish into a nearby cooler he had brought for this specific purpose.

"What are you doing?" There was a tinge of panic in Libby's voice.

"I'm putting him on ice, we'll eat him later."

"We can't eat Leon."

Aron sat back on his heels and looked at her. "Leon?"

"I don't think I could eat him. I've looked him in the eye, and he looked back at me."

Aron scrunched his lips together, desperately trying not to laugh. "Libby, this is not a catch and release lake. It's the McCoy fishing pond. And we eat our fish."

"Please? I'll do unspeakable things to your body." The devilish little gleam in her eye sold him on the concept.

"Come here, Leon." He readily grabbed the slippery fish and returned him to the lake. "Okay, baby – strip. Time for unspeakable things."

"Now?!?" Libby started to run, but Aron tackled her. "What are you thinking?"

"I'm thinking skinny-dipping. We're going swimming with Leon!"

"But what about perch-kisses?" Libby whispered aghast.

"Perch ain't the only thing that's gonna be nibbling on you." Aron stepped back and began shedding his clothes hand over fist. Libby went more slowly, fascinated by the strip show he was putting on. When he was naked, she was captivated. His cock was so engorged and swollen it couldn't even stand up, instead, it hung heavy against his thigh. She felt her loins liquefy in anticipation of being filled by him.

He began to walk slowly toward her, she finished disrobing, stepping slowly backwards. She didn't know why she was retreating when everything she wanted was stalking her like a hungry predator. "You're going to step off the dock, Libbykins." he warned just a microsecond before she stepped off into nothing.

"RAT BUGGERS!" she squealed as her naked form was encased in the cool spring-fed water. Diving in behind her, Aron gathered her close, pushing her hair out of her eyes.

"Refreshing, huh?" She was so cute.

"It's colder than a witch's tit!" she exclaimed. The word 'tit' was the only word he heard, so he held her aloft in the water and fastened his mouth securely to one slightly wrinkled areola.

"Oh, I love that, Aron. Sometimes, I want to just sit in front of the television all night and let you lie in my lap and suck my breasts." The sexy domestic scene she painted had him designing blueprints in his mind. They needed their own house. He wanted to be able to love Libby anytime, anywhere without worrying about his brother's disturbing them. Or maybe, he would just build them another house – yeah that's what he'd do. He was the eldest – he'd keep the big house. Besides, Libby loved the house. It was fast becoming hers – not Bess's and not his own

Mom's. Libby's.

"Mmmmm," he groaned as he chewed softly on her nipple. "I could just eat you up."

He felt her legs wrap around his chest and she began to push against him in a rockin' motion that he longed to share. "Aron, I'm aching. I need you to put him in. Please," she begged.

"Relax and lay back," he instructed her. "You're going to float and I'm going diving." When he had her fixed, and she was lying on top of the water like some erotic mermaid, he brought his lips to her hot-button. With soft swirls, he caressed her pink folds. "You have the prettiest pussy."

"I'm going to sink, Aron. It feels too good, I can't be still." Aron ran his arms underneath her bottom and gave her the support she needed. He'd always give her the support she needed. Kissing her pussy was an absolute delight. She smelled like the body wash she used, something with raspberries. Tunneling deep in her passage, he felt her began to tense. Knowing she was close, he moved the sensual assault to her clitoris. Using the flat of his tongue, he laved the pink pearl until she screamed his name. Before she could recover, he stood her up and walked her to the dock. "Hang on, baby." Butting up to her back, he lifted her bottom and entered her from behind.

"My God, Aron." Almost immediately, she began to push back on him, enveloping him in red-hot velvet, enthusiastically impaling herself on his tumescent organ. "You are so big!" Enclosing one breast with a hand, he reached around her cupping her vulva in the other hand and finding her clitoris with the pad of his forefinger. Then, he went to work. Squeezing her breast, massaging her sex and pumping into her from the rear was a trifecta move. They had both been so heated with desire that in just a few minutes they were writhing in a climax so powerful, the tremors lingered and lingered long after the initial explosion. Without pulling out, he carefully turned her in his arms, running his hands over her damp body. She nestled close to him in complete trust and complete satisfaction.

Well, not completely complete. "I'm hungry, Aron."

"Well, since we won't be having fish for supper. How about a wienie?" Deep within her he wiggled his cock.

"Can we roast them, outside, around a fire?" The enthusiasm in her voice was contagious.

"Is there any other way?"

She was lovely by firelight. Aron couldn't take his eyes off of her. She had taken a quick post-romp shower alone, much to his dismay, and then changed into one of the short sets he had bought her. Seeing her clothed in things he had given her did something to the he-man part of him that wanted to provide for his woman. Her damp hair was loosely braided with a yellow ribbon and her eyes were shining like the brightest of stars. Tonight was the night. He was going to tell her he loved her or die trying.

She had been enthralled with roasting her own wieners on a limb that he had cut and carved just for her. In fact, she had almost made herself sick eating, because she kept wanting to hold another hot-dog over the crackling fire. "Hold off, Libby. Let's have dessert, instead." A warm look of lust came into her eyes and she reached for him.

"Wait, Munchkin. Hammock time is next, but while we've got the fire going, I want to introduce you to Smores."

"That's what I want, too. S'more of you." He almost ditched the graham crackers and hauled her off to his lair, but he knew if he could calm her down she would love the warm chocolaty treat. And he wanted to give her every good experience he could think of. Libby's amazingly sweet innocence was riveting to him. Experiencing new things with her was like enjoying them anew for himself. Everything was fun. Every moment was precious.

"Here put these marshmallows on your stick." He handed her a couple of the big white fluffy ones.

With child-like awe she watched the puffy pillows turn brown, and then Aron showed her how to layer them on graham crackers with a small chocolate bar. The heat from the marshmallows would melt the chocolate and make the combination into a warm gooey sandwich of celestial goodness.

"Oh. My. God," she exclaimed when the flavors melted onto her tongue. "That's the best thing in the whole world!" Seeing his playfully downcast look, she relented. "Except you, of course." She ate two more before deeming it enough.

Catching him in an embrace, she cuddled him close. "Thank you Aron. I have never had this much fun in my whole life. I grew up in the city and never had a chance to do things like this. Later..." her voice trailed off, but she covered it up by letting her lips get preoccupied with kissing his. Aron's own mind was so preoccupied with his coming declaration, he didn't even notice.

"I'm glad you had fun. I enjoy every second I spend with you. There is nowhere else in the world I'd rather be, nor anyone I want to be with more."

"Take a walk with me. The moon is so pretty and full."

Who could resist a man like Aron McCoy? Sometimes when she looked at him, she couldn't believe he was hers. But, he was. By some miraculous means, this perfect man wanted her – Libby Fontaine. She took his outstretched hand, memorizing every feature of his beautifully chiseled face and body. Even though he was a physically perfect specimen, the most beautiful part of him was his heart. Plus, he was smart. And he loved his family; above all, he loved his family. Oh yes, she was lucky. "I'd love to walk with you, Aron."

He led her off the porch and out under the canopy of trees. A field of wild flowers lent its incredible scent to the fresh night air. A dove called in the distance and a lone owl added its haunting voice to the enchanted evening. They strolled past the lake and on down a narrow trail which led to a high bluff overlooking the grand expanse of Tebow land. "This is all McCoy property, Libby." He pulled her back against him and she laid her head on his wide chest. Aron rested his chin on her hair and his hands smoothed up and down her arms. "There is 535,000 acres of land in our holdings and we run nearly 20,000 mama cows for production purposes. We breed horses and cultivate our own hay and grain to feed them all. Primarily, our money comes from oil and natural gas."

Libby slowly stepped out of his arms. What was she doing here? This was a rich man. And who was she? Dirt poor, sickly Libby Fontaine. "I didn't know you had so much."

"Why did you move away?" He reached for her.

Libby held back, not moving to him as readily as in the past. "Aron, you could be with anybody! I have nothing, absolutely nothing to offer you. I am nobody, from nowhere. Why are you wasting your time with me?" Her voice was colored with despair.

Aron was flabbergasted. This was not at all what he had intended to convey with his speech. "Libby, you don't understand what I'm saying." He fell to his knees at her feet. "I have all of these things – this property, livestock, and minerals – but they mean nothing to me, nothing at all compared to how I feel about you."

Libby froze. God, it was happening. What was she going to do?

There were many things she could have done, but Libby decided she didn't want to look eternity in the face having lied to the man she loved. And, God, did she love this man. Taking one step forward, she knelt down with him – joining her hands to his. "I love you, Aron. So much." He held out his arms and she dove into them. Before he could respond, she slipped one hand over his mouth. "I've said it, now. I've told you how I felt, now let me finish."

He knew this was big, but he didn't know what was coming.

"You don't have to say you love me. I know you do. I can feel it stronger than I can feel my own heart beating, but I don't want you to say it out loud. Not yet." Aron moved his mouth under her fingers, needing to say something. "Let me finish." She took a deep, steadying breath. "There's something I have to do in a little over a week. Let me get through it, and if all is well, I'll come home to you. And when I do, the first thing I want to hear out of those sweet lips is how much you love me."

"And if all isn't well?" He had pulled her hand away, and was planting kisses in the soft well of her palm.

"I don't know, I just don't know."

"Why can't you tell me what's wrong? Don't you know I would turn the world upside down for you?" Aron's strong face was compelling; he looked as if he would slay dragons or attempt to pull the moon from the sky for her.

"There are some things beyond even your control, Aron." She grabbed both of his hands in hers and she kissed each finger. "But let me say it again, Sweetheart. I love you. I love you so much. I never knew I would get the chance to say those words to anyone, so let me say them again. I LOVE YOU."

"Let me say it, Libby. For God's sake let me say it."

"No, don't. Things may fall apart. And if you say them, I would never be able to walk away from you."

"Is that why?" Aron was bamboozled. "If I were to say I love you, just saying that will prevent you from leaving me?" Could it be that simple?

"Yes, I'm afraid so."

Libby didn't understand that she was about to be hoisted by her own petard.

Aron rose swiftly, scooped her up and marched back toward the cabin. "Where are we going, Aron?"

"To the blasted hammock, that's where." He looked like a man on a mission.

Libby's heart raced with excitement. She was about to be thoroughly taken by the man she loved. When they reached the hammock, filled with gaily colored pillows and two thin blankets, Aron deposited her in the middle and then stood back. He began taking off his shirt. "Pull off those clothes, Baby. Skim them right off that sweet body. I know you don't have anything on under them, I've been watching the play of light on those puffy little nipples and that sweet shadow between your legs." Raising her hips and then her shoulders, Libby pulled the short-set off. Aron had undressed and he moved over her, blocking out the starlight.

"I'm about to show you how I feel about you, Libby-love." Aron whispered right in her face. "I'm about to worship you with my body." He nudged his nose up the side of her face, then back down. He ran his lips over her eyes and then he kissed the tip end of her nose. "A woman needs to know that she can't always dictate to a man about what he should do or what he should say."

"Really?" Where in the world was he going with this?

"That's right. I'm a man, Libby."

Duh! "Yes, you are." There was no denying that fact or the monster cock that lay up between them. Her private areas were already readying themselves for his possession; they sensed his presence and were preparing a place for him.

"I am your man."

She had no response to that, the knowledge was just too wonderful for words.

"And as your man, I have certain rights."

"Unalienable rights?"

"I don't know what those are." He thought for a moment. "Probably."

"I don't know what it means, either. Go ahead. Sorry, I interrupted you." She smiled. She loved him, so.

"Thank you." He paused. "Damn it, Libby. You made me forget where I was in my speech."

"You were saying, that as my man, (God, what a concept) you have certain rights. Unalienable rights."

He was resting almost on top of her, but he wasn't crushing her. To tell the truth, his proximity made her feel absolutely safe and protected. And the words he was saying were music to her ears. She had thought she didn't want to hear them, but she was wrong.

"Right. Unalienable rights. And one of those rights is to be able to share my heart with you, and my thoughts, and my feelings." He was so sweetly serious.

"Okay, I guess." Was he expecting her to disagree?

Good enough. Shifting her in the hammock, they lay side by side, facing one another. He skated his lips over her forehead, down her cheek and kissed her in the corner of her mouth. "I love you." His tone was so tender, it made her heart melt. This giant of a man was openly declaring his love for her like she was the most precious thing in the world to him. "Did you hear me, Elizabeth? I love you. I love you. I love you." As he said the words, he wrote them on the smooth skin of her back.

I love you. I love you. I love you.

"Yes, I hear you and I feel you." She leaned into him.

"So, what do you have to say?"

"I love you more than I love life." Loaded comment. "I'm honored above all women to be the recipient of your love." Then she grinned at him wickedly – "and my name's not Elizabeth."

"Not Elizabeth? Well, Libby-bell, what is your name? I think as the declared love of your life, I am entitled to that important piece of information."

"Can't you guess?" she teased. "You almost said it just a minute ago."

"What did I say?" He scrunched up his forehead, trying to recall.

"I know it's hard for you to remember, you talk all the time."

"Are you saying I rattle like a two-bit radio?"

"No, I didn't say that."

He pulled at her braid. "Now, what is the last name I called you. You're going to have to help me Libalicious, I'm getting old."

"Libalicious? I see a whole new phase of this game coming on."

He glared at her.

"Okay, you called me Libby-bell."

For a moment, he looked confused and then his eyes widened.

He still didn't say anything, so she sighed. "I feel like my name should be Rumpelstilskin."

At his horrified expression, Libby convulsed in laughter. "I didn't say my name *was* Rumpelstilskin. Think, McCoy! Think!"

Holding her steady, so she wouldn't shake them out of the hammock, he finally said. "I got nothing."

"My name is Liberty. Liberty Bell Fontaine."

Aron roared. He laughed and laughed. He rolled out of the hammock and just had to walk away, laughing all the while. Libby almost got offended. "Hey, it's not that funny."

"Oh, yes it is. Suddenly it all makes sense."

"What makes sense?"

"How I've been acting."

"Run that by me again."

"You've had me chasing you around in circles. And I'm going to catch you and keep you, damn it, I'm entitled. It's my unalienable right."

"What right?" she was growing flustered.

He rejoined her in the hammock, cradling her close. "I am a man, Libby. And I am an American."

Oh, boy - here we go again. Was he about to sing, 'God Bless America'?

"And as an American man, I am entitled to life, Liberty, (that's you) and the pursuit of happiness."

* * *

A little while later the hammock rocked back and forth as Aron pumped hard within the loins of the woman he loved. She had her legs wrapped around him and her hips were working in tandem with his, meeting him thrust for thrust. The delicious friction of his cock sliding in and out of her body hit a spot deep inside of Libby that had her quaking with delight, an incredible sensation of heated desire coursing her veins, his perfect movements sending flickers of raw carnal pleasure all the way to her womb.

Since Aron had told her he loved her, he had developed a voracious sexual appetite. His whole demeanor had changed, and he was more commanding, more demanding of her complete response and her utter surrender. It was as if he had conveyed to her that things had changed, she was now his possession, his responsibility. Libby moved her hands over his chest; she combed her fingers through his chest hair, feeling the small swelling of his nipples. She found this more than exciting. If it were possible she would have rose up into his body, crawled right up into him and made herself at home. Watching the play of emotions on his face, she longed to give back to him the same measure of pleasure he was giving to her. Impulsively, she sat up and mimicked one of his moves. Taking one of his nipples into her mouth, she began to suck on it, tonguing it, scraping it with her teeth. He let out a low, lusty growl, increased the speed of his thrusts and pushed his chest toward her, encouraging Libby in her sensual pursuits. "That's right, baby. Love me…love me with all you've got."

And so, she did.

Their mutual climaxes rushed upon them like a run-a-way mine train. Neither one of them had realized what a difference love made. But, it did. Love released energy and fed hungers. Love built bridges and tore down walls. Love settled doubts and answered questions. Love conquers all.

Chapter Seven

"Let's go in. That big old bed is going to feel really good." She held up her arms like a small child and he picked her up, heading to the cabin. They had dozed off, cuddled up. But the chill of the night air on his skin had awakened him. It was early morning, but they could still enjoy a few hours of sleep wrapped in the soft, warm covers. He had pulled on his jeans, but he hadn't bothered to dress her. They weren't going anywhere but straight to bed. Before he made it to the foot of the steps, he heard an engine.

Pulling up in the yard was Jacob.

As he got out of the pick-up, Aron turned to the side, shielding Libby from his brother's eyes.

He knew something was wrong. It had to be or Jacob wouldn't be here.

"You don't have the satellite phone on." Jacob quietly complained.

"Sorry. What's wrong?"

"Ya'll need to come home."

"What is it, Jacob?" Aron was getting scared.

"It's Joseph."

Libby threw their stuff together. The horse was to be left in the corral and one of them would come back for it later that day. She flew out of the bedroom and joined them as they hurried out the door and into Jacob's truck.

Aron had finally got out of Jacob that Joseph had been hurt. How badly, they didn't know. He had flipped his dirt bike in a freak accident during a race in Marble Falls. The family hadn't been notified immediately. Rather he had been airlifted to Dallas and was undergoing procedures to see what the actual damage really was.

"He takes too many damn risks." Aron suffered with the knowledge that his little brother's life might never be the same. "Is he paralyzed?" This was Aron's greatest fear. Since their parent's death, Joseph had become a dare-devil. Nothing was off-limits or too dangerous. Skydiving had been just one of the wild thrill-seeking interests which had drawn his attention. It wasn't that he had fallen in with a bad crowd. He existed on the periphery of these groups. He joined them for training and races, but did not immerse himself in their lifestyle.

Libby was sitting in between Jacob and Aron. She could feel the worry and tension emanating off their bodies. Any time one of the McCoy brothers was threatened or in trouble, they all rallied to defeat any adversary who might jeopardize their safety. Aron felt for Libby's hand, pulling her against him. "I'm so scared, Libby."

She turned, enclosing him in her arms, offering him all the comfort she could convey with her warmth and her embrace. "He'll be all right, he has to be."

When they pulled into the circular driveway in front of the main house, Jacob whipped his truck in and barreled out. Noah and Isaac stood on the front porch waiting for them. Nathan was nowhere to be seen. Aron helped Libby out and got her onto the porch. "Go in and check on Nathan. If you could put on a strong pot of coffee, I'd appreciate it. We've got to get things in line here and then some of us have got to get to Dallas."

"Anything, I'll do anything." She rose on tip-toe and molded her body to his. "Your family is more than important to me."

"Libby, you help just by being here." Giving her a hard kiss, he strode over to the others to see what the latest word was on Joseph.

Libby was devastated. All she could see in her mind was Joseph's beautiful face. He was so alive. Although like an addict, he constantly had to feed his need for the adrenaline rush he got from the high-risk adventures he lived for. All Libby could think about was how nice he had been to her and how much his brothers loved him.

As she started making preparations for their next meal, Libby began to feel ill. She stopped, afraid to move a muscle. 'No, God, no,' she prayed. From out of nowhere, waves of nausea caused her to break out in a cold sweat. She struggled to get to a chair. Holding her stomach, the panic hit her harder than the nausea. This felt so familiar. She knew what this was. Hello, old enemy. No, no, no. She wanted to run and just keep running—maybe she could outdistance herself from it. Hanging her head, she mourned what could have been. Libby had just found happiness and she didn't want to lose it so soon. Fleeing to the bathroom, she made it to the toilet just in time.

"Libby! Libby? Where are you?" Aron called. Hastily, Libby washed her face with cold water and dried it with a towel. Turning, she ran slap-dab into Aron's hard chest. He enfolded himself around her like a drowning man would cling to a life-line.

"Tell me everything," she encouraged, breathing in his scent as if it were the finest wine.

"He's awake, that's one good thing." His hold on her tightened, and he picked her up squeezing her to him. Libby would have groaned had she not known he was hurting worse than she was. "He's paralyzed, Libby. Oh, God, he's paralyzed." Tears dampened her neck. His tears.

"Oh, no." Libby cried. "How bad is it?"

"They are still running tests. I think he can move his hands and arms, but nothing below the waist." Aron rubbed his face back and forth over her shoulder as if trying to eradicate his painful reality.

"It could be a temporary thing," she sought to reassure him in any way she could.

"No one knows at this point." He let her slide down. "I'm going to go with Jacob and Isaac up to the hospital. Noah will stay here with you and Nathan to keep things going."

She took his face in her hands and rubbed away the trace of tears on his cheeks. "What can I do?"

"Pray, Libby," Aron begged. "I don't know how anymore."

"I will," she promised. "Anything else?"

"Take care of Nathan." Clutching her to him, he held her tight. "Oh, Baby... just knowing you're here and that I have you to come home to, makes all the difference in the world." Their lips met in a tender kiss. "I'll call you every few hours."

"Please, do. I want to know," she assured him.

"I won't be calling you just to inform you about Joseph, I'll be calling to get my Libby-fix. Sweetheart, I'm so sorry this happened just when we brought our love out into the light of day..."

"Don't worry, Aron. My love for you isn't going anywhere."

"And I don't want you to go anywhere, either. Whatever you have going on in your life that's creating this barrier between you and me—just know that I plan on beating the shit out of it. You *will* be mine, Liberty Bell. Do you hear me? And someday, I want to hear exactly how you got that name." He tried to smile, but worry wouldn't let his face muscles relax enough to pull it off.

Libby's mind went back to the bout of nausea which had overtaken her only a little while ago. "Everything will work out. We just have to have a little faith."

"My faith is in you, Libby." He kissed her one more time before heading for the door, and Dallas.

* * *

Joseph lay in the hospital bed and wished he were dead. There was no way he could live like this. The doctors had tried to tell him the paralysis could be temporary due to swelling around the spinal cord. But they were only spouting off guesses. Hell, he couldn't even piss by himself. Every time a nurse came in and wanted to mess with the catheter that was stuck up his dick, he just wanted to throw a fuckin' bedpan at 'em.

Rolling his head from side to side, he tortured himself with a mental list of things he might never do again.

Ride a horse.

Climb a mountain.

Take a shit in anything besides a damn bag.

Walk.

Feel a warm, soft woman beneath him.

Get an erection.

Hell! Damn! Fuck! Joseph heard familiar footsteps coming down the hall - three sets of them. The steel-toed boots and the long determined strides of the McCoy brothers were unmistakable. In anguish, Joseph realized that he might never walk beside them again.

As the hospital room door creaked open, he reset the muscles of his face into a devil-may-care expression. He couldn't let them know he was scared shitless. They didn't deserve to have to put up with a brother in his condition. He would have to see what he could do about that.

* * *

Libby had lain on the bathroom floor for about twenty minutes. She had kept the door locked. Now was no time to cause concern or generate questions—whether with Nathan or Noah. Concern over Joseph must come first. She had not let the time go to waste, however. She used it to reactivate her prayer life. She prayed for Joseph, that he would get well and go back to being the happy-go-lucky man they loved. Libby prayed for the family, that they would hold it together and be strong for Joseph. She especially prayed for Aron, asking God to encase him in a cocoon of warmth and peace. Lastly, she prayed for herself. Libby didn't want to die and leave Aron. Libby wanted to live.

When she was able to resume her work, she returned to the kitchen and put on a big pot of chili. The spicy stew would be perfect, because she could keep it hot and the guys could come in and eat it when they had time and felt hungry. Right now, it was her job to keep the house going and things as normal for Nathan as she could make them.

The phone rang a little after six. Noah grabbed it, anxious to hear news. He spoke quietly for a few minutes, and then handed the phone to Libby. She took the phone and Noah got up, giving her some privacy. "Hey, Baby." Aron's voice sounded tired.

"I love you, Aron." It was the most comforting thing she could think to say. "How's Joseph?"

"I love you, too, more than you'll ever know. I wish you were here...I keep reaching for your hand. Jacob's slapped me twice. He thinks I'm getting fresh with him." Libby laughed at the mental picture. Aron's voice grew serious. "The tests are coming back, and the doctors say that Joseph has a spinal cord injury. They still can't tell us the full extent, but they know there is damage around the T10-L2 level."

"What does that mean?"

"I may be saying it all wrong, but right now Joseph seems to be fine above the waist, but he has very limited sensation below. That's not to say he won't regain some or all of it, but, right now, we just don't know. I can tell he is scared to death." Aron's tone revealed to Libby that he was worried and weary, also.

"What's next?" she asked.

"We're bringing him back to Austin in the morning. I want Dr. Cassidy to see him, as he's the absolute best. Oh, yeah, and I've called a contractor to come out and put in some ramps and do some work on the back wing to make a place for Joseph to have all the room he'll need...for...whatever."

Libby understood. Joseph's ordeal was going to be a long drawn out battle, at best.

"Tell him I love him," Libby whispered.

"I'll do it. You get some rest Libby-pearl. I'll kiss you awake when I get there."

"So, you're coming back tonight?"

"Yes, Jacob is going to stay and come back with Joseph when they transport him. Isaac and I are going to come home and then we'll all meet him at Brackenridge, tomorrow. They have a woman there that's supposedly doing wonders with patients like Joseph."

"Be safe," Libby said softly. "I'll leave the front porch light on."

"I will be, and Doll—keep the bed warm, I need you so badly. It just feels like that if I could get my arms around you, everything would be all right."

"Hurry home, I'll be waiting."

Getting ready for bed, Libby made some decisions. Life was so uncertain, no one was guaranteed tomorrow. What happened to Joseph lent credence to that age-old truth. She decided that she was going to live as if God had sent her a memo and told her that she would break the century barrier. In a few days, she would keep her appointment with Doc Mulligan, but there would be no plans to leave Tebow until the day came when she felt that Aron was ready for her to go.

At the same time, she wanted to cover her bases and mend any fences that might have sagged over the years. Before she lay down, she wrote down the names of two friends she wanted to reconnect with, and she found a Bible in the den that she intended to read through—it had always been a goal of hers. Finally, she thought about making a will. That was funny; she didn't have anything to leave to anybody, except for her one precious piece of Aron's sculpture— 'Freedom'. And the only person she wanted to have that was its creator, Aron. If things looked like they were digressing, she wanted to put it back into his hands and see his face when he realized she had kept it safe for him all of these years.

* * *

Aron gently closed the door behind him. It was good to be home. The helicopter carrying Joseph and Jacob had probably beaten them back to the Hill Country. As soon as morning came, they would head to the hospital as a family. A Dr. Susan Grigsby was going to sit in on the consult with Cassidy and they would evaluate Joseph's test results and recommend what would come next. One thing which worried Aron was the thought of Joseph having to exist in a sterile hospital setting. That was why he intended to build whatever facilities were needed for Joseph to rehabilitate at home. While the contractors were at it, he was going to build a studio for Libby—a place where she could design and create her handbags. It was good to have contacts. He had placed a few phone calls to a man he knew in New York, and soon boxes and boxes of fabrics, decorations, leathers, and all manners of sewing supplies would be delivered to the front steps of Tebow. He had also told Gregory to send state of the art sewing machines and sergers so Libby would have the very best tools to work with. There was nothing too good for his love, and he couldn't wait to see her eyes light up when she saw his surprise. It would all come to pass quickly, because Aron wanted things to settle down and get back to some semblance of normal. Joseph was going to be all right...Aron was determined he would be. Nothing else was acceptable.

Heading up to bed, he found her right where she belonged. "Now, that's what I needed to see." He breathed a sigh as he took in the sight of Libby in bed, curled up on her side. Her hand was underneath her cheek, and the covers were thrown back to reveal the fact that she was waiting on him wrapped only in the beautiful skin God had originally clothed her in. Stripping, he was eager to feel her warmth merge with his.

"Libby-honey, open those arms, I'm home." Immediately, she opened herself to him, fitting her body to his, welcoming him home.

"I'm so glad you're here. How's Joseph?" She didn't give him time to answer. She was so starved for the taste of his kiss that she molded her lips to his and drank greedily. Aron answered in kind. Rolling to his back, he pulled her on top of him, letting his hands move down her body, memorizing every dip and hill. He plunged his tongue in deep, letting it mate with hers. How wonderful it was to be greeted with a homecoming like this.

So glad to be with her, Aron felt playful. Running his hand down her silky back, he let his fingers play lower. Her sweet bottom was beckoning him to caress and mold. Dipping his finger between the clefts of her cheeks, he teased regions that had as of yet gone unexplored. She gasped at the unfamiliar intrusion. Aron just laughed, "Nice crack, Liberty Bell."

Not to be out done, she came back with one of her own. "Why don't you just give me your John Hancock, already?"

"So, you want me to dip my feather in your ink?" Their happy laughter filled the room.

"I'm sure there's a law against patriotic porn on the books somewhere," she teased.

"Just as long as there is no law against loving you." Aron put his hands under her arms and lifted her up, sliding her body over his until he could get one of her nipples in his mouth. Without preliminaries, he began to suckle, seemingly taking comfort from the feel of her breast in his mouth. Libby lay her head on the pillow above his, relaxed, enjoying the tug and pull of his lips and the rasping of his tongue. In a moment, his fingers found her sex and he began to massage her slit, sliding his finger in and out, reminding her why she had been created. His mouth became insistent on her breast, demanding an audible response to his lovemaking. She gave it to him.

"You are making me crazy, Aron." She tightened her sheath around his fingers, moving her hips in a dance of excitement. Pulling one nipple out of his mouth, she shifted and offered him the other. He never missed a beat, consuming the jealous nipple with a devotion equal to what had been lavished on its counterpart. "Bite me, please – just a little."

Chuckling under his breath, and without turning loose of her breast, he nipped at her nipple. The sharp jolt of erotic shock ripped through her, making her wonder at the depths of sexual exploration still available for them to delve into. "Oh, I like that," she praised him. "You are so good."

"Can't wait any longer," he announced. Guiding her to one side, he rolled them over, careful to keep his full weight from crushing her. "Open those legs, Libby. I need to come inside."

Splaying herself open, she lay there eagerly awaiting him. "I ache Aron, fill me up, please." Libby lifted her hips to him, panting for his possession. Slowly, he pushed in. He seemed larger than usual, bigger around, more swollen. She felt her channel stretching to make room for his tremendous girth. Every nerve ending in her vagina was tingling with high-pitch awareness. Even the lips of her vulva were passion-kissed with arousal, seeking to fit themselves around his member, making them one in body as well as spirit.

"Look at me, Libby," Aron demanded as he sank further into her. She lifted her amethyst eyes to him, but they were unseeing, unaware of anything but the wonder of his claiming. "Do you know who you belong to, Libby?"

She managed to nod, but she couldn't verbalize a response. Aron thrust into her hard, as if he were planting a flag, claiming his property. "You are mine, Liberty Bell. I don't want there to be a doubt in your mind." Sitting back on his haunches, he pulled her up and across him, lifting her hips, angling her so that he would drag sensuously across the very place which would drive her insane.

Taking complete control, Aron thrust into her again, slowly, rubbing the distended purple glans at the head of his penis across the spongy spot that was made for just a time as this. What a marvel the human body was, she managed to think. She was created just for him, fashioned to accommodate his male needs and demands. "Mine, Libby. Mine," he chanted as he drove into her, pushing as deep within her heart as he was into her body. He laid his hand flat on her belly, steadying her for his pummeling. Unable to contain the bliss, Libby shattered into a million shards of light and color. Her body fluttered and pulsed around his staff, massaging his phallus until he too, flamed and detonated, pouring himself into her with unequaled vigor. Even after he had emptied himself, Aron kept rocking into her, unwilling to pull out and break the sweet connection.

"I love you, Aron." Libby said it like a prayer, a fitting benediction to a sacred act.

"I worship you, Baby. You don't know what it meant to me, knowing you were here waiting for me." He moved from over her, fitting himself to her back, pressing against her, asserting himself as her protector.

"Can I go with you to see Joseph tomorrow?" she asked, holding her breath. As far as she was concerned, this was a test. Did he consider her a girlfriend or a bedmate?

"Of course. He's already been asking for you. He wants some of your brownies." Before he knew what was happening, she was out of the bed. "Hey!"

Smacking him on the forehead with a loud kiss, she calmed him. "Go to sleep. I'll be back in an hour and a half. If Joseph wants brownies, then he gets brownies." Aron knew there was no use arguing with her. Libby had made up her mind.

As she padded down the stairs, Aron lay there and counted his blessings. Libby made life worth living. If only Joseph were whole again, life would be perfect. Throwing the covers off, he went to the sink and wet a washcloth and wiped off the remnants of his passion. Only six weeks ago, he had been alone and lost, bitter in his celibacy. He had only dreamt of having a companion like Libby—one who was sweet, sexy and eager to show him her love. Stroking himself, he remembered the wonder of Libby's heat engulfing him and he prayed to God that Joseph wouldn't have to go through life and never experience this kind of joy.

When the brownies were done, Libby returned to Aron's arms. Without awakening, he instinctively made a place for her, whispering her name and nuzzling her neck. Before sleeping, she sent up another petition that she be given the gift of health and life so she could spend her days caring for and spoiling the man that she loved.

* * *

Libby and Aron entered the hospital room expecting to find an invalid; instead they found an agitated, unhappy McCoy—which is a fearsome thing. "I want to go home, Aron." Joseph demanded.

Even as he bellowed at his brother, he held his arms open to Libby. She sat the brownies down on the rolling table and hurried to step into Joseph's hug. "How are you?" she whispered for his ears only.

"Holding up," he whispered back.

"I'm getting you out of here as fast as I can," Aron assured him. "I've got two crews who will be there today and they are making all the modifications necessary so we can get you set up for anything you may need."

"Sounds good to me. I'll go crazy if I have to stay in this place very much longer."

"Can I get you anything?" Aron asked.

"How about some coffee to go with those scrumptious smelling brownies?" Joseph wanted to get Aron out of the room. He needed to talk to Libby.

Aron left for the coffee, willing to do anything that would perhaps bring a smile to his brother's face. Once the door shut behind him, Joseph sobered. "Libby, you've got to do something for me."

Libby didn't like the change in his demeanor or his voice. "What would that be, Joseph? You know I'd do anything to help."

"I want the truth. I need you to find out from Aron exactly what my expectations are. They're just feeding me a line of bull. I know I'll never walk again…there's no way. I can't feel my feet. Hell I can't even feel my balls unless I reach down to see if they're still there. I don't know if I can face life as half a man, Libby." He sounded so desperate; she knew he wanted to scream in frustration. Libby knew exactly how he felt. She had felt the exact same way that very day.

Even though it shouldn't be so, with a man it was different. Libby recognized the symptoms. She had seen it more than once. A man's identity was so tied up in his strength, how tall he stands, and in his virility. She heard panic in his voice, raw panic that could eat away at your sanity and leave you questioning the value of facing another day.

Joseph was questioning his legitimacy as a human being. This scared the crap out of her. She had to get through to him.

"Joseph Anthony McCoy, you listen to me—and you listen to me good." Libby got right up in his face, desperate to make him understand. Life is worth living, in whatever state you're offered it. I'm going to level with you. Aron doesn't know this yet, and I shouldn't be telling you before I tell him…but this is an emergency, so…here goes. I have spent the last eight years of my life living on borrowed time." At Joseph's puzzled expression, she sat down beside him and took his hands in hers. "At present, I am in remission. My disease of choice is leukemia. The type I have is fairly aggressive and remission doesn't usually last over two years. Yet during this unexpected and perhaps brief reprieve, I have fallen head over heels in love with your brother. He wants a future with me, a future I have no assurance even exists."

Joseph was flabbergasted. "Libby, you have cancer?" Pulling her to him, he held her close. "No, you've got to be all right! We can't do without you."

"Exactly, my point—and we can't do without you!" she spoke in an adamant, no-nonsense tone. "Joseph, I have hope. It may be stupid, but I don't have a choice. In one week, I'll go and sit down in front of a doctor and he will tell me whether my blood count is still improving or whether it is taking a nose-dive. Just yesterday, I had waves of nausea knock me to my knees. Yet, I can't give up. I want to live too badly to throw my hands up and quit. I love your brother, and I want to live for him. And you, you don't know what the final verdict is, yet. You have to get a grip and find a way to hold on. Joseph, you have got to have hope, also. Your family loves you. I love you. And, there's a woman out there—somewhere, that was meant just for you. She's not here yet, but she's coming. Love is worth holding on for."

Libby could tell she had hit a sore spot. He looked at her sadly. "I don't have anything to offer a woman, Libby. My injury has stolen my manhood."

"Don't say that, Joseph." She clasped his hands. "Let's make a pact. I'll pray for your miracle, if you pray for mine."

"Deal?" She waited, expectantly.

He hesitated for a few long moments. Finally, he answered, "Deal." Solemnly, they shook on it. This is the way that Aron found them.

"I just leave the room, and come back and you two are all lovey-dovey. Should I be jealous?" he asked with a smile.

"Yes, you should." Joseph kissed Libby on the forehead soundly. "If the day ever comes, when you don't want her—I'll be standing, hopefully, standing by."

"I want you standing, Joseph…walking, running, jumping…whatever." Aron assured him. "But you can't have my Liberty Bell."

"Your what?" Joseph wasn't privy to Libby's real name.

"Liberty Bell Fontaine," Libby explained with a smile. "My mom was from Philadelphia, and about the time I was born, I think she was feeling homesick."

* * *

Libby cooked and cleaned around the mess the contractors were making. The hustle and bustle of revamping the back wing of the Tebow main house was exciting in a way. It meant that Joseph could come home as soon as possible, and they could care for him. Libby was nervous. She had endured two more bouts of nausea, complete with throwing up.

But instead of giving up, she was determined to have a positive attitude. Oddly enough, her puniness only seemed to affect her after breakfast, and by noon it was over and she would feel fine. Aron wouldn't let her go back and inspect the work being done. He told her she might get hurt, and on top of that, he wanted it to be a surprise. Why he wanted to surprise her, she didn't know. The work was being done for Joseph.

No one had thought to do it, so Libby did—she called Bess and broke the news to her about their sweet dare-devil. Libby had thought long and hard about calling her. She halfway expected for Bess to say she was on her way back to Tebow and Libby wasn't certain she wanted that. She wasn't ready to leave. Aron might want her to stay, but there were still doubts floating around in her head.

Bess was shocked, to say the least. She said she would call Joseph, but she didn't offer to come home. In fact, she talked as if Libby's time there was indefinite. That sounded like music to Libby's ears, but there was still the dreaded doctor's appointment to get through.

* * *

The work was complete, and Libby couldn't wait to see what Aron had done to accommodate his brother. She had so much planned…they all did, and everyone was anxious to have Joseph home. She had gone to see him almost every day and each time they were alone, Joseph questioned her about how she was feeling. The doctor's appointment was the day after next, and Joseph's support was one of the main things keeping her going. She still hadn't confided in Aron. She just couldn't bring herself to do it. After seeing Doc Mulligan, she would know what she was going to say, anyway.

There were plans to bring Joseph home that very afternoon, so Libby began cooking all of his favorites. She decided to make it her personal mission to keep his spirits as high as possible. At the stove, she worked on a pot of homemade chicken noodle soup. Adding some parsley and cream, she put it on a slow simmer. When two large, warm hands slid around her waist, she didn't even start, his touch bringing her the greatest comfort in the world. Leaning back against him, she breathed a sigh of contentment. "I'm so glad Joseph is coming home." As soon as she said the words, she almost bit her tongue. She had to be careful…she was beginning to talk as if this were her permanent home and she was the matriarch or something.

"Yeah, me too." Kissing the back of her neck, he teased, "You smell almost as good as your soup." Pulling her gently by the hand he walked her to the rear of the house. "Close your eyes. I've got something to show you."

"They're closed. It smells good in here. I love the 'new' stuff smell." Aron was right behind her, his hands moving up and down her arms. When they stopped, he moved to her right side. "Okay, open them." Libby did. For a moment, she didn't understand what she was seeing. This wasn't what she was expecting—not at all. Where she was prepared to see exercise equipment, massage tables, whirlpool baths, and stuff like that—instead, she saw shelves and work tables. Libby put her hand over her mouth and walked forward. There was a sewing machine and a serger. There was equipment to attach jewels and studs. And the wildest part was that the shelves were full of every type of material and fabric imaginable. Boxes of beads, jewels, brads, studs…all types of decorations were in neat little cases. There were scissors and tape measures, threads and cording, enough to make any designer cry. Sweetest of all was the sign on the wall. "Libby's Designer Bags."

Libby began to cry. Turning, she blindly groped for him. She didn't have to move but a few inches when he pulled her close. "Do you like it, Baby?"

"You did this, for *me*?"

"I'd do anything for you, Libby-mine." This was fast becoming his favorite Libbyism. Libby's tears were not fading; in fact she was beginning to sob. Aron didn't know what to do. This was supposed to make her happy—not sad. "Hey, hey." He scooped her up. "Why in God's name are you crying, Sweetheart?"

Little hiccups of tears interfered with her speech patterns. "What….about….if….I….have….to….leave?"

"Leave? Libby, you're not going anywhere."

"I may not have anything to offer you." She sobbed into his shoulder.

"What do you mean? You have the only thing in the world that I

Cowboy Heat

want."

"What is that?" More hiccups. More tears.

"You."

You. His love for her was a miracle. Dare she hope for two? "I may not be able to stay forever."

"I don't know what that means, but I won't settle for anything less. Forever is the only thing that will do. Forever is all I want. It's the only thing I will accept."

She framed his face with her hands and began to smother him with kisses. The passion that always smoldered between them flared up. "Let's christen my sewing table," she suggested with a twinkle.

He carried her over to the wide wooden surface. "Good suggestion, Babe. It's just the right height."

"Right height for what?"

"For this." He laid her down, pushed her skirt up and ripped her lace panties off with one sharp tug. "Do you know what I want to do?"

"Yeah, probably." She hoped.

"I want to shave you. Will you let me?"

"What?" This was a surprise.

"I want you smooth as silk. Do you trust me?"

"With my life." That wasn't a lie.

"Lay right there." He was gone 94 seconds, she counted. When he returned, he had a towel, a razor, some shaving cream and a wash cloth.

"Heavens to Betsy!" she gasped.

"That's right, Libby, I'm about to shave you till you're smooth and soft as a baby's bottom." He proceeded to do just that. With great care, he dampened the area, applied shaving cream and began to pass the sharp blade over the delicate, down-covered skin. She tensed up, not really expecting it to hurt, but fully aware this was a totally new experience. Trust Aron to make it a spectacular experience! He would shave a spot, wipe, then kiss—shave a spot, wipe, then kiss. By the time he had her naked, she was wet and ready for some extra special attention. Aron went a little crazy; he rubbed his face across her smooth mons, bumped her clitoris with his nose and tongued her thoroughly from one end of her slit to the other. By the time he had made two passes, Libby couldn't remember her own name.

"Aron, I swear to God, if you don't get inside of me right now, I'm going to scream." Libby panted with desire. When Aron hesitated, stripping off his clothes, Libby scooted her bottom down the table and made a grab for his business.

Aron dodged, just for fun. "Do you want something Libby-mine?"

"Yes, I do." She made another pass at him, again he side-stepped.

With a wicked gleam in her eye, Libby decided to change tactics. She knew this would work; it had certainly paid off at the stock tank.

Opening her legs, she showed him what he was missing. Thanks to Aron, she was as smooth as silk. Pink, glistening and swollen, it felt as if she were actually pulsing down there. Never taking her eyes off of him, she sucked on her forefinger really slow. Aron almost stopped breathing. She had his attention. Taking the wet, glistening finger, she rimmed her pussy lips, enjoying the new-found smoothness. A little hum of satisfaction escaped her mouth. Aron moved one step closer. Making one circle around her clitoris, Libby made hungry little grunting noises, specifically designed to make Aron sorry he had started the teasing game. "You can go back to work Aron, I've got this one," she spoke in a husky tone. Ignoring the movement she heard at the edge of the table, Libby moved her finger down her slit to the opening that was swollen and puckered, like a hungry little mouth. Sliding her still wet finger inside of herself, she wiggled it around and moved it in and out, letting her hips gyrate to a tune that only she could hear.

"Good God, Libby," Aron breathed.

At his tortured tone, she added another dimension to the performance. Moving her hands away from her pussy for a brief respite, she plumped her breasts and began to tease them. "They want to be sucked, Aron." Taking her nipples in her fingers, she pulled on them, distending them out, then rolling them around between her thumb and forefinger until she drove her own self mad. One hand ventured back down to her desperate little hole, and she slid in – adding another finger to the first, pushing rhythmically in and out of herself until she moaned in pleasure.

"Stop. Stop." Aron ordered. "You're killing me." He clasped both of her hands and stilled their movement. Grabbing her ankles, he pulled her right to the edge of the table and plunged in. There was no preliminaries, no introductions, no warning. Libby literally screamed with relief when he began to hammer inside of her. "You shouldn't tease," he admonished as he gave her just what she craved.

"Good God, Libby," Aron breathed.

"I don't know why not," she panted, "I seemed to be getting what I deserve." Her rapier wit, even in the midst of a good romp amused him no end.

"Oh, you think so, do you?" He didn't know how long he could keep up the banter, but he didn't want to be the first one who slipped into mindlessness. "I think you deserve better than this."

"What do you think I deserve?" He picked up one leg at a time and placed them up on his shoulders. Kissing her ankle, he ran his hands up and down her legs.

"I think you deserve to be deeply and completely –" he paused for effect. Libby thought he was about to talk dirty to her, but instead, he almost made her cry. For the word he growled, was the most precious one he could have enunciated – "loved."

At his sweet words, she lost it. No longer able to say anything, she just laid back and enjoyed herself. The feeling of him loving her was the most wonderful sensation she could ever hope to experience. No doubt about it, she felt taken, possessed, conquered. But mostly, she felt cherished. Her climax overtook her and she trembled like a leaf in a hurricane. "Aron, Aron," she moaned. "Don't stop, for God's sake, don't stop."

He couldn't have stopped if the world had been grinding to a screeching, apocalyptic halt. The feel of her fisting around him in convulsive, tiny movements made him swell until he thought he would literally burst. She watched him take his pleasure, she watched him throw his head back and bow his neck. God, she loved him. She adored him. Wanting to see the wild side of the man she craved, she whispered, "Show me your teeth, Baby." When she said that, he did—he bared his teeth at her and drove inside of her like a raving madman with a jackhammer. Nipping her ankle, he raised her bottom clear off the table and spewed his life-giving essence deep inside of her, marking her forever as his choice.

Needless to say, Libby appreciated her design studio.

Later, he shared with her the haven he had created for Joseph. Now, when they had him home, they would be on the road to recovery.

Chapter Eight

"I hate to bother you Aron, but did you send any money to that address I gave you?" Libby didn't want to have to ask, but if he'd changed his mind, she was going to have to get to the bank and move some money. The last thing she wanted to do was miss a payment to the foundation which had been so generous to her. If it hadn't been for them, she wouldn't have been able to finish school or take the college classes she had enjoyed so much. One day, if her remission held, she was going to finish her degree.

They had spent the day readying Joseph's room for his return. The guys had put handrails in the bathrooms and installed a chairlift on the stairs. Isaac had even moved the furniture around in the den and dining room so Joseph's wheelchair would be able to maneuver through the area easier. Aron had just finished a ramp that would ease Joseph's getting on and off the verandah. Finally, everything that needed to be done for their brother's homecoming had been completed. Libby had walked out to bring him a big glass of iced tea, which he drank thirstily.

Aron looked sheepish. "I'll take care of it as soon as I put up my tools. I've had so much on my mind. I'm sorry I forgot." He picked up her hand and kissed her. She had tried to hide it, but Libby was pale, and her skin was slightly damp. Aron was a little worried about her. Maybe, she was just nervous. She still hadn't told him what the big trip to Austin was about at the end of the week. He knew it was momentous for her, and all he could think of was that she had some type of court appearance or legal problem. She had said there was a battle and an enemy and Aron couldn't think of any other possibility. All Libby would have to do was ask, and Aron would have a battalion of lawyers at her disposal. He was fairly confident it was no big deal, or Libby would have been upfront and honest with him about it. Still, he knew it was important to her, or she wouldn't have gauged their relationship by its boundaries. Whatever it was, she wanted it out of the way before she gave their future a green light.

Libby returned inside and Aron cleaned up his work area. When he entered the house, he looked for Libby and found her curled up on one of the couches in the den. She had dozed off. Lifting her, he carried her to their room and laid her on the bed. At the contact with the mattress, she roused. "Aron, when you come to bed, will you get my fuzzy slippers from the bottom of Bess's closet?"

"Sure thing, Babe. Let me take care of that bill for you and I'll be right back." He intended to do an electronic transfer if he could find the information online. Heading to his office, he found the slip of paper which was still folded, just as she had handed it to him. Sitting down at his computer, Aron flipped the power switch and sat back till the monitor woke up. Taking the paper Libby had given him, he unfolded it and looked at the address. His heart immediately rose up into his throat. The recipient was The Rockwell Foundation. His parent's legacy. This was his company. With shaking fingers, Aron logged into the Foundation Website and entered the account number on the paper.

One Liberty Bell Fontaine had been granted a loan of five thousand for tuition, books and fees. She had made ten payments which had all been mailed on time and in full. Aron's heart was beating a mile a minute. There had to be some mistake. This grant money was only available to those adults who were attempting to get their education while battling cancer. Throwing the paper down as if it burned his fingers, he paced up and down the floor.

There was nothing to do, but go ask her. Surely, there was some explanation. Perhaps she'd gotten the loan in her name, but it was for someone else, someone else who had cancer. It had to be. Throwing open the door to his office he started to his bedroom to beg her to explain the mistake. Halfway there, he remembered the slippers. With shaking hands, he opened Bess's door and went to the closet. There on the floor were the pink bunny slippers which would keep her feet warm. Kneeling down, he reached for them. His hand bumped a pasteboard box which contained something quite heavy. Wondering at its contents, he pulled it to him. Opening the box, he stared at the contents dumbly for a moment, until what he was seeing registered with him.

It couldn't be.

It just couldn't be.

Aron doubled over in pain.

No! No! No! He screamed in his head.

Aron's first bronze was in the box, cradled by a generous nest of tissue paper. Everything the PI had said flashed back through his brain. The buyer of 'Freedom' was someone Martinez had seen on television. The buyer of 'Freedom' was a woman who was battling cancer. Leaving the bunny slippers where they lay, Aron stumbled to his feet. He had to get out of the house.

Now.

Not seeing anything, he plowed through the house, staggering through the door and out on the porch. Still not aware of his destination, Aron began to run. If he ran fast enough, he could get away from the truth. If he ran far enough, he could escape the horror that Libby was sick, maybe dying.

God, Libby had cancer.

Damn! Damn! Damn!

She had told him time and time again . . . .

You don't have to say you love me.

I'll stay until it's time for me to go.

I may not be able to stay forever.

I don't have anything to offer you.

Holy Jesus! He was going to die, right here.

Aron fell to his knees and screamed at the top of his lungs.

"No! No! No!"

First his parents – and Lord in heaven knew he'd prayed they would be found alive. But, no. Three days after their car had been washed off the bridge, their bodies had been found, still trapped in their watery grave. Joseph was paralyzed and Aron's prayers had not changed any of the test results. And now his precious Libby was sick.

What was he going to do?

What had he done?

Aron beat the ground with his fists. He had given his all for his family. Never had he even considered backing away from them or throwing his hands up. He had always put others first.

"Libby! Oh, God – Libby!"

Aron cried until he couldn't cry anymore.

Libby was so cold and sick. Shaking, she made her way to the bathroom. "Aron!" She called. "Aron, where are you?" There was no answer. The house was quiet. Jacob, Isaac, Noah and even Nathan were out with the wranglers finishing up the vaccinations and the branding of the weaned calves. They probably wouldn't be in until the wee hours of the morning. There had been no one in the house but them. Now Aron was gone. She made it to the bathroom, but she couldn't sit up. So, she lay down on the floor near the tub. She would rest her eyes, just for a moment. Then, she would feel better.

Aron sat out under a spreading pecan for over an hour. He had to get control of his mind and his body. Reasoning with himself, he went over his options. Clearly, he had to get Libby to talk to him. Obviously, this had everything to do with the secret appointment she had to keep. Why hadn't she told him? Aron felt betrayed. Didn't she trust him?

What did this mean for them? Holding his head in his hands, Aron tried to think. Offering up one prayer after another, he asked God to calm him enough so he could make the right decisions. Rocking back and forth in agony, he waited for a sign.

Little by little, peace flowed into his soul. And with the peace came a modicum of clarity. It was easy. Libby was his gift from God, so therefore God must intend for him to have her and keep her. They could face this together. They could beat this together. With that revelation easing his mind, Aron went back to the house.

Libby was scared. She felt so bad. Where was Aron? Finally, she heard footsteps coming down the hall. When they entered the bedroom, she heard them pause. He was looking for her in the bed, only she wasn't there. "Libby? Baby?" Walking the few short steps to the bathroom he spotted her. "Baby, oh God!" Kneeling beside her, he lifted her in his arms.

"Would you take me to the doctor, Aron? I'm sick. I feel so bad." Her voice was so small, yet the request was so momentous. Taking just a millisecond to cleave unto her, he vowed to God to do whatever it took to keep her.

He radioed for Jacob. There was no way he could drive and hold her at the same time. And he needed to hold her.

"I'm sorry, Aron." Libby whispered.

"Shhh, Baby." He comforted her. "Everything is going to be okay."

Before long, they were headed to the hospital. Mulligan had been called and he would meet them there. Mulligan! Damn, he should have recognized his name. He was the Chief Oncologist at Brackenridge. Hell, Aron was on the board, but apparently he wasn't on the ball. The name hadn't even rung a bell with him.

"I should have told you," Libby continued to try and make amends. "I thought I would get to feeling better." She held on to his shirt with a tight little fist and buried her head in his shoulder. "I've been living with leukemia for years." When every muscle in his body tensed, she began rubbing his chest and arms and shoulders, anything she could reach. "I've been in remission and I didn't want you to know anything about it until after my check-up." Aron rubbed his lips back and forth across her forehead. When he didn't say anything, she sought to find more words to say to make it all better. "If you don't want to come with me, I'd understand. Who wants to wait at the hospital while all those tests are being taken?"

"Where else would I go, Sweetheart?" Aron asked. His voice was stiff with unshed tears. "My place is by your side. And that's where I'm going to be."

Jacob drove carefully, but at a pace designed to eat up the miles. He kept glancing in the rearview mirror, willing Libby to feel better.

"You knew about this, didn't you? You son-of-a-bitch," he bit out at Jacob, once he realized Libby had dozed off. It had just registered with Aron that this was the secret Jacob had kept for so long.

"Yeah, I didn't want to. But, she begged me to keep her secret. She didn't want you to see her as a sick person; she wanted you to see her as a desirable woman."

That was the stupidest thing Aron had ever heard. Libby was a desirable woman. How else could he ever see her?

"I was the one that headed up most of the fund raisers for Libby." Aron tried to remember if he had ever heard anything about Libby or her sickness. Surely, if his brother had been *that* involved, he would have known something was going on. Wouldn't he? Was he so selfish? Was he so self-absorbed that he would miss something so important?

Jacob was the philanthropist, the community activist. Just this afternoon, the Little League Advisory Board had called him. There had been a break-in at the concession stand, and he was the one who had to go and make sure everything was fixed and accounted for. Who would want to break in a concession stand? A few things had been reported missing, but mostly it was just bread and ketchup. The thief was obviously not a gourmand.

"I'm sorry, Aron. I know this has thrown you for a loop. But, it was her place to tell you, not mine." Jacob watched his brother's face. If he could take away their pain he would have done it in a heartbeat. God, he wished he had that ability – to touch the ones he loved and just take away their pain. Aron. Joseph. Libby. What a miracle it would be if such a gift existed.

"She's going to be fine," Aron assured himself as well as his brother. "She's got to get well and Joseph's got to get to feeling better. We've got a wedding to plan."

At the mention of nuptials, Libby came to life.

"Let's not talk of weddings." Libby urged.

"Oh yes, we must talk of a wedding," Aron assured her.

"Aron, I'm in remission, but the leukemia I have doesn't normally stay in remission very long." Every syllable she let leave her lips shot a dagger through his heart.

"I'm going to marry you, Libby. I want to give you as many new adventures as you can handle: a husband, a home of your own, children, Fourth of July picnics, Easter Egg Hunts – the whole shebang."

"It sounds wonderful, but we just can't count on it." Her voice was so weak it scared the living daylights out of Aron.

"Jacob, write it on the calendar. We're getting married, Libby and I, three months from tonight. What day will that be?"

Jacob did some math in his head and came up with an answer. "October the 16th."

Libby smiled, "The sweetest day."

"What?" Aron was trying to follow, but he was worried sick.

"October the 16th is designated as the sweetest day." Libby's voice was weak, but she was paying attention.

"That sounds about right, Libby-mine. Any day when you became my wife would be the sweetest day that the sun ever rose to brighten the sky."

"Jacob, will you be my best man?" Aron was not leaving anything to chance. Before they reached that hospital, he wanted Libby to realize he was dead-serious about their having a future."

"There are four others who will want in on the festivities." Jacob assured Libby.

"Who do you want to ask to be your bridesmaids?" Aron asked her.

"I don't have anybody to ask." Libby confessed softly.

"That's all right," Aron reassured her. Jacob and the boys will get right on the task of finding themselves some women. We have a need for them; every beautiful bride deserves beautiful bridesmaids."

"We'll get right on it," Jacob assured them.

* * *

Doc Mulligan met them at the hospital. Aron didn't like the worried expression on his face. Libby made the introductions and the Doctor was glad to shake their hands.

Aron wasn't shy about identifying himself as Libby's fiancé. This pleased Doc Mulligan to no end. "Well, I have never been more honored to meet anyone in my life. Did you know we would sit and talk about you?"

Aron wondered at the doctor's comment. Libby smiled a weak little smile and told Aron, "One of the last doctor's orders I received from him was that I should go out and find someone to love."

"This is the sweetest little girl I know." It was obvious the doctor cared more about Libby that just a normal doctor/patient relationship.

"You'll get no argument from me about that." Aron shook hands with the doctor and then introduced him to his brother.

"I have to take her back now, and run a whole mess of tests." He explained to Aron. "You can pass the time out in the waiting room or leave your cell phone number and go to a hotel; I'll have one of the nurses call you when I get some answers."

With hat in hand, Aron stood his ground. "Thanks, but no thanks. I'll be just outside the door."

"So will I," Jacob chimed in.

This didn't sit well with Libby. "Why don't you go get some rest, Aron? It's late. You and Jacob are both tired."

Neither of them would budge. "I can't rest away from you, Libby-mine." He gave her a sweet, slow kiss. "I'll be right here. You hurry back to me."

The doctor took her behind closed doors and the waiting began. "What do you think they're doing to her?" Aron asked Jacob.

"Blood tests, I would think."

"Have you prayed?" Aron knew the answer, but knew Jacob would find a way to make him feel better.

"I have prayed for her every day she has been with us. I knew from the start that you two belonged together. After all you've been through, Libby and her guileless goodness was just what you needed."

"God wouldn't take her from me, would he?" Aron asked the one question that Jacob had no way to answer.

He tried anyway.

"Libby is going to be fine."

Four hours later, a nurse called his name. "Mr. McCoy?" Both he and Jacob jumped, but it was Aron who rose and followed the uniformed woman dressed all in white.

The doctor was sitting on a stool beside Libby.

Aron couldn't read his expression.

"I need to talk to the both of you. I found something."

Aron's heart flipped over. This couldn't be good. Usually, when a doctor says he has found something, it's a tumor or something worse – if that were possible.

"What is it?" Libby's face was more peaceful than he had ever seen it. In fact, there was a glow of contentment to her countenance. Aron thought he knew why. Libby was in love. With him. And no matter what the doctor had found, no matter what the final diagnosis might be, their love would stand unchanged and eternal.

"What did you find?" Aron wondered if he would wish he had never asked the question.

"Well, I have good news." The doctor paused for effect. "The remission is still holding strong." Aron let out a huge sigh of relief. He moved across the room and grabbed his baby. She let him hold her, he could tell she was almost in shock, her whole body was trembling.

After a few moments, Aron's thinking ability began to kick back in. "What about the symptoms, her nausea and lightheadedness?"

"That wasn't all the news I had." The doctor seemed to have a flair for the dramatic.

What other news could there possibly be? Libby's remission was still holding on.

"What else, Doc?" Libby asked nervously. What if he gave her another timetable to worry about counting down?

"The nausea and sickness in question does have a source." Doc had an unreadable expression on his face.

Oh, no. What else could be wrong?

They waited for the verdict.

Throwing up his hands, Doc Mulligan nearly whooped with glee. "Libby's pregnant. She's going to have a baby!"

No one said a word. Noises from down the hall could be heard, but in their room there was nothing.

Finally, Libby broke the silence. "Pregnant?" She couldn't believe it. Putting her hands on her stomach, she moved them over the flat area in disbelief. "I'm pregnant? With a baby?"

Aron was ecstatic. He went to the bed, scooped Libby up and spun her around and around. Doc Mulligan cautioned him. "That might not be the wisest move considering her bouts of morning sickness."

Aron agreed. He slowed her to a halt, and then held her close. "I love you. I love you. I love you," he whispered.

"I never expected this," she looked at him through tear filled eyes. Doc stepped out to give them a bit of privacy and to get the papers ready for them to go.

"My prayers were answered." Aron had no doubt about that.

They held one another for a few more minutes, then Libby thought of his brother. "Jacob's waiting. Go to him."

"Okay, I'll be right back." He sat her carefully on the bed. Aron went out and told Jacob the good news, the first revelation – the remission news. He wanted to save the announcement about the baby until all the brothers could be together, including Joseph.

"Thank goodness, something is going right." Jacob sighed with relief.

He drove the couple back home. Libby slept most of the way, exhausted from the ordeal of testing. Aron held her most of the time, he was content to just watch her sleep.

"You love her don't you?" Jacob observed happily.

"More than my next breath."

"I want what you have. And as God as my witness, I'm going to find it." Jacob vowed.

* * *

All at Tebow Ranch was peacefully still as dawn broke. Not everything was perfect; one of their own still lay in a rehabilitation center, broken from a fall. But time was righting the wrongs and smoothing out the wrinkles. The balance which had been lost years ago was finally righting itself.

Upstairs, in the master bedroom, Aron crooned to Libby. "See, everything is going to be all right." Aron looked deep into her eyes, making sure she digested every word he said.

"Yes, I believe you."

"You said I didn't have to say that I love you, but I did. My love for you is my life's truth." He stroked her hair back from her brow, tracing the beloved features of her face. "Your love defines me. It is my reason for living." Aron hadn't known he could wax poetic, but the words were flowing from him unbidden. He had to make her understand. "You are my reason for existing, Libby. I love you with a love deeper than the sea – a love that will last longer than forever."

Libby turned in his arms and held on to him for dear life. "I often doubted whether or not I would get to live. But now that I know that God has granted me grace-days, I want to put them to the best use. Aron, my love, I devote my life to living just for you."

"There will be decades of days. We're going to grow old together. You, me, our children and all of my brothers and their families – Tebow Ranch is going to be a place of love and laughter." Aron gently unbuttoned Libby's night shirt, opening it all the way so he could lay his head over his unborn child. "I can promise you both one thing, a day will never go by that I don't tell the two of you how much you mean to me. I will tell you I love you every day for the rest of my life."

* * *

Joseph was ready to go home. He had one of the cute little nurses' aides get all of his gear together. Isaac and Noah would be after him and in a matter of hours he would be back on Tebow land.

If he had to live the life of a cripple, at least he could live it at home. The doctors and nurses were optimistic, but an optimistic outlook was hard for him to maintain. Was he going to have to live like this forever? Was there anyone in the world who could help him?

The soundless cry for help rose from his bed and reverberated out into the universe – and lo and behold, as the old fairy tales read – someone was listening. A connection was made. Help was on the way. Sometimes there are wonders in this world that go beyond the realm of understanding.

* * *

Back at the ranch, a door creaked open and a shadow slipped along the wall outside the barn. Several cows lowed in protest. There was a stranger on Tebow land. No one in the house heard anything. The stranger went to the stock tank, stripped quickly and then used the warm water to wash off the day's grime. After a few moments of stolen luxury, the small form slipped back to the barn. There was food in the small refrigerator upstairs. Maybe, no one would miss just a little. The bed was too nice to sleep in. Beggars and thieves didn't have to be totally classless. So after eating a bit of ketchup and bread, she went down to one of the stalls, curled herself down deep into the hay and settled down to sleep. Before dropping off, she made a wish: please keep me safe, please let me find a place in this world, and please let me find someone to love. She prayed her wish would come true.

* * *

The sun rose in a celebration of pinks and oranges as Noah pulled into the hospital parking lot. At the double electric doors, Joseph was already waiting in his wheel chair, accompanied by two doting nurses. One of them leaned over and kissed him goodbye. "Look at that," Isaac chuckled. "Hard-head don't let stuff keep him down for long." Noah wasn't as light-hearted as his brother; he could see the strain around Joseph's mouth and knew this was going to be one long, hard haul.

"About time you two got here, I've been sitting out here for a half-hour." Joseph complained. The little blonde aide shook her head at Isaac, telling him Joseph was stretching the truth quite a bit.

"The sun's just coming up, Knothead." Isaac was affectionate, but not ready to cut his brother much slack. He knew if they started babying Joseph, he might not bounce back as quickly as he would otherwise.

"How's Libby?" Joseph quietly asked as Noah helped him into the front seat of the King Ranch.

"She's home. Aron had to take her to the doctor." Isaac had spouted off the information before Noah could shush him. Even though the news was good, they didn't need to upset him anymore than he already was.

"Doctor? Libby's been to the doctor?" The concern in Joseph's voice was evident. The brother's did not know Libby had confided in Joseph before she had anyone else.

"Way to go asshole!" Noah grumbled good-naturedly at Isaac as he slung Joseph's bag into the back seat. "Libby's fine. She got a good report, but I'll let her or Aron tell you all about it. They got in late last night and went straight to bed. There's a family meeting just as soon as we can get you back to Tebow.

Joseph smiled. If Libby was all right, then maybe the fates would have good things in store for him, also.

* * *

"Wake up, Beautiful." Aron sat by Libby holding a cup of coffee. Opening her eyes a tiny bit, and realizing what Aron held in his hand, she made such a ruckus Aron was afraid he was going to spill hot coffee on her. "Easy, Baby. Easy."

"God, Aron! I'm so sorry, I've overslept." Careful not to jostle him further, she turned to wiggle out on the other side. "I need to fix breakfast!" Glancing at the clock, she squealed. "Look at the time! Joseph will be here any minute!" While she was still scrambling around trying to get out from under the covers, she finally realized Aron was laughing. He was holding the blanket down on both sides of her so all of her attempts to move were fruitless.

"I've already fixed breakfast, Wiggle-worm," Aron sat the coffee on the bedside table and stretched out beside her. "Did you think I would let you get up and work after the hard day you had yesterday?" Bracketing her pillow with his arms, he leaned over to get his good morning kiss.

Libby didn't need much persuading; she gave her kiss as freely as she had given her heart. "You taste so good," she savored Aron's affection, happy in the knowledge she had a future with this glorious man.

"I've been nibbling on the pumpkin pancakes. I used your recipe."

"It's not the pancakes that taste so good to me – it's the love. I can taste love on your lips," she smiled at him with a happiness and hope in her eyes he had never seen before. "I love you, Aron," she said simply.

Aron cradled her body up close to his. "I love you. More than I'll ever be able to tell you. An ole' country boy like me just doesn't have all the pretty words that a woman like you deserves to hear."

"You're perfect and everything you do is perfect." Libby reveled in the adoration she saw in Aron's eyes.

"You're just prejudiced, the general female population doesn't view me through the same pair of rose-colored glasses that you do." He carefully traced her eyes and nose with his lips, relishing the fact that Libby was his, healthy and pregnant.

"You belong to me!" Libby's gruff little tone tickled the heck out of Aron.

"You bet your bottom dollar I do!" He had something to talk to her about, something he just had to understand. "Sweetheart, can I ask you something?" He lay flat on his back and pulled her on top of him, resting her head underneath his chin.

"Sure." Libby sighed against him. No more secrets.

"How did you end up with *Freedom*?" He no more had the words out that she raised up to gauge his expression.

"You found it?" Her voice was small and quiet. She didn't know why she was embarrassed; it wasn't like she had stolen it or anything.

"When I went to look for your slippers, I found it at the bottom of Bess's closet."

Playing with the buttons on his shirt, she refused to look him in the eye. "I bought it at the fair; I used my birthday money from my parents and grandparents."

"I've been looking for it for years. I made it for my Mom; it was never supposed to be sold." There was no judgment in his voice, he was just stating facts.

A stricken look passed over her face, "I'm sorry, I didn't know. I've had it all this time." Before Aron could explain, big tears started rolling down her face. "I wish I'd known; I would have given it back." She said it all so fast, and moved off of him before he could even begin to react. "Let me get it for you."

Cussing a blue streak, Aron followed her. "Wait, Libby. Do you think I care that you have it? Libby! Don't run; you'll hurt yourself!" Aron found her on the floor of the closet, cradling the bronze in her arms. He sank down beside her, berating himself for making her cry. "I love that you have it, Libby. I'm not mad."

She searched his face, trying to read between the lines. "But, you said..." She held it out to him, wordlessly returning her most treasured possession to its rightful owner. "I knew it didn't cost enough, I should never have been able to afford something so beautiful." Aron took *Freedom* from her and sat it down, choosing to draw her into his arms instead.

"Don't you dare cry. Everything I own is yours, including this piece of baked clay." She didn't automatically put her arms around him, and he started trying to do it for her, willing to cut off his hand before he hurt her again. "I just wanted to know why you bought it, Honey – I'm thrilled you've had it all these years. It makes the connection between us just make that much more sense. Fate was binding us together. Did you know The Rockwell Foundation was set up in memory of my mother? All of this time our lives were intertwined."

Crawling up in his lap, she poured out her heart. "I can't believe it. I confess I've wanted you for years. I went to every football game and every rodeo until I..."

"Until what?" He couldn't believe she had been his for all of these years. What damn wasted time!

"Until I got sick," He caught all of her tears, kissing them away. "When I saw that beautiful horse, he looked so wild and free, I thought if I could just have it for my own, some of its power and spirit would pass to me. And it made me feel closer to you." Bowing her head, she whispered. "Silly, wasn't it?"

"I don't think so. Look at us, we're here, we're together. And you are healthy AND pregnant. I'd say it all worked out just about perfect." He stood up and picked her up, statue and all.

"So, I can keep it?" she patted the bronze as they walked down the hall toward his room, sounding exceedingly pleased.

"Libby, everything I own belongs to you. You can have that statue and I will make you a thousand more." Thinking how he thought his world was ending just the night before, made the events of this morning heart-wrenchingly sweet.

"Just give me one when we the baby is born, how's that?" She looked at him so trustingly he thought his chest would burst with love.

"Done. I'll make you something perfect. Promise." Setting her on the bed, he put slippers on her feet. She just marveled at the wonder of having someone like him care so much for someone like her. "Your coffee is cold by now. Let's get your robe and go down and wait on the rest of the family. I bet Nathan and Jacob are down there waiting on us. Nathan has been begging to see you since we got back last night."

A horn blew outside and Libby nearly bounced out of his arms. "Joseph!" she screamed. "Let's go, Aron!" Laughing, he slung her up on his shoulder like a sack of potatoes.

"Libby!" Nathan hugged her before Aron could put her down. "Libby, are you all right?" There was so much concern in his voice that Libby almost cried.

"I'm right as rain." She hugged Nathan till he squirmed, then she went down the line and gave Jacob a hug. "Thanks for going with us last night. I don't know what we would have done without you."

"That's what brothers are for," Jacob kissed her on the end of the nose. Aron allowed it, he was too happy to be grouchy.

As soon as the door opened on the King Ranch everyone was crowded around to help Joseph out. "Hey, give me room, you bums!" Then he spotted Libby. "Not you, Libby! You come here." Joseph pulled her to him and whispered. "You went to the doctor?"

She held the sweet dare-devil close and answered, "Still cancer free." He squeezed her triumphantly.

"Somebody hand me my dang wheelchair." Aron helped his brother, wondering at the secret words which had passed between his beloved and his brother. He wasn't worried, just curious.

They assisted Joseph in and made it as far as the dining table. Aron looked around at his family. His family. Joseph had an uphill battle, but he had plenty of people ready to support him. Aron fixed an eagle eye on Joseph, "What were you and my baby whispering about?"

Everyone was filling their plates and Libby was busy pouring cold glasses of milk for all the oversize McCoy men. Joseph looked at him squarely. "Libby set me straight. Don't be mad at her, but when I was feeling sorry for myself and wondering if life was worth living as half a man – she told me the nightmare she had been facing for over half her life."

Aron felt torn. Part of him wanted to be the only one Libby confided in, but the biggest part of him was relieved she cared enough for his brother to say whatever it took to make him want to give life a chance. Aron slapped his brother on the back. "I'm glad she was there for you. Libby is something else. I'm glad you're home."

After everybody was served, Aron pulled Libby into his lap and looked at his brothers. "We have some announcements to make." Before they even began, Libby started to blush. Aron kissed the rosy glow. "It's okay."

"Are you two getting married?" Nathan's eyes shone with excitement.

"Why do you go and steal my thunder, boy?" Aron playfully cuffed his little brother. "Yes, we are. Libby is going to be a part of this family – AND –," he played it for all it was worth. "You, Mr. Nathan, are going to be an uncle."

At Aron's announcement there was a general ecstatic chaos. Libby was grabbed and passed from brother to brother, receiving kisses and hugs and congratulations. Aron was generally being ignored, but it was all right. "Hey, be gentle with the munchkin."

She was gently placed by Isaac in Joseph's lap for a final hug before she was returned to Aron. "I'm so happy for you. You've had your miracle. Now, let's work on mine."

Jessie listened to the happiness inside of the big, inviting home and wished she were part of it. Pressing her face to the glass like a child at a candy store, she watched the one they called Jacob as he quietly surveyed the celebration. He was the reason she was here. After he had almost caught her at the Little League concession stand, she had hung back and watched him work with the children. Never had she known such a man existed. He was patient and kind, working with the boys as if they were his own. But they weren't. She'd watched him leave alone. The next night when he had come, Jessie hadn't even hesitated. She had stowed away in the back of his truck, not knowing where he was going, but knowing where ever he was, that was where she wanted to be.

The pancakes smelled so good, and her stomach growled so loudly Jessie was afraid they could hear. Most of the ketchup and bread was gone, so she was on short rations. Jessie wasn't stealing; she made sure she did work every day to pay for the food she ate. No one had noticed yet, but she was cleaning the tack and mucking the stalls. Most likely each one of the men would think one of the others was doing it. Nevertheless, it made Jessie feel better.

Taking one last look at the happy family, she sighed. Something wonderful had happened. She could tell by the smiles and the laughter. For a few minutes, she took it in. The beautiful girl was so lucky. She was loved by all six of the men, and Jessie had no one.

Sadly, she backed away and returned to the barn. Now, would be a good time to take a dip in the stock tank. Everyone was safely occupied and there would be no chance she would get caught. Carefully, she opened the barn door. The cows and horses were used to her now. She had made sure to pet each one and even slipped them some of the nuggets which were stored in the feed bin. Now, they looked at her expectantly, but none set off any type of alarm. She had claimed the last stall on the right next to the big Palomino. Speaking to the golden horse, she shed her clothes and folded them neatly in the corner. Only having two sets made her keep everything neat. "Thanks for the use of your blanket, Gorgeous." She spoke to the horse; he looked exactly as if he understood every word. Wrapping the horse blanket around her, Jessie stole away to bathe.

* * *

Nathan was so relieved Libby and Aron had gotten together. He may only be thirteen, but he knew the ropes. He could see it coming a mile away. And now, Libby was pregnant. There was going to be an actual, small human being coming to live on Tebow. For the first time, he wouldn't be the baby. So, it was high time they quit treating him like one. Like now. Noah had lost his cell-phone out of his truck and he had been given the thankless job of backtracking all over the place to hunt it. Making his way to the corral, Nathan passed close to the stock tank. Hearing a splash, he almost jumped out of his skin. Slipping around, Nathan was determined to catch the intruder. Easing close, he stood on tip-toe and what he saw made him gasp.

To a thirteen year old, long hair and glistening water on a near naked female could only mean one thing. Turning to run, he began to holler. "Guys, guys! Come quick!" Of course, no one could hear him, except Jessie, who quickly scrambled to get out of the tank. Racing back to the house, he threw open the kitchen door and found Jacob in the midst of kitchen duty.

"Hey, what's wrong with you? You know you're not supposed to slam the door, and look at the mud you're tracking in on Libby's clean floor." Nathan was panting, and more excited than Jacob could remember seeing him.

"Jacob, come quick!" He tried to pull his brother to the door.

"Why? Is the barn on fire?" Jacob knew how boys could flip out over the least little thing.

"No, you've gotta come see." Nathan was insistent.

"See what buddy?" Nathan's enthusiasm was contagious.

"You just won't believe it." At Jacob's stern expression, Nathan held open the door and motioned his brother to follow him with a pleading look on his face. "You've got to see this, Jacob. It's better than the time Isaac found that two-headed snake."

"If you don't just spit it out, I'm going to ground you from your Wii."

Nathan wasn't worried – he knew Jacob's bark was worse than his bite. "For God's sake, Jacob. I've been trying to tell you! There's a mermaid in the stock tank!"

"Well, you're right." Jacob followed his brother out the door. "This I've got to see."

* * *

Libby's pancakes hadn't set well with her at all. Aron bathed her face and handed her some crackers and coke. She had been sick again, but this time there had been relief and joy in the nausea. For now she knew the sickness stemmed from her pregnancy and not from a relapse into leukemia. "All better?" Aron lifted her chin so he could see her expression clearly.

"Yes, all better," she nodded. "I'm just so tired."

"Why don't you lie down and rest for a while? We've had way too much excitement in the last few days." She wasn't hard to convince, and soon he had her nestled down in the soft covers. "I should be out fixing fence, but I can't seem to drag myself away from you," Aron stroked her face. "I love you, Libby.

She smiled at him, then said something which made his mouth fall open. "You don't have to say you love me, Aron."

Confused, he asked, "We've talked about this, you know I do. Don't you like to hear me say I love you?"

Snuggling up to him, she explained. "Oh, I love to hear about your love for me." Pulling his shirt out of his pants and then proceeding to undo his belt buckle, she went on to clarify her surprising statement. "But you don't have to say it out loud. You say it so clearly in so many other ways." One of those ways was poking up through his underwear.

"What do you mean?" He was fast losing his ability to verbally communicate. His attention and oxygen giving blood supply was all headed south.

"Your eyes tell me you love me." She kissed his eyelids softly. "Your hands tell me you love me." Libby picked up each hand and caressed the palm with her lips. "Your body tells me you love me," she got his total attention when her small hands closed around his stone-hard cock. "But most of all, it's a heart to heart communication." She pressed her breasts to his chest so they could feel one another's quickly elevating heartbeat.

Aron was tearing off his clothes, and then he started on hers. "Non-verbal communication can be very effective." Spreading her legs, he readied her to receive him. "You are so hot, Libby. Your heat burns me alive." Kissing a path down her body, Aron showed Libby how much he cared. "Every day, Liberty Bell, I will make sure you know that I love you – in every way I'm able."

And he was very Able.

Ready. Willing. And definitely Able.

Cowboy Heat.

####

ABOUT THE AUTHOR

Sable's hometown will always be New Orleans. She loves the culture of Louisiana and it permeates everything she does. Now she lives in the big state of Texas, and like most southern women, she loves to cook southern food - especially Cajun and Tex-Mex. She also loves to research the supernatural, but shhhh don't tell anyone. Sable writes romance novels. She lives in New Orleans. She believes that her goal as a writer is to make her readers laugh with joy, cry in sympathy and fan themselves when they read the hot parts - ha!

The worlds she creates in her books are ones where right prevails, love conquers all and holding out for a hero is not an impossible dream.

Visit Sable:
Website: http://www.sablehunter.com
Facebook: https://www.facebook.com/authorsablehunter
Amazon: http://www.amazon.com/author/sablehunter

Hell Yeah! Series Reading Order

Cowboy Heat http://amzn.to/WhY6dw
Hot on Her Trail http://amzn.to/U3zpT1
Her Magic Touch http://amzn.to/11b1aw6
A Brown Eyed Handsome Man (FREE Read available from SCP or contact me via email sablehunter@rocketmail.com)
Badass http://amzn.to/UsrJJ4
Burning Love http://amzn.to/15Z4Lyi
Forget Me Never http://amzn.to/U3PjwK
I'll See You in My Dreams http://amzn.to/11nsvpg
Finding Dandi http://amzn.to/12kK4Kh
Thunderbird (Coming Soon)
Skye Blue (Coming Soon)

*Books in the Hell Yeah! Series are grouped by Hell Yeah! And Hell Yeah! Cajun Style.

Visit: http://www.amazon.com/author/sablehunter

Available from Secret Cravings Publishing

TROUBLE - Texas Heat I
My Aliyah - Heart In Chains - Texas Heat II
A Wishing Moon - Moon Magick I
Sweet Evangeline - Moon Magick II
Unchained Melody - Hill Country Heart I
Scarlet Fever – Hill Country Heart II
Bobby Does Dallas - Hill Country Heart III
Five Hearts - Valentine Anthology - A Hot And Spicy Valentine Cookbook
Sable Does It In The Kitchen
For more info check out…
www.sablehunter.com

~~*~*

Cowboy Jackpot: Christmas
Cowboy Jackpot Series, Book 1
By Randi Alexander

A lucky first kiss in front of a Las Vegas slot machine pays off big for bull rider Boone Hancock and New York college student Gigi Colberg-Staub. During the day they spend together as VIP guests of the casino, an intense attraction develops. Throughout the night they share in the big bed of the comped suite, hot, sensual moves ignite wild climaxes.

When Gigi receives a miscommunication, she believes Boone thinks of her as one-night buckle bunny. She confronts him, but Boone convinces himself it's best for both of them if she goes on believing that, and he lets her walk out of his life. When he realizes his mistake, and then sees the sacrifice Gigi made for him, is it too late to win her back?

Chapter One

"Buckle bunnies to your left."

Boone Hancock turned his head at Dallas's alert.

Two cuties stood at one of the giant slot machines. They both smiled and waved.

Dallas tipped back his cowboy hat. "I'm puttin' dibs on the redhead."

Boone glanced at her, but his gaze shot back to the angel with the long black hair and pale skin. Her curves, packed into a petite little body, captured his complete focus. Her slinky purple dress and black spike-heeled sandals shouted she was ready to party.

"Look at those legs." Dallas raised his hand in a return greeting.

The redhead wore a green dress that showed off her nice breasts and skimmed her thin body. Boone smiled. "You like the tall, leggy ones, buddy. I'm likin' her girlfriend. She's a hot little bundle."

"Let's get 'em." Dallas took a step forward.

"Wait." Boone stopped him with a hand on his shoulder. "Remember, one night. Two at the most."

"Yeah, yeah."

"You say that like you mean it, but we promised to keep each other out of the deep shit."

Dallas looked him square in the eyes. "I learned my lesson the hard way. You don't have to babysit me."

Boone had watched Dallas going through hell two months ago with the girl he thought was the one for him. It had affected his buddy's performance in the arena, and his ability to stay sober.

Boone's little brother, Jayden, caught up to them and busted in between them. "What's going on?"

Dallas nodded toward the two girls. "Couple ladies recognized us and want us to come and say howdy." He flicked the brim of Jaden's cowboy hat. "Now get lost. They're both spoken for."

"Mmm, I'm liking that redhead." Jayden grinned at her.

Boone looked back at the women. The shorter one—his—waved them over.

"Called dibs." Dallas hitched up his jeans and headed toward the girls.

Jayden caught up to him. "We'll see, won't we."

Boone quick-stepped and lined up next to his brother. As they got closer, he saw his cutie's eyes watching him. Hazel. Damn. Beautiful eyes, beautiful face, a body that he needed tight against his. It didn't take any effort to slide into charming cowboy mode. His body warmed, primed and ready to sweet-talk this little honey 'till her toes curled.

****

Gieselle Colberg-Staub leaned against the Birthday Baby slot machine, her knees wobbly and her stomach jittering as she watched Boone Hancock walk toward her. "I can't believe it. They're actually coming over here."

Kira twirled a lock of hair around one finger and made a shy smile at the cowboys. "Of course they're coming over here. How could they resist?"

Gieselle sucked in a calming breath. She'd watched Boone win the bull riding competition this afternoon, and now he—and his big, shiny belt buckle—headed her way. "God, he's cute." Shaggy blonde hair touched his collar at the back of his black cowboy hat. A purple and black print western shirt and the sexiest jeans she'd ever seen on a man.

"That big, dark haired hunk is fucking gorgeous." Kira sipped her vodka tonic.

"That's Dallas Burns. He came in third in bareback riding today." She glanced at her friend. "Weren't you watching?'

Kira sniffed. "You saw that sexy cowboy sitting right behind us. He was worth watching."

Gieselle had picked up a love of rodeo from her college roommate, but this was the first live event she'd attended. Now the sexy stars she'd drooled over headed straight toward her. She held back a nervous giggle. "Dallas is definitely your type with those dark eyes."

"Oh yes, my heart is thumping." Kira stirred the ice in her drink with the straw. "So, we agree? Dallas for me and Boone for you?"

Gieselle licked her lips. She would let herself go a little crazy this holiday break, because what happens in Vegas, hopefully stays in Vegas. "Agreed." She squinted. "What about the third one?"

Kira laughed. "Oh, now you're getting kinky?"

Gieselle sent her a look. "That's your specialty, girl."

The cowboys reached them, sauntering up with wicked grins on their faces, like they expected Kira and her to peel down naked and let them have a quickie right here on the casino floor.

Gieselle liked the cockiness.

"Ladies." Boone touched the brim of his hat. Dallas and the other cowboy did the same.

Kira took a step toward Dallas. "I enjoyed watching you ride today."

He nodded once. "Thank you. I'm...comin' back from a dry spell." He held out his hand. "I'm Dallas Burns."

She smiled. "Oh, I know who you are."

Gieselle had to suppress an eye roll.

Boone shifted closer to Gieselle. "I'm Boone Hancock." His eyes took in the details of her face. "And I'm rightly glad to meet you." He took her hand.

The tingle of sexual desire raced along her arm and down deep inside, shocking her core with an achy, molten quiver.

His eyes opened a little wider. Had he felt it, too?

"I'm Gieselle Colberg-Staub." The words came out in a seductive purr.

Boone grinned. "Three names, wow." He didn't release her hand. "Where are you from?"

She'd worked for years to obliterate her accent. Had she lapsed into New York English in her excitement? "Manhattan."

"New York?" He looked deeper into her eyes. "I think you're the first person I've met from there, but if all the women are as beautiful as you, I've been missing out."

She sucked in an uneven breath. Yes, it was a hokey, overused line, but with his blue eyes looking so sincere, it worked for him—and it worked on her. She felt warmth rush her cheeks. "You're sweet."

He lifted her hand and kissed it, his mouth lingering a couple seconds, his blue gaze locking with hers. "You're delicious."

A double-shot of lust raged through her, and her eyes nearly rolled back in her head.

Kira elbowed her and gave her a warning glance. They'd promised to watch out for each other this vacation, stick together until they felt comfortable that their respective men were harmless and trustworthy. How could her friend tell that Gieselle was nearly ready to drag this cowboy back to the hotel room?

Dallas held out his hand to Gieselle. "Dallas Burns."

Boone released her hand and she shook the cowboy's.

"Gieselle Colberg-Staub. Congratulations on your rides today. It's good to see you back up at the top."

He blinked, surprise showing in his eyes. "You're a rodeo fan?"

She took back her hand and nodded. "I've been watching it for years, but today was my first live event."

The third cowboy stepped closer and held out his hand. "Glad to meet you, Miss Gieselle. Once you've seen us live, you'll be addicted for life." He grinned. "Jayden Hancock."

She shook his hand as she appraised his face. He resembled his older brother but with curly blond hair and inky blue eyes. "Nice to meet you. You rode barebacks today, right?"

He nodded. "Yes, ma'am."

"I heard your name and wondered if you were related."

He stuffed his hands in his jeans pockets. "I don't like to admit to it, but yeah, I'm related to a bull rider."

The cowboys and Gieselle laughed, and Kira smiled, her eyes shifting like she didn't get the joke.

Boone introduced himself to Kira then brought his attention right back to Gieselle. "You look like you could use a drink."

"Can I buy you a drink?" Dallas and Jayden both asked Kira.

"Mmm hmm." Kira smiled and batted her eyes.

Gieselle elbowed her back, giving her a meaningful stare.

Kira ignored her and stepped closer to the two cowboys, out of reach of Gieselle's elbow.

Boone turned, separating them from the group. "What are you drinking?" His voice rolled slow and sexy, and longing stirred inside her.

"Gin and tonic." She gestured to the huge slot machine. "Let me finish my credits and maybe..." She glanced at him, deciding how flirty to be.

He set his hand on her bare arm. "Maybe we can find a quiet spot to talk?"

Shivers of excitement coursed through her. "That'd be nice." It came out on a breath.

"Birthday Baby."

She blinked. "What?" How did he know it was her birthday?

He looked at the six-foot tall slot machine. "You're playing Birthday Baby. I'm guessing it's your birthday."

Gieselle nodded. "Tomorrow."

"Happy birthday, Gieselle." He said it with such warmth, the words flooded her chest with pleasure.

"Thank you." She shifted her attention to the slot machine. The count on the credits had gone from 100—from the $100 dollar bill her grandmother had given her to "throw away in some silly machine"—to just five credits. "I haven't been very lucky." She pressed the One Credit button three times then grabbed the giant handle on the side and pulled it.

The enormous display showed a seven, a blank, and a birthday cake. Nothing.

"Next one will be it." He wagged his eyebrows at her.

"I'll let you pull the last one. Winning the bull riding buckle today, you're probably full of luck."

His hand on her bicep slid up and down, as if he were imparting luck with his touch. "Okay. Set it up."

She pressed the One Credit button twice, but was out of money. Completely. She'd have to hit a cash machine soon. "Oh well, I guess it'll have to be two credits."

"Uh uh. Wait." Boone released her arm and tugged his wallet out of his back pocket. "We need to do this right." He pulled a single from a thin supply of cash and slid it into the machine. Hitting the One Credit button, the machine dinged and showed it was fully loaded.

She crossed her fingers. "Good luck."

He stepped close to her. "I know what will bring us luck." His eyes locked with hers, his pupils dilating, darkening the blue of his irises. "Trust me?"

Licking her lips, she nodded. "I trust you."

He put one hand on the big handle on the side of the machine, and the other on her lower back, pulling her closer to him. He tipped his head and pressed his lips to hers.

Waves of heat surged through her. She grasped his biceps to keep from keeling over.

He kissed her gently, with a sweet brush of his lips and a groan from deep in his chest.

When she parted her lips, he stole his tongue inside while jerking down the slot machine's handle.

Everything went wild inside her as she closed her eyes.

His fingers threaded through her hair, tipping her head at the perfect angle.

The tang of beer lingered on his tongue. She smelled the soap he must have showered with after the rodeo. Pressing her breasts to his chest, her nipples hardened at the warm touch.

Bells went off inside her head and lights flashed against her eyelids as his tongue tickled along hers, and his teeth nipped at her lips. Her pussy lips ached for a touch, a stroke, a fierce release.

"Gieselle!" Kira's voice cut through the sweet haze. "Look! You won!"

She forced open her eyes as Boone slowed the kiss, opened his eyes, and looked at her with a desire so intense, she would have let him take her right here. Right in front of the dinging, bonging, flashing Birthday Baby...

"What?" She jerked her gaze to the slot.

Lights flashed and bells rang on the machine. The window showed three pink, triple-layer birthday cakes in a row. "Oh my God!"

Boone started laughing. "Damned if that kiss didn't work!" He glanced at her. "Congratulations, birthday girl!"

She smiled and wrapped her arms around his neck. "This is so exciting. I've never won anything before in my life." She kissed him smack on the lips. "Thank you."

When she tried to pull away, he tugged her close. "You're welcome." He kissed her, quick and hard, but with all the passion of a man who was deep in the clutches of need.

Against her belly, his arousal pressed hot and hard. She nipped his lower lip. "Looks like we're both going to be lucky today." The words slid from her lips before she could send them through her anti-trampy filter. Oh hell, as long as she'd gone that far, she circled her hips against his and gave him her naughtiest smile.

He grinned. "Seven's my lucky number, so plan on at least that many times." His hips ground into her once, quickly, before he released her.

The promise of this hard cowboy riding her almost eclipsed the excitement of winning whatever prize she'd hit on the slot. She glanced at the chart below her reel. "Okay, three pink cakes…" It was the top prize. She followed the line to the word "Progressive." Glancing at Boone, she noticed him looking, too, and asked him, "What's 'progressive'?"

He looked up above the machine to a digital display. "I think you won that." He pointed.

She looked up. "Two hundred and fifty seven thousand, three hundred and twenty five." Her heart thudded and she met his surprised gaze. "Dollars?"

"Hell yeah!" He picked her up flat against his front and spun her around three times. "You're rich!" He set her down, laughing, his eyes sparkling.

She laughed so hard she got the hiccups.

Kira pulled her in for a hug. "Un-fucking believable." She stepped back and her smile lit her face. "This is so awesome."

Jayden and Dallas grinned. "Congratulations."

A cork popped and an employee in a Western-cut tuxedo walked toward them holding a bottle of champagne. A woman in one of the casino's skimpy cowgirl uniforms followed him, carrying a tray of champagne glasses. "Congratulations, from the Old West Casino, sir." He looked at Boone.

The cowboy immediately pointed to Gieselle. "This is your winner."

The tuxedoed man nodded. "How many in your party?"

"Five." Gieselle's voice quavered. Was she in shock? Things were suddenly spinning around her.

Boone's arm slid across her shoulders. "Okay, Gigi?"

Gigi? She nodded. "Just a little stunned, I guess."

A security guard walked up to the machine. "The manager will be here presently."

A glass of champagne appeared in Gieselle hand.

Boone, Kira, Dallas, and Jayden lifted their glasses, tapping them on hers.

"To Gigi. May luck always ride right beside you." Boone winked at her.

His double meaning set a race of desire through her.

Before she could sip, a casino host had her and Boone stand in front of the machine as a photographer took a dozen pictures.

Behind him, Kira used her phone to snap a couple of her own.

The tuxedoed man set the bottle in a silver stand and looked at Boone. "Enjoy your champagne."

Dallas had the presence of mind to tip the two employees before they walked away.

Boone smacked his friend's shoulder. "Thanks, buddy."

Dallas nodded. "Don't thank me. You're gonna be paying me back."

The cowboy laughed. "Still gotta cash my prize check." He tapped his pocket. "Or we won't have enough to buy the ladies supper."

Gieselle shook her head. "I'll be buying supper. And a limo for all of us to see the city."

Jayden refilled their glasses. "I'll drink to that." Jayden lifted his glass. "To Gigi's lucky day." He winked. "And her generosity."

Gigi, again? Heck, she didn't care. Gigi did sound better than Gieselle coming from a cowboy's lips.

They all touched glasses and drank.

Kira, Dallas, and Jayden walked behind her to look at the slot machine.

Boone leaned in for a brief but steamy kiss.

Her body reacted instantly, her nipples puckering and her core jittering with need.

"To our luck, baby." He looked intently into her eyes. "Both the one-armed bandit and fate bringing us together."

"Fate." She liked this guy. Had watched him on television for years, and couldn't believe her good fortune in finding him. Now they shared the big moment of the jackpot win. Could that be a sign? Would they have more than just one wild night together?

A tired-looking man in a rumpled suit reached them. "Sir?" He held out his hand to Boone.

Her cowboy automatically took it.

"Congratulations. I'm the slot department shift supervisor. If you'll follow—"

"No." Boone stepped back. "I'm not the winner." With his hands on her shoulders, he eased Gieselle forward. "She's the one who was playing the slot. I just pulled the handle for her."

The man looked between the two of them. "We did a quick review of the win." He looked around at the crowd, which had moved in closer to hear. "Let's go back to my office and straighten this out."

Gieselle's heart dropped to her stomach. Crap, was this going to be a problem? She'd already imagined using the money to start her own business instead of having to work for someone else until she had enough to go off on her own.

The casino manager turned and walked away.

"We'll be in the Roundup Bar." Dallas gestured over his shoulder. "Kira and I, that is." He looked at Jayden. "Junior, here, said he had plans." He lifted his brows. "Right?"

Jayden adopted a cocky grin. "Nope. I got nothin' to do." He offered Kira his arm. "I'd be happy to sit and have a drink with you two."

Kira smiled, took his arm, then took Dallas's, too. "Take your time," she threw over her shoulder at Gieselle.

Boone took her hand. "Let's go get your money." He smiled at her. "So we can get that fancy meal you promised."

They walked quickly to catch up to the manager, her anxiety building with each step.

He led them through a nearly invisible door and down a long, brightly lit hallway to a small office. As he sat, he gestured for them to take the guest chairs. "We have the video." He typed at his keyboard then swiveled to look at a television on the wall.

In slow motion, it showed Boone inserting a dollar in the machine, pressing the button, then grabbing the handle. Watching the kiss they shared brought warmth to Gieselle's cheeks and heat to her core. Especially in slow motion, the tangle of their lips and arms took sensual to the next level.

She glanced at the manager. He smiled at her. "How long have you two been together?"

She heaved out a breath. "Would you believe we just met?"

He smiled and turned toward to the television where Boone pulled the handle while their kiss went on. "Ma'am, this is Vegas. I believe anything is possible."

They watched as the three cakes came up, one after another, the lights flashed to life, bells rang, and their kiss went on.

Boone turned in his chair and winked at her.

Gieselle smiled. His presence eased her worry.

The manager stopped the video playback. "So you can see that Mr...." He tipped his head and looked at Boone.

"Boone Hancock," her cowboy supplied

The man wrote then looked up. "Mr. Hancock is legally the prize winner."

"But I don't want it." Boone took her hand. "I want to give it to her." His voice sounded as determined as the tightness in his jaw.

Relief washed through her. Boone could have claimed the money, waved goodbye to her, and left Vegas a rich man.

As the manager looked at her, he sighed. "And your name?"

"Gieselle Colberg-Staub."

He wrote again. "Here's the issue." The manager leaned back in his chair. "There are tax implications here. Ones we can't legally get around."

She sat forward in her chair. "Such as?"

He gestured to Boone. "He may be a tax evader, trying to get out of paying—"

Boone sat up, as stiff as new cowboy boots. "I'm a rodeo bull rider."

Gieselle waited for him to say more, and then snorted as she sucked in air, trying to stifle a laugh. A couple chuckles escaped her.

Boone glared at her.

"Sorry." She suppressed her smile. "I don't understand. What does being a bull rider have to do with honesty?"

He stared into her eyes. "I believe in the American dream. I'm going to make it big on the rodeo circuit and I'm going to start my own business based on the name I make for myself. I'd never do anything to jeopardize the future I've got ahead of me." His face softened, became less intense. "One day, I want to hold public office, work for the community, help those that need it, and punish those who deserve it." He blinked a few times. "I want a family of my own, and a ranch where my kids will learn those same values and ethics."

"Boone. I…" She swallowed the sudden urge to kiss him, to tell him she believed in him. "I'm sorry. I didn't mean to laugh."

A corner of his mouth quirked up. "And I didn't mean to get all righteous on you, Gigi." He glanced at the manager. "My apologies."

The manager's eyes had lost the tired, bored glaze and now held appreciation. "Mr. Hancock, no need to apologize. And I should be the one to ask your forgiveness for blurting out what may have sounded like an accusation." He picked up a piece of paper. "I'll stick to my approved script from now on." He smiled.

Boone nodded.

Gieselle wanted to be on her cowboy's lap, in his arms. But this was neither the time nor the place. This whole jackpot fiasco was spinning

out of control. How could she make this work out for both of them?
　　She turned to the manager. "Could we have a minute, please?" As a plan formulated in her mind, she grew excited to share it with Boone.

Chapter Two

Boone stood and watched the casino manager leave his own office at Gigi's request. Once the door closed, he turned to her. "We're going to have to make this fast, baby." He reached for her with a grin.

She laughed and slapped away his hands. "That's not what this is about, you studly, horny cowboy."

He flexed his muscles and gave her a steamy look. "How about now?"

Smiling, she shook her head. Her beautiful hazel eyes sobered as she stood. "I wanted to make sure this was okay with you." She crinkled her nose.

"Sure. What's on your mind?"

"I want to split the jackpot with you."

His head jerked back. One hundred twenty five thousand dollars, less taxes. He could start the rodeo school he and Dallas and Jayden had talked about. Pay off the money he owed his folks. Buy a decent truck. He looked at Gigi's pretty face. Find a woman to love, and start a family... "No." It just wasn't right to take half her money. "It's generous of you to offer, but I can't accept."

Her mouth opened then closed, and her brow wrinkled. "You have to. It's only fair. I had two dollars in. You had one dollar in, and you—"

"No." He had no right to it. "It should all be yours."

"Listen, please." She stepped closer and placed her little hand over his heart.

Tender feelings slid around his chest while hot, nasty urges grew low in his belly. This woman was sweet and sexy and exactly what he needed. He shook his head to settle his brain in the right place. Exactly what he needed for a couple hot nights. That's all. Looking up at the ceiling, he tamped down the urge to see if it could be more.

She stared at him as if he'd lost some of his lucidity. "Boone?"

"Yeah. Sorry. Listening." He laid his hand on top of hers. Warm and soft.

"I've never won anything before, so I have to give you credit for bringing all the good karma. You had a dollar in, plus all that luck...that adds up to half the jackpot. "

He lifted her hand and kissed her palm. "I appreciate that you're trying to do this, but it just wouldn't be right."

"Please?" She gave him a mewling voice and doe eyes.

How could any guy resist? He shook his head. "Gigi—"

"Where did this 'Gigi' come from?"

He shrugged as he nibbled on the pad of her pinky finger. "Hard to remember that big, fancy name of yours." He needed to get her alone. Get her under him, naked; get their bodies joined, hot and sweaty.

She tugged back her hand. With a patient smile, she sighed. "I know what you're thinking about, but we need to do this first." She sat. "Tell me the reasons you won't take the money."

He sat next to her, his hand on the back of her chair, his fingertips playing with her silky hair. "It was your machine."

"That's it?" She shook her head. "Okay, imagine if I had left two dollars in the machine and walked away. Someone came up, put a dollar in, and won the jackpot."

He nodded. He could tell where she was headed.

"Could I come back and say, 'Oh, excuse me, I get part of that because I left my money in there'?"

"I see what you mean."

She laid her hand on his thigh.

Pulses of lust rushed to his cock. The sooner he got this settled, the sooner he could get *them* settled. In his bed.

"Boone, let me do this for you. It's the only fair way."

He puffed out a breath. "It doesn't seem all that fair, but if you're sure."

She smiled so wide, he nearly lost his breath. "I'm sure."

She had to have a hell of a generous heart to give up half of a small fortune. Everything about her so far lined her up as the perfect woman for him.

He pressed his lips tight together. That line of thinking would only bring him trouble. "Okay then." He stood. "But if you change your mind, you can—"

"I won't." The look in her eyes confirmed her words.

"I'll get the boss back in here." He opened the door and gestured to the manager. "Ready."

Once they were all seated, Gigi explained that she wanted to split the money.

The manager rubbed his eyes. "Okay, here it is one more time. The money belongs to Mr.…." He checked his paper. "Hancock. You…" He looked at Gigi. "Can't take half of what is not yours."

Boone leaned forward. "I want to give Miss Colberg-Staub half the money."

Her head swiveled. "So you can remember Colberg-Staub, but you can't remember Gieselle?" She gave him a glare that she ruined by smiling.

He grinned back at her. "Yup. Just blame it on one too many falls off rank bulls."

The manager cleared his throat. "All right. Here's how this works." He gave them each a serious look. "The Gaming Commission needs to verify the jackpot. It'll take until morning to get this all tidied up, since it's the holiday." He slid a tiny folder with two keycards in it. "You'll have the Gunslinger Suite for two nights." He glanced between them. "It has two bedrooms, since you're not…together."

Boone winked at her.

She bit her lip and blushed.

Damn, he wanted her.

"I also put five hundred dollars casino credit on the suite. Eat at any of our restaurants, drink in the bars, dance in the clubs." He smiled. "Get hitched at the wedding chapel."

Boone's heart double-beat as he pictured Gigi standing next to him in front of a preacher. Then his stomach clenched and an icy wash of panic slid through him. He had to wait until he had his business up and running and profitable before he even got serious with a woman. It could take months. Years. Why the hell was he having goddamn wedding fantasies?

Gigi laughed. "Everything but the wedding part sounds lovely. Thank you."

Boone frowned at her. She didn't want to marry him? She could at least give him a dreamy-eyed stare before she laughed it off.

He blinked. What the fuck was he thinking? No, they weren't getting married. So why did her words nag at him? "Hell."

"Pardon?" The manager watched him.

"Uh, thank you. That'll be great."

He handed them each a couple papers and a pen. "Fill these out and put your phone number at the top. I'll call you tomorrow when we're ready to finalize the payout."

****

Married? Gieselle spent too many minutes thinking about it as she and Boone walked hand in hand to the Roundup Bar. He led her to the corner table where his brother, Kira, and Dallas sat. In front of each of the men, glass mugs in the shape of cowboy boots sat half-empty. Between them, Kira sat sipping from a straw in a margarita glass large enough to wash her hair in.

"Let's see the cash." Jayden slid closer to Kira, making room for them.

"No cash." Gieselle slid in next to the cowboy and Boone took the last spot on the end next to her. "We have to wait until morning."

"What?" Kira pulled out her phone. "I'm calling Daddy. His attorney will—"

"Put that away." Gieselle glanced at Dallas. "How many of these has she had?" She tapped the margarita glass.

Dallas grinned. "Evidently not enough to mellow her out."

Kira glared at him as she set her phone on the table. "Only one." She shrugged. "But the shot of tequila we each did got us kicked off."

The waitress took Gieselle's order of a small margarita, and Boone's order of a beer and a shot of whiskey.

Boone set the folder with their key cards on the table. "We've got a suite for two nights, and five hundo to spend in the hotel."

Kira, Jayden, and Dallas hooted and toasted them.

Boone and Gieselle explained that they were going to split the jackpot, and Dallas and Jayden shared a look before staring at Gieselle.

She met their gazes and saw appreciation in Jayden's, and panic in Dallas's. What the heck did that mean?

After they'd finished their drinks, they got busy making plans for the night.

Kira and Gieselle headed to their room to pack Gieselle's clothes for her move to the suite.

Kira, Dallas, and Jayden refused to stay in the suite with Gieselle and Boone, but promised to help them spend every penny of the casino credit.

Gieselle zipped her bag and hefted it off the bed. "Are you sure you feel safe alone?"

Kira walked out of the bathroom wearing fresh makeup and perfume. "If things go the way I plan, I won't be alone." She dug in her suitcase and moved a box of condoms to the drawer in the bedside table. She paused and glanced at Gieselle. Opening the drawer once again, she pulled off two packets and slid them into her purse. "Since it's Vegas, it's best to be prepared for anything."

Gieselle laughed. "Dallas or Jayden?" She opened the door to the hallway.

"Oh please. Jayden? He's got to be eighteen." She walked past Gieselle and swayed her tush as she sashayed toward the elevator. "Dallas is all man." She pushed the up button to call the elevator. "How about Boone? Is he going to be in his own bedroom tonight? Or in yours?"

Gieselle could almost feel the touch of Boone's hands on her body. Tweaking her nipples then licking and sucking. His mouth drawing wet paths along her ribs and stomach, parting her bare pussy to taste her, lave her, and suck until she shook with climax.

"Don't answer." Kira stepped into the open elevator. "The look on your face tells me that poor bull rider is going to be useless for anything but sleep after you get done with him."

Gieselle grinned. "I hope so."

Opening the door to the suite, both women sucked in startled breaths.

Gieselle expected something Western, but it was sleek and modern. A few cowboy paintings hung on the walls, and rustic accent pieces sat on the heavy wooden tables. But the sleek, brown leather furniture and plush tan and brown patterned carpet invited her to stay. Forever.

Floor to ceiling windows showed an incredible view of the lights of the strip. A huge wood bar filled one corner. On top of it sat a bottle of champagne chilling in a bucket of ice.

"Can I change my mind?" Kira walked into the room and spun around on the acres of carpeting.

"No." Gieselle looked in the first bedroom, then in the second, and chose it for its beautiful view and extra-large bed. "And Kira..." She shouted from the bedroom. "When I give you the sign, you take those other two cowboys and get the hell out of here."

Kira laughed. "Nice."

Gieselle chuckled as she unpacked. "As if you haven't done that to me a couple dozen times." She hung up her dresses and slid her underthings into a drawer.

When she carried her cosmetic bag into the attached bathroom, her mouth dropped open. A walk-in shower with six sprinkler heads took up a whole wall. A ridiculously huge bathtub with jets filled the other. Big enough for two. She quickly turned off the light and walked out to the bedroom before her girlfriend saw it and truly did decide to move in.

Kira came in and flopped backward onto the bed. "This baby'll get a workout tonight."

"Uh huh." Gieselle tucked her own box of condoms into the bedside table. She stashed her suitcase in the closet as the click of the hallway door echoed.

"...and I swear to God..." Dallas's voice boomed through the suite. "I'll hit you over the head and drag you out to the truck if I see you getting attached."

Gieselle's eyes popped open wide as she looked at Kira, whose eyes narrowed.

Her friend pressed a finger against her own lips to shush Gieselle.

"Don't fucking worry about me, asshole." Boone's voice came from the first bedroom. "I know what this is." His voice grew closer. "I'm not going to get suckered into..." He stopped just inside the bedroom door.

"Not going to get suckered into what?" Kira gave him a glare.

"Oh fuck." Dallas's voice came from behind Boone.

Jayden peeked his head into the room then disappeared.

A loud smack sounded and Jayden and Dallas's quiet, angry voices moved off.

Boone smiled at Kira, then at Gieselle.

She saw a flash of something in his eyes, but it was quickly replaced by excitement.

"Not going to give the casino back any of the winnings." He tipped his head toward the living room. "These two cowpokes think the only reason we've got the suite is to keep us here so we'll spend all our money."

Kira glanced at her, a disbelieving look on her face. She slid off the gold satin bedspread and walked past Boone. "Uh huh. Good cover, cowboy." She shut the door behind her.

Boone flipped the lock.

Together, alone with Boone, with a big bed between them, Gieselle's nerves kicked up into a whirl.

He set his duffle bag in the corner. "Are you ready for this?"

Chapter Three

Boone took off his hat and ran his fingers through his hair, lifting it into messy, sexy locks that she wanted to get a hold of. He stalked toward her.

She didn't believe for a minute Dallas had been talking about Boone losing his winnings at the casino. He'd been referring to her, to how quickly their feelings for each other had developed. The way Boone had responded to his buddy, Gieselle didn't know if she should believe the words Boone had said to her about fate and luck, or if his honest thoughts included the fear of getting "suckered in" by her.

Either way, she would be with him as much as she could over the next two days. Something about him pulled her in, made her want to know everything about him. The few guys she'd dated seriously in New York had never made her this…nesty? Could that be it? Had finally meeting a true gentleman, an all-American male, given her ideas of what she was missing in her life?

Gieselle swallowed and looked at the bed. "Ready for what?"

He laughed and set his hat on the dresser. As he reached her, he held out his hand. "For a wild night of…partying?"

Sliding into his arms, she smiled. "Is that what you cowboys call it?" Her body melted against his, her arms wound tightly around his neck.

His lips brushed her jaw and settled at the sensitive skin near her ear. "Call it gettin' to know you, beautiful."

A knock sounded. "Hey you two, we're ordering booze from room service and charging it to your room." Jayden sounded so much like his brother.

"Go ahead," Boone shouted over his shoulder.

"We got beer, whiskey, tequila, and vodka and tonic for Miss Kira. Anything else? Gigi?"

Boone raised his eyebrows. "What's your pleasure tonight?" His hard shaft pressed against her belly.

She shifted her hips against him. "Besides this?"

He groaned and stepped his feet farther apart, hitting her lower with the rise behind his fly. "You know this'll be pleasure for you. As much as you want."

"I want…" You. She couldn't say the word. It sounded too serious. "How about gin? I'd love a gin and tonic."

He nodded and shouted over his shoulder. "Gin. And make it the good stuff, Jay."

"Right." His voice moved away from the door.

Boone ran his knuckles over her cheek. "Where were we?" He tipped his head and moved closer.

"Hey." Jaden's voice came through the door. "It'll be here in ten minutes." He laughed. "Just enough time for you to get it done in there, huh, big brother?"

Boone's lips tightened. "Get away from that door."

Gieselle smiled. "Ten minutes, huh?"

"He's got to die." Boone pressed his lips to hers.

A pop sounded outside the door. It had to be the cork from the champagne bottle.

"There he goes! Didn't even last ten minutes." Jayden shouted.

Somewhere in the living room, Dallas laughed.

Gieselle smiled against Boone's lips. "This isn't going to happen right now, is it."

"No." He stepped back. "But I'm gonna take a great deal of pleasure in thumping my baby brother into that nice carpet out there." He walked to the door and ripped it open.

"Oh fuck." Jayden shot across the living room.

"You need to get some manners, boy." Boone's hands fisted.

Gieselle walked up behind him. "It's okay, Boone." She ran her hand over his forearm. Hard, corded muscles bulged under her fingers.

"No, it ain't." He glared at his brother. "He knows better."

"Let him be." Dallas took off his hat, got up from the couch, and walked behind the bar. "It's close to his bedtime anyway."

Jayden popped up from crouching behind the bar and pointed the champagne bottle at Dallas. "I got a fake ID that says I can drink and gamble all night if I want." Without his cowboy hat, he looked so young.

Setting five tumblers on the bar, Dallas chuckled. "Fill up our glasses. We need to have a real toast to our big winners."

Looking around the room, Gieselle didn't spot Kira.

Dallas nodded toward the closed door of the other bedroom. "She got a call." He narrowed his eyes. "Does she have a man back in New York?"

Boone hefted out a breath. "Dallas?"

Jayden poured champagne into the glasses. "Watch out. He's doing that bonding thing again."

Dallas pounded a fist on the bar. "It's not like that. I just want to make sure I'm not moving in on another man's woman."

Gieselle watched the cowboys' body language, weighing their words. Evidently Dallas had some history with women he was trying to live down.

"No." She took Boone's hand and pulled him with her out of the bedroom. "She doesn't have a man. She's free and clear." Gieselle walked to the bar and slid onto a barstool.

Dallas handed her a glass. "Ma'am."

Boone stepped up behind her, his arm draping across the back of the stool. He picked up a tumbler and touched it to hers. "To tonight." His eyes darkened and his mouth curved slightly. "When we can lock these clowns out of our suite."

She laughed. "The best toast I've ever heard." She sipped her champagne.

"Hey." Jayden walked out from behind the bar and jumped onto the barstool next to hers. "Mom said you were supposed to keep an eye on me." He grabbed a glass and chugged it down.

"Just how young are you?" Gieselle took a closer look at his cute face.

"Almost twenty-one." He glanced at his brother. "He's twenty-three." He looked into her eyes. "How old are you?"

Boone shook his head. "You don't ask a lady that."

"Jayden, damn." Dallas refilled their glasses. "You have no class, dust eater."

"Hey, I landed on my feet today." Jayden's jaw tightened.

"You didn't go more than two seconds on that crow hopper." Dallas leaned on the bar. "You do better at practice than you do at events. Why's that?"

Jayden blushed and shrugged.

Kira came out of the bedroom, pasting a smile on her face. "What are we talking about?"

"How old Gigi is." Jayden grinned.

Gieselle met her girlfriend's gaze with an inquisitive look. Was everything all right?

Kira smiled and nodded at her, then looked at Jayden. "How old do you think she is?"

"I'm gonna say twenty-one."

Gieselle laughed. "I'll be graduating with a masters in business this spring." She glanced at Jayden. "What does that make me?"

He whistled. "Impressive."

She shook her head. "No, I mean—"

"Then what?" Jayden leaned closer to her. "What are you going to do after you graduate?"

"I've got a couple internship offers at companies in Manhattan." She looked at Boone. "But I think I'm going to use the casino's money and go for it. Start my own company."

He nodded, a pensive look in his eyes.

Kira set down her glass. "Prestigious companies in New York. Gieselle's graduating top of her class." She pointed at her friend. "Companies that would look really good on your resume."

Gieselle nodded then frowned. "I can't make the decision right now. I've got too much rattling around in my mind." Top of the list; Boone, and the bedroom so close to them.

"All right, so you start college at eighteen." Jayden calculated on his fingers. "I'd say you'd have to be twenty-three, but you sure don't look it."

She smiled at Boone. "Twenty-five tomorrow." She batted her eyes. "Is that too old for you?"

He let out a laugh. "Practically a cougar." He leaned down and kissed her. "You're perfect."

Something warm and sweet spread through her chest. Perfect. If only.

A knock at the door had Jayden shouting, "Booze!"

****

Six hours later, Boone walked out of the Beefsteak Grill with his arm around Gigi's shoulders and a belly full of the best beef and whiskey he'd ever tasted. "I've never had a Christmas Eve dinner quite like that."

She groaned. "I ate about ten ounces too much beef."

He stopped and tipped his head, kissing her quickly on her pretty lips. "That's what you get for betting Jay you could eat a sixteen ounce steak."

She held up the ten-dollar bill. "I won, didn't I?"

"Baby, you have no idea how impressed I am."

Kira, Dallas, and Jayden stopped next to them. They looked sluggish and bleary-eyed after four hours of drinking in the suite followed by a two hour orgy of food and liquor in the restaurant.

Jayden pointed to his right. "We've got a country bar with dancing this way." He pointed left. "And a rock band playing this way." He looked at all their faces. "Aw, don't tell me you old folks are going home to bed."

Kira shook her head. "Hell no! Let's get country!"

Dallas got them walking toward the Hotfoot Lounge. "It's not even midnight yet. We've got to celebrate Gigi's official birthday."

She smiled at Dallas. "You're so thoughtful."

A burst of jealousy surprised Boone. She'd been kind and playful with both his brother and Dallas all evening, and he loved how she fit into his gang. Boone stopped walking and cursed himself. He was getting too close to her. Hell, she had dreams of being a big New York businesswoman, ready to start a business or work for some major company. Her future didn't include a beat-up bull rider.

"Boone? Are you okay?" Gigi looked up at him with those big hazel eyes.

He got moving again. "Yeah. Just looking forward to getting you back upstairs." He grinned.

She gave him a sly look. "We can duck out through the back—"

"Uh uh. I want at least once dance with you." One slow, sexy dance where he'd let his lust take over again, let it edge out the strange craving filling his heart.

They caught up to the group and found a table near the dance floor. The band was excellent, playing old standards and new songs.

Dallas and Jayden argued over which of them did a better two-step, and Kira volunteered to be the judge. When Dallas took Kira out on the floor, Jayden scoped out the rest of the bar, checking out the honeys.

When it was Jayden's turn on the floor with Kira, Dallas stared at them, a dark scowl on his face. Was his buddy getting too close to Kira? Just like he'd let Gigi mean a little too much to him at a time in his life when he couldn't afford to have any distractions.

The band started a slow song.

"Belly rubbing music." He stood and held out his hand.

Gigi placed her warm little palm in his. "Careful, cowboy. Last time we started rubbing bellies, we almost ended up in bed."

He groaned, picturing her on the golden bedspread, her pale skin glowing, her dark hair fanned out. Her arms reaching for him.

Pulling her close, he nibbled at her ear. "I wanna touch you. Every perfect inch of you."

She shivered and sighed, closing her eyes.

"When I pull off your clothes, I'm going to taste you, slowly, and kiss your breasts until you beg for more."

"More." The word left her mouth on a breath.

In his jeans, his cock pulsed, taking too much blood from his head, making him dizzy with the need to have her. "When I kiss your belly, you'll grab my hair and push my mouth lower, into your sweet, honey lips."

A tiny cry escaped her. Her cheeks glowed pink and her head lolled on her neck.

He ran his tongue from her earlobe down her neck. "You're delicious. I won't be able to get enough of you."

"Boone." She licked her lips and opened her eyes. Her hazel irises had turned to a dark gray. "You have to stop or I'm going to be a puddle on the floor."

He chuckled. "Hold on to me. I'm here for you." Always. He

Cowboy Jackpot: Christmas

blinked and pulled back a few inches. Where the hell had that come from?

She blinked a couple times, too. "Something wrong?"

Yes! "No." Just a fool falling for someone he couldn't have. "Let's get out of here."

Gigi smiled. "Let me talk to Kira quick." She looked around the bar. "Something's wrong. That phone call she got had to be bad news, but she won't admit it."

"Probably because it's your birthday." Her concern for her friend struck a soft spot inside him. He led Gigi back to their table where Kira sat next to Dallas, each of them with a straw stuck in one huge glass of ice water.

"Kira, we should talk before I go—"

She held up a hand. "No. Everything's fine." She shooed them away. "You two go. Have fun and we'll talk tomorrow." She hugged Gigi. "Happy birthday!"

Dallas looked at his phone. "Five minutes to twelve. Better run if you're going to be naked by midnight."

Gigi blushed and swatted him. "You're naughty."

Boone took her hand. "Keep an eye on Jayden, would you?"

Kira said, "Sure."

Dallas scowled at her. "I think he meant me."

Glancing between the two, he let their comments pass. He had better things to do. Naked by midnight sounded like an achievable—and interesting—goal.

He led her through the casino to the bank of elevators. In the car riding up, he pressed her against the elevator wall and kissed her.

Her soft lips parted and he took her, deep and wild, his tongue twisting with hers, their breaths shared back and forth.

When the elevator doors slid open, he picked her up and carried her down the hall to their suite.

She slid in the keycard, and he kicked open the door.

A six-foot Christmas tree filled with twinkling lights and shiny decorations stood in front of the wall of windows.

She gasped. "Boone." Cupping his face with her palms, she kissed him. "Did you do this?"

His chest expanded and his voice choked. "Happy birthday, Gigi. And Merry Christmas." He set her down in front of the tree.

She walked around it, touching a few ornaments and smoothing her hand over the long needles. "It's a real tree." Her face showed surprise.

"I have an uncle who's a tree farmer up north." He shrugged. "I like to support the industry, and I'm partial to the pine scent."

She leaned close to the tree, sniffed deeply, and let out a loud sigh. "It's perfect." Shaking her head, she walked to him and wrapped her arms around his middle. "I would be amazed that you could arrange this, but I've been astounded by you since the moment I met you." Her eyes held a depth of emotion he couldn't let himself name.

Instead, he winked. "This is Vegas, baby. Anything's possible."

****

Gieselle couldn't speak over the catch in her throat. How had he known exactly what to do to make her crazy for him? He didn't have to do this. She would have spent the night with him. What a surprising man her cowboy turned out to be.

He slid his arms around her, linking his fingers at the base of her spine. Bending back to look into her eyes, he asked, "Would you like a drink?"

She shook her head. "I've had enough to drink." Her gaze dropped to his lips. Firm and full, smiling with a naughty smirk, she could drink them up.

"What do you want to do, then?"

Running her hands slowly up his arms, she sighed. "I want to fool around."

Chapter Four

Boone tipped his head back and laughed like a kid. "You're the best Christmas gift I've ever gotten." Against the backdrop of the suite's windows, he reminded her of a package all wrapped in lights.

His hands slid to her butt and he tugged her up.

Holding on to his shoulders, Gieselle balanced herself and wrapped her legs around him. She loved it when he carried her.

"You don't have to ask this cowboy more than once." He strode to the bedroom, bent over the bed, and laid her back on it. Lit only by the lights of the strip, the room wrapped around them, romantic and cozy.

Propping his elbows at her side, his face hovered inches from hers, his breath warm on her skin. "Baby, I've got plans for you."

A hot shiver skittered through her. "Plans?"

"Mm hm." His eyes darkened and his breath came faster. "

She unbuttoned one button of his shirt. "What kind of plans?"

He reached behind his back, tugged off her shoe, and tossed it. "Wicked ones."

Flicking open another button, she asked, "Hot plans?"

"Yeah. And sticky." He took her other shoe and threw it, too.

Opening the rest of his buttons, her mouth watered for a lick of his nice pecs. "God, you're sexy."

"Baby." It came out on a growl and he ripped off his cowboy hat and threw it onto a chair. "You're making me crazy."

She tugged his shirttails from his jeans. "I want to make you naked."

With incredible speed, he removed his shirt and leaned back over her. "Your turn." He slid his hands from her knees down her thighs, his fingers tracing the elastic of her panties around her hips.

The rough calluses on his warm hands rattled lusty heat along her skin and down to her pussy.

Boone gathered her dress under her butt and sat her up, pulling it from under her and up over her head.

He froze, his eyes on her see-through lavender bra. "Oh jeez."

His stare puckered her nipples and tingled chills across her breasts. Gieselle laced her fingers through his hat hair, releasing the blond mop. The softness on her fingers tugged at her heart. A rugged cowboy with the sweet personality of a gentleman.

Boone's mouth covered hers as he laid her back on the bed. He wrapped his arms around her, holding on tight. His big prize buckle chilled her belly.

She traced his lips with her tongue and he dove in, his tongue on hers, on her cheeks, tickling the roof of her mouth.

His overpowering strength did fuzzy things to her brain and wild, jittery things to her core. Her hips made tiny circles, cradling his hard shaft through his jeans.

"Gigi." He whispered against her lips as his hips took up the rhythm of hers.

She scraped her nails lightly down his back. "Boone?"

"When you do that…" His mouth pressed hard and hot on her neck, his teeth nipping, his tongue tracing patterns. Slowly he eased his body lower, dragging his mouth along her skin, tasting as he went.

She closed her eyes and tipped her head back, thrusting her breasts closer to him as desire swirled and puddled low in her belly.

His mouth traced the line of her bra across one breast, then the other. "You're so hot. Your skin is burning my lips."

"Don't stop." Her blood raced through her like solar flares.

"No, ma'am." Boone took her nipple in his mouth through the sheer fabric.

She jumped. "Oh yes."

He moved his lips, scraping the fabric on her tender flesh, sending bolts of electricity to her pussy. When his mouth covered her other nipple, achy contractions pulsed in her core.

With one hand, he unfastened her bra at her back and tugged it off her. He sucked in a breath as he looked at her breasts. "You are too beautiful." He gazed into her eyes. "Not just your body, Gigi. You."

Her heart thumped and she had to swallow before she spoke. "You're an exceptional man."

"I'm coming to think…" He shook his head. "Now isn't the time for words, is it." He lashed his tongue over her nipple.

Flashes radiated from the peak and she grabbed his hair and pulled him to her breast. "No talk."

He chuckled as he took her nipple into his mouth and sucked. His tongue swirled and flicked, his teeth grazed and nipped.

Gieselle grabbed his shoulders to keep herself from sailing out of her body.

Boone licked widening circles around her breast and slid across to the other, licking along the base then narrowing until her came to her areola.

His slow loving eased her race toward climax but jittered hot spikes that wet her pussy lips.

When he took her nipple deep into his mouth, the corresponding tug burned at her slit. She held her breath while he teased and pleased her, heating her until she felt a sheen of sweat on her forehead.

Releasing her nipple, he kissed a trail to her ribs then dipped his tongue into each indentation, moving lower, slowly and painfully teasing. His tongue darted into her belly button.

She lifted her head and watched as he swirled it around, the decadence making her hips jerk.

His eyes shifted and caught her gaze. With a wicked smile, he kissed his way down to the edge of her see-through panties. "I can smell you, sweet and musky, honey and spices." His tongue snuck under the elastic.

"Please, Boone. Oh God. I can't wait." Her thighs shook, needing his lips, his tongue, working magic between them.

"Baby." He kissed her through the fabric, inching lower, slow, open-mouthed kisses that promised everything, hot and lovely all the way down her mound and along her pussy.

The barrier of the fabric made her hungry for the touch of his lips on her bare flesh. She flattened on the bed and grabbed the quilt. "Boone. You're teasing me."

"Damn right I am, woman." His tongue licked hot and hard along the edge of her panties where they met her inner thighs.

She moaned.

He chuckled, but promised relief from her suffering when he slid off her panties.

Opening one eye, she saw him toss the panties onto his cowboy hat. Was he planning to keep them? When he parted her thighs, all concern over her wardrobe ended.

"Your pretty pussy, Gigi. All shaven clean for me." He blew on her lips. "Pink and wet. Mmm, your juices are shining, luring me in for a taste."

"Yes, take it."

"Slow down, baby. Make this last." He kissed and nibbled his way down her tender inner thigh.

Her body shimmied with desire.

He licked behind her knee, then trailed his lips to her feet.

"You've got toes that make me want to spend hours on them."

She rolled her head from side to side. "We don't have hours, Boone."

He laughed. "Your toenail polish matches your panties and bra." Taking her big toe into his mouth, he tickled it with his tongue and scraped his teeth along the bottom.

"Do they?" With his mouth on her that way, she couldn't remember what color they were painted. Or what color her bra was. Nothing filled her head except the pleasure Boone created. Like a string of tracer lights, tingles coursed from her foot to her core. "Oh yes. That's lovely."

He treated each of her toes to the same attention then switched to her other foot. "Sexy feet."

"You like feet?" Her hips rolled, her core wetting with cream, wanting the attention of the lips and tongue that he used to please her toes.

"Yeah." He took her hips in his big hands. "But not as much as I like your other beautiful parts. Roll over."

"Huh?" Was this more of his teasing? She let him turn her onto her stomach.

He held her butt cheeks in his hands and squeezed, then kissed each one. "So sexy. You've got the cutest ass I've ever seen."

Did he really mean it? He'd have seen a heck of a lot of women's butts in his life. She wiggled her tush a little.

With a groan, he licked the bottom of her cheek where it met her thigh, a long, hot taste.

Her core quivered with desire. She was tempted to move her hand lower, pleasure herself, but she'd let him have his fun. She'd be sure to keep him in suspense when it was her turn to be in control.

He licked the other side of her then grabbed her hips and lifted her.

With her face on the quilt, she fisted her hands in the fabric next to her head and hung on. "What are you doing, cowboy?"

"Trust me?" The rumbled words shook her low in her slit.

He'd said the same thing to her at the Birthday Baby machine, and look how well that turned out. "I trust you."

He chuckled. Kneeling behind her, he slid his hands between her thighs and grasped her hips from below, lifting her bottom higher. When his mouth closed over her pussy lips and sucked, she could see the genius of this position.

Blood flowed to her brain, spinning her like a ride at a carnival as his mouth heated and tickled her slit.

His tongue lapped along her folds then deep inside her, slow and hard.

Manic chills raced up her spine, flickering lights in her head, sending her reeling toward climax.

His mouth slid closer to her butt, and his nose pressed against her anus, circling as his tongue and lips continued to eat her with nibbles and sucks.

"Oh God, where did you learn that?" Blasts of heat rocked through her, wildly whipping her toward nirvana.

"Mmm. My signature move."

"So when girls ask you for your signature…"

He laughed. "Just you, Gigi. You're my only fan."

Warmth spread from her heart. He was hers this Christmas. A gift she wished she didn't have to return on the twenty-sixth. She pushed the thought from her mind and concentrated on finding her orgasm.

His mouth slid down and captured her clit. With a suck and a couple flicks, he gave her what she craved.

Wheeling crazily, multicolored flashes blazed in her head. "Boone!" Her core contracted and her hips bucked in rhythm with his tongue. Whirring kaleidoscopes of color and light carried her off for long moments. The blood rushing to her head intensified the orgasm until she felt weightless, ungrounded.

The touch of his lips on her clit gentled her, eased her back from the perfection of the amazing orgasm. He licked her pussy. "You are honey." He sucked. "Sweet spicy cream."

"Haa ahh." Words wouldn't form, but a smile curled her lips.

"Is that a good thing?" His voice held a teasing note.

"So, so good, Boone." Aftershocks rallied through her pussy, climbing her spine to shimmer like fireflies on a dark night. "I'm lifeless."

He kissed her thighs softly and lowered her to the mattress. His body came down half on top of her, warming her as his lips sought hers in a tender kiss. "You are incredibly sensitive." He laid his head next to hers, their noses just inches apart.

She could stay like this forever. She'd never come so quickly or so hard.

"Why did you decide to come to Vegas for Christmas?"

Gieselle sighed. She could go with the story she told her friends at college; that she just needed to do something wild on her birthday this year. Or, she could tell the truth. "My parents were invited to their friends' chalet in Switzerland." She wasn't invited.

His brow creased and his eyes held sympathy. "No brothers or sisters?"

"Only child." She smacked a kiss on his nose. "So, I talked Kira into sin city. And here I am. With you." Karma at its best.

"I'm damn glad you are." His hand trailed up her spine to her neck, brushing back her hair.

"What about you? Siblings? Besides Jayden, of course."

"Two older sisters and another brother who's sixteen." His eyes turned serious. "But, I'm not in the mood for talkin' right now, if you don't mind."

Against her thigh, his erection pulsed, hot and sticky with pre-cum.

"Mmm. I can see why." She trailed a hand down between his body and the quilt until she touched his cock. "We're going to have to do something about this."

"Fuck, yeah!" He grimaced. "Excuse my language, ma'am."

"When we're in bed, you can be a naughty cowboy."

He wagged his eyebrows at her. "Oh, I plan to be, baby. Naughty and wild."

Grasping his thick length in her hand, she whispered, "Condoms in the drawer."

He reached over his head to the nightstand and came back with a foil packet. Ripping it open with his teeth, he sheathed himself in seconds.

"You practice that?" She loved how his every move was sure and commanding.

"Yep. Like bull riding. The more you do it…" He stopped and looked away.

Chapter Five

Gigi smiled. "I appreciate all the practice you've had up 'till this point. I can imagine you've had a long and memorable career in bed."

Boone looked into her eyes, helpless to keep from connecting with her, to keep from wanting more than his two-night limit. Hell, he hadn't even slid his shaft inside her and he was far too attached. "Right this second, Gigi, I can't remember one of them." His heart thumped a feral beat as he opened himself more than he should. In a day or two, he'd say goodbye and whatever was going on in his chest would feel like muscle ripping from bone.

She bit her lower lip and blinked rapidly.

Oh shit, she wasn't going to cry, was she?

It was her turn to look away. With a sigh, she pushed up on her elbows.

He had to change the mood. Wrapping his arms around her, he sat up and pulled her back against his chest. His hands slid to her breasts. "I want you, baby." He kissed her neck. "Want you to ride my cock."

As he tweaked her nipples, her body shivered and arched.

"Mmm, yes." She bent her knees and knelt on each side of his hips.

Skimming his hands down her narrow waist, he lifted her until her pussy touched the tip of his twitching cock.

She braced her hands on his knees and tipped her ass in a gorgeous display. Her hot, wet lips surrounded the head of his shaft.

Boone's balls tightened as flames seared deep in his belly. He had to hang on, cowboy up and give her a long, rowdy ride. But all he wanted to do was pump into her and release his cum.

Gigi sat up, skimming her hands over her thighs in a move so seductive, he nearly shot over the top.

Looking over her shoulder, her eyes dark and heavy lidded, she smiled as she grabbed her ass and spread her cheeks, sliding centimeter by agonizing centimeter down onto his throbbing cock.

"Aw, baby." His words barely more than a breath, his heart raced as air panted through his gritted teeth.

When she bit her lower lip and dropped fully onto him, he shouted a couple curses he couldn't find the memory to remember.

Gigi moved, circled her hips, sliding his cock in amazing patterns that blasted flames up his spine.

His mind flared, wanting to enjoy this, but desperate for release.

Lifting herself, she pulled her sweet pussy nearly off him, then slid back down again, grinding her hips against his.

The pleasure ricocheted through him, heating his flesh, drawing beads of sweat to the surface. "I want you to fuck me, Gigi." He reached for her hair, fisting it with a tug. "Fast and hard, like you can't get enough of me."

She cried out in a sensual moan and lifted her body quickly, dropping again just as fast.

"That's it, baby. Ride it."

She did, her muscles working in beautiful ripples as she pumped her tight slit onto him over and over.

Her hand eased between his legs, cupping his balls.

He had to shake his head to keep the orgasm from overtaking him. "Touch yourself. Play with your clit. I want you to come, want your pussy to suck the cum out of me."

"Boone." It was half sigh, half whine. Her body tensed.

He tugged her hair a little tighter and slid his other hand over her ass, feeling the muscles working to bring him pleasure. He eased his thumb over her pink puckered anal opening and circled gently.

"Uhhhhhh!" Her cry accompanied the stiffening of her body.

Around his cock, her pussy tightened, incredibly hot and fierce.

His mind combusted, shooting backdrafts of heat to his sack. Deep inside his groin, pleasure rocked him and his cum pulsed from his balls and out through his cock. White flames seared inside his mind, licking wildly through his skin as every nerve burst into hot, glowing bliss. Sailing upward like a spark from a bonfire, he let go and felt the pleasure of shooting his load into the perfect woman. "Gigi."

"Boone." Her voice echoed in his head.

Long moments later, he came back to earth, back to reality.

She slowed her ride then stopped, her body shaking and hot.

He eased her down beside him, tugging her close, her head on his shoulder.

She curled in, her legs twining with his, her arm around his middle, holding tightly as if she didn't want to let him go.

He understood the emotion. To find someone so well matched to him, physically and emotionally, but worlds apart in goals. It was just not fair. "If you decide to open a business, are you going to do it in New York?" Not the most romantic cuddling talk, but he needed to know everything about her. Details to keep with him as he traveled the rest of the lonely rodeo tour.

"I love to travel. I'd like to find a way to work from home—wherever that ends up being—and work with customers at their locations." She shook her head. "I thought I'd have years to decide, but now it's actually happening. Too fast, maybe."

"Huh." He felt the same way. Almost as if it wasn't real.

She flattened her palm on his chest and rested her chin on it, gazing into his eyes. "Huh? What does that mean?"

"I'm considering starting my own business, too." Maybe her goals weren't as far from his as he'd thought.

She smiled. "In Reno?"

He nodded. "I've got some land. Inherited from my grandpappy on my mother's side. Grampa Boone."

Gigi smiled. "That's nice that you're named after him."

"My parents farm the land right now, but whenever I'm ready to settle down, they're more than ready to have me take it over."

"Are you going to farm?"

"Nope. Dallas, Jay and me want to open a rodeo school. We can probably get it going part-time in the off-season. If we stay on the rodeo circuit…" He smiled. "…and keep winning, we can finance the business until the school takes off and brings in enough to support us and a staff."

She lifted her head and her eyes opened wide. "What a great idea." Her gaze shifted and her brow furrowed. "Perfect location. The marketing and promotion would be easy because of the draw of the casinos, and because both you and Dallas are big names in the business."

He shook his head. Too much to think about after the major orgasm he'd just experienced. "I don't know anything about that. I'll probably hire that part out."

She batted her eyelashes and grinned. "You'll never guess what type of business I'm going to open."

"Marketing?"

"Uh huh."

His heart lurched. An opportunity to see her again? Reality came down like a boulder. He couldn't get his hopes up. Couldn't risk wanting more than these few days. He'd be busy turning the old barn into a rodeo arena, buying livestock, and trying to get sponsors for his business. And doing all this while making sure he didn't break his neck falling off a bull. He wouldn't have time for a long-distance relationship.

Rolling on top of her, he kissed her. "Something to think about."

Her eyes shadowed. She nodded. "I guess so."

It felt like closing the door on the possibility of a future with her, but it was what he needed to do to keep his focus on his goals. "Be right back." Holding onto the condom that threatened to slip off, he walked into the bathroom. "Holy shit, have you seen this bathtub?"

Her footsteps sounded behind him. Her hands landed on his hips and she kissed his back. "Feel like a bubble bath?"

"Sure do."

While he cleaned up, she filled the tub and poured in crystals that weren't too girly smelling. When she bent over and swished her hand through the water, her ass rounded. Too sexy.

He scooped her up into his arms.

She screeched and wrapped her arms around his neck, smiling. "You're crazy."

"Crazy is right." Crazy for her. And damned if that didn't make a mess of things.

He stepped into the bathtub, careful with his footing. He sat with her on his lap, facing him.

Lacing her hands behind his neck, she sighed. "Oh, Boone. You're so strong." Her voice was a breathy tease.

He chuckled. "You feel like a feather in my big, manly arms."

Running her hands over his shoulders to his biceps, she licked her lips. "You are all man, cowboy. Almost too much for me to handle."

His gut lurched. "Did I hurt you?" He glanced down to where her sweet pussy lay open to his gaze below the waterline.

"No." She ran her fingers slowly down his chest, past his abs, and onto his fully hard cock. "You fit just perfectly."

Relief washed over him. He prided himself on his control, but with Gigi, he seemed to give in to manic desire. "You're tight and hot, baby." His cock jumped. "I could take you again right now."

She held her breath, and her nose crinkled. "You like feet?" A naughty smile curved her lips and sparked in her eyes.

He tipped his head. "Uh huh. Not like a fetish or anything, but I like your little toes and soft skin."

Gieselle took a breath and slid back. "I have a secret talent."

He grinned. "Oh yeah?"

She nodded and leaned back in the tub. She lifted one foot out of the water. "Wanna see it?"

He eased back and stretched his arms along the back of the tub. "Hell yeah!" He laughed. "I'm just imagining what you can do and it's got me rock hard."

A blush climbed her cheeks. "Okay, but stop me if you…"

"No. I'm going to love this." His mouth dropped open as his gut tightened with need. "Do it, baby."

She touched her foot to Boone's cock.

"Uh huh. Yeah. I'm lovin' it."

Bracing herself with her hands, she brought her other foot up and bracketed his shaft with her feet. In the slick water, she slid them up and down, using the space between her first two toes to squeeze his head with each stroke.

His head dropped back as zips of electricity charged up his spine to ricochet around in his head. "Aw fuck."

She worked his cock for long minutes, changing her foot grip on it to horizontal, then one-footed while she pressed her big toe into the spot behind his balls.

Closing his eyes, he experienced the kinkiest rubout he'd ever had. Damn, she was the perfect combination of sweetheart and sexual adventurer.

His mind muddled with snaps and pops as his balls tightened and an extra pump of blood shot into his cock. "Aw, baby."

When he tensed, she switched one foot to horizontal, one foot to vertical and started a fast race.

He jerked, his head fogging over, zaps of heat racing down his spine. His balls shot out, and hot ropes of cum blasted out of the water, landing in floating puddles on the surface. She stroked him until his balls emptied and he returned to consciousness, his body relaxed and melted into the water. "Holy shit, Gigi." He breathed a couple unsteady breaths. "That was truly awesome."

Easing her feet from him, she smiled. "My signature move."

He couldn't move, the warmth spreading through him tempted him to close his eyes and replay the amazing climax. He'd come so quick and hard, his balls felt cramped.

As the pools of cum dispersed into the water, she jumped up.

He blinked. "What's wrong?"

She shrugged. "Paranoid about loose sperm. I'm…not on any contraceptive. It's been so busy at school, I haven't dated much."

Her openness tugged at his heart.

"I know they're probably not viable." She grinned and stepped out onto the bathmat. "But with a big stud like you, a girl can't be too careful."

"Damn right." He pulled the plug to drain the tub. "Bull riders have especially rugged swimmers."

She laughed and started the water flowing in the walk-in shower. "Want to rinse off with me?"

He stood and pinned her with a hot stare. "There are a couple other things I'd like to do with you in a shower."

"So many wicked things to do, and so little time left." Her gaze locked with his, her eyes turning sad.

Damn, he didn't want to think about it.

****

Gieselle watched Boone's face shut down. Was he feeling the time slipping away, too? It made her nervous that they hadn't made plans to see each other again, but maybe that would come later. If he didn't bring it up before they parted ways, she would.

This connection between them was something unique. Compared to Boone, every man she'd dated was a complete asshole. She could get used to being spoiled and pampered, even if she had to travel long distances to do it.

She stepped into the shower. The hot water pulsed on her skin as a delightful shiver from his words ran through her. "What are the things you want to do to me?"

He followed her, closing the glass door. "First one is making you scream my name."

Licking her lips, she backed under one of the showerheads and wet her hair. "I think you've done that already. A few times."

He took her face in his hands. "Not nearly enough to hold me over."

Gieselle moved closer, her hands sliding around his back and sneaking lower, cupping his hard butt. Could she get enough of this man to hold her for their time apart? "I'm all yours, Boone." Her double meaning had to show in her eyes.

He kissed her as the water rushed over them from above and from three sides. His lips were gentle on hers, almost like a farewell kiss, his tongue making love to her mouth.

When he pulled back, his eyes searched hers. He tugged her close and held her for a moment.

She tightened her arms around his middle, not ready to let him go.

He turned her in his arms, her body facing one of the wall showerheads.

The water hit her nipple, taunting it into a hard peak. Slides of lust raced from her breast to her core.

Boone took the nipple in his fingers and played with it, teasing, using the water's pulses to make her quiver with bliss.

She laid her head back on his shoulder.

He slid a hand down her belly to her mound and gently slapped her bare, wet skin. "You like that?"

She nodded and spread her legs for him, wanting him to touch her where her lips swelled and pulsed with need.

He eased his hand lower and slapped her twice.

"Mmm." The sting shivered as a wave of desire through her.

Pushing a finger into her core, he pinched her nipple and bit her neck.

"Oh God." Her mind flooded with the pleasure of his triple assault. Reaching back, she grabbed his thighs. Hard and slick, they ramped up her desire for this man.

He slid his finger deeper in her slit as his other hand brushed across her chest to taunt her other nipple, and his mouth sucked her neck.

Surges of lust roared through her, and her mind began to slide into climax.

When he eased a second finger into her slit, washes of heat shot up her spine. His thumb touched her clit.

Gieselle jumped, the tender flesh already tightened and needy.

On her clit, his thumb rubbed a pattern designed to make her go over the top. "Come, Gigi. Now. Cream all over my fingers." He sucked her earlobe into his mouth and bit. His fingers on her nipple increased their pace to match the rhythm of the finger fucking he gave her, and his thumb's beat on her clit.

A wave of heat struck, swamping her, pulling her under until she couldn't tell up from down, didn't know if she was standing or falling. Sounds muted as she rode the wave, crashing with it in a sensual roll of ecstasy. "Boone!"

His name echoed in the tiled room. She grounded to shore as the wave of delight receded, leaving her weak, wet, and quivering.

He held her, his arms wrapped around her from behind, bearing the weight her legs wouldn't support.

"Boone, you didn't warn me you'd be using another signature move."

He chuckled and kissed her temple. "I'll give you notice right now, baby. All my moves are signature."

"Yay." She turned in his arms and kissed him.

He took over, tasting her deeply, sucking her tongue into his mouth for a nibble.

She slowed the kiss and pulled back. "Damn. You're even an amazing kisser."

He smiled. "I'm good with scalp massage, too." He grabbed the shampoo bottle and turned her to face away from him. "Hang on to your sanity, 'cause this will make you pure loco."

She laughed but was soon moaning in pleasure as his strong fingers did wondrous things to her scalp.

They washed each other, slowly and thoroughly, exploring and tasting. After they dried each other, Boone took the fluffy white hotel robes from their packages, slid her into one, and him into the other. With a towel wrapped around her hair, she held his hand as he led her into the living room.

"Hold on." Boone dragged the loveseat in front of the Christmas tree and flipped the switch on the gas fireplace. He helped her sit then gestured toward the bar. "Gin and tonic?"

"I noticed a bottle of red wine. That sounds nice."

"Anything else, birthday girl?"

She tipped her head. "I'd almost forgotten it was my birthday."

He opened the wine and poured a tall balloon glass for her then put an inch of whiskey into a tumbler for himself. He carried them over, handed her the wine, and set his glass on the end table. Walking back to the bar, he bent over where she couldn't see him.

"What are you doing, cowboy?"

Chapter Six

"Just hold on, city girl." A few seconds later, Boone stood up behind the bar holding a tiny cake with one lit candle. He carried it over to her on the loveseat.

Her breath caught. "Boone." Her eyes misted. "How did you…" She sighed. "No. I don't need to know."

He sat next to her holding the cake and a fork. "I'd sing, but it'd probably spoil the moment." His eyes gleamed a soft blue in the candlelight.

Another chunk of her heart broke off and became his property. "Thank you."

"For not singing?" He grinned. "Make a wish and blow it out."

She closed her eyes, listing all the things she would have wished for before she met Boone, but trashing them all for the one thing she wanted right now. More time with him. She blew out the candle.

He plucked it out of the cake, scraped it across the frosting, and held it out toward her. "Lick it, baby."

She shook her head but smiled. "You're so bad." She wrapped her lips around it and sucked.

"Yeah. That's the way." He laughed. "For some reason, I seem to have a tent in my robe."

"We'll take care of that. After cake."

"Promise?" He forked a piece and held it out to her.

Delicious vanilla butter cream frosting and a dark chocolate cake melted on her tongue. "Mmm hmm. Promise."

"Damn. You're callin' me bad?" He took a bite and nodded. "This is almost as delicious as you."

After they plowed through the cake, she held her wine glass and snuggled close against his chest.

His hand stroked her arm as they watched the cacophony of the Christmas tree lights against the background of the Las Vegas strip.

"Boone?"

"Uh huh."

"Why did you decide to spend Christmas in Vegas?"

"The rodeo."

She glanced up at him. "Your parents didn't object?"

"At first. Then we explained that the Old West Casino Invitational is something new the casino is doing. Put on just to benefit local food shelves."

Gieselle laughed. "Kira and I wondered why people were carrying cans into the arena. At first we thought they were going to open them and pelt you with baked beans."

He chuckled. "Doesn't happen at rodeo. It's a pretty respectful crowd, usually."

"It was so much fun, Boone. I loved it, and I really want to see more live events." Her hint that he could ask her to join him was met with silence.

A few minutes later, Boone set down his empty glass. "Mom made us promise to be back the day after Christmas. She's holding the feast until we return."

"That's nice." When she finished her wine, Boone took her glass and arranged her more snugly against him.

"Does Dallas live close to you?"

"He does. He's on his own, though. Lives in an apartment in town."

The warmth of the fire surrounded her in a cozy, muzzy blur and her eyes slid shut. The next thing she knew, Boone had her in his arms, carrying her into the bedroom.

He stood her next to the bed, tugged off her hair towel and robe, and tucked her in. Before he even slid in next to her, she was half asleep.

Gieselle woke with a start. The bedside clock said four-fifteen a.m. Boone's hand rested on her belly and she slid out from under him. Digging a T-shirt and jeans from the dresser, she grabbed her jogging shoes and walked out to the living room.

The tree, the birthday cake, even the candle were the most thoughtful gifts any man had ever given her. She wanted to surprise him with a little gift. Something that said she needed more than these two amazing days with him.

Grabbing her wallet and phone, she snuck out of the suite and headed down to the twenty-four hour gift shop.

The casino was quiet. Just a few hardcore gamblers played slots. The poker rooms were busy, though. In the shop, she browsed a minute before the sleepy employee walked over and greeted her. When Gieselle explained the type of gift she was looking for, the woman came to life. In minutes, they found the perfect thing.

A replica old West pocket watch. Flipping it open, there was a place to put a photo.

Gieselle touched her phone in her pocket. Kira had sent her the picture. "Is there a place in the hotel to print out a photo?"

The woman smiled. "What a great idea. The business center on the third floor is open twenty-four hours a day. They'll get you all set up, then you come back down here and I'll gift wrap this for you."

Gieselle smiled. "Thank you. He's going to love it."

A half-hour later, she snuck into their suite and set the little package under the tree for him to find. She undressed, slid back into bed, and he rolled over, capturing her in his arms.

"Where'd you go, baby?"

"Just felt the need to gamble." Gamble on offering this man a little more of her life.

****

Boone felt the bed shake. Half-awake, he'd been dreaming of the beautiful woman he'd made love to early this morning, and his cock stood at full mast.

The covers shifted and something warm touched his thigh.

He opened one eye.

Gigi's feet stuck out of the covers on the other side of the bed. She licked and nibbled at his hipbone.

"What's going on here?" His growl set a giggle rolling from her.

"Room service." Her soft hair trailed onto his belly as her breath blew hot against his shaft.

"This is the kind of room service I've been looking for my whole life."

A warm hand grasped the base of his cock and her tongue trailed a path up to his throbbing head. "Only in Vegas, baby."

He laughed.

She giggled, and got very busy under the covers.

A half hour later, after Gigi begged him to get out of bed so they could go down to the buffet and eat, he stepped out of the shower.

"Your phone buzzed." She stood gorgeously naked brushing on mascara in the bathroom mirror.

He walked up behind her, dripping wet, and pressed his hard cock into the crease of her fine ass. "You sure we don't have time for a quick—"

"I'm starving. And it's my birthday." She wiggled her ass against his erection. "Feed me first and I'll spend the rest of the day in bed with you."

He hefted out a breath. He'd hold her to that promise. "Best Christmas ever." Their eyes met in the mirror.

She smiled. "For me, too."

Pushing back, he dried himself and forced his heart to back away, too. No sense in drifting into her pretty hazel eyes and dreaming of things that couldn't be. In the bedroom, he found his phone.

Dallas had sent a text. Did you get $125K worth of nookie out of your buckle bunny?

"Harsh." It was Dallas's way of reminding him not to get involved. Not to fall in... He looked into the bathroom where Gigi blow-dried her hair. No, not love. Just a need for companionship. If he kept telling himself that, sooner or later he'd believe it.

Boone typed his reply. *Less taxes, of course.* He shook his head. This wasn't the conversation he should be having about a woman like Gigi. But if it would keep Dallas from busting in and hauling him back to Reno, he'd play along. He slipped into a clean pair of boxers and jeans.

His phone buzzed again. Dallas texted, *Taxes up the ass, buddy!*

"Crude fucker." He replied, *That's a lot of taxes. Gonna need more lube.* It felt awkward talking about her like that, but Dallas didn't need to know how invested he'd become in Gigi. He read his words again and wished there was a way to recall that last text. "Shit." He set his phone down and walked out to the mini fridge for a bottle of water.

Cracking it open, he stood looking out at Vegas in the morning sunlight. A different world than the nighttime city. This morning, it looked hard and cold, frayed at the edges and dirty all over.

"No." Gigi's soft cry came from the bedroom.

He rushed back in. She wore her robe and held…his phone. "Aw hell."

"Dallas says to take the cost of the lube out of Gigi's half." She looked at him with pain and terror in her eyes. "I read the other messages, too." Her hand shook as she handed it to him.

He set the phone in a dresser drawer as his heart shot a twinge across his chest. "You're reading my messages?" It was the first thing he thought to say, and the last thing he should have spoken out loud.

Tears filled her eyes. "Your phone chimed as I walked past. I picked it up to bring to you and saw my name. I didn't mean to…" She shook her head and turned away.

"Listen, baby, it's just guy talk."

She ripped off the robe and stepped into her jeans, slung on a bra, and pulled her T-shirt over her head. "Guy talk? You really talk about women like that?"

He hefted out a breath. "We just have this thing. This promise. Keeping each other from making a mistake."

With one shoe in her hand, she searched for the other. "A mistake? Treating a woman like a lady is making a mistake?"

His back stiffened. "I treated you like nothing less than a princess."

"You did. And you had me fooled." Her hands fisted at her hips. "I know you think of me as a one nighter, and maybe that's all I am to you. But for you and Dallas to talk about me like I'm a slut…" She dropped her head. "Maybe that's all I am."

The words were said more to herself than to him.

She wiped a tear from her cheek. "Maybe I was fooling myself."

"No. Gigi. Wait a minute." He could diffuse this if he could think of the right things to say.

Spotting her shoe, she reached under the bed and bumped her head on the footboard. "Bitches and whores." Rubbing her scalp, she stood and brushed past him, walking out into the living room.

He followed. "It was inappropriate. Okay? I'm sorry."

She looked at him with such agony in her eyes, he nearly choked.

"I'm sorry, Boone." She picked up her purse and walked to the door. "Sorry you didn't get to take me up the ass the way you wanted." She turned the door handle.

"Now hold on." He stormed over and pushed the door closed. Held it shut. "Forgive me, give me another chance. Let's just hole up here, lock ourselves in, and I'll find a way to make it up to you."

"How, Boone? How can you take this hurt away?" She touched her chest. "Was I just imagining that we had something special? Something more than a couple days?"

Ah shit. This was what Dallas warned him about. Getting in too deep. Falling without thinking first. Making a mistake that'd cost him more than he could afford.

Cold acid swirled in his gut. This was his chance. Break it off clean for both of their sakes without having to do the whole goodbye scene.

"Yeah, baby. I think you were imagining it." The lie rose like bile but it was the best way to handle it. He removed his hand from the door. He turned and walked away.

Silently, she left him.

He nearly collapsed from the pain. Boone walked to the bar and grabbed a tumbler and the half-empty bottle of whiskey. He passed the tree and flopped onto the loveseat. "Merry Christmas, asshole." He poured a shot, added another inch, and set down the bottle.

How did doing the right thing feel like fifteen seconds under a bull's hooves? She needed to move on, finish college, start her business. He needed to focus on his rodeo school. He had Dallas and Jay to think about, not just himself.

Stretching out his legs, he bumped something under the tree. A package? He set down his glass and picked it up. Wrapped in cowboy Christmas wrap, it had to be for him. From her. Should he hand it back to her unopened?

She'd just throw it at him.

He pulled off the paper and opened the cardboard box. A pocket watch. It reminded him of the one his grandpa left to his little brother. The cover had an engraving of a cowboy on a horse. He pushed the button to flip open the top. The time was right. Color caught his eye. He tipped it back.

She'd printed a picture of the two of them standing in front of the Birthday Baby after their win, holding champagne glasses. She smiled, but her eyes looked mostly shocked. He had his arm around her and grinned, proud and happy and...about to fall in love?

"Shit. Fuck me." He snapped it shut and wrapped his hand around it. The gift was sweet, but adding the photo was a message. They'd found something rare and special, and he'd shoved it away because it didn't fit into his timeline. "Asshole."

His phone rang. Was it Gigi? He leapt to his feet and grabbed it. He didn't recognize the number, but it was a Vegas area code. Could she be calling from Kira's room? "Gigi?"

"Ah, no. Is this Mr. Hancock?"

"Yes."

"This is Ray Truman, the slot department manager at the casino. We're ready to distribute the winnings to you and Ms. Colberg-Staub."

He had to get to her before she went to the casino office. "Have you contacted Miss Colberg-Staub yet?"

"Yes. I just hung up from her."

"Damn."

****

Gieselle closed her phone. She stared out the window of Kira's room.

"Was that him?" Kira lay on the bed, her head propped on her bent arm.

"No. The casino office is ready to hand out the money."

"Good. Get your money, and let's get the hell out of this town."

Gieselle's chest gave her pain with every breath. Her stomach churned, and her throat tightened each time she thought of him. He wanted her out of his life.

The words repeated like a bad soundtrack at a cheap casino.

He wanted her gone.

Her phone rang and she checked the number. It wasn't a Vegas number. She sent it right to voicemail.

Kira sat up. "Let me get dressed and I'll go down with you."

The hotel phone rang and Kira picked up the receiver. "Hello?" Her eyes opened wide and she mouthed, "It's him."

Gieselle shook her head. She had nothing left to say to him.

"You're worried about her?" Kira listened for a few seconds. "Is she here?" She looked at Gieselle for an answer.

The decision came in a split second of clarity. She nodded.

Kira wrinkled her brow, giving her a confused look. "Yes, she's here."

Gieselle mouthed, "In the shower."

"But she just got in the shower." She listened for a moment. "Sure. I'll keep her here until you get here." Kira gave the phone the middle finger, and hung up.

"Okay, here's the plan." Gieselle walked to the door. "When he gets here, tell him I'm in the shower. Turn on the water."

"Wait, where are you going?"

"I have to let him go. If I don't, I'll be living with him in my heart for the rest of my life."

Kira rubbed her forehead. "You know I hate it when you talk in riddles."

Gieselle smiled. "Just delay him as long as you can." She left the room and headed for the far bank of elevators, just in case Boone was already on his way. During the ride down to the casino, she listened to her voice message.

"Gigi, this is Boone. I'm sorry. I made a big, stupid mistake. Call me back. Please." He paused. "God I wish I could turn back time to an hour ago."

Her finger hovered over the delete key but she couldn't do it. His voice would haunt her forever, but the message would be a good reminder of why she needed to guard her heart more carefully.

****

Ten minutes later, Boone paced the small room, past the empty, unmade bed that would have been Gigi's last night, and past Kira in sweats, sitting on her rumpled bed with her arms crossed, glaring at him.

"So, Boone, you really said you'd need more lube to take the cost of the taxes out of Gieselle's ass?"

He tugged his hands through his hair. "I told you. It was just trash talk that Dallas and I do. It didn't mean anything."

The bathroom shower still ran. He'd been in the room for—he checked his watch—eight minutes and thirteen seconds and she still hadn't come out.

"So, tell me again why you said you didn't feel anything for her? After she said she felt something for you."

He fisted his hands. "Because I'm a goddamn idiot, okay?" He thumped his fist on his forehead then dropped into a chair. "I thought she'd be better off without me complicating her life. And I thought I'd be better off if she was just a memory. But I was wrong." He dropped his head into his hands. "So fucking wrong."

"Somehow, you're convincing me. But I'm not the one you tossed out of your life."

He caught Kira's gaze. "Do you think she'll ever forgive me?"

"You two seem good together." Kira looked away. "Gieselle was happy." Emotions rolled across her face. "She deserves to be happy, and I think she could be with you."

She stood and opened the door to the hallway. "She's not here."

"What?" He looked at the bathroom door, strode to it, and threw it open.

The shower was empty.

"Where is she?"

"I don't know. She left right after you called here. Asked me to detain you as long as…"

He ran out the door and reached the elevators as her voice trailed off.

"Hey, idiot." Kira shouted down the hall. "Make this right."

"I plan to, ma'am." He jumped into the elevator, making two older ladies screech. He apologized while he pressed the buttons for Casino and Door Close until the damn thing got moving.

He jogged to the business office door and asked to see Ray, the manager. He was shown into an office, empty except for Ray. "Is Miss Colberg-Staub coming?"

"Well…" The manager took his time sitting.

Boone leaned on the desk. "Was she here already?"

"She's been here, and is gone." He smiled. "And you'll be pleased to know she signed a waiver turning over all the winnings to you."

He stepped back, his legs bumped a chair, and he sat. "What? She can't do that, can she?"

"Legally, the money is yours, anyway." He leaned forward. "She wanted you to have it to start your rodeo school." He slid a stack of papers in front of Boone. "She even suggested I talk to you about the casino sponsoring your school. I'd like to set up a meeting for tomorrow with you and our marketing people."

Boone couldn't speak. She'd given him the money. She'd talked them into sponsoring him. His first reaction was to tell the casino to shove the money, but now he wanted to tell her to shove it…into her bank account. His lip curved in a half smile. "She's quite a woman."

"She is, Mr. Hancock. An impressive lady." He handed Boone a pen. "Now, if you'll give me your driver's license, and start completing the paperwork, I'll have you out of here in no time."

Chapter Seven

Gieselle phoned Kira. "I'm in the Roundup Bar drowning my stupidity in margaritas."

"I'm close. Be there in a minute."

She stirred the slushy drink and propped her head on her hand. Boone must have his money by now. Was probably celebrating with a girl on each arm. "Sluts."

The bartender turned. "What?" The place was empty except for the bartender, her, and a guy reading the newspaper in a corner.

"Slush." She twirled her straw in her drink. "Nummy."

He grinned. "You need breakfast? I can order something for you."

"I got my breakfast right here." She sipped from her glass. "Fruit, ice, sugar, and fermented agave." Her voice slurred just a little. It'd be slurring a hell of a lot more in a half hour or so.

"Okay. If you change your mind, I get a break in an hour. I know a great place for omelets."

She sighed. "And so the bullshit begins all over again."

The bartender shrugged. "On second thought, I retract that invitation."

Gieselle slapped her hand down on the bar. "That's probably the smartest thing you'll ever do, Mr. Bartender."

"It's Don. If you care."

"I'm Gigi, if anyone cares."

"Oh, fuck you." Kira's voice carried across the bar. "Stop being a baby. You knew him for less than twenty-four hours."

The man in the corner folded his newspaper and left the bar.

"Don." She gestured to Kira. "This is my good friend Kira, who's come to cheer me up." She sneered at her friend. "Not that anyone could tell by her bitch act."

Kira slid onto the stool next to her. "Hi Don. Please excuse her. She's just given up a huge jackpot to the asshole who dumped her."

Gieselle focused her eyes on Kira. "How did you know?"

"Boone called the room looking for you. Said you're not answering your cell."

"Maybe I should get out of here. Hide out somewhere." She sucked in a breath as an idea came to her. "I should get a flight out today."

"No. Let's wait until tomorrow." Kira looked guilty and wouldn't meet her gaze.

What was going on?

"But maybe some time away from this hotel would be good. After Boone called, I rounded up Dallas and Jayden. They're on their way.

We're all going casino hopping. The four of us. And we're going to have fun." She pushed Gieselle's margarita away.

"No. I'm not going anywhere. I'm going to sit here and drink until Don has to call security to bring me to my room."

"Okay." Don walked over with a slip of paper. "Let me get your room number right now."

She laughed and wrote it on the slip. "I like that you think ahead. Be sure to give yourself a nice, big tip after I pass out." She retrieved her drink and took a healthy sip.

Dallas and Jayden walked in, their boots loud on the wood floor.

"What the hell is going on?" Jayden sat next to Gieselle.

Dallas stood by Kira. "Boone took off in his truck. He's not answering his phone."

Gieselle shrugged. "He's got what he's dreamed of. He's probably halfway to Reno by now."

Jayden narrowed his eyes. "What does that mean?"

Kira explained the whole story, giving the cowboys the evil eye when she mentioned the text messages.

Gieselle swung around on her barstool and faced Dallas. "Do you really think I'm just a slut?" She spun toward Jayden. "Just a trampy buckle bunny?"

Both men shook their heads.

"We know you're not." Jayden looked at Dallas. "It's just guy talk, I guess."

Dallas heaved out a breath. "I'm really sorry you saw those texts, Gigi. It's nothing personal. We'd promised to keep each other on track, which means no women for more than a weekend." He dropped his head. "It was my way of reminding him, but it came out too strong, and I'm sorry."

Kira crossed her arms. "That was a shitty thing to do, Dallas."

"Kira." Gieselle appreciated her friend's loyalty, but this was her issue to tackle.

"Don't 'Kira' me, girl. You're too damn forgiving." She flicked a hand at Dallas. "If it was me? I'd yell and scream until you realized how bad you'd hurt me. But Gieselle's too sweet for that." She gestured toward her friend. "Look at those puppy eyes."

Gieselle groaned. "Shut up, Kira."

Dallas looked at Kira for a moment before glancing at Gieselle. "She's right, Gigi. I'd feel better if you let me have it with both barrels." He lifted a hand then dropped it again. "I wish I could think of a way to make it up to you. To make you believe I didn't mean those things about you."

"Maybe you didn't." Her airway constricted. "But Boone shouldn't have replied the way he did."

Jayden turned her stool. "Boone didn't mean it, either.. He's just runnin' scared right now."

"I wish I could believe that." Gieselle looked at the face so like her Boone. "It wasn't just the text messages, though. It's what he said after that, and he meant every word." Anguish rolled through her.

Dallas swung her stool back to face him. Her head started to spin. "I really like you. I like you for Boone, and I know he does, too. But give him some time."

Shaking her head, she reached for her drink. "It's too late for us."

"I don't think so." Dallas squeezed her shoulder. "He's spent so many years avoiding any emotional connection, that when he found someone he really connected with…" He shrugged. "It just came natural to him to push you away."

She dropped her head. "The way he did it, though." She sucked in a breath, promising herself she wouldn't cry.

Jayden touched her arm. "You want me to beat him up for you?"

Dallas laughed. "I'll help."

She smiled. "Thanks, no. But I appreciate the offer."

Kira rubbed her stomach. "I'm hungry." She looked at the cowboys. "You guys eat yet?"

"Nope." Jayden motioned for the bartender. "You woke us up when you called."

Kira snorted. "No buckle bunnies sleeping next to you?"

"Nope." Dallas echoed Jayden. "We were good boys last night…or this morning. After we walked you to your room, we went right to ours and climbed in our beds."

Kira narrowed her eyes and stared at him.

Was there something happening between the two of them?

Jayden asked for menus and they all ordered breakfast. They sat at the bar and ate, the cowboys washing it down with beer, and Kira and her sipping on margaritas.

It all seemed so normal. As if her heart hadn't been dropkicked across the Vegas strip. She just needed to get through the next twenty-four hours until their flight left for home. "Merry Christmas, guys." Gieselle held up her drink.

"Happy birthday, Gigi." Dallas tapped her glass, Jayden and Kira followed suit.

"Okay, men, let's go." Kira jumped to her feet and slung her purse over her shoulder.

Jayden looked at her. "We can't leave Gigi."

Kira jerked her head to the left.

Gieselle turned to look but Kira grabbed her arm. "You stay here and behave. Promise?"

"You're leaving me? I thought you were my friend." She narrowed her eyes. "You're fired."

Kira laughed. "You'll re-hire me. You always do." She winked.

She didn't blame them for taking off without her. She was a pathetic lump of depression. "You all have fun."

They tossed money onto the bar and left.

She should just go back to her room and sulk alone. It'd be less expensive than soaking herself in tequila. Going from a rich woman back to barely making it again, would take some getting used to.

"Do you have any special drinks for idiots?" A male voice came from her right. Her male.

She swung her head. There he stood, in a light colored cotton shirt, the sleeves rolled up on his muscled forearms. A tan cowboy hat, and his jeans and boots.

Don grinned at him and looked at Gieselle. "Sure do. Arsenic okay?"

"Yep. With a longneck to wash it down." He gestured toward her. "And whatever the smart, lovely lady's having, give her a double."

Gieselle sighed. Her heart thumped and the ache that had cramped her chest all morning doubled in intensity. "I'll pass on that right now, Don."

Boone walked over to her, his body so tense, she barely recognized the normally cocky cowboy. He stood beside her. "Can I sit?"

She'd rather walk away, but facing this head on would speed her healing process. She gestured. "Sure."

Don brought the beer and cleared away the leftovers from the other three.

"Could we have a few minutes alone?" Boone jerked his head toward the door.

Don grimaced. "I'm not allowed to—"

"Hear that?" Boone pulled a wad of cash from his breast pocket, peeled off a fifty, and slid it across the bar. "Your Uncle Ulysses is looking for you."

Grinning at Boone's reference to the president on the bill, he picked it up. "I can hear him calling me." He left the bar.

"Listen." Boone faced her, his elbows on his thighs, leaning close. "I got scared. I panicked."

She swiveled toward him, nodding. "I was scared, too, but I was willing to give it a try."

"You're braver than I am. You see things through the vision of a woman with a graduate degree and a big future." He tipped back his hat. "I'm a high school grad. I know nothing but rodeoing. If this idea of a rodeo school doesn't work out for me, I'm done. I got nothin'."

"I understand. Your commitment to pursuing your dream comes first." She was just a lucky pickup for him, and he was here to apologize before he went on with his life.

"It did." He put his hand on hers on her thigh. "Until I met you."

His touch felt too good. Knowing it was the last one she'd ever experience from him, she savored it for a second before swiveling to face the bar. "I wish I could believe that." She stared at the colorful bottles lined up. How many drinks would it take before the pain eased?

His hand dropped. "I want to try again. I want to make this work."

"Boone, let's not make promises we'll regret. You sent those texts to Dallas." She narrowed her gaze on him. "Can you imagine how disposable that made me feel?"

He lifted his hands, palms up, then let them drop. "Even while I was doing it, I knew it was wrong. I just…" He blinked slowly, his eyes tortured. "I didn't want Dallas to know how I really felt."

"I don't think *you* know how you feel, but your actions speak for you." Her hand fisted. She'd love to knock some sense into him. "You intentionally…" She'd been about to say "broke my heart," but that would reveal too much, give him too much power over her. She softened her voice. "You intentionally let me walk out of your life. Forever."

He nodded and swallowed. "A mistake I regret, and wish I could take back."

"But, that was what your common sense told you to do." Her mouth went dry. "Which means it was the right thing to do. I can see that now."

"No, it wasn't." He reached for her but when she flinched away, he dropped his hand.

"You told me there was nothing there." She locked gazes with him and fought to keep her emotions bottled. "That I was imagining this thing between us." Gigi tipped her head. "Could I be so foolish, so naïve that I just dreamed it up?"

"No, baby, you know I—"

"Boone." She gripped the bar. "Don't." Her chest tightened. "Don't call me that. You lost the right."

He mumbled his own name, followed by what sounded like curses. "You didn't imagine anything, Gigi." His eyes glowed with intensity. "It's there." He touched the spot over his heart. "It may even be here. All I know is that we're meant to be together."

She couldn't let herself slide back into his life. Not with damage to her soul being so likely. "Three hours ago, you said something completely different." Gigi made a face. "Why would I believe what you're saying now?"

He took her hands.

She tried to pull back, but he stood and held tight.

"I've been so goddamn careful to stick to the path I mapped. First, rodeo until I have enough to start a school. Then make it profitable for the long term. Then build a house, find a woman, and settle down." He shook his head. "Hell, I even have this written down and taped to the mirror in my bathroom."

His sincerity chipped a crack in her defenses. His touch warmed her, defrosting a corner of her anger. She should pull back. She should run or he might break through the shield she'd erected around her heart.

Boone's gaze caught hers and locked on. "Wait, let me finish." His thumbs traced softly on her palms. "I was so focused on the things I need to do right now, I missed seeing how having you with me would make everything so much better." He hauled in a long breath and puffed it out. The emotion in his eyes shook her, made her nearly desperate for his next words.

"And I missed seeing…" His hands gripped hers tightly. "…that without you, the rodeo, the school, the ranch; they just don't mean a damn thing."

Gigi closed her eyes and swayed with the powerful words. So much stronger than the harsh words he'd used earlier, his admission set hope racing through her like wild mustangs across a prairie. Looking into his beautiful blue eyes, she searched for any hint of evasiveness. She saw only soul-deep sincerity.

She had to be honest. "I wish I could believe as easily as I want to. But the scars are still there, Boone. It might take some time for me to be able to trust again."

He brushed his fingers along her cheek. "I understand." His jaw tightened. "If I could go back…" He looked away with a mumbled curse. His gaze flew back to hers, his eyes bright in the soft lighting. "I have never in my life felt this way." He didn't move for long moments, just stared at her. "Not about anything. Not about anyone."

Those scars she'd been hiding behind started to melt away. "It feels…amazing to hear you say that."

"But?" Wrinkles formed between his brows.

"But, I want to make sure this time." She smiled, proud of herself for not admitting her deep feelings for him, or for throwing herself into his arms and begging him to carry her to their suite. She would approach this with more reserve, now. No more muzzy blur of infatuation. Eyes wide open. "We've known each other for less than a day. Let's give it a little more time before we decide anything."

His face unreadable, Boone stared at her. "You're kinda smart, aren't you."

She blinked.

His lip twitched in a partial smile.

"Yes." She grinned. "I'm very wise." Warmth spread through her chest. She had another day—another chance—with her cowboy.

"Okay. Let's start over from this morning, before the texts, and before I let you get away from me."

She held out her hand. "Agreed."

He took her fingers in his hand and lifted them to his lips for a slow, warm kiss. "You're amazing, Gigi." He released her hand.

She touched his cheek. "And you're irresistible, cowboy."

He chuckled and kissed her palm, took her hand and held it. With his free hand, he reached into his chest pocket and pulled out the watch.

Searching his eyes for his reaction, she held her breath.

He clutched it in his hand, his head tipped down. "This is probably the nicest gift I've ever been given." He looked at her. "Thank you. It means a lot that you went through all the trouble…for me."

She squeezed his hand. "You're welcome. It was a lot of fun pulling it together."

He dropped his head. "And I messed it up." Shaking his head, he opened the watch and looked at the picture. "I hope I can make it up to you." He closed the watch and slid it back into his pocket.

A lump formed in her throat. His sincerity did so much to heal her wounds. "You can." She winked. "I saw a little ornament in the gift shop that you can buy me. We can hang it on our tree."

He nodded. "Our tree. Sounds nice." He reached into his back pocket and pulled out an envelope. "First, I have something for you." He sat and handed it to her.

She took it, watching his face.

His expression gave nothing away.

Inside were six personal checks from Boone's account. She stared at his heavy cursive and distinctive signature. Her mouth dropped open. Each check was made out to her, each for thirteen thousand dollars.

"The casino manager helped me find a tax accountant who figured this out."

Her brows rose. "Really? On Christmas Day?"

"This is Vegas. Anything's possible."

She scanned through the checks again, calculating the total. "Wow." This was nearly unbelievable. "Why six checks?"

He took a breath. "Since I'm from Nevada, I don't pay state income tax. We figured out how much federal tax I'll have to pay on the winnings."

"Okay." She wished she were a little less emotionally drained.

"If you deposit those checks into separate accounts, you should be safe from paying any more taxes. The amount of each one is under the maximum gift tax exclusion."

She smiled. "You know about all this?"

"Just learned today." He cleared his throat and shifted in his seat. "Since the tax debt will be fully paid on the money, I don't feel that we're doing anything to avoid paying our fair share."

She sobered. That had to be a difficult decision for him. "No, you're right. But what if you do your taxes and realize you've overpaid me?"

He grinned. "Can I contact you?"

She smiled. "I'd like that." She slid the envelope into her purse. "Thank you. This is unexpected. I love all the effort you went through to do this."

"You're welcome." His eyes held an emotion that made her breath catch. He looked away. "Just don't try to deposit those checks until I can get the casino's check into my bank account tomorrow."

She patted her purse. "I'm not heading home until tomorrow afternoon."

A look of worry crossed his face.

****

"I don't want to think about that." A chill raced through Boone. He'd just got her back, and he wasn't ready to let her go. "Can we spend the rest of your birthday together?" He swallowed. "In our suite?"

She slung her purse strap over her shoulder as a sweet expression filled her eyes. "I thought you'd never ask." Her voice was breathy.

He left cash on the bar and they strolled through the casino. Her little hand in his felt too right. He'd missed this during the few hours they were apart.

In their suite, he took off his hat, kicked off his boots, and waited for her to set the pace.

She set down her purse and hung the little gold-plated slot machine ornament on their tree. Turning toward him, she held out her hand.

Boone took it, watching the tree lights reflect in her eyes.

"Bedroom?" Her sweet smile nearly broke his heart.

"Yeah, bedroom." He let her lead him in.

Housekeeping had been in and the bed was made.

Pulling her close, he ran his hands up under her shirt, caressing her back. "I missed you."

Her eyes closed for a second. "I missed you, too." She wrapped her arms around his neck. "Kiss me."

He chuckled. "Don't have to tell this cowboy more than once." He pressed his lips on her soft, warm mouth, breathing in the essence of her.

She sighed, and he inhaled her breath. His tongue did a slow trace on her lips before easing inside her mouth.

She lapped at his tongue, building heat between them.

Her excitement drew on his, and heat flowed to his groin, hardening his shaft.

She slowed her manic kiss and stepped back. "I would like a birthday gift from you."

He blinked. Demanding? Hell yeah! "Anything, Gigi." And he meant anything.

"I want you inside me. Right now."

An earthquake of lust shook him. "As you wish, ma'am." He tugged her shirt up and off her, unfastened her bra, sliding the straps down her arms, and bent to kiss her nipple.

"Oh, Boone." She sighed the words as she ran her fingers through his hair.

He suckled her other breast, the taste rocking him, raising a desperation he'd never known. Kneeling at her feet, he unbuttoned and unzipped her jeans and slid them down her curvy hips. "No underwear?"

A little laugh escaped her. "I couldn't find them this morning when I was stomping around yelling at you."

He kissed her belly. He had her underwear in his pocket. He might give them back. Someday. "You were magnificent, Gigi." He glanced up at her. "A mix of anger and heartbreak that nearly paralyzed me."

"Cowboy." She brushed a wild lock of hair from his forehead. "I'm glad it all happened the way it did."

"You are?" After all she'd endured, how could she be glad?

"If I hadn't lost you…" She sucked in a breath. "I wouldn't have realized how much you mean to me."

"Aw, Gigi." He wrapped his arms around her and pressed his cheek into her stomach. If his heart had any pull over his brain, he'd never let her go again. He tugged her jeans off her and coaxed her to part her legs.

Her scent filled his nostrils and he needed a taste. He bent and lapped her pink pussy lips, sucking them into his mouth.

"Ahh." Her nails dug into his shoulders.

He loved it. Kissing her mound, he nipped at her, finally finding her clit and sucking. The base of his spine tightened, radiating vibrations up his backbone to his brain.

"No." She breathed. "Can't come yet." Her body tensed. "I want you inside me."

Backing off was the hardest thing he'd ever done. "Anything you want."

He stood and tugged the front of his shirt, his gaze locked with hers. The snaps popped open and he slid it off. Unfastening his belt, he silently thanked the bulls that let him win the huge buckle that brought Gigi and him together.

With a grin, he dropped his jeans and boxers, pulled off his socks, and stepped out of the pile of clothes.

She lay back on the bed. "What's the smile for?"

He grabbed a condom and slid it on. "The way we met."

She lifted her arms to him.

He'd never seen anything as beautiful. His chest ached for this. He lay on top of her, his weight on his elbows. "Like all the forces of karma coming together."

Gigi kissed him. "I believe in karma, too." She reached between their bodies and grasped his cock, guiding it to her wet pussy.

He had one overwhelming thought as he slid his erection into her tight slit. This was where he belonged.

Chapter Eight

Gieselle's mind blanked in and out in odd rhythms as Boone slid his hot shaft into her core. Her whole belly heated as he filled her, and her insides shifted to accommodate his length and width.

When he'd entered fully, she spread her legs farther and he pushed inside another incredible inch. "Boone." She rolled her head from side to side as tiny red lights blinked behind her eyelids.

"Gigi." He pulled out and pulsed back in again, his hips quivering as he fought for each additional centimeter. "So tight and hot."

She cracked open her eyes.

His eyes were unfocused, his pupils large. Easing out once more, he locked gazes with her and pumped into her. His eyes rolled back for a second and his breath panted hot on her face.

Bells rang in her ears and she slipped further into the climax that pulled at her. That helped to heal her soul. "I'm almost there."

"Baby, let go. Come for me. I want to see your face when you hit the top." His hips picked up speed as he rammed into her. He slurped her nipple into his mouth.

The lovely jolt from her breast to her pussy tipped her over and she tucked into a wild spin, traveling through time as alarms shimmered up and down her spine, tremors gripped her core, and flashes blipped in her brain.

As she coasted back toward consciousness, the slide of his cock in her rippling slit drew aftershocks that had her whimpering with pleasure. Rolling her hips with his thrusts, she opened her eyes.

His gaze was still on her. "You're incredibly beautiful when you come." He smiled and kissed her jaw. "But then, you're beautiful no matter what you're doing."

She tipped her head, encouraging him to taste her neck. "Coming for you is my favorite."

He slid warm, wet lips across her skin. "Coming in you is mine." He sped his rhythm and his body tensed. "I want you, Gigi."

She couldn't get enough of him. She bit his earlobe. "Show me how much, Boone. Show me what I do to you."

He lifted his head and kissed her hard and desperate, his tongue matching the thrusts of his cock.

Tingles raced through her as a quick-burning orgasm ripped her out of reality.

He broke the kiss and shouted as his pumping hips drove into her, his body tensed and shuddered. His hands gripped her with bruising strength.

Her own body tingled and shook as she accepted his thrusts, welcoming his pulsing heat inside her.

"Best ever…" His dark, heavy-lidded eyes locked onto hers.

She cupped his cheeks. "Gets better each time."

"Might not live through the next one." He pulled out and collapsed next to her, rolling onto his back and bringing her with him.

Her hand rested over his heart, feeling the rapid beats and his labored breathing. "We'd die happy."

He laughed, a slow rolling rumble. "You make me happy, Gigi."

She snuggled in as her stomach jittered with glee. "I'm happy, too."

He sat up. "C'mon."

"No afterglow cuddling?" She faked a pout.

He stood and tugged her up with him. "On the loveseat."

After a quick stop in the bathroom, they wrapped themselves in their robes and snuggled in front of the tree as the fireplace warmed the room.

Her head rested on his shoulder as she took in each one of the ornaments sparkling in the multicolored tree lights. The little slot machine they'd picked up at the gift shop had the casino's name and the year on it, and she reached out and gave it a twirl, watching it reflect the lights. One ornament seemed out of place. A plain black bag about four inches wide.

Boone's tension was the giveaway.

She bit back a smile. "Okay, what is it?" She gestured to the tree. "What did you go spending your money on?"

He laughed as he kissed her. "Took you long enough." He bent forward and his long arm reached out and plucked the bag from the branch.

The brand name on the front of it had her gasping. "Oh, Boone. You didn't do anything crazy, did you?"

"It's Vegas, and I'm a rich man."

She pulled a three-inch square black box from the bag and opened it.

A lovely silver bracelet rested on black velvet. On it, two charms sparkled.

She lifted it out. "It's beautiful." Glancing up at him, she was surprised by the intensity of his gaze.

"You like it?"

"Yes. I've always wanted one of these, but thought I'd have to wait a while." She smiled. "A long while."

He touched the two charms and sent them spinning. "I hope you like these."

She turned the bracelet to see what he'd chosen. "A birthday cake." The silver three-tiered cake had a little gold heart at the top. "And a Christmas tree." All silver except for the gold star on top.

She brushed a kiss on his lips. "They're perfect." A lump of emotion clogged her throat. "They'll always remind me of this time with you."

His brow furrowed. "I'm not ready to end this, Gigi." He hefted out a breath. "I know we said we'd give it a little more time, but I know what I want." He took her hand. "I'll be out east for a few rodeos in January. I'd like to have you there for as many as you can."

She nodded. "I'd love to, if my schedule allows." She crinkled her nose. "I do have a lot of work to do before I graduate."

"I understand. And if it works better for you, I can come to you."

"To New York?" She'd never pictured him in her little on-campus studio apartment.

"Yeah, to New York." He frowned. "They don't allow cowboys there?"

"They do." She laughed. "But only in limited quantities to save the women from melting into lusty pools."

"Okay, then. We'll compare calendars later."

"Okay." So much excitement, she didn't know where to start. Rodeos and college visits. Life would be complicated but she'd make it work. He'd make it work. She held up her bracelet. "Will you help me put this on?"

He sat up. "Sure."

He took the jewelry and opened the clasp. "Here's the thing." He slid it around her wrist and worked to fasten it. "I want to be able to fill this with charms." He looked at her. "Tokens of times we've spent together."

The sweetness of the moment washed through her and moisture gathered in her eyes. "Could take a long time." She held up her wrist. "To fill this, I mean."

He kissed her, pulled her close, and rested his chin on top of her head. "I'm hoping it does."

She closed her eyes and gave in to the joy that filled her. A couple tears escaped, and she let the emotion carry her off into dreams.

Banging sounded and Gigi startled awake.

"What the fuck?" Boone sounded groggy, too.

More banging on the suite door.

He stood and strode over. Even in a robe, he was all macho studly. He opened the door.

Kira burst in and dropped her suitcase. "I'm leaving this town right now." Her voice sounded frantic.

Gieselle raced to her, took her arm. "What happened?"

"Dallas." Her lips tightened.

Boone took her other arm. "What happened? Is he okay?"

"He's fine, besides being an asshole." She shook off both of them and walked to the bar. "That phone call I got yesterday?"

Gieselle sucked in a breath. Something bad? She'd been so involved in her own drama, she'd never asked Kira about it.

Boone led her over to the bar.

Kira found a shot glass. "I'd left a message and asked my dad's attorney to run a background check." She grimaced at Boone.

"On me?" His brows furrowed.

"Sorry. I was worried, with this whole jackpot thing." She smiled at Gieselle. "He's squeaky clean."

She nodded. "I could have told you that."

Boone wrapped his arm around Gieselle's shoulder and kissed the top of her head. "That doesn't explain why you're leaving."

"I got another call today." Kira downed a shot of tequila, choked, then waved a hand. "I don't want to talk about it." She strode to the door. "I'm sorry to leave like this, Gieselle, but I booked the last seat on a flight out in…" She checked her watch. "Shit, I've gotta run."

"Wait." Gieselle grabbed her wrist. "Stay here in the suite tonight and we'll fly back tomorrow."

She snorted. "Right, with you two banging the headboard all night?"

Boone fought a grin. "You're welcome to stay, Kira. We'll keep the banging to a minimum. I'll even keep the asshole out. Jayden, too."

"Thanks for the offer." She smiled at Boone. "I'm leaving, though." Kira gave her a fast hug. "We'll talk when you get home." She opened the door and did a finger wave at Boone. "Have fun. Merry Christmas. And happy birthday, Gieselle."

Gieselle took Boone's hand. "You can call me Gigi." She glanced his way. "It's kind of growing on me."

Kira turned and stepped out the door. "What have you done to her, Boone?" A laugh softened her words.

He closed the door and took her into his arms. "What have I done to you, Gieselle?"

She pressed her hands to his chest, admiring her beautiful bracelet. "More than you can imagine, cowboy."

His stomach rumbled. "We need room service."

"We do. Then more banging of the headboard."

Boone shook his head. "I wonder what that goddamn Dallas did."

"I'm worried about the phone call. Something about him?" She sighed. "I'll find out tomorrow when I get home."

He frowned at her. "About that. I was thinking."

"Uh oh."

"Mom's doing Christmas dinner for the family tomorrow night."

"And you're driving home tomorrow." The thought of saying goodbye stung like a million wasps.

He slid his hand up her spine to her neck and traced his thumb along her jawline. "I'm gonna let Dallas and Jay take my truck back. And…" He stared into her eyes. "I want you to fly back with me."

Everything inside her froze.

"I know it sounds like too much too soon, but I can't let you go yet. I'd like you to be there with me. To meet my parents and the whole damn herd of Hancocks."

She remembered to breathe. "Really? You want me there for your family Christmas?"

He smiled. "I sure as hell do."

Real tears rolled down her cheeks this time. "Boone. I'd love to."

"Woo-hoo!" He picked her up and spun them in circles. When he set her down, he wiped the tears from her cheeks. "No more cryin' until after you see what a weird bunch we are."

"If they're anything like you, I think I'm going to like your family. A lot." She pressed a kiss to his lips. "But what will they think of a buckle bunny from New York?"

He laughed, tipping his head back like a kid. "Aw, Gigi. They're going to love you." He grinned. "Trust me."

####

Would you like to know what happened the next time Dallas and Kira met? They have their own book, the second in the series, Cowboy Jackpot: Valentine's Day. Read the book blurb and find buy links on my website http://RandiAlexander.com. Here's a sneak peek:

Dallas and Kira's Story:
Cowboy Jackpot: Valentine's Day

Chapter One

Dallas Burns shifted on the plush chair in the high-stakes area of the Old West Casino in Las Vegas. He tipped his black cowboy hat back on his head and glanced around the red velvet-lined room.

Hell, he hoped his buddies didn't see him playing roulette. Not that it was a woman's game or anything, but rodeo men only talked about poker. The way they liked to tease each other, this would be a tough one to live down.

"Twenty-four black." The dealer set five more chips on Dallas's bet on Black, and five on his Even bet.

He scooped up his winnings and stacked them in front of him. He'd been fascinated with the game since he was a kid watching an old cowboy movie. Tonight, he was having the best luck of his life. He did a quick count. He had over six thousand dollars in chips and he'd started with three hundred.

He set five chips on First Twelve, and five on Odd. Mixing it up had been working for him tonight. The table was busy. Seven other people stood or sat around the board and placed bets that were quite a bit larger than his. A few wrists flashed diamond-studded watches as they set down their chips.

He glanced around the room and caught a very familiar green gaze.

Kira Morrow. Her eyes opened wide and she leaned toward the strawberry blonde next to her, pointed at him, and said something he knew couldn't be good.

Kira wore a soft-looking blue sleeveless dress and low-heeled white sandals that matched the little purse hanging on her shoulder. It was nearly noon, had they been out on the strip? Her bright red hair hung loose and shimmery halfway down her back. He'd loved running his fingers through it two months ago at Christmas. The day his buddy Boone had met his fiancée, Gigi, right here in this same casino.

Dallas, Boone, and his brother Jayden, had been competing in a rodeo put on for local charities. They'd driven down from Reno for a few days, and had run into Gigi and Kira, who they'd mistaken for buckle bunnies.

Dallas looked back at the table, hoping she would keep walking. He and Kira had gotten into a nasty dust-up on Christmas Day. She'd stormed off and flown back to New York before he'd had a chance to cool down and apologize.

Her unmistakable floral scent threaded through his nostrils and into his brain, making his body remember how he'd wanted her crazily back then. He turned his head. "Kira."

"Dallas." She stood right next to him, too close for safety.

She looked better than ever, her long body slim and graceful, her beautiful breasts large and round.

"Stop staring at my tits."

A couple people at the table laughed.

He met her gaze. "Then get them the heck out of my face."

She lifted a brow. "As charming as ever, I see." She gestured to his other side. "This is my cousin Stormie."

He turned and started to rise.

"Oh, don't get up." Stormie pressed her hand on his shoulder, keeping him down. She was strong. Her denim shorts showed toned legs ending in flip flops, and her white tank top displayed some noticeable but feminine arm muscles.

He held out his hand to her. "My condolences for being attached by blood to this…sweet lady."

Stormie giggled and shook his hand, then leaned closer to Dallas. "She's always been mean, but now I'm big enough to fight back."

He took a closer look at her. Green eyes like Kira's, pale skin with cute freckles. Much too young for him, but he liked her spunk. "Are you here for the bachelorette party?"

"Dallas?" Kira interrupted. "Can I play a chip?"

He turned his head. "Sure." He could afford to lose one chip to get Kira less irritated with him. He needed to work on accomplishing that before they had to walk down the aisle together in New York next week, at Boone and Gigi's wedding.

"I am going to the bachelorette thing." Stormie drew his attention. "I hadn't planned on it so Kira and I were just out shopping. I'm here with my parents for the stock show. When I heard Kira would be here too, we arranged to meet. We had drinks with Gigi last night and she invited me to the party tonight."

Dallas nodded. She worked with stock, probably rode a horse. That's where her well-shaped curves came from.

"What kind of stock do you raise?"

"Horses, mostly, and we've diversified into bucking broncs."

"I've met a few of those." He cracked his neck, relieving the tightness from an old injury.

"Oh right, now it clicks. You're a bronc rider." Stormie grimaced. "When Kira saw you, and told me your name, I didn't place you right away."

More than likely because Kira had been saying something insulting about him.

The dealer spun the wheel and set the ball rolling. "No more bets," he called. "No more bets."

Dallas glanced at the table. All his chips were gone. "What the fuck?"

The chips stood in a tall stack on one spot on the roulette table.

"Kira." His heart palpitated and sweat broke out on his forehead. "Why?"

She smirked. "I put them all on double zero, 'cause you're a big old crusty double zero in my opinion."

Curses rained through his head, followed by a vision of grabbing her long, pale neck and choking the life out of her. Then he felt the need for tears. "Damn it to hell, woman." He grabbed her wrist. "Do you know how much that was?"

She rolled her eyes and tugged her arm free. "You big baby. What was it? Fifty bucks? I'll pay you back." She huffed out a breath and opened her purse.

"More like six thousand."

She froze and her eyes widened. "Say that again."

####

Jayden has his own story, too! Read about how Stormie won his heart in the third book in the series, Cowboy Jackpot: St. Patrick's Day. Read the book blurb and find buy links on my website http://RandiAlexander.com. Here's a sneak peek:

Jayden and Stormie's Story:
Cowboy Jackpot: St. Patrick's Day

Chapter One

Jayden Hancock tucked his hand into the rigging on the back of Chicken Foot, the bay gelding he was about to ride bareback. "Who the hell names a horse Chicken Foot?" The object of his derision lurched in the chute, jamming Jayden's leg against the fencing.

The pain shot up his thigh. He had to get loose. He tightened his grip and shouted, "Okay, okay, okay."

Three point eight seconds later, he lay on his back on the hard packed dirt, staring up at the arena ceiling, his breath knocked out of him. He looked up to see the replay of his ride on the big screen above the ring. When it ended, the shot went live to him lying there, his blond, curly hair full of red dirt.

"Fuck." He was careful not to move his lips when he cussed. Someone could easily read his lips on the screen. He scrambled to his feet, picked up his hat and waved to the crowd in gratitude for the few claps and shouts. He heard women's voices woo-hooing as he walked out through the narrow opening between the gates. Gigi, his brother Boone's wife, and Kira, who was long-distance-dating his friend Dallas, were in the stands for the rodeo.

"Great." He pulled off his gloves and stomped back toward the locker room. Now both Kira and Gigi had witnessed his latest failure.

"Tough luck, Jay." His friend Rance smacked him on the back, stirring up a cloud of dirt. "Chicken Foot is a tricky bastard."

"It ain't the horse, it's the rider." He hadn't won an event in months. He rarely hung on for eight seconds. "My head isn't in the right place anymore."

"Bro, don't jinx yourself." Rance's green eyes locked on his. He was big into superstition, and it was working for him. He was getting close to Jayden's brother, Boone, in the bull riding rankings. "Walk it off."

How many times had he heard that in the five months since his rides had turned bad on him? He jerked off his chaps and stuffed them in his gear bag along with his gloves, vest, and spurs. "I'm gonna get a drink. Come with me?"

"I can't, buddy. I'm in the short go." The riders with the best times in the first round faced off in the final round for the win.

He punched Rance on the arm. "Good luck. I'll be cheering for you from the first bar I find."

"Thanks." Rance pulled off his hat and scratched his head, ruffling his black hair. "I'll meet you for a drink after."

Jayden stuffed his gear bag into a locker and secured it. How long had it been since he'd made it to a short go? Too fucking long. His fist connected with the metal door.

"Hey, you've got another chance tomorrow. Concentrate on that." Rance settled his hat low on his head and walked away.

The two-day rodeo at the Old West Casino in Las Vegas drew some of the best riders. If Jayden didn't pull it together and win tomorrow, he'd drop off the bottom of the ranking charts. His pro rodeo career would be over. His credibility to teach bareback riding would be gone. Yeah, his mind wasn't in the right place. Instead of being set on winning, hollow desperation rode shotgun in his head.

Brushing the dirt out of his hair and off his jeans and his unlucky green "lucky shirt," he walked out of the arena into the casino. Poker would take his mind off his troubles. It was the day before Saint Patrick's Day, and he was half Irish. Things should be going in his favor.

He dusted off his brown cowboy hat and set it on his head the way the buckle bunnies liked it, with his curls showing a little around the edges. Maybe finding a sweetie to spend the night with would help him feel luckier.

The poker room was packed, and he put his name on the waiting list for seven card stud. It'd be a while before a spot opened up. He wandered to the snack bar and had a couple tacos and a beer, then found a comfortable seat at a video poker machine.

"Might as well practice." He pulled a twenty out of his wallet and slid it into the machine. It pinged and chirped a welcome. "Dollar poker. Crap." He'd thought it was quarters. What the hell. It was only twenty bucks. He played the maximum, five dollars, and won a few hands.

After he ordered a beer from the cocktail waitress, he looked around the casino. Both his brother Boone and their friend Dallas had met their women here, under very lucky circumstances.

The two of them had pooled their winnings and were in the process of starting a rodeo school where they lived in Reno. Jayden was supposed to be part of the school, but he had no money to fund his piece of the partnership, and was quickly losing his credibility as an expert. No lucky circumstances for him.

The woman he'd met at the casino on Valentine's Day had turned out to be pretty darn unlucky for him personally—if he remembered correctly. It had been a wild night, what he recalled of it. Had they really gotten…? He pushed the scary memory back again, deep behind the beer fog he'd drunken himself into that night. Right now, he just didn't have the willpower to deal with the bad decision he'd made.

His beer came and he focused on his machine, pressing the maximum button as he took a sip from the red plastic cup. Three aces with a five and a seven. Now this was getting interesting.

"Jayden!" A female voice called from a distance.

He glanced around. A buckle bunny? He spotted Stormie Thompson. "Oh man." It was her, his unlucky charm from February.

####

Connect With Me

Thank you for reading the first Cowboy Jackpot story. It was a pleasure to write, and the characters kept me smiling and blushing the whole time. I'd love to hear from you. I've listed all the places I hang out, and I hope you'll connect with me at one or more of them.

All my best,
Randi
"Rode Hard and Put Up Satisfied"
http://randialexander.com/
https://www.facebook.com/#!/RandiAlexanderAuthor
https://twitter.com/#!/Randi_Alexander
http://www.goodreads.com/author/show/4885056.Randi_Alexander
http://wildandwickedcowboys.wordpress.com/
http://69shadesofsmut.com/

About the Author

Randi Alexander is published with The Wild Rose Press Cowboy Kink line and with Cleis Press. When she's not dreaming of, or writing about, kinky cowboys, she's biking trails along remote rivers, snorkeling the Gulf of Mexico, or practicing her drumming in hopes of someday forming a tropical-rock band.

Other Books by Randi Alexander

Read the first chapters on my website
http://RandiAlexander.com

Chase and Seduction - Country music superstar/actor Chase Tanner has yet to be denied anything—and he's never wanted anything or anyone more than gorgeous screenplay writer Reno Linden. So when the film they are working on is finally finished, Chase decides to turn up the volume on seducing Reno.

Reno Linden lived a quiet, rural life until she was thrust into the Hollywood scene when her book was adapted to film. Chase Tanner is larger than life, sinfully sexy and hell-bent on getting her into bed. Skittish after a failed wedding engagement, Reno risks the plunge into Chase's arms, and is surprised that her good girl self can keep up with bad boy Chase.

Though Chase returns to his cowboy roots often, and Reno cherishes the time spent with him on his ranch, the two find their careers pulling them in different directions. Will their attraction survive the glitz and stress of fame?

Her Cowboy Stud - Trace McGonagall's quiet life on his Houston stud ranch is shaken up when gorgeous Macy Veralta arrives to claim an inheritance left to her in his uncle's will. Trace sees her as just another gold digger, but he also can't resist her curvy body. When she hints at being the perfect submissive to his Dom, he has to have her.

Macy wouldn't have been three months late to claim her inheritance if she'd known Trace was sin in jeans. The cowboy's dominant bearing and the smoldering glint in his eyes send shivers to her toes and stirs images of being bound in his bed and disciplined at his hand. But could Trace's perfect seduction be part of his plan to reclaim her inheritance?

Turn Up the Heat - During the filming of the reality show America's Newest Chef, finalist Mackenzie Jarvis falls desperately in lust with actress Gina Volto. Mackenzie's never been with a woman, and her strict Wyoming upbringing has her questioning whether she can loosen up enough to live out her fantasy.

When Gina shows Mackenzie how sensual their nights could be, Mackenzie ignores her doubts for one wild weekend. Monday morning, she returns home to her ranch, her horses, and her busy career as the owner and chef of a restaurant. But a week later Gina shows up at Mackenzie's home. She's come to Wyoming-for Mackenzie.

Gina teaches Mackenzie the sweet pleasures of loving a woman, the naughty sting of a whip, and the seductive submission of bondage. But Gina admits she wants more than just a few days. Can conservative, family-valued Mackenzie ignore the plans she's made for her life, and find her future in the tender arms of a woman?

Cowboy Bad Boys - Randi Alexander has created ten male/ female (M/F) erotic romances starring sexy cowboys and the ladies in their lives. Each story combines the heart-pounding heat you expect from Randi, as well as the touching romance she does so well. Randi's stories take you from an early summer High Country Ride in the Rockies, to a dangerous buck off a rodeo bull with a Hard Headed Cowboy.

Body Heat – When a rancher and his gorgeous passenger are buried in his truck under an avalanche, they discover a sensual way to keep warm.

Breakfast in Bed – A ranch foreman devises a plan to keep his woman from bolting out of his bed every time they're through making love.

Hard Headed Cowboy – When a rodeo bull rider needs a lift, his sexy equipment sponsor makes him a proposition.

High Country Ride – Fulfilling her father's last wishes, a city girl hires a hot cowboy to guide her into the Rockies.

Kill Me or Kiss Me – With her life in danger, an exotic dancer has to trust a sexy cattle rustler to keep her alive.

No Way Out – The town sheriff and the beautiful bank president he's been lusting after are cornered by a killer.

Private Lessons – When her girlfriends buy her a mechanical bull lesson with a real bull rider, a college girl gets a sensual ride from her high school crush.

Stubborn Redhead – The rancher's woman left him because of rumors of his cheating, but what will it take to make her believe his innocence?

Takin' a Chance – A barrel racer has one last opportunity to seduce the sexy rodeo bullfighter she's fallen for.

Where We Left Off – In desperate need of help, a country veterinarian contacts the man she'd loved but booted out of her life years ago.

Banging the Cowboy (short story in the Cowboy Lust anthology) - Every Saturday for a year, Annie Paris has lusted after Rafe McCord from behind her drumset on stage at the honky tonk. The Big Cowboy, they call him, and rumors say he likes it rough in the bedroom. The thought of banging him makes Annie's pussy tingle and cream.

But Rafe is a one-night-stand kind of guy, and Annie couldn't handle seeing him every Saturday, knowing she'd already had her one night with him. That there'd be no more.

Tonight, something's different. Rafe doesn't leave with a woman. And he's been staring at Annie since he came in the door. At closing time, he sets his longneck on the bar, and swaggers toward her, his gaze locked on hers, his smile pure sexual invitation. Annie's slit contracts and her nipples harden. Oh God, if he asks her to his house for a rough ride on his big, hard cock, where would she find the strength to say "no"?

Double Her Fantasy - At a comic book convention, artist Megan Shore is amazed to find action movie hunk Garret McGatlin sharing the same elevator. Usually reclusive, she jumps on the rare opportunity and flirts shamelessly with the man who has starred in more than one of her sexy fantasies. He responds strong and seductive, and she agrees to meet him for a drink—in his suite. When she arrives, it's his rancher brother, Trey, who opens the door and unleashes Megan's cowboy fantasy. Both men pour on the charm, and she's uncertain which of them she desires more.

The McGatlin brothers have shared many women, but Megan is an irresistible combination of brains, beauty, humor, and sensuality. They want her, need both of their cocks sliding deep inside her. Working together, they execute a potent seduction. When one hot night turns into an amazing week, the three-way relationship becomes emotionally charged. But some bad publicity sends a terrified Megan running, and Garret and Trey have to devise a way to make the headlines disappear. Can they pull off the impossible, or will they lose Megan forever?

FREE READ A Gentleman and a Cowboy - Storeowner Laci Monson can't see that Finn Halliday is just the genuine cowboy she's been looking for until he resorts to using borrowed duds to capture her attention. When things go wrong, will she be able to see the real man behind the clothes? - Free at Amazon, Barnes and Noble, Smashwords, and All Romance Ebooks

~~*~*

Her Fated Cowboy
Harland County Series
Cole
By Donna Michaels

Sorry guys, the lady's with me tonight."

Her heartbeats tripled. She was?

Eyebrows shot up and heads snapped in their direction as the news registered in everyone's brains. Smiling, he guided them towards the food.

"Wait, McCall." She pulled him out of the line.

A big smile split across his face. "You want to get me alone already?" he teased, grazing her hip with his hand.

"Cole, what's going on? Is this a date?"

"Yes."

"You and me?"

"Yes. It generally takes two."

"I know that, but one is generally asked." She raised a brow and waited.

Laughter faded from his eyes. "Are you saying you don't want to be here with me?"

"No, ya big dummy. I'm saying I expected to be asked."

"Oh, I can do that." He grasped her hands and gazed straight into her eyes, his own alight with mischief and hope. "Jordan, I know this has been a very long time coming, but would you do me the honor of being my date for this evening?"

All kidding aside, her heart thudded in her throat. "Are you sure about this Cole? Are you sure you're ready for me?"

"Jordan." Lips twitching, he cupped her chin. "Honey. I don't think I'll ever be ready for you."

Dedication

To fans of hot, sexy cowboy romances, may this be a series you enjoy, starting with the cantankerous Cole.

To my real life hero, my husband Michael, my family, the HOODS, my fellow author and friend JT Schultz for her unending support, and Jimmy Thomas for heating up my cover and putting the *hot* in Cole.

Prologue

…Something's not right.

Heading down the aisle at the corner store, unease bit into Jordan's spine like a swarm of bees. She quickly scanned the area.

Where's Eric?

There—over by the row of coolers. Heat from his gaze lessened her apprehension. *What did I do to deserve him for a husband?*

Looking at her through an opened cooler door, rapidly fogging from the California heat, he raised a can of whipped cream, a mischievous grin claiming his lips.

Rogue! No need to ask if he was ready for round two of their all-nighter.

Her sigh rustled miniature bags of chips on a nearby shelf. It'd been so long since their time off coincided.

Unable to contain a spark of devilment, she winked and raised two fingers. They'd need the extra one for what she had in mind.

Sexy grin broadening, he grabbed a second can, then glanced back at her, and his smile suddenly faded.

What's wrong?

Throat dry, swarm of bees re-attacking her back, she slowly looked down at her hands.

The loaf of bread and jar of peanut butter she had been holding turned to cold steel warmed under her grip as she aimed a loaded 38 Magnum at the man she loved...

Jordan Masters Ryan vaulted upright in her sheet tossed bed, waist-length hair violently jerking forward. She swiped the brown mass from her eyes and bounced her gaze from the cherry armoire to the oversized matching dresser. *Damn!* She drew in a shaky breath while reality returned. *That dream again.*

Wet and firm, an eager nose nudged her dangling wrist and brought a quiver to her lips.

"Oh, Bullet." She slid to the floor and hugged the big German Sheppard to her sweat-soaked body. "I thought they'd stopped."

A whimper tickled her ear. She drew back from his comforting warmth and raised her gaze to compassion-filled, chocolate-brown eyes.

"I know, boy. You miss him, too." She rubbed Bullet's thick, black head and sighed. "No sense in trying to go back to bed. There'll be no sleep coming after that nightmare."

Jordan rubbed her eyes and stood, deciding to get ready for her morning flight a few hours early. Maybe she'd have better luck with sleep in Texas.

Nate Masters stowed his cell phone and didn't stop the smile from spreading across his face. "They're on the plane," he informed, and a collective sigh echoed around the McCall's den. "That was their friend, Megan. She said she'd just dropped the girls at the airport and is sure they don't suspect a thing. Their plane is scheduled to arrive in Houston around one-fifteen; that should put them here around two-thirty."

"Great," his buddy, Alex McCall, exclaimed from across the room.

"I sure hope this works," Alex's wife, Leeann said, a frown marring her brow. "If I wasn't so worried about my sons, especially Cole, I would never have agreed to this scheme." She paced in front of the window overlooking the sprawling south Texas ranch.

Nate understood her tension. Didn't matter if your children were grown and had lives of their own, you always worried about them and wanted to see them happy. Heck, he wanted the best for his daughters, too. That's just how it was.

Alex got up to hug his wife, dwarfing the concerned woman by at least a foot.

"Now Leeann, don't you worry none about this. You're right, those boys need to do more than work themselves to death and I believe—no, I *know* Nate's daughters are perfect for them." He looked down at her and smiled. "Don't you remember how those two girls were never put off no matter what Cole and Connor said or did?"

"Yes."

A smile softened her face for the first time that morning.

"I always thought Cole and Jordan were the perfect match. I just hope it's not too late and she can bring him back to the land of the living. She's our last hope." Despair crept into Leeann's voice as she continued, "He's become so mean and unfeeling since Bess' death. It's been *two years*. It has to stop, Alex. It just has to stop."

Nate shared a look with his wife, Hannah. They'd gone through the same thing with their daughter but she'd snapped out of her reckless despair after a year. His heart twisted. This *scheme* had to work. He shared their hope that his oldest daughter would be the key to Cole's cure. Their children were just too young to be going through such heartache.

"Well, if anyone can get through to Cole, it's our Jordan," Hannah chimed in, echoing his thoughts as she stopped in front of Leeann and touched her arm. "Besides, being near Cole just might benefit Jordan too. She hasn't fully embraced life either since her loss. I'm praying this reunion helps them both."

Leeann nodded and pulled Hannah into a hug. "Let's hope so."

"All right, then." Alex filled four flutes with champagne, handed them out, and then raised his glass. "Here's to the McCall boys and the Masters girls."

Nate grinned. "Let the fireworks begin!"

Chapter One

Cole McCall shot to his feet and shoved a hand through his hair, careful not to loosen the band at his nape. With a thousand and one projects, programs and outlines on his plate, he didn't need a setback. He needed competence like that with which his team put forth. CEO of McCall Enterprises, software specialists, he employed over one hundred twenty-five people, all of whom did their job. He wasn't used to incompetence.

"I don't care if it is Saturday! That shipment was due in yesterday and it hasn't shown up yet," he snapped into the phone. "McCall Enterprises has never had any trouble with your company before, but I have my own deadlines to meet and I can't achieve them with this kind of ineptitude. If it means finding someone else who could get the job done, then so be it." He silently counted to ten. It didn't help. "You have until Monday at noon to deliver. If the equipment isn't here by then, I'll be on the phone with a new supplier at one minute past."

The slamming phone echoed in his otherwise quiet office. He sucked in a breath, trying to get a handle on his annoyance. That didn't help either.

Why was the world full of so much ineffectiveness?

Exhaling, he eyed the iPad on his desk, glaring the day's agenda. *Great.* On top of the mess with this supplier, he had three other projects in the works he himself headed. But could he give them the time they deserve this weekend? No. Why? Because he had to entertain—no, baby sit—the Masters sisters from California. *Christ.* That's the last thing he needed.

Muttering a curse, he strode to the window and gripped the metal sill. Anger prevented him from enjoying the breathtaking view of Houston's skyline. Today, he didn't witness the myriad of skyscrapers vying for the top position against the cloudless blue horizon or the beautiful spring morning. No, instead he stared blindly at the one-thousand-foot Texas Commerce Tower, his mind in turmoil over the promise he'd made to his mother and how it was already interfering with his deadlines.

He hadn't seen those girls in what, ten, almost eleven years now? Kerri had always been sweet but Jordan? Her favorite past-time had been to try to pull one over on him.

A genuine smile, foreign for so long, twitched his lips. Three years younger than him, a beauty with brown hair, brown eyes, a quick wit and one hell of a backbone, she'd always proven to be a challenge. One thing for sure, life had never been dull with her around.

But times have changed…I've changed.

Smile gone, he stiffened and pivoted from the window. That teenage boy who tolerated the carefree antics of a cute but annoying tomboy was long gone. Life had crushed his rose-colored glasses, forcing him to see the harshness of reality, and lay his childhood fancies to rest. His outlook on life dimmed, he no longer sought companionship or warmth from people. *People meant feeling, and feeling equaled pain.* Therefore, he took people right out of the equation. Life was unpredictable and cruel, and the only way to get through it was to work, and work hard. Predictable and constant, work was now his life.

When he wasn't at the office running his multi-million dollar corporation, he'd physically exhaust himself by helping out at the Wild Creek Ranch, his family's ranch. He didn't have time for frolicking little girls right now.

Feeling claustrophobic, he strode to his massive mahogany desk and saved the lines of gaming codes he'd been working on when his supplier had called. Concentration completely shot, Cole switched gears. *Time for open-spaces.*

He packed up his laptop and left his office. The hum of his secretary's computer tower was the only noise emanating from that floor. Since it was the weekend, only he and a few security guards graced the halls of McCall Enterprises. A routine he found both preferable and profitable.

When his father had retired three years ago, he'd handed Cole a very lucrative business. Since then, he'd added PC games to their list of marketable software. Between that addition and his almost constant work ethic, Cole took pride in the fact he'd increased the holdings and net worth of McCall Enterprises by almost a third.

He was young, successful...and miserable.

Cole stopped dead. Where the hell had that thought come from?

Shaking his head, he stepped into the elevator. *Must be from lack of caffeine.*

To clear the unwanted thoughts, he focused his attention on his *Masters* problem. By the time he reached the garage, he'd reasoned out a solution. Another smile cracked his lips. He'd promised his mother he'd be there when the girls arrived but that didn't mean he couldn't work around the ranch.

Something always needed mending or a chore needed attention. Connor, his older brother by one year, ran the Wild Creek Ranch. The two thousand plus acres were not only home to the McCall's but housed over a thousand head of cattle, five prize winning bulls and twenty horses ranging from Quarter to Stallions. And even though his brother employed full-time ranch hands, Connor always welcomed the help.

Feeling slightly better, Cole left the underground parking garage and began his daily sixty-minute southern commute over familiar roads to the ranch. Slipping his sunglasses on, he made a mental list of the things he wanted to accomplish and, visitors or not, he would get them done. Then at least the day wouldn't be a total waste. He'd make it to the ranch by noon and, with any luck, he'd be dirty and grimy by the time the girls arrived.

That should be enough to keep them out of my way.

Jordan shook her head at the familiar southern Texas scenery, her long French-braid grazing her shoulder blades as she turned off the highway, and onto McCall property. Speeding down the two mile-long dirt driveway bordered by bluebonnets and wild daisies, she shifted her glance from the road to the dashboard clock. Two-fifteen. They'd made good time.

"Feels like we're driving down the déjà vu trail."

Her sister Kerri McCall nodded from the passenger seat. "Yeah, it's hard to believe it's been ten years. I can honestly say I didn't expect to ever come back."

Jordan spared her sister a glance. "Come back? We're only here for two weeks to help the McCall's prepare for their 40th Wedding Anniversary Party." Staying? Her grip tightened around the steering wheel. *Hell, no.* They weren't staying. "You make it sound permanent."

"Oh, jeez no." Kerri shuddered before smoothing the violet linen skirt of her spaghetti strapped sundress. "I'm back on that plane to California the day after the party. I hate leaving my kitchen—well, our restaurant—in someone else's hands for that long. I mean, we've only been open a year and a half, what if—"

Jordan grabbed her sister's knotted fingers and gave a gentle squeeze. "Relax. It'll be fine. Mario is more than capable of handling the kitchen for that short period of time. You've trained him well. And I have faith that Leon will take care of all my managerial duties while I'm stuck here too."

Heck, the guy had practically been doing that since the place opened. Jordan was a fulltime L.A. police officer and wasn't always able to be at the restaurant. She worked around her shifts. The man had more than proved himself. She squeezed her sister's fingers one last time before returning her hand to the wheel.

"Believe me, if I could've gotten us out of this visit, I would have. Hell, I was all set to give Mom and Dad the *'our restaurant is too new, we can't leave it'* speech, but they'd already talked to Megan." Her lips twisted. Too bad, too. Jordan had rehearsed that line for three days. She was golden.

"You know, sis…I realize Megan has been your best friend since we moved to California as teenagers but, no offense, I hate her right now," Kerri grumbled, smoothing her unwrinkled skirt for a second time.

Jordan blew out a breath. "Yeah, me too."

Her sister's phone rang out the first few chords of Beethoven's Fifth. They locked gazes and, together, chimed, "*Dad.*"

Smiling, Kerri flipped open her cell.

"Hello, Dad. Yes. We're on the dirt drive. We'll be there shortly. Okay, bye."

"That's the second time he's called since we landed. Mom and Dad have only been here visiting a week, so it can't be because they miss us." Jordan chewed her lip. Intuition poked at her like her Captain's agitated finger. "What do you think he's up to?"

Kerri twirled a smooth strand of shoulder-length brown hair around her finger and turned to her with wide brown eyes. "Up to? W-why would you think he's up to something? You don't think it has to do with Cole and Connor, do you?"

Heart suddenly lodged in her throat, Jordan pulled to the side of the road and jammed the rented car in park. The last thing she needed was her parents playing matchmaker just because she'd once had a crush on the younger McCall. Okay, more like an obsession, but that was years ago. She'd long grown out of her Cole-worshipping ways.

"Oh my gosh. You *do* think this has to do with the boys..." Kerri gripped her skirt and twisted the thin material tightly. "Turn around, Jordan. We're going back to California."

"Whoa, wait a minute. Calm down." She placed a settling hand on her sister's bare shoulder. "We don't know what Dad's problem is…or if he has one. There might be another explanation." *There'd better be another explanation.* "Besides, the guys are probably married with two point five children…well, except Connor—I bet he's multiplied like a rabbit..."

Expecting Kerri's whimsical laugh to echo throughout the closed confines of the car, Jordan's ears met with silence. She glanced at her sister's dazed expression. *What is up with her?* She hadn't been right lately. The divorce had really messed her sister up. When Jordan opened her mouth to ask, Kerri shook her head and reached for her bottled water.

"No. The world's safe from mini McCalls for now. Mom said Cole wasn't dating and Connor was in between *engagements*."

Jordan's heart stopped. "Mom said? When did Mom say this?"

"Last month when we went shopping for the…trip." Kerri choked.

"Oh no. It never occurred to me," she sputtered between bought of coughing.

Jordan patted her sister's back. "Don't worry about it. I doubt that the guys would be interested. We've always been like pesky younger sisters to them anyway."

"You really think so?" Kerri wiped the tears from her face, then leaned back in the seat of their idling car and closed her eyes. "Good because I want to enjoy my career *man-free*."

"Amen, sister."

Jordan laughed. *Man-free* was definitely the best way for both of them to go this time in their lives, especially with their new profession still in its infancy.

Not long after her husband had died Jordan had needed a distraction and jumped at the offer her newly divorced sister had made of opening a restaurant together. *Comets*—the thriving new business they'd poured their hearts and souls into—took up every waking moment. There was no room in their schedules for a social life…or a need.

Any romantic ideas her parents had for them and the McCall brothers were a waste of time. They were barking up the wrong pair of females.

"I wonder if the guys are fat and bald." Kerri mused.

She snorted. "I doubt it."

"Yeah, you're probably right. And it really wouldn't be bad seeing them again if I weren't so darned embarrassed by the things we used to do." Kerri snapped a hopeful glance her way, brushing aside a sweep of dark bangs. "Maybe they won't remember."

"Are you kidding?" Jordan chuckled. "They'll probably throw it in our faces as soon as we step out of the car."

Her sister tossed her hands in the air and turned pink. "Oh, that's just great. I mean for goodness sakes, we once stole their clothes when they were skinny dipping!"

"Ahh. I forgot about that." Jordan slapped a hand to her chest and played with the scooped neck on her sleeveless, navy dress. Grinning, she recalled the whole event clear as day. "Boy, were they mad. I didn't see what the big deal was, though. We gave their clothes back."

Kerri's face headed for crimson. "Yeah, but not before they stalked out of the water buck naked after us!"

So true. Wearing only mischievous, twinkles in their dark eyes, the two teenage brothers had stalked boldly towards them. She still remembered in detail the way the water had glistened and glided off their tanned bodies and dripped from places not so tan. *What an introduction to the male anatomy!* Her adolescent body had tingled with an unknown excitement.

"Well," she cleared her suddenly dry throat to repair her present day body's reaction to the memory. "I would've given the clothes back, but *no*! They got out *knowing* we'd turn tail and run." Jordan's grin broadened. "I could still hear them laughing half a mile up the field."

"Yeah, we sure did get an eyeful."

Kerri keyed right into her thoughts and together their laughter reverberated throughout the stationary car.

Elbowing Jordan's arm her sister continued, "Remember that time Cole was in the barn making out with that well endowed cheerleader? It sure was mysterious how those horses got in there and chased her down the road."

Jordan raised her brows in mock innocence. "Wasn't it though? I never could figure out why the horses all decided to take a stroll through the barn all at the same time." Snickers trickled from their lips and she slapped Kerri's knee. "And you're one to talk. I seem to recall an episode with a very muddy dog and Connor's party date dressed in white."

With a sheepish grin, her sister reluctantly confessed. "I know. I couldn't help it. Ashley had been teasing me about my braces before Connor came downstairs." She raised her hands and shrugged. "The hose was there, the dog was there; I just reacted."

Laughter once again echoed throughout the car and lessoned their tension. Jordan fell back against her seat and sighed.

"Man. Those were the days. Embarrassment and all, I wouldn't trade our past with the McCall brothers for the world."

"You're right, Jordan. I don't know why I'm making a big deal out of it. That was the past. We were kids and we did kid things." Kerri clasped her hands together on her lap, the color in her cheeks returning to its natural glow.

"Exactly. Why don't we fix our faces and get back on the road?"

"Sounds good to me."

They pulled out their makeup, repaired the damage all the laughter and tears had caused, then stowed the makeup in their purses.

"Well I don't know about you but I'm ready to get this reunion over with. You know," Jordan lifted her hands and turned to face her sister. "Until now, I hadn't given Cole a thought in over five years. I really have been doing just fine without him." Even though, that hadn't been the case in the past.

"Yes, and I don't need a man..." Kerri pushed her visor up with a snap. "If Mom and Dad have any matchmaking ideas, they can leave us out of it."

"Amen, sister," Jordan repeated. "Okay. We can do this. We're only here for two weeks to cater and put this event together. After the McCall's Anniversary party we can go back to our lives at home." Jordan stuck the car in drive and sped off in a better frame of mind.

She spotted Kerri's sideways glance, and could guess what was coming.

"Jordan, what are you going to do if you and Cole still have an attraction to each other?"

And there it is.

"Nothing," she answered honestly. "We had our chance in the past. I'm not interested in him now." Her hand shot up to stop Kerri's protest. "Loving, then losing Eric has taken its toll on me. I know Cole and I used to have a kind of connection. We always did and probably always will. But times have changed. *I've changed.* The last thing I'm looking for is to reconnect with Cole McCall."

For most of her life, he'd been a constant shadow hanging over her shoulder, immobilizing her love life with his laughing brown eyes and mischievous grin.

Until, after a secret visit a few years ago, Jordan had managed to put him safely away.

She shifted in her seat. It was nice to be out from under his spell and she was desperate to stay that way.

I will not allow myself to become obsessed with him again. No way. Quieting her mind, she buried wayward emotions and hardened her heart.

"Fate—or our parents—might have other ideas," Kerri pointed out.

Ignoring her sisters' last remark as the ranch came into view, Jordan gazed at the place that long ago used to be their second home. They'd spent equal time between here and their own house, which, back then, had only been ten miles away.

Big and beautiful, the McCall homestead still looked the same. With a backward u-shape, the Spanish two-story had a long porch out front and balconies all around the two jutting wings. Off to the side sat the stables, a garage, ranch-hand quarters and the infamous barn.

She stopped in front of the house, shut off the engine and squared her shoulders. This was only a visit. *I have a new life in California.*

Texas was no longer in her blood.

Then why did it feel like she belonged here; like she'd just driven up to her fire-in-the-fireplace, hot-chocolate-simmering, warm-blanket-waiting...*home*? Why did her soul rejoice at the site of the front patio where she used to chase Cole; at the driveway where he'd taught her to drive before she was old enough for a permit; at the corral where she'd learned to ride; at the property where she had her first kiss?

Because I'm a sentimental fool.

The front door banging open pulled her thoughts and her gaze to her parents rushing out, followed closely by Mr. and Mrs. McCall.

Withdrawing her phone from her purse, she winked at her sister and punched a number. "Hello, Dad?" she said into the phone while leaving the car. "Just wanted to let you know we're here." Smiling, she walked toward him.

"Good to know. Thanks for the call." He grinned, snapped his phone shut and pulled her into a hug. "You're crazy."

"Yeah, I know, but you love me anyway."

"You're darn right I do." He kissed her cheek, then reached for Kerri.

"Hi, Mom," Jordan said. "Did you miss me?"

"You know it."

Hannah Mitchell was a very beautiful woman. Hair shorter and lighter now that she was in her late fifties, she was still very becoming. In fact, her parents made a striking couple, and she realized with a start, they too would be celebrating their 40th anniversary later this fall.

Her mother squeezed her again before she stepped aside to allow her to greet the other couple.

"Mr. and Mrs. McCall." Jordan smiled. "Two more tolerant people I've never known—my parents excluded, of course."

Enveloped into alternating hugs, Jordan returned the favor. As she tried to pull away from Mrs. McCall, however, the woman held tight for a fraction of a second longer.

What in the world was that all about?

"It sure is good to see you again girls. This old place hasn't been the same without you." Mr. McCall chuckled.

"And look at the two of you. You're just beautiful," his wife gushed. "I'm glad you both came. It sure will be nice to have some laughter back in this house again."

Jordon frowned. Why would they stop laughing?

About to ask, she opened her mouth but the sudden appearance of a familiar awareness zapped the words from her lips.

Fastened to her body like a too-tight jumpsuit, a tingling sensation started at the base of her neck and rushed like a current to every extremity. She rubbed her arms, ordered her racing pulse to settle and air to return to her lungs. This strong, engulfing feeling hadn't existed since...*Cole McCall.*

He was there behind her, she knew without looking.

With her sister's indrawn breath cooling the air at her side, Jordan figured she was turning around to face trouble. A gasp bubbled up her throat. Okay, double trouble.

Holy Texans...

With the gasp still clogged in her throat, she inspected the pair of virile men approaching from the stable. Their strides sure, their forms vaguely familiar; their attributes—*wow*.

Even if she hadn't known them, these men would've caught her attention. They had a commanding presence with two distinctly different airs. One, a few inches taller, had a set of broad shoulders that appeared laid back and welcoming, while the other loomed stiff and unyielding.

Damn. She swallowed. This visit would be so much easier if the Brothers McCall had gotten dumpy instead of...wow.

Gaze automatically drawn to Cole, she avoided his face to admire his wide-expanse of chest, biceps and forearms. Who knew building software codes could produce muscles like that? Her throat dried. *Lordy*, his shirt clung to him like a second skin. Stretched possessively over his physique, the material of his grubby white t-shirt rippled as he walked.

Butterflies stirred in her stomach. .

Damn. Leave it to Cole to spark life into her body. *Unwelcomed* life. She didn't want to feel.

The further south she investigated the harder breathing became. Snug jeans hugged lean hips and an awareness of his masculinity stabbed at her core. Slowly warming like a spring thaw, her insides prickled in an explosion of sensations, awakening needs dormant too long.

She pulled in a breath and snapped her gaze to his brother.

Connor...yes, he was much safer.

Though equally handsome, his muscles and good looks didn't have the same mind-boggling effect. Breathing easier, her body relaxed as she focused on the other man.

Taller but not as broad, Connor's jeans and t-shirt showed off his solid, muscular build. *I bet his black book is still thicker than the phone book.* Jordan glanced sideways at Kerri.

Flushed, mouth opened, her sister blinked but made no sound. Apparently, Connor's body had an entirely different affect on her sibling. Feeling sorry for her, she decided to give Kerri a chance to recover.

Unlike her sister, Jordan wasn't the type to shy away from an uncomfortable circumstance. She straightened her shoulders and prepared to meet the situation head on. Planting her hands on her hips, she closed the distance and stopped in front of the taller—*safer*—McCall.

"Wow. It's the *Marlboro* Man." Brown hair with sun-kissed highlights, deep tan and laughing brown eyes, he hadn't changed, just got better. More lethal. She smiled and stepped into his opened arms. He was all cowboy, and she had no trouble envisioning him on that famous billboard. "You sure are a handsome devil. It's so good to see you again,

Connor."

Drawing back from their hug, he bounced his gaze between her and Kerri. A broad grin dimpled his cheeks and lit his brown eyes. "It's the two of you who look great. This time, I think my little brother and I will be the ones doing the chasing."

Cole stiffened as he stood off to the side, making no attempt to join the reunion.

The tall cowboy chuckled and, soon enough, Connor ambled toward Kerri, leaving Jordan to face the person who had introduced her to desire, angst, and her first hint of what kind of pain a heart could endure.

The one man capable of threatening the little of it that was left

Chapter Two

Jordan could handle smiling brown eyes, incessant teasing…the usual. Life in California had proven she could survive without the likes of Cole McCall. He was just a silly childhood crush. One she hadn't thought of in years.

Feeling confident, she transferred her gaze to Cole.

Her heart flopped…all the way to her toes.

Who is this stranger?

His face, although still handsome with a strong chin and high cheekbones, was cold and bitter, marred by lines from a constant frown. She searched his eyes and inwardly winced. They were the worst part. Reflecting his name, his gaze was hard and lifeless. Even his dark hair, once noted canvas to trendy styles, was now longer, the unruly lengths pulled back into a ponytail as if he didn't care.

Shaken to find her friend in such bad shape, she swallowed and took a moment to gather her wits. The person, whose exuberance drew you in and made you feel elated, had vanished. The smart cowboy with a can-do attitude was gone. Standing before her was a hardened man who'd lost his love for life.

She may not recognize the man, but she sure as hell recognized the expression. The same look used to stare back at her in the mirror every single day.

He was a living dead guy.

She didn't know how his wife had died, but one thing was very clear—Cole McCall had shattered.

Was he with his wife when she'd died?

One thing was certain. He blamed himself.

Throat hot, Jordan knew firsthand the weight Cole bared. Black musings like those could strangle a person from the inside out. Her gut twisted at the thought of him suffering the same damnation. This shell of a man was so unlike the Cole she had known and loved that her heart cracked open and bled. God, how she hated to see him like this.

So much for keeping my feelings at bay.

She choked on them. The urge to cradle him in her arms and take away his pain overwhelmed and cancelled any thoughts of keeping her distance.

Clearing her throat, she stepped over to him, and assessed the situation. Body rigid, face unsmiling, he wanted no emotional contact; no physical contact either. He chose to remain detached from the world and those who loved him.

Bad choice. Nothing but pain, loneliness, and self-loathing thrived in that hole. She'd barely made it out. No way could she allow Cole to wallow in that pit.

A deep need to make him react—to show a spark of life, gripped her soul and spurred her into action. Tears held in check, she didn't wait for his arms to open as his brother's had, instead, she slid her hands over his ribs, around his back and pressed into him tightly.

At first she didn't think he'd reciprocate but finally, she felt a very light pat on her back. Her limbs warmed. The sweet smell of hay mingled with his musky essence, and triggered a primal need deep within. She tamped down her newly-awakened libido and stepped back. That's not what she was trying to achieve.

White teeth gleamed from his smile, but his dark brown eyes remained emotionless. Without thought, she cupped his face and kissed his dirt-stained cheek—one lost soul to another.

Lips tingling, she cleared her throat and lifted her chin. "Hey, McCall."

Shock changed to surprise, then eventually settled into irritation. He stepped back and his cold mask slipped into place. "Hello, Jordan. I see you haven't changed much." Tone dismissive, he turned toward her sister. "It's good to see you again, Kerri."

"You too, Cole."

Jordan noticed he hadn't said that to her, but wasn't surprised considering his condition. And if she had him pegged right, he'd leave now—that's what she would've done.

His glance swept over the rest of the gathering. "If you'll excuse me, I have work to do."

And there he goes.

He pivoted on his booted heel and strode back toward the stable.

Her heart squeezed. He needed help and a possible intervention. Having walked that same dark and dangerous path, she recognized the signs and the deep urgency of the situation. Jordan eyed his frowning family. Would they be strong enough?

She prayed they would and turned back to study Cole. He needed to wake up and see what he was doing to himself and his family. And she knew just how to kick-start the process—get in his face, just like old times.

With her shoulders thrown back, she raised her voice loud enough for his retreating form to hear. "My...my...my. Do you think that was an invitation for me to follow?"

He stiffened and stopped dead.

"Ooh, maybe it was," she added.

That got his goat.

Jerking back around, he shook with cold fury. Mouth twisted into a scowl, fists clenching and unclenching. He was one unhappy Texan.

Not good. The man was wrapped tighter than an unstable bomb. Heaven help anyone in his path when he finally *went off*.

Three strides put him in her face.

She stood her ground, unaware of their audience.

"In case you haven't noticed, Jordan, *we* are no longer children. I didn't appreciate the attention back then, and I certainly don't want it now." He poked her shoulder, hard. "I mean it. Leave me alone. Whatever you're playing at…stop. I'm not interested in those games again. Ever." Teeth clenched, he turned and stomped away for the second time.

Did he honestly think she'd let him get away with that?

No way in hell.

Jordan lunged in front of him and cut off his escape. "I know what you're doing." She shook her head and sighed. "Cole, Cole, Cole. Have you forgotten just how stubborn I can be? Honey, that's exactly the wrong thing to do."

"Get out of my way." Tone deadly, he pushed past.

If she had to resort to old tactics to get him to feel again, then so be it. She moved with him. "When I'm done. And I'm not done." Her finger poked the taut, meaty, muscle of his chest as she walked backward. "First of all, we *are* no longer children so why are *you* acting like one? Second, don't you lie to me, Cole McCall. I know exactly how you felt about me back then. And finally," she paused to bat her eyes and lower her voice, "Me thinks you doth protest too much. It gives you away."

A quick tap to his cheek, wink for affect, and she stepped around him. *Let him chew on tha—*

Her gaze met a crowd of wide-eyed Masters and McCalls. She'd forgotten they were there. Hiding her surprise behind a quick grin, she walked into a pregnant silence. *Maybe I pushed too much too soon?*

Laughter exploded from Connor first, startling the horses grazing in a nearby pasture. Their protesting neighs and whinnies garnered chuckles from the rest of the group. Everyone slapped her back as they made their way to the house. Jordan snuck a quick peek behind her. An opened-mouthed Cole stood where she'd left him, staring at her with a mixture of disbelief and undisguised fury.

Her heart sighed. She needed to form a game plan for taking on that man.

Impaling bales with a pitchfork, Cole grumbled and thrust the hay in the horses' stalls. Jesus, he was in for it. This visit was going to be the death of him.

"Never in all my life has there ever been someone so damned annoying as that girl." The chestnut mare's ears twitched, full of his heated words.

A lot like some of the computer viruses he'd encountered, that girl had always overcome every obstacle in her way in order to achieve her goal. Obviously, nothing had changed.

His raised pitchfork stopped, along with his heart.

What if she got it into her head that he needed fixing? *Ah hell.* There'd be no escaping the Jordan Virus then.

Tightening his grip on the pitchfork, he jabbed the hay and finished the last stall. *You're wasting your time on me, Malibu Masters,* he silently insisted. *Save it for some surfer dude. I don't need you.*

With the task completed, he set about replenishing fresh water.

"Why couldn't she have grown into a quiet, demure woman? Someone who only spoke when spoken to."

He stopped short and snorted.

"Yeah, right. What am I saying, that'd be like telling Connor to give up ranching." Water splashed out of the bucket, soaking into his jeans on its way to the ground. "Son-of-a…See, this is what she does!" He backtracked, refilled the bucket and finished the job without losing another drop.

"You can mumble to yourself as much as you want, little brother, but that won't make her go away." Connor chuckled as he lumbered into the stable.

Cole gripped the bucket and let out an oath. "How long have you been standing there?"

"Long enough to hear the ranting and raving of a mad man." A broad smile spread across his brother's face.

Not wise.

"Yeah, well I seem to recall you weren't exactly thrilled at the prospect of Kerri visiting us either." His own smile widened as the grin departed from Connor's face.

"You're crazy. I said no such thing."

"You didn't have to. I know you too well," he continued smugly, going in for the kill. "One look at your face when she gave you a hug and anyone could see you weren't as indifferent to her as you'd like us to believe."

Connor's lips thinned but he didn't respond.

Cole raised a brow. *No come-back barb?* Had his brother gotten wise to his merciless moods? *Better to keep the focus on him and off me.*

"What's wrong, Connor?" Cole's humorless laugh echoed in the stable. "Does the truth hurt?"

Leeann rushed in to join their secret pow-wow in the den, a hope-filled smile lighting her face. "It's safe to talk. Kerri and Jordan are upstairs freshening up."

"Perfect," Nate replied, very happy with that first meeting.

"That was more than I could've hoped for. Did you see Cole? He was speechless," Leeann continued. "For once in the past two years, he actually didn't know what to say!"

Nate turned to his wife sitting next to him on the couch and winked. This scheme was going to work.

"I know he didn't, and he actually showed a spark of life." Alex laughed, hugging his wife as they stood on the other side of the room. "I always said that boy met his match in Jordan. She won't let him get away with anything…not even now."

"Especially now," Nate declared. "She's been in his shoes, knows the moods, the thoughts…he's in big trouble if he thinks he can bully her. She'll be a force of nature."

Alex nodded. "Good. That's just what that boy needs."

"Let's hope he realizes just how important she is and fast. He only has two weeks," Leeann pointed out.

"It's just a matter of time now," Nate said, lacing fingers with his wife.

"I hope you're right, dear." Hannah patted his hand and the four of them nodded in agreement.

Upstairs in the solitude of her room, Jordan slumped on the bed. Emotionally exhausted, she slowly scanned her lovely surroundings. This was the same room she'd often used as a child but it had since been updated and redecorated, no longer exhibiting the childish flare.

During Jordan's youth, her mother had often accompanied her father on his annual business trip to keep up with the current computer trends overseas. Unwilling to disrupt their daughters' schooling, her parents had left Jordan and Kerri in the care of the McCalls.

With no girls of their own, their neighbors had spared no expense in turning two of their many rooms into a girl's paradise. Doted on, Jordan and Kerri had frilly canopy beds, a play house-castle, desk and easel, and their own bathrooms all done in their favorite colors; Jordan's in blue and Kerri's in purple.

Her gaze swept the new decor. Except for the colors, all of that had changed and in its place stood a beautiful, sophisticated area. A queen size four-poster bed with matching cherry furniture hallmarked the room.

Luxuriant bedding of palm leaves mixed with a palate of golds and olives offset by a rich navy background, adorned the bed. Shimmering olive and gold material draped over the corners creating a tropical romantic air. It spoke to Jordan's free spirit and she felt welcomed.

A fireplace with a lounging couch and seating area of deep navy and gold, replaced the play house-castle. No doubt wonderful on a cold winter's night.

She slid off the bed to explore her private bathroom. An oversized stand up shower, sunken whirlpool tub with Italian marble beautifully encasing the countertop, sink and floor, met her gaze. Promising herself she'd take advantage of a nice long bubble bath later, she turned and headed for the one thing that had remained the same; the long, large balcony, accessible from each room on that side through individual French doors.

Stepping outside, she drew in a breath. Heat, dirt, and oh yeah, horses and flowers all mixed to scent the air. Various pieces of patio furniture and freestanding hammocks filled the space. It was homey and inviting and she already felt more relaxed. A set of steps stood at the far end that led to the grounds below. She exhaled through a smile, remembering how she used to sprint down them when Cole tried to sneak off without her.

Out of habit, her feet took her to the railing where she glanced toward the stables. Another childhood routine. Every morning she'd race to this spot, watching Cole do his daily chores, until she was old enough to pitch in. He'd been kind and patient, taking the time to teach her how to feed the animals, brush down a horse and even the proper way to clean out a stall. One time, when he'd tried to replenish the hay she'd missed in a stable, she'd read him the riot act, wanting to prove she could do whatever he did.

She suspected he'd waited until she left, then added hay to her stalls to make up where it lacked.

Her throat swelled. God, she missed that friend. Sure they fought and teased but they challenged each other, making them reach into themselves to do better. Truth be told, they'd shared a bond no one could explain or fill. Standing here again, Jordan longed to have that comradery back…to have her friend back.

She hadn't expected trouble on this visit, just planned to help out, celebrate the anniversary, then return to her west coast life. But she couldn't, in good conscience, turn her back on her friend. Not when a ghost of a man stood in his place. That would never do.

As if fate could feel her loss, at that very moment Cole strode out of the stable and headed for the balcony. Halfway there, he stopped and looked up.

Her heart leapt into her throat. Honest-to-God leapt. An act it hadn't done in a very long time.

They stared at each other for a several beats. Too far away to read his expression, she sensed his inner battle and longed to reach out to him. She held her breath and prayed he'd come to her to open up and talk like they used to.

But with a rigid spine, he pivoted instead, and strode toward the front and out of view. She exhaled her pent up breath, the warmth hitting her bare arms.

"Damn stubborn man. I'm going to help you whether you want it or not," she muttered, saying it out loud to make it real. "I have two weeks to help you come to terms with your past and get on with life, Cole McCall. And by God, I'll do it. I *will* do it."

Resolve set, she went inside to grab her cell and make a few calls. After informing Megan they'd arrive safely and hung up knowing her dog was doing fine, she called the restaurant and spoke to both Leon and Mario, happy to hear they were indeed doing well. She ended the conversation a few minutes later, promising to continue with daily check-ins.

Calls made and suitcase unpacked, she left her room in search of her mother and their host. They had a lot of plans to make and only a short time to carry them out, but first, visiting was in order. As she descended the polished oak staircase, smells, sparking happy memories, greeted her nose. A myriad of taste buds happy danced in anticipation. That heavenly aroma couldn't be mistaken.

Emma's Texas-sized chocolate chip cookies.

Oh hell yeah.

Jordan hurried across the foyer into the kitchen. She was going in battle ready and taking no prisoners.

"I knew I smelled heaven." She salivated at the sight of the freshly baked morsels cooling on the counter. Turning to the other occupant of the kitchen, she smiled. "Emma, it's so good to see you again." Rushing into the older woman's open arms, she received a bear hug she knew only too well. "I've missed you."

The rotund woman's pretty blue eyes misted over as she smiled. "You only missed my cookies."

"That's not true. Well, at least not completely." With a wink, she procured one from the counter and promptly took a bite. Moaning as the chocolate melted in her mouth, she noticed Emma's face light up at her obvious enjoyment.

"Oh it sure is good to see you again, Jordan." As the cook's thoughts changed, so did her smile, casting a shadow over her features. "Maybe now there's hope for Cole." Sighing, Emma wiped her hands in her red and white checkered apron but remained silent.

About to ask her to elaborate, Jordan closed her mouth and curbed her curiosity when her mother and sister waltzed in.

"I thought I might find you in here." Her mother grinned. "You never could resist Emma's cookies."

"Me either," Kerri exclaimed and received an identical bear hug to the one Jordan had gotten a few minutes earlier.

"Kerri! My little Kerri," Emma cried, holding Kerri to her chest before she stepped back to eye her young protégé. She split her glance between them. "You are both just beautiful." She handed Kerri a cookie. "Here. You'd better take this before your sister eats them all."

"Don't laugh. I'd be more than happy to rid you of these delectable morsels," Jordan admitted, biting into her third one.

There they stood, chocolate smeared on their fingers and faces, laughing just like old times when, just like old times, Cole and Connor entered the kitchen.

Smiling brown eyes rolled, while a pair of cold, dark ones scowled. Cole ignored them and dropped his water bottle into the sink. Connor, however, faced them with a lop-sided grin and glaring dimple.

"I guess it'd be foolish to ask if you left me a cookie."

Jordan blinked. "Oh? Was I supposed to save you one, Connor?"

"No." he chuckled. "I remember only too well that when the Masters sisters are around, Emma's chocolate chip cookies are on the endangered list."

"So is peace and quiet," Cole muttered as he passed her on his way to the door.

Knowing the low spoken barb had been meant for her, Jordan tried not to let it hurt and concentrated on the other brother still in the room.

His glance strayed to her sister. Indifference replaced a flash of admiration so fast she almost missed the evidence of his inner battle.

But she hadn't.

"I'll see you all at dinner," Connor muttered quickly before leaving the room.

These McCall brothers are a mess.

Jordan was beginning to think she arrived just in time. They needed her help. Big time.

But would two weeks be enough?

Chapter Three

Visible through a large dining room picture window, a brilliant orange sunset streaked the darkening sky and left him…cold. A few years ago, Cole wouldn't have hesitated to stand there until all light faded—completely in awe, and warmed by nature's beauty. Not now. The scenery didn't produce so much as a flicker of heat. Time was better spent writing code that brought life to a computer screen and profits to the bank.

He didn't need beauty or people or this dinner with the Masters. Exertion was what he needed. He'd much rather spend time with the mountain of work piled in his home office. Although he had no problem with being rude, he wouldn't embarrass his mother by leaving.

Reluctantly, he took his seat around the long oak table set with blue and purple linens, a decoration no doubt for the girls. He snapped out his napkin and shoved it on his lap while the McCalls and Masters talked over old times and caught up on times missed. Everyone contributed to the conversation, except him. His body ached, and the heaviness in his head increased. The day had been long and tiring. He had absolutely no desire to speak.

Too exhausted to even taste Emma's specially prepared roast duck, he stabbed the poultry with his fork and ate anyway. The sooner he finished, the sooner he could leave. Once dinner was through, he'd say a polite goodnight, then retreat as he did every night to his home office down the hall.

At his family's suggestion, he'd sold the house he and Bess had lived in and moved back to the ranch. Not that it had taken much persuasion. He couldn't stand coming home to an empty house every night. All he required then and now was a place to sleep—when he did sleep—and a place to work when he was away from the office.

Sitting across from him in her old seat, Jordan reached for her wine and regarded him as if he were a wounded stray.

He stiffened.

Christ.

He was in trouble. She had that *I'm-going-to-help-you* look. He didn't want her help, didn't need her help…didn't *fuckin' ask* for her help. The pest was in way over her head and couldn't possibly help him. *No one can.*

Teeth clenched, he dropped his gazed to his plate before she could read his thoughts.

When they were young, she was the only one who could tell if he was lying. He'd rarely been able to pull one over on her…a trait he used to admire. She had been a challenge he couldn't resist.

His lips twisted. But not now. The last thing he wanted was Jordan Masters' fuckin' discerning ability to see into his soul.

Earlier, when she'd been on the balcony and their eyes had met, it'd felt like they'd communicated without talking. Warmth and comfort had beckoned, along with a sudden, deep urge to go to her and open up like he used to. Thankfully, common sense had returned in time and he'd strode off in the opposite direction.

No amount of talking would make him happy.

He didn't *deserve* happy.

"So, Jordan."

His father's voice cut through his dire thoughts and he lifted his gaze.

"Your parents tell me you've become quite the business woman, splitting your time between that and the police force."

Jordan was still on the force?

Swallowing his surprise with a mouthful of duck, he wondered how she'd managed. Sympathy squeezed his hard-edged heart. *She must've gone through hell.* Despite himself, his eyes sought her face.

A whooshing sped through his ears.

Her animated expression and the way her lips moved as she responded to the statement, stole his breath. Long, thick, silky dark hair fell to her waist, warm, brown almond-shaped eyes gleamed with life. *God, he could get lost in those eyes*. Not wanting to feel anything for anyone, especially Jordan, Cole tore his gaze away, then stamped out the sympathy and everything else she sparked.

Damn nuisance woman.

She was the only female he knew who could talk about work and make it sound sexy. *Hell!* She could read the ingredients off a bottle of PMS medication and every man in the store would stand in line to buy one. Grabbing his glass, he gulped down half the wine.

Big damn nuisance.

"I hear the restaurant you and your sister opened has established quite a clientele."

His brows wanted to rise. He fought the urge and won, cocking his chin instead. The idea of those two girls in the restaurant business together, made sense to him. When Kerri was a kid, she could always be found shadowing Emma. And Jordan's knack for taking charge and bossing people around was perfect managerial material.

"What's the name of it?" Connor asked between bites.

"Comets," Kerri replied.

His brother chuckled. "What a perfect name for a restaurant owned by you two. Like a comet, you're both beautiful but stubborn and once you're on course, you're unstoppable."

Cole smirked and broke his silence. "Truer words…"

The room stilled for an instant before shouts of laughter filled the air.

"Well," Jordan turned her teasing gaze on him. "I did have a good role model."

He ignored the dig and leaned back in his chair. She could try all she wanted, but he wasn't biting. He wasn't in the mood.

As if sensing the tension, his father set an elbow on the table and shifted closer.

"Jordan, do you do any cooking at the restaurant?"

Thankfully, her upbringing saved him when good manners forced her to transfer her gaze to his father.

"Oh my, no. Kerri is the one with that particular talent. As a matter of fact" —she pointed toward their kitchen— "she got her start right here in your house. Emma sparked that desire in her."

His mother smiled at Kerri, a dinner roll poised in her hand. "I remember many an afternoon I'd see you in there helping Emma out with supper."

"Yes." Light glimmered off Kerri's sleek dark hair as she nodded. "I learned a great many things from her they never taught in school."

Helping himself to more roast duck, his father continued to grill the older sister. "Well then Jordan, I take it you handle the managerial side of the business.

"Yes. I do the books, payroll, order supplies, bartend, hostess and generally fill in where needed, whenever possible around my police shifts, of course. My minor in business has definitely proved to be the right choice."

Like a gust of wind, her gaze fastened on him and air escaped his lungs.

"I hear you've become quite the tycoon, Cole. Maybe you could give me a few pointers?"

Unhappily drawn into the conversation, he answered through tight lips. "I highly doubt you would listen to anything I said, Jordan, so why bother?" He shoved a forkful of garlic potatoes in his mouth, hoping she'd take the hint and drop the conversation.

He should have known better.

"Why, Cole," Jordan began softly, placing her elbows on the table and chin in her hands. "Surely you remember how it used to be my sole practice to listen to you with bated breath?"

The batting of her dark eyes caused an unwelcome tightening in his groin.

Completely irritated by her behavior and, moreover, his body's reaction, Cole dropped his fork and leaned forward. "Quit the games, Jordan. I don't know what you're playing at, but I am *not* interested." He sat back and waited for her anger.

It never came.

Genuine amusement lit her face and his fingers balled into fists. *Christ.* What the hell was wrong with her? The woman was not stupid. She knew he was pissed, but still she kept at him.

"Jeez, lighten up, Cole. I was only joking with you." She had the audacity to laugh. "You do remember how to joke, don't you? Besides, you don't seriously think I'm still interested in you *that* way, do you?" An eat-your-heart-out smile graced her lips. "You should be so lucky."

"Okay, you two," her father said with a smirk "You might as well stop now because neither one of you will get ahead of the other."

Grateful for the intervention, Cole inhaled, then slowly exhaled. He wasn't sure he could keep his cool much longer.

"You're right, dad. But for the record," she paused and pointed a finger. "Cole started it!"

Connor's bark of laughter momentarily drowned out female giggles and their fathers' shared chuckle.

He didn't find Jordan's childishness amusing. How much more nonsense did he have to endure? He was trying his best to stick it out until dessert, but it seemed to be a losing battle.

"Jordan, do you still like to sing?" his mother asked.

Jordan touched the napkin to her lips. "Yes, I do on occasion. We have a piano at the restaurant and on the weekends we showcase local talent. Sometimes I get to sing backup, or play the piano or guitar. Even Kerri joins in once and a while. It's a lot of fun."

"Yeah." Kerri nodded. "All those lessons as a child actually paid off."

Jordan's warm gaze returned to him. "And all of those duets and private lessons Cole gave me were good practice, too."

Private lessons? He reluctantly recalled their combined music instruction.

At Jordan's urging, he'd even taken it upon himself to teach her how to play the guitar. She had a great voice to go with it too, although, back then he'd never admit it, choosing to tease her instead. Of course, she'd tease back.

His lips twitched. One thing was for sure, Jordan Masters always gave as good as she got. Heat invaded his groin as he wondered if that included other venues.

Annoyed with himself, he shifted in his seat. *Jesus*. He did *not* want to be attracted to her. Or anyone. He wasn't worthy. He dropped his gaze and concentrated on the rest of his meal.

"I always thought the two of you sounded great together."

Connor had a death wish.

"I can remember countless barbeques and parties where you two would sing, even if you weren't asked to." His brother's grin spread into a broad smile as a brilliant thought apparently invaded his mind.

Cole cringed.

"Maybe you could do a duet for mom and dad at their party? You know, for old time sake?"

Ah, fuck!

Their dad sat up straight. "What a wonderful idea, Connor. What do you say, you two?" Eyes wide, his father's gaze bounced between him and Jordan.

"Oh Cole, I'd love to hear you sing again. That would be the best present you could give us. Would you please?" his mother begged, eyes full of hope.

Guilt stabbed his heart with dozens of tiny daggers. He glared at his brother, cursing him for making that stupid suggestion and Jordan for bringing up their past.

Snapping his gaze to hers, he noted her furrowed brow and blinking eyes. *Good for her*. It was her fault they were in this situation. She should've kept her pretty mouth shut.

Pretty?

When the hell had he noticed she had a pretty mouth? Lowering his gaze to her lips, he swallowed and revised *pretty* to *perfect*. Her mouth wasn't too wide or too small, too thin or too full. She had the kind of mouth a man would love to kiss and feel caressing his body.

Once upon a time, long ago, he'd had a quick taste…

Her tongue darted out to wet her bottom lip. His groin stirred as did a distinct moment of déjà vu. Sucking in air, he recalled a similar reaction in their past.

A few weeks before she'd moved, they'd taken the horses to the beach as usual, but when they got there and dismounted, she'd grabbed his hat and ran. Forced to tackle after a few minutes of chasing, he'd turned her over and pinned her down in the warm sand. The strongest urge to rub his thumb over her lower lip and taste her sweetness had gripped him, hard. So he did. She'd tasted sweet and hot and innocent and adoring.

It'd knocked him on his ass.

If Connor, Kerri, and their friends hadn't arrived, to this day Cole wasn't sure what else he would've done. He'd thought he had things under control but one look at her wild eyes and invitingly sweet mouth and his control had disappeared. She had nearly been seventeen and he'd been nineteen, and his lust-induced mind had reasoned it was okay. He'd never felt anything so intense before or, if he was honest, since.

Until now.

Mustering strength, he tore his gaze from her mouth and glanced at his plate. *Unacceptable.* He hadn't had a sexual thought for another woman since he'd met Bess. Guilt flooded strong and swift. He sat back and clenched his fists.

What the fuck was wrong with him? He had no right to…

Lifting his gaze, he realized everyone waited for his reply. "I haven't played the guitar or done any singing in years. Besides…." He cocked his head and did his best to get out of the duet. "Haven't you hired a professional for that, Dad?"

"Yes, but I'm sure they wouldn't mind if you both sang a song or two."

His dad was no help. Only one chance left. Jordan. Great. He was forced to rely on an enemy to be an ally. Still, he had to try.

"You forget Jordan is here to help with the catering and set up of this party. She has more than enough work to do. Isn't that right?" He looked at her somewhat startled face. It was all he could come up with and hoped she'd take his lead and nip this stupid idea in the bud. Holding her unblinking gaze, he willed her to take the hint.

Several emotions chased themselves across those exotic-shaped, chocolate-colored eyes. Soon enough determination won out and settled on her pretty features. Relief relaxed Cole's fists. She'd get them out of this.

"Actually," she began. "I don't consider singing to be work."

Shit. His knuckles cracked. That was not at all what he'd expected her to say.

She turned to his mother and smiled. "I'd be honored to sing something for the two of you. Think about what you'd like, then let me know and I'll tell you if it's within my vocal range. It's been awhile but I'll do my best. However"—she turned back to face him—"I think your son is going to wimp out."

Besides determination, her warm gaze held a fair amount of sympathy. *Christ.* What was with her and that stupid emotion? It was a damn sight worse than her pestering attitude.

"Oh, Cole, please don't do that." His mother frowned. "It would really mean a lot to me."

Unable to stand the hurt swimming in his mother's eyes, he softened his resolve…just a little. "I'll think about it, Mom, but I'm not promising anything." He looked at Jordan, keeping his tone neutral, while putting as much fury and disgust as possible into his stare. "I'm sure Jordan would do just fine without me."

Either she didn't get the hint or deliberately ignored it. Probably the latter.

"You're right, Cole. I don't need you. But then again"—her face broke into a mischievous smile—"what fun would that be?"

A living hell.

Cole honestly believed she was there to make his life a living hell...and was enjoying it way too much. His lip curled at her satisfied expression. Time to wipe that grin off of her face.

He leaned across the table for a close-up view. "About as much fun as a funeral."

Swift and intense, pain darkened her gaze.

His pleasure faltered and before he could lean back in his chair, warm, slender fingers curled around his wrist.

"I think we've both had our fair share of that, Cole. It's time to move on."

He jerked his arm free and bolted back, ignoring his tingling skin and her last statement.

"So, Mrs. McCall," Kerri coughed, breaking the uncomfortable silence. "How many people are coming to your party?"

"About a hundred or so. We only invited family and friends." His mother looked at his father with affection. "I would've been happy with just the eight of us here, but Alex wanted to celebrate in grand style."

His father kissed her cheek. "I want to show off my still beautiful bride to all her old boyfriends."

"Alex." His mother blushed, playfully slapping his father. "Don't talk such nonsense. You just wanted the chance to party."

"Well, let's just say I wanted a little of both," his father conceded before planting another quick kiss.

A stabbing sense of loss gripped Cole's chest and tightened his throat as memories of sharing similar actions with his own wife flashed through his mind.

"One thing's for sure," Hannah Masters spoke for the first time that night. "Both of our families could use a happy occasion. I, for one, am looking forward to this party."

"And I'm honored to be helping Emma cook. Thank you for the opportunity," Kerri added, her face alight with pride.

Desperate for a distraction, Cole glanced at his brother.

No help there. Connor, staring at the younger Masters sister, wore the same gut-punched expression he himself had experienced earlier. Cole almost felt sorry for him. Almost. Connor had taken way too much pleasure in his discomfort all day.

Finishing his wine, Cole considered the attraction between Kerri and his brother. It was high time Connor stopped treating every woman he met as if she had the same bad qualities as his worthless ex-fiancés. If only his thickheaded brother would take notice, *he* at least might find happiness and produce an heir to carry on the family name.

Cole swallowed. It certainly wouldn't come from him. His chances had died with his wife.

Loss twisted his insides, again. Shifting in his seat, he only half heard the discussion. He blinked and refocused on the room. Thick slices of black forest cake sat in front of everyone.

Snippets of conversation returned to his ear.

When had Emma cleared the table?

"I think that would be a wonderful entrée, lets add it to the menu. Now if only Cole and Jordan would sing for us at the party, it would be a perfect night."

His mother smiled at him.

"Give him some time to think about it. I'm sure he'll do the right thing." Jordan scraped the cherries off of the top of her slice with her fork.

The familiar action took him back to when she was ten and, hands on her hips, she'd explained to him how this allowed her to enjoy the chocolate by itself.

Strange how that had stuck in his mind.

Cole forced a forkful in his mouth. Emma's black forest cake was the best in Harland County, she'd even won that distinction at the annual fair, and he usually devoured his serving. But not tonight. The day's and evening's events gave the confection a cardboard taste and lay like lead in the pit of his stomach.

Nauseous laughter reverberating around the room. He had to get out.

Dropping his fork, he pulled in a breath and leaned back in his chair. This was becoming the dinner from hell. He drew in another mouthful of air and made the mistake of looking up. Jordan stilled, while the others continued to talk, oblivious to his condition. Eyes full of sadness and sympathy, she gazed at him from across the table.

Torn between anger and grief, he willingly chose the former. Blood pressure shot to the ceiling and numbed his pain. Just who the hell did Jordan think she was to look at him with understanding? *No one understood. No one.*

Walls began to close in, sweat trickled down his temple. He swiped at it, then yanked his collar. Suffocation moments away, he had to get out of there, now. Jumping to his feet, he choked out a curt, "Good night," then strode from the room.

He hadn't let his family and friends pity him and wasn't about to let the pest from his past smother him with compassion now. No matter how much they had in common.

Jordan's heart twisted in her tight chest. She recognized the look of claustrophobia that had crossed Cole's features until he had to bolt from the room.

Part of her wanted to follow and comfort him, and another part argued he needed to be alone. Since it was increasingly apparent he'd been left alone for far too long, she decided to go with *follow*.

Forcing herself to give him a two minute reprieve, she finished her chocolate cake and chewed on the scraped off topping, wondering what subject would get Cole to talk? Forget weather, sports and world news. He'd slam the door in her face. Work. *Yes*. Computers…software. She slid the last of the sweet cherries in her mouth. Software was a bit out of her realm but she did know video games.

Her mood brightened.

"Well, dinner and dessert was delicious as usual. My compliments to Emma," she said. "But if you'll excuse me, I feel the need to go bother Cole. Any idea where he went?"

"That would be his office. I'd be happy to show you." Connor rose to his feet, then rounded the table and pulled out her chair. "Right this way, darlin'."

"Why, thank you, cowboy." Grasping his arm, she stood, then strode with him from the room. "I hadn't meant to make you leave the table, Connor. You could've just told me which door to head for. I know my way around pretty well. I'm sure I would've found it."

"Of that I have no doubt, Jordan." He chuckled. "But I was done eating anyway and needed to get to my own office to check on a feed delivery."

"Okay. Then I don't feel so bad. You're not the McCall I wanted to annoy."

He chuckled again, but didn't laugh as she had expected.

"I hope you know what you're doing, Jordan. My brother doesn't have the same sense of humor as before. In fact, the hay in the loft has more humor than Cole. He's fresh out."

"Don't you think it's high time we rectified that?" She patted his arm. "I've only been here a few hours and I'm already tired of *Attila No*

Fun."

He brought them to a halt and grinned. "Well, here's your chance. This is his office. Holler if you need me. I'll be just down the end of the hall."

"Will do. Thanks." She rose on tiptoes and kissed his handsome cheek. Damn, the man was tall. He had to be close to six-four. "Don't work too hard."

"Never." He winked, then disappeared into his office.

Time to push some buttons.

She turned back to Cole's door, squared her shoulders and knocked.

"What?"

She snickered and entered, shutting the door behind her. "You forgot, where, when, who, why, and how."

"Jordan." He threw his pen down on the desk and hit her with so much fury in his gaze, she nearly stumbled backward. "Is there a reason you're here bugging me when I'm trying to work?"

She crossed the room on shaky legs and dropped into the leather chair in front of his oak desk. "You want the long list or the short list?"

"I don't want any." He glared. "Get out."

"No can do, McCall. That's not on my list."

"*Jordan.*" He pushed back from the desk. "So help me, if you don't—"

"Wow. Did you know the vein in your neck bulges when you're angry? You should do something about that." She shook her head and clasped her hands in an attempt to hide her trembling fingers.

He closed his eyes and sucked in a long breath.

"That's better. Deep cleansing breaths."

His eyes snapped open. "You're still here?"

She laughed. "Yes. You can't will me away, Cole. You know that."

"Damn nuisance." He straightened in his seat, folded his hands on the desk and looked her in the eye. "What do I have to do to get you to leave?"

"Just talk."

"Good. We did, now go." He turned dismissively back to his computer monitor.

"No, I mean talk about you." She crossed her legs and straightened her blouse.

"Sorry, sweetheart. That's not what you said. Now, kindly get the hell out of my office so I can get back to work."

No way. With her heart hammering out of control, she leaned closer. "Are you working on a game?"

"No." He leaned closer, too. "It's a photo's program. Can I please get back to it now?"

"Soon, but first I wanted to tell you I was sorry about Bess."

Okay, that came out clumsy.

Still, she'd expect him to react with sadness, grief, pain, even anger, but the unbridled fury reddening his face was bad. Very bad.

"For the love of Texas! *Go!*" He shot to his feet, rounded the desk and glowered down at her.

Holy cow.

She rose and ordered her body to remain steady despite the murderous look in his eyes. Chest to chest, she stared up at him, refusing to show fear. "Look, Cole. I just want you to know I'm here if you need to talk."

Tight lips and flared nostrils relayed his rage while the rapid, single blink of his eyes gave away his unease.

If he was uncomfortable with her being so close, why didn't he step back? What was she saying? That would force him to show weakness and heaven forbid the mighty Cole McCall should act human.

"I don't want to talk," he ground out through clenched teeth.

"Well, you know where to find me if you do," she said, ignoring the warning voice in her head. "I can help with Bess—"

"I don't need help with Bess! I need help with my program. So get the hell out of here, Jordan! Now!" Fisted knuckles cracked at his sides.

Sorrow, painful and deep, funneled into her heart. *My God, he was a mess.* She had to convey some warmth to him.

Taking her life in her hands, she touched his arm. "I hate to see you like this, Cole. Just remember I have a good ear."

"Fine. Duly noted." Strong fingers clamped tightly around her wrist and pulled her to the door. "Now, kindly leave and take your good ear with you."

She snorted into a laugh. "You made a joke, Cole. Good for you."

"Yeah, hurray for me. Now, leave."

She sandwiched his hand between hers and squeezed. *Let me in*, she willed, staring into his cold gaze, hoping some of her compassion reached past the dark pit where he dwelled.

"Please, I can help you…" Her voice trailed off, leaving the ball in his court.

He volleyed. "I'm fine. Now leave me the hell alone." Yanking free, he glowered before throwing the door open. "Good night, Jordan."

What he'd really meant was *good riddance.*

She smiled. Too bad. The devil inside made her stand tall, lean in and place a noisy, wet kiss on his taut cheek. "Night, McCall."

Chapter Four

Daylight found Cole wide-awake. He'd slept fitfully. Again. When he eventually did fall asleep. Once that pesky Jordan removed herself from his office, he'd managed to calm down, burying himself in codes until the middle of the night.

Now, once again, the need to escape consumed him. It was still the weekend. He'd be expected to entertain and couldn't very well stay in his room all day. Although, that was exactly what he'd love to do. Drapes drawn, lights out, the perfect atmosphere for his mood. Visiting with the Masters, or anyone for that matter, was not a fun prospect.

There had to be some way out of it that wouldn't reflect badly on his parents.

He ran a list of chores through his mind and stopped at the thought of the fence in the unused pasture running along the southern border of the ranch. He tossed the covers aside and sprang out of bed. Connor had mentioned last week's spring storm had damaged that area. Today was a good day for Cole to tend to the mess.

Twenty minutes later, on his way out through the kitchen, he filled a thermos with coffee, grabbed the piping hot breakfast bagel Emma pushed at him, then headed for the barn.

Halfway there, he turned and looked up at the balcony. Maybe he was paranoid but he couldn't break the old habit. It was as if he was fifteen again, trying to sneak out without his twelve-year-old shadow catching him. He never seemed to succeed.

A smile tugged his mouth. No matter what he did, she always spotted him.

Balcony vacant of the twenty-seven-year-old updated version of his shadow, Cole congratulated himself for effectively avoiding the *Jordan-virus* and entered the stable.

"Just where do you think you're going, Cole McCall?"

The smell of hay and horses hung in the air as Jordan stood just inside the stable doors, waiting for Cole to answer. In the habit of getting up early to let her dog out, she was an early riser and happened to overhear Emma talking to Cole. On impulse, she slipped unnoticed out the front door to surprise him.

Judging by his slack-jawed expression, she'd succeeded.

"I said, where do you think you're going?"

He blinked. "Not that it's any of your business but I'm going to mend fences."

Gaze frosting, he brushed past her to his horse. She sighed. His mood hadn't improved since last night.

"Can't it wait till after Sunday Services?" She followed him into the stall, unwilling to give up. Her mouth dried at his effortless act of slinging the saddle onto his mount. Talk about instant dehydration. *That had to weigh…*

"No."

"Why not?"

"Jordan," he growled.

"Cole," she mimicked his tone and fastened her gaze to the play of muscles under his thin T-shirt as he secured the saddle and bridle. *Damn.* She swallowed. And to think she'd thought the teenage Cole had had the perfect body.

Wrong.

Without answering, he shoved several water bottles into the saddlebag, then swung onto the horse.

That wouldn't do.

She crossed her arms over her chest and nodded. "Mending fences is good. As a matter of fact, there are several I think you *need* to mend."

His face darkened. "Back off, Jordan."

"No."

He grumbled a curse. "Move away from the stall door or I'll plow right through you. I swear it."

Defiance stiffened her spine. She placed her hands on her hips and lifted a brow. "Who's gonna make me?"

"Oh, for goodness sakes, Jordan, grow up!" He glared down at her.

"And you need to lighten up, Cole."

Scowling, he spurred his horse forward and gave her no choice but to jump out of the way.

"Quit sticking your nose in my business," he ordered, ducking under the doorframe as he passed. "Go back to California and leave me the hell alone."

"Not on your life, McCall. You're my friend and I'm not giving up on you," she called after him.

Back stiff, he galloped out of sight.

He's worse off than I thought.

Releasing repressed tears, she leaned against the doorway. He couldn't even see the humor in her words. Instead of laughing he'd lashed out. She wiped her face. His actions only managed to firm her resolve. She wasn't going to *back off*. She was going to help him…and *dammit*, she was going to succeed.

Having donned a bikini underneath her jeans and T-shirt, Jordan crossed the driveway after Sunday Service and brunch, eager to get to the stable to start her picnic with Kerri. It had been so long. She could hardly wait.

About to ask her flushed sister if she was feeling alright, the reason for Kerri's rosy cheeks soon came into view. Sporting dimples, a tan Stetson and cowboy boots, the *Marlboro* man led two saddled horses their way.

"This is Cinnamon and this one's Ember," Connor informed, handing over the reins of a pair of chestnut mares. "There's no need to tie them while you have your picnic. They'll just graze nearby."

"Great. Thanks, Connor." She stroked Ember's neck. Coppers, browns and reds shimmered under her fingers. What a perfect name.

"Are you sure you girls will be okay? Do you remember your way around? Maybe I should go with you?" The cowboy frowned towards Kerri.

Jordan looked at her sister and raised her brows. Did Kerri want to spend time with Connor? Deciding to leave it up to her, Jordan remained quiet and busied herself with storing the day's necessities in her saddlebag.

"No!" Kerri cleared her pink throat. "I…I mean, no thank you, Connor. We'll be fine. Jordan and I remember everything."

We sure do. She fought a grin as the image of two naked, brazen McCalls streaked through her mind. Things were so much simpler back then. Everyone was carefree. Even her sister.

Jordan's gaze lifted to a crimson-faced Kerri. Come to think of it, her sister had always been a little sweet on the cowboy, although it had never been public knowledge like Jordan's youthful crush on Cole.

"Well, w-we don't remember *everything*. I mean we don't need anyone. Thanks anyway." Kerri's pleading gaze swiveled her way.

Time to intervene. "Yeah. We'll be fine, Connor. This place is embedded in our minds," Jordan reassured him. "You go ahead and do what you have to do."

"Okay. If you're sure. I'll go give Cole a hand."

"We're sure. Oh, and Connor"—Jordan paused as she swung up onto the mare—"tell Cole he can run but he can't hide."

Smiling, she trotted the horse out of the stable next to Kerri on Cinnamon.

"I'll be sure to do that, Jordan. I'll be sure to do that." Connor's chuckles followed them into the pasture.

Galloping through fields, heavy with the beautiful state flower and its fiery counterpart, Jordan's eyes' delighted at the sight. Blue bonnets grew everywhere and were a soothing contrast to the Indian blankets found alongside. The red wildflowers with yellow tipped petals brightened up the scenery and together they were simply breathtaking.

Cole used to claim Kerri was the Blue Bonnets and she was the Indian Blankets. Her heart sighed. Would he ever find his way back to that state of mind?

Loaming on the horizon, the infamous swimming hole caught her attention. Jordan's heavy thoughts lifted. She met Kerri's glance. They burst out laughing and urged their horses on.

Fifteen minutes later, the roar of the ocean filled her ears and she could see the big oak tree in the distance. Sea breeze scented the air and soft cry of seagulls brought back memories of many childhood outings there at the gulf.

The girls dismounted and allowed the horses to graze. Jordan strolled to the tree to seek out her old handiwork. Goosebumps covered her skin. There, three feet up the trunk, sat the mark she'd made the morning they'd moved. Upset, and with all of the emotions of a love-sick sixteen-year-old, she'd carved out a big heart with the letters J + C in the middle.

Her fingers skimmed over the initials. *They're still here.*

"That was a long time ago."

Jordan jumped at her sister's voice. "Y-yes. A million years," she whispered, dropping her hand and stepping back. "Yet, I remember it as if it were yesterday."

"I know what you mean." Kerri walked in front of her to lean against the tree. "I remember picnicking here with the boys, and Kade, Kevin and Jen before we'd go down to the beach for a swim."

"Those were the days. Hey? Speaking of Kade, Kevin and Jen, I wonder how the Daltons are." She smiled at the memory of their other old neighbors. Kevin and Jen were brother and sister, and Kade was their older cousin. He was also Connor's best friend, just as Kevin was Cole's. Together, the seven of them had had a lot of fun.

"Me too. Maybe they'll be at the party."

"Maybe."

Jordan turned to survey the U-shaped beach ten feet below. The ocean glistened and beckoned with a welcomed bellow. She exhaled and rubbed her arms. This was her favorite part of the McCall ranch. Many a time, she'd lain on this very spot, looking up at the sky, listening to the waves…daydreaming about her future with Cole.

Her heart twisted. Life had had other plans.

Breathing past her tight chest, she acknowledged the grieving process was a long and hard road—a road she still traveled. One everyone who had suffered a loss must take if they're to function in society…including Cole. Jordan squared her shoulders. That sexy, stubborn tycoon was going to get on that path if she had any say about it.

She yanked off her shirt, then jeans. "I don't know about you, Kerri, but I'm ready for a dip in that ocean."

"Yeah. It sure has gotten hot out," her sister agreed, stripping to her bikini.

After applying sunscreen, they grabbed their towels and trekked down the familiar trail to the beach. Just what the doctor ordered to relieve stress and keep thoughts of Cole at bay.

Light-hearted and refreshed a half-hour later, they dried off and climbed up the hill to spread their towels in the grass.

"All of that swimming has made me hungry." Jordan's stomach grumbled in confirmation.

"Not to fear, my dear sister. I anticipated that and stopped by the kitchen on my way out to make us each a sandwich. Emma threw in some of her cookies, too." Kerri strolled to her grazing horse.

"You mean she actually had some left?" Jordan chuckled, spreading her sister's purple towel next to her tie-dyed one.

"No, I think she made these this morning. We depleted yesterday's stash, yesterday."

Kerri returned with an insulated sack and quickly unpacked their lunch. Jordan couldn't recall the last time the two of them had spent an afternoon this way. A tradition they needed to rectify.

Taking the final bite of her ham and cheese sandwich a few minutes later, she washed it down with water and sighed. This was pure bliss and exactly what she needed to regroup before confronting Cole again.

Confronting Cole.

Boy her parents were shrewd, not to mention Mr. and Mrs. McCall. Jordan was under no illusion that this had been their plan all along. The niggling in the back of her mind that they were up to something was suddenly very clear. They knew she'd suffered a similar loss and would never allow Cole to remain closed-up and shut everyone out. They were right. She smiled into the sun. His days of using pain as an excuse to act like a jerk, were numbered.

"Thanks, Kerri. That hit the spot." She re-capped her bottle as well as her troubled thoughts and reached for a cookie. "I've been wondering...did I interrupt something between you and Connor earlier?"

A flush spread across her sibling's face. Choking on her own cookie, Kerri took a swig of water before answering.

"No! My goodness. Why do you ask?"

"It's just that it seemed like I walked in on something at the stable. I wasn't sure if I should've left the two of you alone or not."

"Definitely not. No, no. I can't seem to think straight when I'm around him and I don't like it. Not one bit." Her semi-wet hair shook vigorously.

"I know what you mean. I get that way with Cole. Although right now, I'd like nothing better than to slug him one." Her fists curled as she studied the waves rolling onto the beach below. His behavior was similar to the turbulent water—out of control; tumbling inside until it build up force and crashed to the surface.

She drew in a breath. Next weekend would be a concern. The McCall's were going to exchange their vows and the decorated surroundings, the smells, the cherished words would undoubtedly remind Cole of his own wedding and how happy and excited he and his wife had been that day.

Would he make an effort to be there? In all honesty, she wouldn't blame him if he failed to show.

Jordan understood all too well. She'd been through a similar experience last year when she was maid-of-honor for Megan's wedding. But she'd gotten through it, determined her friend would have the memory of Jordan supporting her on her special day. Although it was hard, very hard, she was glad she'd made the effort because now, she would always have the memory too.

If he didn't go, in a few years, Cole would regret not attending the ceremony for his parents. However, not even Jordan would force him to be there...but she had absolutely no problem railroading his stubborn caboose onto the right track, the healing track.

Last of the cookies finished, she reapplied sunblock and lay on her towel, noting Kerri did the same. Eyes closed, she enjoyed several content minutes of doing absolutely nothing.

Jordan sighed, relishing the feel of the afternoon sun heating her skin. "This is a little bit of heaven."

"Absolute rapture," her sister agreed. "But if we stay much longer, they might send out a search party for us and you know who they'll probably send."

Eyes now reluctantly open, she turned her head toward Kerri, and shrugged. "So let them. I'm not going to allow *Mr. Personality* to spoil our wonderful picnic."

Rising to her feet, she shook her head. This was her time. She wasn't...

Alone.

Jordan stilled. Hair on the back of her neck stood up while goose bumps prickled her spine. *Someone's out there*. Hand to her brow, she squinted against the bright sun and scanned the horizon for movement.

Only trees, pastures, and a few birds met her gaze.

Kerri scrambled to her feet and looked in the same direction. "What is it, Jordan?"

"I don't know. It just felt like someone was watching but I don't see anyone."

"Well, maybe it was just that half a dozen cookies settling in your stomach."

Kerri jabbed her and laughed.

Goosebumps diminishing along with her concern, Jordan transferred her attention to her sister. "You're one to talk, you ate the other half."

Carefree mood restored, she chased her giggling sister back down the trail and right into the ocean.

Stilled to the point of not breathing, Cole halted his horse next to Connor's, under the shade of a willow oak tree. *Damn.* As big as the ranch was, over two thousand fucking acres, and they had to stumble across Jordan and Kerri having a picnic. Pounding increased in his head. The girls squirted on sunscreen and proceeded to rub the lotion all over their nearly naked bodies.

Cole's groin bypassed *tight* and jumped straight to *throb*. Closing his eyes, he cursed his weakness. He hadn't had an erection since before his wife had died; except for the few caused by thoughts of Bess or the dreams she'd haunted.

Not that he'd lacked opportunity the past two years. He knew without conceit he'd had plenty. But he never gave the flirting a second thought. He felt nothing.

Until now.

He swallowed. Now his body betrayed his heart and all at the sight of Jordan who, by the measure of the bikini she wore, was practically naked.

Blood raced to his groin as he gazed at his curvy ex-neighbor. He'd always known she'd grow up beautiful but, taking in her ample curves and long legs, what he saw was a knock out.

And that's exactly what she was doing; knocking out a piece of the carefully built wall he'd erected around his emotions. She attacked his libido like a heavyweight in a title match—he didn't stand a fucking chance.

Leather groaned under the stress of his clenching fists. He didn't want to feel. Not now. Not with her. *Christ.* When had he become such a pansy ass?

Jordan stood and lifted her arms above her head to stretch.

Ah hell.

Hunger ripped through him and gripped tight. Tall and lean, she made him sweat as her curvy ass, barely concealed under her blue bottoms, dried his throat. *Damn near perfect.* Her top, which at that angle didn't cover her abundant, more than a handful bust, twisted his gut. *I take it back.* She *is* perfect. He would've salivated if he had any saliva left. She had him fully aroused without even touching him.

Her hands returned to her sides and everything fell back into place. He expelled the breath he hadn't realized he held and heaven help him, continued to survey her body. A strong urge to place his mouth in the curve of her waist and trail kisses to the bottom of the tiny blue triangle awakened the rest of his long dormant cravings.

Did she taste as hot as she looked?

Hell. He wanted to strip off her bathing suit, experience that incredible kiss again, and feel her supple flesh quivering beneath him. Desire turned fierce so fast, need nearly doubled him over. He couldn't help but wonder if the intense response was from being celibate for the past two years...or just his reaction to Jordan.

His grip tightened on the reins. *I owe Bess.* How the hell could he even think those thoughts, let alone allow himself to be driven to this state?

Self-loathing lessened the intolerable need. He swallowed and turned toward his silent brother. A pulse pounded in Connor's neck as he gazed at Kerri in a similar manor. At least he wasn't alone in his torture.

Another quick glance at the girls and Cole's heart stopped altogether. Incredibly, Jordan shielded her eyes and looked straight in their direction. *Fuck.* Remaining still, he prayed the trees shaded them enough from her view. Now was certainly not a good time for a confrontation.

When Kerri stood and joined her sister in the search, he thought for sure they were busted. Relief swiftly flooded his body when the girls stopped and began to playfully romp with each other before disappearing down the ocean trail.

That's what the hell he needed—a cold soaking.

Giving his head a slight shake, he cleared his dry throat. "I uh vote we high-tail it to the stable. I've seen more than enough."

Connor lifted his hat, swiped an arm across his sweat soaked forehead, then placed the hat back on his head. "I'm with you little brother. Those California bikinis sure don't leave much to the imagination, do they?"

"No, they don't."

"Still." Connor lips grew into a mischievous grin. "Those two sure can fill them out, or should I say—fall out."

Groaning at the images those words conjured, Cole turned his mount. "Let's just go."

Without waiting for his sadistic brother, he galloped toward the stable, putting as much distance as he could between Jordan's sexy curves and his pent up, traitorous body.

Mrs. McCall glanced over at Jordan from across the coffee table later that evening. They'd all convened for pre-dinner drinks in the gathering room.

"I hope you girls will have time to do a little socializing while you're here," their host said.

"Yes." Her mother smiled her agreement. "There are a few old neighbors we'd like you to visit with us this week and some shopping in Houston, of course."

Kerri shifted in her seat next to Jordan on the couch. "That would be lovely."

Liar. Jordan held back a snort. Her sister was as reluctant as she was to waste their days reminiscing when there was a lot of work to do, but they were there to please.

"What about you, Jordan?" her mother asked.

"Of course," she dutifully replied.

The last thing she wanted was to socialize, unless it involved provoking a reaction from a certain dour McCall. Her glance traveled across the room to the silent man standing a few feet away by the corner bar next to his brother, her father and Mr. McCall.

Pale and drawn, his face didn't mask his exhaustion. Her heart squeezed. Cole was working himself to death. She had to find a way to deliver him from his hell.

But not tonight. No, she'd give the poor guy a break from the teasing and prodding tonight. Let him get some sleep, tomorrow was soon enough to start at him to live again.

"Well..." Her father bounced his gaze between her and her sister. "It looks like you both brought back some sun from your outing today."

Kerri smiled. "Yes. It's been so long since we've taken time off. It felt good to just sit and relax at our own leisure."

"I agree." She glanced up and grinned at Cole. "The feel of the warm sun on my skin was heaven."

He paled and averted his gaze.

What's with him?

She glanced at Connor. The twinkle in his eyes and dimples in his cheeks spoke volumes. Her pulse quickened. Those buggers.

They were there. It had been the *brothers McCall* she'd sensed.

Why hadn't they joined the picnic? The four of them used to eat and swim together all the time. She shrugged. Their loss—the water had been pure bliss.

Sipping her Bordeaux, her taste-buds clamored in an almost painful attack on her tongue. Momentarily distracted by the perfect tang, she closed her eyes as the succulent flavor greeted her palate. *Great choice.* Slowly, reluctantly, she licked her lips and reopened her eyes, and her heart slammed straight into her throat.

Cole stared at her lips with what almost looked like longing in those dark depths before he dropped his gaze to the glass in his own hands. She frowned and forced her pulse back to normal. Jeez, she must've gotten too much sun. She was seeing things. Cole didn't feel…he couldn't have…hell, he doesn't even like her right now.

With her eyes still trained on him, she didn't move, didn't breath, just sat there waiting for him to look up. When his gaze finally lifted, she was doubly convinced she'd imagined the desire. His expression was full of disdain.

"It's about time you two girls did some relaxing," her father said.

Returning her attention to the others in the room, she silently laughed off her hallucination. *Cole desiring me…hah!* Poor guy only had two emotions right now; anger and fury.

Another sip of the wonderful wine crossed her tongue and restored her earlier euphoria. Today had been a good day. A great day.

The conversation turned to favorite vacation spots and they discussed the merits of beaches versus snowy mountains, while they finished their pre-dinner drinks.

Cole covered his mouth and yawned.

Jordan regarded his eyes. Red and watery, they confirmed her earlier assessment. This time, he wasn't faking it to get out of socializing. Poor guy was truly exhausted.

Which became increasingly apparent later, when he headed for the stairs, instead of his office after dinner.

"There's a good thriller on TV tonight," his dad said.

"Count me out." Cole shook his head. "I'm heading to bed. I'm tired."

"How about you, Jordan?" her father asked. "It's the one you like about the US Marshall on the train."

"I think I'll pass. We've got a full week ahead of us. I'm going to turn in too." She swiveled to the retreating form. "Wait up, Cole. I'll walk with you."

Broad shoulders rose and fell in a silent show of annoyance, but he stopped at the bottom of the stairs and waited while she said her goodnights.

"Thanks," she told him as they began their ascent. Worried about his pallor and the fatigue slumping his shoulders, she put her hand on his arm when they reached the top. "What are you trying to do? Work yourself to death?"

"Drop it, Jordan." He yanked his arm out of her grasp. "I'm not in the mood."

She brushed his irritation aside and searched his face. "You have to stop doing this to yourself, Cole. You need to slow down."

"And you need to mind your own *damned business*."

She ignored him. "There's more to life than just work. What happened to that mischievous boy I knew?"

"He died."

Her hissed breath echoed down the hall. "Cole McCall! That's a horrible thing to say and I refuse to believe it." She gripped his shoulders, hard and stared into his cold gaze. "He's still in there and I'm going to find him. And when I do…I'm going to kick his ass for letting *you* take over."

"There's nothing wrong with *me*, Jordan," he scoffed. "I grew up. You should try it."

She released him and laughed. "Yeah, you sure got me pegged, McCall. I'm very immature and not responsible at all."

He pinched the bridge of his nose and exhaled. "Maybe you are as far as work is concerned, but you need to stop trying to change me, Jordan." He dropped his hand and his gaze bore into hers, flashing a silent warning.

She hated warnings.

"No."

"What do you mean no?"

"Just what I said. No. I won't stop trying to change you because I don't particularly *like* you. I want *you* gone and the old Cole back."

Firm fingers suddenly dug into her bare arms. "Too damn bad. This is who I am now. The old Cole might've put up with your antics but I won't."

Damn, his hands were strong…and big…and deliciously calloused. And big. They covered most of her upper arms. How would they feel scraping the rest of her body?

She drew in a breath. *Not smart*, her mind screamed while her nose rejoiced. *Mmm…fresh and male.* Hit with a sudden vision of a naked Cole lathered and wet, a small sound escaped her throat. *Damn.* Desire flooded her fluttering stomach and pooled between her legs.

"Did you hear me, Jordan? I won't put up with your nonsense."

He increased the pressure on her arms, and the warmth amplified between her thighs.

Whoa. Back the reaction train up. She wasn't the one who needed to feel.

Her chin lifted. "Oh no? Well, I'm not going to stop just because *you* tell me to, Cole. You're way over due for an emotional overhaul and reality check. So, what are you going to do about it, *Mr. Personality?*"

"This."

In an instant, he had her pinned against the wall and pressed into her with his gorgeous, hard body.

Sensations—hot and frenzied, scorched a path to her lower belly. She was damp and trembling in seconds. *Dammit.* The resulting shudder had her shocked, wide eyes staring up at him.

Triumph gleamed back.

He leaned closer, sexy scruff grazing her cheek, sending a wake-up call to all her good parts, the ones that had gone dormant the past few years. *And damn her nipples, too.* They beaded and tried their hardest to get his attention.

They did.

He glanced down at them and smiled before his warm breath tickled her ear as he whispered, "Apparently, you like *me* after all, Jordan."

Anger, mostly at herself, erupted just enough to tamp down her yearnings.

She pushed out of his hold. "Don't try to turn this all around and put the focus on me, pal. It won't work. I'm not one of your unsuspecting victims. But, you're right. There is something about you I like. Your body. Or should I say *Cole's* body," she corrected, looking him up and down, really, really liking what she saw. *Dammit.* "It's grown up quite nice. But I still don't like *you.*" Pivoting on her heel, she drew in a steadying breath and walked as nonchalantly as she could to her room.

His deep chuckle echoed down the hall and rumbled through her like a Southern California tremor. It was great to hear genuine amusement from him…although she could've done without the *Me thinks she doth protest too much* remark uttered with it.

Damn sexy Texan.

Okay, so she wasn't as immune to him as she'd hoped. That changed nothing. Shivers covered her skin. She ignored them.

Jordan Masters Ryan never failed a case and *Operation Heal McCall* would be no exception.

Chapter Five

By the time Tuesday arrived, Jordan's head spun, filled with old acquaintances and a few dinner invitations she'd politely turned down.

Today's line up of events appeared better. Excitement fluttered in her stomach. They were heading to Houston with a stop at McCall Enterprises to meet Cole for lunch and then shopping at The Galleria to find outfits to wear to the McCall's party.

How Mrs. McCall had managed to convince her son to take time out of his hectic day to do lunch with the four of them, baffled Jordan. But she was glad. It would aid her to be able to observe where he worked, glimpse him in his own environment. She refused to blame her excitement on anything other than research.

Donning a sleeveless white dress trimmed in navy with a boxed neck and a slit up the back, she coiled her long braid at the nape of her neck and secured it with strategically placed sticks. A quick glance in the mirror and she was satisfied enough to leave the room to seek out her sister.

She found Kerri in the kitchen, an apron over her strapless yellow sundress, hair twisted up and clipped, and looking refreshed and full of sunshine—no doubt discussing the menu with Emma for the party to be held a week from this Saturday. Cooking, and all it entailed, always put her sister in a good mood.

Emma smiled. "Jordan you look so pretty. Hey, I'm missing a set of chop sticks, is that what you're using on your hair?"

"Oh, darn. I was hoping you wouldn't notice." Jordan jumped into the joke. "I just couldn't get the spatulas to work right."

Her mother walked in with Leeann McCall. "How lovely you both look. Are you ready?"

"Thank you."

"Yes."

"Good because I told Cole we'd be there around eleven thirty, since he has some phone conferences to attend this afternoon." Mrs. McCall's eyes sparkled.

She was glad Cole granted his mother this outing. She'd noted since her arrival that pleasure rarely found the woman's face. "Well, then by all means, let's not keep his majesty waiting."

An hour later, Jordan was standing in an elevator, soaring to the top floor of McCall Enterprises, wondering once again how Mrs. McCall had roped Cole into this lunch. Before she could formulate any plausible explanation, the polished doors opened to reveal a posh, but regal floor.

Straight ahead in the reception area, wood panels graced the wall.

Two portraits broke the gleaming surface; one of Alex McCall and the other of Cole.

Jordan's heart hit her painted toe-nails. *The picture must've been taken before Bess' death.* He still had life in his eyes. Hair shorter, flopping on his forehead and barely touching his collar. God, the man was gorgeous.

Further into the lobby, a stylish gray haired lady greeted with a warm smile. "Hello, Mrs. McCall, Mrs. Masters."

"Hello, Stella," Leeann and her mother replied warmly.

"You two beautiful ladies must be Jordan and Kerri." The woman rounded her oak desk to stand in front of them. "I'm Mrs. Dixon, Mr. McCall's secretary."

"It's nice to meet you. I'm—"

"No, don't tell me which is which," Stella interrupted. "I want to try to guess for myself."

Standing still, Jordan found the woman's assessment amusing. Mrs. Dixon was cordial but shrewd, exactly what you'd expect of the executive secretary to the CEO of McCall Enterprises.

A well-manicured finger pointed at her sister. "You are definitely Kerri. And you"—Stella paused to transfer her intense blue gaze—"are undoubtedly Jordan."

"Aah…you figured us out. What gave us away?" Jordan laced her voice with fake disappointment.

"Well," the prudent secretary went on to explain. "Kerri has a sweet aura about her and was a bit unnerved by my scrutiny, whereas you…" Mrs. Dixon grinned as she walked around them. "You just stared right back at me without flinching, completely amused. And from what I've heard about the way you used to handle Cole—and apparently still do if his grumbling is any indication—it's a characteristic only Jordan could possess in order to deal with him."

Immediately liking his secretary, Jordan plunked her hands on her hips and cocked her head. "I noticed you left out the word *sweet* when you described me. Does this mean I need to eat more sugar—"

The rest of her words died in her rapidly drying throat. Heat prickled up her spine and settled in a slow tingle at the base of her neck. Their lunch date had, no doubt, just entered the room.

"Jordan," Cole said, his deep tone spreading the tingle down her arms. "You could consume a five pound bag of sugar and you'd still be lacking in the *sweetness* department."

"Stop the presses! Mrs. Dixon, take a memo. Cole McCall still has a sense of humor." Jordan slapped a hand over her heart and turned.

"And you still have a big mouth," he countered smoothly.

Two jokes in a row. Her pulse quickened.

Surrounded by several men wearing suits, he stood out, exuding confidence and authority. Good thing she got that remark out before turning around because *this* Cole McCall stole her breath as she slowly appraised the tycoon.

The superb cut of his Italian suit emphasized broad shoulders and trim waist. *Powerful*. From his stance right on up to the arrogant tilt of his head and cocky smirk on his lips. Fleetingly, Jordan remembered how they'd felt on her lips and couldn't help but wonder how they'd feel on her skin. Butterflies stormed her stomach.

Thoughts of that nature were forbidden. She forced Eric's image to mind and her control returned. That type of involvement she did *not* need.

Stepping forward, realization hit her with a start and she halted. *I've come full circle*. Laughter bubbled up her throat. All those years of comparing her male suitors to Cole, this time, she'd finally compared Cole to someone else. Eric.

Okay, so, he didn't come up lacking. But, he did come up dangerous and that was just as bad.

Finding her voice, she followed his lead and planted a hand back over her heart. "Why Cole, you sure know how to flatter a girl." She walked to him and playfully tapped his cheek. "Do you see why I can't resist this man?"

His colleagues hissed, looking at her like she'd committed a mortal sin. What? No one had enough nerve to talk to Cole that way? Or was their reaction because she'd ventured to touch his majesty—Cole the Conqueror?

A bark of laughter filled the office. "Jordan Masters, you haven't changed one bit."

She searched the sea of faces in the doorway. It didn't take long to find the culprit and her brows shot up. "Kevin? Kevin Dalton, is that you?"

"The one and only." Tall, dark and devastatingly handsome pushed through the men with his hand extended. "It sure is great to see you again. How've you been, sugar?" Smiling, he swallowed her hand in both of his before drawing her in for a big hug.

She returned the hug wholeheartedly, absently noting the man was all muscle under the Armani. He, too, had grown up hot. Cripes, what was in Harland County's water? First, Cole, then Conner, now Kevin? She wasn't sure her fluttering heart could handle seeing Kade again if he'd filled out like these guys. And how could he not? He'd always been cute, with an edge, a dangerous air that'd attracted the opposite sex in droves.

Smiling, she stepped back and winked. "I've been okay but apparently, according to Cole, you can't call me *sugar* since I don't have any sweetness in my body."

"Hold on there, honey." His blue gaze, surrounded by thick, dark lashes, admired her all the way down and back up. "Your body looks sweet to me."

"Well, I guess it's just your boss who doesn't think so."

Kevin pulled her out of earshot and kept his voice low. "Cole's been dead from the waist down for almost two years now."

More than she wanted to know, and disgusted with herself for the burst of joy his words brought, she just smiled and glanced over at Cole. Even at this distance, she could see the spark of irritation in his eyes. A reaction? She didn't know if it was because they were quietly discussing him or because Kevin was paying such close attention to her. Either way, Jordan decided it was a good thing.

Hooking arms with Kevin, she led them back toward the crowd. "How's your sister? And Kade?"

"Jen's just fine. And Kade is on his third deployment."

"Wow. Kade is still in the National Guard?"

She remembered talk of his cousin joining to help make ends meet at the Dalton ranch way back when the cowboy was still in his teens. The once a month drill and two weeks a year annual training were something he'd always looked forward to.

Kevin opened his mouth but never had the chance to continue because Cole spoke.

"Alright, enough with this reunion. I don't pay you to just stand around. Do it on your own time."

Jumping at the order like a bunch of rookies, his men gave her one last curious look before disappearing down the hall.

Except for Kevin.

His attention switched to the other women. "Hello, Mrs. McCall. Mrs. Masters," he said, bending to kiss them each on the cheek before he turned to her sister. "Kerri! It's good to see you, too." Capturing her hand, he brought it to his lips. "You Masters have gone from cute kids to stunning women."

"Kevin," Cole interrupted yet again. "I need you to work up the statistics on the new software account. Socialize on your own time, not mine."

Kevin smiled and turned a hopeful blue gaze upon them.

"You heard my boss. You two will have to come to Shadow Rock on Sunday evening. We're having our annual spring barbeque at the ranch. Jen would love to see both of you again." He glanced at his boss. "I've asked Cole to come repeatedly but he never does. Connor, on the other hand, will be there so maybe you can hitch a ride with him. What do you say? Is it a date?"

"I..." Kerri sent her an uncertain look.

She smiled. "I wouldn't miss it. We all have a lot of catching up to do."

"Great! I'll tell Jen and we'll see you both there. Now, I'd better get to work before the *bossman* has a fit."

He nodded toward Cole, and Jordan watched him until he disappeared down the hall. "Wow. He sure turned out to be gorgeous."

"Yeah, he sure did." Kerri nodded, watching where tall, dark and sexy once stood.

"If you're done discussing the looks of my VP, maybe we could get lunch over with?"

Cole held his elbows out to the two smiling mothers and walked them to the elevator.

Unlike him, however, Jordan didn't ignore his secretary. She strolled to Stella and held out her hand. "It was nice to meet you, Mrs. Dixon. I'd like to chat longer, but if I don't pick up my feet, I wouldn't put it past Cole to leave without me."

His secretary shook her head with a gleam in her eye. "Something tells me that's not possible."

The next morning, Jordan sat in the parlor with Mrs. McCall, discussing the progress of party arrangements.

"Have the two of you decided on the songs you'd like me to sing?"

Her host ripped a paper from the yellow legal pad on her lap. "Yes. Here's our list."

List? She frowned. Hopefully, they won't want too many. She accepted the offered sheet and was relieved to find only a handful of country songs.

"These will be fine. As a matter of fact, I'd already promised my mother I'd do two of them you have listed."

"Wonderful. I think—" Mrs. McCall halted when her phone rang. "Sorry," She said, glancing at the cell. "It's Cole."

"No problem." Jordan stood and walked to the window to give her host some privacy. Besides, she wasn't happy with the woman's son at the moment. He hadn't said much at lunch yesterday and ran back to the office as soon as he'd finished eating, leaving everyone else to have coffee and dessert without him.

Her fingers curled into fists as she stared at the horses grazing in the distance. Dinner that night went as it had every night since she arrived. Cole didn't speak much and when he did, he was unbelievably rude, even to his parents. If they didn't say something to him soon, she would. They needed to stop treating him with kid gloves and put an end to this nonsense. She wasn't going to let him get away with it much longer. He was corralling his emotions and it was high time someone broke past his firewall.

"Oh, Cole, what do you mean, you can't? I was counting on you. I even had Emma make all of your favorite dishes. Are you sure you can't make it?"

Mrs. McCall's raised tone stiffened Jordan's spine. *Now what?*

"Well, if it's unavoidable, then it's unavoidable. All right. No it's okay. I'm sure everyone else will enjoy it."

Shoulders slumped, Mrs. McCall hung up the phone. When she finally turned around, Jordan watched her host fight to hold tears in check.

"What's wrong, Mrs. McCall?" She strode to the unhappy woman and touched her arm.

"Oh, it's nothing, really. Cole just called to say he has to stay late tonight to work on some kind of project of his. You know, he has deadlines and all…" her voice trailed off as she wiped her cheek.

"And this meal is important to you?" Jordan kept her tone soft. When what she really wanted to do was scream.

"Well, you see, his father and I had planned on giving him a little surprise celebratory dinner tonight—for the award the company just received for their latest software innovation."

"So you had Emma make his favorite dishes and everything?"

She smiled weakly and nodded. "We invited his college professor and Kevin, too."

"And now Cole's not coming home."

Mrs. McCall sat back down and picked up her notepad. "Well, he didn't know we had this planned. It's okay. At least I know you'll all enjoy Emma's cooking."

"We *all* sure will," Jordan reassured.

In her room ten minutes later, she picked up her cell and punched in the numbers she found for McCall Enterprises. Mrs. Dixon told Jordan Cole was in a meeting and wasn't taking any calls.

"Please. This is somewhat of an emergency," she said truthfully and was put on hold. Technically, it wasn't a lie. Surely when she explained things to him, he'd rearrange his schedule.

"Sorry, Jordan, he won't take the call."

Why that dirty rotten…

Her temperature rivaled summer in Texas. Jordan hung up and punched her pillow.

An hour later, Stella relayed the same message. *Bastard!* Snapping her phone shut, Jordan shot off the bed and grabbed her purse on the way out of the room. Finding her sister in the kitchen with Emma, she informed the pair she had some errands to do in town and would be back in time for dinner.

"*Won't take my calls?* Well, now he's gonna be sorry he didn't take them," Jordan muttered as she strode to her rental car, jammed the keys in the ignition and started the vehicle. Determination stiffened her spine. With a deep breath, she began the hour's drive north to Houston and the stubborn Texan who was quickly becoming the bane of her visit.

Arriving just before noon, Jordan marched to Mrs. Dixon's desk and smiled as the secretary's shock turned into a grin.

"Why Jordan, let me guess, you're here to see Mr. McCall." She glanced at a set of double doors at the end of the hall. "I'm sorry he's still in his meeting and isn't taking calls or visitors."

"Actually, I'm here to see Cole, *Mr. McCall* is back at the ranch. When Cole does something to earn my respect, I'll address him that way."

Mrs. Dixon raised a brow.

"What kind of a meeting is this?"

"A trouble-shooting meeting."

That didn't help.

"How long do they normally last?"

His secretary sighed and opened a folder. "Sometimes well into the night."

"Do they take breaks?"

"Rarely." The secretary didn't look up, and obviously wasn't going to be much help.

Becoming more aggravated by the minute, Jordan walked to the window and studied the view of the incredible skyline in order to calm down. Buildings glinted in the sun, a stark contrast to the brilliant blue Texas sky behind them. Alone or in a cluster of commerce, the skyscrapers enhanced the image of the city. She had to be that lone building whose sole purpose was to achieve—and achieve she would.

By the time Jordan turned around, she had a plan. The secretary's blue gaze rose, waiting with amusement to see her next move. Shoulders squared, Jordan strolled to a chair and sat down to begin her vigil. No way would she leave without seeing Cole.

"If you don't mind, I'll just stick around awhile, in case they take a break," she informed Mrs. Dixon, and crossed her long bare legs.

Tugging her white denim skirt until it settled a few inches above her knees, she realized she still had on the backless black halter-top trimmed in white, and sandals—clothes she'd donned for a day at the ranch. The last thing on her mind when she'd left in a hurry was her appearance. *Oh well*—she leaned forward to pull her hair from between her back and the chair and dropped the heavy mass over her shoulder—*not much I can do about it now*. Chocolate brown waves cascaded down to her hip as she settled in for a long wait. Jordan glanced at her feet. Pearlized by the sun streaming in through the window, her shell ankle bracelet and matching toe-ring stood out against her tan. She wiggled her toes and smiled. Perfect. Her outfit was more suited for a picnic at the beach, not an afternoon in a stuffy corporate office.

I hope I put a wrinkle in Cole's well-ordered life. Damn, stubborn Texan.

An hour and ten minutes later, her patience eventually paid off. A server from the cafeteria staff wheeled a cart full of sandwiches and coffee off the elevator. With a nod from Mrs. Dixon he pushed the food toward the conference room.

Then the secretary's phone rang.

Fate calling.

Pulse pounding, Jordan waited until Stella, phone cradled on her shoulder, turned her attention to the computer. *Bingo. My window of opportunity*. Sandals in hand, she scurried unnoticed down the hall.

Reaching the conference room at the same time as the cart, she smiled and opened the door so the server could wheel through. Everyone looked up and stared at her, chins dropping to their suited chests. Jordan had all she could do not to burst out laughing. They'd completely ignored the food.

Even Cole, bent over the table pointing to something, looked stunned. He straightened up so fast, he could've slipped a disk.

"What," she said. "You never saw a barefoot woman holding sandals before?"

Kevin was the first to recover as the cafeteria worker disappeared, closing the door behind him.

"Jordan, what a pleasant surprise."

"Hi, Kevin." She waved.

"What do you want?" Cole barked, an angry flush invading his cheeks.

"It's nice to see you too." She dropped her sandals on the floor and slipped her feet into the cool leather before strolling toward him. "Look, I know you're in a meeting and I'm sorry to interrupt but I've tried to talk to you for several hours now. Can we please go somewhere private?"

"No."

"Just for a few minutes?"

"No! Now get out," he said firmly.

The door flew open behind her.

That would be the loyal Mrs. Dixon.

"There you are," Stella exclaimed. "Sorry, Mr. McCall, one minute she was sitting and the next she was gone."

"If it had been anyone else, Stella, I'd be furious. But knowing Jordan as I do, you were out maneuvered." His hard gaze never left her face.

"You didn't give me much choice, Cole. It certainly wasn't Mrs. Dixon's fault." She waved in his secretary's direction as the rest of the men looked on with interest.

"You can go now, Mrs. Dixon, and take Jordan with you." He returned his attention back to the table.

"Sorry, honey," Jordan told him firmly. "I came here with something to say and I will *not* leave until I do."

His men flinched.

"Whatever it is, we can discuss it when I get home."

"When will that be?"

"When I'm good and damn well ready! Now, kindly go away or I'll have you thrown out. The choice is yours, Jordan. I have a business to run." His deadly tone would've scared off any normal person.

Too bad for him, she wasn't a normal person.

"I'm not leaving until we talk. If you want to involve your security guards, then bring them on." She stared him down, ignoring the loud thumping of her heart.

He cocked his head. "Don't think I won't, Jordan."

"All right you two. Go to your corners." Kevin stepped between them.

She snickered, Cole scoffed.

Dropping her arms, she inhaled, then exhaled, trying hard to hold onto her temper. "Look, Cole, what I have to say is very important. Can't you just give me a few minutes while your crew takes a break to eat their lunch?" She waved to their audience.

"No. They're not taking a break. It's a working lunch," he informed tight-lipped as he pulled his chair away from the table and sat down with a flourish. "Now, go nicely and don't give Mrs. Dixon any more trouble or I *will* call security."

Wrong answer. He gave her no choice...

It was drastic measure time.

Moving away from Mrs. Dixon, Jordan conjured a sultry smile and swayed seductively towards Cole.

He stilled.

"But, baby." She pouted and plopped on his lap, tossing her legs over the side of his chair and crossing them at the ankle. "We really need to talk." One hand around his neck, the other fingering his lapel, she laid her face on his shoulder.

He smelled wonderful. The scent of spicy aftershave and musky cologne heated her insides. Sitting on him, Jordan became instantly aware of the hard body concealed beneath his clothes. Yearnings—strong and deep—scampered through her and she fought to keep from melting into him.

Stay focused.

Starting at his jaw, she fingered a path down his neck to his chest. "The sex this morning was great, honey, but I found out the diaphragm I used was broken," she told him in a low, sexy voice.

Cole stiffened and she acknowledged several startled hisses and one distinctive laugh, before she continued with her charade.

"Did you hear me, honey?" She wrapped her finger around his chin and forced him to look at her. "I said the diaphragm was broken and that means all that wild, incredible stuff you did to me last night might've created us a baby!"

A proverbial "Huh!" sounded throughout the room.

Cole sprang them from the chair, grabbed her arm and pulled her roughly through an adjoining door to a massive office.

"Dammit, Jordan," he spat, kicking the door shut behind them. "This is a place of business—my business! You don't just come barging in prancing around in provocative clothing demanding attention. What's wrong with you? Please tell me you don't run your business that way."

She jerked her arm free and held his glare. Provocative? Anger formed a burning ball churning in the middle of her stomach, but she refused to give into the inferno. She needed to remain cool. "No, I do not run my business that way. Only a certain, stiff, pompous Texas tycoon could force me to act unprofessional."

"Force? Jordan! What the hell was that all about?" he choked, clenching and unclenching his fists.

He does that a lot, she noted.

"Well again, you didn't give me much choice, now did you McCall?" she calmly explained, wisely putting his desk between them. "I told you I needed to talk to—"

"Too bad!" He turned to leave.

Oh, hell no!

Beating him to the door, she body-blocked his escape. "You're right. It is too bad. It's *too* bad you wouldn't take my calls this morning. It's *too* bad I was forced to come all the way here and it's *too* bad I had to do that in there." She jabbed her thumb toward the conference room and continued. "It's *too* bad you wouldn't see me when I first arrived almost *two* hours ago, and it's *too* damn bad you're *breaking your mother's heart!*"

His head jerked back. That last remark got through to him.

"What are you talking about, now?"

"Dinner tonight. You need to be there."

"Not that it's any of your business, Jordan, but I already explained to my mother I have a lot of work to do here and she was just fine with that." He grabbed her upper arms in an attempt to move her.

"If she was so fine with it, Cole, why did I witness her crying?"

He stilled. "She cried?"

"Yes. Is it finally getting through to you in there?" She knocked her fisted knuckles off his forehead.

Firm fingers clamped around her wrist. Current after current shot down her arm and tripped her pulse. Sidetracked by this new sensation, Jordan looked up at him and sucked in a breath.

His eyes mirrored her shock.

They stared at each other for a moment before his gaze dropped to her mouth. She forgot to breath. Unable to move, and with her wrist still trapped in his grip, she backed up against the door not quite sure what to do.

On one hand, she longed to drag his mouth to hers and delve inside, finally putting an end to their long overdue *adult* kiss—the one she'd dreamt about for years. On the other hand, she was scared to death, her reaction to this man was way too strong and she wanted to turn tail and run.

The decision was taken from her when Cole suddenly released her and turned his back. The current turned to a tingle, and she remembered how to breathe. Damn, he was potent.

Slumping against the door, she concentrated on his hands as they raked through his hair and loosened the leather band.

Her fingers itched to run through his wavy tresses. *Bad thought. Dangerous thought.*

Deciding it was best to ignore what had just happened, she tried to reason with him while his defenses were still down. "Cole, isn't there any way you could leave in time for dinner tonight? It really is important to both of your parents that you come."

Twisting around, he frowned. "Why, Jordan? What's going on?"

Hair wild about his shoulders, eyes dark and troubled, he made it hard for her to remember why she was there. Or her friggin' name for that matter.

She walked to him and placed her hand on his arm. "I'm sorry, Cole. The only thing I can tell you is that your parents have something special planned and it would mean *so much* to them if you showed up."

With one last imploring look, she turned and left his office through the door opposite the one they'd entered, and found herself back in the reception area.

She crossed to Stella's desk, the plush burgundy carpet eating up her footsteps. "I hope I don't get you in trouble."

"Don't worry, dear. I can handle him." A huge smile spread across Mrs. Dixon's face. "I swear I'll never forget what you did. Oh, Jordan, if you could've seen his face…"

Laughter interrupted the woman's words and she had to take her glasses off to wipe the tears from her eyes.

Smiling, Jordan absently traced a circle on the desk. "I swear that man makes me do the stupidest things."

"It wasn't stupid, it was priceless!" The tears came again as Mrs. Dixon's chest shook with unadulterated amusement.

Boarding the vacant elevator with a smile, Jordan prayed her visit had yielded more fruit than a batch of joyful tears from the CEO's secretary.

Halfway through dinner that night, Jordan was just about at the end of her rope. Cole kept glancing at her, sending her messages she couldn't interpret. She was half sorry she'd managed to persuade him to attend his special dinner. One minute his eyes were frosty, the next they were angry…the next they were heated. He drove her nuts. Napkin clenched on her lap, she was trying, really trying not to embarrass Mrs. McCall in front of Cole's college professor, Mr. Dempsey, but her son's demeanor made it hard.

Right now, the only thing keeping her tongue in check was recalling the excitement on Mrs. McCall's face when Jordan had returned from her *errands*. Her host had rushed to tell her Cole had called and said he'd be home after all and wasn't that great?

Yeah, loads, she thought to herself, grinding a piece of steak between her teeth.

"So tell me, Jordan, how was your day?"

Kevin's question brought her back to the present.

She grinned. He was a welcomed devil. "Okay. I ran some errands but I'll tell you, there are some people out there that are so stubborn…it's a wonder how they stay in business."

"I know what you mean," Mr. Dempsey replied. "I have several students like that."

"No. Really? What a shame." She tsked, glancing at Cole.

He wasn't amused.

"Yes, they think they know it all but they soon learn the hard truth about that." The professor winked. "I never had that trouble with Cole, though."

Jordan nearly choked on her wine. "You never found him stubborn?"

"No. He was always brilliant but never full of himself." Mr. Dempsey shook his head.

Boy, did McCall have him fooled. "Are we talking about the same Cole?" She pointed to the man smirking across from her. "Him?"

"Yes, *him*." Mr. Dempsey chuckled and the room laughed.

Jordan couldn't believe what he was saying. Looking at Cole, she saw the epitome of stubborn; tipped chin, folded arms, cocky grin. "You and I know two completely different people."

Kevin snickered.

"What's so hard for you to believe?" Cole leaned forward and sent her a challenging glare. "I *respect* him."

"Cole." His father frowned. "Apologize to Jordan."

This ought to be good. She sat back in her chair, folded her arms and waited.

"Sorry I don't respect you, Jordan," he told her smoothly.

Not at all what his father wanted to hear, she wagered but she thought it was funny as hell.

"That's okay, Cole. I don't respect you either." She shrugged, smiling along with Kevin and Connor's laughter.

Thankfully, the rest of the meal went by without the barb exchange. Mr. Dempsey made his apologies for not being able to stay for dessert because of a prior engagement, congratulated Cole again, then left.

Jordan breathed a sigh of relief. Not because she didn't like the man, he was very smart and funny. No, she was relieved because now she didn't have to worry about embarrassing Mrs. McCall in front of her special guest, which meant, no more curbing her tongue where Cole was concerned.

Dessert was served. She smiled. *Mmm…blueberries.* Her mouth watered but her skin prickled when she caught Cole staring at her almost…hungrily. She stilled. *Damn mind was playing tricks again.* She blinked and found him glaring.

That was it.

Fork sticking out of her fist, she brought the handle down on the table—hard. "Don't you have work to do?" Twisting the fork around, she jabbed a piece of her sister's scrumptious blueberry pie, and slid the confection into her mouth, all while staring defiantly at him.

Kevin and Connor both snickered while Cole's eyes hardened so much they glittered.

It's a wonder he doesn't explode.

"As a matter of fact, I do have work to do." Cole sent her one last furious look, then got up and left the room.

"Good, now maybe I can enjoy my dessert in peace," she said, loud enough for his rigid form to hear.

After dessert, Kevin announced he was going to help Cole put some finishing touches on their latest project and disappeared into his boss's home office while the others gathered in the den to watch a comedy. Tonight, she decided a funny movie was just what she needed and joined them.

A few hours later, she left the room in a lighter mood.

"Hey, Jordan," Kevin greeted in the hall, closing Cole's office door behind him. "Walk me to my truck?" He took her hand, and once outside, chuckled as they strolled to his pick up. "Girl, I can't thank you enough for what you're doing to Cole."

She twisted her lips and talked out of the side of her mouth. "Yeah, right. That guy's too stubborn to notice his family's concerned. There's no way my pestering has made a dent in his control…yet."

"Oh, darlin', you are so wrong. He doesn't know whether he's coming or going and those rumors are the icing on the cake!" A satisfied smile spread across his face as he released her hand to gleefully drum the hood of his truck.

Her heart stopped. *Rumors?* "Kevin, exactly what kind of rumors are you talking about?"

"Well, little lady," he grinned, crossing his arms over his broad chest while he leaned back against the cab. "I can't imagine how it got started but it seems Cole is not only involved with a bombshell—who, by the way is a nymphomaniac," he snickered, "but it seems she's also carrying his baby."

Baby? *Oh no! The meeting…* Groaning, Jordan clamped a hand over her mouth to keep the chuckle inside.

Didn't work.

"Oh, Kevin. Please tell me you're just joking." She laughed.

"Nope. I kid you not." His grin broadened and he turned to happily drum his roof again. "Our buddy Cole is now officially a hot tamale."

"No wonder he kept glaring at me all night. Oh cripes, I certainly didn't mean for this to happen. I just wanted five damn minutes of his time and he wouldn't give it to me." Jordan sobered. "Man, he must be so angry with me."

"All I can say is thank you, thank you, thank you for being you, Jordan." Kevin placed both hands on her shoulders. "You're so good for him. He needs you."

"Maybe, but I don't think he needs that rumor." She couldn't stop the chuckle.

"Don't be so sure. That stiff demeanor of his is now officially cracked and he's back down to our level—human. He's even been getting a lot of back slapping and thumbs up from his male staff members," Kevin informed with a big smile, then kissed her forehead. "Got to go. *Bossman* expects me to be in bright and early tomorrow."

He waved before driving out of sight.

I am so dead.

She turned and rushed around the side and up the balcony steps. With luck, Cole would still be downstairs in his office and she'd avoid the retribution she knew he'd demand.

In her hopes for a reaction, retribution wasn't one of them.

"Not so fast, Jordan." The deep steely voice hit her ears just as she reached her door. "I want a word with you. *Now!*"

Chapter Six

Busted. *Damn.*

"Look, Cole. Whatever it is, can't it wait until tomorrow?" Jordan hoped by some miracle he'd postpone his rant. Maybe he'd be calmer by the morning.

"No, Jordan. It can't wait," he snapped, coming out of the shadows to glare.

Barefoot and bare-chested, Cole wore nothing but a pair of jeans. Her throat dried. *Holy friggin' torsos.*

Water dripped off his loose hair, and ran unchecked down solid pecks, then followed the tight ruts of his abs, sporting a happy trail to jeans slung low on his lean hips. The naked expanse of his chest glistened from the droplets as moonlight caught them in its glow.

She swallowed and searched for her voice. "F-fine."

He scowled. "No, it's not *fine*, Jordan. You had no right to treat me like that in front of my staff today. People I work with day in and day out." He drew in a hissed breath. "People I demand respect from. I will not tolerate that kind of behavior again."

Sighing, she stepped toward him and looked into his narrowed eyes. "You're right, Cole. I shouldn't have and I'm sorry. But I tried all morning and most of the afternoon to get you to talk to me in private so it's as much your fault as it is mine," she finished with a tilt of her chin.

"Ah, hell no! Don't even try to blame your wild behavior on me, Jordan. Thanks to you, there are all sorts of rumors circulating at my company."

She bit back a smile and remained silent, letting him vent. He had a point. She should've found another way. If she had it to do over again…she wouldn't change a damn thing. Mrs. McCall's gleaming face popped into her mind. The results were worth his baby rumors. She bit harder and tasted blood as she swallowed a giggle.

"I'm glad you're amused by this, Jordan, because if you ever step foot inside McCall Enterprises again, I'll have you physically removed!"

Okay, now that was really amusing. She smiled outright. Funny, that only made his frown deepen. *My God,* he was serious. Straightening, she shoved her hands on her hips and tilted her head back to stare him down.

"You and what army?"

Oops, there went her mouth again.

His face darkened. She swallowed and backed away—straight into the railing. One quick stride and he had her trapped with his body. His half naked, wet, mouth-watering body. *Damn.* Her body immediately rejoiced.

Bad body.

Jaw tight enough to crack, and it did, he glared down at her. "No army. Just me."

Intending to push free, her hands met the bare flesh of his chest. Solid. Smooth. Deliciously warm. Her knees wanted to buckle. She refused. He's just a man. A very well-proportioned man. Arousal, unwanted yet strong, rippled through her, instantly stalling her need to flee. Cole stilled. His incredible broad expanse begged her palms to explore. She drew in a breath. *Damn man was too friggin' sexy for her health.* Fresh scented soap and shampoo tickled her senses and she eyed his wet torso. *Lucky droplets.* A tremor of desire slipped past her dwindling control as she slowly lifted her gaze.

Stormy brown eyes widened a fraction before locking on hers. With each heartbeat that passed, breathing became a chore.

"Maybe we should make good on those rumors…nymph." Thrusting his fingers in her loose hair, he held her head immobile.

Sanity returned with his sudden movement. "No," she protested through clenched teeth, trying to push out of his arms again. There was no way she could survive. No way.

"Yes, Jordan," he replied in a rough voice before claiming her mouth.

Hot liquid sensations shot down her spine then back up. Half of her wanted to melt into his magnificent body while the other half wanted to fight. The best compromise to her rebellious libido was to keep her lips closed.

Her good parts tingled and wanted to know where the hell he'd been for the past decade, but she immediately told them to shut the *frig* up. He made her feel. She did *not* want to feel. Not yet. Jeez, they needed to straighten him out, and right now, she was so damn mixed up.

Without warning, his kiss changed from savage to soft and seeking and lazy.

Dammit.

Nibbling, teasing, nipping, he didn't play fair. His tongue glided over the seam of her lips. She couldn't help it, she moaned, involuntarily giving him access to her mouth. *Oops.* He tasted of mint and desire. He was so hot. So very, very hot.

Jordan's control deserted her. Snapped. Left her alone to deal with an unhealthy, wild hunger buried so long ago. Maybe a little taste. What harm was there? She touched her tongue to his.

Mmm…adult Cole tasted better than she'd ever imagined.

He groaned into her mouth, body heating under her touch, and heaven help her, she wanted more. Sliding her hands over his shoulders, she stopped at the back of his neck where her fingers tangled in his thick, wet strands. His hold on her tightened. She took advantage of the better angle and boldly plunged her tongue into his mouth, savoring his intense taste as her eyes drifted closed and she melted into him.

All the longing she'd had for Cole during her youth hit her full force but in a much stronger, womanly form. Completely overcome, coupled with the pent up yearnings of the past few days, Jordan's common sense joined her control and took a hike. A long hike.

His lips tantalized, kissing, seeking, drinking, drawing a throbbing response from deep inside. Bodies aligned. Mouths aligned. She rediscovered his taste, experienced the mind-drugging stroke of his tongue, basked in his warmth.

Hot damn, the man could kiss. He was so hot. So was she. They were on fire.

Never breaking the kiss, he released her head to skim his hands over her peaked nipples to the curve of her waist before sliding over her ass where he gripped tight as he rocked into her. *Oh, yeah…that*. Shards of heat shot out in all directions, weakening her knees, forcing a whimper from her throat. He did it again, and oh God, she was in heaven. Of their own accord, her eager hands slid over his muscles, descending lower until they hit the waist of his jeans.

He stiffened, then abruptly pushed away with a curse.

Jordan's eyes flew opened at the absence of his mouth and warmth of his flesh. Panting, she sucked in air, and common sense returned with a flood of guilt and shame.

Eric.

With a hand on her quaking stomach, she drew in more air and fought a wave of nausea.

If Cole hadn't stepped away…

She shuddered, refusing to think about what she'd almost allowed to happen.

"I'm sorry, Jordan," he said unsteadily. "I didn't mean to let that get so out of control." Thrusting a hand through his hair, he tugged at the back of his head before dropping his arm to his side with a thump. "But I think you've learned your lesson. Good night."

Before she could respond, Cole retreated to his room, locking the door, effectively shutting her out. If only she could shut out guilt. Her stomach churned.

How could I betray my husband like that?

Okay, so she was technically no longer married. But she'd never been with anyone but Eric. Sure, she'd gone on a few dates and kissed a few men the past six months. But that had been to please her family and friends; to put on a show of moving on. Those embraces meant nothing and left her cold, keeping her heart true to Eric.

Not this time. God, no. Not this time. This time she was ready to jump up, wrap her legs around the sexy CEO cowboy and take in every hard, delectable inch she felt bulging behind his zipper. All because of one damn, heated kiss.

Mouth souring, she continued to hold her lurching stomach and walked blindly toward her room.

This time, Lord help her, she wanted much more.

Cole couldn't believe what had just happened. What he'd almost *let* happen. Jesus, the woman made him nuts. Their exchange just proved he had zero control where Jordan was concerned. Zip. Zilch. Nil.

And he certainly had no business kissing her. What the hell was wrong with him?

She was what was wrong with him. She had him so mad he couldn't see straight and the next thing he knew he had her soft curves pinned against the railing, his tongue in her luscious mouth wanting to prove, God knows what, when all it proved was he wanted her more than his next breath.

Christ.

He stripped out of his jeans and stepped back into the shower, violently twisting the cold tap. Even thoughts of Bess and his near betrayal hadn't lessened his arousal.

And that pissed him off.

He did *not* want to be attracted to Jordan. Did not want this unhealthy need eating him up, making him yearn to kiss her long and slow, to lick her from head to toe…to thrust deep inside her until she clenched tight and called out his name.

Ah hell…

The cold shower wasn't helping. He was so hard he could crack the Italian marble lining the walls. *Damn woman!* He was going to have to take matters into his own hands, something he hadn't done since his teenage years. And yes, that pissed him off, too. What was worse was the fleeting thought that right now, at that moment if he hadn't stopped Jordan, her sweet heat could've brought his release. *Son-of-a-bitch*, if *that* wasn't the very image that flashed in his mind when he let loose.

Now he was good and pissed.

He slumped against the wall. She had to go. Just had to. He wanted her gone. Now. But that wasn't possible. He expelled a breath and stepped back under the cold spray. He was stuck with her until after the party. Didn't mean he had to be nice. Hell, he was done being nice, even though he knew he'd pretty much been an ass since she'd arrived.

Well, things were about to get worse. He loved his mother, he really did, but he was done holding back to keep the peace. Right now, he needed to think of himself. He washed up, rinsed, then shut off the water before he towel dried with brisk strokes. If he wasn't careful, Jordan was going to knock down his wall. The hell if he was going to let that happen. No way was he ready to feel. Especially with that…that…*her*.

Two minutes later, Cole crawled into bed and forced himself to relax. He could get through the next week and a half. It was just a matter of control. Jordan wasn't going to be a problem. Truth be told, he had to admit, she wasn't even the biggest problem. *He* was. And the person he was most furious with was himself for not being strong enough to fight their attraction.

Why the hell did his control disappear around that woman? That's all she was. A woman, for Christ's sakes.

A sweet, sexy, giving woman who nagged and challenged and wouldn't let up. Deep down Cole knew Jordan did it because she cared. He didn't want her concern. She understood his pain. He didn't want her understanding. She felt the same fierce hunger and need ripping him open from the inside out. Lord help him, her eyes had smoldered. They'd *fucking* smoldered.

Ah hell…he was hard again.

Sitting atop Ember Friday afternoon, Jordan turned the horse's canter into a trot. She was in no hurry to reach the ranch or its growing tension. Cole had been an even bigger bear since they'd kissed two nights ago. His family was walking on eggshells around him and the kid-glove treatment was ticking her off.

Big time.

Needing a break after doing her follow-ups on the party arrangements, she'd snuck to her favorite spot, enjoying the sun and sand, until her conscience told her it was time to head back. She took the long way, though, reluctant for her stress-free time to end.

Up ahead, near the road, the brush started to shake. Her back stiffened. Snake? She tugged on the reigns and brought Ember to a halt.

The shaking stopped. She frowned and held her breath, waiting to see if the critter would reveal itself, hesitant to go past if it would put her horse in danger. Sweat gathered on her brow and ran down the side of her face.

Bursting into the road a moment later, a roadrunner shot from the brush and scurried to the other side. Jordan jumped, then laughed. The bird was a common sight around there, dining on insects, spiders, scorpions, small snakes and lizards. Ranchers welcomed them because of their varied menu.

As the roadrunner disappeared once again into the brush, she nudged Ember back into her trotting pace and contemplated her long week so far.

She'd planned, ordered, and arranged all that she could for the party. Spent several days visiting old friends with her mother, sister and Mrs. McCall. Met Cole's secretary. Crashed a meeting, jump started his reputation as a satisfying sex partner, and avoided him like a California mudslide, ever since their eye-opening adult kiss.

Embarrassed by her lack of control, she'd been reluctant to face him yesterday. She needn't have worried. He acted like their kiss never happened. The responsive, hot man who'd shuddered with passion two nights ago didn't exist. Whenever she walked into the room his lips thinned and face darkened, and he'd nearly jumped down Connor's throat for suggesting he take up Kevin's offer on this weekend's barbeque.

Stupid, stubborn jerk.

Cole was just as hard and unfeeling as before, maybe even more so. By responding to their kiss, he'd shown need and that meant weakness. And heaven forbid the mighty Cole McCall should show weakness. Why act human when he could be a mean, ornery bastard?

The leather rein crackled under her clenched fists. If he didn't snap out of it soon, she'd haul off and pop him one. For the life of her, Jordan couldn't figure out how come no one had done that yet.

As the ranch came into view, the roar of a powerful engine and dirt-eating sound of a car tearing up the road behind her met Jordan's ears. She glanced over her shoulder and barely had enough time to close her eyes before a tornado of dust engulfed her and Ember, as a black BMW sped by.

"Son-of-a…" She coughed. "Dammit, Cole!"

When the cloud cleared, she drew in a few clean breaths, and galloped straight to the stable. Bringing Ember to a halt just outside the stable doors, she eyed the building across the drive.

Briefcase in hand, Cole came out of the garage without so much as an apology or inquiry to see if she was all right.

Jumping off the mare, she bit back an unladylike curse and strode to him. No way was he getting away with that stunt. She wasn't family and not at all intimidated. Not caring if she dirtied his expensive suit, she grabbed his arm and twisted him around. "Not so fast, McCall. Just where do you think you're going?"

"I'm sorry. Do I know you?" he had the audacity to ask.

"You son-of-a—"

"Jordan? Is that you?" He cut her off, eyes widening in mock innocence. "I didn't recognize you under all that dirt."

White hot steam replaced her blood, evaporating her retort, leaving an instant throbbing in her head. When the heat lessened enough for speech, she shoved a stray strand of hair off her face and spat, "What's wrong with you, Cole? You were driving like a maniac! Do you want to have an accident?"

Blood drained from his face while his gaze took on a deadly glare. "Try riding in a field next time," he ground out and ripped his arm free with such force Jordan had to step backward to avoid falling over. "And mind your own damned business!" With a white-knuckled grip on his briefcase, he pivoted around and strode to the house.

If not for the horse to take care of, she would've taken care of him. Jordan unclenched her fists and marched back to Ember. Grumbling, she guided the mare into the stable, removed the saddle and slammed it on the rack as if it were a feather. Tremendously ticked-off, she probably could've lifted the horse with one hand. A pinky.

Stupid, no-brain, McCall.

Imagining the reins to be Cole's neck, Jordan led Ember to the back of the stable with her own white-knuckled grip. Prying her fingers loose, she inhaled and threw her unbridled energy into ridding the horse of the coating of dirt—courtesy of *Jerk* McCall. That man better not even think of pushing her further tonight because she was done babying him. Done with a capital *D-on't even think about it!* Venting her frustration with every brisk movement, she finished up the task just as Connor entered the barn.

He stopped dead, brows disappearing under the brown brim of his well-worn work hat. "What in the world happened to you?"

"Your brother, that's what." She motioned with the hose, nearly spraying Connor's jeans. "He came tearing up the road as I was riding. Didn't slow down…didn't swerve…just drove like a bat out of hell. Does he always drive that fast?" She turned off the water and looked up at him.

Connor sighed. "Unfortunately, yes, every once in awhile, the past two years."

"Two years?" She reeled back, dropping the hose. "Why don't you all do something about it, for goodness sake? He can get hurt. Or hurt someone else. This has to stop, Connor. I can't stomach the way he talks to all of you or the way he treats you. He's the same way with his staff, and I'll tell you right now," she said, pointed to the house again. "If someone doesn't say something soon, then *I* will."

Unease emanated from the quiet cowboy. He removed his hat, swiped his forehead with his sleeve, then set the hat back on. "Cole's been through so much and lost so much, Jordan. We don't want to add to his burden."

His concern for his brother took some of the bite from her demeanor and softened her ruffled edges. "Oh, Connor, don't you see?" She stepped closer and touched his arm, tipping her head back to look him straight in the eyes. "You're all only compounding the problem. He needs to open up and get it out. Not hold on so it can fester inside."

Connor's large hand gently covered hers and squeezed. "I've tried, but he blames himself for Bess's accident and won't listen to reason."

Jordan's heart rocked hard against her ribs. She'd known that the second she'd looked into Cole's eyes. Now it was time to find out why. "He blames himself?"

Connor nodded. "He was working late and Bess was on her way to the office, bringing him supper so he could finish up the code to a new software program." He dropped his hand and drew in a breath. "She was hit head on by a tractor trailer. The driver had fallen asleep at the wheel. Bess died at the hospital later that night."

Oh God…Cole.

Eyes stinging, Jordan blinked, sending a lone tear down her face. "What an awful thing for him to have carried around all these years." She swallowed, hating that her theory was right. "It certainly wasn't Cole's fault, but I know what he's feeling."

Hugging herself, she turned away. Eric's death still haunted her. It was her fault. With all of her training she should've been able to stop it. Her family, friends, superiors—even her head, insisted it wasn't true, but her heart never believed them.

"Jordan, are you okay?" Big, warm hand reassuring on her shoulder, Connor twisted her to face him.

He was such a sweetheart.

"Yes." She nodded, and with a sigh, released her turmoil to jump into Cole's. "We have to do something, Connor. The accident was two years ago. Cole needs to get on with his life and that isn't going to happen unless you and your parents help him."

He dropped his hands and shook his head. "I told you, Jordan, we already tried that. It didn't work. He bit our heads off and retreated further into himself. We don't want to lose any more of him than we already have or make him hate us."

"I don't think that would happen but in any case, I'm not afraid of him or his hatred." She moved to the horse and picked up a brush. "It'd be worth it to get him to open up."

The handsome cowboy stepped forward, gently removed the grooming tool from her hand and graced her with a glimpse of his dimples. "I'll do that, darlin'. You'd better go inside and hose *yourself* down…unless you plan on eating dinner in a coating of dirt with streaks down your face."

Taking a cue from his playful tone, she spread her arms out and twirled. "What's wrong with the way I look?"

He sent her a lop-sided grin. "Nothing, if you were out cattle rustling with me."

Jordan had always considered herself tolerant. A pillar of strength and restraint when needed. Her job demanded it. Her nature imbedded it. But tonight, *strength* and *restraint* gave her permission to take on *Billy-Bad-Ass* sitting across from her. She'd just about reached her limit where Cole was concerned.

Holding her tongue for the tenth time that night, Jordan stared at the sexy SOB, refusing to endure any more of his bad temper.

With an arrogant tilt to his head, sarcasm flowed from his lips deliberately trying to push her buttons. *That*, she could put up with, but when he talked cruelly to his family, her patience thinned.

"Cole," his mother began, looking up from her plate to smile at him. "Have you given any more thought to singing with Jordan at the party?"

He cursed. "Mom, I've already told you I'd think about it. Besides—," he jabbed his fork in her direction. "Jordan is more than capable of handling it herself. Why don't you get off my back and just let her do it?"

Silence halted all movement, conversation…breathing from the room. Everyone just stilled.

Oh, no he didn't!

Air hissed into Jordan's lungs. She waited, teeth clenched tighter than her fists, to see if the McCall's would do anything. Her gaze bounced to the three members of his family. They all sat with their hands on their laps and their eyes downcast. Why? Surely there weren't going to let him get away with that? But after several more seconds passed and they remained in that pose, it became obvious that was exactly what they were going to do—let him get away with being a miserable SOB.

Not her. Not tonight. Not anymore.

Her fork clanked a violent protest onto her plate. His days of getting away with a mean attitude were done. They ended with her!

"That's it! I'm done." She shot to her feet, jammed her hands her hips and fixed Cole with an unwavering stare. "Apologize to your mother right *now*."

His gaze slowly met hers and he lifted a brow. "What?"

"You heard me. I said, apologize to your mother, and then you and I need to go somewhere and have a talk."

His lips curled into a scowl. "I have absolutely nothing to say to *you*."

"That's okay, Cole, because I have plenty to say to you. So you can just shut up and listen, but first…" She pointed to his mother. "Apologize to her *right now!*"

Mrs. McCall shifted in her seat and twisted her napkin. "Jordan, it's all right, really. He doesn't have to."

Heat rushed into Jordan's face and she barely choked out, "Cole," through clenched teeth.

His eyes narrowed and he hesitated a moment before he turned to his mother. "I'm sorry, Mom, if I hurt your feelings. I didn't mean to." His gaze snapped back to her, daring her to find fault with his words.

"Fine. Now, I have a few things to say to you that should have been said a *long* time ago." She pushed in her chair then headed toward the door.

"You'll just have to say them to me here, Jordan because I'm not leaving."

She stopped and turned around to find him adding more meat to his plate. *Why that…* She shook her head and sighed. "You have to make this difficult, don't you, Cole?"

"Make what difficult? I'm just trying to eat my dinner," he said matter-of-factly, putting a forkful of roast in his mouth.

She tried one last time. "Cole, I'm serious, can we please go somewhere private to talk?"

His fists hit the table, rattling the china. "Look, Jordan, I'm not going anywhere so if you have something to say, then just say it! If not, shut up and let us eat."

"Don't think I won't, McCall." She crossed the carpet in three strides and stood across from him again. *Stubborn fool.* Her gaze fell to each of the silent onlookers. "I apologize in advance for what I am about to say. It may seem harsh but it needs to be said. It's not my wish to do this in front of you all but since Cole won't leave..."

She noted identical frowns on Connor and his father, while Mrs. McCall clutched the napkin on her lap and bit her lower lip. Jordan's parents and sister, on the other hand, all sat back with a nod.

Her gaze returned to Cole. He was not going to like this but she had to do it. Jordan straightened her spine and her heart stopped as she forced the hard truth from her lips.

"Cole, Bess is dead."

He paled and dropped his fork. Someone sucked in a breath but the rest remained quiet. She continued with his lesson on harsh reality.

"Bess is dead, but *you're* not."

Leaping to his feet, Cole's chair flew backwards with such force it skidded across the wooden floor and crashed into the wall.

"Jordan, I swear to God if you were a guy I'd punch your lights out!" His hands curled into fists at his sides.

She was thankful for the table between them because by the time she finished, Cole probably wouldn't care what gender she was.

Connor stood and grabbed his brother's arm. "Cole. Calm down. I think you should listen to what Jordan has to say."

"I will *not* stand here and listen to any more of this." He shook Connor off and twisted to raise a white-knuckled fist at his brother. "Back off."

"Yes, you will, Cole." She waited until his focus returned to her.

"Give it a rest, Malibu."

"No. I'm not done with you." She held his glare.

He cursed and stepped closer. "Just who the hell do you think you are, Jordan?" Both fists connected with the table, sending the plates and silverware into the air again before they set down with a jolt. "What makes you think you know what I need? You don't know the first damn thing about pain!"

Her heart froze mid-beat. *Don't know pain?* Blood rushed through her ears with magnum force as it swiftly drained to her toes. *My God, he was asking for it!* She sucked air into her lungs before exploding.

"Don't you *dare* tell me that I don't know *pain*!" Her voice was low and hoarse as her fingernails bit into her shaking palms. "I *know* what it's like to watch the person you love die right before your eyes. I *know* the horrible, helplessness of not being able to do anything about it!" Her stare never wavered from his face as she pointed to herself. "And I *know*...I *know* what it is like to be covered with his blood as I watch him take his last breath. So don't you *dare* stand there, Cole McCall, and tell me I don't know pain."

Silence filled the room as a single tear fell down her cheek. She thrust her finger at him and continued, "About time, my friend, you realize you don't have the corner on that market."

When he remained quiet, she went on with a little less anger.

"You also have to realize, like I did, that you need your family." She moved to stand behind her sister and placed her hands on Kerri's shoulders. "It was only with their help that I made it through those horrible times. Don't you see, Cole? Everyone here has felt a loss." She stepped back to her spot and when he looked blankly at her she continued with more compassion. "Your brother lost a sister-in-law and your parents lost a daughter-in-law, whom they all loved very much. And Cole," her voice wobbled as she placed her hands on the table and leaned toward him. "Somewhere along the way, they lost *you* too."

Her heart cracked open and bled as understanding dawned and emotions filled his eyes.

He turned to his family. "God, I'm sorry. I had no idea. I didn't realize…"

His mother and father rose at the same time and pulled him into an embrace.

"It's all right, son. It's okay," his dad reassured.

"We miss her too, Cole." His mother buried her face in his shoulder and they grieved together.

Connor joined the embrace, looking over their heads at her, gratitude lining his face as he mouthed a *thank you*.

She nodded and turned to slip out the door with her family, praying her legs had the strength to carry her from the room. Once in the hallway, she collapsed in the nearest chair and began to shake.

At least now, the McCall's could finally begin the long process of healing.

Chapter Seven

Screen door shut and balcony door opened, Jordan crawled restlessly into bed that night, hoping the breeze might help calm her quaking nerves. It was going to take a hell of a lot more than that. She'd learned long ago there was no remedy. In fact, given her history, she was pretty much guaranteed a crappy night.

She didn't want to go to sleep.

No. Dredging up the past like she had at dinner was a sure-fire trigger to her nightmare. *God, I wish Bullet was here.*

Maybe, by some miracle, it would pass tonight. With her arms folded across her stomach, she listened to the soothing sounds of the night, willing the tension from her body. Her last thought was a prayer for Cole to have an easier night than the one she knew lay ahead for her.

Sure enough, a little while later, Jordan screamed herself awake. Dammit!

Sitting up, she fought to breathe, tears rolling off her chin in a steady stream.

"Jordan? Are you all right?" Cole's voice hit her ears, along with the sound of the screen door sliding into place.

"Yes." She tossed her legs over the side of the bed, drew in another shaky breath, and stood. "Just give me a minute."

Suddenly claustrophobic, she charged passed him onto the balcony outside, the slight breeze cool on her heated flesh. *Was this ever going to stop?* Leaning on the rail, she closed her eyes, and breathed deep, until her trembling subsided.

Once a semblance of control returned, she twisted around and looked at Cole who stood just outside her room. Squinting through the semi-darkness of the night, she studied him.

With his hair falling loosely onto bare shoulders and wearing nothing but silk pajama bottoms, he appeared more human than he had the whole trip.

"I'm sorry, Cole. Did I wake you?"

"No, you didn't." He nodded. "I couldn't sleep so I was just sitting out here thinking, when I heard you scream."

She dropped her gaze as embarrassment stabbed her heart. "Sorry about that."

He made no sound and she hadn't realized he'd moved until his feet came into view in front of hers.

"Hey, don't be sorry." He bent at the knee, dipped down, and fingers under her chin, gently tipped her face to bring her gaze to his understanding brown eyes. "How long have you been having the nightmare?"

She swallowed. "Ever since Eric died. How about you? Are you plagued by them too?"

He hesitated, then nodded before he dropped his hand and moved to the railing. Her heart literally ached at the thought of him going through the same hell. She joined him, and together they looked over the moonlit land, blue bonnets appearing white under the glow.

"Have you told it to anyone?"

"No." He turned and walked to a hammock where he lay down.

Waiting to see if he'd offer on his own, she watched as he slung his hands behind his head and stared at the stars. She glanced up; seemed like a trillion lit the night sky. She missed their brilliance in California. Her gaze settled back to earth, and Cole.

Wanting to tread softly, she chose the chair closest to him and sat down, unsteady legs thankful for the respite. She lifted her hair and dropped it over the seat before leaning back and closing her eyes. This felt almost like old times.

And like old times, she had to try to get him to talk. Heart back in her throat, she willed a calm to her voice and took a chance. "Do you want to tell me?"

After a few minutes of silence, Jordan figured Cole wasn't ready to reveal that pain yet, which was okay. It had been worth a shot.

Her pulse jumped when his low voice filled the night.

"I'm sitting in my office, working at my desk. Then all of the sudden, I'm driving a semi and I can't see because there are computers and codes and CD's falling from the sky. I flip on the wipers to try to clear my window but it's too late. By the time I see the car coming I can't even swerve to avoid it."

He fell silent.

She slid off the chair and knelt down by the hammock, the balcony cool on her knees and shins. Her fingers curled around the hand he'd placed by his side and she squeezed in silent encouragement.

He drew in a deep, shaky breath, then exhaled. "After pulling over, I run to the car and Bess is there in the driver seat, barely conscious. She looks up at me and whispers, *"Why Cole? Why?"*...and then she dies."

Jordan closed her eyes and swallowed around a lump in her throat as tears burned hot and heavy down her face. God, how she'd give anything to make this better for him. The thought of all his pain and self-loathing was too much. She laid her head on his arm and squeezed his hand again.

"Cole, if I could take this pain from you, I swear I would," she choked out.

His breath hissed and his hand squeezed back. Knowing there was nothing else she could say to ease his pain, she remained silent, holding onto him while he came to terms with his emotions.

A few minutes later, he placed his free hand on her head and gently played with her hair. "What about you, Jordan? What's your nightmare?"

She swallowed again, and nodded into his arm. It was only fair to share and it might help him to know he wasn't the only one plagued with guilt.

"It's night, and Eric and I are at the corner store picking up a few things. All of a sudden, he stops and looks at me with a horrified expression. I glance down and the bread and peanut butter I'd been holding turn into a gun and bullets. Shots are fired." She closed her eyes against the full force of her dream.

The hand playing with her hair stilled before warm, gentle fingers grazed her shoulder, as if waiting for her to continue.

She drew in a breath, tightening the vise clamped around her chest. "The can he'd been holding rolls straight to me through his pooled blood and then I lower my spent weapon."

Releasing him, she twisted her back to the hammock and sat with her arms around her bent knees, hugging them tightly to her shaking body. When her tears dried and her shuddering subsided, Cole lightly touched her hair again. "What really happened? How did Eric die?"

She leaned her head back and looked up at the stars. "We finally both had the same weekend off. It was eleven o'clock at night and we decided to run to the corner store for a couple of things. I did have bread and peanut butter in my hands and Eric was at the cooler when the robbery started. God, I can still see his face through that glass door, worried about me because we were unarmed." Fresh tears wet her face. "This crack-head yelled to the cashier, then turned his gun on Eric and shot. Just like that, no warning. Glass shattered; Eric flew backward into the cooler, then slid to the floor. I ran to him, the cashier was screaming, the guy grabbed the money, looked at me as I cradled my husband in my arms, then he left. He just left. Why didn't he shoot me too, Cole? Why the hell didn't he shoot me, too?"

That very question had plagued her life ever since that night.

Pain and misery rushed through her body and propelled her to her feet. She picked up a chair and threw it. "I don't get it. He looked at me...he had the gun...why the hell didn't he shoot me too?" Strength suddenly left her legs and she crumbled to her knees.

Cole was by her side in an instant, grabbing her shoulders and bringing her to her feet before he crushed her into his solid chest. "No, Jordan. God...don't think like that. Don't ever think like that." His arms wrapped around her tight, surrounding her with warmth as she cried into his neck.

"But I don't understand. Why did he have to shoot Eric? I was closer, the cashier was closer, why Eric? He didn't have his gun. He never provoked him."

The strong arms holding her close squeezed tighter. "No one knows why those things happen, Jordan. There was nothing you could've done. You have no control over other people's actions. You have to give yourself a break."

She stilled. He was right. She knew this, but did he? Jumping at the chance to help him, she pushed her grief aside and pulled back to look into his compassionate face. "You're right, Cole. We have no control over other people's actions. That includes Bess' desire to see you that night and the truck driver's lack of sleep."

His jaw clenched and his grip on her tightened. Anger and self-hatred flashed in his eyes, and for a moment, she thought he'd revert back into his old tyrannical self.

Instead, he let her go gently and moved to the railing. "Connor talks too much."

"He's just worried about you." She put her arm around his back and leaned her head on his shoulder. "We all are. You need to give *yourself* that break you mentioned."

He glanced sideways at her. "I know and I've tried, believe me. It's just that…" His voice trailed off and he shook his head.

"Let me guess, your mind understands it's not your fault but your heart doesn't." She lifted her head to look into his eyes as she spoke her motto.

"Yes." He put his arm around her shoulders and expelled a breath.

"Man, McCall, we're a mess." She sighed, transferring her grip to his hip as they stood side-by-side, staring out over the land. Who would've thought two such level-headed, optimistic people could lose touch with themselves this way. Life was nuts. She dropped her head on his shoulder. "Thanks for talking to me and for listening."

"Anytime, Jordan, and thanks for doing the same."

Strong fingers curled around her upper arm as he twisted them around and walked them back to the oversized hammock. If her heart could smile it would have. The gratitude in his tone actually matched his words. Dark, arrogant, Cole seemed to have disappeared. *That's a good change*, she thought as they settled into the swaying cloth.

Lying next to him on her back, head pillowed comfortably in the crook of his arm, warmth replaced the deep chill that had invaded her body. Overlooking the tingling sensations where their flesh met, she concentrated on the night sky.

"Jordan?" His low voice interrupted her thoughts. "How did you do it?"

"Do what?"

"Get on with your life?"

Her gut twisted. "Oh, Cole, I won't kid you. It wasn't easy. It still isn't at times, as you can see. But I know it's what Eric would've wanted me to do...and what Bess would've wanted you to do, too. So I'll let you in on a secret," she said into the darkness. "I couldn't have done it without my family. That's why it was so important for me to convey that to you at dinner tonight. I'm just sorry I had to be so brutal."

"Don't be," he gave her a quick squeeze. "It opened my eyes—big time. Thanks."

"You're welcome," she managed to get out before her throat closed and tears rolled across her cheekbones. When her ability to talk returned, she decided to share one more piece of advice. "Over the next few weeks, the urge to retreat back into yourself to stave off the pain is going to be strong," she told him honestly. "Worrying about how that would affect my family and friends was the only thing that grounded me those first few weeks after my breakthrough."

She felt him nod.

"I was so wrapped up in myself and my grief, I failed to see theirs," he admitted quietly. "From now on, I'm going to do my best to remember that."

Her heart shed some of its heaviness. "Good, Cole. I'm glad." She smiled and gave him a slight squeeze.

He responded in kind before a large palm covered her hand, calluses scraping her knuckles as he held her fingers in place over his chest. And just like that, the relaxation she sought only an hour before finally made an appearance.

With their hearts and minds opened to each other again, Jordan felt their old connection and friendship re-establishing itself. Strong. Binding. Tight. Under her ear, his heart beat steady and strong and sure. For the first time in years, a satisfying contentment washed through clear to her soul and she closed her eyes and sighed.

Voices and snickering filtered into Jordan's sleepy mind. Slowly opening her eyes she found Kerri and Connor staring down at her with matching grins.

What are they doing in my bedroom? And who let the birds in? Birds?

Flying in the background, their chirping appearance tripped her pulse and snapped her fully awake. She glanced at Cole, aware of his warm flesh beneath her clinging body. *Clinging?* Sometime throughout the night she'd thrown her leg over both of his and her arm hugged a sleekly muscled chest. He stiffened, signaling he too was aware of their entanglement and audience.

She stretched up to look into his confused face.

Guess it's up to me.

Mischief made her wink, before she dipped her head to kiss his cheek. "Thanks for last night, Cole. You were wonderful. That was the best night I've had in years…if not ever."

His lips twitched into a smile. "Anytime."

She got to her feet and walked as nonchalantly as possible to her room, shutting the door, leaving Kerri and Connor to draw their own conclusions.

Sunday evening, Jordan was pleasantly surprised to see Cole standing next to Connor in the foyer. She and Kerri had made plans to meet the older McCall brother to hitch a ride with him to the Dalton's barbeque.

"Jordan, Kerri, you both sure are a picture." Connor removed his black Stetson and gave her peach dress and Kerri's lavender sundress the once over. "I hope you're up to dancing because your cards will be full tonight."

Cole smiled at them, black Stetson in his hand as well. "A breath of spring."

"Thank you, boys. You don't look too shabby yourself." She eyed the blue-jeaned cowboy-booted men.

Connor wore a red and white plaid shirt. *God bless Texas* this cowboy truly belonged on a billboard. "I hope you're part of my full dance card, Connor." She smiled as she crossed the foyer.

"You bet, sunshine." He slung the Stetson back on his head.

Turning her attention to Cole, Jordan's heart warmed. Wearing a gray-striped shirt with the sleeves rolled up, he appeared much more relaxed than the stiff man who just two days ago gave her and Ember a dirt bath. Extremely pleased he was putting forth an effort to socialize but not wanting to make a big deal out of it, she nodded. "I'm glad you're going, too, Cole."

"I thought I'd give it a try," he said quietly, then opened the front door and they all headed to the land rover.

By the time they arrived, the Dalton's barbeque was in full swing. Guests walked around the side of the sprawling, two-story, wooden ranch with wrap-around porch, complete with swing, into the back where picnic tables dotted the yard along with strung up lights.

Shadow Rock Ranch, though not quite as large as Wild Creek,

boasted fourteen hundred impressive acres but wasn't home to one single calf. The operation was primarily to train and sell stock horses, although Kevin had told her they also fostered rescued and abused horses. A cause near and dear to her and a few friends out west.

Familiar people and some not so familiar greeted them warmly, lingering on Cole. After the initial entrance, his awkwardness subsided, and shoulders lost their stiffness. For the second time that night, his efforts encouraged her to believe he was on the right path.

"Kerri, Jordan, so great to see you again and you too, Cole," was the repeated greeting they received for five minutes straight.

"Once again, I'm chopped liver," Connor stated, hat in his hand. The dejected look a little too playful to be taken serious.

"Not you, Connor. You're more like a thick steak." Jordan joked, looping arms as they headed for the food line.

With their plates full of barbequed delights, they made their way to a waving Jen sitting with a handsome light-haired cowboy and cute little boy. Their black-haired, blue-eyed, friend only got prettier. Two months younger than Kerri, Jen had often hung out with them, and the three girls had had lot of fun shadowing the guys.

"It's great to see you all again." Jen got up from the table to give them each a tight hug, then turned to the good-looking stocky man who stood up with her. "This is my husband, Brock, he's the ranch manager here, and this is our son, Cory." She ruffled the high-chaired toddler's fair head. "Brock, this is Kerri and Jordan. They used to be our neighbors. And you know Connor and Cole."

"It's nice to meet you both." Brock shook their hands, then greeted the McCall's like old friends before everyone settled at the table while Kerri and Jordan gushed over Cory.

Kevin appeared from the crowd in faded jeans, blue and white checkered shirt, black Stetson, mirrored aviator sunglasses and that perpetual mischievous grin tugging his lips until his lone dimple showed. Heads turned of the female persuasion as he strolled toward them carrying two pitchers of beer.

"I thought I spotted you all walking in." Their gorgeous host set the beer down, then laid a hand on Cole's shoulder. "Glad to see you could make it, buddy."

Cole nodded.

"You spotted the hot Masters sisters, that's who you spotted," Connor teased, helping their friend pour out the beer.

"Well, who can blame me?" Kevin winked, slipping onto the bench between her and Kerri, making them move a little so he could fit.

Connor laughed and she noted a smile from Cole. Sandwiched

between him and Kevin, she received several envious glances from female guests. *Yeah…today, it's good to be me.*

"Jordan," Jen said, when the table quieted down. "I'm sorry about your husband. I wish I could've met him. He must've been something to have captured your heart." Her friend's hand snaked out to deftly grab the sippy cup her son aimed at the ground.

"Thanks, Jen," she replied, her heart giving a slight tug. "Eric was something else and I know he would've liked you all too."

"How did you meet? If you don't mind me asking." Kevin surprised her with the question.

"No. I don't mind." She turned to him. "Eric was giving a lecture on Criminal Justice at the college I attended. Let's just say that by the time the class was over, he caught me." She smiled at the memory, more and more thankful everyday for the good ones.

Jen eyed her from across the table. "How long ago did he die?"

"It was two years last month."

"Jeez." Jen blinked. "That's around the time Bess died, isn't it Cole?"

He cleared his throat and nodded. "Yes, I guess it was."

"Did you know Kerri and Jordan own and operate a restaurant now?" Connor asked with a grin.

Jordan could've kissed the cowboy's cheek for deftly changing the subject.

"You two own a restaurant?" Brock's eyes held interest as he handed a fidgeting Cody an apple slice.

"Yes and it's doing fairly well, I might add," Kerri spoke up between bites.

True. They'd had a pretty good year so far. Clientele had increased. Profits were up. Between them and their staff, they were doing something right. Plus, her sister was a genius.

"That's because of your wonderful cooking," Jordan boasted. "As you will all get a chance to taste for yourself at the anniversary party next weekend."

Brock stood up to remove his fussy son from the highchair. "I'm looking forward to it. Now, if you'll excuse me, somebody needs to be changed."

"Thanks, hun," Jen said, touching her husband's arm.

He smiled down, adoration clearly visible in his green gaze. "Enjoy your visit." A quick kiss to Jen's cheek and he was gone, squirming toddler in his big hands. Truly a sweet sight.

The happy couple reminded Jordan of Megan and her husband Shawn and their soon-to-be little one. Had Eric been alive, she might've been pregnant right now. A small pang of envy rippled deep. She caught Cole looking at her, a measure of encouragement in his gaze. Clever man no doubt read her thoughts. Expression gentle, smile reassuring, *yep, he did*. It sure was nice to see his sweet side again. And it was time to take her own advice and move on. She smiled back, then returned her concentration to her meal.

"Kerri, I can remember way back how you were always helping Emma cook and bake while Jordan and I helped eat," Jen said with a laugh. "Of course, we had to before these two McCalls or my brother or cousin came by, then there would've been nothing left."

"You're right." Jordan laughed too while the whole table smiled. "Speaking of cousins, how is Kade?"

"Good. We *web-called* last night." Jen smiled, although, worry clouded her gaze.

"I can't believe he's still in the Guard," Kerri remarked.

Jen nodded. "Going on fourteen years, now."

Kade Dalton had joined the National Guard while he was senior in high school. Jordan vaguely remembered him saying something about the extra income helping around the ranch. Jen's mom had raised him when his own mother had run off with a rodeo clown two years after his dad had died in the first Gulf War. Kade had already been living on the ranch, his mother running off only made it permanent. Something the eleven year old boy had needed. Stability. All things she'd grown up to know as fact since she'd barely been five and too young to actually remember the events as they'd happened.

Jordan reached across the table to squeeze Jen's hand. "He'll be okay. He's smart."

Kerri added her hand. "And capable."

"I know." Jen nodded and managed a smile. "He was promoted to Captain after his last tour."

"Don't forget tenacious," Connor added, grin tugging his mouth.

Yes, Jordan could certainly see that description fitting the young cowboy she remembered. And despite the edge that had shadowed him, he was also the most helpful person she'd ever met.

Kevin chuckled. "True. My cuz could stare down the most ornery stallion."

"And win," Cole stated firmly, lifting his beer. "To Kade."

Everyone tipped their drink to their missing buddy and Jordan decided to lighten the mood.

"Well, now I know why I haven't seen him kicking Connor's butt in basketball at Wild Creek."

"Hey!" Connor sat up straight and frowned, half-eaten rib in his hand. "I kick ass, too."

"No, buddy, you *grab* ass," Kevin said, causing the table to laugh. "My cousin is the one out of all four of us who oozes athletic ability."

"True, although, I can out-ride him." Connor nodded, before bringing his cup to his lips.

Jordan knew from her parents what he said to be true. Connor held several records at the local rodeo.

"You'd better give him that one, Kevin or he'll whine like a baby all night." Cole smirked at his brother's frowning form.

"Bullshit, I do not whine. I do not," Connor insisted and they all broke out laughing.

As the taller McCall had predicted, the dance requests started to come in for both her and Kerri, putting an end to their conversation and meal.

Several dances with Kevin, a couple with Connor and a few with some other guests later, Jordan joined Cole in the food line for a pick-me-up, happy to find herself alone with him as they headed to an empty table. He poured them both a cold beer. After taking a much needed sip, she studied him.

"How are you doing, Cole? Do you want to leave?"

"No. I'm having a good time." He blinked, sounding surprised by his answer. "I've been talking with some of my co-workers and I even made plans with a few of them to go fishing next month," he said, smiling into his beer.

A second later, his gaze lifted and he sent her a sincere look across the table. *Damn her pulse for leaping.* She really needed to do something about that. Cole was her dear friend. Nothing more. She'd do well to remember that.

"Thanks for asking, Jordan."

Damn her pulse for racing.

Two short days since his breakthrough and she already noticed a few small changes in him. The best one was in his eyes. Her heart swelled just thinking about the difference. Incredibly, they no longer reflected his hard name and, although they still held sadness, there were smidges of hope and amusement flickering through the warm, brown depths.

Those were the eyes that were dangerous to her heart. They were the ones that had haunted her since she'd moved to California, coming between other boys, then eventually men. Except for Eric. She inhaled and found a sense of calm.

Every bit of that was in her past.

Moving on…

Falling into a companionable silence, they ate their barbeque and watched the dancers. Connor and Kerri two-stepped past their table. They looked good together. No, they actually looked great together. Jordan was struck by how naturally they moved, not to mention the flush in her sister's face and sparkle in Connor's eyes.

"Your brother and my sister sure stand out among the crowd."

"That they do," Cole agreed with a smile and a nod.

The next hour and a half fulfilled her imaginary dance card. Sure were a lot of eager cowboys. Jordan figured she'd pretty much danced with them all, except Cole. But he wasn't dancing and she hadn't asked. It was enough that he came. She certainly hadn't expected him to jump into normal mode. Besides, the last thing she wanted, okay, maybe *wanted* wasn't exactly the right word, the last thing she *needed* were his hands on her. She wasn't stupid. This version of Cole was a danger to her healing heart.

As the party began to break up, Jordan stood next to Cole, Kerri, and Connor, and said goodbye to their hosts.

Kevin drew close and grabbed both her hands. "Have dinner with me this week, Jordan."

He gazed down at her, sunglasses residing in his pocket now that the sun had gone down, a hopeful, yet mischievous glint in his blue eyes.

Caught off guard, she blinked. Kevin was a fun friend, an extremely handsome, fun friend and she liked him a lot, but not that way and didn't want to give him false hope. About to decline, Cole stepped toward them.

"Did you forget about the conference in Dallas this week, Kevin?"

The blue-eyed cowboy frowned and released her hands to turn to his boss. "I thought Bob's team was going?"

"They are but I want you to go to keep an eye on things and make sure we're well-represented," Cole explained, a slight tilt to his head.

Jordan couldn't help but wonder if Kevin's dinner invitation had been issued to get a rise out of Cole. She certainly wouldn't put it past the bugger.

"If you think that's best, *Bossman*." Kevin shrugged, then recaptured one of her hands and brought it to his lips. "Until I get back then."

Yanked out of Kevin's grasp by a grumbling Cole, she had no time to respond as he quickly ushered her to the car. Although dying to discover what prompted his strange behavior, she curbed her curiosity since his actions had ultimately helped her get off the hook.

If Jordan didn't know better she'd swear Cole was jealous. She smiled. *How absurd*. Her heart rocked into her ribs. Cole…jealous. That would be a first.

Saturday. The day of the anniversary party had finally arrived. Jordan stood in the driveway, computer tablet in hand, directing the incoming workers to their various locations. What hadn't been done yesterday was being finished now.

Where had the week gone, she wondered, steering the flower deliverers to the florist busy inside.

Free of tension, the days had flown by and the mood in the house had reflected the change. The atmosphere no longer held that walking-on-egg-shell feel. Almost cheerful, the ranch appeared brighter—as if someone had upped the wattage on the light bulbs. And even though Cole came home late from work a few nights, she was happy to note *Mr. Gloom and Doom* had been deleted.

Couldn't happen to a nicer guy.

Following the band's set up crew inside, she allowed herself a moment of peace and slipped into the deserted dining room unnoticed. She placed her tablet on the table and strolled to the window to look out.

Alive with pre-party activity, the backyard slowly transformed from ranch to festival. Tables received their white linens and yellow rose centerpieces, lights strung overhead would give the night a romantic air, the band was setting up in the far corner and in another, a group of men constructed the champagne fountain. She glanced at her watch. Everything was on schedule.

Someone placed a basket of Mrs. McCall's favorite flowers near the make-shift stage. Staring at the white lilies, Jordan's mind turned to the service that morning.

Mr. and Mrs. McCall had re-affirmed their vows in a beautiful but simple ceremony. Surrounded by family and a few select friends, the occasion was made all the more special by the attendance of Cole.

Sitting next to him, Jordan had been extremely proud of his effort. Having reservations about the service herself, she was surprised when she looked back on it now. Eric, and their wedding, had flashed through her head but her stomach hadn't hollowed out with the usual intense pain.

Peace had settled over her heart and she'd viewed the memories as a blessing. A smile tugged her lips. Happiness for the McCall's and concern for their youngest son had prevailed. When Cole's parents had stood at the altar, his hand had tightened into a fist on his lap. Recognizing the signs of his inner battle, she grabbed his hand, laced their fingers together, and kept the contact, until the end of the service.

The snap of spreading tablecloths outside broke through her

thoughts. Jordan pulled her mind back to the present and the many tasks needing attention before the reception party that afternoon. With a lighter heart, she grabbed her tablet off the table and hurried from the room.

Time to check on the food. Detouring to the kitchen to see if they needed anything, she stopped and inhaled slow and deep.

"Mmm…it smells incredible in here, ladies." The heavenly aroma drew her to where Emma stood sprinkling herbs and parmesan cheese on freshly baked breadsticks.

"I was wondering when that nose of yours would make an appearance." Emma chuckled, shoving a breadstick at her. "Here take this, *before* you grab."

"Don't mind if I do. Thanks." Jordan chuckled and glanced around at the various stages of cooking and baking overtaking the kitchen from wall to wall. She sidestepped a server as she approached Kerri.

Her sister spooned some sort of thick, white sauce onto baked chicken. "What do you need?"

"Nothing. I came in to see if you needed anything."

Her stomach growled and Kerri stopped spooning to raise a brow at Jordan's midsection.

"You should feed that thing before it attacks."

She saluted. "Yes, ma'am." Then shoved the breadstick in her mouth.

Smiling, Kerri shook her head and returned to her poultry dish.

Exiting the kitchen, Jordan said a silent goodbye to the teasing aromas and headed for the back of the house. The delicious bread melted in her mouth as she stepped outside and gazed at the transformation that had already taken place.

Pale yellow napkins and place settings decorated the table. The fountain was finished. Someone was putting the yellow rose petals she'd ordered in the pool and, later that night, floating candles would join them.

One by one, the set up crews started to leave. She stood back to survey their work… Pride covered her arms in the form of goosebumps. This was exactly what she'd promised her hosts. *Ladies and gentlemen, I give you…the McCall Celebration.*

"Well done, Jordan." Mr. McCall's voiced boomed from behind.

Twisting around, she smiled at the happy couple crossing the patio. "I'm glad you're pleased."

"It's absolutely incredible." Mrs. McCall put her hands to her mouth as she slowly turned around. Diamonds shimmered on her wrist.

"Wow. What a beautiful bracelet," she remarked.

Her host's eyes sparkled brighter than the gems. "Thank you. Alex just gave it to me for our anniversary."

He hugged his wife. "There's a diamond for every year we've been married."

"Why, Mr. McCall." Jordan tipped her head and grinned. "What a romantic you are."

Clearing his throat, he neither admitted nor denied but instead, changed the subject by nodding towards the band. "I understand you got together with them this week and practiced the songs for tonight."

"Yes. They were very nice." She waved at them and smiled. "They even invited me to sing a few more throughout the evening."

"Wonderful. How about Cole? Has he said anything to you about that duet?" Mr. McCall asked quietly.

"No, I'm sorry. He hasn't said a word." She touched his sleeve. "I think it might be too soon to expect him to sing."

"Yes. I think you're right. We're just happy to have him on the mend and can't thank you enough, Jordan." He pulled her into a hug and soon Mrs. McCall wrapped her arms around Jordan's waist.

"God bless you, Jordan. You've given us our Cole back."

Swallowing past a hot throat, she squeezed the McCalls, then drew away. "You're welcome. I had to do something. That stranger was asking for my fist."

Mr. McCall chuckled. "I could tell you had trouble holding back several times."

"You have no idea how close I came." She shuddered in an attempt to dispel those memories. *Good riddance, Mr. Personality*. Refusing to waste one more iota of energy on the past, Jordan raised her tablet and asked, "Do you need anything else?"

"No, my dear. You've done so much for us already." Mrs. McCall touched her hand and smiled.

"You've always been wonderful to Kerri and me. This has been my pleasure." She patted the woman's hand and, with the start of the party drawing nearer and everything on her list completed, Jordan excused herself to go upstairs to change.

Halfway through the party that night, Jordan leaned against the corner of the house to take a breather.

"Jordan, you look absolutely beautiful tonight."

A short lived breather.

Kevin appeared out of nowhere, dimples blaring. "How about a dance?"

All evening, his waylaid attempts to get to her had kept her amused. "Thank you. I'd love to." She took his hand and followed him to the patio dance floor.

No matter how hard he'd tried, someone had always cut him off. If not Cole, it was a cute brunette or blonde intercepting his course. Not that she lacked partners. Between dancing, making sure everything went smoothly and a bit of socializing, she was ready for bed. Too bad there were a good two hours of party left.

Kevin nodded toward Cole doing the two-step with a pretty little redhead across the floor from them.

"Well, would you look at that. You're a miracle worker, Jordan."

Her feet faltered. "Sorry." She picked up the rhythm and they continued the dance, but for some reason, the shimmering lights and flickering candles in the pool lost some of their luster.

What was wrong with her? She swallowed and forced her gaze to the other couple. This was a big step for Cole and she should be proud of him. She *was* proud of him.

He still had a long road of healing ahead, but she was amazed at the difference in him since last week. He glanced over at her and smiled. Her heart expanded, killing her unrealistic jealousy. He deserved to have fun and so did she. They broke no laws or rules and weren't committing a lifetime to their dance partners, simply enjoying the moment.

Exhaling, she vowed to enjoy the evening for what it was—entertainment with family and friends.

"What's the smile for?" Kevin looked down at her, eyes twinkling as he led her smoothly around the floor.

She grinned up at him. "Because I'm having a good time."

"Good. So am I."

The tune got livelier. So did Kevin.

The cute prankster began to spin her, taking advantage of every upbeat the song offered, until her right blurred into her left and she didn't know east from west anymore. By the time the song ended, her head ached to the beat of the band. Literally.

"How about we switch."

Cole's face suddenly materialized in front of her and she eagerly focused on his swaying features. Unsure what happened to Kevin and the redhead, Jordan put the pair out of her mind, grateful for Cole's reassuring strength when his warm arms wrapped around her back and he led her in a slow dance.

"Thanks," she said, party coming back into focus. "And please, whatever you do, don't let go of me right now. I'm so dizzy I think I'd fall down and throw up and not necessarily in that order."

"Don't worry, I've got you." He tightened his grip, his heat and strength a steady support. "I was wondering how much more of that you were going to take."

His deep laugh rumbled through her. She shivered and pulled back to meet his gaze.

Big mistake.

Chapter Eight

Jordan's legs buckled. Cole quickly tightened his hold, but wasn't prepared for the swift, flood of awareness rushing through him as their bodies touched. And her eyes, damn, those beautiful, brown eyes, full of warmth and fire knock his heart clean into his ribs.

Jesus, he was in trouble.

All week. All damn week he'd been fighting this attraction, doing his best to resist. He knew it was too soon. She wasn't ready. Hell, he wasn't ready, especially for something so strong it knocked the sense right of him. Wiped out his control. Kept him off kilter.

But tonight? *Ah hell*, tonight Jordan mesmerized, tempted…ripped the hell out of his gut and sent his dwindling control out to pasture. Her baby blue, backless dress…*backless, Jesus*…it looked soft, almost dreamy with no belt or discernable indenture at the waist, hinting at her incredible body with every damn step. The slight glimpse of her hip, swell of her breast when she moved was slowly driving him insane. Did she wear a bra? How the hell could she with no back? The thought of her unhindered made him sweat. He couldn't take it. He was done, to the point where he had to touch her, couldn't keep his distance any longer, hence his rescue from Kevin.

And, God…it was worth it.

She felt like heaven brushing against him, all soft and warm, smelling of sunshine and fresh citrus. Placing a hand on his chest, she opened her mouth to reply but gasped instead. His heart jumped under her palm. *Jumped*. Hell yeah it jumped, because he remembered that mouth and how responsive and hot and delicious it had been when they'd kissed a little over a week ago. Grin slowly leaving her face, she stared up at him through arousal and need darkened-eyes. And hot damn, *yes*, he was ready to throw away all his reasons for keeping his distance and leap on board except…there was one more emotion blatant in those beautiful eyes. Terror.

God help him, he could never live with himself for putting that look there.

This is crazy.

She'd spent most of her adolescence chasing after him and he'd let her because, well he was just as smitten. Now, *hell*, he could tell this awareness plumb terrified her. She wasn't ready.

He blinked and shook his head.

Neither was he, his mind reasoned again.

This…whatever it was between them was too damn powerful, engrossing. Not something he wanted in his life. Much too dangerous for his not-yet healed heart. *Christ*, he had to do something.

Releasing her with a jerk, he quickly grabbed her arm and led them to the fountain of bubbly. "We need a drink," he said, roughly.

Relief swam in her eyes. She filled her glass and drank the whole flute. "I guess that'll teach me to spin too much."

"Yeah, I guess." He laughed, deciding to take the out she'd given.

A moment later, the band called her up to the stage, much to their mutual relief. Because Cole knew, and he knew *she* knew, if they'd stayed near each other too long, all bets and best intentions were off.

Grateful for the rescue from her rescuer, Jordan performed her songs for the McCall's and happily hung around to sing a couple requests.

Every so often, Cole's broad frame appeared out on the dance floor with a new partner. It was good to see him dancing. Really…it was. Explaining away the tightness in her chest as a reaction to singing nonstop for thirty minutes, Jordan *told* herself she was happy things return back to normal.

That man was more dangerous to her equilibrium than Kevin's dancing.

With her set completed, she thanked everyone for their kind words. And before she could blink, Connor's large hands wrapped around her waist and he whisked her off the stage. Lifting her like she was a feather instead of a solid one-hundred-thirty-three pounds.

"You were great, Jordan." He winked down at her, dimples increasing in depth as they began to slow dance. Dressed in new jeans, hugging low on his lean hips, red snap-front western shirt and his black Stetson, the man was very easy on the eyes. And smooth. She couldn't forget smooth. They practically glided across the floor.

"Thanks. It's a fun hobby." Her gaze traveled over the backyard, noting the glow of lights and candles softening the atmosphere since the setting sun had disappeared an hour ago. From a corner table, a bevy of frowning beauties pointed to her and she held back a laugh. "Connor, don't look now, but your fan club isn't too happy with me at the moment."

His gaze shot to the corner and he smirked. "Don't worry about them, darling'. There's plenty of me to go around. And, I'm not the only McCall with a fan club. Cole's got them lining up, too."

He pointed to several smiling ladies standing on the side of the dance floor, ogling her former crush.

"I must say you're surprising me, though."

She frowned and looked up at him. "Me? Why?"

"The Jordan I knew would've sent in a stampede of horses to rid the party of that particular line."

His chuckle spurred her laugh.

"True. I guess I've outgrown those tendencies."

"That's too bad." He sobered. "I think you're perfect for Cole. Was a time you used to think that too."

Her heart squeezed. Tight. "I know. I'm just happy to see him interacting with people in a socialized setting." A smile, bursting with whimsy, tugged at her lips. "He's had a good start this week."

"Yes. Thanks to your eye-opening words, he's on the road to heal. But just imagine how much easier his journey would be if you stuck around to help him along." Connor stared down at her, gaze hopeful, squeezing her hand as they danced. "I know you still feel something for him, Jordan."

Her back stiffened. She wanted off this dangerous subject. Now. "Connor, I do still feel a connection to your brother. But I don't want to." The truth in her words strengthened her voice. "We had our chance. I was obsessed with him once, I don't plan on heading down that restrictive road again. Besides, he's not over his wife and until he is, he won't move forward. Any relationships he has won't last. I'd be a fool to try and start something now, even if I was ready, which I'm not."

"You could be if you stayed in Texas." His brows rose, rounding his puppy-dog eyes.

Oh…he was a dangerous one, this one.

"Nope."

"You'd be around for the fair…"

Yes, dangerous indeed. Bugger knew a young Jordan had lived for the county's annual fair in late May. Livestock, auctions, rodeo, games, rides, food…a venue to spend time with Cole. Fond adolescent memories flooded her mind of walking hand-in-hand, from booth to booth, riding rides, sharing funnel cake. Her insides warmed. Oh, yeah, the *Marlboro* man did not play fair.

"No. Now, shut up and dance." She chuckled and slapped his chest.

"Yes, ma'am."

Lop-sided grin in place, he led her around the floor, keeping time with the beat like a pro. Another reason for a fan club, Jordan thought wryly as she glanced at the crowd of beauties all wearing an identical look of envy.

Happy to have dropped the subject of his brother, she had just started to relax and enjoy the dance when they literally—and knowing Connor—purposefully, bumped into Cole.

"Hey, bro," the cowboy said to his startled sibling, both dimples making an appearance.

Bastard.

If her shoes didn't happen to be her favorite pair, she'd plant her heel in the middle of his leather boot, and cheerfully provide him with a well-deserved foot ornament.

"What'd you say we switch partners?"

Without hesitating, Connor grabbed the smiling brunette from Cole and pushed Jordan into his brother's arms

Son-of-a…

She glared at Connor's back, her mind calling him several unladylike names. "Sorry, Cole. It's okay if you want to sit this one out."

"Now, why would I want to do that?" Cole pulled her close. He smelled of woodsy aftershave and…alcohol.

She frowned. Just how many had he had?

His eyes were still alert. He wasn't completely drunk, yet.

"I like holding you best of all."

Warm hands caressed her bare back and she clenched her teeth against her body's need to respond. Oh, her good parts were good and happy now. Very happy. So damn happy she vibrated. And, damn, he was just so irresistible.

"Is that right?" She couldn't help but smile at him.

Stinking McCalls.

"Yes, you've been driving me crazy all night." He crushed her closer, hips to hips, as he nuzzled her neck.

Heaven help her.

Desire spiked in an almost painful shower of need. He felt good. It'd be so easy to give in and explore the man Cole had grown to be—she re-clenched her jaw and immediately derailed that dangerous train of thought. This was wrong. That was the beer talking. He didn't know what he was doing. Hell, *she* didn't know what she was doing.

Note to self; strangle Conner McCall.

Staying put for fear if she moved back Cole would try to kiss her, Jordan swallowed and closed her eyes.

I will not give into this.

He swayed seductively to the music, holding her tight so they moved as one, placing open-mouthed kisses over her neck and collarbone. *Holy hell*. Her temperature hit unsafe.

She liked safe. *Safe was good. Unsafe bad. Cole unsafe. Great*. He'd reduced her to thinking in caveman.

Damn Texan was depleting her brain cells faster than drugs. And she needed her brain because her heart was vulnerable and her body was way out of control. So were his hands. They glided over the space left uncovered by her backless dress, sending shivers down her spine.

She swallowed her moan, but couldn't prevent the tremor. *This has to stop.*

"I want you, Jordan."

He whispered so low, she'd barely heard the admission. Well, her body heard it and God help her, now she was damp.

"Come to my room tonight." Warm breath fanned her ear and neck and stopped her heart.

How was she supposed to be their voice of reason when she longed to be mute?

She opened her eyes and the first thing she saw were both sets of parents watching them with identical grins on their faces. Great, more matchmakers. Didn't they get it? He wasn't ready. And she didn't want to be used.

The song stopped. Alleluia…praise be.

Inhaling, she lifted her head and pushed out of his arms. "Thanks for the dance, Cole, but I think we should leave it at that for now."

Disappointment darkened his desire-laden eyes. "I'm not sure I can." He grabbed her hand and didn't let go until they were alone on the side of the house. "What's wrong, Jordan? I know I'm feeling something from you. You can't deny it."

"I don't deny it, Cole. I've always been attracted to you, you know that. If you hadn't stopped that kiss the other night…" her voice trailed off. She leaned against the house and sighed.

Hand on the house near her head, he leaned in and touched her cheek, his warmth zeroing in on her heart. "Then what's the problem?"

She turned her face into his hand and brushed his palm with her lips before looking into his eyes. "Cole, it's just too soon. It would only end up in disaster. Don't you see? I don't want to be a substitute for Bess and you don't deserve to be one for Eric." She reached up and gently cupped the hand he still held to her face. "That's exactly what would happen if we took this any further tonight."

Stiffening, he jerked from her grasp and turned away. Her throat tightened and burned. She stepped toward him then halted. What could she say? Nothing came to mind that would ease the stiffness from the man who stood staring at the shadows of the night, hands shoved deep in his pockets as if the world's weight rested on his shoulders.

Words of wisdom wouldn't help. What he needed was a friend. A truthful friend.

Unable to bear the silence anymore, she walked to him and touched his back. "I'm sorry, Cole. I didn't mean to lead you on in any way. As great as you make me feel, I know I'm not ready for what you're offering. I don't think you really are either." When he sighed, Jordan felt she was actually getting through to him. "You need to go slowly, Cole. Date a few times, you know, sort of wet your feet a little?"

He turned to her, a crooked grin on his lips. "Wet my feet, huh?"

"Yeah. You know what I mean."

He caressed her cheek again. "You're something else, Jordan Masters."

She returned his grin. "I've been telling you that for years now, Cole McCall."

He dropped his hand to hers and entwined their fingers. The unexpected gesture increased her pulse. *He's just being friendly. All you want is friendly.* Body ordered to play neutral, she was proud of her control, until he lifted her captured fingers to his mouth.

"And so you have. Thanks, Jordan."

She cleared her throat and fought the warmth of his gaze. "F-for what?"

"Your friendship. Your strength." He lowered their hands and squeezed. "Now, what do you say we go back and sing that song for my parents?"

Her eyes narrowed. "Are you sure, Cole?"

"Yes, I'm sure. Thanks to you, I know I can do this. I *want* to do this." His tone held no strain or forced gaiety. He genuinely wanted to do this for his parents.

Admiration swelled her heart. "Okay." She grinned. "Let's go sing."

Hand in hand, they strolled back to the party, discussing his parents' chosen song and agreed on which key would suit their voices. When the band consented, they took the stage.

"Good evening everyone. My parents have asked the two of us to sing a special song for them," Cole told the euphoric crowd. "Jordan and I would like to do that now."

He started the song and the rich timber of his voice—much deeper than when they were younger—sent chills over her entire body. Carefree memories of their childhood came flooding back and at that moment, Jordan was happy to be alive... really happy to be alive for the first time in years.

Later that night, after she returned to her room and got ready for bed, Jordan slipped under the cool covers and willed her frayed nerves and tired bones to give into the slumber that beckoned. No such luck.

One minute her body ached with need for Cole and the sensations his touch induced, the next guilt seized her heart and stomach, squeezing until she could barely breathe. Her pounding head was her punishment.

She knew she wasn't really betraying Eric by having thoughts and feelings for another man, but couldn't stop the guilt, just the same. It'd been over two years. He'd want her to be happy. She just wasn't ready to be. Not with Cole, anyway. That man made her feel way too deep, too strong, too dangerous.

Trying not to think about that part, she rubbed her temples and closed her eyes. Thank goodness she was leaving tomorrow. With all her mixed up emotions and confused heart, it was time to get out of *vulnerable city*. Maybe somewhere down the line she'd come back for a visit or he'd take a trip out to the coast. But for now, they definitely needed to part ways.

Even though they were both single again and fate had thrown them together *again*, the timing for her and Cole, as always, stunk.

Jordan was starting to think maybe Fate had never really been on her side.

The next morning, Nate, his wife and the McCalls gathered in the dining room to make more plans. Round one had gone well. Now, they needed to discus, round two.

"Are they coming yet?" Leeann asked from behind.

Nate peeked out the dining room to find the hall empty. "No." He shut the door, sealing the four of them in before he turned around. "They must still be packing."

Alex shook his head and walked toward him from across the room. "Well, my friend, since my two thickheaded sons are actually letting your daughters head back to the coast, I think we need to go to plan B."

"I agree." Nate slapped Alex's upper arm. "I'll put the bid in this morning."

"At least Jordan got Cole to open up. Did you see him last night?" Leeann smiled.

Face brighter than it had been since he and his wife had arrived a few weeks ago, his friend's wife walked with a lighter step as well. He understood her euphoria. Amazing how your children's moods affected your own. Nate's heart warmed. Tricking his oldest daughter into this visit had been the best idea he'd ever had.

His wife touched Leeann's hand. "And don't forget that last dance they shared."

About to comment on how great the couple had looked together, he swallowed his words when the door opened up and their children walked in, bringing their conversation to an end.

Chapter Nine

Seven days had gone by since she and Kerri had returned to California…alone. Now, gathered at her sister's house for a welcome home dinner for their parents, the four of them, plus Shawn and Megan, were seated at the cherry table set elegantly with white linens, heirloom china, and crystal.

"We're moving back to Texas."

Jordan's heart hit the floor and Kerri's fork clatter onto her plate as they stared at their smiling parents.

"What?"

"You're moving to Texas?"

More than once this past week, a nagging prickle had nudged Jordan's mind. Why hadn't her parents returned with them? She hadn't bought off on their 'we want to visit longer' excuse.

She sat back in her seat, gaze bouncing from her silent friends, shocked sister, to her bomb-dropping parents. "I knew you stayed in Texas for another reason."

A flash of worry crossed her father's face as he busied himself with moving his fork to the other side of his knife. Jordan's nagging prickle returned.

His fidgeting stopped and he lifted his gaze. "We never could pull one over on you, sweetheart."

She regarded him closely. Genuine warmth shone from his eyes. All traces of worry, gone. *Maybe I imagined it.*

Spine easing away from the chair, she relaxed. "True. And don't you forget it."

"Wait a minute." Kerri lifted her hand and waved. "Hello? Freaking out daughter here. Why are you moving? When? You just got back today."

"I know." Dad nodded. "We stayed that extra week to put a bid on our old homestead. The place just went back on the market." He smiled and squeezed their mother's hand. "Our bid was accepted and the closing is in a few weeks."

"You're leaving in a few weeks?" Kerri's tone shot up two octaves.

"What about your job, Dad?" Jordan frowned.

Quite the unusual behavior for her 'plotter' father, she suspected his motives. He had a flowchart for everything. Heck, he had flowcharts for creating flowcharts. No way could this be an impulsive buy. This was related to a plan. Question was…plan for what?

Warm fingers gently touched her arm. She turned to her left and met her mother's smiling gaze. "He's semi-retiring."

Oh…that plan. Never heard of it.

"What?" Her sister voice rose along with her brow. "First you're moving back to Texas—in our old house no less—and now you're retiring?" Kerri reached past her coffee to grab her wine. "Do you have any more surprises in store for us or will you leave that to fate?"

Their parents exchanged a look and chuckled. "No, no more surprises or news. That's it."

"Thank goodness." Kerri sighed.

Jordan agreed. Wholeheartedly. The Texas trip had been quite trying, even for her. Although, she had to admit, she felt better, stronger, more at peace than she had in a very long time. She smiled. Helping Cole had somehow helped her, too.

A few other things stood out about the trip. Like Kerri was even more quiet than usual. Instinct told her it had to have something to do with Connor but Jordan had no idea what and her sister wasn't talking. Then there were her parents. Seeing them in that environment, surrounded by old friends and distant relatives, Jordan knew Texas was where they belonged.

She held up her wine. "Well, as long as you're happy, I guess congratulations are in order."

A round of cheers and clinking cemented the toast.

"Nate, does your house need a lot of work?" Shawn asked while they dug into their dessert.

"Well, it needs updating. The previous owners didn't do anything since we sold it to them."

Kerri gasped. "You mean my bedroom still has purple walls with the bright yellow flowers I painted when I was ten?" Hand paused in midair, a strawberry pitched precariously on her sister's fork.

"Yes, and Jordan's still has the bright orange stripes she experimented with before we left." Her mother bit her twitching lower lip.

Jordan grimaced at the memory. "Oh mom, that *has to be* one of the first rooms you do over."

Her dad sat back with a *here's-the-plan* gleam in his eyes.

"Actually, when your mother and I walked through the house, we decided every room needed updating, starting with the kitchen."

Jordan stared at her parents. "All of them? Are you going to move in before or after you tackle the remolding?"

"After it's finished," her mother replied. "Alex and Leeann said we could stay with them while the renovations are going on. We already have a storage facility lined up for our things."

Megan raised her coffee mug and they toasted again. "Then here's to the new, old Masters house."

An hour later, her mother hugged Kerri. "Thanks for the lovely dinner, sweetheart."

"You're welcome, Mom. I'm glad you enjoyed it"

"Now, I hope you realize this means you two have to come to Texas this September for our fortieth anniversary party." Their dad dropped that bombshell as he rose to his feet.

Kerri frowned. "What? You said no more surprises."

"Sorry, hun, I forgot about this one." He shrugged. "The McCall's insisted on throwing it for us and I'm hoping you'll both work your magic like you did for them."

Forgot my ass.

"The fall is busy. We won't be able to spare two weeks. It'll have to be one," Kerri quickly replied, hugging them one at a time.

"That's fine, dear. We know you're busy." Her mom patted her hand, then turned to Jordan for a hug. "How about you, hun? Will you be able to get more leave?"

She drew back and shrugged. "Not sure. But, being that September is in a new fiscal year, I can probably swing another week."

Her mom smiled. "I'm so glad."

"Yeah," her dad said, giving her hug. "See what you can do, sweetheart."

"Will do."

Her dad pulled back and faced Megan and Shawn. "That goes for the two of you as well."

"Yes," her mom chimed in. "I hope your doctor will allow you to come. It wouldn't be the same without you."

"I hope so too. I'll ask him on my next visit." Megan patted her bulging tummy and grinned.

"Well." Her father looked at his watch. "We'd better get going. It's been a long day of travelling."

"I'll walk out with you two. I go on duty in a half hour so I have to leave now as well." Shawn kissed Megan then carefully touched her swollen belly. "You take care of your mom while I'm gone."

"We'll be fine." Her friend cupped his face. "You just worry about yourself."

Jordan's chest tightened. She remembered having similar conversations with Eric. It never got easier.

"Always." He kissed his wife's hand then turned to Kerri. "Dinner was delicious as usual."

"Thanks," Kerri replied, her face turning pink.

"And you." Shawn winked. Strong arms enveloped her, tightening for a hug. "Make sure you give my wife the *Cole* scoop. She thinks you haven't told her everything yet." He rolled his eyes. "I'm tired of hearing about the McCall brothers and would *love* to get a decent night sleep."

"Not sure I can help you there, pal." She returned his squeeze and stepped back. "I'll do my best."

"Bless you," he said before rushing from the house with her parents.

"Come on, Kerri. I'll help you clean up." Jordan slung her arm around her sister's shoulders and walked them back into her dining room.

Megan followed. "Me too."

A half hour later, table cleared, dishes washed, the three of them sat in the kitchen and talked over coffee.

"Okay, ladies. Like my husband said. I need the scoop. You two never did tell me much about Cole and Connor." Megan picked up her mug and smiled. "So?"

"So, what? There's nothing more to tell." Jordan rolled her eyes. "They're gorgeous, stubborn and still single."

"Don't forget conceited."

Kerri's tone oozed sarcasm. Jordan frowned. Where'd that come from? Her sister never had a bad thing to say about anyone. Ever.

"I don't think Cole acted conceited, maybe arrogant, but not conceited…at least, not yet." She sipped her coffee, the hot liquid warming her throat as she thought about their visit.

Kerri's head snapped back with a snort. "Not Cole. I'm talking about Connor."

"Oh. Well, with all those women throwing themselves at him, I guess it would be tough not to develop that flaw." Jordan snickered.

"Develop it?" Kerri snorted again. "He was *born* with the defect."

Jordan exchanged a look with Megan, who raised her brows before they both transferred their gazes back to Kerri. Her sister had been more indecisive than usual this past week, unable to pin down specials or choose a wine when asked to recommend one. Unusual behavior for an accomplished chef. When it came to food, Kerri excelled and ruled the kitchen.

Not this week.

Of course, her sister's ex-husband showing up at Comets for dinner few nights ago hadn't helped. Jordan had attributed Kerri's lack of self confidence to that visit. Now, she wasn't so sure.

She watched Kerri hug her mug with two hands and sip her coffee, scowling at a seam in her kitchen table.

Jordan leaned forward. "Kerri? Did something happen between you and Connor?"

Cheeks suddenly pink, her sister's mug clunked on the table as she avoided her gaze. "H-he...um sort of kissed me on the night of the party."

"Hah! I knew it!" Megan slapped the table wearing a pleased-with-herself grin on the pretty heart-shaped face.

Jordan reached across the table and touched Kerri's hand. "Was this a good thing?"

"Not really." Kerri sighed. "We were cleaning up...and...it just sort of happened."

"You said he kissed you. Does that mean you didn't kiss him back?" Jordan prodded gently, worried about the pallor under her sister's blush.

"Not really," Kerri repeated with a shudder. "It-it caught me off guard and, to be honest, I think it startled him, too." Freeing her hand, her sister sat back. "Before I even *had* a chance to respond, he pushed me away. But that's okay. It reaffirmed what I'd been saying all along." Chin and voice rose in unison.

Jordan recognized the action. Kerri wasn't only trying to convince her and Megan, she was trying to convince herself, too.

"I don't need that kind of complication. I'm happy with my life just as it is."

She didn't look happy, but Jordan kept her comments to herself. "Me too."

Megan sat back in her chair and folded her arms across her extended tummy. "So, Jordan, you're telling me you didn't kiss *Mr. Yummy Tycoon*?"

Kerri sat up straight, eyes wide. "Did you, Jordan?"

She looked from one direct gaze to the other. *Damn. No getting out of this.* Her shoulders lifted. "Yes, we kissed."

"And?" Megan's brows disappeared under her bangs. "Come on! You're killing me. What happened?"

"And that's it. I'm here." She got up and washed her mug.

"Oooh, no."

Her friend shot from her chair and joined her at the sink, leaning her back against the counter.

I didn't know a pregnant woman could move that fast.

"That is *not* it, Jordan Masters Ryan. You pined over this guy for almost half a decade, compared every Tom, Dick and Harry to him and then sent them packing because they were never better than Cole."

"Which was just about all of them." Kerri spoke from her right, sticking her mug in the sink.

Megan peered at her. "Yes. It was just about all of them, so...I want to know if it was worth keeping all those guys at bay. Well? How was it?"

"How was what?" She scrubbed her mug so hard she nearly put a hole in it. *Cripes*, the last thing she wanted to discuss was the heated kiss she'd shared with Cole. For the past few weeks she'd barely managed to put it out of her mind. She really didn't want to dissect it.

"Jordan!" Megan's eyes almost bugged out of her head.

Her sister lightly touched her arm, gaze hopeful. "How was Cole's kiss?"

What a complete turnaround from the *trying-to-convince-myself* thing her sister had going on a few moments ago.

"Well?"

Jordan stopped rubbing the cup and stared at her hands, remembering how Cole had felt under them. "Incredible."

"Yeah? Really?" Kerri's face brightened.

"Incredible what? Incredible toe-curling. Incredible heart-pounding…what? Tell me," Megan pleaded, grabbing her other arm.

"Incredibly stirring, core-melting, leg-weakening, every hair on my body vibrating as if next to a television screen, can't think straight kind of kiss." She pulled in a breath, then released it in a gush.

"Wow." Kerri sighed.

Megan blinked, then felt Jordan's forehead. "Are you ill?"

"No. I don't think so. Why?"

"Then what the hell are you doing in California? Why didn't you stay with him?"

Jordan brushed her friend's hand aside and strode to the table to straighten their chairs. "The timing was all wrong. Neither of us are ready for that strong of a feeling. I mean, sure the sex would be mind-blowing—"

"Mind-blowing's great!" Megan threw her hands in the air. "What's wrong with mind-blowing?"

"But then we'd feel horribly guilty afterwards." Jordan continued as if uninterrupted. "And would always associate the other with that negative feeling. No, I needed to come home. I *wanted* to come home." And she meant it. "We're not ready."

"What about in the fall?" Kerri spoke from her perch on the island.

Jordan stilled, caught off guard by the question.

"Yeah. A lot can happen in five months, Jordan." Megan cocked her head. "Do you think you'll both be ready for a relationship by the time you go back to Texas for your parent's anniversary party in September?"

Good question. She chewed her lower lip.

Would her guilt be gone by then? Would Cole's?

The day was unseasonably cool for the first Friday in September, which suited Cole. He was playing one on one-on one with Connor and

Kevin behind the stable at Wild Creek. A west wind blew lightly across the court, refreshing their overexerted bodies.

Connor was winning three baskets to two. That's because his brother was a fucking brick wall. A towering brick wall. Impossible to go through, and if you did manage to get around him, his reach was illegal, easily blocking their shots or knocking the ball out of their grasp. Which he just proved, once again, to Cole's perfectly timed layup.

"Oh-ho-ho..." Kevin taunted. "Struck down by *Long-arm* McCall. What's wrong, Cole? Mind still on that cute blonde I saw you with last month?"

"Blonde?" Connor threw the ball a good four feet over their heads to swish unhindered into the basket...all net. Four to two. "I saw him with a redhead."

Cole just smiled at them and shook his head. They were both right, although, the redhead was seven weeks ago. Since the Spring, he'd started dating again. Ended his celibacy. Learned to have fun and relax. None of his four 'dates' were long term, and he made sure the women knew that up front. He only wanted companionship and a warm body once in awhile. And never with the same woman twice.

Jordan had been right. He hadn't wanted more. He hadn't been ready. Getting involved with her back then would've been a huge mistake. But now? Now, he felt different.

Hell, he *was* different.

Guilt no longer clawed at his gut, and he'd even entertained starting an actual relationship. That blonde Kevin had mentioned had gone on a second date with him, then a third. But when he kept comparing the poor girl to Jordan, even seeing Jordan when they had sex, well, he had to cut her lose. It wasn't fair to the girl, and she certainly wasn't who he wanted. Her kisses weren't as hot and consuming as Jordan's. And she didn't inspire the deep, fierce need that had wracked his body like at his parent's anniversary party. Hell, even just thinking about Jordan and that damn backless dress got him hard.

"It's great to see you dating again, buddy. But your basketball is a bit rusty," his friend said, as he recovered the ball, doing some fancy footwork and dribbling behind his back as he stupidly took on Connor. "Let me show you how it's done. You went about it wrong," he claimed before executing a perfect drive down the middle, jumping up, no doubt intending to foul Connor and sink the basket.

But Connor had his feet planted and it was Kevin who hit the ground a second before the ball bounced next to his head.

"Jesus, Connor," Kevin uttered. "What are you? A fucking brick wall?"

Cole laughed at his friend's echoing thought as he watched his brother help Kevin to his feet.

"No." Connor chuckled, slapping the fallen man's shoulder before he released him to walk toward their water bottles, nestled in a small patch of shade. "You're just a pansy-ass, Dalton."

"*Pansy-ass*, my ass," Kevin muttered.

Connor snickered. "I think that's what I just said."

"Fuck you, Connor," Kevin countered.

"Sorry, Dalton, but you're not my type," came his brother's easy reply.

The three of them laughed before taking a moment to drink what was left of their water. Cole opened the cooler and tossed them each another. It felt good to laugh. Good to play. Good to not have an overwhelming, crushing weight on his shoulders. To just relax and have fun.

"So, tomorrow's the day, huh? The girls are coming back," Kevin said, recapping his drink, bouncing his gaze between him and the *fucking brick wall*.

Cole noted his brother's arm still a moment before he continued to drink. Pretty much how Connor had acted before the last visit, although, if anything, now he seemed a little more put out. Not Cole. No. He'd actually done a complete one-eighty. Unlike the Spring visit from the Masters sisters, this one he looked forward to very much. Hell, he was actually excited. It'd been years since that emotion had rushed through him. Leave it to Jordan. Damn woman was responsible for a lot of emotions running through him, lately. He couldn't get her off his mind, and after awhile, he stopped trying. Thoughts of her warmed him from within, and he realized two things. One…he liked the feeling. And, two…

He deserved it.

"Yeah, sometime in the afternoon, I think," he replied, non committal.

He preferred to keep his thoughts to himself at the moment. To keep his plans a secret. She was only there for a week this time, and he had plans for six out of the seven days.

Unfortunately, he had a commitment he couldn't get out of tomorrow night, but the rest of the time… *oh hell yeah*, he had plans for Jordan Masters Ryan.

Chapter Ten

Nate sat in the McCall's den chatting to his wife and Leeann, waiting for Alex to finish his conversation with his oldest son. Once Connor left, they had their own agenda to discuss. Tomorrow, finally, round two would start. It had been a long but fruitful summer. The old homestead was coming along and so was Cole.

The younger McCall had shed his cold demeanor and embraced life again. He smiled more. Worked less. Joked, laughed, dated. Nate's own heart warmed at the transformation. He could only imagine how wonderful his friends felt at having their son back.

Leeann's laughter echoed through the room, mixing with his wife's, and the sound brought a bit of peace to the ranch that had been absent back in the Spring. Even Alex and Connor stopped talking to look over at the women and smile. *Yes*, it was good to have a lighter air about the ranch.

"Okay, son," Alex said. "I'll take care of it. You go ahead and enjoy the rodeo. We'll see you on Sunday." His friend slapped his oldest on the back and winked.

Connor grinned. "That's a given, dad. That's a given."

If ever there was a more easy-going fella Nate sure never met him. Girls loved Connor. His ranch hands respected him. The boy had a lot of friends and worked just as hard as he played. Of course, that could be the reason he hadn't been able to hold onto his three former fiancés.

He watched as the boy ambled across the room to his mother.

"You two ladies are music to this old dog's ears."

Leeann smiled. "Oh, Connor, you're not old." Her smile broadened as her son bent down to kiss her cheek. "You behave yourself now. Okay?" She touched his face then frowned. "I wish Kade was going with you boys. He'd keep you all out of trouble. I hate the thought of him fighting in the war again."

"I do, too, mom." Connor straightened and a rare bit of sadness clouded his gaze. "But, Kade's tough. He'll be fine."

"He's right, Leeann. Don't you worry none about him," Alex said, hand on Connor's back as he walked him to the door. "Kade's smart and resourceful. It'll be February and he'll be back from deployment before you know it."

Nate had to admit, he'd be happy to see that day too. The Dalton boy was a good egg. Poor kid had had one hell of a childhood but according to Alex, he'd turned out all right. God bless Sarah Dalton. She took him in and raised him alongside her own when his mom had run off.

"Okay," Connor said, turning to face Alex when he reached the door. "If there's any problems, Cole said he'd take care of them. So, that should do it. Sorry I won't be here when the girls arrive tomorrow. But, I'll see you all on Sunday."

"Bye, Connor," Nate said, echoing the others.

Alex waited until his son disappeared into the hall, then shut the door and turned to face them. "Okay, now, about the girls."

Nate stood and pulled his phone from his pocket. "I was waiting for Connor to leave before I called Jordan to confirm their flight." He dialed his daughter and waited for her to pick up.

"Hello, dad," she answered with a laugh. "I was wondering when you were going to call."

He smiled. "Hi, sweetheart. Just checking to see if everything is okay."

"Everything is fine. I'm on duty, catching up on some paperwork."

As usual, his stomach clenched tight whenever he thought about his oldest and her job. He knew the world needed police and his daughter did a damn fine job, but…she was his daughter. He'd much rather her cooks like Kerri and not patrol the streets of L.A. So far, she'd managed without incident, but…five years…she was pushing her luck.

His gaze wandered to the other three people in the room. They all looked at him, eager for a report. He cleared his throat and got to the point.

"Then I won't keep you, hun. Just wanted to double-check your flight time for tomorrow."

"I'm sure you have it memorized better than I do." She laughed in his ear. "We're due in to Houston at two-ten, so we should arrive at Wild Creek by three-thirty," she answered.

"Okay. Good." He gave the others a thumbs up, to which they all smiled.

"Ut, I've got to go, dad. We just got a call, burglary in progress. Love ya, see ya tomorrow."

"Okay, sweetheart. We'll see you then," he said, and would've added his wish for her to be careful but she'd already hung up.

This just had to work. He wanted to see her settled here with Cole working for the local police. It had been bad enough when he'd lived in L.A., but being several states away was a lot harder than he had expected, especially given her occupation.

Alex handed them all their customary flutes of champagne and raised his glass. "To round two."

Nate answered the toast and reaffirmed his resolve. Come hell or high water, his girls were going to settle down here in Harland County again.

Jordan couldn't believe how fast the time had passed since they'd driven under the *Wild Creek Ranch* sign. She glanced at the passenger seat. Kerri sat chewing her bottom lip. Déjà vu. Shivers shot down her spine. Their Spring visit had started off this way.

"Is it just me, or is this trip even more nerve-racking than the last one?" She smirked, trying to break the tension.

"It's not just you, believe me. This trip is definitely worse."

Her sister flicked her hair away from her face with a shaky hand. The kiss she'd received from Connor no doubt running through her mind. Just as Cole's ran through Jordan's.

"I have to admit, though," Kerri said. "I am a little curious to see Cole."

At the mention of his name, Jordan's gaze snapped fully to her sister. "Why?"

"Well, mom said he's changed so much in the last few months we might not recognize him. He's even started dating." Kerri looked at her and frowned. "I'm sorry, Jordan. I probably shouldn't have told you that."

She laughed, her tone slightly off. "No. It's okay. I knew he'd been dating. Mom told me too. It's what he needs to do. I'm glad he's doing better."

And she was glad…and jealous…and mad because she was jealous. She gripped the steering wheel and continued down the drive. *Jeez.* She was on the ranch less than one minute and already Cole had her confused.

Not that she hadn't suffered that affliction back in California the past few months. Because she had…thanks to him—stealing into her thoughts at the most inopportune moments; like when she'd kiss her dates goodnight. *Damn Texan.* She'd thought she'd overcome the Cole-comparison stage. Wrong. Her heart squeezed. Now that she'd tasted his recent kiss and the promise of fire, the rest of the male population held no spark.

"I hope you're ready for round two because we're here."

Kerri's words brought Jordan back to the present. She straightened in her seat and forced her gloomy thoughts away.

"I'm ready. We're here for mom and dad. This is going to be a great trip. No room for doom," she said, more for herself than her sister.

"You're right." Kerri nodded. "We won't allow the McCall brothers to ruin our fun."

The only problem with that statement, Jordan thought, was that Cole *was* her fun.

They pulled up in front of the ranch to find both sets of parents waiting with hugs and kisses.

"Sorry the boys aren't here to greet you this time, girls. Cole's out for the afternoon and Connor is at a rodeo with a few friends and won't be back until tomorrow," Mr. McCall explained while they walked inside.

Jordan exhaled the stiffness from her body and noted color had returned to Kerri's face at the news.

"That's okay. It's not necessary for them to be here." She flipped her loose braid behind her back and switched her attention to her parents. "So, Mom, Dad, when do we get to see the old house?"

"How about right after you're settled?" Her dad smiled.

"Great," Kerri's reply echoed her own.

Forty-minutes later, they piled into their dad's car with their parents and made the ten-minute trip to their old two-story Spanish-style house.

Several pickup trucks and vans dotted the driveway. Workers dodged about, some heaving sheetrock inside, their biceps bulging under the weight. Childhood memories flooded her brain as she stepped out of the car and stared at the house that had once been her home for the first sixteen years of her life. If it were possible for her heart to smile, it just did.

The whine of dueling saws echoed in the background as workers cut a pile of two-by-four boards.

"Wow, renovations are in full swing." Kerri glanced at the hustling, muscled men, blushing when a few smiled at her. "Let's see the inside."

"Yes, lets." Jordan put her arm on her sister's shoulder and together they entered the noisy house.

The sweet smell of spackling and paint immediately tickled her nose. The overhauled entrance sported fresh umber colored walls and a new hardwood floor shot straight into the opened great room in the back.

"You knocked down a wall." She blinked at the transformation. "This is great. It's more open."

"Yes, and we took down the one between the dining room and kitchen as well." Her mother's eyes sparkled. "Wait till you see."

Jordan stepped into the dining room and gasped. "Wow. Look at that kitchen."

"Pinch me. Am I dreaming?" Kerri floated toward the industrial size stainless steel gas stove without glancing at the incredible view from the wall of floor-to-ceiling windows in the back. "I think I'm in heaven," Kerri sighed. "Look at this monster. It has four burners, a griddle and even a warming rack built in. I can't take it!" Her sister shook her head in awe.

"We hoped you'd like it. After all, you'll probably be the one to cook our holiday dinners on it." Their mother walked over and hugged her sister.

Kerri turned, passion sparkled in her eyes. "I can't wait until Christmas!"

Jordan laughed with her parents. "And look at this refrigerator." She strolled to the other stainless steel giant occupying a full corner of the kitchen and peered inside. "What in the world do you need with such a big thing?"

"Well, the two of you will eventually have families and I assume, come for long visits..." her mother's hopeful voice trailed off.

"I'm not sure children are in my cards," Jordan replied. Not with Cole in possession of her deck.

The hair on the back of her neck tingled and spread over her shoulders then down her back. *Speaking of the possessor...* She stiffened, butterflies suddenly swarming her knotted stomach.

"Jordan with children? Now that's a scary thought," came the amused reply from down the hall.

She swiveled around and scanned the faces, until they centered on Cole. *Holy Transformations.* Her throat dried. They weren't kidding when they said she wouldn't recognize him. She almost hadn't.

He'd cut his hair. Short around his ears and neck, a little longer on top where it carelessly flopped onto his forehead. The style suited him and increased her pulse to super-sonic. Gripping the handle on the refrigerator, she continued to size up the approaching man.

Dark and sexy in jeans and a dusty black t-shirt stretched thin over his muscles, it was obvious he'd been working on something in the house. She'd question that in a minute, first, she needed to catch her breath.

As he neared, she studied his eyes. *He's back.* Her heart turned over, then soared. The only thing hard on Cole was his fit form. The coldness and almost constant frown he'd worn during her last visit had disappeared. *Gone. Adios.* Sadness no longer lurked in the warm brown depths. His gaze was reminiscent of the mischievous look of his childhood. He looked younger, happy even. Like a man who enjoyed life again.

"Cole?" Kerri stared opened-mouthed at him. "Is that really you?"

"Yeah, it's really me."

He chuckled and picked her sister up to twirl her in a circle. Kerri's laughter filled the room. Recovered from her shock, Jordan pushed from the refrigerator and walked around him, resisting the urge to hug.

"Wow, Cole, you look so different."

This was the Cole she'd been afraid to find five months ago. The one she was terrified of and longed for at the same time. Her stomached fluttered with ripple upon ripple of awareness.

Ah, hell. She was in trouble.

Still smiling, he released her sister to place a hand over his heart. "I can assure you, it's me."

Even his stance was different; confident yet relaxed, not stiff and unyielding. He stepped closer and all the hammering, sawing and voices faded into the background. The only hammering she heard now was the beating of her own heart.

"Welcome back, Jordan." Longing darkened his eyes as he held his arms open.

Oh God, yeah. Big trouble.

She swallowed. "I was going to say the same thing to you."

They stepped toward each other and Jordan found herself engulfed in heat and muscle...*and heaven help her,* never wanted to leave. Ever. She melted into him and sighed, burying her face in his neck. Damn, he smelled good, like spackle and hot man and musky aftershave. The sexy scruff dusting his face grazed her cheek, sending goosebumps down her right side.

"God, I've missed you," he whispered in her ear, sending more of those delicious shivers south to all her good parts.

She smiled against his throat. "I'm glad." His chuckle vibrated through her before she drew back slightly to look into his warm brown gaze and add, "I missed you, too."

Returning her smile, he brushed his thumb across her cheek. "I'm glad," he said, and they just stood there, staring for several beats.

Her father stepped forward and slapped Cole's shoulder. Dust departed in a puff of smoke. "Cole and Connor have been a big help. They've worked on several of the rooms in this house."

Forcing herself to step out of Cole's embrace, she focused on her father, and as nonchalantly as possible, backed up to lean against the countertop for support. Cole's eyes sparkled knowingly. *Bastard*. He knew his blatant interest had knocked her off balance.

"Heck, I spent half my youth here messing up the place. It's the least I can do." His appreciative gaze never left her face.

Blatant attraction. He was no longer hiding his feelings. *Damn*, she could use some water. A cup. Bottle. Gallon. Her throat was parched. Maybe Cole *was* ready. Was she? Thoughts of Eric and what they'd had—love, trust, commitment, great sex, and fun, crowded her head. She looked into Cole's warm brown eyes and sucked in a breath. *I want all those things with him.* She waited for the hand of guilt to grip her gut. It never showed. Not even a tug. Her pulse leapt.

Maybe their time had finally come.

Fingers relaxing, her grip on the round edge of the counter eased as that notion took root. *Their time*. Excitement shivered to her toes. Maybe it was okay to have a little fun. Her lips split into a grin. "Wow, McCall. You not only transformed yourself, you're transforming this house as well?"

"Only in a small way. Your father is too generous with his compliments. I've only given him some of my weekends."

"You're the one being modest, Cole," her mother insisted with a smile. "You should see what a terrific job he and Kevin are doing in the bathroom down here."

"Kevin's here, too?"

"Yes. Come on and say hi." He grabbed her hand and Kerri's, and led them down the hall. Heat shot up her arm and she suddenly wished their destination to be more private so she could hold onto him longer.

"Hey, Kev, look what I found for us in the kitchen," he addressed the man busy installing a burnt umber ceramic floor tile.

Kevin glanced up from his task and his blue eyes lit with warmth.

"Hi, Jordan, Kerri. It's great to see you both again." He stood and wiped his hands on a rag before hugging them. "You're back just in time, too. We're having our *good-bye-to-summer-barbeque* tomorrow."

Jordan smiled. "Talk about timing. Sounds great."

"I'm sure you can hitch a ride with Cole and Connor again. Right buddy?" Kevin patted Cole's chest and winked.

Kerri turned wide eyes to Cole. "You mean you don't already have a date?"

"Nope. I don't have one for tomorrow but I do, however"—he glanced at his watch—"have one in two hours. If you girls will excuse us working guys, we need to get back to the job at hand."

With a teasing smile he unceremoniously shoed them out the door.

Shock, hurt and jealousy took turns stabbing Jordan's gut. What kind of game was he playing? Or had she just imagined his interest? She forced her smile to remain on her lips. "All right, we can take a hint. We know when we're not wanted."

Cole's gaze snapped to hers, dark, serious, heated. "I didn't say that."

Her heart slammed in her chest. Did her wishful thinking put the longing in his eyes? Or was his need real?

"Come on, Jordan. Let's take a look at the rest of the house," Kerri called from behind.

Gaze still locked to his, she replied, "Yes, by all means, lets."

Turning on her heel, she broke eye contact and waltzed from the room head held high.

If he was going to show interest one minute, then dangle women in front of her the next…this week was going to be the week from hell.

Vowing to enjoy her short stay at the ranch, Jordan refused to think about Cole and his date. She was the one who'd encouraged him in the Spring. He was dating. Good. It was none of her business. *That's my story and I'm sticking to it.*

She needn't have worried.

"I'm sorry Cole couldn't be here for your first night back, but it's his company's annual dinner," Mrs. McCall explained with a tip of her head as they sat on the porch, enjoying a glass of lemonade while they waited for dinner.

"That's all right. He did say something about a date," Kerri replied.

"A date?" His mother laughed. "He's escorting his secretary, Mrs. Dixon because her husband's currently away on business."

Stella?

Relief flushed away Jordan's unhappiness with the force of a rogue wave. The thought of him deliberately ditching her for a night on the town with a faceless bombshell disappeared into dust.

That devious bugger.

Heart infinitely lighter, she hid a smile as she digested this welcomed news. He'd led her to believe he had an actual date. She sipped her drink, a plan forming in the back of her mind. Tomorrow, she'd get back at him.

"I'm glad to hear he's getting out and living a little again," she remarked, concentrating on the slow, setting sun.

Mr. McCall laughed. "He's certainly doing that. I swear that boy is making up for lost time. He hit the dating scene like those earthquakes you get out on the west coast—unexpected and hard."

Emma's wonderful fresh squeezed drink turned to pure sour in Jordan's stomach. She should be happy for Cole, but a surge of jealousy and disappointment invaded. Her foolish emotions made her favorite drink tough to swallow.

Desperate to change the subject, she turned to her parents. "What else do you plan to do to the house?"

Her father went on to explain the rather extensive remodeling still to be done before they could move in.

"That sounds like it'll take several more months," Kerri said, a slight frown to her brow.

"Yes. The projected date should be around the beginning of

December. Poor Alex and Leeann, they'll be thoroughly tired of us by then." Her mother sighed.

"That could never happen," Mrs. McCall promptly reassured.

The rest of the evening was enjoyable. Good meal, good company. A fruitful discussion on the preparations needed for the anniversary party next weekend. All things to keep Jordan's mind occupied. *Not.* Her damn thoughts strayed to Cole.

Just how many dates had he been on? Did he compare their kisses to mine?

Sunlight poured in through a stain glass window, casting a glow of blues, reds, greens and yellows over the pages of the hymnbook Cole shared with Jordan. She glanced at him from under her long lashes. Dark hair, dark eyes, perfect cheekbones, perfect smile. *God, she was breathtaking.* Wind blew in from the open pane, stirring her hair while her sweet voice stirred his soul. His heart warmed with a sense of peace he hadn't felt in years. If ever.

Afterward, they drove back to the ranch to find Emma ready to serve their brunch.

"I understand you girls are going to the Dalton's barbeque tonight," his father remarked, digging into his eggs and salsa.

"Yes. Kevin was nice enough to invite us yesterday," Kerri replied before sipping her orange juice.

"Then you'll be riding over with the boys?"

His mother's tone held a hint of…hope. Jordan glanced at him, then his mother. She'd heard it too. His mother dropped her gaze, picked up a knife and fumbled with Emma's prize winning jam already spread on her toast. *Nope.* Not imagining it. They were up to something.

"Yes," he finally answered. "That's the plan."

He had lots of plans and surprises for this week, and they all centered on a certain beautiful woman who stole his breath, challenged, and turned him on and inside out.

"Provided they don't have dates," Jordan said, a small grin tugging her kissable lips.

And God help him, he wanted to kiss them again. The right way. Their first one had been unexpected and way too short. Their second had been just as unexpected but spurred by anger, despite being the hottest, out of control experience of his life. Now, he was ready, and if he didn't miss his guess, she was ready, too. Anticipation heated his body. Tonight. He would see to it everything was perfect for Jordan, tonight.

"Nope. No dates," he answered her, a smirk tugged the corner of his mouth. "I think I already told you that."

"Yes, you did. But that was yesterday." She stabbed a piece of chicken with her fork and continued with her teasing. "For all we know, you might've already asked the girl you dated last night to go with you."

He couldn't tell if she knew he'd taken Stella last night or if she was fishing. Either way, he was more than happy to play her game. "True. But I didn't."

Mr. Masters chuckled, covering his mouth with a napkin. His father chewed his eggs while his mother and Mrs. Masters both smiled down at their plates.

"Why not?" Jordan's gaze grew serious. "Didn't your date go well?"

"It was fine," he said candidly, pushing away from the table and the subject. "Connor's due back by four. Meet us in the foyer at five. Now, if you'll excuse me..." He stood. "I've been neglecting my preliminary reports for too long. They need my attention." With a nod and a smile, he headed for his office before he decided to ditch work in favor of play.

Two hours after brunch, enjoying a lazy afternoon of swimming and relaxing in the sun with Kerri, Jordan found herself alone when her sister went inside to shower, claiming she needed to discuss a few party entrées with Emma.

Enjoying the peace and quiet of solitude, she adjusted her lounge chair, laid back and closed her eyes. Water lapped gently against the side of the pool, birds chirped in the nearby trees and the sun warmed her body. *Ah, serenity.* She'd missed this. Her busy schedule at the precinct and restaurant rarely allowed such a luxury.

The screen door opened and closed. In an instant, the air changed, crackled, attacking her nerve endings with a prickle.

"You're going to burn if you don't put on some lotion." Cole's deep tone shot a thrill down her spine.

A smile tugged her lips. "Sorry to disappoint you but I've already done that," she replied without opening her eyes.

"Spoil sport."

She could hear the grin in his voice and a chair scrapping concrete as he sat next to her.

"Are you sure?" His voice turned low and quiet and friggin' sexy as hell. "Maybe you missed a spot."

She opened her eyes and put a hand to her forehead to block the sun in order to see him better. *Yeah,* sexy as hell. "Oh, I'm sure, but I do give you an A for effort, McCall."

He shrugged his broad shoulders and the devil danced in his eyes. "You can't blame a guy for trying."

"True." She chuckled. "If you want to make yourself useful, you could poor me a glass of lemonade." After repositioning her chair to sitting, she glanced sideways at him. Grin lifting his lips, teasing gleam in his dark eyes. Her heart fluttered. Lord help her, he was irresistible when he was like this.

"Here you go, my *Masters*. But I'm sure you could come up with some other use for me." Head cocked, he grinned endearingly and handed her a glass, deliberately grazing fingers.

Her heart knocked into her ribs. He was playing a dangerous game, and heaven help her, she was all for it. "You're right. I could, but I won't." She sipped her drink, then pointed at him. "Don't think you can go out carousing with some bimbo one night, then expect me to allow you to massage sunscreen on me the next afternoon, Cole McCall."

He leaned toward the small table separating them, delight sparkling in his eyes. "Why Jordan, I do believe you're jealous."

"Yeah, I am. I'm also disappointed in you." She bit her lip to keep from laughing when he frowned.

"Why?"

"I never thought you'd go for a married woman, Cole, let alone an older employee."

His killer smile stopped her pulse. "Who told you it was Stella?"

She shrugged, enjoying herself far too much.

"Fine." He sat back in his chair and crossed his arms over his chest. "Now I don't know if I should give you the present I bought you."

Oh, he was so good.

She narrowed her eyes. "What present?"

"This one." He withdrew a small white box from his pocket and placed it on the table.

Her gaze lifted from the gift to his face. He grinned from ear to ear. *And not to be trusted.* She frowned. *What the hell was the sexy bugger up to now?*

"It's too small for a snake to jump out." She thrust her chin in the air. "Don't think I've forgotten that trick you played on me when I was ten."

"I promise it's not a snake. Go on, open it." He pushed it closer.

She hesitated, well aware of all the jokes he use to play…and that she'd enjoyed every last one. Fighting a grin, she picked up the box and gave a careful shake. Something rattled inside. *Too big to be jewelry*. Her gaze flew to his. Eyes, dark and mischievous, out-sparkled the sun. *He's definitely up to something*. Adrenaline heated her veins. Jordan Masters never backed away once Cole McCall threw down the gauntlet. With one last glance in his direction, she slowly opened the box.

A blue diaphragm met her cautious gaze.

She screamed and dropped the box. *Crazy bastard*. She loved it! Unrestrained amusement slackened her body. Jordan fell back in her chair and dissolved into fits of laughter. Never in a million years did she expect a diaphragm. Dragging in air, she reached for the box again.

"Oh Cole. You've outdone yourself. That was your best one yet," she managed between giggles.

He laughed with her. "I'm glad you liked it. You should've seen your face."

"It couldn't have been anywhere near as priceless as yours was in the Spring. I swear, when I sat on your lap and told you we had broken one of these during a night of wonderful sex, your jaw nearly hit the floor." Her body shook with renewed mirth at the memory.

"I still can't believe you did that." He shook his head and chuckled. "What am I saying? Of course I can believe it."

She wiped the tears from her face and held up the birth control device. "Do I even want to know where you got this?"

"Now, Jordan, don't be jealous. It's from a doctor friend of mine and I can assure you it isn't used. At least, not yet," he added, hope gleaming in his eyes.

Her heart slammed into her chest, sucking the smile from her lips. Excitement and panic gripped. What exactly was he saying?

Thoughtful, she watched as his gaze travel leisurely down her body and back again, caressing every inch of her languid flesh. By the time their eyes met, her goose-bumped skin and hardened nipples ached for his touch. And damn, was she wet.

"Sorry to disturb you, Cole." Emma's voice stopped Jordan's heart. "But there's a call for you from overseas."

He cleared his throat. "I'll take it in my office." Regret filled his gaze as he stood. "We'll finish this *conversation* later," he promised, sending her one last rueful look before he disappeared into the house.

Inhaling a deep, steadying breath, she closed her eyes and lay back in her chair. *Okay, Cole. Two can play at this game.* Body shivering in disappointment, a plan formed in her head.

Smiling, she gathered her things.

This should be one interesting barbeque.

Standing back from her mirror an hour later, Jordan couldn't stop the wide grin from spreading across her face. In keeping with their teasing, she donned the exact outfit she'd worn to Cole's office in the Spring. She'd thrown the *provocative* clothing in her suitcase last minute—because the clothes made her smile. Her fingers skimmed the gold necklace around her neck, sparkling like the matching heart-encrusted bracelet on her wrist—both gifts from Cole a lifetime ago. Her heart warmed at the memories.

The bracelet had arrived Special Delivery for her seventeenth birthday. Not long after they'd moved from Texas. He'd sent her the matching necklace for her high school graduation. A day fate had turned bittersweet. His parents had delivered his gift because he'd stayed behind to take over temporary reign of McCall Enterprises while his father took his first ever leave of absence. Too bad it had been to attend her graduation and visit California for a month. In the space of Mr. McCall's innocuous decision, her two year countdown to see her Texan again, had significantly altered. Jordan had understood the trial run of operating the company had been an important honor for Cole and she'd been happy for him, but disappointed at the same time.

After that, they'd conversed less and less, and other than her secret visit a few years later—one even Cole knew nothing about—they'd lost touch. Until now.

Heart pumping a familiar *Texas* tune, she stared at her reflection. Was this really finally happening? Did she want it too?

Oh, hell yeah!

Laughing, she twisted her hair up and clasped it with a clip. She couldn't wait to see Cole's expression.

Wearing a salmon colored sundress, her sister stepped into the hall at the same time and had her hair twisted off her neck to help alleviate the late summer heat, too.

Jordan wanted to tell her sister how stunning she looked but knew Kerri would high-tail it back into her room to change.

"You look cool," she said instead.

"So do you." Her sister's eyes widened. "Are you trying to give Cole a heart-attack?"

"No. Just a good laugh." She winked.

As Jordan and Kerri descended the stairs, the waiting cowboys removed their hats and watched with interest. Her gaze devoured Cole. Tucked into his jeans, his short-sleeved blue/gray shirt had the first three buttons undone, hinting at the broad chest she knew lay underneath. She could barely breathe, thanks to the heart hammering in her dried throat.

"Hmm. Now where have I seen that outfit before?" He grinned wickedly, smoldering gaze following her every move.

"What? This old thing?" She batted her lashes and his laughter increased the tempo of her heart.

"Hello, Jordan." Connor cleared his throat. "Jordan? It's nice to see you again, too. Hello-o-o."

The sound of snapping fingers cut through her haze.

"Hello-o-o? Other McCall here..."

Pulling her attention from Cole she smiled at his older brother. "Sorry, Connor. I um…didn't see you there."

"I noticed." He chuckled as they hugged. "You sure know how to deflate a man's ego."

"No one could deflate your ego, Connor. Who are you trying to kid?" Kerri spoke from behind.

Connor threw his head back and laughed.

Poor Kerri. Instead of embracing the humor in her comment, her hands flew to her flushed cheeks.

"I'm sorry, Connor. I can't believe I just said that."

Cole snickered. "Don't be, Kerri. You're absolutely right."

Stepping in to rescue her sister, he dropped an arm around Kerri's shoulder and led her toward the door. "That was a good one."

Jordan's heart warmed for the man even further. His sweet gesture touched her beyond reason. The old Cole was back. And Jordan was falling for him again, big time.

"Connor has a big ego. Who knew?" She linked arms with the still smiling cowboy, noting the deep tan and sun-streaked hair he'd acquired during the summer.

Why wasn't he spoken for? He was gorgeous. Gaze straying to his younger brother walking ahead, she swallowed. Gorgeous was a McCall trait—a strong one.

When they reached the vehicle, Cole released Kerri to open both the front and back doors. Before Jordan could blink, slim fingers clamped around her elbow and yanked her into the back. Slack-jawed, eyes wide, Cole stared at them from the driveway. She hiccupped a giggle and promptly sank her teeth into her lower lip to thwart the rest. He obviously never expected Kerri to be sharing her seat. *I never expected Kerri to be sharing my seat.* She glanced at her sister busily rearranging the dress around her knees.

Where was self-assured Kerri Masters? This woman fidgeting next to her as they headed down the drive wasn't her. Not by a long shot. Jordan's chest tightened. Why wouldn't she want to sit up front with Connor? Because of their mistaken kiss last Spring? She pursed her lips and tried to put herself in her sister's shoes. Maybe.

Divorced a year-and-a-half now—thanks to an unfaithful ex-husband—Kerri gave *shy* and *reserved* a new meaning. Jordan suspected there was more but try as she might, she couldn't get her sister to talk.

All this happened a few weeks after Eric had died. *Too occupied with my own grief. I missed something.* She sighed inwardly. Kerri had always been outgoing and popular. That and her natural beauty had attracted many admiring glances and she always took it in her stride. Her gaze dropped to her sister's knotted hands. Now, Kerri was like a scared rabbit too afraid to come out of her hole. Why?

As they drove under the Shadow Rock Ranch sign, Jordan made a promise. Once they got back to California, she'd sit Kerri down and get to the root of the problem.

California.

Her heart rocked. The prospect of returning there next week flooded her body with waves of forlorn. She eyed the sexy dark haired man sitting in front. Suddenly, Jordan wasn't so sure she wanted to leave. Not if the old Cole was truly back.

"Big turnout this year," Connor said as he parked the car in a field full of vehicles.

California promptly tucked to the back of her mind, Jordan squared her shoulders. Right now, she'd enjoy the time she had in Texas and not worry about leaving until next week.

Cole opened her door, helped her out but didn't release her hand. Warm and firm, his fingers, entwined with hers, felt right but still, doubt returned. She glanced sideways at him. Was five months long enough for Cole to come to grips with moving on? He squeezed her hand and smiled. Her heart fell into her fluttering stomach.

God, I hope so.

When several familiar men approached and asked her to reserve them a dance, Cole dropped her hand. Disappointed, she opened her mouth to reply but her voice evaporated as he draped an arm around her shoulder and drew her against his side.

"Sorry guys, the lady's with me tonight."

Her heartbeats tripled. She was?

Eyebrows shot up and heads snapped in their direction as the news registered in everyone's brains. Smiling, he guided them towards the food.

"Wait, McCall." She pulled him out of the line.

A big smile split across his face. "You want to get me alone already?" he teased, grazing her hip with his hand.

"Cole, what's going on? Is this a date?"

"Yes."

"You and me?"

"Yes. It generally takes two."

"I know that, but one is generally asked." She raised a brow and waited.

Laughter faded from his eyes. "Are you saying you don't want to be here with me?"

"No, ya big dummy. I'm saying I expected to be asked."

"Oh, I can do that." He grasped her hands and gazed straight into her eyes, his own alight with mischief and hope. "Jordan, I know this has been a very long time coming, but would you do me the honor of being my date for this evening?"

All kidding aside, her heart thudded in her throat. "Are you sure about this Cole? Are you sure you're ready for me?"

"Jordan." Lips twitching, he cupped her chin. "Honey. I don't think I'll ever be ready for you."

She laughed. "You've got that right, Cole McCall. You've got that right."

Kevin approached with a grin. "Cole is right about something?"

"Yes." She laughed.

Cole slipped his arm around her waist and grinned. "You've got to start sometime."

"That you do, my friend. That you do." Kevin slapped Cole on the shoulder and smiled broadly. "Carry on," he added, giving them a wink before he sauntered off toward Kerri.

The next few hours turned into one of the best nights of Jordan's life.

How could it not be? She was there with Cole. After all those years of wishing and waiting, it finally happened. Cole had asked her out on a date. She could barely breathe as the reality of the momentous occasion sank in.

He twirled *her* on the dance floor; held *her* body close on the slow songs; called *her* up onto the stage to sing with and laughed and joked with *her* all evening.

She'd treasure the night forever.

Later on, as they piled into the SUV to head back to the ranch, Jordan beat her sister to the punch. Wrapping her fingers around the taut muscle of Cole's bicep, she quickly tugged him into the backseat, forcing Kerri to sit up front next to Connor. It was either that, or all three stuffed in the back. She couldn't bring herself to leave Cole's side. Not even for the brief ten minute ride to the McCall's. Guilt pricked her conscience until Cole's warm hand found her knee. Thumb lightly rubbing across her leg, he stroked and stroked, and desire simmered.

Kerri's a big girl…she'll survive.

Air, thick with humidity, blew in from the opened windows and clung to her already heated skin. With her head on his shoulder, she looped her arm through his, listening to the hum of the vehicle and the sound of country music playing softly on the radio as they silently made their way to the ranch.

Where Kerri and Connor disappeared to once they got back, Jordan had no idea. She was only aware of Cole's warm fingers still entwined with hers as he led the way up the outside stairs to the balcony.

"I don't know about you but I'm not ready for this night to end just yet." His twinkling eyes outshone the starry sky.

Her pulse jumped. "What are you up to?"

He shrugged, guiding her to the other end of the balcony just outside her door.

She stopped dead and gasped.

Chapter Eleven

Candles lit the balcony, while soft music played in the background. Jordan gazed in amazement. A bottle of champagne chilled on ice and two empty glasses beckoned as a single red rose sat in a crystal vase in the middle of a white-linen table. Balancing out the romantic setting, sat a silver-covered dish.

She turned to him and blinked. "How did you manage all of this, Cole?"

"I asked Emma to set it up for us." He grinned slowly, hope lighting the dark depths of his eyes. "Do you like it?"

"Like it?" Her stomach dipped. "I love it. And that would explain the knowing glances she kept throwing my way today."

"I just wanted things to be perfect."

Barely recovered, her stomach dipped again. "They are."

Unable to wrap her mind around the fact he'd gone through all this trouble just to please her, Jordan remained rooted to the spot. The whole evening had been surreal, yet *so real*.

He handed her a glass of champagne, fingers grazing in the process. She drew in a breath, his fresh, sporty scent filling her nose.

He's real. He's very real.

"To us." Cole raised his glass, and her temperature, with a look of intense longing.

Her heart slammed against her ribs. Hard. "To us," she replied a little breathless, touching flutes.

As she sipped the bubbly, his gaze devoured her, making it difficult to swallow. She was a strong person, sometimes damn immovable. But not with this man. God, not with Cole. Excitement and anticipation hitched her breath and weakened her knees. The full force of his attraction was damn potent. She didn't resist when he took the nearly full glass out of her hand and placed both flutes on the table.

"Dance with me?" he asked softly.

Unable to speak, she nodded and he pulled her gently into his arms. Quickly becoming her favorite place. Her eyes fluttered closed and she melted against him, reveling in his warm strength. This was right. This was Cole. His heart thundered under her chin and matched her hammering pulse. More alive than ever, her body buzzed with awareness, and for the first time since Eric's death, she allowed her heart to *feel* another man.

For several minutes the two of them dwelled in a special, private place.

A short time later, Cole jarred her senses by doing the

unthinkable—he stopped and drew back. Jordan nearly cried out in protest but when her eyes flew open she promptly forgot her objection—and how to breathe. Hunger darkened his eyes to coal.

"Jordan, things were all screwed up on your last visit. This time I want to do them the right way." Voice husky, he lightly caressed the side of her face. "I'm going to kiss you now. I hope that's okay?"

Okay? She swallowed past her dried throat, and acknowledged her mind, body, and heart where finally all in agreement.

"You bet it is, cowboy." She lifted the Stetson off his head and tossed it on the chair behind him. "I've waited a lifetime for this kiss."

Desire blazed in his eyes as he cupped her face with both hands and slowly lowered his head. "So have I, Jordan."

Hot breath hit her mouth a mere second before his lips.

A charged tremor instantly rippled to her toes. *Wow.* They both pulled back, the awe she felt reflecting in his eyes.

"Jordan…"

He lowered his mouth to hers again and this time, as the current ran through her, she didn't draw away but rejoiced at their incredible connection and moved closer.

Different than the angry, heated, kiss they'd shared in the spring, this one was stronger, more concentrated, more…potent.

Cole gathered her nearer still and she moaned at the new sensations wracking her body. Liquid fire replaced her blood, heating her from the inside out—while goosebumps shivered her flesh at the same time. Taking advantage of her opened mouth, he deepened the kiss, causing Jordan's insides to flutter. He tasted of champagne and passion, making her heady for more. Much more.

Running her tongue inside his mouth, she swallowed his groan and cupped his jaw for a better angle. They kissed long and deep and she didn't want to stop. If she hadn't needed to get air into her lungs, she would never have ended their first *real* kiss.

Resting her head on his shoulder, she looked down at her feet and grinned at her curled toes. "Man, Cole, you sure do pack a punch." She lifted her head and touched her fingers to her mouth. "That was better than our last one."

Chest heaving, he answered her smile. "You're the one who packs a punch, Jordan. You took the breath right out of me. And…" A regretful look crossed his face. "I'm sorry about that other kiss. It shouldn't have happened."

Eager to dispel his guilt, she touched his face and held his gaze. "Don't be sorry. I certainly didn't complain. Now," —Grinning, she pulled his head down to hers— "Let's see what I can do to give you back your breath."

Kissing him with a fervor she hadn't known she possessed, Jordan embraced the passion he induced. Finally, her opportunity to taste the man who'd haunted her life for so long. Strong fingers raked through her hair and sent the clip clanging to the balcony. He drew back panting and she used the break to suck in air.

Enthralled, he stared wide-eyed at the wavy tresses sliding through his fingers. Her chest swelled with a heady dose of triumph, and she glorified at being the woman responsible for his mesmerized expression. *About damn time*. She smiled, until he lifted his gaze. All the oxygen she just managed to put into her lungs dissipated by the raw need in his eyes.

"You're so beautiful, Jordan."

Emotions burned her throat.

"Hey, don't cry." He brushed an escaped tear. "You haven't even seen the feast I asked Emma to create."

His mischievous gleam had her beyond curious. Hand-in-hand he led her to the table. When he lifted the silver lid off the dish, she laughed at the plate of freshly baked chocolate chip cookies awaiting their demise.

"Oh Cole. You don't play fair, do you?"

He smiled, bringing one of the warm morsels to her lips. "Nope."

Neither do I.

Nibbling the cookie, her mouth deliberately brushed his hand. Desire burst into his gaze. She placed the remainder of the confection on the table to turn her attention to the chocolate on his finger and gently licked it off.

He drew in a sharp breath. "*Jordan.* God, do you have any idea what you do to me?"

He didn't give her a chance to answer as he devoured her strength with a greedy kiss. Fully aroused, her body was ready to take things further, to go where they should've gone years ago, but her mind threw up a roadblock to the fast lane they traveled.

"Cole, w-we need to slow down," she told him breathlessly, putting some space between them. "I-I haven't been...with another man since Eric died. In fact, h-he's the only man I've ever been with." She held up her hand to stop whatever words he was about to say. "Please, let me finish. Sharing my body is not something I take lightly, and although I've always wanted to share it with you—and still do—I just don't want to screw things up. I mean, once we give in to this, there's no turning back."

Her heated body promptly protested. She glanced at his full lips and questioned her decision. The talent she'd tasted was not easy to walk away from. But her mind niggled and Jordan had learned never to question that niggling. They just needed to make sure they were on the same page. It didn't mean they wouldn't make love, it just meant they'd realize what a big step they were taking, and take it together. She searched his face for understanding, hoping he wasn't angry or felt she'd lead him on.

He stepped closer and tipped her chin. "It's okay, sweetheart. I'd never rush or pressure you. I want to do this right."

Her pulse jumped at the endearment, and the gentleness in his eyes and voice warmed her heart.

"I'm glad you told me, Jordan, because it does change things. I'm sorry if I came on too strong." His index finger glided over her cheekbone. "But I honestly can't seem to control myself around you."

Relief washed away her stiffness and she lifted her palms to splay his chest. "It's alright, Cole. You toss me into a frenzy too. But at the same time, my head's telling me this is big, this is different than just physical and we need to acknowledge it."

"Then that's what we'll do."

He led her over to the table for a much needed glass of champagne. No protesting. No pressuring. It would only take one more of his delicious kisses to change her mind and send her back on that fast track. But this was the old Cole who'd always put other's needs before his own. The one thing she always coveted was his kindness. She loved him all the more for his sweet actions.

Jordan stilled. *Love?*

Her gaze met his over her poised glass. *Yes*, she loved Cole McCall. After all these years, her suppressed feelings for him had finally blossomed into love. This was no crush. And it certainly wasn't just physical attraction, although that was major. No. Her heart ached when his ached; soared when his soared; raced with passion when his raced. Hell, they were so intuned right now he could probably breathe for her.

She nibbled another cookie and decided to keep the news to herself for the time being. No sense in scaring the poor bugger away.

Not after she'd finally caught him.

Besides, this revelation was momentous and required time to sink in. The *L* word changed everything and Cole was right, this time, they needed to do things the right way.

"What do you say we simply spend the night together under the stars again?" He pointed to the hammock they'd shared in the spring. "I promise I'll behave."

Pleased, she smiled broadly. "I'd like that, Cole." Although, she wasn't sure she could behave.

A little while later, after a long, lazy, body warming kiss that had her trembling from head to toe and back again, he tucked her into the crook of his arm and covered them with a light blanket. Despite the warmth of the late summer night, she snuggled closer and sighed. Ear to his chest, she listened while his heartbeats slowed to a steady beat. Feeling his kiss on the top of her head, she gave his body a squeeze in response.

"Night, Cole."

"Good night, Jordan."

Before drifting off, she promised her deprived body she'd let Cole satisfy it very…very soon.

Waking up alone the next morning, Jordan groaned in disappointment. She'd hoped to see Cole before he left for work. Opening her eyes fully, she spied a rose in her hand with an attached note.

Lips instantly spreading into a grin that could grow no wider, she sprang into a sitting position and devoured his words.

Morning, sweetheart.

Thanks for last night. Know that I wouldn't have gone into work today if it hadn't been absolutely necessary. Please come to Houston and meet me for lunch. There's no way I can wait until tonight to see you again. I'll call you in a few hours to persuade you further.

Yours,

Cole

Jordan read and reread his note several times. *Please come to Houston...*He couldn't wait to see her. *Joy* chased *thrill* down her spine. He certainly didn't need to persuade her. She was eager to see him, too.

With a happiness too wondrous for words, she skipped inside to get ready. After a quick shower, she slipped into a pale aqua, strapless sundress, the prettiest dress she'd brought, and was just brushing her hair when her cell phone rang.

"Hello?"

"Morning, beautiful."

The intimate timbre of Cole's voice raced her heart and she closed her eyes and shivered. "Mmm…morning, handsome."

"Did you sleep well?"

"Yes. And you?"

"Oh yes," he stated firmly. "Are you going to meet me for lunch or do I need to persuade you?"

"Well, since my mother didn't raise a dummy, I'll go for the persuasion." Grinning, she twisted a strand of hair around her finger then frowned and pulled free. Dang sexy Texan had her acting like a schoolgirl.

"I figured you'd choose that." Cole chuckled. "Are you in your room?"

"Yes…why?" She stiffened and glanced around, searching for anything he might have done.

"Don't bother looking around, Jordan. You won't find it." His deep, smug tone tickled her ear and she giggled.

"Brat!"

"Try under your pillow."

She raced to her bed, lifted the pillow, and found a napkin wrapped around a chocolate chip cookie and another note.

Sweetheart,

Since the promise of my company wasn't enough, I hope this will be. If you'd like more, I'm holding eleven of its relatives hostage at McCall Enterprises. Come alone. Don't call the police for backup or I'll be forced to make the cookies disappear without a trace. Follow my instructions and I'll release the hostages into your custody.

Yours,
Cole

Laughing, Jordan shook her head. "You're crazy, do you know that?"

"Crazy about you," he boldly proclaimed. "So what's it going to be? You hold the fate of these defenseless morsels in your hands."

"Well, far be it for me to turn my back on them. When and where?"

"My office, one o'clock."

"I'll be there. And Cole?" She eyed the cookie in her hand. "There better not be any chips missing on them or you'll have me to deal with."

"Yes, ma'am. You fulfill your end of the bargain and I'll fulfill mine."

"Deal."

"I'll see you at one. Bye, Jordan."

"Bye, Cole."

Still smiling, she hung up and bit into her cookie. Having set the time for their date, she went down stairs to work on the arrangements for her parent's party, praying they would keep her mind occupied until it was time to leave.

Thankfully, they did.

At five to one, Jordan stepped off the elevator and strolled towards Stella.

"Well hello, Jordan." Cole's secretary smiled up at her.

"Hello, Stella."

"It would seem Mr. McCall has caught the same virus as you." The woman laughed when Jordan frowned. "You're both afflicted with the same sickening grin and light footedness."

"Ah, yes, the dreaded light-footed virus." She grinned down at the secretary. "He probably caught it from me when we kissed."

Stella shook her head, pointing to Jordan's face. "There's that sickening grin again. I'll tell Mr. McCall you're here."

An idea popped into her head. "No, wait. Is he alone?"

"Yes," Stella said slowly.

"Is he on the phone?"

"No." She sat back in her chair, her face full of curiosity.

"Good. Then I think it would behoove you to hold all his calls and make sure he isn't disturbed," Jordan informed, whipping a pair of handcuffs out of her purse.

Stella's eyes nearly popped out of her head.

"Jordan! What in the world are you going to do with those?"

She spun at Kevin's voice and grinned wide.

"Why, teach Cole a lesson, of course. He shouldn't mess with my cookies."

"I'm not even going to ask…I want to…but I won't." Kevin snickered, then sobered. "I'm really glad things have finally worked out for you two."

She cocked her head. "Forgive my bluntness, Kevin, but if you feel that way, why did you ask me out to dinner in the Spring?"

He winked. "To get a rise out of Cole. I would've explained it to you, had he actually *allowed* us to go out."

She laughed. "You're trouble, Kevin Dalton. Pure trouble."

"Yeah, well, I try." He straightened his collar and grinned.

"You don't need to try," Stella said under her breath.

Chuckling, Jordan walked to Cole's door, then turned. "If I'm not out in ten minutes"—she bounced her glance between them—"I'll be out in eleven."

Cole had never worked so hard or intensely all his years at McCall Enterprises—all to clear his schedule for lunch. For Jordan. He hit send, closed his computer and leaned back in his chair. The woman was never far from his mind. He wanted to give her his undivided attention. No distractions, no interruptions. Just them.

She was special, and as expected, given half the chance, he was falling for her, hard. A fact that thrilled and terrified at the same time. But he was so tired of terror, fear, pain. He wanted the joy, fun…pleasure her smiling eyes and open, honest heart promised. She deserved happiness, and he was beginning to realize he deserved happiness, too.

A light rap on the door and a second later Jordan breezed into his office and stole his breath. God, she was gorgeous in a strapless green dress, hugging and flowing in all the right places.

Laughter drifted in from behind her, before she shut the door and smiled. Not just any smile. No, heaven help him, it was sweet and mischievous at the same time and had his heart kicking the shit out of his ribs. He thought he heard her locking the door but couldn't be sure since his pulse thundered in his ears.

"Hi, beautiful." He pushed his chair back and was about to stand when she stopped him.

"Wait. Don't get up." She sent him a wicked grin.

Only too happy to oblige, he sat back in his seat, and watched her sway toward him, throat suddenly parched. The air crackled as she dropped her purse on his desk. This woman was up to something, and by God, he couldn't wait to find out. Anticipation sparkled in her dark eyes and, still grinning, she carefully lowered her sweet ass to the middle of his lap, dangling her sexy, supple legs over his right thigh, reminding him of that day she'd burst into his conference room.

She ran a hand up his chest and played with his lapel. "Now, tell me what I need to do to save those eleven cookies?"

Cookies were furthest from his mind as he ran a hand down her leg. *Damn, she was so soft.* "I can think of several things," he joked, all of them immature. He couldn't help it. He felt like a horny teenager around her. "A kiss would be nice, though."

He leaned closer but she pushed him gently back and slowly brought her face to his. "A kiss *would* be nice but first, we have business to take care of."

A sharp, snap echoed the instant cold steel closed around his wrist and a second before she stood.

"What the...?"

He looked down at his arm and frowned at the handcuffs locking him to the chair. A quick tug proved they were real.

"Now, what about those *hostages*, Mr. McCall? Where are they?" She glanced around.

Son-of-a-bitch! She handcuffed him to his chair. If that didn't fucking turn him on.

Big.

Time.

Heat rushed through his body, zapping every inch of him to life. Oh, he was more than up for her challenge.

"Maybe you should've thought to ask before you restrained me to my chair." He tipped his chin and held her sparkling gaze, issuing a challenge of his own. "I'm not going to tell you where they are unless you give me that kiss."

She shook her head and sighed. "Boy…the things a girl has to do for her cookies."

"I know. It's a damn shame what this world is coming to." He ran his free hand up her arm and tugged her back on his lap.

"Yes. Damn shame." Straddling him, she brushed the corner of his mouth with hers and drew his lower lip between her teeth for a nibble.

He cupped the back of her head and deepened the kiss, groaning when she thrust her hand through his hair and brushed the back of his neck with her thumb. She tasted hot and wild, her tongue teasing his before darting away. That wouldn't do. He needed more. The sound of protesting metal hit his ears as pain stung his restrained wrist. He grunted. If she hadn't immobilized that hand, he could crush her closer. That didn't stop him, though. He thrust his tongue inside her mouth and she moaned deep in her throat.

"The heck with the cookies…I'll take eleven more of those," she breathlessly exclaimed a minute later, just as lost and heated as him.

Cole chuckled. "That could be arranged." He kissed her again, long and wet, releasing her head to run his hand down her back to cup her sweet ass and pull her up against his zipper.

She let out a sexy, little sound before breaking the kiss to graze his jaw with her teeth while she unbuttoned his shirt from the tie down, and hungrily stroked and caressed in a frenzy of moves that nearly drove him mad. "God, you're so hot," she said against his jaw.

He closed his eyes in pure pleasure when she bit his neck and soothed the ache with her tongue. "Jordan—" He hissed out a breath when she sucked his earlobe into her warm, wet mouth.

"Hmm." She continued to kiss and lick.

"If you don't stop, I'm not going to be able to keep this thing between us slow."

She drew back and blinked at him. "Do you recognize this as more than physical?" she asked, waving a hand between them.

It was his turn to blink. "Yes." Hell yeah. She'd always meant more to him.

"Good, then to hell with slow," she said against his ear, tugging on the lobe again with her teeth, stroking his ribs with her wicked fingers, and his heart gave one hard lurch.

Fast track it is.

He kissed the side of her neck, loving the way her breath hitched.

"Did you lock the door?" Needing to feel her everywhere, he ran his hand down her leg, stroking the soft spot behind her knee.

She stilled, then drew back to look at him through heated eyes again. "What?"

"The door," he repeated, skimming his hand down her throat over her breasts, lingering on her beaded nipples. *God*, she was perfect. "Did you lock it?"

"Yes," she replied, rocking against him, head thrown back, eyes fluttering closed.

And just like that, he was a goner. She had him but good. Truth be told, she'd gotten under his skin a long, long time ago.

In less than a second, he had the top of her dress pulled down and, *oh yeah*, her warm, full breast in his hand while he sucked the tip of the other into his mouth.

So damn perfect.

She gasped and arched into him, driving him crazy. "Cole."

"I know," he said, switching to her other breast, rasping his tongue over her nipple, drawing another hissed breath from her throat.

Licking and nipping, he continued to answer her wordless pleas. Not letting his restrained arm slow him down, he slipped his free hand under the hem of her dress, running his fingers up her hot, trembling thigh until he found, *oh hell yeah*...her lace panties.

They were wet. Soaked.

She was destroying him.

He traced the lace with the pad of his finger and she whimpered and rocked against him. Back and forth he outlined, and her hands cupped his face and pulled him toward her mouth for a heated, hot, wet kiss. And when he slipped behind the lace to stroke her creamy, wet center, she mewed and thrust her tongue into his mouth while she rocked against his hand.

Ah hell, she was hot. *So fucking hot*. He slid a finger into her and pulled out on a long, sure stroke. She released his mouth to pant his name. *That sound... damn*, he loved the sound. So he did it again, and again with deliberate, careful, concentration.

"Cole," she panted. "You have to—"

"Take care of you, and I will." He upped the pace, and increased the pressure. She was so close. He could tell by the way she trembled over him.

"No, wait...it's not...fair..."

"Yes, it is. Come for me, Jordan. I want to feel you," he urged, adding a second finger, stroking her longer, faster.

"Please...don't stop."

He didn't. He leaned forward and licked her nipple, and her fingers dug into his biceps as she rode his hand. Looking up, his heart clutched at the absolute rapture covering her face, head back, eyes closed, lower lip caught between her teeth. *God*, she was a sight. Hair wild about her shoulders, falling across one breast, nipple peeking out as she moved.

Never had he ever seen anything so beautiful, it made him hotter and he nearly lost it when she gasped out his name and tightened around him as she burst.

Staying with her, he let her down slowly before removing his touch, completely thrilled he could bring her such pleasure…barely hanging on from how hot the experience made him. She opened her eyes and looked down at him, her panting filling the space between them.

"Damn, Cole…" She leaned forward and kissed him before drawing back to suck in more air.

He caressed her jaw and chuckled. "Imagine what I could do with both hands."

Her grin disappeared and gaze shot to his restrained hand. "Oh my God, Cole. I'm so sorry." She grabbed her purse from his desk and fished out the key. "I forgot."

As soon as she released him, he surged up, plopped her sweet ass on his desk and ran his newly freed hand over her breast, thrilling at her gasp. "I wasn't complaining," he said against her neck, biting the sweet spot behind her ear, making her cling to him. "And you weren't either."

"No way," she said breathlessly, running her hand down his chest to his lower abs, and if she just—

Yeah. Hell yeah, *that*. She outlined his erection with her finger cupping him, making him groan and press closer. He wasn't going to last much longer. As he ripped a condom from his pocket, she unhooked his belt and pants, and a second later freed him.

Something unintelligible sounded from her throat as her eyes devoured the part of him she gripped with her hands. She was destroying him.

Destroying.

Him.

He grabbed onto the desk and sucked in a breath. "Jordan." His voice was rough, because *damn*, he was barely holding on. He removed her hand, sucking in another breath, or three, while he tore the packet open and protected them.

Her hand was back on him, stroking, caressing, and when she leaned forward to lick his nipple he hissed in another breath.

"I need to have you inside me, Cole, please…" She leaned back on her elbows, looking up at him with so much heat it was a wonder he didn't disintegrate into ash. "Make me yours…"

With a sound hovering between a growl and groan, he grabbed her hips, drew her to the edge of the desk and thrust into her wetness in one quick drive. *Oh, sweet mercy.* "You feel so good." So fucking good. He gripped her thighs and held her still. If she even moved a hair, he was a goner.

A low moan sounded deep in her chest as she clenched her jaw and closed her eyes. Then heaven help him, she sat up, wrapped her legs around his hips and drew him in further. "Cole, I swear if you don't move soon I'm going to have to kill you." She nipped his chin, then his lower lip, her glorious breasts brushing his chest. A shudder racked through her and straight into him.

"Yes, my Masters," he managed to reply, brushing his mouth over her smile and he began to move. Slow didn't last long. They were far beyond that pace. And God, she felt good. *So damn, fucking good*. He'd never felt anything so exquisite.

Finally joined in the most primal, basic of ways, he closed his eyes, wishing he could stay that way and savor her forever.

Chapter Twelve

When Jordan said his name again, Cole opened his eyes to find her head tipped back, looking at him through dark pools of desire, bounce rippling through her breasts with each thrust. She was breathtaking. His heart split open and he felt hers. Connected. He was no longer drowning, needing, seeking something just out of reach. Hands on his shoulders, she looked down to where they joined, and he watched, too as he thrust into her, hard.

He felt her tremble, and it was too much. With a groan, he kissed her long and wet, nearing the edge, needing to end the long climb they started over ten years ago. Cupping her ass with one hand, he ground against her, and reached between them with the other to brush his thumb over her center. In an instant, she exploded and he immediately followed.

They collapsed on the desk, spent, breathing hard. *Christ*, he couldn't feel his legs. He angled his body to the side so he didn't crush her.

She smiled big and broad as she traced his face. "Damn, Cole. That…"

He kissed her hand. "Shouldn't have happened. I'm sorry, Jordan. I wanted our first time to be perfect."

She blinked and leaned up on her elbows to stare at him. "Are you kidding me? That *was* perfect. You and I have always been frantic and wild and out of control."

Now he smiled. "True. How could our first time be anything else?"

"Exactly." She cupped his face and kissed him lightly on the lips.

He drew back to look into her eyes. "You were worth the wait."

"Mmm…so were you," she said, trailing a finger down his abs. "And I can't wait to do that again."

Jesus, he was already half hard. And completely on board. "Me, too…but not here." He glanced around his office, his gaze settling on the conference room door. *Christ.* He stilled. "I forgot about locking that." He pulled out of her warmth, missing it immediately as he grabbed a piece of paper and disposed of the condom in the trash, before buckling his pants.

Her gaze bounced to the unlocked door. "Oh well." She shrugged, slid off the desk, and *damn*, fixed her dress, covering all her glorious secrets. "So, someone would've seen you programming my software with your hardware."

He laughed and pulled her close, loving how her arms immediately went around his neck and she leaned into him. "Yeah, they certainly would've seen that. Let's hope they didn't hear it. You weren't exactly quiet, you know." Smiling, he kissed her jaw.

"Yeah, well, neither were you," she said, running her hand up his bared torso, awakening the heat that had barely settled. "And don't think I forgot about my cookies, either." She released him to grab her handcuffs, key and panties from the floor. "Hmm, looks like you owe me more than cookies, McCall," she said, holding up piece of ripped, white lace.

"What can I say? It's not my fault you're so hot." He grabbed her hips and rocked into her. At her intake of breath, he smiled. "I couldn't get you naked fast enough."

A wicked grin crossed her lips as she slid her hands up around his neck. "Well, you just insured it won't take as long next time. Now, how about those cookies?"

He reached around her, opened the top drawer and pull out a white bag. "Here you go. Eleven cookies with all their chips intact as promised."

She stored the bag in her purse, along with her handcuffs, key and…panties.

Panties. Next time…

"Jordan." He looked from her to her purse then back again, blood rushing through his ears. "What about your…" He glanced down at her hips and swallowed. Didn't matter if she had a dress on. She was naked underneath. Naked.

A warm finger crooked under his chin and lifted his face. Devilment danced in her dark eyes. *Dear God, she was going to go the rest of the day…commando.* "That's right, McCall, thanks to you—" She buttoned his shirt, tucked it in and fixed his tie, then slapped his chest and smiled. "I'll be completely naked under here."

Another slap to his chest and she took advantage of his surprise, grabbing her purse from the desk before heading for the door. He was still staring at her sweet ass, zipper tightening painfully across his erection at the thought of it unencumbered. *Fuck.* He was doomed. He wouldn't last till lunch.

She stood by the door, waiting for him, smoothing her hair down but no amount of primping was going to erase the satisfied look on her beautiful face. A look he put there. He straightened and walked a little taller. Hell, he wanted to beat his chest. But he refrained, barely. Mostly because she opened the door.

Kevin straightened from Stella's desk and stared at Cole's hands. *Christ.* He hoped his friend hadn't heard them.

Jordan laughed. "It's okay. I've already released him."

Hell yeah, and what a release!

"I take it he behaved?" Kevin's blue eyes sparkled.

She glanced up at Cole and grinned. "No."

"No? Then why are you smiling?"

Stella sighed and smacked Kevin's arm. "Because he *didn't* behave, you big dope!"

"Oh." His friend's goofy smile broadened. "Kerri doesn't happen to have a set of handcuffs too, does she?"

"No. Her specialty is knives and meat cleavers."

Kevin shuddered. "Just not the same."

Cole slung his arm around Jordan's shoulder and led her to the elevator. Enough talk. He wanted to get her alone again. Hell, it'd already been two minutes.

"I'll be back in an hour," he tossed to the others.

"Don't forget we have that Network Security Dinner tonight," Kevin called back.

Cole stiffened. "Damn. I did forget." His gaze met hers. "I don't suppose you'd be interested in going with me? There'll be lots of boring talk of software and the latest computer innovations?"

"Well, since you put it that way, how can a girl resist?" She placed a hand on his shoulder and smiled. "I'd love to."

He chuckled and hit the down button. "Doesn't take much to make you happy, does it?"

Withholding nothing from her gaze, she looked up at him, emotions warm in her incredible eyes. "No…just you."

His chest suddenly ached. "You've got me."

"Stella," Kevin began. "If you're looking for me I'll be in the bathroom throwing up."

Jordan and Cole snickered, turning their attention to the retreating man, walking backwards down the hall.

"I'll see you two later. Cocktails start at six. And, Cole, I don't want to see you until then."

"Listen to that." Cole raised a brow, quite happy to oblige. "My VP giving me orders."

"He's right," Stella agreed. "You already finished your important business. There's nothing pressing for the rest of the day."

Jordan leaned closer. "Seems he's in cahoots with your secretary. What are you going to do about it?"

He grinned as the elevator opened behind them. "Make an executive decision, of course—I'm going to take the afternoon off and spend it with you."

"I was hoping you'd say that." She tugged him inside before the doors closed.

"Let me fix it so we get an express to the street." He shoved a key in a slot and pressed a button then crossed his arms and leaned back against the wall. "Now, there's something I've just got to know."

"What?"

"Why do you carry handcuffs in your purse? I mean, if you're off duty, can you carry them?"

She chuckled. "They're my personal ones."

"Oh?" His heart knocked his ribs.

She hit his arm. "For my dog."

"Your dog?" A smile tugged at his mouth. He hadn't expected that.

"Bullet, my German Sheppard."

He grabbed her hands, twisted their positions, and pressed her into the wall. *Oh yeah, this was much better.* And if it weren't for the damn security cameras, he'd take her against the wall. "Dogs don't have hands, Jordan," he murmured, trailing kisses down her throat to her breasts…naked under her dress.

"Really? Well…nobody told *me*." She gasped when he nibbled near her ear. "I use them to chain Bullet's leash to the fence behind the restaurant. They're stronger than the hook."

He chuckled. She was too much. "Only you would find a way to use handcuffs on a dog," he said into the curve of her delectable shoulder.

By the time they reached the bottom he was famished—but not for food. She sent him a knowing smile…an *agreeing* smile and straightened her dress as the doors opened. *Sexy, damn Masters*. He fixed his tie, offered his arm, and together they walked out into the lobby full of curious looks from his employees.

Let them look. He didn't care. He was happy and satisfied and whole. Feelings he hadn't felt in so long. Hadn't wanted to feel…until now.

Until Jordan.

He stared at the beautiful woman holding his arm, leaning close, smiling, brushing her luscious curves against him. And as usually happened when he allowed her behind his wall, his heart leapt with pure, unaltered joy. He wanted her near. Plain and simple. He wanted her near.

"Where are the keys to your car?" Not about to waste one minute of their day in separate vehicles, he brought them to a halt in front of reception. "I'll have someone drive it back to the ranch."

"Actually," she said, digging in her purse. His gut tightened when he caught sight of lace, before she dropped the keys into his hand. "This is a good opportunity to take the rental back to the airport. I don't need it. Kerri and I will be driving back with Shawn and Megan, and mom said I can borrow hers if I need one." Sadness flashed through her eyes before she blinked the emotion away.

His gut suddenly twisted for a completely different reason. Next week at this time, she'd be gone. Back to her life in California.

Maybe he could persuade her to stay longer, he thought forcing himself to breath normally. "Good idea. Are the papers in the glove compartment?"

"Yes."

"Then I'll have someone return it to the airport."

He handed the keys to the receptionist while Jordan told the lady where the car was parked. She turned to Cole, determination straightening her shoulders. *That's his Jordan*. She wasn't going to let her eminent departure ruined their time together. Besides, a lot could happen in a week.

She grabbed his hand, smiled up at him and squeezed. "Now, how formal is this dinner party?"

Half past midnight, they pulled up to the ranch and neared the end of their second date. Warm fingers laced with Jordan's as Cole helped her out of the car. The Network Security Dinner had actually been fun. She glanced at him as they strolled toward the house hand-in-hand under the moonlight. Beyond gorgeous in his black tuxedo, he stole her breath, much as he had the whole night. Hell, the whole day.

Intelligent, witty, and charming, he handled his speech with ease and had everyone, including her, eating out of the palm of his hands. The man swept her off her feet and she never wanted to set foot on earth again.

Tired but not wanting to part, she slowed her steps. "Do you think Emma's left anything in the kitchen for us to snack on?"

His teeth gleamed under the Texas moon. "I'm sure we can find something. And if not, I'm completely available."

Damn, but that man was irresistible. She'd already *snacked* on him twice today…and he on her three times. Heat shot low in her belly just thinking about their day. The sexy Texan couldn't keep his hands to himself. Seems her lack of undergarments tormented him. *Ah, poor baby*. Lucky her. He had big hands. Great hands. Damn talented hands.

Jordan always knew when they finally got together it would be explosive, but hell…she hadn't realized just how fiery and all out consuming their union would be.

And heaven help her, she was ready for more.

She swayed closer, pressing into his hot, rock hard form while caressing the five-o'clock shadow now covering his strong jaw. How would it feel against her skin?

"And I'm completely game." She smiled, pulling his mouth to hers for a long, wet, deep kiss. Her new, favorite kind.

His hands crushed her close, grinding into her, cupping her ass because, *oh yeah*, she didn't have anything on underneath the black Halston Heritage gown she'd bought today. The gown he offered to buy but she wouldn't let him. The gown from the store who's fitting room proved just how great Cole *fit* inside her.

"Jesus, Jordan, you drive me crazy," he said against her ear.

He said that a lot.

"I can't get enough of you."

And that, too. And she certainly felt the same way.

"Hmm…" She drew back and nodded. "Ditto."

Smiling as they entered the house, she warned her body to remain cool. This was the McCall household. She would not disrespect them by devouring their youngest son in the kitchen.

Four pairs of startled eyes looked up from the table as they entered.

"Wow, look at the two of you." Mrs. McCall's hand flew to her mouth.

Her mother smiled. "Jordan, you look lovely. And you look very handsome, Cole."

"Thank you. But anyone would look good next to your daughter." He released her fingers to slide his hand tantalizingly slow across her back until he cupped her hip and squeezed.

"How did your presentation go, son?" Mr. McCall set his coffee on the table and waited for his son to reply.

Cole shrugged. "Good."

"He's being modest," Jordan told them proudly. "It went better than that. His software met with a standing ovation and high praise."

Impressed beyond words when he'd given his presentation, she'd sat there enthralled. His speech was strong, eloquent, informative and even humorous at times. When he'd made a statement that the only virus his software couldn't prevent was the *Jordan Virus*, she'd nearly choked on her wine. Confusion had rumbled through the guests, until he cleared the matter up by asking her to stand and introduced her as his *Jordan Virus*.

"That's wonderful, Cole. Congratulations." His mother stood and gave him a kiss on his cheek, bringing Jordan's mind back to the present.

"Yes. Good job, son."

His dad and her parents all slapped Cole's back on their way out and, in a blink of an eye, they were alone.

"Wow, we sure know how to clear a room." She chuckled, looking around the deserted kitchen.

"Now that they're gone…"

Strong hands tenderly cupped her face as he gazed warmly into her eyes. Her heart fluttered.

Yay, more snacking.

Her palms glided over sinew from his chest to shoulders on her way to tangle in the thick hair at the back of his head. "Yes?"

Smiling, full lips brushed hers ever so slightly, turning one tantalizing second into two before they grew bold and deepened the kiss. Tongues explored and teased, bodies pressed closer, straining to touch. She was addicted to the taste of his wild abandonment.

Just when her lungs threatened to burst, he broke the embrace and buried his face in her neck while they both drew in several deep breaths.

Holy smokes, could the man kiss.

The sound of the kitchen door opening had her taking one step back from Cole and gaze shooting to Connor's large form.

"Wow, look at you two." He stopped dead. "Did you just get back from the prom or something?"

They laughed.

"You know…I wanted Cole to take me to my prom but…he wouldn't," Jordan pouted, enjoying the dazed looked in her cowboy's eyes.

"I was several states away." He frowned. "You didn't miss out going, did you?"

"My goodness, no. The star quarterback asked me."

His body stiffened. "Oh."

Connor grinned, grabbing a bottle of beer from the refrigerator. "Built was he?"

"Yes, and blond in a California kind of way." Biting her lip, she turned her back to Cole and busied herself with rinsing their parents' cups. She knew she was bad, but couldn't resist falling in line with Connor's teasing.

"He was probably a surfer, too," Cole muttered.

She swiveled to face him with innocent surprise. "How'd you know? He won several tournaments and everything."

"Wow, he must've been good," Connor exclaimed.

"He *was* good. I was life-guarding at a few of those tournaments. I believe he set some record or other."

"Wait a minute." Connor's beer bottle paused in mid air. "You were a lifeguard? Like on that television show?"

She rolled her eyes and glanced down at her chest. "Not exactly. The *girls* never could get that bounce just right."

Muttering an oath, Cole yanked the fridge open and swiped a bottle of water from the shelf.

Mischief hovered in Connor's brown gaze. "So what ever happened to the star quarterback/surfer and the lifeguard?"

She fought her smile. "He asked her to go steady."

"And what did the lifeguard say?" Connor prodded.

Cole slammed the refrigerator shut, rattling the jars in the door. "She said, no."

"No?" Connor's bottle clanked onto the counter. "Why ever not?"

She moved to stand in front of her brooding date. "Because he wasn't Cole."

Delight replaced the dark expression as her words sunk in. The corner of his mouth lifted. "He wasn't?"

She traced his jaw. "Nope, none of them could compare to you. Ever."

Deep affection and heat combined to smolder in his gaze as he pressed her against the counter, cupped her face and kissed her slow and sweet.

Connor cleared his throat. "Don't mind me. You all go ahead…have some fun. I'll be fine."

Cole broke the kiss and dropped his forehead to hers. "Did you hear something?"

"Nope." She smiled, playing with his collar. "But maybe your brother did."

They laughed, including Connor. She released Cole and walked to her purse, withdrawing the white bag.

"Anyone care for a cookie?"

Connor blinked a second before his hand shot into the air. "Hold on a cotton-pickin'-minute. First Cole's grinning like the Cheshire cat and now Jordan's sharing cookies?" His gaze bounced between them. "Wow. You two *are* good for each other."

"I tried to tell your brother that over a decade ago." She nodded toward Cole.

He stepped to her, settled his hands around her waist, then said softly, "I'm listening now," before brushing her mouth with his.

"Okay, I can take a hint," Connor joked good-naturedly and headed toward the door. "Night, you two."

"Good night, Connor." Cole chuckled, hugging her head to his chest.

"Night, Connor," she echoed, preoccupied by the pounding of Cole's heart beneath her ear as Connor disappeared through the swinging door, leaving them alone in the silence.

"I hate to say it, but I better get you up to your room."

Goosebumps raced his fingers, skimming a path down her arms on the way to her hands.

"Yes, it's getting late," she replied, reluctant to leave him.

Arms around each other's waists, they walked silently to her room. What a day it had been. She didn't want it to end, and wondered if it must. Again, she didn't want to disrespect his parents, but…*God,* she just couldn't let go of this man.

When they arrived at her room, she twisted her back to her door and looked up expectantly as he leaned his hand on the doorframe and gazed down.

"I had such a wonderful day today, Cole." Her body wanted his again with a hunger so fierce the passion admittedly scared her, but the new intimacy—the tenderness harboring such promise and hope was too special to ignore. They'd already taken the first step. It was too late to turn back. And she was so happy he felt the same way and took a chance on her. How could she possibly not take a chance on the man she'd always known she belonged with—even before she'd been old enough to vote?

"I had an incredible day, too." His finger trailed a streak of fire up her neck to her lower lip. "I hope you'll have dinner with me tomorrow. I did have a nice one planned for tonight, until Kevin reminded me about that presentation."

She eyed his hovering lips. "I'd love to." Anticipation flowed like a river rushing over rapids.

"Good," he whispered into her mouth.

Kissing her slow and deep, he turned her legs to liquid, and forced her to cling tightly to his solid frame. Over and over he delved, taking his time, thoroughly attacking her brain cells. When it ended, he pressed his forehead to hers and took a deep breath.

"Jordan..." His voice was rough with need, as he slowly stroked her bottom lip with his thumb. "I had every intention of kissing you goodnight and heading to my room, but I can't seem to let you go."

"God, I was hoping you'd say that. I don't want you to go, either." She opened her door and drew him inside, holding his smoldering gaze. "Stay with me tonight, Cole."

With that sexy growl-like groan, he thrust his hands in her hair and covered her mouth with his as he closed the door behind them.

The next night, Jordan had no idea where they were going for dinner so she opted for casual and donned a pale blue halter sundress. Hair clipped up because of the heat, she added the jewelry Cole had given her and came downstairs as he entered the house.

"Mmm…mmm…mmm. You look great." He dropped his briefcase on the table by the door to take her in his arms. "I've been dreaming of this all day."

"Me too." She met his kiss head on. He was hot and hard and delicious and her body craved all of him. The greedy bugger.

"Okay, the sooner I get changed the sooner we can go." His voice matched the reluctance in his eyes as he released her and turned to take the stairs two at a time.

She hoped he changed just as fast. With a smirk on her lips she stepped into the kitchen to chat with Kerri and Emma in an attempt to occupy her mind—she'd never been good at waiting. And now that she'd been with him a few times, her body was already highly charged for his touch.

When Cole strode in fifteen minutes later, her throat dried. *Holy cowboys*. Sleeves rolled up on his tapered white buttoned-down shirt, his lean form and bronzed muscled arms toppled her heart. She couldn't believe he was hers. Finally hers. Black Stetson and boots completed the package she wanted to open and use and ride…and if she didn't get off at the next station the train she was on was going to take her straight to orgasm.

Every inch of him was male and every inch would be hers. Again. Tonight. She trembled but kept her need in check. They had an audience. She slid off the stool and swayed toward him.

"That looks wonderful." He smiled.

At first she thought he'd meant her, then followed his gaze to the food Kerri and Emma were packing.

Packing?

The two women place fried chicken and a few other finger foods into a soft insulated pouch. She'd just spent the past fifteen minutes with the cooks and hadn't realized the food they were preparing had been for her and Cole.

Jordan pursed her lips and fought a grin. *There goes another round of brain cells lost to the likes of Cole McCall.* At this rate, she'd be a blubbering idiot by the end of the week.

"That should do it, Cole." Emma zipped the bag, then handed it to him with a smile.

"Thanks, Emma, Kerri," he said, grabbing the cooler.

Kerri smiled. "Anytime. You two have fun."

"We will." He turned to Jordan and held out his elbow. "Shall we?"

"Yes." She grinned and together they left the house.

When they appeared to be heading for the stables, she glanced sideways at him. "Okay, you've got me. The sun is almost down, we're not taking the car and you're carrying a basket of food. Where exactly are we going?"

He led her to the last stall where Connor was busy saddling Cole's horse.

"Someplace special."

His gaze softened and her questions disappeared. As long as it was with him, it was special. Her glance fell to his lips. "Lead the way."

"Jordan," he groaned thru clenched teeth. "Stop looking at me like that or we're not going to leave this stable."

"Yes, *please*, Jordan." Connor grimaced. "I'm glad you two are finally seeing each other but I don't need to witness it firsthand. A kiss is one thing, but that?"

"Yeah…yeah, Connor. We're going." Smirking, she helped Cole secure their dinner and a blanket before he swung into the saddle and held out his hand.

Her pulse leapt at the intimacy a shared mount would bring. Thankful the skirt of her dress was loose fitting, she had no trouble joining him on the horse. Breathing, however, was an entirely different story.

"Don't do anything I wouldn't do," his brother preached.

"That leaves the slate *wide* open," she said on an expelled breath.

"You're darn right, darlin'. You're darn, right." Connor winked, then slapped the hind end of the horse.

The creature lurched forward and soon Jordan rode off into the setting sun and to her fate with Cole McCall.

Light-hearted and light-headed at the same time, she wrapped her arms around his broad form and pressed her body into his back. Her nipples beaded against him from the friction of the gallop's erotic bounce. Their fast paced knocked away her hair clip, and she closed her eyes and enjoyed the sense of freedom as her locks flounced in the wind.

When the horse slowed to a trot and eventually stopped, she opened her eyes and gasped. They'd reached the big oak tree overlooking the ocean. *Their tree.* And at the base sat a romantic picnic for two with a red-and-white-checkered blanket and hurricane lamp.

Playing their song, the ocean roared in the distance and swallowed the setting sun, leaving the sky streaked in a mass of deep purples and blues.

"Cole, this is incredible…" Her breathless tone faded into his back. Once again, she couldn't believe he'd gone through all of this…for her.

The warmth of his palm seeped into the hand she'd clamped around his hip.

"I'm glad you approve," he said before dismounting with ease.

Turning to her, he looked up, and his sucked-in breath dropped his jaw and hissed into the breeze. Hunger—instant and fierce—entered his gaze as he held his arms out to help her down.

Pulse roaring louder than the surf, she slid off the horse and into his arms, his large hands brushing the sides of her breasts on her way down.

"You're so beautiful, Jordan," he breathed, his voice husky and full of emotion. Finger tenderly touching her skin, he traced a path from her chest to her shoulder as he pushed back a strand of hair. "So damn beautiful."

The rising and falling of her chest increased when he continued to trace a path to her parted lips. Her tongue snaked to touch his finger and hot breath hissed through his teeth. Empowered, she repeated the action. He groaned and brought his mouth down on hers.

Finally.

Wrapping her arms around his neck, she inadvertently knocked his hat off but neither of them cared. Long and deep and wet, they kissed with wild abandon flowing in their veins. Seemed like this could be their common way of kissing. *Yay!* By the time they came up for air, her body ached for release. A release only he could give.

He sucked in air and stared down at her through smoldering eyes. "If you kiss me like that I won't be able to keep the promise I made to myself to take things slow. To make tonight special."

His dark hair captured a glimmer of the sun's disappearing glow, while his words captured her heart. She loved him, always had, and the fact he was trying to keep his promise surely must mean his feelings for her ran deep. This was more than physical; more than great sex on a desk or fitting room or bed. She wanted to give him all of her and was ready to take whatever he would give in return.

Convinced she was right, a calmness swept over her. The time for holding back had passed and the time for Cole and Jordan had arrived.

She cupped his face and stared into his incredible eyes. "Tonight is already special, Cole. We're together. That's all I need." Her gaze dropped to his full, talented lips and a tremor shook through her. "And right now, I need you, very, *very* much."

To prove it, she pulled his face down to lick lightly across his lower lip. A rough sound rumbled in his throat and he crushed her close, exploring her mouth with a bold and oh-so-talented tongue. Heat shot through her body and she made a rough sound of her own. *More, please.* She had to have more. Wet and throbbing, she longed to have other parts of him inside.

Only because she was about to burst did she break away to drag in a breath. "Let's get out of these clothes…and onto…the blanket."

"Wait." He backed up and thrust both hands through his hair. "Jordan, I don't have any protection with me. Taking it slow…I wasn't expecting to…"

"That's okay."

"Awe, hell, Jordan. I'm sorry." A hand shot through his hair again.

"No." She stepped closer and caressed his jaw. "I mean, I'm on the pill, have a clean bill of health."

"Me, too."

She smiled. "So…I'm okay with not using protection…if you are."

He blinked as realization dawned. "What if…"

"We make a baby?" She giggled and kissed his chin. "I'm okay with that too." This was the man she belonged with, the man she wanted to have children with so if it happened sooner than later, she saw no problem. "What do you say, McCall? You willing to take the chance?"

His eyes blazed the reply his words confirmed. "Yes, ma'am."

He had the lamp lit and his boots off before she could blink. While he worked on his belt, she helped him with his shirt, snapping it open and yanking it off with a quick jerk. Bared for her eyes and touch, his glorious abs, chiseled chest, and broad shoulders begged for attention.

She willing obliged.

Running her hands over his carved muscles, she yearned to feel and taste every last ridge. It had been nearly sixteen hours. Sixteen long hours. And although they'd already had sex several times now, they hadn't been completely naked out in the open before. He disposed of the rest of his clothes and stood before her in the naked splendor she'd glimpse at that watering hole many years ago.

Boy, had the years been kind.

All muscle, no fat and a whole hell-of-a-lot of Cole. She swallowed, boldly taking his erection in her hand.

"Jordan…*dammit* woman." His hot words matched his breath as he sunk his teeth into her neck.

Heat rushed in shards low in her belly and just like that she went damp. She needed to have him inside. Now. Releasing him, she stepped back to slip out of her sandals and rip off her dress.

His sharp intake of breath stilled her hands as they fingered the band of her baby blue silk thong.

"You're so damn beautiful."

Dark eyes devoured and caressed her body, peaking her nipples even further.

He swallowed and nudged her hands aside. "Allow me."

Chapter Thirteen

Gifted fingers, full of magic and fire, scorched Jordan's skin as they grazed her hips, thighs and calves before she stepped out of her final piece of clothing.

"So damn beautiful," he repeated, staring up at her.

Exploring hands started their ascent, along with his lips and she trembled under his touch as he kissed her body from toe to head. When his mouth found hers, she wrapped her arms around him and crushed their bodies together. Hard, ripped and hot, he felt so good pressed close her legs nearly buckled.

Cole picked her up and laid her on the blanket, then ended their kiss to tease and torture her nipples, rasping them one by one against the roof of his mouth. She drew in a breath and arched, desperate to feel his hot touch on more of her sensitized skin. As if he knew, his wandering fingers found her wetness and slid inside.

"So wet." He made a rough, sexy sound deep in his chest while his finger stroked slow and deep. She moaned. *Damn* he was good. But she wasn't ready to burst…well, *hell yeah*, she was, but didn't want to lose control just yet.

Breath hitched, she pushed his shoulder and flipped him over. "My turn," she panted, straddling him.

His eyes sparkled and erection throbbed against the inside of her upper thigh—deliciously close to her own throbbing zone. Leaning down, she kissed his lips, tugging on the lower one before trailing to his earlobe, then pulled back to puff air over his moistened skin. He hissed her name, tightened his grip on her waist and rocked his hips in a sensual rhythm. *His* rhythm. A rhythm she now knew and would never forget.

"Somebody likes that," she teased, sinking her teeth into his neck, while she ran her hand down his heated skin and thumbed his abs just below his belly button. Taught and hard and quivering, his body was magnificent.

Finding his hot length, she stroked and squeezed, and he let go another of those sexy, deep rumbles while she kissed his torso on her way down. Need burned her body with trembling force as her breasts skimmed his muscles. *Mmm…he was lickable. So damn lickable.* Riding the frenzied tide, she covered his thick tip with her lips.

"Christ, Jordan," his hoarse gasp filled the evening air and blew away with the ocean breeze. Strong fingers tangled in her hair to lightly grip her head. Delighting in his thrusts, she took in more until he grabbed her shoulders and drew her back up his body. "Enough. I'm not done with you yet."

Capturing her mouth, he rolled her onto her back. Heat pooled low in her belly along with rapidly building pressure. She spread her legs to welcome him. He drew back and looked down at her through smoldering eyes. "God, you're so beautiful."

But he didn't enter her. No. He bent down and kissed her long, and lazy, and hot. She was so on fire. This unhurried, smoldering he had going on was slowly consuming every inch of her trembling being, driving her out of her mind.

"Slow this time," he murmured against her neck, collarbone, over her breasts where he lingered and had her pleading in seconds. "Soon." He headed south to the curve of her hip before placing open-mouthed kisses across her belly. His breath was warm, his chin deliciously rough against her skin and finally, finally he brushed her thighs. She closed her eyes and drew in a breath, need ripping through her. He nudged them open with his shoulders and settled her legs where he wanted them.

"Cole, I..."

"I know," he said, his gaze dark and fierce with the same need. "I'll give you anything you want, Jordan. Anything."

She wanted...she wanted...him. Just him and his love. But she wouldn't ask. Not exactly. "Love me," she begged instead.

His gaze grew wickedly indecent and that in itself nearly set her off. "With pleasure," he promised an instant before he traced a finger over her center.

She jerked with a gasp, but he wouldn't be rushed. The bugger kissed her inner thigh, his chin grazing her sensitive skin in a delicious rasp. She moaned her approval. "Somebody likes that," he said, repeating her words from earlier, then kissed her other thigh. "Me, too."

Without warning, he slid a finger inside and she cried out and arched right up off the blanket. A rough sound ripped from his throat. "You're so wet."

He settled her back down, ragged breath warm and tantalizing on her sensitive skin. *Cripes*, she was wound so tight a few more puffs of air and she was going to burst.

"I have to taste you," he said, and then did.

"Yes..." That was what she wanted, too. She was quivering and hot and he was right there, his mouth warm and seeking on her damp folds. "Please..." And he did, sucking her into his mouth while he slid a finger inside her, then another. It was too much. Too incredible. Perfect. He was perfect, and on his second stroke she burst with a powerful release.

He brought her down gently, and when he lifted his head after taking one last lick, his eyes were so dark and so heated she lost her breath all over again. Holding her gaze, he entwined their fingers and with one thrust, drove deep inside her. She cried out, lost in the incredible feel of him filling her so completely.

All Cole. Raw Cole. No barriers.

And there were no barriers in the emotions she saw in his eyes. Their hearts connected, bodies connect…souls connected in that very moment. She wrapped her legs around him, drawing him in further, and he slowly lowered himself down. They were chest to chest, heart to heart, nothing separated them, not even air. He held her tight, as if she was his very life, and he certainly was hers. Continuing to hold her gaze, he began to move, pulling nearly all the way out before thrusting in to the hilt.

Hunger took over. Need rushed through her body, blazing where they touched. Everywhere. Eyes dark, he continued the slow thrusting, their ragged breathes combining to form rough spurts competing with the distant roar of the ocean. She was falling, drowning with this man…in this man, and nothing else mattered. Not their unspoken words, their past, their future. Nothing but right now. The unhurried drag of their bodies and the fierce connection they shared.

She was not going to be able to let him go next week. No way could she walk away from this man.

But what if what she was seeing in his gaze and feeling in his touch wasn't enough for him to want her to stay?

Tears burned behind her eyes and she closed them, not wanting him to see the depths of her emotions for fear it would scare him off.

"Jordan."

They were supposed to take it slow, but she'd jumped straight to light speed.

"Jordan, look at me."

Somehow she managed to open her eyes and meet his gaze, hoping she'd toned down her emotions. But the look in his eyes told her she needn't bother.

Gaze soft and warm, he gently touched her lip, brining tears back to her eyes. *God*, she loved this man.

"Cole I..."Emotions clogged her throat.

"I know," he said. Moonlight glistened off his heated skin and a trillion stars twinkled above as he began to move again, reigniting the blaze. "Me, too." He kissed her deeply, completing the connection, intensifying the burn.

He upped the pace, thrusting harder and faster, breaking the kiss to look down at her, holding her gaze as he slid almost all the way out then drove all the way home. That's when she burst and took him with her.

Warm, languid, and tingling, she lay under him, watching his shoulders rise with each ragged breath. He pulled out but didn't leave her arms.

"You were incredible, Jordan," he said against her collarbone, lips brushing her skin in a soft caress.

She smiled and hugged him closer. "Yes, you were, Cole."

He made a noise in his throat but otherwise was quiet as he kissed her neck, her temple, her eyes. She could've stayed like that forever. Lavishing his back with caresses, she loved the feel of his hard muscle under her fingers. He leaned on his elbows, lifting some of his weight but not his gaze. Dark eyes gleamed as a warm finger grazed over her breast.

"I'm not done with you yet."

His words and his touch brought a delicious shiver to her skin and anticipation tingled in all her good parts.

"But I need some food to replenish my strength. I say we dig into that meal. You wait here," he said, giving her a quick kiss on the lips before headed for the basket.

Feeling more content than anyone had a right to, she stretched and waited for his return. Her stomach growled. Maybe eating wasn't such a bad idea. The cowboy certainly helped her work up an appetite. When he approached with their food, she sat up and pulled in a breath.

He really was beautiful. Naked. Lean. Ripped.

Naked.

Eyes gleaming dark and delicious under the glow of the nearby hurricane lamp, he placed the food and cooler on the blanket, then kissed her hard, running his hands down her torso. "I think we'd better eat quick. I need to be inside you again."

She trembled, completely on track with his plan. "Yes, very quick."

He poured wine while she made them each a plate of chicken and raw vegetable, leaving the dessert for last. She smiled. Her sister would be getting a big hug tomorrow.

"What's that grin for?" He raised a brow as he ate.

"Wait till you see dessert."

His drumstick poised mid air. "Oh?"

"Yes, eat up." She had several bites of chicken before nibbling on a piece of celery.

He skimmed a slice of carrot up her arm and circled her shoulder before he popped the vegetable in his mouth. She was still shivering when he spoke. "Tastes much better with Jordan on it."

She ran her gaze down his naked splendor and smiled. "Well I know you'll *enhance* dessert."

His gaze darkened and he pushed their plates aside. "Bring it."

"Oh, believe me, McCall, that's exactly what I intend to do." She winked, pushed him onto his back, then pulled out the strawberries and chocolate sauce.

He stilled. "Oh-ho-ho, man. You can keep the strawberries, give me that sauce!"

She slapped his reaching hand. "Nope. Me first."

Taking a dipped strawberry to his chest, she swirled it around before biting the bottom of the berry. "Not bad." She leaned down to lick the chocolate from his skin, lingering to scrape her teeth over his nipple, smiling when he uttered an oath. "Mmm, that's good, too."

His tortured gaze darkened further. "When do I get to taste?"

She rubbed the berry across her chest. He groaned. Smiling, she brought the strawberry to his lips. He bit into the fruit, then licked the juice and sauce from her finger.

"That was delicious." Then before she knew it, he had her on her back and was licking the chocolate off her breasts, lapping and licking until she writhed under him.

They spent the next ten minutes sampling each other's bodies, until they ran out of dessert. Hot, demanding lips found hers. He tasted of chocolate, berries, wine, and a whole lot of passion—bringing a whole new meaning to the term *passion fruit*.

Fully erect, he was as ready as her trembling form. Wanting to shift their foray down to the beach, she moved from underneath him and stood, while her mind still harbored a few brain cells.

"We need to clean up." She winked, nodding toward the ocean.

He rose to his feet and opened his mouth to speak, then stilled when a fat rain drop hit his shoulder. "I've the feeling that's not going to be a problem."

Following his gaze to the sky, she noticed the moon and stars had disappeared and a rumble of thunder shook the night.

She frowned. "When did that happen?"

"Must've been when you were ravishing me." He grinned, running a bold hand down her back.

"Mmm, yes. I guess I was preoccupied." She smiled and would've returned the caress but he stopped her.

"Sorry, sweetheart. We really should head back before everyone worries about us out in the storm."

She sighed. "I guess you're right."

Late summer storms in Texas were nothing to take lightly.

Dressed quickly, they were halfway through packing up when it started to drizzle. As fast as possible, they finished their tasks and galloped for the ranch.

Completely soaked by the time they reached the stable, Jordan's body hummed with need. Their frantic pace forced her to cling to Cole, and the frenzied contact of brushing up and down his slick, warm back fogged her mind with a haze of delight. Sliding her hands under his wet shirt, she stroked the hard, hot flesh of his chest and abs. *Mmm…yes, please.* Trembling into him, she inhaled the scent of ocean and rain. Images of the two of them naked and entangled increased her ache. She needed to finish what they'd started. Needed him and his unrivaled release. Nothing else mattered.

Legs quivering, center heavy with desire, she was eager to face the front of him when she lost her grip and fell from the horse to the stable floor.

"Jordan? Jordan, are you all right?" He was kneeling at her side in an instant, eyes dark and tortured as they swept over her body. "Wait! Don't move. Let me check you first."

"I'm fine, Cole…although, I wouldn't mind if your hands ran all over me to make sure."

"I'm serious, Jordan." Brows knitted together in a face seemingly devoid of blood, he muttered an oath. "Look how close your head is to the damn pitchfork someone left laying out." His fist shook around the handle before he propelled the pitchfork across the stable.

Her heart lurched.

"Hey." She sat up, grasped his chin and looked straight into his wild, darting gaze. "I'm fine, Cole. Nothing bruised but my ego."

Pressing her lips to his, she kissed him until he took over the embrace. She never wanted to see that crazed, worried look in his eyes again. Ever.

He rolled her on top of him and granted her wish when his hands roamed all over her fevered body. Desire returned in a rush of heat. She knew they needed to get inside but…

His horse whinnied.

Cole stiffened and she reluctantly lifted her mouth.

"I…uh…guess I should take care of him," he said without enthusiasm.

The light on the porch flicked on in the distance. She sighed. "I was hoping you'd take care of me but looks like you were right. Our parents are up and no doubt worried."

"Yeah, but don't worry, Jordan." He smiled and helped her to her feet. "I have a special day planned for you tomorrow."

She shivered despite the heat of his gaze. "You do, do ya?"

"Yep." His smile turned smug as he readied his horse for the night.

Her gaze followed the rippling muscles in his arms and shoulders as he unhooked the saddle. "You care to elaborate?"

"Nope."

Cold under her wet clothes, she hugged herself and threw him a pout. "That's not fair, you know."

"I know." Finished, he sauntered toward her, eyes bright with mischief.

"You're bold, McCall."

"I know," he repeated, grabbed the cooler, then dropped a kiss on her nose. "You ready to get wet?"

She snickered. "Yes, because obviously I'm not wet enough."

Smiling, he reached for her hand and together they raced through the rain to the house, surprised to find Connor in the foyer.

"Just the guy I was looking for." Connor clasped a hand around Cole's shoulder, his face unusually serious. "I could use your help," he claimed before turning an apologetic gaze at Jordan. "Sorry, darlin'. I hate to cut your night short but the storm rolling in has shifted, instead of centering north, it's now tracking south, which means I have cattle to move."

"It's okay," she reassured. "You just take care of the cattle. And be careful."

The famous *Marlboro* grin appeared, dimples and all. "Always. And I promise to bring him back in one piece."

"You'd better or you'll have me to answer to."

Connor shuddered. "Yes, ma'am. Will do." He turned to Cole. "The guys and I are meeting in the stable in five to mount up."

"I'll be there in a minute," Cole replied.

Connor nodded then left the house.

Shivering and beyond soaked, she'd hoped Cole would've joined her for a long, hot shower, but those plans just took a hike. Or a gallop. "You'd better get going," she said. "I'll take care of the cooler."

"Thanks." He set his hat on the container on the floor, and cupping her face with both hands, backed her up against the door where he leaned into her with his incredible, wet body. A delicious tremor shot to her toes and she gripped his hips for support.

"Don't wait up," he said, caressing her cheek, regret filling is gaze. "Even with all of Connor's men, it'll take awhile."

She sighed, not bothering to hide her disappointment or her worry. "Just be safe." Her mind refused to entertain the alternative. This was a common Texas occurrence. *Cole will be fine. Connor will be fine. Everyone will be fine.*

Thunder boomed, closer than before, causing her to jump, and a few seconds later lightening lit up the sky visible through the windows.

He pressed his forehead to hers. "No worrying, okay?" His gaze held steady, waiting for a reply.

"I'll try not to, but I...care very deeply for one of the cowboys," she said, almost dropping the *L* word.

A smile spread across his face. "Yeah? He cares very deeply for you, too." His words and the affection in his gaze warmed the chill from her body. "Good night, Jordan," he whispered, mouth slowly drawing closer.

"Night, Cole." More than ever, she longed to spend the night in his arms.

He traced her mouth with his. "Pleasant dreams."

...Cole looked at the clock on his office wall. Quarter to eight. Where is she? She called and said she'd bring supper. What could be keeping her? His gaze fell to the codes on his desk and he drew his chair closer.

The desk suddenly faded and he found himself inside the cab of a stuffy truck. Rain pelted the mist-covered window. He couldn't see. Squinting, he flipped on the defroster, then flinched when something whacked the windshield. The mist slowly disappeared.

Smack!

What the hell?

He leaned closer. CD's and flash drives pummeled the semi like rain. He switched the wipers to high. It didn't help.

Crack!

Pitchforks and computers fell from the sky.

He swerved the truck but couldn't avoid all of the falling objects. Smash. The windshield spider-webbed.

Son-of-a-bitch!

Pressing the brakes, his foot hit the floor.

No brakes.

A set of headlights suddenly appeared in front of him.

His heart rocked hard in his chest. Where the hell did that come from? He tried the air brakes. Nothing. Reaching for the shift to down-shift, he found air. That's gone, too. The truck picked up speed and headed straight for the car.

"Get out of the way! I can't stop!"

Heart in his throat, he jerked the wheel—hard. Tires screeched. A sickening crash and crunching filled his ears.

In the next second, the computer rain had stopped. Everything stilled. Cole opened the door and, stumbled outside, pulse hammering at the sight of a smashed up car lying in a mangled heap against a tree. He raced across the deserted road—weaving his way around the computers, pitchforks, flash drives and CD's. He reached the driver's side and gasped.

"Jordan! Oh God! I have to get you out of there. Jordan? Talk to me. Are you alright? Please talk to me!"

"I'm alright, Cole," she miraculously proclaimed.

"Thank God." His eyes closed momentarily. "I have to get you out. I'm sorry. I couldn't stop the truck. I'm so sorry, Jordan." Tears burned his eyes as he pushed her blood soaked hair from her face. "It'll be okay. I'll get you out."

Her lips twitched. "I know you will, Cole. I'll be fine but the door won't budge."

"I'll take care of it. There's a crow bar in the truck. I'll be right back."

"Okay. I know you won't let me down. You sure do pack a punch, though." She smiled weakly. "I knew you'd come to me. It was worth the wait."

"I'll be right back. Hang in there." He leaned in through the broken window to gently kiss her cheek before racing across the street.

Back at the truck, he thrust the seat forward, and as his fingers curled around the cold metal of the crow bar an explosion rocked him hard from behind.

Jordan!

Swiveling around, he dropped the bar, and watched helplessly as the car burned out of control—with Jordan still inside.

No! Jordan! Please, God no!

Vaulting upright in bed with such force, Cole knocked the alarm clock off the nightstand and joined his comforter on the floor. *Oh God...* Intense pain ripped through his heart and shredded in all directions. *Not again. Not again.* Ramming his face in his hands, hot tears burned behind his eyes. God, he couldn't go through that again. Not with her. Not with Jordan.

He'd known her since she was born. Cared about her since she was born. And, although they only had three dates, he was definitely falling for the incredible woman. Hard. She made him feel things he never felt before, not even with his wife.

The unrelenting grip of guilt didn't seize him, so he continued to assess his feelings for Jordan.

Recalling the way her body melted against his as they made love had him growing hard. She was now truly imprinted on his soul. The fact she had invaded his nightmare was proof. He hadn't had the damn dream in months. Now it was back.

With Jordan as his victim.

Another wave of intense pain ripped through him. He gripped his stomach. *I can't do this again.* He couldn't handle the thought of loving, then losing Jordan the way he'd lost Bess. He couldn't live with himself if he caused her death, too. And now he was beginning to wonder if he could deal with her profession. Being a cop put her in danger's path every day. He leaned back against the bed and swallowed. With a deep ache in his heart, he started to realize what all of this meant.

He had to end this relationship before it went any further.

Dragging a shaky hand down his face, he thought hard. He was so tired of the hurt. So tired. It had been his constant companion for years. He slammed his head into his fists and prayed for strength. How did he give up her laughter, teasing, challenges...kisses?

You will if you want her to live.

That woman would do anything for him. Wouldn't hesitate to put herself in harm's way for him. He knew this to be true, his heart knew without a doubt, but instead of rejoicing, it ached. The image from his dream of her face, bloodied and in pain, shot through his mind. Deep anguish squeezed his chest and choked the air from his lungs. He coughed repeatedly.

"I'm sorry, Jordan. I can't do this again."

With a heavy heart, he pulled on some clothes, grabbed an unopened bottle of whiskey and drove to his office.

Chapter Fourteen

Jordan awoke the next morning content and deliciously sore. She'd slept wonderfully again. Since the start of this trip, her slumber had been uninterrupted…once she'd fallen asleep of course. She smiled, reaching for the pillow Cole had laid on two nights ago. For the first time in a long time, she was incredibly happy to be alive. Images of last night flooded her mind. Her smile widened and she stretched out in bed.

Cole.

Making love near the tree, *their tree*, had really been a fantasy come true. She'd fantasized about that moment for over a decade. Up until that point, sex with Cole had been mind-blowing, but last night? Last night she'd truly felt his heart. He'd opened up and shared, and so had she, and that was what made last night so special. It wasn't just the coming together of their bodies. It was the coming together of their hearts and souls, too.

Cripes, she sounded like a greeting card. But it was true.

Gripped with an intense need to see him, she looked at the clock on the bedside table. Six AM. She smiled and hopped out of bed. It was early enough to catch him before he went to work. If he was going in. Who knew what time his cattle-roundup had ended. Her stomach instantly knotted and she chewed her lower lip. Hopefully, everything had gone well.

She washed up, yanked on some clothes and raced downstairs to the kitchen. Disappointment rippled in waves as Emma told her he'd left even before she arose.

Left? Did he even get any sleep?

"Since you're here, how about some chocolate chip pancakes?" Emma smiled, wiping her hands in her apron.

"Sounds good." Jordan grinned, hoping the unease fluttering in her stomach was just hunger.

Sitting at the table, she contemplated her disquiet. A sense of urgency settled over her like a blanket.

Something was wrong. But what?

"Thanks for the picnic meal you made for us, Emma." She grabbed onto the happy memory, letting it warm the chill her insides had taken.

"Oh, my goodness. You're welcome, my dear." The woman smiled, placing a tall glass of orange juice in front of her. "To be truthful, I'm surprised you're up this early."

"I was hoping to catch Cole before he went to work," she admitted, keeping her voice light.

He'd given her the impression yesterday that he was going to take the day off. The fact he went to work, and earlier than normal, just didn't feel right.

"He must've gone to work very early," Emma confirmed her thoughts. "I found a note telling me not to worry about making him breakfast."

Maybe he went in early so he could leave early.

Her apprehension lightened along with her mood as Emma placed a small stack of warm, chocolate smelling, pancakes in front of her.

Feeling better, she dug into her breakfast, deciding it was best if she didn't dwell on Cole. Her impatience could cause her to jump to the wrong conclusion. Her parents' party was in three days; she had enough work to deal with to keep her busy, until he came home.

Kerri and Emma had the catering covered. She had an appointment with the florist to double-check details and okay the centerpieces before her second appointment with the set up crew. Her errands could keep her occupied all day. Best to keep Cole simmering in the background and concentrate on the party.

What difference could a few hours make?

By dinner that night, Jordan's heart sank lower than all the oil in Texas. No sign of Cole. Oh, he'd called—left a nice, simple message for his mother that he wouldn't be home for dinner because he was working late on a project. Never asked for her, though. Why should he? Just because they'd shared several mind blowing days this week, not to mention their special time last night? Tears burned hot in her throat. She knew what he was doing…

Avoiding her.

With no appetite and a pounding head, she excused herself halfway through the main course and went upstairs. *This isn't happening.* She paced her large, lonely room. Three-hundred and two footsteps separated the walls.

What was wrong? Why was Cole doing this?

Her chest tightened. She couldn't breathe.

After they'd made love last night, she was his, heart, body and soul and he'd given himself to her in the same way. Their connection had strengthened. Hadn't it?

She stopped pacing and clenched her fists.

"Why are you doing this, Cole?"

She needed answers. Having left a few messages for him throughout the day, his silence tore at her heart. The longer he stayed away the clearer things became. Cole was backing out.

Why? What happened? What scared him off?

Dread filled her soul. She had to see him. Short of sitting on his bed to wait for him, she only had one other choice. Stakeout the balcony. Deciding it would be best to wait until the house quieted down for the night, she noted the time and sighed. She had a few hours to kill.

The option of driving to his office had crossed her mind...several times that day. She'd even gotten as far as the interstate but had turned around. Unlike in the Spring, she wasn't in a teasing mood and needed to keep this confrontation private.

When walking didn't help, she plopped onto her bed and rubbed her throbbing temples. She wished Bullet was there. His love and affection were needed and missed. Big time. Sun sliced through the crack in her curtains and cast an orange glow into the room as it slipped from the horizon. Her mind drifted to yesterday's sunset...when Cole had given her a glimpse of paradise.

She wouldn't give up on him without a fight.

He owed her an explanation and she intended to get one.

At eleven o'clock sharp, she stepped onto the balcony, quietly passed Kerri's door, then settled in a chair near Cole's room to begin her vigil.

A warm breeze blew strands of hair in her face, but she remained cold to the core. Hugging herself, she fought the reoccurring stinging behind her eyes.

Two hours later, too jittery to sit anymore, she paced the balcony, stopping short when she heard Cole's car. Finally. A few nerve-racking minutes later, the light came on in his room. Chest tight, stomach fluttering, she was halfway to his door when it opened.

He stepped outside and stiffened. "Jordan."

"Yes, it's me—unless I'm not the only one you're avoiding. What's going on?" She hurried to him and touched his arm. "You never returned one call today."

He tugged from her grasp. "I had work to do."

Her heart sank. "Don't give me that. When I woke up today, my first thought was to find you. Your first thought, on the other hand, was to run. Why? What's going on?"

His jaw twitched. He looked exhausted. Tie and jacket missing, his shirt was half unbuttoned and eyes bloodshot. He hadn't sleep last night. Why? She had. Like a log. Satiated and spent. Why hadn't he? Unable to fight her need to erase his worry, she stepped to him and touched his face. He jerked back.

She winced. "Cole, talk to me. *Please!*"

He wandered to the railing and stared at the yard without a word. Her throat burned, but she refused to give into her emotions until he explained himself. She deserved at least that much. His hand tunneled through his hair and down to grip the back of his neck before he slowly expelled a breath.

"You're right Jordan. I owe you an explanation." His voice held no emotion as he faced her. "I had time to think about what's happening between us and I think it was a big mistake."

"What?" Heart cracked and bleeding, she rocked back. "You can't possibly mean that, Cole?"

"I do mean it, Jordan. I'm sorry. I never should have started anything with you. I don't know what the hell I was thinking! You have a settled life several states away. It was dumb. It was a mistake," he repeated sternly.

Almost doubled over with pain, she gripped the back of a chair, a lone tear escaping from her burning eyes. How could his lips say that? Lips that had devoured hers and trailed hot kisses over her skin, called her beautiful and couldn't get enough of her…

This is crazy. I won't accept this.

She strode to him but kept her hands to herself. "I *know* you felt the same things I did. This doesn't make sense."

"Look Jordan, I can't take back what already happened but I can nip it in the bud and that's what I'm trying to do." He stared down at her, pity and guilt darkening his gaze.

"You're scared, Cole." She pounded her chest. "Don't you think I'm scared too?"

Pain entered his eyes. Finally, tangible proof she wasn't the only one hurting. He opened his mouth, then clamp it shut.

What she wouldn't give for him to voice the battle going on in his head. *Damn, stubborn Texan.* Her childhood friend, Cole McCall, was fading away—right in front of her. She had to do something…but what?

Stoic and quiet, he rubbed the ring finger on his left hand and suddenly she knew. That crap about her living in another state was just that—bullshit. This was about him being scared. Of her getting hurt. *Dammit!* If only she hadn't fallen from that damn horse last night. She stepped closer, needing to make him see he wasn't the only one afraid.

"Cole, the mere thought of something happening to you kills me." She touched his cheek. "But going through life without at least giving us a chance, is just as bad. Don't you see that?"

Fear and intense pain consumed his expression. She thought she had gotten through to him, until his blank mask fell into place.

"Then you're far stronger than I am Jordan, because I can't take a chance like that again. *I won't.*" He pushed past and stalked to his door. "I'm trying to make this as painless as possible for both of us. Just let me be."

"I can't," she choked.

"You have to."

He turned at the door. She followed, until he held up a hand to halt her approach.

"You'll be back in California in a few days. Just forget what happened between us and go on with your life as before. You don't need me in it and I *don't* need you in mine."

Pain squeezed her chest, tight. Drawing on it, her hand shot out to grasp a fistful of shirt and twist hard before thrusting him backward against the house, forearm pressed firmly under his chin. "Now you listen to me, Cole. You keep telling yourself that and maybe you just might believe it. But I don't. I *know* better. And if you think that all of this"—she waved a hand between them—"will disappear when I go back to California, then you're sadly mistaken. These feelings we share are embedded in our hearts and our souls." She poked his chest and forehead, emphasizing her words.

"Are you done?" he asked quietly, without moving.

"No, I'm not. You think I'm just ranting don't you, but I *know* how this works, Cole because *I* tried to forget *you* when I moved away but I couldn't. Just before my junior year in college I flew to Houston...to you."

His head jerked to the side. "You did?"

"Yes. I didn't tell anyone. Saved my life-guarding money, bought a ticket and flew to see Cole McCall."

He shook his head. "But I never saw you."

"You're right, you didn't." She released him and stepped back, wrapping her arms around her middle. "I was about to cross the street to McCall Enterprises when I saw a beautiful blonde run into your arms."

"Bess..." His eyes widened. "I remember that day," he said quietly. "I thought I felt..."

His voice trailed off and her eyes closed then opened as she drew in a ragged breath.

"Yeah, well, doesn't matter. I didn't stick around. I heard fate laughing so I got on the next plane and licked my wounds."

"Then do that now." His chin lifted. "You did it once, you can do it again."

"Are you crazy?" She gave a mirthless laugh, jammed her hands on her hips, and frowned until it hurt. "You think...after what we shared this week...*last night*, that I could ever recover? Cole, no amount of time can heal me now."

"Then find something else. We're done." He turned to leave.

"Oh, no you don't. I'm not done, McCall. I have one more thing to say." Surprising him, she pinned his hands against the house and brushed her lips to his.

Current coursed between them, heated and fierce. She felt a change in his body. He came alive, and to her immense satisfaction, he crushed her to him, taking control of the kiss. Hot lips devoured and demanded—urgent, rougher than normal. She responded in kind, rejoicing in the desire she induced in him.

A moment later, he stiffened, and thrusting her aside, he strode to his door.

Her hand shot to the wall to keep from falling. "Tell me, Cole, how are you going to forget that?"

He gripped the door handle and turned to her. "It doesn't matter. I *will* do it."

Without another word or glance, he stepped inside and the click of his lock resounded like gunfire from her piece in her safe at home.

Home…

For a little while this week, she'd entertained thoughts of possibly transferring to Harland County, or at the very least, Houston.

Rapidly turning numb, Jordan stood there for several minutes, stucco pressed into her cheek. Hot tears emptied her soul as her heart up and died.

Megan and Shawn, with Bullet in tow, weren't due in until around six. It was Friday, the day before the party. With things set up as far as they could be for the day, Jordan had nothing on her agenda until they arrived. Tired of putting up a front, she opted for a light lunch and a horseback ride. It would be good to be alone.

An hour later, Ember halted and Jordan found herself staring at the *J + C* carved in the tree overlooking the ocean. *How did I end up here?* She blinked and dismounted. Guess her heart needed to be where it was happiest. As thoughts of the last time she was here began to invade her mind, tears streamed down her face.

"Damn it. I am not going to do that again." She swiped at her cheeks and turned to face the ocean.

Feeling lower than she had in years, Jordan sank to her knees and squeezed back more tears. She was returning to California in two days. Two days.

What am I going to do?

She'd hoped Cole would've come to his senses by now, but judging by the way he avoided looking at her when they ended up in the same room, she knew he'd made up his mind to shut her out. The cold tyrant was back...and his indifference hurt like hell.

Dragging in a shaky breath, she opened her eyes and watched absently as Ember grazed nearby. Hoof beats pounded in the distance, the sound hitting her ears and stopping her heart. *Cole?* She jumped to her feet. *No. Connor*. Pulse returning to normal, she slumped back against the tree as he approached.

"Jordan, I thought that was you," he said pleasantly as he dismounted and sent his steed to graze near hers.

"Hello, Connor," she greeted, determined to keep the disappointment from her voice. "What brings you out here?"

He frowned. "I'll be honest with you, Jordan. It's about Cole."

Heart flopping, she vaulted upright. "What's wrong? Is he okay?"

"He's okay, Jordan. Nothing happened—at least not physically." He gasped both her arms and lightly squeezed. "I was just hoping you could enlighten me as to my brother's strange behavior the past three days. And yours too, for that matter," he added, looking at her through narrowed eyes.

The lump in her throat kept her quiet.

"I mean the two of you were so cozy the first few days and now you're barely in the same room for more than five seconds. What gives?" He released her to cross his arms over his chest. His normally friendly, pleasant gaze was serious and intense.

No sense in making something up, the cowboy was too astute. She lifted her shoulders. "I wish I knew, Connor. Those first four days were incredible and now Cole expects me to forget them and go on with my life as I did before." She tossed her hands in the air while tears filled her eyes. "Well, I can't *do that*. I didn't do such a good job of forgetting Cole before, except for Eric. But this time it's worse. Much, much worse."

Gaze full of compassion, Connor remained silent.

She walked to Ember and stroked the mare's flowing mane. "God, Connor." Her hands stilled and she turned in his direction, unable to keep the ache from her voice. "What am I supposed to do? How am I supposed to go on without him?"

In two strides, he was at her side, wrapping his strong arms around her, pulling her against his broad chest. "It'll be okay, Jordan. You'll see."

Calmed by his strength and his friendly embrace, she looked up at him. "You sound so sure."

"I am sure, darlin'." He brushed the hair from her cheek as he spoke. "Because from what you've just told me, Cole is running scared right now. Give him some time and he'll come to his senses." He winked down at her.

She hiccupped. "It didn't work the last time."

He tapped her nose. "Because you were both very young." His confidence and gesture made her smile. "That's better. Just trust me, Jordan. I know my brother. His feelings for you are very strong."

"I know." Nodding, she pulled in a breath. "That's why this hurts so much."

He snorted. "My brother is in for a rude awakening if he thinks his feelings for you are going to disappear when you go back to California."

"I told him that." She eyed Connor. It almost sounded as if he was speaking from experience. Putting her troubles aside, she placed her hands on his shoulders and reached up on tiptoes to kiss his cheek. "You know, Connor, you're something else. Those ex-fiancés of yours were damn fools. Don't you for one minute think those breakups were all your fault."

He dropped her gaze and cleared his throat. "Thanks."

"You're welcome." She smiled for the second time in three days. And both had happened in the last two minutes, thanks to the *Marlboro* man.

He nodded and ambled to his horse. "Just, remember what I said, Jordan. Don't give up on Cole." He swung his large frame into the saddle. "He'll come to his senses just give him some time."

"I will, Connor. I've waited almost eleven years already, what's a few more weeks?" She believed this down to her toes, and yet...

Her throat heated. What if she was wrong?

When the silver Subaru drew to a stop, Jordan ran to greet its occupants. Smiling, she helped Megan from the front seat and looked at her friend's swollen belly.

"Not much longer now, huh, sweetheart?"

"I sure hope not," came Shawn's impassioned reply from the other side of the vehicle.

She laughed and met him in front of the car for a hug. "Are you trying to say she's getting hard to live with?"

Shawn put his hands up. "I am not going there." His gaze fell lovingly on his wife. "No, she's been wonderful through all of this."

Pain crushed Jordan's already flattened heart. She turned her attention to the barking in the back seat and opened the door. Kneeling down, she hugged her dog, tight. *God, she'd missed him.* She rubbed his belly then hugged him some more, while Bullet whined and lavished her with love for a good two minutes.

"It's good to see you too, boy." She held him close and fought back tears. Time for that later. She swallowed and stood to walk her friends to the veranda where everyone sat sipping lemonade.

"Megan, Shawn. I'm so glad you could make it." Her mother shot to her feet and greeted them with a hug as they stepped onto the porch.

"Yes, it wouldn't be the same without you here," her father said, standing behind her mother.

"Oh, we wouldn't miss it." Megan beamed, elbowing Shawn. "Right, honey?"

"Right." He nodded, rubbing his gut. "You must be Mr. and Mrs. McCall." Turning to the other couple, he extended his hand.

"It's nice to have you here, son." Mr. McCall pumped Shawn's arm and slapped his shoulder while Mrs. McCall gingerly hugged Megan.

"So nice to finally meet you."

"Likewise," Megan said with a grin.

Jordan scratched her temple. The way they all greeted, you'd swear they'd talked before. Which was ridiculous, of course…wasn't it? She stepped forward, eager to get through the rest of the introductions.

"Kerri's inside cooking so let—."

"Where else would she be?" Her friend cut her off and chuckled.

"Indeed," Connor said under his breath.

Megan's gaze flew to hers and she slowly raised a brow.

Jordan swallowed a snort. *Yeah, that's the cowboy.* "Connor, I'd like you to meet my friend Megan and her husband, Shawn."

"Nice to meet you, ma'am. Shawn," he said, shaking each of their hands.

"Ma'am? I've never been called that before."

"That's a darn shame," Connor said, tipping his hat. "A pretty, married woman like you deserves some respect."

Well I'll be… A flush crept into her friend's cheeks, deepening the green of her eyes.

"I could get used to it here." Megan turned to touch her husband's arm. "Texas is good for my ego."

"And I'm not?" Shawn frowned.

"Of course you are, but you have to say things like that to me. You're my husband."

Megan patted Shawn's arm and his gaze softened to a look of complete devotion. Jordan's inside squeezed tight. *Deep breaths…* She shifted her stance to combat the pain and glanced over at Cole.

He stood just outside of the crowd, regarding her with the bleakest expression she'd ever seen. Her heart lurched but shouldn't have bothered because his cold mask immediately fell into place.

"You must be, Cole." Shawn stepped forward, taking the lead again.

"Yes." Cole shook his hand. "How was your drive in?"

"Surprisingly good."

"Good?" Megan snorted, one hand on her belly the other rubbing her back. "Not from where I was sitting, watermelon pressing my bladder every time we hit a pebble. Yeah, it was a complete joy ride."

"Sorry, hun." Shawn dropped an arm around her shoulder and drew her near. "I'll do my best to avoid the pebbles on the way home. Okay?" He kissed the top of her head then turned to Cole. "This beautiful, pregnant ball of fun is my wife, Megan."

"Nice to meet you, Megan," Cole said, shaking her hand. "I've heard a lot about you."

"Yeah? I've heard a lot about you, too." Her gaze shot to Jordan, flush back in her cheeks again. "You're right, Jordan, they do grow them big in Texas."

The McCall's laughed, along with her parents, Shawn and Connor. Jordan did her best to turn her lips up appropriately, noticing Cole had trouble doing the same.

"Okay," Mrs. McCall said, clasping her hands. "Let me show you to your room. I'm sure you'd like to freshen up, or perhaps, stretch out after that long drive."

She ushered them inside and everyone retook their seats. Jordan settled down next to her father, Bullet immediately dropping to lie at her feet. The warmth of his fur on her ankle was a comfort and she happily stroked his broad head.

"Thanks, again for allowing Bullet to visit," she told Mr. McCall.

"No problem, Jordan. He's quite an animal," he exclaimed, admiring the dog.

"Yes, he's something else." A smile tugged her lips as Bullet looked up with unconditional love and happily wagged his tail. "Eric and I adopted him through the K-9 unit of our precinct. He was past his prime and retired out with honors. I'm very lucky to have him."

Especially these past two years. Bullet had been a rock and a constant companion through some very rough times. She glanced at Cole from under her lashes. Her chest tightened. More tough times loomed ahead. She was going to need to lean on Bullet once again.

Leaving his perch by her side, he padded over to Cole, placed his head on a jean clad knee and whimpered.

Startled, Cole looked at her for an explanation. She had none. Bullet had never done that before. Could he tell the man held the pieces of her heart? Sense their connection?

The rest of the evening was pleasant but Jordan was thankful to escape the weight of Cole's silence and walk into her bedroom that night.

Her Fated Cowboy

Coming out of the bathroom, she spotted Bullet sprawled out on the floor at the foot of her bed, as if he'd been there for years. She stopped dead, struck by how comfortable he was at the ranch. Sensing her attention, he sat up and wagged his tail.

She put her hands on her hips. "Look at you. You look like King Farouche." Bullet's wagging tail swayed his back end as he trotted to her. She knelt down and received her own wet praise. Laughing, she scratched under his collar. "I've missed you boy. I've missed you so much." Hugging him, she allowed her tears to fall. "I've done it again, Bullet. Just when I thought I put all the pieces back together, my heart is shattered again."

Whimpering, he turned his head to lick her tears. She swallowed and pulled back to look him in the eyes. "I know I've left you twice, boy, but I'm not going to leave you again. Just you and me, pal." She received a kiss as a reward.

A knock rattled her door, causing a small growl from Bullet and a racing heart in Jordan. Maybe it was Cole. She swiped her face, straightened her clothes and rushed to the door.

Disappointment flooded her body but she forced her lips to smile at her friend. "Hi, Megan, come in."

Tail wagging, Bullet nudged Megan's hand. She bent slightly to rub his head.

"Judging by her reaction," her friend talked to the dog as if she wasn't there, "Jordan was hoping for someone else, boy. Who could that be?"

Bullet whimpered.

Shaking her head, Jordan headed to the chair, leaving the sofa for her pregnant friend. She knew Megan was dying to talk about the infamous McCall brothers after hearing about them all these years.

"Well? What are your thoughts, Megan? Come on. I know you're dying to dish."

Once seated, her friend's green eyes became as big as saucers. "Holy *manflesh*! No wonder the two of you used to chase these guys." She fanned herself with her hand and lowered her voice. "I couldn't say anything in front of Shawn of course. He wouldn't understand it's just a girly reaction but...wow!"

Jordan laughed. "Yeah, Cole and Connor seem to have that affect on women."

Megan snapped a sober gaze to her. "So, what's going on between you and Cole? He's reserved when you're looking but when you're not, it's a whole other program," her friend informed with a shake of her red curls.

This was news to Jordan. She searched Megan's face as if it held the answers, then realized her friend was waiting for her to reply. She drew in a breath and sat back. "I think he's afraid to love again."

"Then he's a fool. Doesn't he know how lucky he'd be to have you?"

Damn those tears.

She swallowed. "I guess not."

Megan softened her tone. "You've done more than kiss this time, haven't you?"

"Yes." She couldn't bring herself to say more. Jordan sighed as she wiped her wet face, then patted Bullet who'd come to see why she was upset.

"So? What's the problem?"

"That *is* the problem," Jordan corrected. "The connection we have is strong. It can be all consuming and I think that's what he's afraid of. He said he's putting a stop to things before it's too late."

Megan reached out and touched her arm. "It's already too late, isn't it?"

"Hell yeah…at least it is for me. But I'll tell you, Megan. Cole's going to find it just as hard to live without me. He just doesn't know it yet." She finished with a small laugh and a whole lot of hope.

"You've got that right, honey." Megan's chin lifted. "The way he looks at you when you're not looking is as if he's trying to memorize everything about you."

"I keep telling myself to be patient and he'll come to his senses. I just hope that it happens before we leave on Sunday." She closed her eyes and swallowed.

"Well, then. I suggest you use your time wisely. You know, show him what he's going to be *missing*." Megan snickered.

Jordan's eyes flew open. Her friend's words made enormous sense. "You're absolutely right, Megan. Not counting tonight, I've only got one night left—and hell if I'll go softly."

Megan slapped Jordan's knee. "Good for you! Now, if you'll excuse me I'm feeling a bit tired," she said, and promptly yawned.

"Yes. You go get some sleep and I'll see you tomorrow. I've some planning to do."

Chapter Fifteen

Cole wasn't at the bottom of the stairs when Jordan came down for the party the following evening. Why should he be? They weren't together. The party was for her parents. It was her mom and dad who stood there greeting the guests as they arrived.

She put on a bright smile and hugged them. "Happy Fortieth, Mom and Dad."

"Thanks, sweetheart. And thank you again for the cruise." Her dad smiled.

Jordan and Kerri had privately presented them with their gift two hours ago. "Well, the two of you deserve it. And since your present situation finds you in between homes, it seemed like the perfect gift." She squeezed their hands.

"You look lovely tonight, honey," her mom said.

Smiling, she pushed Jordan's hair over her shoulder, worn loose and styled to bounce with fat curls—courtesy of Megan's hot rollers.

"Thank you."

"And this color is perfect for you."

Jordan glanced down at her mauve organza dress cut to hug her bodice and accentuate her cleavage.

"Cole doesn't know what he's missing." Her mother touched her cheek. "Don't look so shocked. I know there's something going on between the two of you but I won't pry—for now."

"Thanks, Mom."

The door opened, saving her from having to say anything further. Leaving her parents to greet the new arrivals, she headed toward the outdoor party, alone.

Stepping onto the patio, her gaze immediately drew to Cole's commanding presence. Impeccable black suit, another white shirt like the one...

She inhaled and lifted her chin. *I can do this.*

With his back to her, he was leaning on the bar, talking to Connor, Kevin, Shawn and Megan. A moment later, his spine stiffened and he slowly straightened from the bar to stand tall.

Jordan willed him to turn around and held her breath when he did. Dark eyes widened a fraction before he turned away and downed his drink in one gulp.

Good, McCall. I'm just getting started. Keeping his dark head and broad shoulders in her sight, she strolled straight for him.

"Jordan, you look incredible." It was the heartfelt compliment she wanted to hear but from the wrong handsome Texan.

"Thank you, Kevin." She smiled and looked him over when she reached the group. Dressed in a cobalt blue dress shirt and navy pants, he could stop traffic. "You look quite dapper yourself."

"Jordan always looks great." Megan's smile held mischief. "Back in college, you should have seen how many fake drownings they had at the beach on the days she worked. They kept a record and the only thing those days had in common was Jordan Masters on lifeguard duty."

Kevin winked. "Can't say as I blame them."

"Maybe those California guys aren't as dumb as they look, no offense Shawn." Connor grinned.

"None taken." Shawn lifted his beer and laughed. "Eric was smitten the first time she walked into that classroom. He said it felt as if someone sucker-punched him in the gut."

"Okay. You can all stop talking as if I'm not here." Jordan noted Cole was the only one to remain silent. In fact, he hadn't even turned to look at her. Undeterred, she leaned between him and Connor, making sure to brush against him as she asked the bartender for a glass of wine.

He stiffened again, the air instantly heating between them. *Let's see him ignore that.* Sipping her rosé, she looked up to find his eyes finally on her. Blood rushed through her veins as she deliberately ran her tongue across her bottom lip, pretending to catch a stray drop of wine. His jaw clenched.

Score.

Chest tight with emotions, she allowed them to enter her eyes and willed him to say something.

He didn't, choosing as always, to run instead.

"Excuse me, folks. I see my secretary and her husband have just arrived." Without another word he walked away.

"You're doing great, Jordan. Keep it up." Megan smiled reassuringly.

"Yeah. I thought he was going to faint for a minute there." Connor snorted. "Man, it was priceless!"

"Okay. Would someone like to tell me what's going on?" Kevin chimed in, bouncing his gaze around them.

Jordan just smiled and walked away allowing the others to fill him in. The night was young and she was far from through with Cole McCall.

Hours later, disappointed and distraught, she sat on her bed and clenched her teeth, on the cusp of a breakdown. She didn't want to sleep. Doing so would put her that much closer to morning and her departure. She was nowhere near ready for that moment.

Still in her dress, she sat absently petting Bullet, wondering what she could have said or done differently to sway Cole.

Nothing. There was not one thing she hadn't tried.

She'd touched and brushed him more than a dozen times and had even corned him for a dance, completely shocked when he'd agreed.

She'd blinked, expecting a refusal.

The band had started to play a slow song. Cole had grabbed her hand, walked them to the middle of the floor where he'd pulled her fully into his arms. Surprised, yet pleased, she'd rested her head on his shoulder and slowly closed her eyes. Heartbeat strong and reassuring, his body warm and welcoming, she didn't want to leave. She belonged there. Did he feel it too?

Apparently not, because when the dance had finished, he'd simply let her go without a word.

Shaking her head, she looked down at her dog. "Well, boy, looks like we're going home tomorrow, like it or not."

He whimpered.

Sick of thinking about it, she jumped to her feet instead. "Come on, Bullet. Let's go for a walk." And with his excited bark, she led him outside and down the balcony steps.

The air helped but not the scenery. Everywhere she looked, she saw Cole. Young or present day, he was all over, haunting her steps and her heart. He was young and in the barn with the cheerleader being chased by stampeding horses. He was in the driveway, yelling at her to mind her own business. He was in the stable, helping her on his horse for their picnic.

She swallowed and wiped her face. "Maybe this wasn't such a good idea, boy." Hugging her arms, she walked back to the steps and up to the balcony with Bullet at her feet.

The hair on her neck instantly tingled.

Cole.

Bullet wagged his tail and left her side.

On a chair outside his room, he sat still dressed in his party clothes, minus the suit coat with his shirt completely unbuttoned.

Her heart squeezed. He looked so incredibly sexy...and so incredibly tired. She wanted to do and say so many things but it was useless. He was the one with the problem. *He* needed to come to terms with his fears. She finally realized she couldn't do that for him.

Refusing to make any more of a fool out of herself than she already had, she called to her dog. "Come on, Bullet. Let Cole alone. It's time for bed."

He whimpered but didn't move.

Trying again, she came closer. "Let's go boy. Cole wants to be alone."

Another whimper but no movement.

Close to tears, she went over to him. Bending down she looked her dog in the eyes. "It's okay. We have to go. Cole doesn't want us here."

Cole's breath hissed into the night and pushed the tears down her face.

Bullet rose and began to lick. "Thanks, boy," she said softly, then stood.

A cold, hand gripped her wrist. "Look, Jordan. I said I was sorry."

"Yeah. Well, I'm sorry too, Cole." She shook him off. "I'm sorry you're not strong enough to deal with us. I'm sorry you're feelings for me aren't strong enough to want me here. I'm sorry I've fallen in love with you and I'm damned sorry it hurts like hell!"

He closed his eyes and swallowed. The pulse in his neck throbbed but when he opened his eyes, they were blank. And still he remained silent.

"You seem to be under this misconception that when I leave, you'll be able to forget me. That just isn't true." She leaned closer. "Everywhere you go you're going to see me. Every woman you kiss, you're going to compare her to me because no one"—she lifted his chin to lock gazes—"and I mean no one, is going to make you feel the things that I can." He swallowed and she held on tighter. "I already told you, when I moved to California you came with me. You haunted me all through my high school years and right into college. I couldn't form any lasting relationships because *your* memory wouldn't let me."

He cleared his throat. "If that's true, then how did you manage one with Eric?"

She released him and stood straight. "Because of that little trip six years ago. I guess I have you and Bess to thank," she stated. "On my flight home I'd promised myself never to look back. I met Eric later that fall, and because I knew you were happy with Bess, I let you go and allowed him into my heart."

His head cocked. "You can do that again."

She closed her eyes and expelled a harsh breath before opening them again. "God, you're so thick. No. I already told you. It's different now. Because of what we shared this week you're a part of me now—ingrained, not only in my heart but my soul. Our connection is much stronger, deeper…straight through." Her gaze fell to his mouth. *God*, how she longed to kiss him back to last Tuesday. "Now I can never be satisfied with anyone else...and I know it'll be the same for you."

It has to be. I can't love this hard and painfully all on my own.

Cole stood and ran a hand through his hair while he cursed.

He turned to leave but she stepped in front of him. "We're meant to be together, Cole. Why don't you see that? You're making a big mistake and it's ripping our hearts apart." He remained quiet so she cupped his face and looked deep into his eyes. "Don't let me walk out of your life, Cole. Please don't let me go tomorrow." Pressing her mouth very lightly to his, she tasted the salt of her own heartache as a tear spilled out and found its way between their lips. She drew back. "I love you, Cole. Don't let me go."

Sorrow and pain swam in his eyes, while a tentative hand brushed her cheek. "I *can't* give you forever, Jordan. But I can give you tonight."

Her heart thudded out of control at the words torn from his throat. She searched his face and weighed her options.

She didn't want just tonight, she wanted forever. But…maybe, if she took up his offer, he'd find it that much harder to let her go in the morning. And even if he did let her go, it would be one more memory to haunt him, one more memory to make him see reason, one more memory to make him seek her out.

Even as her mind conjured more pluses, she knew her answer. If they made love again and he walked away, the last pieces of her world would crumple into dust.

Several tears raced down her face, easing the lump in her throat enough to allow her to speak. Drawing in a breath, she looked straight into his tormented eyes.

"I *can't* give you tonight, Cole. It's not enough."

She turned and walked blindly to her room, her life completely shattered.

Dawn broke the horizon, sending sunlight onto her face. Lying on the bedroom floor, arm draped around Bullet, Jordan watched quietly as the sun rose further into the sky.

Departure day.

Panic seized her body. *I should've taken Cole up on his offer!* No... It would've killed her. She snickered without mirth. So? She was already dead.

Her mind had fought the same argument all night long. Over and over. She'd even gotten up to open her screen door, but a shred of common sense kept her rooted to the room.

Unable to go to him, she did the only thing she could do, drop to her knees and sob uncontrollably while she held onto her dog.

Bullet licked her face.

She reminded herself to breath. "We're going home in a few hours, boy. I guess I should get up and pack."

Concentrating on the mundane routine of getting ready, she emerged out of the bathroom a half hour later, dressed for her trip home.

A knock sounded on her door. Her spirits rose. She answered it to find her sister standing there with a cheerful smile.

"Good morning Jord—" Kerri stopped her greeting and frowned, pushing into the room. "Jordan, why are you doing this to yourself?"

Kicking the door shut, her sister pulled her into a much needed hug. Throat hot, Jordan gave in to the tears prickling behind her eyes. When she finished crying her sister took her hands and squeezed.

"Why don't you stay longer? I'm sure mom and dad could use your help with the house."

Jordan blinked. That would give her a legitimate reason to stay. *But is that the right thing to do?* She shook her head. No.

"Thanks, Kerri, but I have to go. Actually," she corrected. "I need to go." Seeing her sister's confused frown, she explained, "Cole seems to think that if I leave, his dilemma will disappear too. I have to go in order to prove to him that we are meant to be together."

"Well then," Kerri said, dabbing Jordan's face with a tissue. "You get packed and give him a good-bye he won't forget!"

Jordan hugged her. "Thanks, Kerri. I love you,"

"I love you, too." With one last squeeze and a kiss on the cheek, her sister smiled. "I'll see you downstairs."

An hour later, the car was packed and ready to go and Bullet had been given sufficient time to run. There was only one thing left to do—say their good-byes.

Where was Cole?

She hadn't seen him all morning. God, she hoped he was still on the ranch. Her heart dipped. What if he wasn't? *I can't leave without talking to him.* Just as hyperventilation loomed on her horizon, he strode from the house to join the group on the veranda. Blank expression plastered on his pale, drawn face, he stood off to the side and refused to look her way.

Shawn and Megan started things off. They thanked everyone and promised to send pictures of the baby when the time came, then made their way to the car.

After Jordan said good-bye to Mr. and Mrs. McCall, Emma thrust a bag in her hand and squeezed her tight.

"I put something extra in yours because you didn't eat much at breakfast and I thought you might need it later."

"Thanks Emma. You're too good to me." Jordan smiled as brightly as possible and kissed the woman's cheek. She had no intensions of eating now or later, even if Emma had packed her nothing but chocolate chip cookies.

Receiving hugs and kisses from both her parents and promising to call them when they made it back home, Jordan found herself in front of the McCall brothers along with her sister. Unable to face fate yet, she stepped to Connor as Kerri said her good-byes to Cole.

Her throat burned. "Connor, I'm going to miss you." She hugged him tightly.

"It'll be okay, darlin'," he whispered in her ear. "I promise you. I know my brother. He'll come around. Just try to be patient. Give him some time."

"I will," she told him quietly. "That's why I'm leaving."

Jordan returned his wink and stepped back. *You can do this. You have to do this.* Mustering her floundering strength, she traded places with her sister and faced the man who held her heart.

Hunched shoulders, blank eyes, pale face…Cole looked as miserable as she felt.

A part of him doesn't want me to go.

Hope flickered in her heart. Could she reach that part? She had so much she wanted to say to him—feelings she needed to share. Mouth opened, she drew in a breath but the words refused to come.

His throat rippled and a muscled worked in his jaw. Silence stretched between them.

Say something, Cole…please.

Connor and Kerri exchanged an awkward good-bye before her sister walked to the car and everyone else went inside the house.

She stood alone with Cole.

Swallowing, she wished with all her might he'd take her in his arms and never let her go. Fate once again had different plans.

Through sheer strength of will, she forced herself to speak. "I guess they think we need some time alone."

His shoulder lifted. "I guess so," he replied, then bent down to pet Bullet who pawed his foot.

Seeing the bond they'd made in just a few days, Jordan realized she wasn't the only one who'd fallen for Cole. Long fingers stroked the dog's black and tan fur. Yearning gripped deep. Her body already missed his caress.

He gave Bullet a final pat before he stood to face her. "Well, you don't want to keep them waiting. I know you have a long journey ahead of you."

"Yes…good luck with your journey too, Cole." She nodded, waiting to see if her meaning sunk in.

His shoulders dropped. "Jordan, I alrea—"

Her fingers pressed into his warm lips. "I know what you told me,

Cole. You just need to remember what I *told* you. Besides, I'm giving you what you wanted. I'm leaving. You won't have to look at me anymore. You won't have to touch me anymore," her voice was low as she caressed the side of his face. "You won't have to taste me anymore, either."

His jaw clenched, but he remained silent.

Don't let me go, Cole. Don't let me get in that car and drive out of your life.

Her silent pleas went unanswered.

She pulled in a breath and summoned her trusty in-your-face attitude. "You sure are stubborn, Cole McCall." Linking their arms, she began to walk to the steps of the veranda. "Now, you have my cell phone number and my parents can give you directions to my house when you finally come to your senses," she told him matter-of-factly

He shook his head, a small smile tugging his mouth. "Who's stubborn?"

Stopping at the bottom she let go of his arm and turned to him. "I guess it's time. Do I get a good-bye kiss?" She looked up at him, anticipation racing her pulse as she waited for his answer.

Miraculously, he tipped her chin and brought his mouth to hers. Taking full advantage of the opportunity, she held his face, pouring all the love she had for him in this—their last kiss. Her lips caressed and worshiped and his answering touch told her all he refused to say. When it was over, tears burned her eyes.

She blinked and cleared her throat. "Good-bye, Cole." With superhuman effort, she turned her back and walked toward the car.

A few feet away, she stopped. Her heart hurt so bad her legs refused to listen. *Get in the car, Jordan. He didn't stop you. He needs you to leave.*

Head held high, she put one foot in front of the other and made it to the car. Bullet jumped in and she turned to glance at Cole one last time. *I love you,* she mouthed before getting in the back of the car as he stood, hands shoved deep in his pockets, shoulders slumped, misery on his face.

At least she wasn't in hell alone.

Chapter Sixteen

Four weeks had gone by. Four weeks of hell. And Cole still wasn't sure he'd done the right thing. He didn't feel any better. In fact, he felt worse. Much worse. Jordan had been right. He saw her everywhere. At home. At work. Hell, he couldn't even use his office anymore.

Muttering a curse, he jumped up and strode to look out the conference room window. He'd taken to using a laptop in there, not that Jordan hadn't haunted him in this room, too. The memories just weren't as painful as the ones in his office. No way could he sit in his chair or face the desk where he'd gotten his first taste of Jordan and what it had felt like to be inside the hot, giving woman. To experience a fierce, unrelenting passion that stole his breath and liquefied his bones. His grip tightened around the sill.

God help him, he missed her. He missed her so damn much it hurt to breathe.

And things were no better at home. Jordan haunted him everywhere on the ranch. Inside and out. He thought he'd at least find sanctuary in his room, but *son-of-a-bitch* if he didn't find himself straying just a few doors down to sit on her bed and fumble with the hairclip she'd left on the nightstand. He wondered if she'd left it on purpose. It didn't matter. He still visited almost daily.

"Figured you'd be here," Kevin said, strolling in from the door attached to Cole's office. "You need help moving your things?"

Cole frowned, turning to face his VP fully. "What are you talking about?"

"You're office. It's great. Much better view than mine. Shame to waste it. Thought we'd move your things out, then move mine in…seeing as you're not using it."

"Fuck you. Get out of here."

Kevin chuckled, leaning next to him against the window not at all put off by his tone. "No can do. *Bossman* expects me here. He's a tough SOB."

"He needs to be in order to handle the likes of you." Cole sighed. "What do you want, Kevin. I'm not in the mood."

"That's because you let Jordan get away."

"I didn't *let* anything."

Kevin held his hands up. "That's right, my mistake. You *sent* her away. What the fuck's wrong with you, man?"

"You wouldn't understand."

"Oh, but I do, buddy. I do," Kevin insisted. "You've been in love with that girl since we were kids. Why'd you push her away?"

He didn't bother to explain. There was no easy answer.

"Surely, you're not going to deny you love her?" Kevin raised a brow and waited.

Seemed his buddy was in full *pain-in-the-fuckin'-ass* mode today. "No, I don't deny it."

"Deny what?"

Cole pushed away from the window with another curse. "Jesus, Kevin. Go away."

"No." The man with a death-wish moved with him. "Deny what, Cole?"

"That I love her, okay?" Cole twisted back to face Kevin. "There. I said it. Are you happy?"

"No. I'm not. And neither are you." Kevin frowned, clamping a hand on Cole's shoulder. "You're my friend. You're like a brother to me. I hate to see you hurting. Jordan's my friend too and it sucks that you're ripping that girl's heart out over some misguided sense of something or other." Cole grumbled and made to move but Kevin's grip tightened. "People die whether you're with them or not, Cole. Life is too damn short not to take what comes your way and enjoy it before it's too late. Before you screw up. No one knows that better than me."

Now Cole felt like a complete ass. Some of his irritation dissipated with his friend's statement. Kevin was speaking from experience. He'd waited too long to ask his college sweetheart to marry him. Back then, his friend had been taking care of his invalid mother, teenage sister and was trying to keep the family ranch afloat at the same time. Thinking he was doing the girl a favor by not wanting to saddle her with his problems, he didn't give her the commitment she wanted so she found someone else. He never had a serious relationship since, even though his mother had long passed, his sister was happily married and the ranch was booming.

Cole sighed. "I can't go through it again, Kevin. I can't open up and let her in only to lose her."

Kevin's head jerked back. "What makes you think you'll lose her?"

"She's a cop, for Christ's sake!" Cole shook out of Kevin's grasp and brushed past him. "She'll always be in danger." He'd worry constantly. Hell, they weren't together, she was several states away and he still worried about her on the job.

"So, ask her to quit."

"What?" Cole reeled around to gape at his friend. "Hell no. That's her choice. It's who she is. I'd never ask her to choose between me and her career."

His buddy leaned back against the window, crossed his arms and studied him quietly. "Because she'd choose you in a heartbeat. Then what would you do?"

Cole frowned. "I don't follow you."

"I know Jordan. She'd give her eye teeth to have that choice. Yes, she'd gladly choose you. And you know this. So…what's really eating at you, Cole?"

He sank down in his chair, pressed his fingers and thumb to his eyes and released a long, drawn out breath. There were only three people Cole could never pull one over on. Jordan, Connor and Kevin.

"I don't want her dying because of me."

Kevin uttered a curse. Then another. "God, Cole…you're not still blaming yourself over Bess?"

He dropped his hand and stared up at his buddy now standing next to his chair. "Of course I am. I always will."

"Then stop." Kevin frowned down at him, his expression as fierce as Cole had ever seen. "It wasn't your fuckin' fault. You weren't driving the damn truck."

Cole's breath hissed and stomach clenched while the nightmare flashed through his mind. Only…it was the one with Jordan in the car.

"It was me she was coming to see. And you know full well Jordan would be no different. Hell, she was already here several times."

And he refused to think about that last incredible visit.

"So?" Kevin shrugged. "That's what happens in relationships. People generally drive to see each other. Even in friendships. Don't sit there tell me you'd feel the same way if I was hit by a drunk driver on my way to your ranch?"

"Christ, Kevin," he snapped. "Why are we even on this subject?"

"Because you're being a stupid ass, that's why. Now answer the damn question."

Cole grated his back teeth together. "Yes, I would feel responsible if it were me you were coming to see."

"Well then, listen up." Kevin leaned against the table and stared down at him, arms crossed over his chest. "You are not responsible for other people's actions. Not now. Not ever. You need to worry about you, and what you do. Not what other people do."

"Not going to happen."

"Then you need to pull out your responsibility, whack it against the damn table a few times to shake out the misguided sense of duty and shit, then shove it back in and get the fuck over yourself."

And wasn't that just the problem. Cole was born with a *misguided sense of duty and shit*. He didn't possess the ability to turn a blind eye. It was ingrained in him. Imbedded. By no one in particular, although he was told it was a McCall trait. Passed down generations from the first McCall who fought to claim the land they call Wild Creek Ranch, then provided for those he conquered. No. His misguided sense of duty wasn't something he could easily shake.

Or could he?

Walking into Megan's family room, Jordan felt some of her tension dissipate. The past seven weeks had been difficult. She wasn't sleeping, barely had an appetite, and couldn't focus. All detrimental and potentially deadly in her profession, not only to her but to her partner and those around her. So she did the only thing she could…took a leave of absence. Still unsure how she felt about that because she certainly was no quitter, she just knew it was the right thing to do.

When Eric had died, she'd turned to the job, threw herself into her work, and buried herself in case after case. But not this time. The job held no appeal, no promise to lure her away from her problems and heartache. No, it wasn't going to work. She was pretty much shattered. And a shattered cop was a liability. She was much better off splitting her time between Comets' and Megan's. Especially now that the baby had arrived.

Snapping out of her funk, she handed her friend a blue and white bag with playful dinosaurs on it. This was quickly becoming her favorite time of the day. She could hardly wait to see the little guy.

"Where is that cute little godson of mine?"

"Oh, Jordan, he's only four weeks old and you've already got him spoiled." Her friend smiled. "He's taking a nap but should be waking up soon."

Eric Shawn Corbett had arrived a week early on September thirtieth. Honored and touched, Jordan had cried happy tears when Shawn had named his son after her dead husband—his late partner. Her heart swelled. Eric would've been so proud.

"I enjoy doing things for him and you," she replied.

Jordan and Kerri had pitched in wherever possible. Her sister happily cooked meals and froze for reheating later—a task even Shawn could handle.

Since the birth, Jordan had made a point of running to the store and doing any errand her friends required during her free time. Not only did this give Megan time to bond with her son but also occupied Jordan and kept her mind off Cole.

"Hey, it's not every day that a cute guy comes into my life." Jordan stole the bag back from Megan. "Besides, little Eric told me the other day he just *had* to have this costume for his first Halloween. Apparently, it's all the rage among his peers this year."

"Costume!" Her friend swiped the gift again. "Let me see! Oooh…" Megan gushed when she pulled out a pumpkin-faced little orange sleeper with a matching hat topped with a brown felt stem. "Jordan, it's perfect. Wait till Shawn sees this! He's on duty right now, but I know he'll love it, too."

"Well, your little one does have good taste." Her grin broadened as the baby monitor carried his cries down to them.

Megan chuckled. "What did I tell you? I swear he knows when you're here, Jordan." Smirking, her friend went upstairs to get her son. Ten minutes later, she carried the wriggling bundle into the family room. "Okay, Auntie Jordan. Here he is, all changed and fed."

Arms outstretched, she waited for Megan to transfer the fidgeting baby boy and carefully supported his head. "Hey there, handsome. I get the fun part. The rocking." Smiling at the little sweetheart, she began her duty, marveling over the small miracle when his tiny hand grasped her finger. Cries subsided, he fell asleep within seconds.

Megan smiled. "Jordan, you look so natural. You're going to make a great mom."

She felt the blood drain from her face and settle in her tight chest. "I hope so," she managed to say, never taking her eyes off her godson.

Since his arrival, her maternal instincts had kicked in big time. *If only Cole and I had created our own miracle.* Pain squeezed hard at her heart. More than once this past month, Jordan thought about their unprotected sex and the possibility of having a baby. Granted, the circumstances weren't perfect, but she would've loved to have carried his child. Fate, as usual, had other ideas and time had supplied the proof. Immense loss hollowed her gut. Again. She clenched her teeth and forced those unhealthy thoughts aside.

"You'll hear from him, Jordan. I know it," Megan said softly, laying a hand on her knee.

"I hope so," Jordan repeated. "It's been seven weeks. I thought Cole would've cracked by now. I guess he wasn't as in love with me as I thought." She sighed. "Once again, it was all on my part."

"No. It wasn't just on your part. We all saw how he looked at you and acted around you. That night at the party, Jordan, you had that poor guy going nuts. He didn't know whether to run *from* you or *to* you."

"Well, it looks like he's chosen the former and I don't know what I'm going to do." She shook her head. "I haven't had a decent night's sleep since we got back because I keep having dreams with Cole in them."

Megan stiffened. "What kind of dreams?"

Continuing to rock Eric, Jordan glanced at her friend and wondered if she should answer.

"Jordan?"

"Alright." She nodded. "The nightmares are back, but now, instead of Eric lying there...it's Cole." Closing her eyes she saw her strong Texan plain as day, lying in her arms, blood everywhere...

"Let me take the baby and put him down so we can talk."

"Don't. Please." Jordan looked into the face of the sleeping angel with the dusting of red hair. "He's been the only comfort I've had these past few weeks."

"Alright." Megan sighed, then squeezed Jordan's knee again. "I've got a few phone calls to make, if you don't mind?"

She smiled. "No. I don't mind. Go ahead. We'll be fine."

Megan left the room and Jordan closed her eyes, cherishing the comforting snuggles of the innocent little boy in her arms.

Since his bags were packed for his annual Tokyo trip with Kevin and three others in the morning, Cole spent the better part of the afternoon tackling ranch chores. It was Wednesday, but he had no reason to head to the office. Besides, he needed physical labor right now. He was edgy. So damn edgy. His presentation was cultivated, tight...perfect. McCall Enterprises would be well represented at the Software Development Expo. God, he looked forward to a change of scenery.

As for other business, there were no budgets, projects, programs, outlines, awaiting his approval. Hell, he'd even tackled next year's projected expenses. He was tapped out. Done. Completely depleted. Finding material to occupy his mind was becoming more and more sparse. Not that any of it had worked, anyway. *Christ.* There wasn't a day...not one damn day that Jordan hadn't haunted him. The memory of her laughter, warm brown eyes, sweet smile...wicked grin, sexy little mews, panting breaths, throaty sounds of approval when he thrust deep inside—they all followed him, shadowed, invaded his subconscious at every turn.

So, no. He needed to put his back into some physical work. Once again, he turned to the Wild Creek Ranch and Connor's to-do list. Nothing better than throwing himself into repairs. Exactly what he needed to go *brain-dead* for a few hours. At least, he hoped so.

Whack! The nail slipped easily into the post at the insistence of the hammer gripped tightly in his hand. A crisp, November wind blew away the echo.

"I think that one's in far enough, Cole—unless you want to hammer it clear out the other side?" Connor laughed as he slid off his horse.

Great. Just what he needed, the peanut gallery.

Ignoring the grinning man, he grabbed another nail and began to beat the next post into submission. Finally, he'd found an outlet for his pent-up energy, and it was useful, too. He wasn't about to let his brother ruin it, even though he could feel Connor watching as he repeated the process three more times.

"Cole, why don't you just call Jordan?"

"Son-of-a…"

Thumb throbbing, Cole twisted his lips and grit his teeth against the pain of inadvertently substituting an appendage for the nail he had been pounding.

What the hell was his brother's problem?

Connor shook his head in amusement. "I know. I know. She has that kind of effect on you."

"Fuck," Cole ground out, looking at his swollen thumb. The fingernail already began to purple from the blood trapped underneath. "Thanks a lot, Connor! Why'd you even mention her name?"

More laughter met his ears, but with a lot less mirth. "Because you're too damn stubborn to swallow your pride and call her." Connor grabbed for his hat before the wind knocked it off.

He'd like to knock it off, along with his brother's head. "Pride has nothing to do with it. Mind your own damn business."

Again, with the laughter. Was the idiot looking to get punched? Because Cole was only too happy to oblige. Hell, he was barely holding back.

"Sorry, but I can't do that, little brother. It's been two months since she's left and you've been a bear ever since. You don't eat, I doubt that you sleep and I think this has gone on long enough."

He simmered quietly as Connor stood there, gaze intense as he gave a sermon.

"Everyone could tell you love her and she loves you. It's high time you came to terms with that instead of running from your feelings." Arms folded across his chest, Connor dared him to deny the claim.

There'd be no denying. He'd already been through all this with Kevin a few weeks back. He didn't deny he loved Jordan, because he did, with all his heart. Call it a matter of self-preservation, survival, whatever. He just knew Jordan was the key to both his happiness and destruction. Why didn't anyone get that?

"It's *because* of my feelings for Jordan that I won't call," he explained with all the patience of a nat. "I can't get involved with her and it's not fair to string her along."

Irritation skidded across his brother's face. If Cole hadn't been in so much pain, both physically and emotionally, he would've taken stock in the very rare occurrence.

"Ah, for the love of Pete! *Why* can't you get involved with her?" Strong hands clamped like a vise around his upper arms and dug into his skin. "What the hell is going on in that head of yours, little brother?"

What indeed. He yanked free and stomped back a few feet. "You don't understand."

Christ, it was déjà vu all over again.

If only Stella had been present during his *Kevin conversation*, she could've taken down the minutes then forwarded them to Connor and he could have avoided a repeat discussion. It was painful enough the first time. Gaze skidding across the pasture, he wondered if he could make it to his horse before Connor let loose.

"You're right, Cole, I don't understand. It doesn't make a lick of sense why you're not jumping at this chance you've been given." His brother narrowed his eyes and apparently decided it was okay to get back in his face. "Don't you see how lucky you are? Not once, but *twice* you've found a terrific woman who loves you with all her heart. Some men don't even find that once in a lifetime, no matter how hard they try."

The last sentence—spoken with envy, stopped him cold. *Yep*, another repeat, complete with guilt over how damn inconsiderate he'd become toward others. Connor had three failed engagements. Not something he wanted his brother to dwell on, and Cole hated the fact he was the cause of the reminder. Exhaling long and deep, he took off his hat. He hadn't meant to be insensitive. Jesus, he had no focus lately. Thrusting his uninjured hand through his hair, he shivered as the breeze cooled his head.

"You're right. I have been lucky."

After spending several of the most incredible days of his life with Jordan, he'd barely found enough strength to let her go. And that goodbye kiss? *Damn.* She'd given herself so freely and completely, it touched him deep down. He'd felt…worshipped. In turn, he'd done his best to show her how much he loved her before he let her go. He had to let her go.

"Then why don't you make things right?" Connor's brows dipped.

Ah hell…

"No! Don't you see?" He jammed his hat on his head, and this time, grabbed his brother's arm. "I can't be loved like that and then have it ripped away from me again. I just can't. I didn't do so well the first time. I'd never survive a second. Not with Jordan." God, never with Jordan. He released Connor and swallowed back his threatening emotions. "The further from me she is, the safer she'll be." She was better off without him and he had to live with those terms.

Connor scratched his temple and stared at him. "What makes you so sure Jordan's going to die?"

Jesus!

Cole sucked in a breath but his tight throat wouldn't grant passage. "Christ, Connor." Cole gripped the beam and breathed through the indiscernible fist punching his gut. "I'm not. But I can't take that chance."

"I see." Once again, Connor closed the space between them and placed a hand on his shoulder. "Cole, I need you to answer me truthfully."

He grunted. Hell, he still hadn't recovered from that last question. "What?"

"If you knew ahead of time that Bess was going to die, would you have gotten involved with her in the first place?"

"Yes," Cole answered without hesitation.

Remembered touches and special feelings filled his heart with gratitude. Their relationship had made him a better person. The time they'd shared was special. He wouldn't trade it to avoid the heartache. No way in hell.

And just like that, an invisible weight lifted off his shoulders and he stood taller. "I would never give up the time we had together."

A satisfied gleam entered his brother's gaze as he squeezed Cole's shoulder. "Then, little brother, how could it possibly be any different with Jordan?"

In the stock room at Comets, Jordan and Kerri checked their inventory and were making the regular Sunday list for the weekly order she'd place later that day. A task Jordan normally handled herself but Cole's *haunting* had gotten stronger and she didn't want to be alone. She needed someone to keep her mind occupied so she dragged her sister out of bed to help…and because she had this strange feeling she needed Kerri with her today.

"I can hardly believe Thanksgiving is only four days away," Kerri said with a slight shake to her head. "Where in the world did the year go?"

"Got me," Jordan replied, not wanting to think about any of the upcoming holidays. "Are you sure you have everything you need?"

"I'm sure," Kerri replied.

Bullet's incessant barking burst through the silence of the restaurant from his perch out back. *What's with him today?* In all the time she'd had him, he'd never barked this much.

"Jordan, why exactly did you bring Bullet with you?"

She tossed her hand with the list in the air and stared at her sister. "I didn't have a choice. He's acting so weird this morning. He wouldn't let me leave without him."

When they'd arrived, she'd chained him to the fence behind the restaurant—his usual spot, and expected him to put nose to pavement in search of invisible trails as always. He had a long lead, was away from traffic and loved to explore as well as guard the back door. But not even his favorite stomping ground had satisfied his restless, unsettled behavior today.

When he began to howl, they both turned their heads toward the back of the restaurant. "See what I mean?"

Suddenly, the room started to shake and a deep rumbling filled their ears. Cans danced across shelves and clattered to the floor. The smashing of glasses and dishes echoed from the dining room.

"*Earthquake!*" Jordan sank her fingers around her sister's arm and yanked her toward the hall, as their stock rained down on them.

Bullet's behavior suddenly made a lot of sense.

Chapter Seventeen

The ground pitched beneath Jordan as they scramble from the stockroom off the kitchen. Falling utensils and culinary objects made it far too dangerous for them to remain in the doorway. Pots and pans bounced off the floor and into their path as they ran with staggered steps through the kitchen and out the back to a barking Bullet.

Moving as far away from the building as possible, they tried to catch their breath. The shaking stopped. Alarms blared throughout the street, including their restaurant. Other dogs joined in Bullet's howls.

Jordan eyed Kerri with concern. "Are you alright?"

"Yes, I think so. How about you? You're bleeding!"

Kerry pointed to Jordan's temple and she fingered her aching head. "It's just a scratch."

Turning her attention to Bullet, she bent down. "It's okay, boy. This is what you were trying to warn me about, huh?" She received a bark and a few kisses as his ears twitched.

She unlocked the handcuffs and unhooked his long leash. He stayed close as they made their way around to the front of the restaurant.

Confusion greeted them. People crowded the streets and parking lots. Some walked around in a daze while others ran about helping. Busted water mains gushed into the air. Hissing and sirens sounded in the distance while a haze hung like a cloud as dust tried to settle. Small fires burned, and when the hissing noise became more apparent, Jordan's heart stopped.

"Hold Bullet for me, Kerri." She thrust the leash at her sister and turned toward the building.

"Where are you going? Jordan! You can't go in there. It's not safe," Kerri yelled.

"I'm not. I have to shut off the gas in the back," she shouted over her shoulder, running as fast as she could.

"Jordan, no," Kerri screamed while Bullet barked.

A second later, the strong hissing and pungent odor exploded with a terrible boom. The powerful blast hurt her ears while the percussion knocked her to the ground—hard. *I'm too late*, her mind cried as the area shook and what was left of the windows flew out followed by a cloud of fire that engulfed her restaurant and headed straight toward her wounded body.

The Expo was in full swing. Cole could always count on the convention to grab his interest. The place was crowded with the industries leaders and up-and-comers. Booth after booth held the latest innovations in technology and software. His life's work. Which would be great except…work no longer was his life…and he suddenly wondered what the hell he was doing there.

He didn't want to be in Japan.

He wanted to be with Jordan.

It all became so clear.

Everything his brother and Kevin had said was true. Taking a chance, opening his heart and life to Jordan didn't guarantee eternal happiness. Life was too unpredictable. But it did guarantee *right now* happiness. No one knew what was around the corner, and unless he came out from behind the protective wall he'd built around his heart, he wasn't really living. He didn't regret loving then losing Bess and it would certainly be no different with Jordan. The regret would be to do nothing at all. It would be a mistake not taking a chance on Jordan, to *not* let her into his life. Hell, she *was* his life.

How could he have been so stupid?

He couldn't control the actions of others, but he sure as hell could control his own. Starting right now. He strode through the crowd, straight to the McCall Enterprises booth where several of his employees were dulling out demonstrations and a smiling Kevin who was surrounded by three identical Japanese women.

Cole's lips twitched. Leave it to his friend. Even in the middle of a convention, in a foreign country, surrounded by technology, his buddy managed to attract female attention.

"Until later, darlins'," Kevin drawled, tipping his hat with a slight bow and received three soft giggles before the beauties disappeared into the crowd. He turned his gaze to Cole. "Before you say anything. I can assure you we were talking shop…mostly."

"No need," he reassured, stepping past him and through the blue curtain behind their booth. Kevin followed. "I get it. They're interested in your software."

His buddy flinched. "See? Now that's just plain mean. My *hardware*, man. They're interested in my *hardware*. And I've got a date with them tonight…all *three* of them, for a private presentation to show them exactly how it works."

Cole slapped him on the shoulder and smiled. "Good for you."

A startled blue gaze narrowed on him. "Who are you and what the hell have you done with my friend? He's six foot, dark hair, brown eyes, looks suspiciously like you but walks around with a pole stuck up his ass."

Cole threw his head back and laughed. "I gave him the boot."

"Good."

"And now I'm giving you the booth. I'm leaving," he said, packing his laptop. Kevin had his own with the same presentation and all the information he needed to represent McCall Enterprises.

"Leaving?" Kevin stepped closer and frowned. "Look, if it's because of the triplets—"

"No." He shook his head, cupping his friend's shoulder. "It's not about you. It's about me, not only removing the pole you mentioned, but my head as well."

Kevin cocked his head and narrowed his eyes again. "You're not going to Texas, are you?"

"Nope. California to grovel at Jordan's feet and beg her forgiveness."

Kevin let out a whoop, grasped Cole's shoulders and smiled. "Bout damn time!"

"I know. Thanks, man."

"For what?"

"For riding my ass and making me realize I can't control other people's actions and that I need to take a chance before it's too late." His heart suddenly stopped as the deep foreboding that had been plaguing him the past twenty-four hours returned. "At least, I hope I'm not too late."

"Nah, man," his friend said. "That girl loves you and would wait forever for you. Hell, she's already waited ten years."

Thirteen hours later, Cole continued to glance at his watch as if that would make time go faster. He'd spent most of those hours in the air. Now that he'd finally made up his mind, he wanted to get to Jordan, make amends and start their new life together. He pulled out the jeweler's box from his pocket and stared at the diamond ring he'd purchased while his pilot had readied the jet.

The store, though popular and exclusive, housing only the world's top diamonds, didn't have one big enough to represent all the feelings he had for Jordan. But he didn't go for the biggest or the prettiest. That wasn't Jordan's style.

The ring he'd given Bess was simple and elegant. It had suited her. Not at all the right fit for Jordan. He had no idea what kind of ring Eric had given her, he just wanted to choose something different. Something to represent the woman and how he felt. He eventually decided on a unique, one-of-a-kind ring with an interwoven band to form a love knot with a heart-shaped diamond in the middle. A three karat diamond. Okay, so he went a little ornate. He wanted people to know she was taken, *dammit*.

He certainly was.

The pilot announced their decent. *Thank, Christ.* He was going nuts.

Slipping the ring back in his pocket he contemplated calling her for the tenth time, but then vetoed the idea. Again. He wanted to surprise her. Besides, what he had to say needed to be said face-to-face. If she wasn't home, he'd try Comets', Kerri's, even Megan's if he had to. He'd stored all their addresses and phone numbers in his phone a few months back, not ever intending to use them, but now, he was glad he had. He just hoped he wasn't too late and that she would find it in her heart to forgive him.

Opting to rent a car instead of hailing a taxi since he didn't know how long he'd be staying, Cole punched in Jordan's address on the GPS and headed through L.A., his pulse beating erratic in his chest. God, he couldn't wait to see her and wished he hadn't waited this damn long.

Those same thoughts raged in his head a half hour later as he drove through streets, around road blocks, passed houses devastated as if a bomb had gone off. Cole parked in Jordan's driveway and vaulted from the car, staring at the yellow caution tape blocking her door. Her house was one of the few intact, with only a busted window or two, which were now boarded up. But the others...*Jesus*, they were leveled, tilted, one had even slid half off its stilts and was perched, ready to crumble with the slightest breeze.

He drew out his phone and called Jordan, willing her to pick up. Nothing. He dialed her house and got her machine. Next he called, Kerri. Nothing. Comets. Still nothing. *Christ.*

"Cole?"

He spun around, noting two officers getting out of a police cruiser, one with a familiar face. "Shawn. What the hell happened?"

"Earthquake. Almost two days ago. Where've you been?"

Cole slumped against the car as Shawn's words knocked the strength from his legs. Heart stopping mid-beat, he inhaled sharply while blood drained to his feet as if sucked by a vacuum. The foreboding hovering over the past thirty some hours, suddenly became clear.

"Japan," he vaguely replied, checking his phone. Sure enough, he had several missed calls from Connor. Cole always kept it on silent during conventions. Hell he hadn't even checked his emails.

"That would explain it." Shawn nodded.

Didn't explain why Jordan hadn't answered her phone...unless... *I'm too late.*

Fear took root and propelled him forward. He grasped Shawn by the shoulders and studied his face. "Jordan, where is she? Is she okay?"

"Relax. Yes, she's okay," Shawn reassured.

Cole released him with a nod, doing his best to hold onto his dwindling control.

"So is Kerri. Thankfully she was with Jordan at Comets when the quake struck. That's her house there. Or, what's left of it." The other officer pointed to the house half off the stilts.

"Jesus."

"Yeah. Although, Comets is completely gone, too. Gas main busted and leveled the place." Shawn held up his hand when Cole opened his mouth, his heart back in his throat. "They weren't inside, but did get hit with flying debris. Jordan suffered a slight concussion and they both had cuts and bruises. Still, it could've been much worse."

Cole's chest was so tight he could hardly breathe as Shawn's words sunk in and painted a horrid picture. "Where is she? At your place? I take it you and Megan and the baby are okay."

"We're fine. We happened to be up north visiting my mother-in-law when the quake hit Sunday morning. Our house is good. Only a few broken pictures and lamps. As for Jordan, she's not here."

He reeled back. "Not here? What do you mean?"

"Her parents flew in on one of your father's private jets this morning and took Jordan and Kerri back to Texas with them about two hours ago."

Jordan wasn't there.

He flew to California for nothing.

Jordan was in Texas.

He let out a laugh. *Fucking fate.* "It was nice seeing you, Shawn. Give my best to Megan and the baby. I've got to run?"

A knowing smile spread across the cop's face. "I take it you've come to your senses then?"

"Yes," Cole replied, opening the car door before he repeated what he'd told Kevin the day before. "I'm going to grovel at Jordan's feet and beg her forgiveness."

Chapter Eighteen

Jordan stood on the bluff overlooking the gulf, wind whipping her hair in her face and sending a chill through her bones. She shoved her hands deep in the pocket of the coat she'd borrowed from her mother. Her own clothes weren't exactly fit for a Texas winter. Although, half of the chill had nothing to do with the weather.

God, she couldn't believe she was in Harland County again.

Oh, she wanted to come back, just not under these circumstances. No. She'd wanted Cole to come get her. To profess his undying love and beg her to come home. Her chest tightened with a painful ripple. At least he was in Japan until the end of the week and not there to glower. She couldn't have handled that at the moment. And if he was miserable when he returned, she'd already made up her mind to go stay at her parents' house. She'd sleep in a damn sleeping bag on the floor amongst the renovations if she had to. No way could she stay at the McCall's with Cole so close yet untouchable. She just couldn't.

Unable to stand near the tree, yet unwilling to go back to the ranch just yet, she made her way down to the beach and stared at the waves crashing into the shore. Turbulent. Like her life at the moment. She had no job, be it the force or Comets. But, at least she had her house, although she still had to wait for it to be deemed safe. Unlike poor Kerri. Man, she felt so bad for her sister. The business she loved, poured everything into, had been reduced to ash. Then there was her house. Gone. Collapsed.

Fate sucked sometimes. Took everything away…

Wait a minute.

She straightened and even let out a laugh. No. *My God*, she had it all wrong. How could she not see this before? All the pain, Cole's rebuff, her going back to California…it all made sense.

"Jordan."

Cole?

She stilled. That couldn't have been him. He was in Japan. *Great*, now she was hearing things she wanted to hear. But it did suddenly feel like he was behind her.

"Jordan, please turn around."

She closed her eyes, heart instantly pounding right out of her tight chest. He *was* there. But how? She opened her eyes and slowly turned around. A hiccup escaped her throat at the sight of him standing on the beach in Armani, arms full of roses and chocolate.

"My God!" His gifts hit the sand as he rushed forward, concern darkening his eyes. "Are you okay?" he asked in a rough voice, lightly touching the bandage on her forehead.

She nodded. "Yes, I'm fine."

A second later, a strangled sound ripped from his throat as he drew her into his arms and held tight. Strong, warm, wonderful arms she wanted around her for the rest of her life. *God*, she didn't know why he was there or how, but she burrowed in and took what he gave. It didn't matter. He was here. That's all that mattered. And even if it was just her imagination. She didn't care. Right now, she was happy.

"I'm sorry, Jordan. I'm so damn sorry. I *never* should have let you go," he said near her ear, head buried against her neck. "Now you're hurt because of me. If I would've listened to you and asked you to stay in Texas, then you wouldn't have almost…" his voice trailed off and she felt him swallow.

"Hey, no." She drew back to cup his face and held his tortured gaze. "You did *not* cause the earthquake, Cole. Don't you dare try to take the blame for my injuries."

"But, if I hadn't sent you away…"

She placed a finger on his lips and smiled. "I'm so glad you did."

"You're glad?"

Eyebrows disappearing under his hair, he looked thoroughly confused and utterly adorable. Her hand dropped to his shoulder but she didn't leave his arms.

"I was right where I was supposed to be. Believe it or not, fate had actually been helping this time. If you hadn't sent me away, then I wouldn't have been in California last Sunday to insist Kerri come help me out at Comets." She stopped to draw in a breath as the full force of her realization hit hard. "Kerri's house…" That was all she could get out as emotions clogged her throat.

"I know," he said quietly, catching a tear on his thumb. "I saw it."

She blinked up at him. "You did? How? When?"

"A few hours ago. I flew to California to beg your forgiveness and found devastation instead."

Her heart hit the sand then bounced back into her chest, racing out of control. "Y-you came to California…for me?"

"Yes." He smiled, caressing her face. "But it had nothing to do with the quake. I didn't even know about it. No. I came because I finally got a damn clue. I was in Japan, in the middle of the convention when it hit me. I would never regret loving then losing you if something happened. Never. The regret would be to *not* take the damn chance in the first place."

She smiled and nodded, sending more happy tears down her face. He did get it. *Oh, thank you God*, he finally did understand.

He kissed her forehead then drew back, still holding her face gently in his hands. "I knew that I loved you and wanted to be with you for the rest of my life. Once I figured that out, I couldn't get to you fast enough. But when I did, you weren't there."

"You love me?" The smile in her heart matched the one on her face. Big. Wide. Consuming.

"Yes, with all my heart." He fell to his knees, grabbed her hands and stared up at her. "Please say you'll forgive me, Jordan. I promise I'll make you happy from now on."

"What are you doing? Get up." She tugged but he wouldn't budge.

"No, you deserve groveling. I was an ass."

She hit her knees and got down to his level. "No. You weren't. You were scared, Cole. I understood that. I'm scared too, but like you said, the bigger regret would be to not take the chance."

In one swift move, he brought them both to their feet and crushed her close, burying his face in her neck again. "God, I don't deserve you."

"Don't say that. Don't you *ever* say that. Yes, you do. You deserve to be happy. We both do. And you know I'm the only one who can do that, right? I've told you that since our first kiss here on this very beach."

Drawing back, he smiled down at her, lightly tracing her lip with his thumb. "So you did."

"It's about damn time you believe me."

"Oh, I believe you," he said, then got down on one knee this time and pulled out a jeweler's box.

Her heart slammed into her ribs.

"Jordan Masters Ryan, I love you more than life itself. You saved me, lured me back to the light. Taught me how to feel…*boy*, did you teach me how to feel." He opened the box and held it up to reveal the most beautiful diamond ring she'd ever seen. "Will you marry me?"

Happiness burst clear to her toes faster than the gas explosion that'd leveled her restaurant. "Yes. Yes, I'll marry you, Cole McCall. You've always been my world. I love you so much it hurts."

His *whoop* echoed in the wind a second before he surged up and spun her around. Then he slipped the ring on her finger and finally, finally he kissed her long and slow and so sweet those damn tears wouldn't stop.

Then he buried his head in her neck again and just held her. He held her a good long time and she didn't ever want to let go.

"If this is a dream, please don't wake me," she said against his collar, squeezing him tighter.

"It's not." He shivered. "It's too damn cold to be a dream."

She laughed. "Well, you're the silly one standing here in a suit.

What were you thinking?"

"That I couldn't wait to get to you," he said, drawing back to smile at her. "I got back, raced inside the house. Everyone told me you'd gone for a ride, so I rushed to the barn, saddled up and here I am."

"Crazy man."

"Crazy for you." He bent down to pick up the flowers and candy then handed them to her.

She sniffed the roses, loving their scent and the promise they represented. "Thank you, but you didn't have to go through so much trouble for me, Cole."

"I wanted to." He drew her against him and she felt him shiver again.

"What do you say we head to ranch and I *warm* you up?" she asked.

His gaze was hot and just a bit hopeful.

"Yes, ma'am. And, maybe we can move your things into my room, or mine into yours? I don't want to be apart from you anymore, Jordan. Please say that's okay?"

Was he serious? Of course it was okay. She couldn't agree more.

"As long as you think your parents wouldn't mind, that's better than okay. I'll move mine into yours since I'm not even unpacked yet."

"Perfect. And trust me, the way both of our parents were smiling when I tore out of there after you, I know they won't mind," he said, leading her up the trail toward their tree. "What are you going to do about work? Can you transfer here or Houston?"

She stopped and turned to face him. "Probably, but right now, I'm on leave."

He nodded. "Because of the earthquake."

"No, back in September, I took a leave of absence," she said, watching his face darken. "My head wasn't in the right place."

"God, I'm sorry, Jordan. It's all—"

"Don't you even finish that sentence, McCall. It was all me." She dropped her flowers and candy to poke him in the chest. "And I'm glad I did it. I threw myself into work at Comets and found I really enjoyed it. So, I'm not sure what I'm going to do. And right now, you know, I don't think I'm going to worry about it. I'd like to just concentrate on us for a bit."

"Yeah?" He grabbed her hips and grinned.

"Yeah." She smiled back.

His grip tightened as he set his forehead to hers. "I hope you'll marry me soon, Jordan. I can't wait to make you my wife."

Her heart did a crazy little flip. "Whenever you want." She wrapped her hands around his neck and stroked his hair. "I can't wait, either."

He kissed her then, long and intense, with all the passion and heat she remembered. Hot and desperate, his taste surely matched her own. His tongue stroked and hips ground close, and *oh yeah*, her whole body was deliciously on fire and trembling by the time he pulled back.

"Damn, I missed you." He gave her a quick kiss and turned her around so her back was to him. "What do you think of this spot?"

"Oh…I think all kinds of things," she replied, twisting back to face him. "Like you really should take me up against that tree." Sliding her arms around his back, she leaned into him and bit his chin. "You know, if we only free the essentials…"

"Jesus, woman." He closed his eyes a moment then opened them to stare at her with enough heat to keep her toasty. "I hadn't meant that but now that's all I'm going to think about."

She chuckled. "Then what did you mean?"

"Hmm…" he said, kissing her neck and throat. "Oh. I'm going to subdivide several acres here so when the weather breaks we can start building our house. If…that's what you want."

"What I want?" She drew back and held him at arm's length to stare into his warm eyes. "Oh, Cole, that would be perfect!"

Then she lunged at him and kissed him hard and wild and deep. He jumped right on board and eventually she felt the tree against her back.

They broke apart for air. His gaze blazed. "Now, about this tree…"

She grinned and trailed a hand down his thundering chest. "You, me and this tree make me very happy."

He brushed a piece of hair from her face, gaze suddenly serious. "That's all I want, Jordan. That's all I want." Tenderly and oh so slow, he touched his lips to hers and Jordan's soul rejoiced with a vigor she wished her vocal chords possessed. He drew back and smiled, tracing her lower lip with a teasing finger. "Guess we've proved there's no escape for *fated hearts*, my Masters."

"Mmm…I like the sound of that."

"Good, because I'm yours, Jordan. All yours," he said, bending slightly at the knee to look her straight in the eyes. "I mean it. Anything you want, anything you need, just ask."

She touched his jaw. "All I need is for you to love me, Cole."

"Then sweetheart…," he cupped her face, gaze smoldering with so much love and deep emotions her chest ached. "Prepare to be the happiest damn woman in Texas, because I'm going to love the *hell* out of you."

Epilogue

Connor McCall raised his glass, joy piercing his heart for the first time in months. "Here's to my brother and Jordan and a marriage many, many, many, *many,* years in the making." He'd just witness his younger brother ride off in a suit, of all things, after Jordan...not doubt to beg forgiveness and propose. Good. *'Bout damn time Cole came to his senses and let Jordan catch him.* "If ever two people belonged together, it's those two."

"I agree." His mother nodded, lifting her flute, eyes shining as bright as her bubbly.

"Hear, hear," Mr. Masters and his father agreed in unison.

Mrs. Masters smiled. "Amen."

"To Jordan and Cole." Emma nodded, clinking the group of raised glasses.

"Now,"—his dad lowered his hand and looked over his rim at him—"that's one McCall son and Masters daughter union."

"Yep," Mr. Masters said, slamming him with a direct gaze. "Which leaves only one more to go."

"Hear, hear," his mother and Mrs. Masters agreed.

"Amen," Emma said, turning to face him.

Ah hell no!

His heart stopped and practically fell from his hollowed chest. What the hell happened to all the air in the room? It evaporated. Like their common sense. He tugged at his collar. *Is this what a calf feels like before branding*? In one gulp, he drained his champagne and set the empty glass on the nearby table with a thud.

Thank God Kerri was still upstairs unpacking. She'd no doubt high-tail it out of there before he could. The woman had barely said two words to him, looking so fragile and lost, his gut was twisted up something fierce. Still, that didn't mean he was interested.

Damn, by the looks both sets of folks were giving him, they didn't care.

"Hold on a dog-gone minute. Whatever it is you five are thinking...you can just forget it right now." He back up toward the door, nearly stumbling in his haste to escape.

"Ah, come on now, Connor. It's not that bad." His mother smiled. Smiled!

"Yeah, son," his dad said. "It'll be less painful if you don't fight it."

"Fight it? There's no need to fight it 'cause it ain't happening," he said, door knob slipping in his sweaty palm but he managed to wrench the door open anyway, then turned to stare down the five smiling matchmakers. "Three failed engagements prove I'm one *unbrandable* cowboy."

####

Also by Donna Michaels

~Novels~
Captive Hero (Time-shift Heroes Series-Book One)
The Spy Who Fanged Me
Her Unbridled Cowboy (Book 2-Connor)
She Does Know Jack
~Novellas~
Cowboy-Sexy
Thanks for Giving
Ten Things I'd Do for a Cowboy
Vampire Kristmas
~Short Stories~
The Hunted
Negative Image
The Truth About Daydreams
Holiday Spirit
~Do-Over Series~
Valentine's Day Do-Over
Valentine's Day Do-Over Part II: The Siblings

UPCOMING RELEASES:
Cowboy Daddy Squared (Sequel to Cowboy-Sexy)
~Time-shift Heroes Series~
Future Hero—Book Two
~Harland County Series~
Her Uniform Cowboy (Book 3/Kade)
~Dangerous Curves Series~
Locke and Load—Book One

Donna Michaels

Harland County Series
…Unruly cowboys and the women who tame them…

Visit my Harland County Series Page
http://www.donnamichaelsauthor.com/index_files/Page3317.htm
for release information and updates!
Book One: Her Fated Cowboy
http://www.amazon.com/dp/B00BWAD5KE
Book Two: Her Unbridled Cowboy
http://www.amazon.com/dp/B00D4846AK
Book Three: Her Uniform Cowboy
Book Four: Her Forever Cowboy

♥

Kerri promised herself she'd wait until next spring
to return to Harland County
but fate and a California earthquake
had a completely different timeframe in mind…

♥

On the next page is a preview of

Her Unbridled Cowboy

Available Now

http://www.amazon.com/dp/B00D4846AK

Chapter One—Her Unbridled Cowboy

Homeless and unemployed.

West Coast Chef Kerri Masters silently summed up her current life situation. Her *sucky* life situation. *Would she ever catch a break*, she wondered as she stood in a roomful gathered at the Wild Creek Ranch, home of longtime family friends, the McCall's.

The last place she wanted to be. Ever. She had hoped not to suffer this fate again until, oh…say *never*. Okay, not true. She loved her parents, and since they'd recently moved back to Harland County Texas and were currently staying with the McCalls until renovations were completed on their old homestead, *never* wasn't an option.

But, next summer worked for her. *Yes*, she'd had that timeframe in mind. Not now. Not the day before *flippin'* Thanksgiving.

Leave it to fate.

She swallowed a sneer but was unable to stop a slight twist from reaching her top lip. *Yeah*, leave it to fate to take another swing at her life with a blasted butcher knife. Felt more like a meat cleaver. *Two* meat cleavers.

Didn't she already have enough deep cuts? *Criminy*. Was she walking around with an invisible sign on her back saying '*Come on, is that all you've got'*?

"We're just thankful you and Jordan are all right," her mother, Hannah Masters said, pulling her into a hug.

Again.

This one made number seven since she'd arrived from California with her sister Jordan a little over four hours ago. She'd spent most of that time in her room avoiding…well, everyone, while Jordan did the same by saddling a horse and going for a ride.

But that was okay. She'd understood her sister's need to be alone. Coming here had been painful for Jordan until Cole had shown up and gone after her sister to profess his love.

Finally.

A good size helping of warmth invaded the almost constant chill in Kerri's body. If ever two people were meant to be together, it was Jordan and Cole. Both had lost a spouse, and it was that shared pain, plus a long history of attraction that had brought them together at last.

It did her heart good to know at least her sister would have a happy life.

She also understood her mother's worry and immediately returned the hug. It couldn't have been easy hearing about the earthquake that had destroyed Kerri's home and restaurant, while residing several states away.

The sweet fragrance of jasmine filled her nose and instantly calmed the aggravation from her soul. The smell of her mother's perfume always brought with it an invisible hug and strong sense of reassurance. Something Kerri hadn't realized she needed until that moment.

"I'm fine," she said, holding back a sigh.

"Thank goodness." Her mother's trim frame shook slightly while she tightened her hug. "Things would've been a lot different if you were home when the quake hit."

Everyone in the room knew Kerri's stilted house had crumbled in the disaster. Kind of similar to what was left of her life.

She'd laugh if it wasn't so *flippin'* tragic.

"And we thank God both you and your sister got out of your restaurant before it blew up," her father, Nate Masters added from behind, his hand warm and reassuring as it closed around her shoulder in a soft squeeze.

God, if they only knew...

Kerri closed her eyes and recalled the image forever burned into her mind. The image of Jordan rushing across the pavement intent on turning off the gas to their restaurant despite the danger. Terror, unlike anything she'd ever felt before, had resembled a sharp skewer, piercing the air from her lungs. All she had been able to manage was a panicked cry for her sister to stop.

It was the worst moment of her life.

"We certainly had a guardian angel watching over us that day. Didn't we, Kerri?" Jordan cut through her thoughts from across the spacious gathering room.

Kerri opened her eyes and smiled at her sister, now safe and sound, happily cocooned in Cole's arms. Matching expressions of love and wonderment adorned their faces as they stood in front of a stone fireplace, warm fire crackling in the background.

Okay, forget *love* and *wonderment*. Heck, given her sister's soft smile and relaxed posture—extremely satisfied was a better description. *Jeez Louise*, Cole had only taken off after Jordan an hour ago. Ride time alone was close to forty minutes. How the heck did they fit in sex, let alone satisfying sex?

It usually took Kerri that long just to concentrate when Lance used to...

"What do you mean?" their father asked, removing his hand from her shoulder, and her mind stumbled a bit to get back in the conversation. "What guardian angel?"

Jordan burrowed in a little closer to Cole and he gathered her sister tighter. "Well, I just think we were both lucky that day."

"I don't know about me." Kerri stepped out of her mother's embrace to answer her sister. "But you definitely have a guardian angel. I remember calling out to you as you ran toward the restaurant. But you didn't stop. That's when the most amazing thing happened." She paused to glance around the room, a little uncomfortable with being the center of attention.

That was more a Jordan thing.

"Go on. Tell us what happened next," her father prodded.

Kerri swallowed, then forced herself to continue. "Something…or someone, I can't be sure, mysteriously yanked Jordan to the ground right before *Comets* exploded. No one was there. Just the two of us, but it was as if an invisible pair of hands had reached up from nowhere and pulled her down, out of harms' way."

"Wow…do you think it was Eric?" her mom asked, eyes wide and unblinking.

Jordan's late husband Eric had died in a convenient store robbery almost three years ago. Kerri had to admit, the thought had crossed her mind more than once in the last two days. But she honestly didn't know.

"Could've been my Cole," Leeann McCall said, a look of pride lighting her eyes. "I bet he kept her safe through sheer willpower that day."

"True," her husband, Alex McCall chimed in, draping an arm around his petite wife. "No one's more stubborn than our boys."

Whatever it was, Kerri was forever grateful for whatever caused her sister to hit the pavement at that exact moment. And, she had to admit, now she was just a tad envious, too. Envious that her sister had found such a strong love twice in her life, while she couldn't find it even once. All she'd managed was a disastrous marriage that had left her hurt, confused and divorced, doubting there were any good men left in the world.

"That's not entirely true." A deep baritone with a hint of humor cut through the room, captivating the air into a silence of unadulterated anticipation, and sent her heart tail-spinning into her ribs.

Typical Connor McCall fashion.

There wasn't an unattached female in the tri-county area safe from his sex appeal. That's why Kerri kept her gaze glued to the worn-out sole of his left boot. She knew her place. He was way out of her league. She was under no illusion as to where she stood against such a virile man. Heck, she didn't even qualify to kiss the sole of his worn-out left boot. But that's where her gaze remained. Much safer than traveling upward.

She hadn't really said more than a quick hello. He'd headed to the stables shortly after they'd arrived and she'd happily retreated to her room to regroup. To summon strength, because she was a vulnerable mess at the moment. If she could just gather some willpower, even just a smidge, in order to resist the gorgeous cowboy…because heck, he made her *feel* things she had no business feeling.

Yes, staring at Connor's boot was about all she could handle at the moment. Anything higher…

Heat shot through her body, settling in her face and other parts further south. Parts that liked to be called good, but she preferred to call them *closed for the season*. No way could she allow her gaze to take in the whole man. *Jeez*, the toned scenery of his northern terrain could make a girl want to get lost. And stay lost. Forever. He sported a very sexy landscape restricted for equally sexy women…of which she was not.

The reality of those words hit her with the force of an icy, cold blast. She blinked until his boot came back into focus.

"There is someone more stubborn than us," he continued, that darn sexy drawl sending shivers to her toes, while an unwelcomed heat pooled low in her belly.

And she'd only just cooled off.

"Who?" his father asked.

"Jordan," came his humorous reply.

Laughter filled the room. No one would argue that fact. Once her sister made up her mind about anything, she didn't let go. Kerri laughed, too. When the cowboy was right, he was right.

Maybe she could allow herself a small peek.

Tall, broad shoulders and chest, muscles bulging out from under his red, rolled up sleeves, brown hair, dancing brown eyes and those darn dimples…he was six-foot-four-inches of Texas testosterone. The equivalent of saturated fat.

Tasted good but wasn't good for you.

Granted, she'd only had a little taste when he'd briefly kissed her at her parent's anniversary party back in September. But, it had been enough for Kerri to scratch him off her menu—permanently.

Besides, she preferred men with class, who'd picked her up for a date wearing a suit and enjoyed the fine arts. Not a brash, long-haired cowboy whose favorite pastime was teasing and never took anything serious. One who thought dressing up was donning a new pair of jeans. Whose idea of culture was the black velvet painting of a pack of poker playing, cigar smoking bulldogs hanging in his office.

Maybe she'd gotten this all wrong. Maybe *he* was out of *her* league…

####

http://www.amazon.com/dp/B00D4846AK

About the Author

As I state on my website, it's all my mother's fault. She read to me before I could read and opened up that magical world where I still reside today. Then came television and movies. Now I had three avenues to feed my imagination...and boy could I eat!

As you no doubt figured out, this lead to my writing career. I'm multi-published in e-book and print with several publishers, four self-published novels, and a ton of voices in my head.

I'm an author of *Romaginative Fiction*. From short to epic, sweet to very hot, I writes all lengths and most romance genres—Contemporary; Comedy; Sci-fi; Paranormal; Fantasy; Action/Adventure and Suspense. One thing that is constant, all of my novels are Romance through the H's—Hot, Humorous and Heartwarming.

Happily married to a military man for over twenty-seven years, I live in Northeastern Pennsylvania with my husband, our four children and several rescued cats. It is only natural for the military to spill into some of my writing, as well as humorous episodes from our full family life.

This book is my second self-published novel. If you enjoyed this story, please leave a quick review. It would be much appreciated. All of my books are available in eBook, and my novels are also available in print.

For more information about me, my titles or to join my newsletter visit: www.donnamichaelsauthor.com

Thanks for reading!
~Donna

~~*~*

Ride of Her Life
The Buckle Bunnies Series, Book 1
By Paige Tyler

This ride lasts a lot longer than eight seconds.

Barrel rider Daisy Hollins has run into bronc riders Sawyer Jones and Beau Monroe quite a few times on the rodeo circuit. She's flirted with both of them, but things have never gone any further than that. Before an event, they're all too focused on the competition, and afterward, they're usually too sore and tired to do anything but fall into bed.

When she runs into the two hot cowboys in the hotel bar at the Rodeo Finals in Las Vegas, however, there's a different vibe in the air. When the flirting starts this time, it doesn't stop, and Daisy goes upstairs with both of them for a completely different kind of rodeo ride.

Dedication

With special thanks to my extremely patient and understanding husband, without whose help and support I couldn't have pursued my dream job of becoming a writer. You're my sounding board, my idea man, my critique partner, and the absolute best research assistant any girl could ask for!

Thank you.

And thank you to the wonderful girls on my Street Team. You all rock!

Ride of Her Life

Chapter One

The barrel riding competition might be over, but Daisy Hollins was still buzzing as she walked into the hotel bar two hours later. Simply qualifying for the National Rodeo Finals in Las Vegas had been a dream come true, but she'd ended up doing better than she ever imagined. Even though she didn't win the championship buckle, she'd finished pretty damn cl, coming in second behind a perennial championship winner. After an already amazing season on the circuit, and a nearly perfect week at the finals, tonight's ride had been icing on the cake, and she was ready to celebrate. All she needed was a cold beer and a hot guy. The first was easy to get her hands on. The second could be a bit more difficult—though not for the usual reason. The Professional Rodeo Cowboys Association Finals was in town—there were a lot of hot guys around. How the heck was a girl supposed to pick just one?

Keeping her eye out for the perfect hunk, she smiled and flirted her way over to the bar, complimenting each and every cowboy on his rodeo ride as she went. They flirted right back, flashing her sexy grins and telling her she'd looked damn fine out there herself.

Daisy sighed as she leaned back against the bar and waited for her beer. Dang. Narrowing down the field tonight was going to be even harder than she thought. This place was packed to the rafters with serious cowboy beef. Half the fun of being a professional rodeo rider was all the hot cowboys she got to work with. Nothing finer than a man who knew how to ride.

She turned back to the bar just as Britt Miles, one of her fellow barrel riders, limped over. Daisy winced at the woman's painful gait. She held out the untouched bottle of beer to her friend.

"Here. You look like you could use this."

Britt smiled as she accepted the offering. "You're a lifesaver."

Daisy frowned as the dark-haired woman tipped the bottle up and took a long swallow. "Shouldn't you be in bed with your leg wrapped in ice?"

"Nah. The doc said it won't start to swell up until I lie down. Then it will turn into a watermelon. I want to get a few drinks in me and have a little fun before that."

Daisy grimaced. She'd already finished her run and been watching from the fence when Britt had crushed her lower leg against one of the barrels in the arena. "I thought you'd broken it for sure."

"Me, too." Britt took another swig from the bottle. "Fortunately, Dippin' Dots is a lot smarter than I am. He jerked out of the line I'd put him in at the last second. If not for that horse, I'd be in a cast up to my ass. Of course, the worst part is that I got DQ'd on that run." She grinned. "I think I might have caught up to you if I hadn't been."

Knocking over a barrel meant an automatic disqualification for the round. Something like that could drop the best rider from first to worst dang fast.

Daisy laughed. "Probably." She chewed on her lip as her friend took another long draught. "Are you sure you should be drinking that? Didn't the doctor give you something for your leg?"

"Yeah, but he only gave me a quarter dose of the pain meds, because he knew I'd be out drinking tonight. He promised he'd give me the rest tomorrow—once I sobered up." She lifted the bottle in a toast. "Thanks for the beer, girlfriend. I owe you one. Catch you later. I'm going to get hammered and then find a cowboy who'll be willing to help me get my boots off. Have a fun night."

Daisy shook her head. Britt was a cowgirl through and through. Ride hard, play hard, wake up in time to head for the next rodeo.

She started to turn back to the bar, only to stop when someone called her name. She spun around to see a group of girls hurrying over to her. They had to be over twenty-one to get in the bar, but not by much.

"Can we get your autograph?" the redhead asked excitedly.

Daisy laughed as they each held out 8 x 10 glossy photos of her. "Sure."

The redhead pulled out a Pro-Rodeo T-shirt next, while one of her friends begged Daisy to sign her rodeo programs. Dang, this was so unreal. It wasn't that long ago when she was just a farm girl from Oklahoma no older than they were. Now, she was on the circuit playing the big lights of Vegas, signing autographs. She was definitely living the dream.

By the time the girls left and she turned back to the bar, it was packed with people. As she patiently waited for the bartender to get to her, she noticed Britt sitting on a stool with her bum leg in the lap of an equally sore-looking but totally hot bull rider named Clay Winters. He was slowly massaging his way up Britt's inner thigh, and she didn't look like she was planning on stopping that wandering hand anytime soon.

Dang, that woman worked fast. Daisy couldn't blame her. She'd seen that particular bull buster around a few times, and wouldn't have minded a little of his attention herself. But Britt deserved it. There were still a lot of hunky cowboys out there for Daisy to pick from. And a lot of them were looking her way. All she had to do was give one of them a nod and she'd be set for the night.

After she got her beer.

"Bud Light, right?"

Ride of Her Life

The warm, sexy voice in her ear made Daisy's breath hitch. She turned to find Sawyer Jones standing there, a bottle of beer in each hand. Tall with dark blonde hair long enough to brush the collar of his shirt, scruff on his jaw and amazing blue eyes, he was one of the best bareback bronc riders on the circuit. And standing right behind him was Beau Monroe, another bronc rider. He didn't ride in as many events as Sawyer, but when Beau rode, he rode well. And with silky, black hair, a chiseled jaw and eyes the color of deep, dark chocolate, he was handsome as sin.

Sawyer's mouth curved into a devastating grin as he held out one of the bottles. "This is the kind of beer you drink, right?"

She took it from his outstretched hand with a smile. "It is. But how did you know?"

"I remembered you drinking it the night we ran into you at that bar in Amarillo a while back."

Daisy knew the occasion was talking about. It had been the last night of the rodeo and all the riders were at Dusty's Bar either nursing their wounds or celebrating their wins. She and the two men had been in the first group. They'd run into each other a few times since them, and while they'd flirted with her, things hadn't gone any further. She couldn't really say why, especially since she was attracted as hell to both men. Bad timing, maybe. Before an event, she was too focused on the competition and everything that went into it to put much energy into hooking up. Afterward, she was usually too sore and tired. Having to get up early the next morning to head to the next rodeo tended to put a damper on things, too.

But she had nowhere she had to be tomorrow because the season was over—for her anyway. The professional circuit ran year round, but a lot of riders took a few months off after the finals to rest and heal up, and after the big paycheck she'd gotten this time around, that's exactly what she was going to do. Which meant she didn't have to be in bed anytime soon. Unless it was with Sawyer or Beau. And honestly? She'd be dang happy to end up in either man's bed. It'd be a perfect way to end the night, and the season.

She raised the bottle in a toast, then tipped it back and took a swallow. "Thank you, Sawyer. That was mighty sweet of you."

He jerked his chin toward the man beside him. "Beau saw you standing in the back of the line and figured grabbing you a drink would be the gentlemanly thing to do. Especially after the week of riding you've had."

She flashed the dark-haired cowboy a smile. "Well, thanks to you too, Beau."

"What do you say we grab a table?" he suggested.

"Sounds good to me."

They found one in the back corner, but it only had a single stool. Both men gestured for her to sit. Gentlemen to the core. She liked that.

Beau leaned his forearms on the table, his bottle of beer dangling from his fingers. "We got a chance to see your last ride. You looked good out there. If you'd had another few rounds, I think you could have caught up to Katie Carlyle."

Daisy didn't know about that. Katie'd won a lot of championship belt buckles. "Maybe. I was in the groove for dang sure, but Katie was, too. She won it fair and square."

"Well, she may have won the buckle, but you had everyone cheering for you," Sawyer said. "I don't think I've ever seen a barrel rider take her turns so tight."

Dang. When Beau said she looked good out there, she'd thought he'd meant it in the general sense, like when a football player slaps another on the back and says, "Good game." But they'd actually been paying attention.

She sipped her beer. "It didn't know you two were that into barrel riding."

"We're not." Sawyer grinned. "We just like watching you. Isn't that right, Beau?"

Beau gave her a wink. "That's right."

Daisy blinked. Double dang. She figured there'd be a few more empty beer bottles on the table—and maybe some shot glasses, too—before either man came onto her.

Not that she was complaining. Especially if she ended up roping one of these two studs into her bed tonight. Although it wasn't a given she'd be bedding either of them yet. While they were both smokin' hot, she didn't know if they had the one thing in particular she looked for in a man—the ability to carry on a conversation. And she didn't mean about the weather.

She liked a guy who could talk dirty to her.

She wasn't referring to a guy using nasty words to describe how he wanted to have sex with her—though that certainly had its time and place, too. No, she was looking for a man who took verbal foreplay just as seriously as the physical kind.

She'd first realized the power of a man's voice and how it could arouse her at the impressionable age of sixteen when she'd gotten her hands on a set of audio romance books. The man on the tape had a voice as smooth as honey, and before she knew it, her hand was down her panties and she was touching herself to her first orgasm. Ever since then, a man with a smooth voice and a knack for whispering just the right

Ride of Her Life

naughty words in her ear could get her hotter than a tin roof in August.

Conversely, her attraction to a man tended to drop drastically when she discovered he couldn't talk it up.

As kinks went, it was rather tame, but it was one of her things.

So, while she wouldn't turn her nose up her at a good old-fashioned roll in the hay, she always kept her ears open for a man who knew exactly what to say to get her all hot and bothered. Sawyer and Beau were equally attractive, but if one of them talked dirty to her that would certainly help tip the scales in his favor.

"You mean you like watching the way Playdough and I work the course?" She absently ran her finger around the mouth of the bottle. "Yeah, we're really good as a team."

Daisy couldn't care less what they thought about her and Playdough's teamwork. She just wanted to see if one of the men would step up and engage her in a little saucy repartee, or if they'd both get tongue-tied.

Beau chuckled. "Not saying that watching you and your horse work isn't fun, but speaking truthfully, it's watching your ass bounce up and down in the saddle that really gets my attention. Isn't that about right, Sawyer?"

"I do love watching you ride, not gonna lie about that. And I sure as hell don't mind taking a long look at that behind of yours." The blond cowboy grinned at her. "But since we're being straight here, I sort of have a thing for the way those mighty fine legs of yours look in those tight-ass jeans you wear. Damn if I can't see every muscle flex as you ride. You've got the best-looking legs that ever wrapped themselves around a horse."

Well, dang. They were both interested in her. And they both were willing to talk about it. She might just have a competition on her hands.

She demurely dropped her gaze to study her bottle of Bud. Mostly so she could collect herself. Guys liked women for all kinds of reasons, but it was nice to have two men as hot as Sawyer and Beau tell you they were fixated on a particular part of your body.

When she lifted her head, both men were eyeing her as if they thought they'd said too much. She smiled to let them know they hadn't offended her.

"So, you like my butt? And you like my legs?" She looked at first one man, then the other. "I guess I should take it as a compliment. But if you're so enamored with my below-the-belt assets, why haven't you ever said anything before?"

Both men grinned, visibly relaxing. As one, they moved closer to where she sat perched on the stool. At this proximity, she could almost feel the heat coming off their bodies.

"You may not know this," Sawyer drawled. "But you're pretty damn focused on your profession. Everyone knows you don't let anything distract you during the season."

Daisy opened her mouth to deny it, but stopped herself. It was true. She'd always been a woman who went after what she wanted, and her goal this season had been the finals.

"I guess you're right," she admitted. "What made you decide to say something now?"

Beau shrugged. "Figured since the finals were over and all, we owed it to you to tell you how we felt about you. Let you decide where it went from there."

She liked a man who wasn't afraid to put his cards on the table. "Fair enough. But tell me something. You two aren't so fixated on my bottom half that the parts above the belt have escaped your attention, have they?"

Okay, so she was fishing for compliments. But she had to keep them talking dirty, didn't she?

"Oh, they rate for damn sure." Sawyer gave her an appreciative look. "You are one well put together filly. But we all have our soft spots, that one thing that makes us go weak in the knees. Mine just happens to be a pair of long, well-toned legs."

"Whereas I'm a sucker for a perfect ass," Beau said. "And yours is absolutely perfect. My obsession isn't anything I feel I need to apologize for. It's just the way I'm wired. Doesn't mean Sawyer and I don't appreciate your other feminine attributes. Like your pert breasts and long, silky hair. It just means we have a fondness for certain parts of your body—sort of like having a hankering for apple pie over pecan. Doesn't mean there's anything wrong with pecan, but given my druthers…"

"You'd rather feast on my apples." Daisy laughed, not quite sure what the apple analogy said about her ass.

The two men chuckled.

"Something like that," Sawyer said.

He motioned to a passing waitress, and pointed at Daisy's almost empty bottle. How did guys get waitresses to see them when they did that? She could never get anyone's attention in a crowded place.

"You two aren't planning on getting me drunk and taking advantage of me, are you?" she teased.

"Can't speak for Beau, but I'd prefer for you to be sober, so that we can properly take advantage of each other." Sawyer blue eyes twinkled. "Much more fun that way."

Daisy opened her mouth to ask him specifically what kind of things he'd like her to be sober for, but just then three women walked by. They gave both men the eye, but moved on without stopping. Daisy frowned as she realized several other women were looking in their direction as well. She'd better decide what she was going to do with Sawyer and Beau before some buckle bunny tried to move in on these two. Daisy'd never had a problem with the groupies who hung around so they could hook up with the rodeo riders. She thought cowboys were pretty damn hot, too. Her only gripe was that there never seemed to be as many attractive male groupies as there were of the female variety. The world was cosmically unfair, even on the circuit.

At that particular moment, however, she wasn't as accepting of buckle bunnies as she was at other times. Right now, she was feeling rather possessive of her two hunky cowboys, especially since she hadn't decided which one she was going to sleep with tonight.

"Something catch your eye, Daisy?" Beau asked.

"I couldn't help but notice that there are an awful lot of buckle bunnies here tonight." She gave the men a coy look. "Hope you two don't mind wasting your time standing here talking to me?"

Sawyer shook his head. "Don't think I call talking to you a waste of time. You have that sexy kind of voice I could listen to all night. What about you, Beau?"

"Oh, hell yeah." His eyes smoldered. "I'd listen to just about any sound you'd care to make, Daisy, any sound at all. In fact, why don't we go someplace that isn't quite so loud so we can talk or…whatever?"

Her pulse broke into a gallop. Maybe Beau was going to step up and make her decision for her. "What do you have in mind?"

Beau smiled. "I was thinking about the restaurant on the other side of the lobby. I could use something to eat, and it's definitely quieter there."

"Sounds good to me," Sawyer agreed. "I'm starving."

What the hell? The conversation had moved so fast she felt like she had whiplash. She thought one of them had been about to ask her to come up to their room for the night. Now they wanted to have a late dinner?

Beau took her hand and tugged her off the stool. She went willingly, if for no other reason than to see where this was going.

Daisy heard a whoop as they left, and she turned to see Britt's chosen bull buster carrying her piggy-back style out the other door. Britt was laughing and swatting Clay's ass with her hat, telling him to "git along little dogie." Daisy laughed. Obviously, her friend had found that cowboy to help take off her boots. And everything else, too.

As Beau had promised, the restaurant was a lot quieter than the bar.

More private, too, thanks to the mood lighting and heavy fabric draping the booths. Daisy had eaten there a couple times already. It was good, but pricey.

The hostess led them to booth in the back. Sawyer and Beau waited for her to pick a side. Daisy slid in, slightly disappointed when both men decided to sit down opposite her. She'd hoped one of them would slide in beside her.

Sawyer ordered her another Bud Light for her before she could ask. When the waitress brought it to the table, she let it sit there. She'd had enough alcohol for a while.

The men barely looked at the menus before ordering Kansas City strip steaks—rare. Figured. Cowboys and steaks went together like milk and cookies.

Daisy wasn't really hungry—for food anyway. But she didn't want to sit there and stare at them while they ate, so she ordered a plate of nachos. That way, she could nibble.

After the waitress left, Daisy leaned back and regarded her two men. "Okay, we found a place that's not as loud as the bar. What exactly did you want to talk about?"

Beau's eyes held hers. "About getting you naked later and spending the evening make you moan and scream."

That made both her brows and her blood pressure rise. *That* was what she'd been looking for. She just couldn't believe Beau had said what he'd said right in front of Sawyer.

But Sawyer didn't even bat an eye.

"So Daisy, would you describe yourself as a moaner or a screamer?" he asked so casually the three of them might have been taking about a rodeo event.

Actually, now that she thought about it, she was starting to feel like this was a rodeo event—team roping. And Sawyer and Beau were in the process of roping her up and taking her down like a well-oiled team.

Chapter Two

Daisy sipped her beer, deliberately wrapping her mouth around the opening of the bottle. When she was done, she slowly licked her lips, then set down the bottle with a sultry look.

"I tend to be a moaner, I guess," she said, finally answering their question. "Unless the guy I'm with is exceptionally good, that is."

"What make a man exceptional in your eyes?" Sawyer asked.

"Or exceptional in your bed?" Beau asked.

Both men settled back, their long legs brushing against hers as they got comfortable. The innocent—or maybe not so innocent—move made her warm all over.

"It's not anything specific," she said. "I mean it's not like I look for a certain size cock, or like to do it in a particular sexual position."

She glanced around the restaurant. The booth they were in was situated in such a way that it would be difficult for anyone to see under the table. Unless they knelt down, of course. But why would anyone do that? She carefully kicked off her boots under the table. It wasn't that hard. Her boots were her prized possessions and cost more than all the jewelry and fancy dresses she owned combined. They fit like fine gloves, but slid on and off like a pair of fur-lined slippers. They were so comfy she never even wore socks with them, which was—in her opinion—the sign of a perfect pair of boots.

"I just need a man who's confident and knows how to touch a woman the way she wants to be touched."

"And is there a particular way you like to be touched?" Beau questioned.

How had this turned into her talking and them listening? It was supposed to be the other way around.

As Daisy pondered the turnabout, she settled a bare foot in each man's lap before they even knew what she was up to.

To their credit, they didn't even blink, not even when she started to slowly rub the ball of each foot against the sizeable bulges in their jeans.

"We'll get around to how I like to be touched later." She smiled. "Right now, why don't I just sit here and…well, do what I'm doing…while you two tell me how you want to touch me. Remember, I said I like a man who's confident."

She put a little more pressure against each of their cocks, rotating her feet in slow circles. Men had told her before that her toes were very dexterous. Sawyer and Beau seemed to think so—or at least the cocks did. Their erections had practically doubled.

"You don't mind if I just sit here and focus on what I'm doing while you two talk, do you?"

Both men murmured they were fine with that plan, though they looked around the restaurant to see if anyone had a clue as to what was going on. Daisy did a quick survey of the other tables. No one was paying attention.

"Let's start with you, Sawyer," she said. "You mentioned you like my legs. I don't remember you ever even seeing my legs, except in jeans. I'd love to hear where your fascination with them comes from. And what you have in mind for them."

Daisy did little, rhythmic scrunches with her toes against the material of their jeans, like she was massaging them. She could feel the outline of their shafts quite clearly under her tootsies, and figured it was better than even odds that both men weren't wearing any underwear under those jeans. Two hunky cowboys with incredible bodies, clearly impressive cocks, a penchant for talking dirty, and who went commando? It was going to dang near impossible deciding between them.

But she didn't have to make that decision yet. Right now, all she had to do was play with their cocks and listen to those sinfully arousing voices of theirs.

"I doubt you remember it, Daisy," Sawyer said in that sexy drawl of his. His tone was so firm and controlled it was hard to believe she was giving him a foot job under the table. "But back in July, at the Jubilee Days Rodeo in Laramie, you showed up on the steps of the registration office that first day wearing a yellow sundress and a pair of cowboy boots. I was sitting on the grass outside filling out my form, and when I raised my head, there you were perfectly silhouetted by the setting sun. The dress was pretty thin, and with the sun shining through it and the breeze pushing it up against you? Well, let me just say, it didn't leave much to the imagination. I could see every line and shadow from the tops of your boots to the junction of your thighs." He swigged his beer. "It may have been a trick of the light, but I swore I could see the color of those barely-there panties you were wearing. They were pink—the most perfect, soft pink I'd ever seen."

Sawyer stared down at the table, as if reliving the moment. When he lifted his head, again, his eyes were filled with what could only be called awe. "Daisy, no bullshit—that was the most beautiful moment in my life, and I take it as proof that Heaven must exist."

Okay, that left her completely speechless—and somewhat taken aback. She actually felt the heat rising to her face at learning she'd been part of such a moving tableau for a man without even knowing it. And while she didn't remember seeing him that day, she did recall wearing

Ride of Her Life

that dress. And yes, she usually wore light pink panties with it. Clearly, the material was thinner than she'd thought.

"He's been obsessed with those legs of yours ever since." Beau's deep voice made her jump. "Talks about them all the time."

Sawyer shrugged. "What can I say? They're perfect."

Daisy's color deepened. No pressure there, huh? She supposed her legs were okay. Years of riding saw to that. But she doubted they were perfect—whatever that actually meant. It was nice to know a stud like Sawyer worshipped them, though—even if he hadn't ever seen them for real.

"That's quite a compliment." Her voice sounded huskier than normal and she cleared her throat. "Let's assume—just for the heck of it—you and I end up in bed tonight, Sawyer. What would you do with these legs that you so adore, given the chance?"

As he opened his mouth to reply, Daisy started rubbing her big toe right up and down the center of Sawyer's shaft. She wasn't doing the same to Beau, so he had no idea why his friend didn't answer. If he had, he probably would have been jealous. But he'd get his later. Right now, she was busy with Sawyer.

She wondered if her toes were nimble enough to undo the buttons on his 501s. All it would take was one or two of them and she'd be able to slip her tootsies right in there.

"Something tells me you like to have a man pay attention to your feet," Sawyer said. "Is that right, Daisy?"

Well, dang. Sawyer got himself together surprisingly quickly. Maybe her toes weren't as devastating as she thought.

Or maybe Sawyer was one hell of a disciplined man.

"I think we can assume that's correct," Beau answered for her.

Daisy rewarded him for his perceptiveness by giving him an extra firm rub with the bottom of her foot. He shifted in his seat, grinding against her. Could she actually make either man come just from doing what she was doing?

"Have you ever had a man give you a real foot massage, Daisy?" Sawyer asked.

Daisy could only shake her head. How the heck had he known she liked to have her feet touched? Or that they were one of the most erogenous parts of her body? The thought of lying back on the bed while Sawyer rubbed her feet was enough to made her little kitty purr with contentment.

"No, I haven't, but it sounds like fun." She caught her lower lip between her teeth. "Are you offering?"

"Damn right." He glanced down pointedly at her foot nestled in his crotch. "As far as I'm concerned, your feet are just as perfect as your legs."

"Amen to that," Beau groaned.

She thanked them for the compliment by wrapping her toes around their bulging erections and giving them a squeeze.

"Before I say yes to a foot massage, I want to know how good you are at giving one, Sawyer."

He chuckled, low and sexy. "So good I can make you moan."

She lifted a brow. "You really think you can make me moan simply from a foot massage?"

"I have very good hands."

"Uh-huh."

His mouth quirked. "Is that a dare?"

The sudden heat in his eyes made it hard to breathe. "No, I'm just saying…"

The rest of what she'd been going to say trailed off as Sawyer reached down and grabbed her foot where it rested in his lap and started rubbing.

Daisy caught her breath. Oh dang, that felt good. No, it felt better than good. It felt fantastic. So fantastic she found it impossible to keep massaging Beau with her other foot. She felt terrible about it, but her muscles refused to listen to her head.

Sawyer slowly and firmly ran the tip of one thumb over her heel, then along the inside of her arch, before finally moving up to the ball of her foot. He dawdled there, rhythmically digging his fingers into the muscles between her toes.

She had no clue a foot rub could feel like this. She bit her lip to stifle that moan Sawyer had mentioned.

Movement out of the corner of her eye abruptly caught her attention, and she turned to see the waitress approaching their table with a tray loaded with plates.

Daisy shook herself and sat up. She would have pulled her feet off the guys' laps, too, but they wouldn't let her. She gave them a sharp look. Didn't they realize the waitress could see them? But Sawyer and Beau simply sat there calmly.

The woman plunked the plate of nachos down in front of her. "Anything else?"

"No, thanks," Daisy said quickly. "I'm fine."

The waitress winked at her. "I bet you are."

Oh God, the waitress had seen what she was doing. Heat suffused Daisy's face.

At least Sawyer waited until the woman was gone before he started

Ride of Her Life

rubbing her foot again.

Daisy looked around, sure the whole restaurant was watching them now. But no one was paying any attention to them at all. She tried to focus on her cheese-covered chips, but Sawyers hands made that impossible. The fingers of one hand pressed firmly into the bottom of her foot, while the other slid under the cuff of her jeans and massaged her calf.

She moaned. Just a little, but she couldn't help herself.

To her dismay, Sawyer immediately stopped and released her foot. She stared at him. "Why'd you stop?"

He shrugged. "You wondered if I could make you moan by giving you a foot rub. You moaned." She opened her mouth to protest, but he cut her off. "The idea was to give you a little taste—not the whole treat. You want more, you'll have to wait until later. Besides, I figured you might get a tad embarrassed if the whole restaurant turned to see why you were pulling a Meg Ryan in the middle of the dinner."

Her face colored again. She let out an embarrassed. "Okay. I concede on that point. You have magical hands." She unearthed a chip from the stack. "You've only told me what you have planned for my feet. I have a lot of other body parts that need attention. What about them?"

Sawyer's mouth quirked as he picked up his knife and fork. "Can I tell you while we eat?"

She smiled. "A man who's good at multi-tasking. I like it."

Watching the men dig into their steaks made Daisy realize she was a lot hungrier than she'd thought. Sawyer and Beau must have seen the look of longing on her face because they took turns feeding her little pieces of steak off their forks. It was very sweet, and kind of romantic. More than a few women in the restaurant threw her jealous glances.

"First," Sawyer drawled, "I'd slowly kiss, nibble and lick my way up your legs from your toes to the junction of your thighs until I got to that sweet pussy of yours."

Heat pooled between her legs at the image, and she squirmed in the seat, wiggling her toes against the men's jean-clad cocks. Sawyer and Beau reached down to rub the tops of her feet. She'd long since given up on the notion that she might make them come. Though she had no doubt they both loved what she was doing, they treated it more like a relaxing back massage. Enjoyable? Yes. Orgasm-inducing? Not so much.

A naughty, little voice whispered in her ear that both men could probably go half the night without popping off—no matter what she did. Rather than be disappointed, she was intrigued. How much stamina did they have?

The fact that she kept thinking about everything in terms of *they* and *them* was a bit disconcerting. How was she supposed to figure out which one she was going to sleep with tonight if they both kept being so perfect?

It wasn't as if she could bed both of them.

If she was forced to choose at that very second, it was going to be hard to not take Sawyer. The guy had just about talked her panties off—or at least gotten them extremely wet.

She nibbled on another chip. "And then?"

"Well," Sawyer continued, "I prefer to work a woman's pussy slowly, staying away from her clit until she's really ready for it."

"Words to live by, partner," Beau agreed as he pushed back his empty plate.

Daisy couldn't believe Beau was so relaxed with the way his friend was talking about licking her. Wasn't he the least bit jealous?

"I don't mind a little teasing," she said. "But it's possible to have too much of a good thing. You make a girl wait for it too long, and when you finally get down to it, it's too late and the moment's gone."

"I get that. The key is paying attention to the little signs that a woman is just about as aroused as she can handle." Sawyer speared the last piece of steak with his fork and offered it to her. "How wet she is, how plump her clit gets, her sighs, her moans, the way her stomach muscles flex as I run my tongue up first one side of her pussy lips and then down the other."

Daisy bit back a moan as a surge of wetness flooded her panties.

"Then," Sawyer's voice was husky. "When all the signs are there, when I've gotten her hot as hell, that's when I give in and start really lapping her clit. And I don't stop until I make her come. Over and over and over."

Daisy didn't doubt him. She was practically on the verge of orgasm sitting there listening to Sawyer tell her what he was going to do to her. A few swipes of a warm, soft tongue and she'd go off like a bottle rocket on the Fourth of July.

Across the table, both men were regarding her expectantly, clearly waiting for her to say something. Daisy wet her suddenly dry lips, not sure she could manage to speak quite yet. Luckily, the waitress appeared to refill their water glasses.

"Did you three save any room for dessert? Or do you already have other plans for that?"

The waitress looked pointedly at Daisy, then slid a sly glance toward both men sitting across from her. Good God, the woman thought she was planning on having sex with both Sawyer and Beau!

Did Daisy look that kinky?

Ride of Her Life

She decided the answer to that question was probably yes. The waitress had almost certainly caught Daisy giving the foot jobs under the table. The woman had probably heard snippets of their conversation when she'd walked by the table—snippets that likely included references to foot massages, pussy licking and orgasms.

So yeah, the waitress had good reason to think Daisy was a kinky-ass cowgirl ready to drag two rodeo hunks off to her bed for a night of threesome frolicking.

Little did she know that Daisy had never even entertained such a thought in her life. She was just about to open her mouth with the intentions of telling the woman—somehow—that she wouldn't be sleeping with both men, when Beau spoke.

"I'd love to see your dessert menu, ma'am." His gaze went to Daisy. "I'm dying for something sweet and sticky."

The woman gave her a wink, then turned to Beau. "I just bet you are." She pulled three thin folders from her apron and arranged them on the table. "I'll give you some time to look through the menu and pick what you like. I'll be back for your order in a few minutes."

Daisy pinned Beau with a glare after the waitress had left. "Something sweet and sticky, huh? Think you could have been a little more subtle?"

Beau chuckled, grinding his crotch against her foot. "Probably, but what fun would that be?"

"Are you seriously still hungry?" She wiggled her toes on him. "You just about licked the plate clean."

"I'm always hungry for dessert." He glanced at her as he picked up the menu. "Besides, we spent the entire dinner listening to Sawyer talk about how he plans on making love to you and those hot legs of yours. Only seems fair I get some time to talk about what I'd like to do to your cute, little ass."

Listening to a man talk about her butt and what he'd like to do it? What woman wouldn't want to hear that?

But Beau and Sawyer suddenly seemed more interested in debating the pros and cons of the dessert selections than in discussing her derriere at the moment. Daisy snatched the menus out of their hands and waved the waitress over. No reason to dilly-dally around with it. She wanted to hear what Beau had to say.

"We'll all have your chocolate cake," she told the woman.

"Hey," Sawyer protested. "I was still trying to decide what I wanted."

Daisy handed the menus to the waitress. "Cake. Chocolate. Thank you."

As the waitress walked away, both men eyed her in amusement.

"You must seriously like chocolate cake," Beau said.

"You can never go wrong with chocolate cake, for sure," Daisy agreed. "But that's not why I ordered it. I ordered it because I didn't feel like waiting while you two screwed around with those stupid menus. So, let's hear it. What do you have in mind for my behind?"

Beau laughed. "Sure you don't want to wait until the waitress brings your cake out?"

At the look from Daisy—and a nudge with her foot on his groin—he held up his hands. "Okay, no more stalling." He lowered his voice and leaned forward. "Let's assume for the sake of convenience that Sawyer just finished licking your pussy. That way, you're already naked and hot as hell. That work for you?"

Did that work for her? That worked for her in so many ways.

Ride of Her Life

Chapter Three

So did the idea of Beau watching Sawyer lick her to orgasm. That gave her a jolt—mostly because she'd never had a thought like that. She was a long ways from being a prude. She'd always laughed with all the other cowgirls on the circuit when they sat around drinking and telling stories about banging two or more guys at once. But it had never been something she considered doing. It had always just seemed too impersonal. If a woman were with two guys at the same time, how could she ever hope to focus on the intense personal connection that made sex so wonderful?

But now Beau had planted the image in her head—and it seemed anything but impersonal and mechanical.

"Daisy?"

She jerked. Both men were looking at her curiously.

"You okay?" Beau asked.

She mentally smacked her horse on the rump. How long had she been wool gathering? "Of course. Why wouldn't I be?"

"I thought maybe I said something that bothered you."

"No. I was just…picturing the scene you described. You know, Sawyer licking me to orgasm, then turning me over to you."

Putting the image into words made a seriously warm sensation flood the space in her jeans just below her belt buckle.

"So, does it work for you?" Beau prompted.

Had she zoned out again? They must think she was a whack-job.

"Yeah, for sure!"

Sawyer and Beau exchanged amused looks.

She quickly picked up her beer and took a sip, scrambling to cover up how flustered she was. "What's first on your agenda, Beau? How would you show my bottom some love?"

Beau sat back, a sexy grin on his handsome face. Beside him, Sawyer reached under the table to gently play with her toes.

"Well, when presented with an absolutely perfect ass, I think the best way to start is with a good, old-fashioned, spanking," Beau said.

Daisy's jaw didn't drop. Okay, maybe it did. She must have heard wrong. Beau couldn't have just said he wanted to spank her bare ass. She waited for him to laugh and admit he'd been teasing her, but he didn't.

"You're serious? You want to spank me?"

"Hell, yeah. Don't tell me you've never had that ass of yours smacked really good?"

Before Daisy could answer that question, the waitress came over with dessert. She gave Sawyer and Beau theirs first.

"Here you go, boys. Enjoy."

The woman smiled at Daisy as she set the piece of cake in front of her. "You let me know if you need anything, honey. Anything at all."

Giving Daisy a wink, she turned and left. Daisy picked up her fork. Across from her, Sawyer and Beau dug into their desserts, too. She almost laughed when she realized Beau was eating the cake from between the frosting layers first. Leaving the best part for last. Definitely said a lot about the man.

"You didn't answer my question," he said, pulling her attention back to the topic of her ass and the silly concept of spanking a grown woman.

She put a piece of cake in her mouth and chewed before answering. "Because the answer should be obvious."

"If you've never let a man spank you before, how do you know whether you'd like it?"

"I'm a cowgirl, Beau. It doesn't take a lot of sense to figure out that if my butt is sore after a good hard ride on a horse, then a spanking would be ten times worse."

Beau shook his head. "It's not even close to being the same thing."

"Close enough for me."

He started on the next layer of cake. "Answer me this then, Daisy. Have you ever gotten hot and wet riding your horse? And I don't mean from sweat. I mean has your pussy ever gotten completely dripping wet and throbbing with excitement?"

There was that time back years ago when she and her boyfriend at the time had ridden out to the farthest edges of her family's farm to have sex in an open field. She'd been wet then, but that probably wasn't what Beau was talking about.

"While horseback riding? No, I can't say that I have."

"Further proof that I'm right, then," he insisted. "Because every woman I've ever spanked ended up getting soaking wet."

She frowned at that. She didn't want to know how many woman Beau had spanked. That was under the category of too much information. But still, his logic didn't even make sense.

"Maybe you just hang out with bizarre women."

"Maybe." He glanced up from his cake. "Or maybe you simply don't understand what a spanking is all about."

Beau didn't sound mad, or even offended. If anything, he seemed to enjoy trying to convert her to his fetish.

"You're right. I don't," she said. "Why don't you explain exactly how you'd spank me?"

Now that all the actual cake part was gone, Beau started in on his frosting. Sawyer was licking his fork off—there wasn't even a crumb left on the plate. He eyed her cake. She warned him off with a look—she'd barely started.

"Hey," he protested. "I shared my steak with you."

"That was steak. This is chocolate cake. Completely different." She took another forkful. "No sane woman would share her chocolate cake with a man—even after he promised to give her pussy a tongue bath."

He gave her the most forlorn puppy dog eyes she'd ever seen. Powerless against them, Daisy sighed and extended her fork, a big piece of cake on it. Sawyer closed his mouth over it with a groan that made her tummy all fluttery.

Beau pointedly cleared his throat. "Back to the spanking I want to give you. First, I'd pull you gently over my lap."

She lifted a brow as she loaded her fork with more cake, this time for her. "Gently huh? Because you wouldn't want to rough me up before you spank me, right?"

"Exactly." A smile tugged at the corner of his mouth. "Now you're getting it. Anyway, after I get you comfortably settled across my lap, I'd spend a little time giving your ass cheeks a deep, firm massage."

Hmm. A butt massage? Now Beau was talking her kind of language. She'd never considered her ass to be one of her top erogenous zone. It wasn't at the bottom of the list—no pun intended—but there were a few places ahead of it. Still, the thought of Beau giving her derriere a massage sounded extremely appealing, especially after the hard riding she'd done the past few days.

"Now," Beau continued, "while I'm sure you're thinking a little massage sounds nice and relaxing, that's not the real reason for it. The purpose of the massage is to get the blood pumping in your bottom so you'll be ready for the spanking."

Daisy groaned. "You're a tease."

"True. But trust me, after getting a firm massage, your ass will be primed and begging for that spanking."

"Yeah, right. Whatever you say." She rolled her eyes. "So the ass-whooping comes next?"

"No, not yet. Stop rushing the experience." Beau licked the last of the chocolate frosting off his fork. "Besides, I haven't mentioned the best part of the massage. In between rubbing that beautiful ass, I'd slip my hand between your legs and run my fingers up and down the folds of your pussy. Once you're good and wet, I'll sneak forward to tease your clit. Not enough to make you come, but I guarantee you'll like it."

That part of her anatomy purred approvingly. "I think I can state with a fair amount of certainty that I'd definitely like it."

He grinned. "Thought you might. If you're really good little cowgirl, maybe I'll even slide a finger right into your anus. Would you like that, too?"

That gave Daisy pause. The moment Beau had confessed to being in love with her ass, she knew he'd get around to sticking something in there at some point. She'd had a few dalliances with anal sex before, and the results had been fairly positive. Nothing earth-shattering, but good enough that she was still curious about how amazing it could be—with the right guy. It was one of the reasons Beau's attraction to her backside had piqued her interest.

"Let's assume for now that you're still in the like category. Tell me more."

Beau smiled. "I'll finger your tight, little rosebud oh-so-slowly until your whole body goes all soft and gooey. Only then, when you're perfectly relaxed and seriously excited, will I even consider spanking you."

Her breathing came a little faster. "And how exactly does this spanking thing go?"

"First, I'll place one hand right in the center of your lower back. No matter how enjoyable you find the spanking, it's only natural to wiggle around a bit. My hand on your back is there to make sure you don't fall off my lap."

She wouldn't have thought it, but from the crazy way her body was reacting, it clearly liked the idea of being held down by the big, strong cowboy. "Can't have that."

Out of the corner of her eye, she caught sight of their waitress cleaning a nearby table—one that was already clean. Was she listening in on their conversation? Daisy couldn't help but smile. If the woman got off on hearing the guys talk nasty, good for her.

"I'll start off gently, a little harder than a love pat," Beau explained. "Hard enough for you to feel it, but not hard enough to sting yet. I'll go back and forth from one cheek to the other, setting up a nice rhythm that will almost be hypnotizing."

Daisy tried to imagine what those light smacks on the tender flesh of her bottom would feel like, but couldn't. She simply didn't have a frame of reference to go on.

"After I have you warmed up, I'll start to smack your ass a bit harder. You probably won't even notice at first, but at some point you'll pick up on the fact that the spanks are louder, and your ass is starting to tingle."

"Won't that hurt?"

She hated sounding naïve, but this was so new to her, and she was curious.

"Not at all," Beau assured her. "It will be a pleasant, warming tingle at this point. You might even want me to spank you harder."

She frowned. "Why would I want to be spanked harder?"

"Because your skin will actually be getting used to the sensation. Some women have even told me their ass gets a little numb. They claim they can't feel the smacks as much unless I spank them harder."

"Really?"

That sounded almost right. She knew when she rode Playdough for a long time, her ass actually did go numb. Once that happened, she could ride almost all day. She'd feel it later, but at that moment, not so much.

"Really." He gave her a slow, sexy grin. "In fact, I have a hunch you're the type of girl who'd get to this point sooner rather than later. I also think you probably wouldn't be too embarrassed to let me know it."

She wasn't so sure of that, but took it as a compliment anyway.

"That's when I'll really start spanking you. Making sure I concentrate on those perfectly padded sit spots." Beau leaned in close. "And guess what? You'll be wiggling all over the place and loving it."

Daisy bit her lip. She had sort of a conceptual idea of where her sit spots were—though she wasn't so sure she liked the idea of him calling them padded—but Beau seemed to like them that way. He was also starting to bring her around to the dark side. Maybe she'd actually let him spank her—if he was the one who ended up in her bed that night.

"Okay," she said. "You definitely have my attention. Tell me, how does this spanking come to an end—what's the big finish?"

His dark eyes glinted. "Well, just when I have your ass good and hot, and you're really starting to feel it, I'll grab one of those rosy cheeks in each hand and give them a firm squeeze. The sensations will blow your mind."

She squirmed in the seat. "And if they don't?"

"If they don't, you'll definitely explode when I slide two fingers in your very wet pussy and start finger fucking your G-spot while I spank you with my other hand."

Daisy caught her breath. Man, he was getting her going big time.

"Would you come again if I do that?"

She nodded, not trusting herself to speak. Her clit was throbbing in her jeans. Damn, she really needed to get touched—ASAP.

The only question was which man was going to be doing the touching. She opened her mouth ask, but the dang waitress interrupted her.

"How was everything? That cake was scrumptious wasn't it?"

Daisy pulled her feet out of both men's laps and looked up. The woman's eyes danced with amusement—and no small amount of envy. She'd obviously overheard everything Beau said, including the part about G-spots, finger-fucking and coming.

"It was wonderful, thank you," Daisy told her.

On the other side of the table, Sawyer and Beau murmured their agreement.

The waitress placed the bill on the table. "I hope you have a wonderful evening."

The woman gave Daisy a sly wink and a smile before she left.

Across from her, Beau and Sawyer began to argue over who should pay the bill. Daisy reached out and placed her hand on top of theirs.

"Before you two decide on who's going to cover the check, I think we need to talk about who's getting dessert tonight. That might decide who pays, don't you think?"

Beau frowned in confusion. "We just had dessert."

Daisy heard a thud as Sawyer kicked Beau under the table. "Not that dessert, you stupid cow patty. She's talking about the take-me-upstairs kind of dessert."

"Ah, that dessert." Beau gave her a wink that said he'd known what she meant all along. "Sorry. I got kicked in the head today by a horse and my brain bucket is moving slow."

Both men eyed her, as if waiting for her to say something. Daisy suddenly felt very self-conscious—way more than she did in the middle of packed barrel riding arena.

She took a deep breath. "Look guys, I don't know how you two normally decide these types of things. I know you're good friends and all, and I don't want to cause any friction, but it's getting late and I'm about as ready to head up stairs as I've ever been in my life."

The men only continued to regard her without saying a word, which wasn't helpful at all.

"Um, how do you want do this—rock, paper, scissor or something? Because I think you're both great and I don't think I can go wrong with either one of you."

She didn't mention she'd never been talked up better by a guy in her life. Both men had turned her on with their words like never before.

"I don't think we need to play rock, paper, scissor," Sawyer said. "In fact, we don't really have any decision to make at all."

"You don't?"

Did that mean they'd decided before this evening had even started which one would sleep with her? That was planning ahead. How did they know which one of them she'd like?

Or did they think she was supposed to decide between them

completely on her own? That was going to be impossible for her to do.

Then another thought struck her so hard she almost gasped. What if Sawyer meant that neither of them intended to sleep with her? What if they weren't interested in having sex with her at all?

If that was true, why had they been flirting with her. Were they just a couple of pussy teases?

"No, we don't," Beau grinned. "Because we figured you wouldn't mind if we both got to have dessert."

Chapter Four

Daisy was going to hyperventilate.

She tried to tell herself she'd heard Beau wrong, but she knew she hadn't. He and Sawyer wanted to have a threesome with her. She should have expected it. Things had been heading in this direction the whole night. Still...

"You okay, Daisy?" Sawyer asked.

"Um, yeah." She struggled for breath. "Just a little...surprised. I'm not sure what to say."

"You don't need to say anything," Beau said. "Just slip out of that booth and go upstairs with us."

"But..."

She stopped, not knowing what the hell she'd been about to say. But what? Was she going to confess to them that she'd never been with two guys at once? Too late—they'd already figured that one out on their own.

Was she going to tell them that she wasn't that kind of woman? That was a crock. She'd been giving both of them foot jobs for about an hour and a half while they told her stories about all the dirty things they wanted to do to her body. And she'd gotten horny as hell. She'd be lucky if there wasn't a wet spot soaked all the way through her jeans by now.

She was definitely that kind of woman.

"You don't want to sleep with both of us?" Beau asked.

"No... I mean, yes!"

It was true. She ached to slide her ass out of the booth and go upstairs with both of them. She just didn't know how.

The men exchanged a glance.

"This isn't something you can sit on the fence about, Daisy," Sawyer pointed out.

"I know." She tucked her long hair behind her ear. "I want to, I do. You two have been great. It's just that this is new for me. I'm not sure what to do."

Sawyer exchanged looks with Beau again, then slid out of the booth to stand in front of her. Beau joined him.

"First step—put your boots back on," Sawyer instructed.

Her boots? She stared at him in confusion for what must have been a full minute before finally comprehending what the hell he was talking about. Then she remembered—she'd taken off her boots to play with their cocks under the table.

Glad to have something to do that didn't require too much thought, she reached under the table and found her soft boots, then pulled them on.

She looked up. Both men stood there with their hands outstretched. All she had to do was reach out and accept what they were offering.

She took a deep breath and did just that.

Their warm hands closed around hers and they pulled her out of the seat as easily as she'd slid on her boots.

She let them lead her out of the restaurant like that, Sawyer holding one hand, and Beau holding the other, like they were really good friends.

Or two guys and a girl about to go have a threesome.

Daisy's confidence and commitment grew with every step she took. By the time the waitress waved an envious goodnight to them, she was actually a little ahead of the two men, leading the way.

She was really going to do this.

As they waited for the elevator, she had this crazy urge to pull one or both men close for a kiss. But that was insane. She wasn't like Britt—she never went for public displays of affection.

But that could always change.

She was saved by the bell as the elevator doors slid open. She dashed inside.

"I'm on the twelfth floor," she told Beau, who was standing nearest to the controls.

He pushed the button for the fifth floor. "I'm closer."

That worked for her.

Daisy prayed they wouldn't take the scenic route and stop on every floor. They didn't. When the elevator chimed and the doors slid open, Daisy darted out and almost ran into a family of four waiting to get on.

"Hey!" the teenage girl said. "I know you. You're that barrel rider. You were awesome tonight. Can I have your autograph and a get a picture with you?"

There was such a look of adoration on the girl's face, Daisy couldn't refuse, no matter how eager she was to get to Beau's room. Thanks to that soft spot for her fans, what followed was the most excruciating five minutes of Daisy's life as she and the guys took pictures and signed autographs with the Keene family in from Wyoming to see the rodeo.

Finally—after Beau had practically shoved the family on the elevator while Sawyer pushed the down button repeatedly—they were alone in the hallway.

Daisy turned to ask Beau which way his room was and found him standing six inches from her.

"I can't wait any longer," he growled, pushing her up against the wall beside the elevator and kissing her hard.

She kissed him back, even though she knew the elevator door could open at any moment, or that someone—another family even—could come down the hall. She couldn't wait any longer, either.

Beau twined his fingers in her hair and pulled her mouth tighter against his own, his tongue bulling its way in. She met him halfway, giving as good as she got. One of her hands slid down his side to his grab his ass and yanked his crotch into perfect contact with hers. She wrapped one leg around his thigh and ground against him.

Dear God, she'd never been this hot in her life. She might just explode on the spot.

Beside her, Sawyer cleared his throat. She ignored him, moaning into Beau's mouth. Sawyer cleared his throat again, louder this time.

She dragged herself away from Beau to see Sawyer leaning against the wall beside them.

"Sorry for the interruption, Daisy," he drawled. "It's not that I'm concerned you're grinding against Beau out here in the hallway where anyone can see you—it's that you're doing it without me."

Daisy laughed and reached out with her free hand to grab Sawyer's shirt front and pull him in for a kiss.

His style of kissing was completely different from Beau, but no less captivating. His mouth slowly moved over hers, his tongue teasing hers. She would have kissed him harder, but still trapped in Beau's arms like she was, she had no choice but to let Sawyer take the kiss where he wanted it to go. The effect was intoxicating.

She felt Beau's mouth on the side of her exposed neck, trailing kisses up and down from her earlobe to the top of her shirt collar. Between the warmth of his lips and the light scrape of his scruff, she thought she was going to go crazy.

She whimpered, close to tearing off both men's clothes right there where they stood.

Fortunately, the two women coming down the hall made enough noise for the three of them to drag themselves apart just in time. Sawyer still waited until the very last moment, and when he did, it was so abrupt she was left reeling. Daisy leaned back against the wall, trying to look as casual as possible.

The elderly woman smiled politely at Daisy and her two cowboys as she poked the elevator button, but other than that she took no notice of them. The younger girl with her, however, immediately sensed something was up. She looked at Daisy, then at Sawyer and Beau, then back to Daisy again. Her expression went from curious to knowing in the blink of an eye. A huge smile spread across her face.

"Ride 'em, cowgirl," she said with a barely controlled laugh.

Heat suffused Daisy's face. How the hell had the girl known? Were her lips plump from Beau and Sawyer's kisses? Had she drooled on her shirt? Did she have an I'll-be-getting-it-from-two-hot-studs-within-the-next-fifteen-minutes expression on face?

The older woman turned to look questioningly at the girl. "What was that, hun?"

A smile played around the girl's lips as she motioned to Daisy. "She's with the rodeo, Aunt Margaret. I just told her to have a good ride."

The woman looked at Daisy closely, her eyes searching behind her big glasses. "They let women in the rodeo now? That's nice. Do you get to ride ponies?"

Thank God the elevator arrived before Daisy could answer. If she had, a comment about how women could even vote now may have popped out.

The girl quickly hustled her aunt onto the elevator, then turned to give Daisy a wave. "Have fun riding your ponies!"

Daisy heard the aunt murmur something just as the elevator doors closed.

"Can you believe that?" was all Daisy could say.

Beau's mouth quirked. "The part where Aunt Margaret thinks you ride ponies, or the part where her niece figured out you're going to be riding the two of us?"

Daisy groaned. "Both. But enough about them. Where the hell is your room, Beau?"

The two men grabbed her hands and practically dragged her down the hall. Beau fumbled with the key card for a second before getting it straight. Daisy felt like snatching it out of his hand, but was concerned hers would shake so much it would take even longer to get inside the room.

The moment the door swung open, Sawyer had his hands on her ass herding her in. As it closed behind them, he gave one of her belt loops a yank, spinning her around to face him. She melted in his arms as his mouth captured hers. Beau moved up behind her, pressing his jean-covered cock against her ass as he swept her hair off her neck and began to nibble.

Their hands roamed over her body freely, touching her anywhere and everywhere they wished as they used their lips and tongue to drive her crazy. She wasn't sure if she'd survive the incredible sensations racing through her body.

She dragged her mouth away from Sawyer's. "Whoa there, boys. Let's slow down before I pass out. This isn't supposed to be one of your eight second rides, you know?"

Both men laughed, but backed off, giving her room to breathe. She felt a little chilled without the heat of their bodies pressed up against her. She had no doubt she'd be wedged back between them soon enough.

Daisy took the opportunity to look around the room, and was immediately struck by something total unfair.

"Hey, why is your room so much bigger than mine?" she asked.

The bed was a king-size monster, complete with four posts that ran as high as the ceiling, gauzy curtains and half a dozen ornate throw pillows.

She wandered over to peek into the bathroom, and gaped.

"Dang, you have a Jacuzzi tub, too?"

Daisy had seen swimming pools smaller than the big heart-shaped thing.

"They didn't have anything else left," Beau's said from the bedroom, "so they gave me a honeymoon suite."

"Huh."

She wished they'd offered her one. It would have been nice to have that tub to soak in every night after riding.

She walked out and looked around the rest of the suite. It was obvious to anyone who walked in that Beau was a rodeo rider. The room was filled with the unmistakable scent of leather and horse. There was also a saddle sitting on the small couch, along with a pile of tack piled beside it. She walked over to look at the gear. It was pretty standard rodeo stuff—bridles, bits, halters and a surcingle rig that bareback riders used to stay on their horses. It was the saddle that threw her. It was damn nice. Well worn, but expensive looking.

"I thought you only rode bareback, Beau. What's the saddle for?"

He came up behind her, casually resting his hand on her ass as if reminding her of his fascination with that part of her body. Would he do what he'd described downstairs to her bottom soon?

"Rodeo riding doesn't pay all the bills. I do a little ranch work here and there when I can get it. I don't trust leaving my saddle down in the trailer."

She ran her hand over the smooth leather. "I can understand why. It's beautiful."

Beau chuckled in her ear. "Not that I don't appreciate the compliment, but do you really want to talk about my saddle right now?"

Daisy turned to see both men standing side by side regarding her with evident heat in their eyes.

She smiled. "I do love a nice saddle, but you're right. How about you show me some of your other gear instead?"

Without waiting for an answer, she reached out and unbuttoned Beau's shirt. As the band of bronzed skin became exposed, she had to

Ride of Her Life

fight the urge to lean forward and kiss it. She had two men to think about now.

So she moved over to Sawyer and did the same thing to him.

Once both shirts were unbuttoned, she stepped back and raised an eyebrow. "You two aren't going to make me do all the work, are you?"

The men shrugged off their shirts, then stood there looking buff and magnificent. They were both of the same build—long and lean with wiry muscles—and Daisy couldn't help but stand there and admire them. Dang, they were something to behold.

Daisy stepped closer and placed a hand on each of their chests. The muscular planes of their pecs gave way to equally hard abs as she trailed her hands down. This close, she could define the slight differences between the two men. Sawyer was just a bit broader than Beau, and had a light trace of dark hair that ran down his happy trail from just above his belly button and disappearing into his jeans. Beau's abs were more defined, and she had a crazy urge to drop to her knees in front of him and trace her tongue along every nook and cranny. The idea of being on her knees in front of both of them was doing all kinds of wild things to her tummy.

She was about to do just that when Beau slipped a finger under her chin and tilted her head up.

"Do I need to remind you about the basic rule?"

"Rule?"

He grinned. "You show us yours if we show you ours?"

It took a moment for that to sink in—she was a bit distracted by all the manliness on display. But when it did, she laughed.

"No problem." She reached for the buttons of her shirt. "Fair's fair."

"And go slow." Sawyer gave her a lazy smile. "I like a girl who takes her time."

Daisy was surprised they still wanted to take it slow, especially after all the verbal foreplay and downright scorching hot kisses. But if they wanted her to take it slow, she could do that.

She started at the bottom of her shirt, undoing one button slowly, then taking a good, long time working her fingers up to the next button, making sure they got a good look at the skin she was exposing.

"Mmm," Beau groaned. "That belly button of yours looks good enough to eat."

She let out a husky laugh. "I thought you were more of an ass man?"

"I am." His mouth twitched. "Doesn't mean I don't appreciate all the other fine parts."

Probably sooner than the two men would have liked, she had her shirt off and was standing there in her lacy bra. She reached around to take it off, but Sawyer stopped her.

"Allow me," he said, walking around behind her.

As Sawyer undid the clasp, Beau stood in front of her, gazing down into her eyes. The intensity in his was so mesmerizing she was barely even aware Sawyer had taken off her bra. Until Beau pulled her into his arms and her bare breasts came into contact with the hard planes of his chest. Her nipples felt so hard against him that they hurt, and she gasped against his mouth.

Sawyer immediately sandwiched her between them, his chest warm against her back, his hands reaching around to caress the sides of her breasts. She shivered, moaning her approval.

Beau let out a groan and pulled away. Eyes smoldering, he slid his hands down to the waistband of her jeans.

Sawyer took advantage of the opportunity—and the space—by cupping her breasts. He massaged them firmly, tweaking her nipples as he nibbled on her neck.

In front of her, Beau worked her belt buckle loose. A moment later, she heard a pop as he roughly yanked each button through its hole. Then he shoved his hands inside her jeans and slowly worked them over her hips and down her thighs. When he was done, he stepped back to admire his handiwork. Sawyer pressed a kiss to her shoulder, then walked around to join him.

Daisy felt like a beauty queen as she stood there in nothing but her tiny scrap of panties, the object of a whole lot of desire.

"Damn, Daisy." Sawyer's gaze lingered on her long legs. "You're even more beautiful than I dreamed."

She blushed. These two were good for her ego.

"Beautiful, huh?" She gave them a naughty smile. "Wonder what you'll have to say when these panties come off."

Beau eyed her wolfishly. "Only one way to know for sure."

Daisy hooked her thumbs in the waistband of her panties and slowly pushed them down, letting them flutter to the floor. There was something so powerful about being completely naked in front of two awe-struck studs, especially when they were still half dressed.

Their eyes slid up and down her body so hungrily she had to laugh. "Whoa boys, you just ate like fifteen minutes ago."

"Suddenly I'm hungry again," Sawyer growled.

His blue eyes locked on the tiny triangle of downy hair at the juncture of her thighs, and Daisy couldn't help but remember his description of the pussy licking he had in store for her. The thought of his tongue on her clit made a fresh burst of moisture surge to the surface.

Ride of Her Life

She had no doubt that if she slid her hand between her legs, her fingers'd come away covered in goo.

Both men came toward her, but Daisy held up her hand.

"Do I need to remind you about the basic rule?" she asked, throwing Beau's earlier words back at them. "You show me yours if I show you mine."

Sawyer's mouth twitched. "Fair's fair."

"And go slow, fellas." She gave them a sultry look as they reached for their huge belt buckles. "I like a man who takes his time."

Daisy licked her lips in anticipation as both men slowly unbuckled their belts, then unbuttoned their jeans. As she'd thought, both were going commando and their erections immediately began to fight for freedom. They weren't nearly as graceful about dropping their jeans as she'd been, instead shoving them down their well-muscled legs in one hurried motion. Still, there was something to be said for seeing those nice size cocks spring out all hard and ready for her.

Closing the distance between her and the men, she wrapped a hand around each of their rock-hard shafts. They were throbbing and more than a little sticky from the hour-long foot job she'd given them downstairs. She knew exactly how to take care of that. But for the moment, she was content to give them a nice, sexy hand massage.

Despite their similar body types, their cocks were surprisingly different. They were both long, but Sawyer's was a tad thinner and had a slight upward curve to it. She couldn't wait to feel that in her pussy. It'd hit her G-spot just right. Beau's penis, on the other hand, was a lot thicker. If he thought that thing was going in her ass at any point tonight, he'd better have a few drinks ready to relax her some more.

She'd worry about the logistics later, though. Right now, she had two hand jobs to give. Tightening her grip a little, she moved her hand up and down their shafts, making sure she didn't pay too much attention to the sensitive heads. She didn't think it would be a problem with these two, but she'd had her fair share of guys who'd popped their corks before she was ready.

As she jerked them, she kissed first one on the mouth, then the other, slowly and sensually. Sawyer and Beau kissed her back with the same passion. Since they'd entered the room, there'd been a light, bantering undertone to the sexual tension. But sometime between now and then, that had changed. These cowboys were ready to fuck her senseless.

She rubbed her thumbs over their sticky cockheads. This was going to be one messy night, she had no doubt.

Sawyer leaned in to lay claim to her mouth when she pulled away from Beau, but Daisy released their cocks and stepped back to look at both of them. Their shafts seemed to bob gently in time with their heartbeats.

"You know what I want to do now?" she asked.

Sawyer grinned. "What's that?"

He couldn't seem to decide where to fix his eyes—her legs, the hot pussy between them, or her heaving breasts.

"I want to take a bath in that Jacuzzi of yours."

Daisy tried, but couldn't quite stifle the giggle that escaped as she skipped into the big bathroom. She had the stopper down, hotel-provided bubble bath poured and was adjusting the water temperature before the two cowboys finally followed her in, their two extremely hard cocks leading the way.

She turned and gave them a big, innocent smile. "They have champagne-scented bubble bath. Is that cool or what?"

Without waiting for answer, she leaned over to test the water filling the heart-shaped tub. Yeah, she was giving them one hell of a view of her behind, but they needed the enticement. Men in general—most especially cowboys—weren't known for their love of bathtubs. At least not the guys she'd been with. They were usually in and out of the shower before the water even had a chance to get warm.

"You're not seriously going to take a bath, are you?" Sawyer asked.

"Yeah," Beau added. "We sort of had a slightly different plan for what we'd do next."

Daisy turned and rubbed some of the water on her legs, as if testing the temperature. Sawyer's eyes followed her hand like a hawk.

"I know," she said softly. "But do you two know the last time I got a chance to take a bubble bath? It's been a really long time."

Once again, she didn't wait for an answer, but simply stepped in the tub, bent over and filled her hands full of water and bubbles, then dumped the combination over her breasts. The men's eyes feasted on her foam-covered nipples.

She gave them her best sultry look. "I promise I'll be very grateful for it."

She eased down in the tub, groaning as the warm, sudsy water covered her body. Dang, that felt good. She hadn't been kidding—she hadn't had a bubble bath in years.

Once she was settled, she crooked a finger at them and motioned to the two curved sections at the top of the heart-shaped tub. "Care to join me?"

Sawyer and Beau looked at each other for maybe half a second before both men raced to be the first one in. Water sloshed everywhere.

"Careful," she laughed as they sat down across from her.

Daisy stretched out her legs and ran a foot up the inside of each man's thigh. Her toes found a nice, comfortable resting place atop each of their cocks and wiggled. She leaned back, making sure her nipples poked out of the bubbles.

"Baths can be nice, huh?" she said.

They both groaned in answer. Of course, that probably had something to do with the fact that she was massaging their cocks with her tootsies.

"I'll take that as a yes."

"You have really good feet for a cowgirl," Sawyer eyed her from the other side of the tub. "Any chance you were a ballerina before you started barrel riding?"

She twirled her big toes over the head of their cocks. They each sucked in a breath.

"Nope, I've just always had clever toes."

"That's for damn sure." Beau rasped.

Under the water, she trailed her feet all the way down to the base of their shafts. Then she carefully tucked her toes under their balls and gently juggled those big babies up and down. Beau and Sawyer responded completely differently to the playful touch. Beau dropped his head back and let out another groan. Sawyer locked eyes with her and stared.

She switched back and forth between their balls and the head of their cocks, making their entire bodies jerk out of the water each time she did. More water sloshed onto the bathroom floor. She had no intention of making them come yet. Still, it might be interesting to try.

They took the decision away from her by reaching down and grabbing her feet at the same time.

"Okay. Enough of that." Sawyer's voice was hoarse.

"What's wrong?" she asked innocently.

They didn't answer. Instead, Beau stood up and motioned her forward. His tanned skin glistened with water, making him look like some sun-bronzed god.

"Slide forward, so I can sit behind you," he instructed her.

Daisy obeyed, wondering what he was up to. She found out a moment later when Beau sat down with his muscular legs positioned to either side of her.

On the far side of the tub, Sawyer dug the pads of both thumbs into the arch of her foot he was holding and started massaging. She didn't even have a chance to moan before Beau reached around to cup a breast in each hand, giving her a completely different kind of massage.

"I think you've teased us enough," he breathed in her ear. "It's our turn."

As if to emphasize his words, Beau tweaked both nipples. His touch sent electric shocks through her body, and she moaned as much from that as the foot massage Sawyer was giving her. The man definitely knew how to give a foot massage. No timid poking and tickling for him. He knew just the right amount of pressure to apply and where to apply it.

She let her head fall back against Beau's chest and gave into the sensations of having two men touch her. She thought she'd just about dissolve into the warm water when Beau nudged her head to the side so he could nuzzle her neck. Mmm, that was nice. Had to admit his hard cock felt mighty fine pressed against her ass, too.

"This feels so good," she moaned. "Where the hell have you two been all season? I could have used a little TLC like this after every rodeo."

Beau laughed softly in her ear. "If you decide you like how the rest of the evening goes, maybe that's something we can arrange. We can be your very own personal cowboy massage team. You okay with that, Sawyer?"

Sawyer grinned, his fingers traveling over her right heel and up her calf. "I think that's something I could look forward to."

Daisy was already mentally penciling it in her calendar when Sawyer spread her legs wide and draped them over the edge of the tub. Then he scooted between her legs and moved those exquisite hands of his up the inside of her thighs. Oh God, she knew where he was heading.

Behind her, Beau released one of her well-handled breasts and slipped his hand slowly down her quivering stomach. Apparently, Beau was heading there, too.

Question was, who'd get there first?

But it turned out her cowboy lovers weren't done tormenting her quite yet. Sawyer's hands stopped just short of her pussy to gently caress the insides of her thighs, while Beau's searching fingers stopped their southern travel as soon as they reached her belly button.

"Ah guys, you're killing me here." She sat up in the tub. "Stop all the teasing and get down to it."

"I'm not teasing." Beau gently but firmly pulled her back down. "I'm simply playing with your very sexy belly button. You can't really blame me—it's the sexiest one I've ever seen."

Daisy had no idea what made her belly button any sexier than the next woman's, but she supposed she had no choice but to sit back and make the most of it. Not every day a cowgirl got her belly button toyed with. Who knew? It might just lead to a whole new love affair with that part of her anatomy.

She closed her eyes, resting her head back on Beau's chest again and focused on what he and Sawyer were doing. She had the sneaking suspicion the men had played this game before—they were too good at it not to. She pushed down her naturally competitive jealousy and decided she didn't care. They'd learned to play well together from somebody, and she was dang grateful.

Sawyer worked her inner thighs with the same prefect touch he'd used earlier on her feet, never too much pressure, but never too light and wimpy either. Every few moments, one or both hands would slip under her legs all the way down to the cheeks of her ass and give them a firm squeeze.

She mentally begged him to move that last inch or so to her pussy, but he wouldn't give in. As if that wasn't enough torture, he raised the bar when he leaned forward and pressed his lips to the sensitive skin just above her knee. He moved down her inner thigh, nibbling and tonguing every inch of bare flesh.

He probably would have gone farther, but since he wasn't wearing a snorkel, she supposed that was out of the question. Dang.

While Sawyer was busy below the beltline, Beau was having a fine time exploring every inch of her stomach and torso. He always kept at least one hand on her breast, but he let the other roam free, stroking her abs, her belly button, the sides of her ass, and every once in a while, he'd venture down to the curly hair between her legs. Those naughty sojourns made her gasp every time he did it, which he seemed to find quite amusing.

Her belly button was a heck of a lot more sensitive than she'd realized, too. Beau would slide down under the water, twirl a single finger lightly around the outside of her navel, then dart off before she could really get a groove going, but the fleeting touches made the skin of her belly tingle. She suddenly wished they were out of the tub and in bed—she wanted to know what his touch felt like on dry skin.

As he dipped his hand into the water to tease her belly button again, she closed her eyes and slowly rocked her hips like she was getting fucked. She didn't realize how wildly she was moving until a wave of water splashed up and doused her face. She sputtered as champagne-scented foam went up her nose.

Beau chuckled. "Thought you were about to rock yourself to sleep on us there."

She wiped the soap bubbles from her face with an embarrassed laugh. "I can't help it. You guys are relaxing me so much, I'm turning into a limp noodle in here."

"Then maybe it's time we move on to the next event in our little rodeo," Sawyer said from between her legs. His breath tickled her inner thighs, making her shiver. "If you've had enough bath time, that is?"

She sat up quickly, every nerve ending in her body quivering with anticipation. "What event is next on the schedule?"

Beau's chuckle was soft and sinfully delicious in her ear. "You let us worry about that."

Chapter Five

Beau pressed a hot kiss to the curve of her shoulder, then helped her out of the tub. Both men's cocks were just as hard and throbbing as they'd been before the bubble bath.

Daisy automatically reached for one of the big, fluffy towels draped over the rack, but he and Sawyer beat her to it. It took quite a while to get all the wet skin dried off. She wanted to point out that, while her pussy was obviously very wet, rubbing it lovingly with the towels wasn't necessary, but she liked what they were doing way too much for that.

Taking her hand, Sawyer led her into the bedroom. Beau was right on her tail. Of course, he'd be behind her—he was obsessed with her ass. Not that she was complaining.

When they got to the bed, Sawyer turned to face her. Daisy thought he was going to pull her into his arms for some more of those delectable kisses of his, but he nudged her backward until her knees hit the edge of the bed. Then he gave her a little push. She got the idea, and quickly scooted back so that she was lying right in the center of the big, comfy bed. Giving him a smile, she spread her legs wide for him. She hadn't forgotten what he'd promised to do to her.

Thankfully, he hadn't, either. He grabbed her legs, pulled them wide and kissed his way up from her ankle.

"Are you going to lick my pussy now, Sawyer?" she asked breathlessly.

He paused long enough to climb on the bed with her. Then he smiled as he trailed his tongue past her knee and toward her inner thigh.

"Yes, Daisy. I'm going to lick your pussy until you come all over my face."

She was still a little damp from the bath, but that was nothing compared to how wet her pussy got after hearing those words.

Beau came around the bed and clambered up beside her just as Sawyer reached her pussy. He reclined beside her, his head propped on his hand and a smile on his face.

"You don't mind if I watch, do you, Daisy?"

She opened her mouth to tell Beau she didn't, but Sawyer chose that moment to swipe his tongue all the way from the bottom of her pussy to the very top of her clit, in one, long, tummy-twisting lick. All that came out was a moan as she arched off the bed.

"Oh, fuck me!"

"Not yet," Sawyer chuckled. "But we will."

Giving her a wink, he went back to licking, moving the tip of his tongue up one side of her pussy, then down the other. Every few rotations, he would dip his tongue in her pussy, or swipe it across her clit. It was never enough to make her explode immediately, but it was definitely enough to make her jerk and spasm like she was holding onto a live electrical wire.

It was official. Sawyer had a tongue worthy of a championship buckle. He knew exactly how to lick a woman's pussy, and wasn't shy about letting her know it.

Just when she was sure it couldn't possibly get any better, Beau leaned over and traced his tongue around her belly button. She'd thought his finger had felt good earlier, but his tongue was even better.

"Oh God, that's good," she breathed. "Right there."

The most amazing thing about what Beau was doing to her stomach was that it didn't distract her from what was happening between her legs. She felt every lick, touch and nibble of Sawyer's mouth on her pussy. Beau's teasing only served to heighten her pleasure, not overwhelm her.

Sawyer was careful not to focus too much on her clit. If he had, she would have gone off like a bottle rocket in just a few minutes. Instead, he spent just as much time tracing his nimble tongue up and down her folds as tempting the tender, sweet pea at the top of her pussy. Even that leisurely pace had her whole body tingling. Dang, this was going to be a big one.

For the first time in her life, Daisy actually fought to hold back her orgasm. She didn't want this sweet pleasure to end one second before it had to. It felt too good.

Beside her, Beau slowly made his way up from her belly button to fasten his hungry mouth onto her left nipple. She inhaled sharply.

"Oh, God!"

Beau popped her nipple out long enough to give a deep chuckle. Then he latched onto her pulsing nipple again as if he was starving for it. Apparently not wanting to leave her other breast and nipple unattended, he brought a hand up and firmly massaged that one just as he had earlier in the bathtub.

Daisy reached a hand down and weaved her fingers into Beau's thick hair. She simply intended to make sure he didn't go anywhere, but he must not have wanted her so actively involved because he grabbed her wrist with his free hand and pinned it down to the bed over her head.

She reached up with her other hand to pry his fingers loose, which only got that one captured, too.

So, there she was, pinned to the bed while one hunky cowboy feasted on her nipples, and the other one ate her pussy.

Could anyone really expect her to hold back after that?

She clenched her teeth, stomach muscles and just about every other part of her anatomy—anything to keep the bottled lightening that was her climax from slipping out.

The sensation of two long, wiggling fingers sliding in her pussy to tease her inner walls was her undoing.

She shrieked as she fell off that really big-ass horse called orgasm. And she never hit the ground. Instead, she just kept going and going—moaning, bucking, cussing and coming so hard she thought she was going to explode.

Having her hands pinned down turned out to be a first class mind-bender. It almost felt as if she couldn't escape her own orgasm. It ravaged her like a living thing, making her come harder and longer than she ever had.

She didn't even realize the ride was over until she got her wits back together and discovered she was lying on the bed gasping for breath, a hot cowboy on either side of her. Once her vision uncrossed, she noticed both men were wearing the biggest cat-who-ate-the-canary smiles she'd ever seen.

"Pleased with yourselves?" She pushed herself up on her elbows. "Well, you should be because that was amazing. I can't imagine ever coming that hard again."

Beau's mouth edged up. "I think it's time we work on that imagination of yours because we're going to have you coming like that all night."

Daisy wasn't sure she'd survive too many more orgasms like the one she'd just had. But it sure as hell was going to be fun finding out.

Beau took her hand and pulled her to her feet, eyes smoldering. Her pulse skipped a beat. She knew exactly where he was leading her, and she didn't resist at all. Not even when he sat on the edge of the bed and guided her over his lap. She might have been a bit leery of a spanking when he'd described it earlier. But after all the pampering they'd shown her thus far, she was nothing but curious now. They sure hadn't done anything but please her up to this point, so there was no reason they weren't about to do more of the same.

The position she was in put her upper body on one side of his lap and her legs on the other, with her ass high up in the air. She folded her arms under her head and wiggled around a bit more, getting situated exactly right.

This was sort of nice, cozy even. It certainly didn't hurt that she could feel his thick, hard cock pressing up against her left hip. It almost made her feel bad he and Sawyer were spending all this time pleasuring her. She promised herself she'd make it up to them.

Beau ran his hand across her lower back, then over her ass, and down her legs. It wasn't really a massage, just a light rubbing. Regardless, it felt dang good.

Sawyer sat on the edge of the bed a foot or so away from her folded arms. She tilted her head and smiled up at him. His face was still glistening with her juices. Why the hell was that such a turn on?

"You two really like to watch each other work, don't you?"

He smiled. "Trust me, it's not Beau I'll be watching—it's you. It's fun to watch a woman who knows how to let go and really enjoy herself. Not many women can."

She didn't know about other women, but she supposed he was right about her. She'd never been the kind of girl who held back in bed.

As she turned back to lay her cheek on her forearms, she caught sight of Sawyer's erection. Dang, it was actually pulsing there in his lap it was so hard.

She would have reached out and wrapped her hand it, but something told her he wouldn't let her. He'd probably pin her arms down like Beau had and tell her to be good and enjoy her spanking.

That didn't stop her from taking another quick peek out of the corner of her eye. There was a pearl of pre-cum beaded up right at the tip of Sawyer's cock. She found herself licking her lips in a frustrated need to taste the little offering.

She quickly looked away and closed her eyes before she could give into the urge. She supposed she could be good and control herself just a little longer. But it was only because she knew she would soon be tasting that cock.

Beau's hand came to a stop on her lower back and he applied just a bit more pressure. She remembered what he said about having to hold her steady because she was going to wiggle around during the spanking. She suddenly hoped she didn't disappoint him.

"Are you ready, Daisy?" he asked softly.

The words sent a shiver through her that had her pussy trembling all over again.

She didn't move, or look back him. She just answered honestly. "Yes, I'm ready."

Beau gave no other warning than that. He didn't tighten up, take a breath or anything. He just swung his hand and smacked her right ass cheek.

It seemed to echo in the room. She tensed, expecting to feel an immediate sting but it never came. Instead, she felt a gentle warmth spreading from the place Beau's hand had landed. It wasn't that bad at all. Heck, she'd had harder smacks on the ass while riding a horse.

She was still trying to compare the first spank to something she was familiar with, when the second one fell on the other cheek. The same pleasant heat accompanied it. She sighed as Beau started a slow, steady rhythm—one cheek, then the other, back and forth like a metronome. Dang if he hadn't been right. This was nice.

But then, just as she really started getting into it—anticipating each perfectly timed smack—he stopped.

She turned her head to voice her complaint, but could only moan as Beau squeezed her ass.

"Oh God, that's nice," she whispered.

"You didn't think I'd forgotten about that massage did you?" he asked as he caressed her cheeks.

"Actually, I kind of forgot myself," she managed in between the moans. God, he had good hands. "Having an orgasm can make a girl forget things. But I'm glad you remembered. I wouldn't want to feel like I was missing out on anything."

Sawyer chuckled. "Don't worry about that. You're getting the full package."

Daisy wanted to ask how the two of them had come up with this full package, but right now, she couldn't concentrate on anything except what Beau was doing. He alternated between deep, firm pressure and light caresses, his fingers working just about every square inch of her ass. He even massaged the tops of her thighs. But as much as she would have liked it, he seemed to purposely be ignoring the cleft between her cheeks. And he didn't show her pussy any love at all. He was such a tease.

He gave her no warning before spanking her again. One second he was squeezing her ass, the next he was popping her another good one. This smack felt a tad harder than the first ones. Not really stingy, but heavier nonetheless.

Beau went right into the same back and forth rhythm as before, using the hand on her back to gently rock her back and forth on his lap. He was spanking her harder now—she could feel her butt actually start to tingle. Before she knew it, that tingle turned into a sting. And dang if Beau hadn't been right again. The sensation was pleasant. In fact, it was more than pleasant—it felt unbelievably good.

There was something else Beau had been right about, too. She was gushing wet. She could feel her pussy lips sliding back and forth against each other as he moved from side to side. Her clit had perked back up after her oral-induced orgasm, too. She involuntarily squeezed her thighs together in time with the movements, trying to get a little friction on her nub.

Her wiggling made her hip buck up against Beau's shaft over and over. That felt good, too, but not nearly as good as when she a little dribble of pre-cum landed on her ass cheek. He was as turned on as she was.

As if he somehow knew she was onto him—and didn't like it one bit—his hand began to fall noticeably harder. The tingle-slash-sting turned into a serious burn.

And it felt freaking great.

She laughed out loud, or maybe moaned—she wasn't sure which. She would never have thought in a million years that she'd get this turned on from having her ass spanked.

As if on cue, Beau hit the brakes again. Daisy growled her disapproval.

When he started that firm ass massaging again, all was forgiven. The electric shocks his touch provoked were so intense, she felt it down to her toes. More importantly, she felt it between her legs.

That wasn't the only thing that ended up down there, either.

Beau's fingers snaked between her thighs to glide across her folds. She buried her face in her arms and whimpered.

"Did you know that your pussy is soaking wet?" he asked.

She couldn't answer, because coherent words couldn't find their way out. It wasn't her fault. What woman could talk rationally when a man pushed two fingers in her pussy?

Beau didn't seem to mind her non-response. He only slid his fingers in deeper and pumped them in and out.

"I tend to remember telling you that you'd be dripping wet after I spanked you."

He eased up his slow finger fuck longer enough to let her mumble an answer. "Yes, you did."

"If I wasn't so interested in making you feel good, I might be tempted to say I told you so. But I'll be the bigger person here."

She let out a husky moan. "You can be anything you want, just keep moving those fingers."

She was so hot she couldn't help humping up and down on those fingers of his. She might just be able to come again if he kept doing what he was doing.

But he didn't. Instead, Beau slid his two fingers out with a wet, needy sound and trailed them up the crack of her ass.

Daisy thought he might play with her anus some—he had basically promised, hadn't he? She pushed her ass out, making the offer pretty blatant. But after a quick teasing circle around her sensitive asshole with the tip of a single finger, Beau went back to spanking her.

Even though the smacks were much harder now, Daisy didn't really feel them too much. What she really felt was the absence of those fingers in her pussy. Even her anus was clenching in desperate need to feel them.

She couldn't take it anymore. Lifting her head, she turned to stab her ass-obsessed cowboy with what she hoped was a firm and determined look.

"Okay. I admit that I'm loving your spanking more than I ever dreamed, but don't you think it's time you get back to my pussy? If I get any more excited, I'm going to catch on fire."

He ignored her, laying into her bottom with a dozen firm swats. Okay, she felt those. But she didn't turn back around. She was serious, dang him. She was getting so turned on, it was getting uncomfortable. She was on the edge of some flat-out begging here.

"Beau? I promise if you slide those fingers back where they were, I'll make it up to you."

When Beau stopped mid-spank, she thought he was going to give in, but instead he looked at Sawyer.

"I think Daisy could use a little something to keep her mouth busy while I'm working back here. She seems bound and determined to rush the experience. Can you help a partner out?"

Daisy turned back around to see Sawyer get to his feet. Positioning his left foot on the floor, he rested his right knee on the bed—which put his very hard cock right in front of her face.

He gave her a roguish grin. "I don't have anything little to keep her mouth busy, but I definitely have something that will do the job."

She was so distracted by the innuendo of Sawyer's words—not to mention the firm spanking Beau was giving her—she didn't have time for a snappy comeback before Sawyer slipped his cock in her mouth.

Her reaction was immediate and completely instinctive. She lifted up on one elbow to support herself, then wrapped her other hand around Sawyer's thick shaft to pull him closer. She sucked hard, her tongue twirling rapidly around the head of that beautiful cock.

After waiting for so long to taste one of her cowboy studs, now that she finally had him in her mouth, she was in heaven.

She knew it was probably all in her head, but Sawyer's pre-cum tasted sweet—like chocolate cake. She took him even deeper, then slid back up, milking his shaft with her hand as she did. That earned her both a groan of appreciation and another spurt of pre-cum.

She was enjoying blowing Sawyer so much she almost forgot she was getting a spanking, too. But when she turned her mind in that direction as she idly flicked the tip of Sawyer's cock with her tongue, she realized Beau was really tanning her ass good at the moment—and it wasn't bad at all. Sure, her ass was on fire, but in a good way. It was like when you took a bite of really hot, spicy chili. It burned your mouth, but you couldn't wait to take another bite.

Beau's spanking was exactly like that. Every smack burned like sin, but she found herself still lifting her ass in desperate hunger to more.

Then he stopped again.

She would have screamed in frustration, but there was something in her mouth. And even cowgirls knew they weren't supposed to talk with their mouth full.

Beau slid one hand between her legs to toy with her pussy again while the other went back to that devastating ass massage she was quickly becoming addicted to. After a few rapid passes up and down the folds of her pussy to lube up his fingers, he slipped two sneaky digits deep inside her. Even though she knew it was coming, it was hard not to be shocked at how good it felt when those fingers started wiggling. Beau was one of those rare men who seemed to instinctively know where a woman needed to be touched.

Beau's finger fucking was a tad distracting, a fact Sawyer probably couldn't help but notice. It wasn't her fault. Even the world's best multi-tasker would have had a hard time focusing on giving a champion blowjob at the same time her pussy was being fingered and her ass squeezed.

Sawyer quickly took care of the problem by gently knocking away the hand that had been lazily pumping his shaft, and weaving his fingers into the hair on both sides of her head. Getting a firm grip, he pumped into her mouth. She wasn't normally the kind of woman to take a passive role in when it came to blowjobs, but in this case, she was okay with Sawyer taking the reins. It allowed her to dedicate the proper attention to the sensations that were building between her legs, while still pleasuring Sawyer. If the growls he spit out as he causally fucked her throat were any indication, he was definitely enjoying her suddenly submissive role. She had admit she was pretty dang happy with it herself. Getting a thick cock thrust down her throat while her head was head captive? Pretty freaking intense. Kinky, for sure, but definitely enjoyable. And getting two fingers stuffed up her pussy at the same time? Wow.

She was getting seriously turned on by the raw, wanton things these two hot cowboys were doing to her—which was pretty much anything they wanted.

While Sawyer fucked her mouth, Beau thrust his two fingers in and out of her pussy with perfect rhythm, tapping her G-spot every time. He must have decided her cheeks had been suitably massaged, because he stopped and slid that hand down between her legs, too.

She tensed a little. Whoa, she hoped he didn't think she had room for extra fingers in there. But he only ran a single finger around her pussy a few times, then up the crack of her ass to circle her anus with it. He didn't slide in, but just used his now very wet finger to make rapid, little circles around the sensitive opening.

Daisy groaned around Sawyer's cock. If her eyes had been open, they probably would have rolled back in her head. Happy honking horse balls, that felt unreal.

"I think she likes that," Sawyer commented.

Beau eased the tip of his finger in her ass and made slow, stirring motions. Daisy involuntarily pushed back against that amazing probing digit.

"I think you're right," he said to Sawyer. "What do you say, Daisy? Do you like my finger in your ass?"

She had no idea how he expected her to answer that question since saying anything with Sawyer's cock this deep in her throat was a physical impossibility. However, Sawyer was sweet enough to slide his cock out for her. She'd been drooling over that hunk of love muscle so much her lips were covered in saliva.

"Hell yeah, I like it." Her voice sounded huskier than usual. She supposed getting over stimulated could do that. "Stop teasing me already and give me more."

Sawyer must have decided that was answer enough because he placed the head of his shaft against her lips. She got the message and hungrily opened her mouth. Sawyer slid in deep and held himself there.

Beau got the message, too. He pushed that glorious finger of his deeper in her ass even as he continued to thrust his other finger into her pussy. The dual sensation—not to mention the incredible burning tingle running over both ass cheeks—started her down that path to orgasm.

Praying Beau wouldn't stop what he was doing for another round of spanking—she couldn't take any more teasing—Daisy bucked and wiggled like a mad woman.

"Her pussy and her ass are both squeezing my fingers," Beau said conversationally. "I think she's going to come soon."

"Think I should stop what I'm doing?" Sawyer asked. "I wouldn't want to distract her."

That Sawyer was asking Beau what he should do instead of her was hilarious. She wasn't going to let either man decide what they should do—that was her prerogative. And there was no way she wanted Sawyer's cock anywhere other than where it was right at that second, especially while she was climaxing. Coming while having a big cock stuffed in her mouth sounded like a little slice of heaven to her, particularly if she could make him to come at the same time.

She reached out and grabbed a handful of Sawyer's muscular ass, yanking him in tighter. Now that should clearly signify her desire.

Sawyer chuckled. "Okay, guess she wants me in her throat when she comes. Let's grant her wish, Beau."

"Sure thing, partner."

Beau slid that lone finger at least another two inches deeper in her ass, until it felt like it couldn't possibly go any more. Then he gyrated it in counterpoint to the two fingers flexing in her pussy. Daisy whimpered. Oh yeah, just like that. Just another minute of that. She ground against those three fingers, grunting in time with her movements.

Heedless of her approaching climax—or maybe because he knew it would only make things better—Sawyer thrust more forcefully into her mouth. She couldn't swallow all of him—she was a barrel rider in the rodeo, not a sword swallower in the circus—but he seemed determined to find out exactly how much she could take.

She was beyond questioning why his tightly clenched fingers in her hair turned her on so much, or why she felt almost euphoric as the head of his cock nudged down her throat. All she knew was that she loved it.

Sawyer suddenly pulled all the way out of her mouth. She instinctively took a big gulp of air, about to demand he give her his cock again when he shoved that perfect shaft deep in her throat. That show of dominance was all it took to push her over the edge. Her pussy spasmed around Beau's fingers in one of the very few non-clitoral orgasms she'd had in her life.

She bounced up and down on those fingers wildly, moaning like crazy and mentally begging for Sawyer to shoot his cum down her throat.

Beau's finger plunging in and out of her ass drew her orgasm out longer than she thought possible. Or maybe it was just the unfamiliar pleasure of being serviced by two men at once. Regardless, she came harder than she normally would have considering she'd already come once tonight during Sawyer's oral demonstration.

Just when she started to get dizzy from it, both men stopped.

Sawyer slid from her mouth without leaving her hoped-for present, and Beau slowed the movement of his fingers before gently pulling out of both of her very happy orifices.

Daisy groaned in disappointment. If her body could have survived it, she would have happily let them stay exactly where they'd been forever. But since they couldn't, she closed her eyes and went all noodle on Beau's lap. His lap would make a really nice place for a nap.

But a pop on the ass snapped her out of that.

"No time for sleeping, cowgirl," he reprimanded her. "The night's young and we've just gotten started with this private rodeo."

She pushed herself off his lap and dropped her feet to the floor, then stretched her arms over her head with a groan. She was so gooey after all the finger fucking that her pussy actually felt squishy.

Sawyer's mouth curved into a smile. "Damn, that is one well-warmed ass."

Daisy looked over her shoulder, trying to get a good look at her butt. When she couldn't, she hurried into the bathroom. Being careful not to slip on the wet floor—yikes, they'd made one hell of a mess—she turned so she could get a good look at herself in the two bathroom mirrors.

Freaking galloping gophers. Her ass wasn't just red—it was crimson! Her derriere was glowing all the way from the top of cheeks to the top of her thighs, from one hip to the other.

Catching her bottom lip in her teeth, she hesitantly reached down and cupped her right butt cheek. Her scarlet skin tingled where she touched it. Hot, too.

It shouldn't be possible for her ass to be this dang red and feel this dang good.

She was so entranced by the glow coming off her ass she barely noticed the men had joined her in the bathroom until Sawyer reached down to rest his hand beside hers on her cheek.

"Your ass is so hot," he whispered.

His touch was like little streaks of lightening, and so different than her own. She took a breath and held it, watching his fingers move back and forth across her bottom in the mirror. She was mesmerized by the lines even the light touch of his fingertips left.

Then Beau was there on her other side, kissing her neck and whispering to her. "What did you think of your first spanking?"

She opened her mouth to answer, but couldn't seem to find the right words. So, she did the next best thing—she turned and pulled his mouth down to hers for a kiss she hoped told him everything she wanted to say.

Their tongues tangled and danced for a time, and she dug her fingers in his hair to extend the contact. When he finally lifted his head, the words she'd been looking for earlier found their way to her lips.

"What did I think of my first spanking?" She smiled. "That I can't wait for my second one."

That earned her chuckles from both men, and she pulled Sawyer into her arms for a thank you kiss of his own. The way he'd treated her mouth had been a novel experience for her, and was at least partially responsible for the wonderful orgasm she'd had.

Instead of weaving her fingers in his hair, she dropped both hands down to cup his balls and stroke his cock. He was still rock hard—and still wet with her saliva and his essence. It only reminded her she hadn't been able to make him come.

She pulled back and frowned up at him. "I'm sorry I couldn't get you off. I really wanted to."

Sawyer grinned. Beside him, Beau chuckled softly. "Oh, believe me, I know you wanted me to come. But like Beau said, this rodeo's just getting started."

Her frown deepened. "You held back on purpose?"

He nodded. "You made it damn tough, too. I about lost it three or four times. You have an amazing mouth."

She blushed. "I guess I should take that as a compliment."

"You should."

As they took her hands and led her back into the bedroom, she realized they'd done every naughty thing they'd talked about downstairs.

"What might the next event in our little rodeo be?" she asked when they got to the bed.

Beau's eyes were like melted chocolate. "I was hoping you wouldn't mind letting me have a little taste of that blowjob you gave Sawyer."

That was exactly what she'd been thinking. After two world-class orgasms, it was well past time to show her two cowboys a little attention.

She looked from Beau to Sawyer. She really wanted to get him off, too. "How about I do both of you that way?"

Sawyer shook his head. "I think I'll just relax for a few and watch you take care of Beau, if you don't mind."

Daisy wanted to argue, but didn't. These two seemed bound and determined to last the rest of the night.

She turned back to Beau, ready to drop to her knees in front of him, but he had other ideas.

"Lie down on the bed on your stomach." Beau grinned. "That way, I can see that beautiful red ass of yours as you lick me."

Daisy laughed. That made complete sense considering he was obsessed with her ass. She went up on tiptoe to give him a kiss, then quickly obeyed. The bed was high enough that her belly-down position put her mouth just about at crotch level as Beau stood there with his hard-on in hand.

She raised herself up on her elbows, resting her chin in the palm of one hand and motioning him forward with the other. "Okay, then cowboy. Let's get a look at what we have to work with here."

As Beau stepped forward, Sawyer climbed onto the other side of the bed and sat back against the headboard. She couldn't believe he could sit there and watch her suck off Beau, especially since his own cock looked as hard as on old fence post.

Oh well.

Sighing, she turned back to find Beau's equally hard cock about two

Ride of Her Life

inches from her face. She had to pull her head back a bit to get a good look at him. Either that or go crossed-eyed.

She wrapped her free hand around the thickest part of the shaft and hefted it up and down a few times. Oh yeah, Beau was thicker than Sawyer by quite a bit, though maybe not as long. He definitely looked just as delectable, though. As she watched, a little clear pearl of precum bubbled up from his depths to cling to the head.

Resisting the urge to reach out her tongue and lap it right up, she turned her attention to the big, lightly-furred balls hanging just below his shaft. Clearly this called for two hands. She took the one out from under her chin and reached down to cup those dangling baby. They were warm and heavy in her hand—real heavy.

"If you're done inspecting the beef, maybe you could get on with the taste-testing?" Beau prompted.

"Don't rush the experience, cowboy."

She couldn't resist using Beau's line against him. But to please him, she leaned forward and swirled her tongue around the very tip top of that beautiful, cock.

"Mmmm." He tasted delicious.

Wanting more, she captured the head in her mouth, sucking gently while milking his shaft with one hand and carefully palming his balls with the other. She was immediately rewarded with another burst of sweet pre-cum. He didn't just taste delicious—he tasted unreal. She couldn't imagine what it would be like when he came.

Daisy swore right then that there was no way in hell she was going to let him get away without coming in her mouth.

She wiggled closer to the edge of the bed and tugged his cock, silently letting him know she wanted more. Since he was thicker than Sawyer, she wasn't going to be able to take him as deep, but she wasn't going to let that keep her from giving him the best blowjob he'd ever had in his life.

She was going to need plenty of hand action to take care of the part of his erection her mouth wouldn't be able to get to, though. Fortunately, multi-tasking was her oral specialty. She took him as deep as she could manage, then bobbed her mouth up and down while mimicking the motion with her hand around the base of his cock. She twisted her hand as she jerked him off, moving her mouth in the opposite direction. Then, just so they wouldn't get lonely, she began to lovingly juggle his twins with the pads of her fingertips. Nothing too rough, just rolling them from finger to finger like a magician's treat.

"Damn, Sawyer," Beau rasped. "You weren't kidding. She's amazing."

"I told you. You better cowboy up, or she's going to have you blowing it before we get serious about this."

Daisy didn't know what that last part meant, but Beau took Sawyer at his word. He threaded his fingers in her hair and pulled her back to a slow trot.

"There you go, cowgirl. Let's take our time and enjoy this ride."

She backed off, intending to let Beau know a blowjob did not equal a "ride" in her book, but just as she was about to speak, she felt the bed shift under her. She turned to see what Sawyer was up to and realized he wasn't leaning against the headboard anymore. Instead, he was across the room, playing with Beau's pile of tack.

"What're you up to over there?" she asked.

He didn't stop what he was doing, or even turn to look at her. "Just getting something we need for the next event."

Okay, that piqued her curiosity. And while she felt bad about ignoring Beau when she'd promised him an out-of-this-world blowjob just a minute ago, she couldn't drag her gaze away from Sawyer. When he turned around, her eyes went wide.

He was holding a surcingle strap. Bareback rider's used the two-inch-wide band of leather when they rode in competitions, to give them something to hold onto. In the old days, bronc busters would just grab a hold of a horse's mane and hold on for dear life. These days, they used the surcingle. It wasn't much more than a big belt that went around a horse's chest, with a tiny loop at the top where a rider would slip a single hand.

Last time she checked they didn't allow horses into the hotel. So, what the hell did Sawyer plan to do with it?

"What's that for?" she asked.

"This—" He grinned wickedly at her as adjusted the straps. "—is for riding you."

Ride of Her Life

Chapter Six

Daisy laughed. "I've been known to buck a little bit, but that thing is never going to fit me. I'm not as big as a horse, thank God."

He returned her laugh with a deep chuckle. "Beau had this one made special. It adjusts down as small as he likes—even small enough for you. If you're so inclined, I mean."

"Seriously?"

He arched a brow. "You telling me a rodeo cowgirl such as yourself doesn't like a good, hard ride? That you're scared of a little piece of leather?"

Well, that was a challenge if she'd ever heard one. Above her, Beau's mouth quirked in amusement.

Daisy chewed on her lower lip as Sawyer made the leather contraption smaller. She could visualize how the leather belt would cinch around her waist, creating a handle for him to grip while he took her from behind. It wasn't hard to imagine what kind of fucking she'd get with a belt like that on.

She scrambled up onto her knees and elbows before she could change her mind.

"Okay, I'll give your little toy a go as long as you promise I won't be getting one of those eight second rides all you rodeo boys are famous for."

Beau laughed.

Sawyer let out a snort of derision. "Don't you worry about that, Daisy. This ride is going to last a lot longer than eight seconds, I promise you that."

"And if he doesn't live up to your standards," Beau said, "let me know and I'll step in for him."

Sawyer snorted again, louder this time. "Please. You'll have enough problems lasting more than eight seconds in Daisy's mouth once she goes down on you."

"We'll see about that," Beau said.

Sawyer was all business as he climbed on the bed and strapped her into the modified surcingle with sure, confident moves. Clearly, he'd used it before. Not that she was bothered. She wasn't naive enough to think cowboys as hot as these two were lying around their rooms every night watching *SportsCenter*. But while they might have been with other cowgirls before, they were with her now—and after her, they'd never want to play with another woman on the circuit, she'd see to that.

Daisy leaned back and wiggled a little to get the leather harness arrangement settled into a comfortable position. She had to admit, when he cinched up the last buckle, pulling the belt tight against her waistline and stomach, she felt a delicious tremor ripple through her body. She'd been cinching saddles on horses for most of her life, but this was the first time anyone had ever cinched her into something—and it felt good. Who knew she'd get so seriously turned on by the sensation of being strapped into Beau's sex harness?

Sawyer gave the loop on top of the harness a good yank. The force of the movement was immediately transferred through the straps to her hips and she rocked back and forth. Oh yeah, this was going to be good.

Behind her, Sawyer climbed off the bed and walked into the bathroom. She heard him digging through a suitcase or something—hopefully for a condom.

She took the momentary pause to turn and give Beau's cock a little more oral attention. Not that he'd waned in the slightest. Still, no need to waste time. She flicked her tongue rapidly back and forth over the tip, licking up more of his delectable pre-cum. Heck, if she could make a bar drink that tasted like him, she'd be rich. Not that she'd ever let another woman have any of it, of course.

"Damn Daisy, your tongue is heavenly," Beau breathed.

She decided then and there that Beau was definitely good for her self-image. She tilted her head to look up at him as she kept licking his cockhead. "And I'm just starting, baby."

Giving him a wink, she wrapped her lips around him and swallowed him deep. His width made it tough for her to get him to the back of her throat, but she was motivated to impress him. So, she breathed through her nose and pushed a bit harder, using one hand behind his ass to urge him in even more.

He maybe made it another inch. Not an honest-to-goodness deep throat by any means, but apparently more than enough to make him happy.

"Fuuuuck," he growled.

"Shit, Beau," Sawyer's voice came from the bathroom. "You going to pop your cork already?"

Certainly not wanting to make Beau come this soon—though she really didn't think he was that close—Daisy pulled him out of her mouth with a slightly audible slurp.

She turned to look at Sawyer as he came out of the bathroom, rolling a condom down his shaft. Thank God someone had thought to bring them. She was a firm believer in the no-glove-no-love rule.

"Not yet, partner," Beau said as Sawyer climbed. "But that reaction was purely involuntary. She's beyond talented."

Beau caressed her cheek with his hand. Daisy cooed and pressed a

Ride of Her Life

kiss to his palm. She never thought being touched like that could be so emotional, but it was.

Behind her, Sawyer's hands closed over her hips. She turned to look over her shoulder at him. "You going to give me a hard ride, babe?"

His eyes glinted like sapphires. "You want it hard?"

After two orgasms already, she should be looking forward to a nice, relaxed boffing. But now that she had the leather strap around her waist, she realized she was looking for something completely different. She wanted to be seriously fucked.

"Mm-hmm. You'd better give it to me good, unless you want me to get my boots on and show you how a real cowgirl uses her spurs."

Sawyer grinned. "Yes, ma'am."

Preparing for a seriously hard banging, Daisy spread her thighs and slunk down lower on the bed until her nipples grazed the sheets. Then she gripped the edge with both hands. She felt Sawyer shift behind her and knew he was lining up his condom-wrapped shaft with her pussy.

In front of her, Beau spread his legs so that his cock was again perfectly lined up with her lips. She obediently opened her mouth and Beau slid right in. He wrapped one hand in the hair on the back of her head and cupped her chin with the other. It should have felt confining, but it didn't. In fact, Beau's hands were the most comforting thing she'd felt in a long time.

Beau didn't take advantage of the dominant position she'd granted him. Instead, he thrust his cock slowly into her mouth, giving her just enough. She wanted more, but she waited, knowing she would get it as Beau got more excited.

Daisy was so engaged in the blowjob she was giving Beau she almost forgot Sawyer—until she felt the tip of his cock sliding up and down her wet folds. She moaned around Beau's cock and wiggled back against Sawyer, eager to let him know he didn't have to tease her any more. She was more than ready.

She knew the moment he slipped his hand into the loop of the surcingle harness because she wasn't able to wiggle freely anymore. Sawyer used it to hold her steady as he slowly slid in his cock.

Her moans grew louder as his cock slid in inch by excruciating inch. It was murder not being able to thrust back onto him. But he wouldn't let her.

Sawyer was halfway in when he abruptly abandoned his slow approach and yanked her down hard on the rest of his cock using his leather handle. The strap around her waist bit into her skin in the most delicious way as his cock buried itself to her core. The slight upward curve of his cock had him touching her in places that had rarely been touched in this position.

On the down side, Sawyer's sudden movement had practically pulled her mouth completely off Beau's cock.

Beau simply pulled her back, sending his shaft deep enough that she actually felt it slip a little down her throat. Probably because she hadn't been thinking about it. Her eyes widened. Not at the sensation of Beau's cock being that deep in her mouth—that was so natural she hardly noticed. The thing that had really gotten her attention was the realization that she really had two men inside her at the same time. Not the fingers of one and the cock of another, but two hard, pulsing cocks.

The feeling was breathtaking in so many ways.

But before she fully contemplated the enormity of the situation, Sawyer yanked her hard back down on his cock, pulling Beau from her throat again. She gasped as Sawyer's hips slapped hard against her still tingling ass. He didn't stop with just a single hard thrust either, but fucked her with the intensity of a jack hammer. She'd asked for it hard, and she was getting it hard.

She tried to hold onto the amazing, arousing sensation of being two men's play toy, but it became almost impossible to do much beyond hang onto the edge of the bed and submit to the fucking they'd obviously been waiting to give her. Deep thinking had to take a back seat.

She still had enough animalistic mental capacity to recognize Beau's surcingle harness was possibly the greatest sexual invention since the vibrator. She'd never been taken so hard in her life. This ride was definitely going to last longer than eight seconds.

Not only that, but it came with a special added bonus, too. With her legs spread wide, her clit was completely exposed, and as Sawyer pounded into her over and over, his balls swung forward and slapped her sensitive nub with every thrust. It was like her clit was getting spanked now—with a warm, soft paddle. The sensation was so new and different she couldn't even begin to describe how it felt. She only knew she loved it.

Before she realized it, the lips of her pussy began to tingle, then her clit. After that, her whole insides started to melt into a big, gooey mess of pleasure. This was going to be one for the record books.

And it wasn't just the plundering she was getting from Sawyer that had her body quaking.

After a moment or two of trying to actively take part in the oral sex she was giving to Beau, she gave up and let him take control. She still wiggled her tongue back and forth along the underside of his thrusting cock, but for the most part, Beau was doing all the work, fucking her mouth and throat with the same passion and urgency as Sawyer was doing to her pussy.

She had never, ever, had a man do this to her mouth. It felt so dang amazing.

Maybe it was lack of oxygen, or maybe she was just overwhelmed with all the erotic emotions that came with being double-teamed like this, but she felt like she was in cowgirl heaven. Seriously, there was nothing that could be better than this.

There were so many sensations roaring through her body at once it was hard to catalogue them all—the tight harness around her waist; the long cock pumping in and out of her pussy; the heavy balls slapping her clit; the thick cock filling her mouth and sliding down her throat; her nipples scraping back and forth over the fabric of the sheets; the hands in her hair. It was more pleasure than she'd ever felt before, and she found herself slipping into a primal place of pure animal instinct, where all she did was respond unthinking to the things happening around her. Thrusting back toward the pleasure behind her, opening her mouth wider for the other source of pleasure.

Daisy stopped thinking, stopped trying to analyze why these new things felt so spectacular, and just let them happen, let herself go.

Maybe she moaned, maybe she even screamed—she couldn't really register that level of detail.

All she knew was that she was close to something so powerful it seemed like it could be more than she could handle.

Sawyer's thrusts were so forceful now that the whole bed rocked under her—or was it the whole world? The slap of his balls against her clit was so continuous it could have been a vibrator down there for all she knew.

The tingle of her impending orgasm grew and grew, and then grew some more, until every square inch of her body felt like it was seconds away from exploding.

But no matter how incredible it felt, or how close to the precipice it shoved her, she couldn't seem to get that last little millimeter that would take her to Nirvana. Her climax stayed just out of reach until it seemed like she would die with pleasure.

It was as if the harness around her waist that was responsible for bringing her so much pleasure, was also somehow holding her climax at bay. It was like some kind of medieval torture device—allowing her pleasure to build to unbelievable levels, but not letting it reach the pinnacle.

Beau's cock thrust farther down her throat than she would have ever thought possible, and she could feel his pace quickening. He'd better not stop, not after a build-up like she'd been through. She so wanted him to come in her mouth at the same time she orgasmed—assuming her climax found a way to escape from the bonds holding it back.

Did she have enough control left over her body to reach down and tweak her clit? Surely that would push her over the edge, wouldn't it?

There was only one problem—she didn't think she could get her hand and arm to work in the required coordinated fashion. She was too far past delirious to do it.

But fate—or in this case, Sawyer—chose that moment to intercede. Maybe he knew she needed something to push her over the edge, or maybe he was damn close to coming himself and needed a push of his own. Either way, he chose that exact moment to swing one hand down and smack her on the ass—hard.

"Come for us, Daisy," he groaned through clenched teeth.

After all of Beau's spankings, this one didn't really sting. But like the proverbial straw that broke the camel's back, Sawyer's one hard swat was enough to break the dam and release the flood.

Trapped between her two cowboy lovers, Daisy couldn't thrash and buck her way through the orgasm as she normally would have, and that only made her climax that much more intense. Lights flashed behind her tightly closed eyes, and her vision went fuzzy as every muscle inside her spasmed with a force that threatened to drive her crazy. But still she couldn't move, All she could do tremble and moan as Sawyer shoved his cock deep and held it there, yanking her hard against his hips with the leather loop of the harness around her.

She knew Sawyer was coming hard. She could dimly hear his grunts of pleasure overlaying her own. And though he wore a condom, she swore she could feel the heat of his cum inside her. The notion pushed her orgasm even higher.

Then a burst of warmth in her throat brought her back to the reality that another man was coming as well. Beau's hands tightly twisted in her hair, holding her firm as his creamy cum jetted down her throat. Then he pulled back some, letting the rest of his essence wash over her tongue.

Locked in the throes of orgasm as she was, tasting him that way still registered as one of the most delicious flavor that had every touched her tongue, and she moaned even louder as she reveled in the sensation of having her mouth awash in his cum.

Two men grunting and growling as they succumbed to the same pleasure as she was? Priceless.

Sawyer and Beau stayed buried deep inside her for a long time, making her body quake and tremble as her orgasm ebbed and flowed through her. When they finally slid out as one, she collapsed to the bed on her side like a scarecrow with its supports pulled out. She felt like a boneless mush, like she was unconscious.

But she was far from unconscious. Her body was still responding to the fucking she'd just gotten from her two cowboys, even though their cocks were no longer inside her.

Daisy felt hands soothing her body, then move to the leather harness tightly cinched around her waist. It took her a moment to realize one of the men was trying to remove it. She pushed the offending hands away.

"Leave it," she whispered.

She didn't want it to come off yet. It felt warm and comfortable, like the hands of her two lovers.

The bed moved as Sawyer and Beau men settled down on either side of her. The warm sheen of sweat that covered her body was already beginning to cool, and she snuggled into the combined body heat of both men.

Since she had her eyes closed, she had no idea who was behind her and who was in front of her. She didn't care. She simply lay there breathing in their masculine scent and replaying what had just happened. Even now, it seemed like a dream.

The taste of Beau's come was still present in her mouth and she ran her tongue around, savoring every little trace, not bothering to hide the moan that escaped her lips. Her pussy and clit continued to tremble from the rough fuck she'd just gotten, and she could still feel the place on her ass where Sawyer spanked her and sent her off into this current state of bliss. She luxuriated in the knowledge that she'd just experienced the best sex she was likely ever going to have.

The sheer awesome magnitude of how good that sex had been was so overwhelming, she laughed.

"Okay," Sawyer drawled in her ear. "That's not exactly the response I expected."

She couldn't help it. She laughed some more.

Daisy rolled onto her back. Both men had propped themselves up on their elbows and were regarding her with concern.

"Maybe we shouldn't have been so rough," Beau said to Sawyer. "Maybe we gave her a concussion or something."

Sawyer frowned. "You okay, Daisy?"

She forced herself to stop laughing and calm herself. "I'm fine. And no, you didn't damage me, except maybe for every other man I might ever have sex with. I was laughing because I think I'm still high from all the orgasms you gave me."

Sawyer eyed her skeptically. "Do you always laugh after you orgasm that hard?"

"I wouldn't know." She giggled again. "I've never come that hard before."

That seemed to mollify both men—and please them.

"So, you're saying you enjoyed yourself?" Beau asked.

Daisy shook her head. Typical male—just wanted hear how good he was in bed. Well, in this case, she didn't have a problem stroking their egos a little, not after all the stroking they'd given hers.

"Yes, you two. I enjoyed the hell out of myself."

She leaned forward and kissed first Sawyer, then Beau, making sure she rubbed her breast up against their chests to help convey her true appreciation. As much as she liked being between them like this, it was difficult to carry on a conversation. Sitting up, she spun around and sat cross-legged between them. She traced her fingers across both of their muscular chests and down their tight abs to their dormant cocks.

"I've never been taken so fiercely in my life. You made me come so hard, I thought I was going to pass out."

She ran a finger on each hand down their still very wet and sticky shafts, careful to avoid the sensitive heads. She didn't necessarily want to get them hard again just yet—she was simply doodling as she enjoyed their post-sex pillow talk.

"I hope I didn't…you know…overdo it…in your mouth?" Beau asked.

Daisy couldn't help but laugh again. After the serious fucking these two had given her, now Beau decided to get coy?

"You mean when you were shoving your thick cock so far down my throat I could barely breathe?"

Beau winced, clearly not realizing she was teasing him.

Daisy leaned over and kissed him. "No, you definitely didn't overdo it. In fact, I think having your cock so far down my throat is part of what made me come so hard. It was so raw and animalistic. Like I was a sex toy for you and Sawyer to take however you wanted." She bit her lip. "That doesn't make me sound too submissive, does it?"

A smile tugged at Beau's mouth. "Daisy, you're far from submissive. You may have been getting spanked and wearing the leather harness, but you were the one setting the tone and running the show." He brushed her long hair back. "You're one amazing woman, you know that?"

"Yeah, I know, but thanks for reminding me." She grinned. "And you have my permission to shove that cock of yours as far down my throat as you think it will fit—anytime you feel like it."

Both men's cocks stirred at her naughty words. They obviously liked a girl who could talk as nasty as they could.

Sawyer glided his hand from her nipple down to the leather harness she was still wearing. "I take from those statements that you enjoyed wearing Beau's surcingle harness?"

She reached down and fondly stroked the leather and metal buckles. Just remembering how it had felt to be yanked around and controlled by the harness made her pussy melt inside again. It was impossible to think she could ever want more sex after that fucking, but her pussy didn't seem to know that.

"Oh, yeah. This thing is a dream," she said. "And it wasn't just the fact that you could fuck me so hard while I had it on, though that was pretty spectacular. The way it felt wrapped around my waist was just plain sexy."

Sawyer gaze caressed the leather around her waist. "You definitely look damn sexy wearing it, that's for sure."

Daisy casually wrapped a hand around each of the men's semi-erect shafts. Even in this state, they were both impressive. Still feeling playful, she lightly massaged them up and down a few times. They both hardened immediately. There was still a lot of life left in those bad boys. But was she up for any more?

"So Beau, I have to know. Where the hell did you come up with the idea for this thing?" she asked, motioning toward the harness with her chin.

Beau's cock stiffened even more as her hand slowly moved up and down. Well, regardless of whether she was ready for more cock tonight, it looked like she was going to get it. Her pussy purred approvingly at the thought.

"I sort of stumbled across it by accident, I'd suppose you'd say." Beau grinned. "I used to go out with a woman who really liked to get it from behind—sort of like you do, I'm guessing?"

"Good guess." She rubbed the pad of her thumb over his cockhead. "But go on, you have me curious now. How do you get from a girl liking it doggie-style to resizing an expensive bareback harness?"

"We were playing around one night after she'd fallen off a horse and bruised up her hip pretty good. It hurt when I tried to hold on to her there, but she really wanted me to do her hard. She just up and grabbed my roping lasso and wrapped her around her waist three or four times. It definitely gave me a good handhold and it didn't hurt her as much. She loved it, and so did I. Unfortunately, that lasso is pretty coarse, and she ended up with some bad rope burns."

"Ouch." Daisy winced. "That doesn't sound sexy."

"She didn't care, but it bothered the hell out of me," Beau said. "The next day I went to go see a leather and tack guy I know who works the circuit."

"Hold on." Daisy blinked. "You walked into a tack shop and asked for a sex harness?"

Beau shrugged. "Pretty much. He had that surcingle you're wearing and modified it for me. It cost me a small fortune, but I'm sure you'd say it was worth it."

"I couldn't agree more. What did your girlfriend think of it?"

"She loved it. When I first brought it home, we didn't leave my apartment for three days." He frowned. "Unfortunately, it turned out that she liked my harness more than she did me. Wanted to know if she could use it with another guy—without me being there."

"Dang. Sorry about that." Daisy leaned over and kissed him. "But her loss is my gain."

Beau groaned as Daisy slipped her hand over the top of his cock and twirled it a few times around the rim of his head.

"I guess so," he rasped.

She went back to rubbing her hand up and down his shaft. "How often have you had a chance to use this thing?"

She wasn't necessarily asking out of jealousy, but some catty part of her wanted to make sure she wasn't in too long a line of harness-wearing cowgirls.

He gave her a sly grin. "I assume you don't want me to include the horses that have worn it?"

She reached down and lightly thumped his balls. While he was still groaning from that, she bent over and kissed the tip of Sawyer's cock, then gave him a flick of the tongue. Lifting her head, she gave Beau a mock-stern look.

"More snarky comments like that and you'll just watch me lick Sawyer for the rest of the night while you go play with yourself in the corner."

He held up his hands in surrender, a smile playing at the corner of his mouth. "Sorry, but it had to be said. To be truthful though, I haven't used it with that many women. It takes a certain kind of cowgirl to handle something like that."

He hadn't given her an actual number, but the answer suitably satisfied her anyway.

She ran her thumb over the head of his cock again. "I couldn't help noticing Sawyer certainly knew how to use it."

Beau shrugged. "What can I say—friends share. I wouldn't keep a discovery like this to myself. It wouldn't be right."

"A fact I'm truly appreciative of," Sawyer said.

Daisy stopped massaging their cocks long enough to run her hands back and forth along the hard leather and steel buckles. Just watching her do that made the men's cock twitch a bit. They were so bad. She had a mind to lean over and take each of them in her mouth again.

But she was still curious about something. "Were you two planning to use this on me the whole time we were talking downstairs?"

Sawyer shook his head. "Not really. Like Beau said, the opportunity to use it doesn't come along very often. I was hopeful, though. I figured a cowgirl who rode as hard as you might be game for something a little kinky, but that was mostly just wishful thinking on my part."

She reached down between their legs again, except this time she gently cupped both their balls. In her experience, most women tended to spend far too little time on this part of a man's body. She'd discovered it was an excellent way to guarantee a devoted man toy.

Sawyer and Beau definitely seemed to appreciate it.

"Or really good instincts," she said in response to Sawyer's comment. "What made you decide to pull it out for me once we got up here?"

"Can't rightly say for certain." Sawyer's voice was husky. "But the way you handled yourself once we stepped through that door—dragging us into the tub for a bath, handling that spanking like you'd done it before, taking me on at the same time. I figured you were a pretty adventurous girl who wouldn't shy away from something a little different."

Sawyer slid his hand up her thigh, massaging and teasing. Beau soon followed suit. Though neither could reach any further—their recumbent position on the bed limited how far they could get those naughty hands of theirs—it still felt mighty good. Made her wonder if perhaps she might be up for another round of real sex with these two.

She was a little surprised by that thought. A few minutes ago she was feeling satiated. Even after the two cowboys had started to harden again under her gently caressing fingers, she'd seriously only considered maybe giving each of them a blowjob, if not just a hand job. Now she was starting to seriously reconsider. This talk about their leather sex toy was getting her warm and fuzzy all over.

She gave the men her best doe-eyed look. "I hope you don't mind if I keep this little, ol' thing on for a while. Just in case something comes up and we need to use it again?"

Both their cocks hardened perceptively in her hands.

"That's a good idea." Beau grinned. "I get the feeling that another opportunity might present itself real soon."

She slanted him a smile that was far from innocent as she shifted to her knees. "Maybe sooner than you think."

That said, she leaned forward and took the head of his cock in her mouth.

Chapter Seven

As Daisy licked Beau, she kept one hand casually draped around Sawyer's cock—didn't want the fella to get lonesome.

While Beau was getting firmer by the second, he wasn't rock hard quite yet. That gave her a few moments to work on him while his cock was a little more manageable. She loved sucking guys at this moment, when they were getting hard, but weren't stiff as a fence post. She pushed his semi-erect cock down her throat and pumped it up and down, caressing him with her tongue. This was the only chance she'd ever have to deep throat a cock this big, and she was going to take her time. But even semi-hard as he was, she still couldn't get him all the way down, even if it was a lot further than before. Baby steps, cowgirl.

Once she had him as deep as he could go, she stopped and enjoyed the sinful sensation of him getting hard in her throat.

Beau groaned deep in his chest.

And went from semi-erect to hard as a rock. Daisy was forced to pull back off his cock much sooner than she'd intended to. It was either that or risk a dislocated jaw. Dang, he was thick.

She immediately hopped over to give Sawyer some of the same treatment. Fair was fair.

Watching her deep throat Beau had gotten him quite a bit harder, so she didn't have the opportunity to get him down her throat while he was still semi-erect. She satisfied herself with running her tongue round and round the rim of his cockhead before taking him deep enough to let the tip graze the back of her throat. Then she wrapped her lips tightly around him and pulled back oh-so-slowly. He bucked under her.

"Damn, Daisy," he breathed. "That's so good. Don't stop."

She didn't want to, but she forced herself to pop her mouth the rest of the way off him and sat back on her heels. She looked from side to side, judging their arousal. Both men were now stiff as could be and seemed more than ready for whatever came next.

"Sorry, Sawyer, but I have something else in mind for these big boys."

Beau's grin was positively wicked. "And what's that?"

"Well, I'm still wearing this." She motioned at the leather harness that was nice and snug around her waist. "Might as well get some use out of it."

"Now that's a plan I can get behind." Sawyer agreed.

Beau was off the bed and in the bathroom in a shot. Daisy heard him rustling around and figured he was getting another condom. Dang right. Sawyer took her from behind the first time—now it was Beau's turn. She

Ride of Her Life

could already feel herself getting aroused at the idea of him sliding his thick cock into her already well-fucked pussy.

But when Beau walked out, he tossed the condom to Sawyer, who immediately tore open the foil packet.

Okay, it looked like Sawyer was going to be taking her again. Did that mean Beau would be slipping back in her throat, or would he wait and do her after Sawyer had already taken another turn? Now, that sounded interesting. Could she take a back-to-back pounding from these two—especially now that both of them had already come once already?

Daisy leaned over and helped Sawyer roll the condom down his shaft as he knelt on the bed. She rarely had a chance to do this—guys were always so territorial when it came to their raincoats, so it was fun. A little sticky maybe, since the thing was pre-lubed, but still fun.

She didn't realize she'd giggled until Sawyer cleared his throat. "I'm glad you're having so much fun putting on the condom, but it's really a lot more entertaining if you let me use it for its intended purpose."

She straightened up and gave him a quick kiss. "Sure thing, babe. Ready when you are."

Daisy spun around and quickly assumed the same wide-spread, knees and elbows position they'd used the first time. She slipped a quick hand down between her legs to do a moisture check. Pretty wet, but still…

"Guys," she called over her shoulder. "Do you have some lube by any chance? I think I might need it."

"Already ahead of you," Beau told her.

Excellent. These two cowboys were the greatest. She was going to have to remember to do something extra special for them—besides have sex with them, that is.

She wiggled her ass back and forth while she waited for Sawyer to get a firm grip on that harness loop. Since Beau was still behind her, she figured he was going to take a turn at her pussy next instead of fuck her mouth. She was game.

But just then, she felt the bed shift right beside her. She turned her head to find Sawyer getting comfy—on his back. Her brow furrowed in confusion.

"What are you—?" she started to ask, but he reached out and grabbed her waist, dragging her astride his hips and sitting her right down on his erection.

The breath left her lungs in a gasp as the tip of that perfectly curved cock slid along the inside wall of her pussy, straight across her G-spot and deep inside her. It was so unexpected she actually felt a little dizzy.

She fell onto Sawyer's broad chest, barely catching herself with her hands before doing a face-plant. Beneath her, Sawyer didn't move, didn't thrust. He simply held her down firmly against his cock and waited for her to get a grip on herself.

His blue eyes glittered. "You were about to ask a question?"

It took a moment to get her head screwed back on straight and figure out what he was talking about. "Oh…yeah… You just caught me by surprise. I thought since I was wearing the harness that we'd get a chance to use it again. But don't get me wrong. This is nice, too."

Sawyer chuckled. "I wouldn't worry too much, Daisy. That leather harness is still going to get a good workout—a real good workout."

She started to ask what the heck that meant when she felt the bed shift again, this time behind her. She turned to look over her shoulder and saw Beau there, his cock sheathed in a condom and glistening with lube. The bottle was in his hand.

She might be a little out of it, but she was a real bright girl. Sawyer's comment and that bottle of lube in Beau's hand could mean only one thing—and she wasn't entirely sure she was up for that.

"Whoa there, cowboy." Daisy twisted as much as she could with Sawyer's penis already wedged deep in her pussy. It was difficult to believe, but Beau's cock seemed even bigger than it had when he'd plundered her throat. That wasn't necessarily impossible since the man was a self-professed ass-freak—and he currently had said ass in his crosshairs. She pointed at Beau's hard-on. "Where exactly do you think you're putting that thing?"

Beau positioned himself right behind her ass, resting one hand on her hip, the other casually holding the bottle of lube. The fact that he was able to easily work around Sawyer's legs told her everything she needed to know. This was definitely not their first rodeo when it came to this particular position. She'd been set up.

"I thought you wanted to use my harness again?" Beau asked innocently.

"I did, but I didn't mean both of you at once."

Beau didn't say anything. All he did was carefully squirt some lube onto his finger and reach for the crack of her ass. It was hard to defend her backdoor territory, what with Sawyer holding tightly onto her hips and slowly rotating his hips under her.

But she successfully managed to knock Beau's hand aside anyway.

Beau didn't seem the least bit offended. Or deterred. "You've already handled the two of us together once before," he said as he slipped his wet fingers between her cheeks.

Daisy had to bite her lip to keep from groaning as his lubed fingers began to circle her anus just like they had when she'd been over his lap before. It was getting dang hard to think straight, and Sawyer's light thrusting wasn't helping matters at all.

She turned and whacked Sawyer's shoulder. "Stop that for a minute. I'm trying to talk here."

"Yes, ma'am," he said in that sexy drawl of his. Dang, his voice did crazy things to her. But at least he stopped thrusting—mostly. He still held her hips and ground against her gently.

She turned back to face Beau. "I know what you're thinking, but this isn't going to work. Taking you in my mouth while Sawyer fucked me isn't anything like what you have planned. It wouldn't work."

She braced herself, sure he was going to get upset at her logic, but he only nodded and tipped the bottle up to squirt more lube directly on her asshole. She expected it to be cold, but it was surprisingly warm. Where the hell had he been keeping that, it a hot water bath?

"I wouldn't be so sure of that, Daisy. You seem to be awfully fond of having my fingers in there earlier."

Beau slid his finger deeper into her ass, pulling an involuntary moan out of her and forcing her to buck a few times on Sawyer's cock. The dual assault on her senses felt exquisite and she was once again at a loss for words.

Then Beau slid a second finger into her ass to join the first. She didn't know what shocked her the most—the second finger itself, or how good it felt. She had to get hold of herself. Fighting for control, she turned and leveled her gaze at Beau.

"Yeah, your fingers feel good, really good. And if you want to keep doing that while I fuck Sawyer, I'll be in heaven. But I can't fit your thick cock in my ass—not while Sawyer is in my pussy already. It's just too much cock in too small of a space."

Beau leaned forward, and putting one hand on her shoulder, pulled her back toward him so she was sitting up straight on Sawyer's seriously hard cock. Sliding his hand under her chin, he tilted her face up and kissed her. Then he wiggled the two fingers in her ass as Sawyer moved her hips up and down.

When he lifted his head, she was left gasping with a need for more than air.

"You really sure my cock won't fit in here, Daisy?" He wiggled his fingers again. "After all the new and erotic things you've done already tonight, are you really ready to state for a fact that my nice, hard cock won't fit in here?"

That kiss had been pure blackmail.

So had the wiggling fingers.

And the cock thrusting slowly in and out of her soaking wet pussy.

This was patently unfair—getting her this turned on and then asking if she was sure she didn't want the pleasure to go even further. How could she make a sane decision under these circumstances?

"But you won't fit… Will you?" The statement finished as a question.

Ah hell, who was she kidding? Downstairs, she'd toyed with the idea of letting Beau take her in the ass. But once she'd gotten her first look at his thick cock, she'd naturally changed her mind, telling herself he simply wouldn't fit. And the notion that she could take both of them inside her like at the same time? That hadn't even entered into her thought processes.

But now, in the heat of the moment, with so many sinful sensations racing over her body, her thought processes were rapidly being reprogrammed.

Maybe she could do this?

She kissed him again, then whispered, "You'll go slowly, right? And stop the second I say it isn't working?"

"Of course." He caressed her cheek. "But you already knew that, didn't you?"

She nodded. "Yeah."

Taking a deep breath, she turned back to face Sawyer. She leaned forward again so that her breasts were pressed against his chest and her face was inches from his. The position left her ass completely exposed to Beau.

Daisy wasn't tense about this, really she wasn't. She'd done anal before. Maybe not with a guy as big as Beau, or while another cock was already in her pussy. But the basic concept was still the same. Just relax and enjoy it.

Beau helped by not rushing it. He kept working his fingers in her ass, occasionally adding more lube from the bottle when he felt he needed it. The whole time, Sawyer gazed into her eyes and slowly rocked her back and forth by the hips. She appreciated that he hadn't tried to cajole her while she'd still been undecided.

It didn't take long before her whatever doubts she had left disappeared amidst an avalanche of pleasurable feelings spreading out from her anus. Beau had unbelievably talented fingers.

"You ready, Daisy?"

The question came from Sawyer, not Beau. Maybe because he could see in her eyes that she was totally relaxed now.

She bent her head and kissed him. "I'm ready."

Daisy wasn't sure if Beau actually heard her whispered words, or if Sawyer gave him some kind of signal. Either way, Beau gently slid his fingers out of her ass. The loss of stimulation was immediate and startling, and she whimpered against Sawyer's mouth. Maybe she craved anal sex more than she thought.

Behind her, Beau moved closer. Even though Sawyer was doing an excellent job of distracting her with his mouth, she couldn't help but stiffen. Sawyer's hands glided up from her hips, stroking her back and side until the tension dissolved away. When it had, those hands slid back down to her hips and gripped her ass, his fingers spreading her cheeks wide so Beau could slide in. The move should have made her tense all over again, but instead it only relaxed her more. She didn't even jump when she felt Beau's cockhead press against the tight barrier of her anus.

She shouldn't have worried about whether he would fit or not. Beau wasn't the kind of man to rush a woman into taking his cock. He pushed with gentle pressure against the tight ring of her anus, all the while running his hands over her back and across her ass checks.

Just because Sawyer stayed completely still, letting his partner have the time he needed to get firmly lodged in her ass, didn't mean he wasn't busy. He kissed her the whole time, tracing his fingers casually along the sides of her breasts and over her hips. With him already in her pussy, her ass was tighter than it normally would have been, so it took Beau a little while to slide in. But as both men worked together, she realized she was more at ease getting it from her two cowboys at the same time than she'd ever been with any single guy.

So, when Beau's cockhead slipped right in her ass and pushed in the first inch or two immediately, she wasn't even surprised.

She was surprised by how good it felt, though. She was used to there being some discomfort when a guy first slid in her bottom. It was only natural—things as big as a guy's cock weren't intended to go up there. And she'd really expected more than a bit of discomfort with Beau's cock simply because he was so big.

But Beau's cock didn't hurt at all. In fact, it felt dang good—like she-couldn't-wait-to-feel-more kind of good.

Daisy tried to wiggle back against him a bit, but Sawyer wasn't having any of that. He gripped her ass tighter, refusing to let her move.

"Don't rush the experience."

So, she had no choice but to wait there impatiently as Beau slowly pumped in and out of her ass. The short thrusts made her anus tingle. She moaned and tried to wiggle her hips again, more vigorously this time.

"I think you can let her loose, Sawyer," Beau said. "I'd say she's ready."

Sawyer immediately released her hips, only to reach up and place them on either side of her face. "Is Beau right? Are you ready for more?"

She nodded, then, before either man could stop her, she shoved back onto Beau's cock.

He grunted. "Well, I guess that answers that question."

Daisy would have tried to work herself back even more, but something suddenly immobilized her, putting a stop to her sneaky thrusting attempts. A little thrill went through her. Beau had grabbed hold of the loop atop her harness and was holding her completely still. Between his grip on her booty leash and Sawyer's pogo stick wedged inside her, she couldn't move much at all.

She didn't have time to complain, though. As soon as Beau had properly demonstrated he was the one in charge of this fucking, he slid deeper in her asshole.

And sliding.

And sliding.

And sliding.

Beau pressed in with slow, steady, inexorable force. Her tight anus spread wide to take everything he had to offer, and by the time she felt his hips come into contact with her ass cheeks, she was gasping for breath. Sparks went off deep inside her bottom. Good heavens, this was beyond unreal.

Then he leaned into her, moving that last little bit and pushing her down hard on Sawyer's shaft. Being that stuffed with two cocks pushed her beyond the gasping-for-breath point, and she started hyperventilating.

Sawyer saved her by pulling her face down for a kiss that made her realize breathing was highly overrated anyway. His fingers twisted in her hair and he kissed her like a man who truly wanted to consume her.

That was when the serious fucking started.

Beau pulled his thick cock almost all the way out, then shoved it back in, using the surcingle harness to devastating effect. He thrust at the same time that he jerked her toward him with the leather belt. His aggressive hand on the harness pulled her halfway off Sawyer's erection just as his own slammed back into her ass. Then Beau shoved her forward, jamming her down hard onto Sawyer until just the very tip of his shaft remained buried in her spasming ass. Under Beau's forceful push, Sawyer's dick thumped into a place that no man's penis had ever visited.

"Oh, God!" she screamed.

Stars were exploding around her after only a few thrusts. The concern she couldn't handle two big cocks inside her at the same was overcome by a new fear—that she'd pass out from the overwhelming pleasure long before she could ever orgasm.

No woman could handle this much ecstasy. It wasn't possible.

Ride of Her Life

"Slow... Slow down," she begged breathlessly. "Too...much."

Wordlessly—thankfully—Beau complied with her request, slowing his thrusts and easing up on the force he was applying to the harness. He didn't push her quite so far down on Sawyer's cock, instead giving her time to regain her breath and collect her wits in between.

"Sorry, sweetheart," he said hoarsely. "I didn't mean to be so rough."

"You weren't," she gasped. "It felt amazing... Just too much."

He eased his shaft in and out. "This better?"

"Oh yeah, that's it." She rested her cheek on Sawyer's broad chest with a sigh. "Just like that."

Now that she wasn't fighting to keep the air in her lungs, she could focus on how good Beau felt moving in her ass. Maybe it was how relaxed she'd been before they'd started, or maybe it was just all the lube they'd used. Either way, this was stacking up to be the best ass fucking she'd ever received.

No, skip that. This ass fucking was going to leave every other foray into the land of anal sex choking in the dust.

Her tight anus clutched in vain at the thick intruder moving back and forth, involuntarily trying to trap it inside. But Beau's cock was too strong, too demanding. He moved in and out like a fine-tuned machine. If anything, her desperate attempt to clench down on his shaft only made the tremors vibrating through her bottom more intense.

She wrapped her arms around Sawyer's shoulders, holding on for dear life and pulling her face up until it was snuggled into the crook of his neck. Then she nibbled on his neck like a contented kitty. He must have taken that as a message of some sort because he started making short, rhythmic jabs up into her pussy. She didn't know how he could move like that with her weight and Beau's crushing down against him, but he did. And it was heavenly.

As if they'd done this together a million times—although she hoped they hadn't—Beau and Sawyer developed this perfect little double-penetration rhythm, one cock sliding in as the other slid out. The motion guaranteed that one of her openings was being plundered constantly.

And if the non-stop dual penetration wasn't erotic enough, she was also the beneficiary of the hottest sound she'd ever heard—two men growling and groaning their hearts out as they fucked her happy body. Knowing she was giving them as much pleasure as she was getting was music to her ears.

The feel of a hand gripping her left ass cheek filtered through her fuzzy mind. She entertained herself trying to figure out whose it was, but that was harder to do than she thought. Her head couldn't quite focus on any one sensation for more than a second or two before being distracted by some other out-of-the-world feeling.

She finally decided it was Beau. Of course, she only figured that out after realizing two hands were already firmly holding her hips, and that those two hands must belong to Sawyer. Unless there was a third guy in the room she didn't know about.

"Shit, Daisy." Beau's growl made goose bumps rise up all over her body. "Your ass is so tight, you're killing me."

She stopped nibbling on Sawyer's neck to look at Beau over her shoulder. "That might have something to do with having the two of you inside me at the same time."

"Maybe." Beau plunged in especially hard and deep, making all three of them to gasp out loud. Then he held himself deep inside her, letting Sawyer thrust alone for a bit. "Or maybe you just have the sweetest ass ever to straddle a horse."

That was a compliment she could live with, though it took a while to tell Beau as much since Sawyer was doing some deep thrusting of his own. The base of his shaft was doing devastating things to her clit at the moment.

"That's sweet of you to say, Beau," she finally managed. ""But I have to give you credit. You ride my ass better than it's ever been ridden. It's completely in love with your cock."

She left unspoken the other thought in her head—that Beau could fuck her bottom like this anytime he wanted—as long as Sawyer was in her pussy. She'd bring that little offer up later.

"Speaking of tight," Sawyer said from beneath her. "You think you can handle a little faster pace?"

Daisy raised up enough to look him in the face, worried Sawyer's question meant he was on the edge. He didn't look like a man about to explode, but she couldn't tell for sure.

"Don't you even think about coming yet." She wasn't anywhere near ready for this rodeo ride to end.

He chuckled. "Wouldn't dream of it. I just wanted to feel what it's like being inside your pussy when you come."

Whew. Okay, crisis adverted.

She glanced over her shoulder at Beau. He looked dang good back there covered in a light sheen of sweat while rocking gently back and forth in her ass.

"You think you can handle Sawyer's request?" she asked with a grin.

He returned her cocky smile with one of his own. "I can. The question is whether you can handle it?"

Ride of Her Life

She wiggled her ass. "I can handle it now. Just pick up the pace a little at a time."

Turning back around, she snuggled her face back into place in the crook of Sawyer's neck and shoulder. "Fuck me good, Sawyer," she whispered in his ear.

He gripped her ass tighter. "Sure thing, darlin'."

Daisy smiled to herself at the sweet term of endearment. After tonight, Sawyer could call her darlin' anytime he wanted.

Beau picked up the pace first, with Sawyer quickly following suit. While Beau drove into her deep and slow, Sawyer shortened his thrusts, spending more time grinding on her clit.

"Oh yeah, boys. Do it like that."

Daisy had no idea if they could hear her muffled words, and she really didn't care. She simply had to talk at a time like this—it felt too good to just keep to herself.

"Harder," she begged. "Fuck me harder."

Beau took her at her word, grabbing the loop of her harness and yanking her back fiercely on the pulsing width of cock.

"More," she demanded. "Give it to me, Beau."

He took that as permission to take her ass any way he wanted, which turned out to be long and hard. But instead of batting her nerve endings to near-unconsciousness, his deep pumping felt better than anything in her life.

Shaking under his forceful fucking, she leaned in and whispered in Sawyer's ear again. "You're not going to let him get away with just fucking my ass hard, are you, babe?"

Sawyer didn't answer. He only grabbed her hips in a grip that was going to leave fabulous fingerprints on her creamy skin come morning and shoved his cock up into her pussy until he was banging her G-spot like a drum.

Within seconds, she was being jerked around like a cock-filled ragdoll as two full grown men had their way with both of her nether openings. Dang, this was unreal.

Daisy didn't try to communicate anything intelligent after that. Instead, she moaned over and over. And then, because she couldn't control herself, she sank her teeth into Sawyer's shoulder—for no other reason than because this fucking they were giving her was going to drive her insane.

She didn't know how long she screamed—Seconds? Minutes?—before she realized she was coming.

Between the cockhead poking her G-spot, and the thick, brawny shaft sawing in and out of her hyper-sensitive asshole, she came harder than a human being should ever come—and she didn't stop.

Some primitive part of her animal senses recognized the signs that told her both men were coming, too—the super-tight muscles, the low pitched grunts, the way they gripped her body like they were afraid she might get away.

They were filling her up and she loved every second of it. These two cowboys, and their perfect cocks, were all hers.

At some point, their strenuous thrusting stopped. Her orgasm didn't. Instead, it subsided to a constant rippling spasm between her ass and pussy that was out of this world. Thank God, Sawyer and Beau didn't jerk their hard-ons out of her at that moment. She would have likely considered violence if they had.

Instead, they stayed where they were, pulsing their cocks into her gently, letting her glide down from her place among the clouds in a nice, gentle descent.

Chapter Eight

When they slid out, it was so relaxed and natural she barely noticed it. What finally intruded on her senses at some point was the realization that her back was chilly. Where was Beau?

"Cold," she mumbled.

The word sounded muffled, like there was something in her mouth. She slowly opened her eyes to discover that her teeth were still firmly planted in Sawyer's shoulder muscles.

She jerked back in alarm. Dang, she'd had actually broken skin. "Oh, crap! I bit you. I'm so sorry!"

She moved to climb off him so she could run to the bathroom and get a towel, but strong arms encircled her and held her right where she was.

"You're not going anywhere, darlin'," Sawyer whispered in that drowsy tone of a man who had come just come long and hard.

"B-but I bit you. Let me at least go get a towel."

"I don't need a towel. And if I do, Beau can get it. I like you right where you are. Besides, it's no worse than any of the scrapes I've gotten from being tossed off a horse." His sensuous mouth curved. "And riding broncs, I've been tossed off a bunch."

Daisy frowned at the mark on his shoulder. Now that she looked at it more closely, she saw the skin wasn't really broken, just red where her teeth had dug in.

A deep chuckle came from behind her. She turned to see Beau sitting back on his heels shaking his head. "Relax, sweetheart. You were in the throes of passion when you did it. Besides, I kind of think Sawyer liked it. He definitely seemed to be enjoying himself."

She turned back to Sawyer. He was lying there with a blissed-out look on his face. She re-examined his neck. So, maybe it wasn't quite as bad as she'd thought, especially if he liked it. "Are you sure it's okay?"

He grinned up at her. "I'm sure. In fact, I may have to get you to do it next time."

Daisy wasn't going to promise to bite him, but she definitely liked the idea of them getting together again. She cuddled back on Sawyer's chest and kissed his shoulder in apology. Beau stretched out beside them and threw his arm over her, immediately warming her sweat-cooled skin.

She closed her eyes and savored the warm pulse throb between her legs. Her pussy and her ass were both throbbing gently, tiny orgasmic tremors in time with her heartbeat. She had an almost uncontrollable urge to reach down and finger herself, just to see if she could tweak a few more spasms out of her exhausted body. She didn't bother—why mess with perfection?

But while the orgasms had been off the charts incredible, it was the pure physical contact that had her purring with contentment. She'd had sex with men before—though not two of them at the same time—but she'd never felt this close to any of them. Beau and Sawyer were connected to her in a way no other man would ever be.

Without understanding exactly what, she knew something monumental had taken place tonight. What they'd shared was something special and unique that needed to be explored.

She felt movement behind her and then Beau's mouth was near her ear. "So how was that ride?"

Daisy peeked over her shoulder to look at him. He was smiling—probably because he already knew the answer to that silly-ass question. Still, lovin' that good deserved a response.

She pressed a kiss to his scruff-roughened jaw. "That was the ride of my life."

Beau cupped her chin, turning her to face him so he could kiss her mouth. When he was done, Sawyer did the same. She ran her tongue over her lips, enjoying the taste of them as she rolled onto her back to lie between them. Both men pushed themselves up on their elbows. She ran her gaze over their naked bodies.

Both men had made their condoms disappear in that mysterious way only men seem to have a grip on. Their cocks looked…happy.

"You're amazing," Beau said softly.

"I'll second that" Sawyer agreed.

She smiled. "Thank you for the compliment. I think you guys are pretty dang amazing, too. And all three of us together? Well, that's something altogether special."

Beau grinned. "I won't disagree with that."

"Me, either." Sawyer regarded her thoughtfully. "What d'ya say we make this more than a one-time thing?"

Her pulse skipped a beat. She'd been thinking that very thing. "You mean you want to get together at the next rodeo we all ride in?"

He inclined his head.

"You don't know how much I'd love that, but I'm taking the next few months off. I won't be riding again until spring."

She couldn't imagine waiting that long to see these two.

Sawyer looked at Beau, and it seemed to Daisy that some kind of unspoken message passed between them. Beau nodded, then looked at her.

"We were both planning on taking some time off ourselves," he said. "I know it's forward and all, but we were hoping to get together

Ride of Her Life

before the next rodeo. Even if you weren't planning to take some time off."

Daisy looked at Sawyer. "Is that the way of it?"

His mouth curved. "Hell, yeah. Three months is way too long to wait to see you."

She leaned over and kissed each of them, hoping she made her sudden and complete attraction to both man very clear.

She wasn't usually an impulsive type of woman. Whether working, competing or just plain shopping for a new dress, she usually thought everything out thoroughly before acting on it. A few extraordinary hours in a rather extraordinary day was about to change all that.

"I live just south of Oklahoma City." She couldn't believe that hadn't come up in their conversation. She tended to remember that both of these boys lived in Texas, but she didn't know where—Texas was big place. "What about you guys?"

"I live in Amarillo," Beau said.

"Lubbock," Sawyer added. "Both pretty close to Oklahoma City."

She chewed on her lower lip. "You know, I have a good amount of space at my ranch, if you two want to hang your hats there for a bit."

Whoa. She couldn't believe she'd thrown that out there. Pretty freaking bold.

The two men didn't even look at each other this time before they answered.

Sawyer smiled. "I've always liked Oklahoma City, darlin'."

Beau grinned. "Sweetheart, I'd be there if you told us you lived in Alaska."

Daisy sighed, relief and pleasure coursing through her in equal amounts. "I'm sure you both have stuff to do before you come up, but you're welcome anytime—"

Beau leaned over and put a finger to her lips. "If it's okay with you, we'll just tag along behind you when you drive back."

That was definitely okay with her, though she couldn't help but be kind of amused that Sawyer apparently had no problem with Beau answering for him.

She kissed them both long and lingeringly on the mouth, then scooted to the foot of the bed and hopped off.

"Where you going?" Sawyer asked. "Aren't you going to sleep here with us?"

She turned to give them a huge grin. "I'm definitely sleeping here, you can bet those gorgeous muscles of yours on it. I just need to get my toothbrush and stuff."

They chuckled, lying on the bed and watching as she gathered up her clothes.

"Daisy." She turned at Beau's voice, cowboy boots in hand. "You're going to have to take my surcingle off before you get dressed, you know."

She looked down at the leather harness, her brow furrowing in disappointment. Maybe she could figure out a way to get dressed without taking the thing off. But if there was one, she couldn't think of it. With a sigh, she walked over to stand beside the bed so Beau could undo the buckles and take off her new favorite sex toy.

She felt naked without the wide piece of leather, and she couldn't help looking at the harness longingly as Beau draped it across the bottom of the bed.

Sawyer chuckled. "No worries, sweetheart. It'll still be here when you get back."

She blushed, but couldn't help laughing as she yanked on her jeans and boots. She threw on her shirt without a bra.

"I'll be back in a few minutes. Keep the bed warm for me," she called over her shoulder as she hurried to the door.

Once there, she stopped, and whirled around, her hand on the doorknob. Both of her cowboys were lounging on the bed watching her with what she could only describe as contented expressions.

On impulse, she ran back over and kissed both fabulously naked men. God, she could just rip off her clothes and throw herself on them right now. Not to have sex again, but just to rub herself all over them like a cat in heat.

"This is going to be so good, isn't it?"

She hadn't even realized she'd said the words out loud until both men grinned.

"Something special," Sawyer agreed.

Beside him, Beau nodded, his dark eyes full of promise.

She couldn't help herself—she leaned down for another kiss.

"Daisy," Beau interrupted her mid-kiss. "Go get your toothbrush now, or you might not get out of here until morning."

Would that be such a bad thing? But they did need to get some sleep. Hauling Playdough behind her, it would take two days minimum to get back home. That was a lot of driving without rest.

"Okay."

She headed for the door, but found herself stopping again—this time at the foot of the bed. She scooped up the leather harness she'd been wearing for the last two hours or so and draped it over her shoulder.

"Okay, now I'm ready." She blew them a kiss. "Back in a flash."

"Daisy, what are you going to say if someone asks you what that harness is for?" Beau called out.

She leaned back in the door and gave both men a grin. "I'll tell them this is what a real cowgirl wears—when they're getting ridden by two hot cowboys. All the fashionable buckle bunnies will want one by next season."

The men were still laughing as the door closed behind her. Daisy ran for the elevator. She couldn't get that toothbrush fast enough.

Read on for a sexy excerpt from TEAM ROPING, the second book in Paige Tyler's Buckle Bunnies Series!

Available now!

TEAM ROPING

Copyright © 2012 by Paige Tyler

Dallas's gaze went to Mack and Ked. They were both lounging back on their bar stools, looking more handsome than two men had a right to be. Since they'd hung around this long, they obviously weren't going anywhere. For the first time, she started thinking she might really end up with company for the evening.

But which one would she take home with her? Whoever it was, they were definitely going to her place. She wasn't a hotel kind of girl.

She gave them a careful perusal as she rinsed out the blender she'd used to make the cosmic screwdriver. They were both damn hot, each in his own unique way.

Mack was broader and more muscular. Ked had that lean, wiry look that so many rodeo riders possessed. Mack's hair was a bit shorter than Ked's, but she'd have no problem getting her fingers lost in either man's.

Both men were at least a foot taller than she was—that was important. She liked a guy who could pull her into his arms and make her melt. That didn't work out so well when a woman was taller than her man.

Both had that slight stubble on their jaws she found so attractive. Her hand just itched to caress all that scruff.

Both had very interesting bulges in their jeans, too—bulges that made her mouth water with delight at the thought of how well-endowed they must be.

Hell, both men even had damn near perfect boots on—she'd caught a glimpse when she'd leaned over the bar to talk to them earlier.

So how was she supposed to decide between them?

She didn't know, but figured she couldn't go wrong either way. Something told her both men would be championship buckle material in the sack. The image made her pussy suddenly throb. She would have slid her hand down for a caress or two, but the customers probably would have noticed her playing with herself.

Dallas bit her lip to stifle a moan and glanced at the clock again. One-thirty. It was a little early to give last call, but she did it anyway. The regulars grumbled at that, but she pacified them quickly enough by announcing the final round was on the house.

Mack and Ked both looked relieved to hear it was closing time. To her surprise, they grabbed some towels from behind the bar and wiped down the tables as customers slowly trickled out. They sure were eager to get her into bed, weren't they? She almost told them they didn't have to help, but then she got a look at their jean-clad butts as they turned to put the chairs up on the tables and forgot what she'd been going to say. Damn, those were some great asses.

Since she had two men more than willing to help clean up the place, Dallas let Caleb and the waitresses go early. Her cook, Marsala, left as soon as she cleaned up the kitchen and put away the leftovers.

As Dallas watched the two men sweep the floor—and eye each other like a pair of ornery bulls—she called cabs for the patrons too blasted to walk home, much less drive. She was grateful to Mack and Ked for helping her get those who'd over-imbibed into their rides when they got there. That was usually the worst job of the night, but for the rodeo cowboys rustling drunks was probably nothing compared to manhandling a couple hundred pounds of pissed-off steer.

"I need to do some paperwork before I leave," she said as they closed the door behind the last of the customers. "You'll both be here when I come out of the office, right?"

"I can't speak for Ked, but I'm not going anywhere," Mack said.

"Me, either," Ked agreed.

Her lips curved. She hoped that'd be their answer.

Dallas quickly counted up the credit card receipts and cash, then locked everything in the safe in her office. It took a few more minutes to handle the accounting books. Mostly because she was preoccupied with the two horny cowboys out there cleaning up for her as she marked down Sara as being out while throwing some overtime cash to her other workers for handling the big rodeo rush so well. What the heck was she going to do with Mack and Ked?

They were both gorgeous as sin, both obviously interested in her, and both just looking for a night of no-strings-attached fun. In other words, both were perfect for her. Unfortunately, there was no practical way to choose between them.

She supposed she could ask each man for a kiss and see which was better. Kind of like test driving a car. Then again, maybe that wasn't the best idea. As competitive as these two were, it'd likely start a fist fight between them, and she'd be left with a busted up bar and no sex.

Sighing, she turned off the light and walked out of her office to find her potential bedmates leaning casually back against the bar and looking good enough to eat. It was useless. There was no way she could choose between them.

So why should she have to?

Dallas almost gasped at the thought. What was she saying, that she wanted to have a threesome with them? It was something she'd always fantasized about—didn't every woman? Here was her chance to do it for real. Only a fool would pass that up.

Of course, she had no idea if these two cowboys would go for it.

They'd turned down the lights in the bar until the place felt more like an old-fashioned speakeasy than a modern cowboy bar. She liked it—the darkened room set the perfect ambience for what she intended.

They had also flipped the switch on the welcome light in the front window. Now it read *Closed—Come Back Real Soon!*

These two thought of everything.

Everything except the possibility that she wanted to sleep with both of them, she'd wager.

Dallas put a little extra wiggle in her walk as she approached the two men. Their gazes slid down her body like warm honey to settle on her swaying hips. She had their undivided attention—good.

She came to a halt in front of them, then made a point of looking at the bar which they'd not only cleaned, but polished, as well as the stacks of crated glassed they'd washed and dried.

"Thanks for all the help," she said. "If you hadn't, I'd be stuck here for another hour."

"No problem." Mack grinned. "I think I can speak for Ked when I say we definitely had an ulterior motive."

She let a slow, sexy smile pull up the corners of her lips. "Really? And what motive is that?"

Mack pushed away from the bar to close the distance between them. This near, she could smell his cologne and that unmistakable scent of pure masculine yumminess. Dang, it was amazing how arousing a man's scent could be.

"Oh, I think you know," he said in that soft rumbling voice of his. "The sooner we close up this bar, the sooner one of us gets your clothes off."

The blatant confidence in his words made little goose bumps chase each other across her skin. She licked her lips.

"That's a pretty good motive."

"Yeah, it is." Ked nudged Mack aside and moved in front of her. "And I think you're as interested in getting your clothes off as we are. The only thing you have to decide is who's going to get to see you naked—me or Mack?"

Dallas laughed and pushed past both of them to walk over to the bar. Stepped up on the foot rail, she turned and leveled herself up until she was seated on the highly polished wood. She wiggled back and forth on top of the bar, wondering briefly what it would be like to get fucked up there.

But right now she had to focus on this next part—or she might not be getting fucked tonight at all.

She lounged back on the palms of her hands, kicking her booted feet and giving them her naughtiest smile.

"That part is easy. I'm not going to sleep with either of you." She gave them a sultry look. "Unless I sleep with both of you."

Both men stood there staring at her in stunned silence. From the looks on their faces, they clearly didn't like the idea. Damn. Maybe this hadn't been such a good suggestion.

Ked's eyes narrowed. "Are you serious?"

Then again, maybe this might still work. She nodded. "I'm very serious. You two have spent the whole night trying to charm my pants off, and I'm more than willing to let that happen."

She moved her hands to her belt buckle and slowly began to undo it. Their eyes locked on her movements as if she'd reached for a gun.

"But I've decided it'd be wrong to choose between you—and that I shouldn't have to. If you both want me, you can have me, but you have to be willing to work together. Is that something you can do?"

The way the two men eyed each other made her seriously doubt her sexual magnetism. They looked as if they'd rather shoot each other than bed her together.

She stopped working her buckle and looked at her watch instead.

"If you two can't handle that, you might want to hurry on down the street to The Last Chance Saloon. They stay open a little later than the rest, and there might be a few lonely girls left looking for a cowboy to ride."

Mack and Ked looked at each other again. After a moment, Ked nodded. Mack nodded back.

"We agree—on one condition," Ked said. "At the end of the night, you have to honestly tell us which one of us is better in the sack."

"And no wimping out with one of those, *you were both so wonderful* lines," Mack added. "We want an honest answer."

Dallas felt her whole body start to vibrate. Two hunky cowboys competing to prove themselves the best lover? How could a girl lose in a situation like this? "Deal," she said.

She was lying through her teeth, of course. There was no way she was going to give them the answer they were looking for, but she'd deal with that later. If things went the way she hoped, both men would be so exhausted after she was done with them they wouldn't have enough energy to worry about their silly sexual competition.

####

Ride of Her Life

Other Books by Paige Tyler

SERIES

The Buckle Bunnies Series
Ride of Her Life
Team Roping
Ride 'em Hard

The Badge Bunnies Series
Seducing Officer Barlowe
Two Cops, A Girl and A Pair of Handcuffs
A Cop, His Wife and Her Best Friend
Ride-Along
Hands-On Training

The Cowboy Series
Karleigh's Cowboys
And The Ranch Hand Makes Three
More Than a Cowboy (Special Two-Book Set)

Alaskan Werewolves Series
Animal Attraction
Animal Instinct

The Cutler Brothers Series
Cade
Madoc
The Cutler Brides

Modern Day Vampires
Vampire 101

The Friends Series
Spicing Up Her Marriage
Taking Her Friends Advice
It's Just a Job

Paige Tyler

INDIVIDUAL BOOKS

Western
Kayla and the Rancher

Paranormal
Dead Sexy
Just Right
The Magic Spell
Contemporary
Security Risk
The Postman Always Comes Twice
Good Cop, Bad Girl
Mr. Right-Now
Erotic Exposure
Unmasked
Sexy Secret Santa
If You Dare
Librarian By Day
Protective Custody
Samantha and the Detective
Nosy By Nature
All She Wants for Christmas
The Trouble with New Year's Resolutions
Austin Malone, Private Eye
The Girl Next Door
Bridezilla
A Date for the Wedding

Sci-Fi
Cindra's Bounty Hunter
Pirate's Woman
The Ambassador's Daughter
Not the Man She Thought

Free-Read
Caught Red Handed

~~*~*

Sex Ed Cowboy Style

Ugly Stick Saloon Series, Book 1

By Myla Jackson

Kendall has loved sexy cowboy Ed Judson since the first time she saw him taming wild horses. Now Kendall is twenty-one, legal and ready to be more than friends. In her bid to win his affections she asks Ed to give her a few Sex Education lessons about what makes a cowboy hot.

Ed promised Kendall's brother he'd keep an eye on his little sister while he's away defending their country. But Ed's pretty darn certain Sex Education lessons aren't what big brother had in mind. Caught between his pledge and a recently matured little sex kitten, Ed struggles to keep his word, while giving Kendall what she wants, Sex Ed.

Warning: Determined young woman, unsuspecting cowboy and a feisty roommate add up to fun lessons on how to make a cowboy hot.

Chapter One

Edward Judson slapped his dusty cowboy hat against his leg as he led his black gelding into the barn. The sun baked the weathered boards of the exterior, while the interior remained relatively cool. It took a few moments for his eyes to adjust to the shadows. "I traded that stock yesterday, made enough to pay off my land and put a hefty chunk of cash down on a house."

"Good move." Grant Fowler slung a leg over the pinto mare and dropped to the ground.

Ed owed Grant a lot for teaching him everything he knew about trading shares on the stock market. The man owned a 5,000-acre ranch for a reason. Not because he was good at raising horses, but because he was damned good at managing money.

"You don't need my advice anymore, Ed," Grant said. "You could go into financial planning yourself with a few courses for certification."

"Not interested." Ed had just begun to understand the stock market's full potential and seeing the fruits of his trades pay off. But he didn't need a lot of money, just enough for his own purposes.

"You gonna work training horses for other people like me the rest of your life?"

"Nope." Ed grinned. "Not that I don't appreciate the work and all, but I got plans of my own."

"Whatcha gonna do with two hundred acres, Ed?"

"Get married someday, settle down, raise a family and some horses. It's what I'm good at." He shifted his boots in the loose dirt of the barn floor. "The horses part."

"You're good at day-trading, dude."

"I'll do that on the side so that I can afford my horses too."

Grant shook his head, a smile spreading across his face. "Okay, I get it. Can't say that I blame you. At least when you're trading for yourself, you don't have the responsibility of other people's money hanging over you."

"You hit the nail on the head."

"So how is babysitting Connor Mason's sister? Saw her at the Ugly Stick Saloon last night." Grant whistled. "Looks to me like you got yourself a hot little handful in that one."

Ed's muscles tightened, his pulse kicking up a notch as he stepped around the end of the stall. "What do you mean?"

Grant held up his hands. "Nothing, buddy. Not a thing. Just that she's a pretty girl."

"Yeah and every man in the building was drooling over her. I get it.

Sex Ed

Don't add to the crowd, will ya?" He should never have offered to look out for Kendall Mason. Especially now that she was over twenty-one and legal in every way. As far as Ed was concerned, her body should be considered a class-one felony.

Every time he looked at her, he wanted to commit all kinds of lewd and lascivious acts. With two hard pulls, he yanked the leather strap from the girth around the horse's belly and let it fall, swinging to the other side.

Grant leaned on his saddle, apparently in no hurry whatsoever to groom his own horse or end the current conversation. "I don't see how you do it."

"Do what?" As far as Ed was concerned, Grant talked too much. If he wasn't the boss, he'd probably tell him so. Hell, he might anyway.

"I don't know how you can keep your hands off her."

For the past six months, Ed had been fighting that very urge. "Grant, you talk too much." His hands ached to get hold of Kendall and touch her in ways that had nothing to do with brotherly love.

Grant laughed out loud, then continued to rub it in.

Much to Ed's agony.

"With that body and those boobs, the temptation would kill me."

"Resist, or I might just have to kill you. And I'd hate to lose my job because I killed the boss." Ed tossed the saddle onto a nearby saddle rack and grabbed a brush from the shelf, eager to get the task done and get home.

When Grant made no move to remove his horse's saddle, it was all Ed could do not to throw the brush at the man. With quick, calming strokes, Ed curried his gelding, refusing to respond to any other conversation from Grant.

"Okay, okay, I get the hint." Grant finally turned toward his saddle and removed the strap around the horse's belly. "I'm just saying you're a better man than I am."

Ed snorted. As he ran the brush over the horse's hindquarters, his cell phone vibrated his back pocket. He pulled it out and clicked the talk button. "Yeah."

"Ed?"

Every red blood cell leaped to attention at the sound of Kendall's voice. Then they all sped south to pool in his groin. Grant had it right. Keeping his hands off Kendall was only half his problem. Keeping his mind off her had become an impossibility.

"What do you need Kendall?"

"When are you coming home? I have a project I need your help on."

"I'm not much good with school projects. Get one of your

classmates to help you out."

"I would, but I'd rather you help me on this one. It's special and you're my best choice," her breath whooshed out slowly before she continued, "the only man I trust."

Ed sucked in a deep breath, his imagination running rampant over the close quarters they'd be working in. He couldn't do it. No way. *Just tell her*. "I'll be home in fifteen minutes."

"Oh, good. I'll be waiting," she whispered into his ear, and the phone went silent.

Ed had a good start on a full-blown erection by the time he climbed into his truck and turned it toward Temptation, Texas, the little backwater town he'd been born and raised in.

The short ride home from the Rockin' G Ranch wasn't nearly long enough to cool the heat building in his loins. Tomorrow, he'd start looking for a different place to live. He'd planned on living in the apartment below Kendall's until he had his own house built, but the way things were going, the way he felt about his best friend's little sister…He couldn't last much longer without doing something stupid.

As he turned onto the street where the old Ross house stood, a convertible backed out of the driveway he shared with the other two occupants. A muscular, bare-chested young man smiled and waved as he passed by with the top down, his long, bright blond hair blowing in the breeze.

His fingers tightened on the steering wheel and a frown settled between Ed's brows. Who the hell was that leaving the house he shared with Kendall and Lacey? Better be one of Lacey's conquests. She was old enough to manage her own affairs. Kendall, on the other hand, had barely been twenty-one for a few weeks. She'd better not be messing around on Ed's watch.

As he shifted into park, he glanced up at the window to Kendall's apartment. The blinds were open and Kendall stood with her side to the window, wearing nothing but a thin, lace bra and thong panties. She turned her back to the window and unclipped the bra, letting it fall down over her arms to the floor.

She might as well be naked—the thin strap of the thong cutting a line between her butt cheeks hid nothing.

Ed moaned, his cock twitched, and blood rushed in to make it swell behind his zipper. He forced anger to follow the powerful rush of lust. Did the girl have so little sense as to leave her window wide open so that any peeping Tom could look in?

With the storm of lust and righteous anger driving him forward, Ed leaped out of the car, passed the door to his apartment on the first floor and took the steps two at a time to the upper apartment where Kendall lived. He hammered on the door until Kendall flung it open.

"Oh, Ed." She cupped her hands over her naked breasts, like that did anything to hide their beautiful, lush fullness from Ed's vision. "Where's the fire?"

Ed pushed past her and marched to the window on the other side of the apartment, yanking the string on the shade so hard, the shade popped out of its slot and clattered to the floor.

Kendall giggled behind him, her eyes going wide when Ed glared.

He gathered the shade from the floor, fit the ends into the slot and lowered it with more precision and care this time. When he was done, he faced Kendall, and breathed a sigh to find her clutching a shirt to her chest. "Don't undress in front of the window. I thought your mother taught you better than that."

"There's not anyone on this street who'd care but Old Man Frantzen." She tossed her hair. "I'm sure he's so blind he couldn't see that far anyway."

Ed jerked his thumb toward the window. "You never know what perverts are lurking out there looking for an eyeful. And honey, you were giving an eyeful and then some."

Her eyelids closed to half-mast and she sidled close. "Perverts? Hum…sounds interesting." Slim fingers climbed up his chest and the shirt she held slipped lower, letting one perky nipple peek through.

Ed reached out and lifted the shirt to cover her flesh, realizing his mistake as soon as the backs of his fingers brushed over her naked skin. Stifling a groan, he jumped back. "Just close the blinds before you strip, will ya?"

"Yes, sir!" Kendall popped a salute.

That pesky shirt slipped down again to expose the other pretty breast.

A moan escaped Ed's throat and he dove for the door.

***

Kendall stood at her door as Ed beat a hasty retreat down the steps to his apartment. No sooner had his door slammed than Lacey's door opened across the hall from Kendall.

"Well?" Lacey pushed Kendall into her apartment and closed the door behind her. "How'd it go?"

"I don't know." Kendall frowned. "He came in all angry and left like a cat with his tail on fire."

Lacey's face split in a grin. "Did you show him some boobs?"

Heat flooded Kendall's cheeks. She held her tank top in front of her like she had positioned it for Ed. "I did this side first." She switched to let the other side be exposed. "I did this side and when he answered the door, all I had was this." She dropped the shirt altogether and covered her breasts with her hands.

"Did he touch them?"

"Yes, and no." Kendall's chest rose and fell on a heartfelt sigh. "Only to cover them."

"Did he mention Cory leaving with his shirt off?"

"Not a word." Kendal dropped onto the sofa. "What am I doing wrong?"

Lacey laughed out loud. "Honey, you did it all right."

"Then why isn't he taking the hint?"

"Oh, he took it all right. I'll bet he's taking a really cold shower right now. Shh. Listen." Lacey cupped her fingers around her ear, a smile curling the corners of her lips. "Yup, he's in the shower." She clapped her hands together. "Now, as soon as the water shuts off, be at his door ready to launch Plan B."

"I don't know. He didn't seem too excited by the idea of me being naked."

"Of course, he isn't excited by the idea of you getting naked with anyone else. I take it he closed the blinds based on the noise I heard a minute ago?" She stood with her arms crossed.

"Yeah, so?" Kendall shrugged. "My brother would have done the same. Face it, the man has a brother complex. He can't touch me because he thinks of me as his kid sister."

"Then your job is to show him you're neither his sister, nor a kid."

The pipes clanked in the wall beside Kendall, indicating the shower had been turned off below. Kendall dragged in a deep breath and let it slowly in an attempt to slow her pulse. It didn't work.

Lacey's mouth set in a firm line. "That's your cue." She herded Kendall to the door, grabbing the tank top from the floor. "Don't be too obvious too fast, it tends to scare men off. Remember Plan B. Make him think you're after someone else. Make him jealous enough to cross the brother line. Trust me, there will be no returning."

Lacey practically shoved her down the stairs.

Halfway down, Kendall got cold feet. Really cold feet. Okay, so the cool wood against her bare feet felt good compared to the heat rising up her neck into her face. She couldn't do this. She'd never been this forward in her entire life, always playing the good girl, refusing to give her brother any trouble after he'd taken on the huge responsibility of raising her when their parents had died in a car crash. Having just graduated high school, he'd barely been able to tie his own shoelaces and he'd never tied hers.

Sex Ed

But Connor learned and attended the small college in town while showing up at all of her school events, shuttling her to and from soccer practice like any other soccer mom. He'd grown up before he'd had a chance to be a kid.

Kendall made life as easy on him as possible. She understood the sacrifice he'd made by giving up a scholarship to the University of Texas to stay home and care for his kid sister.

As soon as she graduated and was safely accepted to the local college, he'd gotten his commission into the U.S. Army and left Temptation, Texas. He'd only agreed to go on the condition his best friend would look out for his little sister.

Therein lay the problem. Some of the reasons for which Kendall had fallen in love with Ed were the same reasons he wouldn't look at her as other than Connor's little sister. He was loyal to his friends, protective to a fault, and he kept his word no matter what. And four years later, he was no different. Connor had managed to miss being deployed for the first three of Kendall's college years, but now he was deployed and Kendall was about to graduate. If she was going to get Ed to notice her, it had to be soon.

She'd hoped when she turned twenty-one, Ed would start seeing her as a grown woman, not a kid sister. Two months had passed since her birthday and nothing had changed. After a come-to-Temptation meeting with her best friend, Lacey, she'd made the decision to take matters into her own hands and push the issue.

Thus Plan A of Operation Sex Ed. Let him see what he's missing.

Kendall still wasn't all that sure that standing practically naked in the window had done the trick. Ed had reacted just like Ed always reacted, all protective and big-brotherly.

Enter Plan B.

Kendall stood in front of Ed's door, her hand poised over the wood. "I can't do this."

From above, Lacey called out, "Yes. You. Can."

Kendall jumped and knocked on the door before she could change her mind. As she waited for Ed to answer, she realized she was still naked and carrying the tank top. Her heart palpitated as she shoved her arms through the shirt. She'd just pulled it down over her breasts when Ed jerked open the door.

He wore nothing but a towel wrapped around his middle, his hair and body dripping from his recent shower.

Desire slammed into her belly, spreading like wildfire, frying every brain cell to a crisp. For a moment, she couldn't remember why she'd come down the stairs, then Lacey's words echoed in her head. *Remember*

Plan B. Smoothing the panic out of her face and voice, she smiled up at him. "Got a minute?" Without waiting for a response, she waltzed past him, inhaling the fresh scent of soap and Ed. As she sidled by, she swung her hips in such a manner as to invite just about any hot-blooded male to rutting season with a grown woman, not a little girl. She'd purposely not pulled her shirt over her rear, leaving her naked ass exposed to his view. The thong between her butt cheeks didn't count for anything.

"Got any clothes?" Ed asked, searching the hallway before he closed the door, turned and leaned on it. "Please tell me you don't run around like that in front of the kid that left as I was getting home?"

"Cory?" She faced Ed, twisting the hem of her tank top, drawing it up enough Ed could see the triangle of black lace that was the bulk of material in the thong panties. "He likes it when I dress like this." She stood straighter, her unbound breasts naturally jutting forward. "I didn't come to talk about Cory, I came to ask for your help."

"My help?" Ed glanced down at his towel. "Could it wait until I'm dressed?"

Kendall shrugged, her lips twisting in a teasing smile. "Dressed or undressed doesn't matter to me. I need lessons, and I can't think of anyone that I trust as much as I trust you to teach me."

"Exactly what kind of lessons did you have in mind?" Ed pushed away from the door and strode through the living room to the bedroom.

Kendall had to resist the urge to grab the towel and yank it loose. Her blood raced through her veins, molten hot for the man, and he wasn't aware she existed as anything other than Connor's sister. Why was fate so cruel?

She followed him, standing in the doorway of his bedroom, imagining lying naked in his bed, making mad passionate love. An ache built in her core, fortifying her determination to make Operation Sex Ed work.

Ed reached into his closet for a pair of jeans.

Kendall launched Plan B. "I need lessons on how to attract a man."

He spun to face her, dropping the jeans to the floor. His towel slipped and he barely caught it before it ended up with the jeans around his ankles. "What?"

Her gaze swept over his thick thighs and narrow hips, her pulse pounding in the vein at the base of her throat. "I want lessons on how to attract a man," she repeated more slowly, as if speaking to someone with limited faculties.

"I heard what you said, but what are you talking about?" He clutched his towel in front of him, the effect displaying a significant amount of leg, thigh, hips and groin.

Sex Ed

Kendall licked her lips, her gaze fixed on the position still covered by the towel, willing Ed to expose even more. Her pussy creamed at the mere thought of seeing his cock. How would it be to hold it in her hands? Kendall's breath caught in her throat. In an attempt to concentrate, she pulled her glance up to his face. "I think I'm in love with a guy, but he doesn't have a clue I exist. I want you to help me attract his attention."

"Aren't you a little young for playing games with guys?"

"I'm not seventeen anymore, in case you hadn't noticed, and these," she pointed to her breasts, the nipples puckering on cue through the thin material of the tank top, "aren't getting any action. I need help."

Ed ran a hand through his hair, his gaze glancing off her breasts and hitting every corner of the room without looking back. "Tell me you didn't just say your...your...oh, hell, aren't getting any action."

"Boobs?" She raised her brows and stared at him. "I'm all grown up, Mr. Judson, not the little girl that used to follow you and Connor around."

"I know you're all grown up, but—"

"I'm twenty-one, single and almost finished with college." She jammed her hands onto her hips. "I deserve a sex-life just like anyone else. If you aren't going to help me figure this out, I'll find someone who will."

"Whoa, wait a minute." Ed held up his hands. "Just exactly what is it you want me to teach you? Not that I'm agreeing to this lunacy."

"I want you to show me what turns on a guy. Kind of like a sex education class for dummies. Only I'm not planning on practicing the abstinence part." Her hands skimmed over her breasts, curving down over her hips. "I want the full-blown, how-to-make-him-hot-for-me lessons."

"Holy Hell, you're kidding, right?"

"Do I look like I'm kidding?" She tapped a bare foot, realizing it probably wasn't making a big impression with her bright pink toenail polish. "Not only am I not kidding, I want lessons to begin tonight. And in payment for lessons, the pizza is on me."

"Pizza?"

The knock on the door couldn't have been timed better.

"Right on time." She smiled and fished the twenty-dollar bill out of the triangle of her panties. "I'll be right back. Don't go anywhere, we have work to do."

"Pizza?" Ed stood for a moment as though rooted to the floor, his hand still clutching the towel around his middle, his face pale, probably in shock.

Good. Kendall turned toward the door and called out, "Coming!"

She hadn't taken two steps when Ed caught up with her, ripped the twenty from her fingers and shoved her back in the bedroom. "Stay," he commanded.

Then, wearing nothing but the towel and carrying the twenty, he opened the door to the apartment for Jason, the pizza delivery boy.

"Nice towel." Jason shoved the pizza box at Ed.

For a moment, Ed fumbled with the towel, the twenty and the pizza box.

Kendall fought back the urge to giggle, silently praying he'd slip and drop the towel.

Sadly, Ed managed to pay for the pizza and close the door behind Jason, towel intact around his middle.

Kendall came out into the living room, crossed her arms beneath her chest, giving them a little added lift. "So what's it to be? Will you teach me everything you know about making love, or do I take my pizza elsewhere?"

Chapter Two

Ed's cock twitched, tenting the terrycloth draped around his middle. He felt like an idiot, dressed in a towel, holding a pizza and answering a dynamite-loaded question from the little girl whom he'd promised to protect from lecherous males.

Only Kendall wasn't a little girl anymore and she wanted his help to seduce a man. His tongue wouldn't work, he couldn't find the words needed to talk her out of her cockamamie plan. Instead, he nodded. "Let's have pizza and talk about it."

"First, your promise." She threw her shoulders back and braced her bare feet apart. "I don't want to waste my time and pizza if I need to find someone else who has the experience to teach me what I want to know. Are you up to the challenge or should I check with Whitey Ross. I'm sure he'd show me a thing or two."

Anger boiled up in Ed's craw. "You will do no such thing."

"In case you didn't hear me, I'm single, over twenty-one and capable of making all of my own decisions." She ticked off the list on her fingers. "I just thought that you might be a better choice, given you're not interested in me, and I can trust you not to take advantage. Any more than I deem necessary to learn, of course."

He carried the pizza into the small kitchen and laid it on the counter, immediately regretting his decision. Without the box to run interference, the tent his dick caused jutted out prominently. How could he talk Kendall out of this crazy scheme? He needed time to think through this, time to come up with some plausible reason she should abstain.

"You do realize having sex can lead to—"

"Spare me, will ya?" She rolled her eyes. "I had this conversation with my brother ages ago. I'm on the pill, I have my own supply of condoms, and you will not talk me out of this." She marched toward him, her breasts bouncing with each step.

Ed held his breath, his cock swelling even more the closer she came.

She stopped in front of him. "Are you in, or not?" She planted both hands on her hips and tipped her head to the side. Her determination made the light in her green eyes dance.

Ed wanted nothing more than to be in, all right. But she was Connor's *little sister*.

"Fine. I'll take my pizza elsewhere." She made a grab for the box, leaning past him, her arm sliding across his naked torso.

At the contact, Ed groaned and grabbed her wrist. "Okay, okay. I'll do it. Against my better judgment and barring any lightning bolts from heaven."

Kendall straightened, facing Ed, her breasts pressing against his skin through the thin tank top, the tips, poking out as though teasing him for being weak and agreeing to her scheme.

Was he out of his mind to agree to this? The little girl had definitely grown up. Hell, she sported what...a size D cup, more than a mouthful and...and...he sniffed. A light, citrusy scent curled around his senses, tempting him past redemption. Normally, he hated perfumes, found them usually too strong and annoying, preferring the natural aromas of living things like roses and horse manure. "What's that smell?"

"Must be my perfume. Do you like it?" She tipped her chin and pulled her long blond hair to the side, exposing the graceful line of her neck.

Oh, yeah, he liked.

Too much.

He grabbed her arms and set her away from him. "Quit wearing it. Wear something like Chanel or Candies. Your man should like that." *If he didn't gag first*. "And apply it thick."

Kendall frowned. "Are you sure. Don't you want to smell it again, just to be certain?" She closed the distance and stood on her toes, her body snug against him from her hips to her breasts.

Jaw tight, Ed fought the urge to press her even closer. His cock nudged against her belly as if taking on a life of its own. "Who is this guy?" Ed said through gritted teeth. He grasped her arms and pushed her a safe distance away from him and his randy dick.

She smiled down at the tent his towel made. "Are you always this...um...agitated after a shower?"

He glanced down at the embarrassing tent. "Yes."

"Why don't you lose the towel? I'll need to get used to seeing a man naked. You might as well be the man. One male body looks pretty much like the rest." Her lips twitched, her gaze rising from his stiff member up to his dropped jaw. "Don't you agree?"

"No." Ed's mouth snapped shut. "Not all men are built alike."

"So, how are you different from other men?"

He liked to think he was larger—hell, he'd seen other guys in the locker room after football practice—he had the right to think it. Looking down into little Kendall Mason's bright blue eyes, he coughed. "It's not just the equipment but what you do with it." He shook his head. "Really, are you seriously going through with this?"

Kendall pouted. "Absolutely. I think this is the real deal. I'm in love with a guy that doesn't quite know I exist. I need help attracting him and I don't want to risk screwing it up."

"If he doesn't love you based on your personality, the sex won't be

Sex Ed

enough. Why don't you try abstinence to begin with?"

"Ed, honey, for your information, I'm not a virgin anymore. I got my cherry popped way back when I was eighteen."

Ed's hands fisted, a surge of red-hot rage roaring through his brain, frying a few brain cells along the way. "Who popped your cherry?" He'd find the bastard and wring his virginity-stealing neck.

With a laugh, Kendall reached for a slice of pizza and sat on the edge of the kitchen table. Her legs parted, displaying the silky smooth skin of the inside of her thighs and the triangular wedge of her midnight black thong panties.

Ed's groin tightened even more, and he had to force himself to turn away before he did or said something that indicated the gutter where his mind had fallen. He couldn't get over the image of her pert little ass pressed against the smooth surface of his kitchen table. Ed spun toward the pizza box, grabbed a slice and stared at the shape—a triangle just like the wedge of fabric over Kendall's pussy. He bit in, his tongue slurping the sauce from the sides of his lips—warm, wet, tasty.

"Umm, this is orgasmic, don't you think?"

Kendall's voice was low, silky and spot-on with the way Ed felt at the moment. "It's pizza." He chewed and swallowed, dragging in a deep breath before turning back to face Kendall. "I can't talk you out of this?"

She shook her head, a splash of tomato sauce falling from her lips to the V between her breasts. She giggled, tugged her tank low and scooped the sauce out with a finger, and then looked up at Ed. "You like the sauce more than I do. Want it?" She held out her finger, dripping with the rich sauce that had been warmed by her breasts.

Ed's mouth opened automatically and he sucked her finger into it, licking off the sauce before he came to his senses and realized this was Connor's sister sitting on his table, practically naked, sticking her finger in his mouth and teasing him with triangular wedges. *Holy Hell.* He couldn't do this. Not to his friend, a man fighting for their country in Afghanistan.

Ed grabbed her hand and pulled the finger from his mouth, fully intending on telling her he couldn't, and wouldn't, give her lessons in sex. "Where do you want to start?"

Kendall grinned and clapped her hands. "Tell me what makes a man look at a woman twice."

Full breasts, miniscule tank tops and G-string panties. Ed shook his head. "A pretty smile. Guys like a woman who can make them laugh."

Her forehead puckered into a frown. "That's it? What kind of clothing? What about how she walks?" Kendall hopped off the table and walked across the floor. "Does a man like a woman with a little sway to her hips like this?" She walked sedately across the floor.

No matter how controlled Kendall walked, she was sexy, her hips swaying naturally from side to side. Dressed in nothing but a very loose tank top, that rode up her hips, exposing her ass, the strap of her G-string buried deep between her cheeks. Ed stifled another groan. "A guy would like that." Any man would be a fool or gay not to like what Ed saw.

"Really?" She turned, her brows crinkling again. "Or should I add a little oomph to the hips?" She vamped across the length of the tiny kitchen, one foot crossing over the other, her hips rocking from side to side in an exaggerated swing. Her bra-less breasts swayed, the nipples rubbing against the thin ribbed fabric.

Ed's mouth watered. His dick couldn't get much harder and not explode.

"You liked that, didn't you?" Kendall grinned. "I can tell." She touched the tip of the towel. "That's settled, I'll do that kind of walk to get his attention."

He pulled away from the tip of her finger. "No." Ed grabbed her hips to hold them steady.

"Why not?"

He tried to engage his brain, despite the rush of blood flowing to the lower regions of his body. "Too much of a good thing only makes you look easy."

"And being easy isn't a good thing?" She touched his naked chest with her finger. "Doesn't a guy want to know he stands a chance with the girl?"

His skin heated. Ed captured her finger, his body tense. "Yes, but not all at once."

"Okay then. Minimize the swing of my hips." She smiled up at him. "What about kissing? I've had some experience kissing. Seems most guys start with the tongue. Is that really the right way to begin?"

"Kissing?" Ed gulped. This was going way past anything he could imagine. Think of Connor. Breaking his promise and disappointing his best friend would make him less likely to lose control. "Okay." He closed his eyes and puckered his lips.

"Oh, Ed, please, you look like you're about to suck on a pickle. Be serious and show me what a real first-date kiss should be like." She planted her hands on her hips, pulling the tank taut over her breasts. "I'll bet Whitey would have no problem whatsoever showing me anything I want."

"Whitey has no finesse," Ed growled. "Okay, fine." He gripped her upper arms and pecked her lips with a very chaste, brotherly kiss. "That's good for a first date."

Sex Ed

Kendall's brows rose and she crossed her arms beneath her breasts, lifting them up enough to emphasize the pointy tips. "Really, Ed? That's the best you can do for a first date kiss? I need to know what to expect? How to react?"

"A good knee to the groin would be perfect."

"I'm trying to get the man to fall in love with me, not hit me up with assault and battery charges."

Her full, lovely lips formed a straight line, which on Kendall looked just as sexy as a smile. His determination to stay distant wavered.

"Either show me what to expect or I'll find a better teacher."

"Fine." Frustration exploded inside Ed and he cupped the back of Kendall's head crushing her lips with his. Kendall's mouth parted on a gasp, her tongue meeting his, twisting and stroking, the tang of tomato sauce whetting his appetite for more. She had him kissing her, something he would never have dreamed of, given his promise to her brother.

Her hands circled the back of Ed's neck, feathering through his hair. "How's this?" she said against his mouth. "Do you like this? Will my guy like this?"

"Umm." One hand slid down to cup her ass, pulling her hard against the terrycloth towel and his rock-hard erection. All that stood between his cock and her pussy was a towel, a string and a promise.

"Or, would he prefer this?" She nibbled at his lower lip, then slid her mouth across his chin and down to the pulse beating wildly at the base of his throat. Based on his heart rate and the erection, he couldn't deny his attraction.

So far, so good. But Lacey had said not to push him too far the first day. Go easy, make him want to come to her.

Oh, but she wanted more...now. For the past five years, she'd been in love with her brother's best friend, an awkward place to be. For most of that time, Ed had only seen her as Connor's kid sister. This plan had better work and show Ed she wasn't a little girl anymore.

Reluctantly, Kendall pulled away from Ed and forced an innocent smile to her lips. "Would he like that?"

Ed scrubbed a hand down over his face, his eyes glazed, the point of his cock pressing hard against her belly. "Uh..." He shook his head. "No."

"No?" She feigned surprise. "What *does* get a man excited?"

"Getting naked." Ed's eyes rounded and he clapped a hand over his lips.

Kendall swallowed the big grin fighting for a chance to swamp her face. "Really?" She reached for the hem of her shirt and dragged it halfway up her torso.

Ed's hand shot out, stopping any further ascent. "There are other ways to get a man excited besides getting naked."

"I figured as much. Show me." She let go of the shirt and waited for him to make the next move.

"A woman's hands can be very sexy," Ed blurted.

"You mean like this?" She reached out and circled his cock, towel and all.

Ed sucked in his breath and disengaged her fingers. "Not quite that obvious, although that would get his attention all right. You might save that for the proposal night."

"What about this?" She ran her fingers up his naked torso, something she'd wanted to do for so long. The feel of his muscled skin was so good, she thought she'd died and gone to heaven. Her insides were on fire and she couldn't wait for this plan to take complete affect.

"Yes, maybe tweak the nipples."

She pinched his nipples ever so slightly. "You like that? I mean, a man likes that?"

"With the right woman, anything goes. I don't know why you need me to...to..."

Kendall leaned forward and nibbled his nipple with her teeth.

Ed stiffened, his breathing stopping altogether until she released the nipple. Then all of the air whooshed out of his lungs. "Baby, you don't need me to show you what a man likes."

"Oh, but I do. There's such a fine line between enticing a man and looking like a slut. This man is marriage material. I don't want him to think he can fuck me and ditch me." Her fingers skimmed along his shoulder and downward, weaving into the hairs on his chest. "I want *him* to want *me* enough to work for my affection."

"Okay then, save the nipple sucking for at least the fourth date."

She tipped her head. "Too much too soon?"

He nodded. "Yeah, too much too soon."

Kendall almost laughed. The man had a shell-shocked expression on his face, as if he didn't know how to react to Kendall's come-ons. She almost clapped her hands with her excitement, but she had a long way to go to make him want her badly enough to step completely over the line of loyalty to his best friend.

"Okay, then. Maybe tomorrow we can try the kissing again. I'm on my way to work at the Ugly Stick Saloon." She nodded toward the pizza box. "You can have the rest, but save me one piece I might be hungry when I get back. I have some studying to do late into the night."

"I'll be asleep," Ed said.

His words shot out a little too fast. Probably wanting to discourage her late-night visit. "Not to worry. I have a key. I'll let myself in." She twisted her shirt, making sure she pulled it tight enough to expose the full curve of her breasts. "Don't worry, I'll be very quiet."

His chest rose and fell, the muscle in his jaw twitching.

Oh, yeah, he was barely hanging on by a thread.

She nodded toward his towel. "You might want to do something about that. I'm sure it's not healthy to have a hard-on for that long." Kendall giggled and ran for the door.

The snap of a towel preceded a sharp sting to her butt.

"Ow." She jumped and spun in time to see Ed retracting the towel and holding it over his penis. "What was that for?"

"Forcing me into this crazy scheme of yours. You haven't even told me who this guy is. I've a mind to have a talk with him."

"Oh, no. That wouldn't do at all. I don't want him to know I'm after him. He'd think I was a stalker or something."

"If you don't tell me who he is, I won't continue with the lessons."

"There's always Whitey."

He stepped forward. "I'll kill him if he offers."

"Then I'll find someone else and I won't tell you about him."

His mouth opened and snapped shut. "Brat."

"You love me and you know it." She blew him a kiss and fled through the open door, sure to give him a healthy look at her bare bottom.

If she wasn't mistaken, she'd made the man completely uncomfortable. Based on his continued hard-on throughout the session, the state was exactly the kind of uncomfortable she wanted him to be. Round one: Kendall 1, Ed 0.

Chapter Three

Ed wadded the towel into a tight knot and flung it across the room. What was he thinking by agreeing to Kendall's crazy scheme? It could only lead to trouble, and he'd promised Connor he'd keep his little sister out of trouble until Connor made it back from deployment.

After a glance down at his throbbing boner, he shook his head. Images of Kendall in the window, Kendall in her G-string panties and that damned see-through tank top kept flashing through his mind. He'd never get any relief at this point.

Maybe another cold shower would do it for him. Maybe two or three cold showers. Oh, hell, he didn't want a cold shower, he wanted a satisfying fuck. He grabbed his cell phone and spun through his contacts.

Allison? He shook his head. She'd gotten married two months ago to some guy from Austin.

Danielle? He hit her number and waited for the phone to ring. A piercing tone grated against his ear. "This number has been disconnected or is no longer is service."

Damn!

What about Frankie? Surely, she'd be home and wouldn't mind a quick tumble in bed. He hit her number and waited, his cock twitching.

"Yeah." Frankie answered on the third ring. Children screamed in the background.

"Hi Frankie, it's Ed."

"Oh, Ed, it's been a long time since I heard from you. What's up? Lindsey, put your brother down! Bryan, stop tormenting your sister!"

Ed held the phone away from his ear until the screaming stopped. He'd forgotten she had joint custody of her four children. "Your week to have the kids, is it?"

"Sure is, and Lance gave them to me all hyped up on sugar."

"You're busy. I'll call another time." He started to hit the off button.

"Wait, Ed, I'm free next Saturday. Wanna go out for old time's sake?"

Now that he had her on the phone, seeing Frankie didn't seem such a great idea. She had the grace of a biker babe and the shrill voice of a fishwife, especially when she was mad at someone. "Uh...I'm sorry, Frankie, I'm all tied up next Saturday. Maybe next time."

"Maybe so. Call me."

The hopeful, almost desperate, tone of her voice resonated with his own feelings. Wasn't he just as desperate to find a woman willing to jump in the sack at a moment's notice? Geez had it been that long since he'd gone out on a date? He flung his phone on the couch and marched to the bathroom. Giving the shower handle a vicious twist, he waited for the water to warm, then stepped beneath the spray.

Ed lathered up with soap then his hand closed around his aching dick, sliding up and down, thrusting long and hard, faster and faster until he burst over the edge, his body shuddering with the intensity of his release. Not the best release a man could have, but it would have to do. He had to do something about his lack of female companionship or these crazy, mixed-up sex education sessions with Kendall would kill him.

As he stepped out of the shower, he heard his phone ringing in the other room. God, he hoped it wasn't Frankie. Or worse, Kendall. After jerking off in the shower, he didn't want a repeat hard-on. He wrapped a towel around his waist and ran to catch the call, dripping across the floor. Ed pulled the phone out from under a throw pillow and checked the caller ID. Connor Mason flashed across the screen.

Damn.

Guilt gnawing a hole in his gut, he hit the talk button. Was it fate that had Connor calling tonight of all nights? Or was he psychic and reading Ed's lust-filled thoughts of his baby sister? Ed swallowed hard and forced a cheerful tone. "Hey, buddy, when you comin' home?"

Connor laughed. "I just got here a month ago, and the tour's for no less than fourteen months, you know that. Why? Things getting to you back home?"

"No, no. Nothin' like that. Just askin'." He ran a hand through his wet hair, trying to pull himself together. Connor needed to know everything was going great at home. He had enough to worry about dodging bullets in the Middle East.

"How's that kid sister of mine? Causing you any grief?"

Ed stifled the groan that immediately rose in his chest at the "grief" Kendall had caused him in the past two hours. Keeping in mind the need to keep Connor oblivious to any strife on the home-front, Ed gritted his teeth and lied, "No, not at all. She's being a perfect angel."

"Ha! Now I *know* you're lying."

Crap, he'd laid it on too thick. "Really, she hasn't dropped out of college, she's still working nights and I check on her every day. I'd know if something was up." Ed crossed his fingers and prayed his friend wouldn't question him about Kendall's love life.

"What about guys? Is she seeing anyone?"

"She may have a crush on some guy from one of her classes."

"Really?" Connor's voice tightened.

Ed could kick himself for even mentioning it. "Yeah, they study together at her place."

"Damn. She needs to finish her degree before she gets involved with some jerk."

"Not to worry." Not to worry much, and not at all if Ed could help it. "I'm keeping a close eye on her."

"Got a feeling it'll take more than that. Kendall is too pretty for her own good. She doesn't need to be alone with a guy. You know guys are only thinking about one thing—gettin' some."

Ed's cock throbbed in agreement. "Yeah, pretty much. Although I really think they're studying." But he wasn't sure and he couldn't be sure unless he was at the house all the time. "Besides, she's twenty-one and legal. She can do whatever she wants. No matter what we say."

"I know. I just wish I was there to advise her." Connor sighed. "That's why I asked you to look out for her. She respects you and turns to you like a brother. I know I can trust you to take care of her."

That wad of guilt twisted in Ed's gut. "You can count on me, buddy."

"Do me a favor, will ya?" Connor asked.

"Yeah, anything?"

"Check out this guy. Let him know her brother carries a big gun and has friends who'll take him out back if he doesn't treat Kendall nice."

"Will do."

"Well, I gotta go. Tell Kendall I said hello. I'll try to call when she's not at work. Damn, I miss you guys."

"Same here." Ed missed his friend. Right now, the best he could do for Connor was assure him that he'd take care of his only living relative, Kendall. He ran a hand through his hair. "Don't worry about Kendall, I'll make sure she stays out of trouble."

"Thanks, Ed. I feel better already."

Ed could hear voices in the background over the phone line.

"Hey, Ed, I gotta go. We're moving out for patrol."

His mouth dried and he swallowed hard. "Stay low and come back safe." Ed's words sounded so trite, but he meant them from the bottom of his heart.

"I plan on it. I don't know when I'll get the chance to call again. I will as soon as I can. Later."

Ed hit the off button and stared down at the cell phone, more depressed than when they'd started their conversation. Connor was like the brother he never had. He and Kendall were the only family he had since both his parents had died. If anything happened to Connor...Well, that possibility didn't bear thinking about.

Not one to wallow in depression, Ed pulled on a clean pair of shorts, a t-shirt and jogging shoes. He'd worked hard all day at the ranch and didn't need the exercise to keep in shape. Instead, he needed to walk, to get out and think through everything that had happened that day.

He set off down the street, casting a quick glance up at Kendall's apartment window above his. She'd be at work now, serving beer and shooters to patrons of the Ugly Stick Saloon. Would her new boyfriend be there, waiting to see her after work? Ed walked faster, the frustration he'd felt earlier returning instead of receding.

Kendall was headstrong, stubborn and beautiful. A killer combination to try to keep up with. The kicker was that she had every right to do whatever the hell she pleased. Ed could do nothing to stop her. If he told her not to do something, she'd probably go out and do it, just to spite him. His only option for coming between her and this mystery boy was to plant himself right in the middle. If they didn't have time alone together, they couldn't build a relationship. And they sure as hell wouldn't have time to get it on.

If playing the part of Kendall's sex education teacher kept her too busy to pursue her new love interest, so be it. He'd take on that responsibility, no matter how many cold showers required to get through it or how many times he had to masturbate.

By the time he turned and headed back to the house, he realized he'd been walking for over two hours. He might actually sleep better, but he'd be exhausted at work the next day. At least, his libido had calmed and he wasn't thinking of a naked Kendall anymore. Just the comfort of his bed where he planned to fall to sleep immediately.

As Ed approached the house, he noted the light on in Kendall's window. The shade was drawn, but he could see her moving around, the silhouette of her body clearly outlined. She reached behind her back and unclasped her bra, letting it slide down her arms.

Ed groaned. He didn't need to see that. All the walking he'd done to get his lust back in line just flew out the window. His cock sprang to attention, pressing against the thin fabric of his jogging shorts. *Holy Hell.* The next thirteen months would be the death of him.

With heavy resignation, he trudged up the steps and entered the house, going directly to his apartment and an icy cold shower.

***

Kendall stripped naked and stepped into the shower. Tuesday nights tended to be slow at work and her boss had sent her home early. She'd had far too much time to think through her first sex education lesson with Ed, and she didn't know if she could maintain a teasing distance for long. Lacey assured her that keeping Ed on the edge was a surefire way to make him want her as much as she wanted him. With the added jealousy angle with a potential boyfriend in the background, she'd have his love, or at the very least, Ed's lust in the bag, or sack, by the end of the week.

In the meantime, her body ached with a need so powerful, she thought she might explode if she didn't get some relief.

The warm shower spray only made her hotter and more excited as soap suds sluiced over her breasts and down her ribs. Her fingers brushed over her nipples, the taut, nubs begging to be suckled by a man. One man…Ed.

Her hand slipped lower, the soap slick and smooth, catching in the fluff of hairs over her pussy. How she'd love to have Ed's hands stroking her as she stroked herself. She parted her folds, flicking at her clit, pretending it was Ed's tongue, lapping at her core, drinking in her juices, nipping and nibbling at that oh-so-sensitive bit of flesh, over and over, until she screamed out her release.

Kendall could imagine taking a sudsy shower with Ed. Naked, foaming, incredibly hot. He'd push her up against the cool tiles, wrap her legs around his muscular waist and thrust into her, hard and fast, his cock thick, stretching her channel, their bodies sliding together under the shower's spray. They'd make love until the water turned cold, then he'd dry every inch of her body, and carry her to his bed where they'd make love all night long.

Oh, sweet Jesus. She couldn't wait until her next lesson.

Kendall turned off the shower, grabbed for a towel, barely even dried her body as she headed for the door to her apartment. When she yanked open the door, she yelped and jumped back.

Lacey stood with her hand raised ready to knock. Her brows rose and her gaze swept the length of Kendall's naked body. "Going somewhere?"

"I have to have him now. I can't wait." Kendall pushed past Lacey but was stopped by an elbow hooked into her arm.

Lacey yanked her to a stop. "Oh, no you don't."

Her skin cooled as the air dried the water droplets. "But I can't remain celibate for an entire week, when he's right downstairs." She tugged against the arm holding her. "Let me go."

"No way." Lacey put herself between Kendall and the staircase and pushed Kendall back into her apartment. "Take a deep breath and tell me what happened with Plan B."

Kendall stared at her apartment door, her blood raging through her veins. The fact that she stood in front of her friend without a stitch of clothing on should have been an indication she was losing it. She was past caring, her rampant desire pushing her to the brink of sanity. "I'm on fire." Kendall's hands crossed over her breasts and ran down to the apex of her thighs. "All I can think about is him taking me, again and again. This sex education plan is making me even more crazy than before. How

Sex Ed

is that helping me?"

Lacey took Kendall into her arms and hugged her. "Shh, baby. It'll be okay."

"How, when all I can think about is sex? I barely functioned at work, I can't focus on homework. I couldn't even shower without getting the female equivalent of a hard-on. I need him." Kendall wailed. "Now!"

"What you need is a good vibrator with fresh batteries."

"No, I need Ed, his cock between my legs, fucking me like there was no tomorrow."

Lacey's eyes widened. "My, my. We are in a tizzy, aren't we?"

"I'm going down there." Kendall headed for the door again. "Don't get in my way."

"Okay, go ahead." Lacey crossed her arms over her chest, her lips pressing into a thin line. "And if you go down there like you are now, you'll frighten the poor boy into the next county."

Kendall's hand closed around the doorknob before she froze. "Sweet Jesus." She leaned her head against the wood paneling. "I can't take this."

Lacey's hand smoothed along her back. "Let me help you take the edge off."

Kendall turned and leaned against the door. "How?"

"Close your eyes."

Kendall looked at her friend skeptically then shrugged. "Fine, whatever." She closed her eyes and waited. "But I don't see how that's going to help."

"Just pretend I'm Ed." Lacey's lips closed around one of Kendall's taut nipples, sucking the tip into her warm, moist mouth.

Desire tugged at Kendall's core, and her eyes opened wide. "What are you doing?"

"Saving you from making a big mistake." Lacey grinned up at her. "You liked that, didn't you?"

Kendall frowned at Lacey, but she couldn't deny it. "That doesn't make me love Ed any less."

"I don't want you to love him less, and I have no intention of stealing you away. I'm just helping you keep your sanity until phase two of Plan B." Lacey tweaked the hard little button on the tip of her nipple. "Now shut up and close your eyes again. I'll even lower my voice if that helps."

"No, no." Kendall sucked in a quick breath as Lacey's lips closed on the other nipple and she bit down gently. Her breasts flushed, and swirling heat gripped her low in the belly. "This is doing it."

"Good." Lacey continued to suckle on her breasts.

Kendall moaned. "This is only making me hotter."

Lacey straightened, her brow furrowing. "I guess there's nothing to it but to give you the works."

Kendall's heart skipped several beats. "The works?" she said, her voice breathless, her pussy creaming at the thought.

Lacey pulled her shirt up over her head and dropped it where she stood. She turned her back to Kendall. "Would you get the clasp on my bra?"

Was Lacey a lesbian? She'd always shown interest in sexy men. This was Kendall's first inclination that her best friend might have different tastes in sexual partners.

The thought titillated Kendall. She'd never been with a woman before. She reached out and unhooked the bra while Lacey shimmied out of her denim skirt, revealing a decadent lack of panties, her smooth, creamy ass bared to Kendall's view.

"Oh, this can't be right," Kendall whispered.

"Why not?" Lacey faced her, a hand on her hip, her full, rounded breasts pushed out, ripe and ready for tasting. "You need release, and it's been a long time for me too. What's wrong with helping out each other? We're friends, aren't we?"

"I've never been with a woman."

"That makes two of us." Lacey's lips twitched. "But when you marched through that door all wet and naked..." She shrugged. "I have to admit, you turned me on." She held up her hands. "Don't worry, it's just a sex thing. I know how much you love Ed, and I'd never do a thing to come between you two. But damn, girl, I'm so horny I could die."

"Well...your breasts are...wow...gorgeous...and I am...fuckin' hot, but..."

"Wait." Lacey held up her hand. "Hold that thought. I have something that will help."

She tore open the door and raced across the hall and into her own apartment. The cool night air filtered through the open door, curling around Kendall's breasts and pussy, making her excruciatingly aware of her own nakedness. And damned if she didn't like it. Maybe she'd walk around naked more often.

Lacey returned in seconds, carrying a bright silver thick dildo, no less than a foot long. "Watch this." She twisted the bottom and the dildo vibrated. "It has five speeds."

"You actually own one of those?"

With a raised brow, Lacey looked at Kendall. "Doesn't every girl? Good grief, Kendall. I've got to take you shopping." She grabbed Kendall's hand and led her to the bedroom. "Get in the bed."

Kendall dragged her feet. "I don't think I can do this."

Sex Ed

"Well if you can't, will you at least watch so I can get myself off?" Lacey held the vibrating dildo between her breasts, the motion making her boobs jiggle. "Please."

Chapter Four

Kendall couldn't tear her gaze from the jiggle of Lacey's breasts. When she should have been saying, *hell no*, her mouth opened and she said, "Okay, just this once, and only because I'm still so keyed up I won't sleep anyway."

"Oh, baby. That man has you tied in knots. Let's start by getting you relaxed. Lay down on your stomach and I'll rub your back." Lacey turned Kendall toward the bed and gave her a nudge.

Not entirely comfortable with getting in bed with a naked woman, Kendall lay down on her stomach, her body tense, not fully convinced this was a good idea.

Lacey switched off the dildo and laid it on the bed. "We can do that later." She straddled Kendall's hips, the fuzz of her pussy brushing against Kendall's buttocks, sending shockwaves throughout her body.

Tension and heat filled Kendall's core, drenching her pussy with desire. *Sweet Jesus.* She was lusting after a woman—her friend, no less. She shot a glance over her shoulder at Lacey. "I have a feeling that after tonight, I won't be able to look at you the same."

"As long as you respect me in the morning." Lacey laughed and squirted lotion onto her hands. "If you don't make a big deal out of it, you'll be fine." She rubbed her hands across Kendall's shoulder. "How's that?"

Kendall moaned. "Magic. I need this every day after work." Her friend's hands slipped lower, rubbing lotion into the middle of her back.

Lacey scooted down over her legs and bent closer, her breasts sliding over Kendall's shoulders. "I'm game if you return the favor."

"I'm halfway to considering it." Kendall surprised herself by her response.

"Can't leave you halfway there." Lacey slipped lower still, her fingers skimming across Kendall's lower back to the rounded curve of her ass.

Kendall's tension went to an entirely different level. Part of her wanted Lacey to keep it impersonal, the other part wanted her to take it a step further.

Lacey's fingers slid down the line of Kendall's ass.

That move wasn't impersonal. Kendall sucked in a breath, too shocked and turned-on to say anything. She lay there, letting her friend do what she was doing, helpless to stop her. Unwilling to try.

With the tip of her finger, Lacey traced the tight ring of her ass. Then her finger slid to Kendall's pussy where she swirled it around and around the opening until she had it nice and wet.

Her breath catching in her throat, Kendall couldn't resist hiking up her ass.

"That's right, honey, come up on your hands and knees. It'll be so much easier." Lacey rose to stand on her knees between Kendall's legs.

So far gone to the far side of girl-on-girl sex, Kendall rose to her hands and knees and waited impatiently for whatever Lacey had in store next.

"Mmm, you're pussy is so pretty."

Kendall laughed. "And you would know this *how*?"

Lacey snorted. "I have videos and a mirror. I know what a pussy looks like."

"You have videos?" Why was it she didn't know these things about her very best friend?

"Oh, sweetheart, you have so much to learn. Make a note to have our own Sex Ed show you his collection."

Kendall looked back, her brows rising. "How do you know he has a collection?"

"Seriously?" Lacey shook her head. "Trust me, he has a collection." She slid her finger in and out of Kendall's vagina. When her finger was slick with juices, she traced a line to Kendall's asshole. "Ever been finger-fucked in the ass?"

Kendall's ass puckered, her core tingling in anticipation. "No." Kendall said, sure she was about to experience it.

"Be sure to have Ed do this when you two finally get together. It'll feel even better with bigger..." she pressed her finger into the hole, "...fingers."

All the air in Kendall's lungs whooshed out. "Wow." A rush of juices drenched her pussy.

"Pretty cool, huh? Wait, it gets better."

The hum of a miniature motor filled the air and Kendall looked over her shoulder. "What are you doing?"

"What do you think I'm doing?" Lacey pressed the vibrating dildo to Kendall's clit, while her thumb slid into Kendall's pussy.

With the vibrator stimulating her clit and Lacey's thumb in her pussy and her finger in her ass, Kendall couldn't talk. Every breath she took hitched and released before it could make it into her lungs. "Sweet Jesus. That feels so good."

Lacey increased the pace, thrusting her finger and thumb in and out. Tension spread from her core throughout her body as Kendall moaned and cried out, "Yes! There! Oh, God, yes!" Right on the edge of orgasm, Lacey's sweet torture ended abruptly.

"Oh, please." Kendall's body sagged, her pussy still tingling. "Don't stop now."

Lacey slapped Kendall's ass. "I have no intention of stopping now. But I want some of this too." She lay down on the bed, head pointed to the foot of the bed, opposite of Kendall. Lacey scooted close, lifted Kendall's knee and slid her head beneath Kendall's pussy. "Now, we both get to have a little fun. And remember, the louder the better. Count it as all part of the plan to make Ed wish he was the one." Lacey nudged Kendall's knees wider and wider until her pussy hovered over Lacey's mouth.

A warm breath of air blew across Kendall's hot wetness. A groan rose from her throat as she stared down at Lacey's furry mound.

"Go ahead, touch me. But I'll warn you, I'm ready to come any moment." Lacey let her knees fall to the side, the light brown hair curling over her folds, springy and tempting Kendall.

Balancing on one hand, she parted the folds to find Lacey's clit, the little sliver of flesh making her curious. Kendall knew what turned herself on. She flicked the nubbin with the tip of her finger.

Lacey's heels dug into the mattress and her ass lifted off the bed. "Oh, baby, do that again," she moaned.

The folds were warm but dry. Lacey's clit needed more lubricant to make it easy to rub. Kendall leaned forward, hesitant but driven by her own need for release. She touched Lacey's clit with the tip of her tongue. She tasted mildly of scented body wash and womanly musk. Kendall licked the length of her clit and sucked it into her mouth.

Lacey pressed her feet into the mattress again, thrusting upward, forcing Kendall to take more. At the same time, she parted Kendall's folds and tongued her clit, flicking and licking her until Kendall squirmed, her knees scooting wider, pressing her pussy closer to the source of sweet torture.

"Oh my god, that feels so good," Kendall moaned, breathing a stream of air over Lacey's pussy, much as Lacey had done to hers. She licked Lacey's clit, while pressing her finger into her thoroughly drenched pussy. The pace of her tongue matched that of Lacey's, increasing the tempo and force of her thrusts.

Lacey's fingers clutched at Kendall's ass, her tongue sliding into Kendall's pussy and then returning to her swollen, throbbing, sensitive clit.

Kendall's body tightened like a bowstring, every nerve on fire, her focus centered on the crazy things Lacey was doing. She found that the whole effect intensified when she followed Lacey's lead, repeating her moves until Lacey cried out, "Yes! There! Oh, God, yes!" Her friend's body tensed, pelvis thrusting spasmodically, fingernails digging into

Kendall's skin.

Kendall teetered on the edge, that final climax within reach, her body ready.

Lacey reached for the dildo, switched it on and thrust it into Kendall's pussy. Her tongue stroked her clit while the vibrator filled her channel, the overwhelming sensations catapulted her over the edge, her mind and body exploding with wave after wave of her orgasm. Her breathing grew ragged and her arms and legs shook.

When she finally came back to earth, Kendall collapsed on the bed beside Lacey, the dildo still inside her vibrating. "I gotta get one of these."

***

Ed lay on top of his bed, wearing nothing. He usually slept in the nude, but tonight he couldn't even lie beneath the sheets. The slightest bit of friction against his dick had him rock hard in seconds. That's what that little brat upstairs had reduced him to—a quivering mass of hypersensitive nerves. He couldn't masturbate every time he got a hard on, he'd wear out his hand and his cock. The inside of a vagina was so much softer and lubricated just right.

Ed groaned and glanced over at the clock. Midnight and he was still awake. How in hell was he going to work tomorrow without sleep?

A dull thud made his head jerk up off the pillow. It sounded like it came from Kendall's apartment above him. Then another thump reverberated through the ceiling, followed by a low moan.

Ed leaped out of bed and strained to hear more. Was someone in Kendall's apartment? He was halfway to his bedroom door when he heard another moan, and the soft sound of feminine laughter. What the hell was going on up there?

If Kendall was laughing, she wasn't being attacked. But the moans...

Another moan preceded a muffled scream, "Yes! There! Oh, God, yes!"

Kendall was making love with someone in her apartment.

A flash of rage ripped through Ed, surprising the hell out of him. He marched across his living room, ready to rip a new asshole out of the guy who'd crossed the line.

Ed hadn't gone a day from his most recent promise to get in the way of Kendall and her new lover and he'd already failed. More than that, Ed couldn't stand the thought of Kendall lying beneath another man, his cock inside her, fucking her. Making love to her when Ed himself couldn't.

No fucking way!

His hand closed around the doorknob before he came to his senses enough to realize he couldn't go up there and confront the man while he himself was still naked. With a jerk, he grabbed his jogging shorts from where he'd left them on the living room floor and jammed his legs into them as he pushed through the door. Taking the steps two at a time, he made it to the top in record time and slammed his fist against Kendall's door. "Kendall Mason, open this damned door."

A long pause ensued.

Ed hammered on the door again. "Kendall, come open this door."

The door opened and Kendall stood with a sheet loosely wrapped around her, toga-style.

Her appearance hit him in the chest. Her blond hair was mussed and sexy, her cheeks pink with a faint blush.

"Ed?" She glanced over her shoulder and closed the door a little. "What are you doing up here?"

"Get him out."

"Get who out?" Kendall's brows furrowed. "What are you talking about?"

"The man in your bedroom. Get him out." Ed pushed against the door, fully intending to march into Kendall's bedroom and throw out the bastard.

Kendall planted herself in front of him, her hold on the door firm. "First of all, I don't have a man in my bedroom. Second...I'm twenty-one and can have a man in my bedroom if I choose to." The edge of the sheet slipped down, revealing a dusky nipple. She hiked the corner of the sheet back up to cover herself.

But the damage was done.

Ed's cock sprang to life, his entire body on fire with anger and lust. "I'll count to five and that man better leave before I kick his ass from here to tomorrow. One..."

"Ed, I'm warning you."

"Two..."

"You aren't my father."

"Three..." His hands fisted.

"This is ridiculous."

"Four..."

"Ed Judson...is that you making all that noise out here?" Kendall's friend, Lacey appeared in the doorway, dressed in jeans and a T-shirt, her hair pulled back in a ponytail, her feet bare. "Wanna join the party? We were just watching a video." Her lips twisted into a sexy, secretive smile.

All of the air left Ed's sails and he stared at Lacey, his brow wrinkling, wondering what the hell was going on. "Is there a man in Kendall's bedroom?"

"No men in here?" Lacey stepped to the side. "You can come look if you want. Oh, Kendall, quit teasing the man. Let him in."

Kendall's eyes narrowed. "As long as he understands, that he doesn't have the right to chase men out of my apartment."

Lacey waved Kendall's words aside with a flick of her wrist. "Ed understands, don't you, sweetie?"

He didn't respond, his brain working hard to determine if he was being had or not.

"Whatever, come see for yourself." Kendall shifted the sheet and held the door wide.

Ed strode across the room and peered into the bedroom. As far as he could see, there wasn't a man anywhere in sight.

"Want to check under the bed and in the closet?" Lacey asked, standing in the doorway.

Ed turned sideways and squeezed between Lacey and the doorframe, rubbing against her breasts in the process.

A devilish smile curled her lips.

When he made it through, a sharp sting bit into his ass. He spun, gaze narrowed.

Lacey's hand fell to her side. "Sorry. I just had to know if it was as hard as it looked."

"And?"

"Oh, it is, all right." She winked at Kendall and laughed.

Ed squatted beside the bed and looked beneath. Nothing there but Kendall's shoes and a plastic storage container.

"Don't forget the closet. A girl can hide a lot of sin in a closet," Kendall prodded, standing beside Lacey, still holding that damned sheet over her nakedness.

Uncomfortable with the two women watching him, Ed opened the closet door to a mass of shirts, pants, dresses and shoes. There were boxes and belts, a bicycle helmet, basketball, volleyball and just about everything else under the sun...except a man.

"Satisfied?"

The sarcasm in Kendall's voice couldn't be mistaken. Ed turned and faced the women across the bed, defeated. Confusion spun through Ed's mind. He didn't have a clue what was going on. "If there isn't a man in that bedroom, what was all that moaning?"

That's when he saw it. Light from the bedside table glinted off its sleek silver casing, winking at him like a beacon in a sea of rumpled sheets. He'd almost rather have found a man in Kendall's bed than that.

A man he could pick up by his scrawny neck and kick his ass out with a great deal of pleasure.

A vibrator would remain unchallenged, untouched by Ed's hands and left behind in a room with two women. *Holy Hell.*

Kendall's lips turned up in a Mona-Lisa-smile. "Were we keeping you awake?" She pressed a hand to her mouth, her eyes widening. "I'm sooo sorry. We were just getting into the movie. We promise to keep it down from now on."

Ed glared at Kendall, wanting to say something, but his brain couldn't put words to his thoughts. Finally he managed, "Do that. I have to work in the morning."

"We'll be quiet." Kendall moved away from the door, motioning for Ed to follow. "I wouldn't want you to be too tired for tomorrow night's lesson."

Sex education was the last thing Ed wanted to think about before he attempted to sleep in what was left of the night.

Kendall walked him to the door and held it open, a smile playing around her lips. "I hope to use tonight's lesson on my guy tomorrow. I'll be sure to let you know how it goes." She started to close the door, clearly indicating an end to his visit.

When Ed didn't move, she looked at him wide-eyed. "Is there something else?"

Ed stared down into the eyes of a woman he wasn't sure he knew anymore. She sure as hell wasn't the kid sister of his friend. No sirree, she'd grown into a woman, full of mischief and feminine wiles. "No. Just keep it down." He turned and left.

If he wasn't mistaken, Kendall giggled as she shut the door.

What the hell was that about?

And what was Lacey doing in Kendall's bedroom while Kendall was wearing nothing more than a sheet? And whose vibrator was that on the bed? What were they doing with it while watching a movie?

If he thought images of a naked Kendall were enough to keep him up all night, the images inspired by the two women together doomed him to sleeplessness for the week. *Holy Hell.* Why did Connor have to get deployed now? Why couldn't he wait until his little sister was safely married off to some farmer?

Ed stomped down the stairs to his apartment and slammed the door behind him.

For the next hour, he paced his bedroom floor, his ears straining to hear what was going on upstairs. Other than a few loud giggles, the thumping had stopped. At one point, he thought he heard the faint hum of a tiny motor. But that could have been his overactive imagination.

What was Kendall up to with Lacey? And why was she interested in a man when she was doing God-knows-what with a woman?

Sex Ed

His mind still spinning, Ed stripped out of his shorts and laid on top of his sheets, his dick hard as a rock, the clock displaying bright green as if mocking him. *One-fucking-thirty in the fucking morning.* Ed couldn't believe he was lusting after Kendall Mason—his best friend's little sister. He had half a mind to pay a visit to the doctor for a mild sedative to keep him from getting a boner every time he was near Kendall. Was there such a thing as anti-Viagra?

And to think, some men couldn't get it up. Not Ed. He couldn't keep the poor boy down. He lifted his head. Moonlight shone off his stiff cock. Giving it a silver sheen much like the dildo in Kendall's bed.

Holy Hell.

Chapter Five

For the tenth time, Ed paced the length of the barn. He'd yet to round-up his horse, much less saddle him for the day's work. His eyes burned from lack of sleep and he'd taken not one but three cold showers during the night to shake the effect of Kendall's crazy request. Not to mention the silver vibrator mystery he wasn't sure he wanted to know about.

"Hey Ed, I thought you'd be out in the pen with Ranger by now."

"I should be." He performed a sharp about-face and marched to the other end of the barn, away from Grant.

"My, my. I don't think I've ever seen the great Ed Judson this riled. What's eating you?" Grant leaned against a stall door and crossed his arms over his chest.

"Kendall Mason."

"Is she out carousing with an undesirable?"

Guilt and desire warred in Ed's gut. "I can't say."

"Spit it out."

"No, it's something I gotta work out for myself."

"Suit yourself. I'm here if you need to talk." Grant grabbed a bridle and was almost out the door when Ed broke.

"She wants me to give her sex education lessons," Ed blurted out through clenched teeth.

Grant spun to face Ed, his brows practically meeting his hairline. "She what?"

"You heard me. She wants me to teach her how to attract a man, what a man likes from first date to all-the-way."

Grant stood with his jaw hanging down around his chest.

"Damn it, Grant, shut your mouth before I put a fist in it!" Ed spun on his boot heels, grabbed a bridle and headed out to the corral where Ranger awaited his scheduled morning exercise.

"Wait, wait," Grant trotted to keep up with Ed. "Let me understand this. You mean to tell me little Kendall Mason asked *you* to teach her all about what a man likes?" Grant removed his hat and ran a hand through his hair. "So what's your problem? You've been handed a gift from God."

"The Devil's temptation is more like it." Ed kicked at the ground. He needed a fight, wanting to punch something or someone. "I'm not fit to train horses in my current state of mind."

"Tell me how you managed to land this gig, I want one of my own."

"Not with Kendall, you don't." He glared at his boss and flung the bridle over the fence rail. "I didn't ask for it. She propositioned me and threatened to take her request to Whitey Ross if I turned her down." Ed slapped a palm on the rail so hard it stung.

Ranger flung his head back and trotted to the far side of the pen.

"Hell, I'm not fit to train horses today."

Grant laughed. "No, my friend, you'll get yourself thrown at this rate." The older man leaned his arms on the top rail of the fence and grinned out at Ranger. "Kendall Mason asked you to give her lessons in sex."

Ed growled.

"You know, she's not a baby anymore."

"You think I didn't notice?" Ed tipped his head backward, his eyes closed to the morning sun. His mind replayed Kendall's breast peeking out from the poorly wrapped sheet, the line of her G-string panties disappearing between her butt cheeks, the way her nipples poked at the thin fabric of her tank top. "Hell, she's a full grown woman."

"With the figure and desires to prove it." Grant shook his head. "Think she'd go out with me?"

He sucked in a breath through his nose before speaking. "I'm a hair's breadth away from landing my fist in your face, boss or no boss."

Grant held out his hands in front of his face and laughed aloud. "Sorry, just had to poke at you. You're wound tighter than a bowstring."

"You have no idea. I don't think I slept more than fifteen minutes last night."

"Maybe you should take the day off."

"No. I need to do something to keep my mind off Kendall and the lessons she'll expect from me tonight." Ed leaned his forehead against the fence rail, pressing against the rough wood. "I promised Connor I'd look out for her."

"Wow, you are in a bind."

"Yeah. I'm damned if I give her what she wants, and damned if Whitey takes over."

"Did she say why she wanted lessons?"

Ed's frown deepened, a snarl curling his lip. "She's hot over some guy and wants to use the lessons to attract his attention."

"Did she say who the guy was?"

"No. But I think I have an idea." He swallowed hard against a tight throat. God, he hated to admit this. "She's been studying with some jerk from her college. I see him leaving as I get home from work."

"Maybe you need to get home early and check it out." Grant slapped a hand on Ed's back. "Personally, I'd love to be in your shoes, buddy. Kendall is one hot little filly."

"Grannttt," Ed warned.

Grant raised his hands again. "I'm just saying. She's a grown woman and fair game in the eyes of every male in town. I'm surprised she's held off this long from latching onto a man. Can't be from lack of some guys trying. You're a lucky dog that she picked you."

"Yeah, but Connor trusts me to look out for her, not fuck her. And she only wants sex education lessons to help her land another guy." A burst of red-hot rage slammed through his bloodstream, surging its way straight to his chest. "I gotta find out who this guy is and tell him to fuck off."

"Be careful, Ed. Sometimes telling a guy to back off only makes him want the girl more. It could backfire on you."

"I don't care. Connor's only been gone a month. A goddamn month! I have thirteen more to go before I can walk away from this stupid promise."

Grant looked out across the paddock. "Don't know what to tell you. A cowboy's word is his honor."

"Yeah." Ed drew in a long breath and let it out slowly. "That's the problem. That and some randy boy poking around Kendall while she's as hot as a cat in heat."

"Stop. You're getting me all worked up." A grin spread across Grant's face. "I can just picture Kendall in that tight little jean skirt she wore the other night serving at the Ugly Stick Saloon." Grant shook his head. "She had every male in the building panting after her."

Ed groaned. "You see what I have to put up with?"

"Yeah, I don't envy your promise. Plus I really don't see a way around these lessons you're supposed to teach her. How will you show her what a man likes without actually...showing her?"

"I was hoping you had some suggestions." Ed looked at his boss hopefully.

"Short of buying a blow-up doll with anatomically correct parts, I can't think of a thing."

"A blow-up doll?" Ed's brows rose. "Can I get one of those from that adult shop out on the county line?"

"I'm almost positive they'll have them. I know they have the female dolls. Not so certain about the males." Grant shook his head. "Really, though, you should just go for her body."

"What?" Ed stared at his friend. Had he lost his mind? "I can't do that, she's Connor's *little* sister."

"Are you attracted to her?" Grant's gaze locked on Ed's,

His boss's stare refused to let him shy away from the answer to that loaded question. "Damn it, yes." Ed looked out across the barnyard. "That's the problem. She's too damned pretty for my own good."

"Does the attraction go deeper than just the physical?"

Sex Ed

His chest tightened, breathing becoming more difficult, and his head swam. "What do you mean?"

"Do you love the girl?"

"Of course I do. She's Connor's sister."

"No, do you L.O.V.E. the girl? As in willing to take her to the altar kind of love?" Grant stared hard.

A stare lasting long enough to make him squirm. Ed looked away first. "I don't know."

"Think about it. Can you see her dating another man without getting mad about it?"

"No."

"Can you picture her in bed with someone other than you?"

"Hell, no." Ed shoved his hand through his hair, his body tense, visions of Kendall lying naked in bed rampaging through his head. *Holy Hell*, he wanted her. And he didn't want any man planting himself inside her. "Hell, no," he repeated.

Grant shrugged. "Then go for her. Connor will understand and probably be happy she'd settle for his best friend, rather than a low-life like Whitey."

"I don't know if I'm ready to commit." Ed shook his head. "And I'd bet my leather chaps Connor didn't have *fuck my sister* in mind when he said take care of Kendall."

"Yeah, but if you told him about Kendall's little deal and Whitey, he'd switch gears real quick."

"I don't know. I talked to him last night. He was going out on maneuvers, probably getting shot at. How can I tell him anything that will have him so worried his head wouldn't be in the fight?" Ed leaned back against the corral fence.

"You're right. He doesn't need the worry." Grant's lips twisted. "Do you think your attraction to Kendall is more than because she's pretty?"

"I don't know. I spent most of my life thinking of her as a sister."

"And now?"

Ed's shoulders sagged. "Not at all. She's not the same kid in ponytails and she's got great..." He held his hands out at breast level, his thoughts on the perfect shape and size of her boobs. Then he remembered where he was and who he was talking to. "...skin. She's got great skin."

Grant laughed. "Go for the girl. You have it bad for her already."

Ed hooked his thumbs in his back pockets and stared at his boots. "She's having me show her what a guy likes for some other dude, not me."

"Then in the process of showing her, let her see what a great catch you are."

Ed snorted.

" As far as I see it, you got two choices. Check out the doll situation at the adult toy store, or go for the girl. Either way something's gotta give."

"Yeah."

"In the meantime, how about pounding some T-posts? There's a fence down on the northern edge of the ranch. Do some manual labor to burn off some of that testosterone."

"You're right." Ed smiled at his boss and friend. "Thanks. At least, I have some options to think about."

"Yeah, and I'll have a very vivid image of Kendall Mason in her tight skirt, asking you to give her sex lessons to keep me warm all day in this ninety-degree weather." Grant's lips pressed into a line. "Not sure I'm going to make it to lunch."

"She was wearing a tank top and thong panties." Ed's eyes narrowed. "But get your mind out of the gutter with my girl."

"Your girl, is it?" Grant's eyes widened. "Getting territorial all the sudden?"

"Shuddup." Ed nodded at Ranger. "You got him?"

"Yeah, take the four-wheeler for the day." His boss laughed. "I don't think any of the horses would put up with you today."

Ed gathered a pole pounder, T-posts wire and ties, loaded them onto the four-wheeler and headed out across the ranch, the wind blowing in his face, the sun warming his skin. Yeah, pounding a few T-posts would help for a while. At least until he got home that afternoon, after a detour to the X-rated Adult store on the county line.

***

Near the end of the day, Ed was hot, sweaty and exhausted, certain he'd have no trouble fighting his desire for Kendall. Especially with a blow-up doll he hoped to pick up on the way home.

His first stone wall hit him square in the face when the lady at the adult store told him they only carried the female blow-up dolls. If he wanted, they could order a male, but it would take two weeks to get it in.

Kendall wouldn't wait two weeks for him to continue lessons, she'd pull up stakes and march on over to Whitey's to continue her education.

His frustration made him angry. By the time he reached the house, he was in no mood to see Kendall's window wide open, music blaring loud enough even Old Man Frantzen could hear it, and that blond-haired gigolo gyrating to the beat in nothing but a pair of fancy leather chaps and a G-string.

Ed's blood pressure shot through the roof. He slammed his truck

Sex Ed

into Park and leaped out before the engine had a chance to come to a full stop.

Kendall swung into full view through her window, twisting and gyrating to the music like one of the topless dancers at the Ugly Stick Saloon on a Friday night.

Ed took the stairs two at a time, tripping on the last one when his boot missed it and slipped down a step. He racked his shin on the corner of the top stair and issued a string of curse words that would have made his mother wash his mouth out with soap for a week.

"Ed?" Lacey flung open her door and stepped out. "Are you okay?"

"I'm fine, just clumsy. He picked himself up and dusted his hands on his dirty jeans. "What the hell's going on in Kendall's apartment?"

Lacey smiled. "She's having a little study session with Cory."

"Study session, my ass." He raised a hand to pound it against the door.

Lacey grabbed his wrist before he could. "Hey, before you go breaking up her fun, I wanted to talk to you."

The music inside the apartment was so loud the walls shook. Ed couldn't think past his desire to strangle the dude inside dirty-dancing with Kendall, much less have a conversation with Lacey over God knew what. "What." The one word shot out like a bullet, sharp, and to the point.

"You like Kendall, don't you?" Lacey inserted herself between him and the door, garnering his full attention.

"Yeah, she's my best friend's sister. I've known her all my life."

"You've known her, but have you *known* her since she's now all grown up?"

Ed's groin tightened. "What's your point?"

"You're not her brother, and that's bothering you, isn't it?"

"I'm her brother's best friend. He asked me to keep her out of trouble." Unease skittered along his skin. What was she leading up to?

"Does he know you're in love with her?"

Ed staggered backward and almost fell down the steps. "What are you talking about?"

Lacey grinned and her eyes danced. "You don't even realize it yourself, do you?"

"I can't love her, she's my—"

"—best friend's little sister." Lacey waved his words aside with a flick of her hand. "Does she look like a little girl?" The woman shook her head and poked a finger into his chest. "No. And she's not. She knows what she wants and isn't afraid to go after it. She learned that from you." Tilting her head, Lacey planted a fist on her hip. "So what are you going to do about it?"

"About what?" Ed's head spun. How could he make astute trades in the stock market amassing a small fortune in a short amount of time, but he couldn't begin to understand the workings of a woman's mind?

A loud sigh echoed in the hallway. "Kendall. What are you going to do about Kendall?"

"She's in love with some jerk. Probably the guy in her apartment right now." Ed pushed forward, his determination renewed to break up Kendall's little dance party.

Lacey laid a hand on his chest. "Breaking them up isn't the way to win Kendall."

"No, but I'd get great satisfaction from punching the boy's lights out."

"And Kendall would love him all the more for taking the fall." Lacey shook her head. "Did you ever think Kendall might still think of you as her other big brother?"

"Yeah. So?"

"If you want her to see you as a potential lover, you have to show her how incredible it the chemistry could be between the two of you."

"You mean make love to her?" Ed shook his head, his heart hammering double-time. "I promised to keep her out of trouble, not get her into it."

"No, no. You need to make her notice you by being with another woman. That way she would see you as a very desirable man, not at all a brotherly figure."

Ed's brows pulled together. "Wouldn't that just make her jealous?"

Lacey shrugged. "Yes, possibly. Just depends on how you present it."

Ed scrubbed a hand through his hair, standing it on end. "I'm just a dumb cowboy. Spell it out before I grow old, will ya?"

With a laugh, Lacey leaned back against Kendall's door. "I know Kendall asked you to give her sex education lessons."

Ed couldn't meet Lacey's direct gaze, not liking where this conversation was going. "Yeah, and?"

"And you're probably feeling uncomfortable having her practice the things a man likes on you."

"More like...frustrating...go on." Intrigued, he forced the music out of the forefront of his mind and listened to Lacey. Maybe the woman had a solution to his problem.

"What you need is a demo dummy."

"I thought of that." Ed crossed both arms over his chest. "I tried to find a blow up doll at the adult store. They were out of male models. It'll be two weeks before they get one in."

"You're on the right track, but I have a proposal even better than that." Her lips curled into a secret smile.

Ed braced himself.

"What you need is a live model."

"That's me." Ed poked a thumb at his chest.

"Right, but you need a live female model to demonstrate with so that Kendall won't be demonstrating on you." A grin spread across her face and she held out her hands, like a magician having pulled a bunny out of his hat. "What do you think?"

"That you're crazy as hell, and I'm even crazier for listening." Ed nodded toward the door. "Move, or be moved."

"Promise me you'll think about it. At the least, you don't break your promise to Connor. At best, you make Kendall jealous enough to notice you as the hunky cowboy you are."

Ed breathed in and out several times before he finally spoke. "Fine."

"You'll do it?" Lacey's face lit with a big smile.

"No. I'll think about it."

Lacey nodded. "Fair enough."

The door behind Lacey jerked open and she fell backward into the blond guy's arms. "Oops!" She smiled up at him. "Hi, Cory."

"Hey, Lacey." Cory helped her to stand on her own then stuck out his hand. "You must be Ed. Kendall's told me all about you."

Ed glared at the young man with the light blond hair and shirtless body. With all the restraint of a pit bull on a leash, he held out his hand. "Sorry to say she hasn't mentioned a word about you." His fingers tightened around Cory's in a punishing grip.

Kendall stepped up behind Cory, her brows raised. "Ed? You're home early."

"Apparently not early enough. I was just saying hello to your friend."

Cory's face turned a deep shade of red, his body bending under the pressure on Ed's grip. "Yeah, just saying hello."

With a frown, Kendall said, "Ed, let go of Cory's hand."

"Of course." He immediately released his grip, a smirk tugging at his lips as the boy shook blood back into his fingers.

"Look, I gotta go." Cory smiled at Kendall. "We're on for tonight, right?"

"It's a date."

"Great. See you then." Cory eased past Ed, hurried down the stairs, and the front door slammed shut behind him.

Kendall crossed her arms over her chest, her eyes narrowing. "What are you two doing out here lurking in the hallway?"

Lacey leaned into Ed. "I was just asking Ed if he'd give me sex education lessons along with you. You know, a two-fer deal?"

Ed opened his mouth to tell Lacey what she could do with her deal then stopped. The frown pressing Kendall's pretty brows together had him rethinking Lacey's offer.

"Two-fer?" Kendall stared from Ed to Lacey and back.

"Yeah." Lacey draped a hand on Ed's arm. "Two-fer-one. I volunteered to be his dummy so he could show us both what a man really wants."

Kendall's frown deepened.

A thrill of excitement sped through Ed's veins and he made his decision. Having Lacey as his personal dummy might just work on either front. If Kendall was interested, she'd be jealous. If she wasn't, Ed would be guilt-free with his buddy, Connor.

And it would give him time to sort through his own feelings for Kendall.

Sex Ed

Chapter Six

"How long until you're ready for our lesson?" Kendall directed her question to Ed. Anger warred with anticipation; anticipation winning. She'd deal with Lacey after Ed left.

"I need a shower. Give me thirty minutes. Are you providing dinner?" He grinned.

The man looked far too happy about the situation. "I'll figure out something. Go on and get your shower."

Ed winked at Lacey. "See you in thirty minutes."

"Can't wait." Lacey smiled brightly.

Kendall gritted her teeth, wanting to scratch out her ex-friend's eyes.

Instead, she pasted a smile on her face and wiggled her fingers at Ed, her gaze following him to the bottom of the stairs. She held her tongue until his door shut with a thud behind him. Then she grabbed Lacey's arm in a punishing clutch and yanked her into her apartment, slamming the door. "What the hell are you trying to do? I thought you were my friend?"

"I am, sweetie." Lacey winced at the fingers squeezing her arm. "Mind letting up on me so I can explain?"

Kendall's hands dropped to her sides, her fists clenching and unclenching, her chest rising and falling with each angry breath. "Start explaining, and this better be good."

Lacey smiled. "It is. It'll work out perfectly."

"Yeah, yeah, you haven't gotten to the part where I agree." Kendall crossed both arms over her chest and stood ramrod straight. "Continue."

"Ed was hesitant to touch you, wasn't he?"

Hadn't they already discussed this? Kendall's skin tingled with impatience. "So, the plan was for him to give me sex education lessons, and get used to the idea."

"But don't you see?" Lacey waved a hand. "He's torn by his loyalty to your brother. Involving me in the Sex Ed lessons gets him used to the idea of being with you."

Kendall shook her head. "I'm not seeing it."

"Just give it a chance. If it doesn't work out the way you think it should, I'll back out. No harm, no foul."

Kendall stared at her friend for a long time before she sighed. "One lesson. Then I call it."

"Fair enough." Lacey hugged Kendall. "You'll see, this'll all work out."

Kendall remained stiff. "I don't know. I feel more like I'm losing ground with Ed than gaining."

"Look, let's make a bet."

"I don't need a wager." Her shoulders slumped. "I need Ed."

Lacey smiled. "I bet you ten dollars that by the end of this week, that one-hundred-percent-red-blooded-hubba-hubba male will be all yours."

Kendall hoped so. She'd loved him so long. When she'd set out to win over Ed, she'd promised herself that if the attempt didn't work out, she'd move on. She'd have her degree in a month. If she and Ed weren't together, Kendall had plans to move to Austin and get a life without the man.

"What have you got in your frig that would feed a man with a big appetite?" Kendall asked.

Lacey clapped her hands. "You won't regret it, Kendall."

"I hope not. I'd hate to lose a friend."

Her friend headed for the door. "I have a casserole I can pop in the microwave and have it ready in fifteen minutes." She stopped and faced Kendall. "Did you make up the banana pudding like I told you to?"

"Check." Kendall had it chilling in her refrigerator.

"Spray can of whipped cream?" Lacey asked.

"Check."

"Cherries?"

"Check." Kendall shook her head. "I don't know why we need dessert. Ed rarely eats dessert."

"Oh, honey, he'll be all into it tonight." She smiled and flounced out the door. "Oh, and wear that sleeveless cotton blouse that's so sheer you can see through it with your micro-mini denim skirt. No under things." The door closed behind her, the last three words echoing through Kendall's living room.

No under things.

Her pussy creamed in anticipation of the next sex lesson with Ed. If all went well, she'd see a little action tonight.

Kendall raced around the apartment, digging through her closet, searching for the skirt and sheer blouse. When she couldn't find them immediately, she had a near panic attack. Then she remembered hanging them on the back of the bathroom door, just for this occasion. She stripped naked, tucked her hair up in towel and stepped beneath the shower's spray, rinsing off the sweat from her dance session with Cory.

He was coming along much quicker than she'd anticipated. So quickly, she knew he'd be ready for Ladies Night tonight.

After her lesson with Ed, she planned to make it to the Ugly Stick for Cory's debut performance. The women were going to love him. Kendall had taught him all of the best dance moves she'd observed from the men who came every week for Ladies Night.

Lacey had assured her that going to Cory's debut wouldn't set her back on her campaign to win over Ed. She'd insisted this early in the plan was too soon to stay the night with Ed.

Kendall wasn't so certain. She wanted to spend every night with Ed. For the rest of her life, starting now.

Turning the shower setting to cold, she rinsed off the body wash, the chill making her nipples pucker nicely. She shoved aside the shower curtain and squealed when she noticed the clock. She had only two minutes to comb her hair and dress. She wanted to beat Lacey to Ed's apartment.

Still slightly damp, she yanked the denim skirt over her hips and shimmied into the floral, sleeveless cotton blouse, only buttoning the middle three buttons. Barefoot, she raced through the door and teetered at the top of the stairs when Lacey's door opened and she emerged carrying a casserole dish and wearing a form-fitting ribbed knit tank mini dress that wasn't much more than a shirt barely covering her ass.

A burst of rage roared through Kendall. "Remember, he's mine."

Lacey laughed out loud. "Oh, honey, I know that, and I wouldn't dream of taking him from you. Not that I could. You look absolutely yummy in that outfit. I can see your nipples plain as day. It's perfect." Her brows furrowed. "Where's the dessert?"

"Damn, I forgot." Kendall spun, racing for her apartment, fully aware Lacey would now arrive at Ed's before she could gather the pudding, whipped cream and cherries. Why did she have to be so forgetful?

Her feet slowed. What was she worried about? Ed and Lacey wouldn't start without her...would they?

Kendall grabbed the dessert items and ran for the stairs, almost tripping over the first one. She righted herself and took a deep breath. This was insane. Lacey was her friend. She wouldn't come between them.

Forcing herself to calm, she descended the steps carefully and knocked on Ed's door. As soon as her knuckles hit the wood, her pulse raced and her breathing grew more ragged. Session two of Sex Ed was about to begin.

A full minute elapsed from the time she knocked before Kendall gave up and twisted the knob.

Lacey's laugh could be heard from Ed's kitchen.

Anger pushed Kendall forward. When she rounded the corner, the sight before her made her want to throw the pudding, whipped cream and jar of cherries right at Ed and Lacey.

Lacey leaned up on tip-toe, reaching for plates in the cabinet, her dress hem rising high enough to expose one naked butt cheek. Ed stood behind her, damned near on top of her, reaching high to gather the plates. The fan over the stove roared over a tray of burned toast.

Neither of them had heard her enter.

Ed reached the plates before Lacey and pulled them from the cabinet.

Before he could back away, Lacey spun to face him, laughter shining from her face. "I could have gotten them."

"Face it, you're short." He laid the plates on the counter, then swatted Lacey's fanny. "But nice ass."

Lacey laughed and grabbed for the plates. "Thanks." When she turned toward Kendall, she grinned. "Hey, K. About time you got here. We're hungry and ready to eat."

That wasn't all they were, but Kendall held her tongue, reminding herself Ed thought she wanted to learn about sex to entice another man. She wasn't supposed to be after him. The idea was to make him jealous enough to want her.

Her brows knit. And whose idea had that been?

Lacey's.

And whose idea was it to be a sex dummy for the Sex Ed lessons?

Lacey's.

And who was the patsy here?

Blood pounded in her eyes. Kendall suspected she was being played.

Well, she didn't plan on letting Lacey have her way with Ed. Friend or no friend, Kendall had plans of her own for the night. And top on her list was to show Ed just how sexy and grown up she'd become, even if it meant jumping over Lacey to get to him.

Lacey loaded a plate with the casserole and handed one to Kendall. She loaded another and handed it to Ed. "You two go on into the living room and get started. I want to make another stab at toast. Hopefully, not burning it this time."

Ed grabbed forks from the drawer and nodded at Kendall. "Come on. I'm starving and this smells good enough to eat. That Lacey is a great cook."

A knot formed in Kendall's gut. Strike one up for Lacey. Kendall couldn't cook her way out of a pizza box. She stared after Ed as he left the kitchen.

"What are you waiting for? Don't you know food can be very sexy?" Lacey gave her a push.

"Casserole?" Kendall stared at the chicken with gooey cheese sauce

Sex Ed

on her plate.

"Honey, any kind of food. Go on, get started without me."

"I don't get it."

"Good lord, girl. Use your imagination. Drop some somewhere suggestive."

Kendall carried her plate into the living room and sat on the couch with Ed, her mind spinning around Lacey's suggestion. She lifted a forkful of casserole, a string of cheese stretching from her plate up to her fork. "What are we going to cover tonight in our lesson?" How was she going to make this look sexy? She popped the food in her mouth and chewed.

Ed's hand paused on its way to his mouth. "How about how to make a man hot while on a dinner date?"

For once, they seemed to be on the same page. Kendall smiled. "Enlighten me."

"Start by licking the cheese off your lips."

His voice rasped in her ears and heat rose in her cheeks. "How embarrassing."

"Not at all. Not with the right man. One who can envision the possibilities."

Kendall slid her tongue out along her lips.

"Slowly." Ed's blue eyes flared, his own tongue sweeping out across his own lips as slow as he wanted her to. "You missed it. Here. Let me." He leaned close and pressed both lips to her lower lip, sucking it in.

At his touch, Kendall's heart skipped several beats then crashed against her ribs.

He nibbled at her lip and released it, a smile spreading across his face. "Your turn. Try something different."

Kendall dipped her fork into her food, dizzy from the last demonstration, but determined to pass this lesson with flying colors. She aimed to drop a little of the cheese sauce on her chest, but it wouldn't slip easily off her fork. With a little jerk, she tried flicking it. A glob of chicken and cheese jumped in the air and landed on her thigh, at the edge of her skirt hem and then the warm mixture slid down between her legs.

Her eyes widened, her breath hitching in her lungs.

"I'd say you're catching on quickly." Ed cleared his throat. "Allow me." Eyelids lowered, he bent toward her.

Kendall's legs parted automatically, the anticipation of Ed licking the cheese sauce off her inner thigh more than she could have dreamed of so soon into the lesson.

"Look at you two, getting off to a roaring start without me." Lacey carried her plate into the room.

Ed straightened, a slow red burn rising up from the collar of his black T-shirt.

Once again, Kendall could kill Lacey for even being in the same room.

"If you're not going to get that, let me." Lacey laid her plate on the coffee table and slid a finger over Kendall's thigh, scooping the cheese from her leg. She held it out to Ed.

Without a moment's hesitation, the man sucked the finger into his mouth and licked it clean.

Kendall sat silent, stunned, turned on and furious all at once. If Lacey hadn't entered the room, Ed just might have licked that cheese off the inside of her thigh.

"Let Lacey show you the one where you drop something down your cleavage. A man goes wild for a woman's breasts." Ed turned to Lacey and nodded. "Do it."

Lacey took a forkful of cheese sauce and tipped it carefully.

Of course, the cheese slipped right off her fork and landed as pretty as you please in the cleavage between her breasts.

"Oops." She batted her eyes at Ed.

Kendall gripped her fork, ready to stick it into Lacey's leg.

"Perfect." Ed grinned. "If you and your guy are alone, you can ask him to help you out like this." He leaned close to Lacey.

Lacey tugged on the neckline, drawing it down low enough to display the trail of cheese sauce.

Kendall leaned forward to see what he was doing, half-jealous, and fully excited.

Ed braced his hands on Lacey's rounded breasts and licked the cheese from between them, coming up smacking his lips. "See? Easy and the act gets a guy off like nothing you can begin to imagine."

"Let me try." Kendall dug her fork into her plate.

Scooting back on the couch, Ed shrugged. "No need. I think you have the hang of it."

"No, I want to get it right, and practice makes perfect," Kendall insisted. She swirled her fork around her plate, searching for the perfect combination of wet and cheesy sauce.

When she lifted the fork, the cheese dripped off before she could make it to the V of her shirt. Instead, the glob landed on her nipple. "Great." She looked up at Ed and grimaced. "I can't even spill food right."

Ed's gaze zeroed in on the drop of cheese. He didn't respond to Kendall's lament. The muscles in his neck worked several times before he cleared his throat and looked up. "No, baby, you got it right." He leaned over and sucked the cheese into his mouth, nipple and all through the thin fabric of her shirt.

Kendall's back arched, pressing the breast closer to Ed, her breath hitching in her chest. Oh, yeah, she'd gotten it right. Her hands reached out for Ed's head to hold him closer.

Before Kendall could dig her fingers into his hair, Lacey giggled. "Kendall gets an A for effort on that lesson. Ready for dessert?"

Ed's mouth released Kendall's nipple and he straightened. "Well, done," he said, his voice rough. "And yes, let's move on. I believe you brought dessert?"

The loss of his mouth's warmth sent a pang straight through her core. Kendall could easily have shot Lacey right between the eyes. She'd been so close to...to...to what? Having Ed suck on her boob? Okay, so he'd gone past kissing, that was a step in the right direction. But when would he take her to his bed and make love to her into the night? She wanted to move the lessons along a lot faster than Lacey had dictated. But she didn't want to appear to be easy. She was supposed to be learning all this to entice another man. Well, in Ed's eyes. The added jealousy angle.

"Your guy will definitely like the food on the boob trick."

Ed patted her back like a big brother patting his little sister. So much for jealousy. Kendall wanted to strip off her clothing and stand in front of Ed and say, "Look at me! I'm a woman and I want you." She actually reached for the buttons on her blouse when she glanced across at her friend.

Lacey shook her head. "Go get the dessert, we won't need bowls or spoons."

"For pudding?" Kendall tipped her head sideways.

"Trust me. We won't need them."

Ed grinned across at Lacey, sending another bolt of green-eyed envy through Kendall. Why couldn't he be that sexy and natural around her? What was she doing wrong?

She trudged to the kitchen, returning with the pudding, spray can of whipped cream and the jar of maraschino cherries.

Lacey sat so close to Ed, she was practically in his lap.

Kendall set down the dessert items with a thump on the table.

"Thanks, Kendall." Ed stuck his finger into the banana pudding, dipped out a nice, big dollop and stuck it in his mouth. "Umm. That's perfect for what I had planned next. We're stepping up the pace on the lessons. We'll assume you are past the first few awkward, getting-to-know-you dates. I think you can get through the kissing and dinner. Remember to progress slowly. Men don't like a woman to come on to them too strong at first."

"Really?" Kendall caught herself before snapping, *you could have fooled me*. She waited until Ed wasn't looking then glared at Lacey.

Lacey had the gall to wink at her.

"As I was saying," Ed continued. "We'll move right into the first bedroom contact."

Kendall plopped down on the couch next to Ed. "Now, you're talking."

"You're ready for the next lesson?" Ed nodded toward the dessert. "A man likes it when a woman tastes sweet, no matter where he tastes her. Lacey, if you would, dip a finger into the pudding and stick it into your mouth."

"I've been dying for some of this." She dipped her finger into the pudding and poked it into her mouth.

"Hold it there and make it look like you're having an orgasm."

Lacey's eyelids drooped and she thrust her finger in and out of her mouth, moaning softly.

"Good. Very good." Ed watched her a moment longer then turned to Kendall. "Now, Kendall, dip your finger."

She did.

"Now put it in my mouth." Ed smiled. "Go ahead."

Kendall pressed the tip of her pudding-drenched finger into his mouth. At the same time, her own opened, her tongue sliding across her suddenly dry lips.

He sucked her finger into his mouth, tonguing the pudding with firm licks. When he had it cleaned, he pulled back. "Dip again."

His blue eyes glowed with an intensity Kendall couldn't resist. She dipped her finger into the pudding and raised it to his lips.

He kept his mouth closed and shook his head, his body so tight already he couldn't imagine taking this lesson any farther. But he would.

"No." He guided her finger to the side of her neck and spread pudding down to the base of her throat where her pulse beat erratically. His gut clenched, his penis throbbing painfully. She was aroused as much as he was.

"If a man is interested, he'll see this as an offering and accept, like this." He cupped the back of her neck, tugging at her hair, pulling her head back to expose her throat and the long line of pudding. He licked the pudding from just below her chin, down the column of her neck to the base where he lingered, tonguing the pulse beneath her pale skin.

"I do believe you two have that one down."

Kendall's eyes narrowed.

Ed straightened. "Right. Lacey, your turn. Dip out some of the pudding."

She did and held out her finger.

Next to him, Kendall frowned, leaning into him, her gaze on Lacey's finger.

Ed guided Lacey's finger to her thigh and ran it from the inside of her knee to the hem of her dress. "Now it gets more interesting. When a woman traces a path of sweets along the inside of her thigh, the act tells a guy she's ready for the next step. Come and get me."

With his large, calloused hands, Ed parted Lacey's legs. He dropped to his knees and moved between them, dipping his head to lick the pudding from her knee along her inner thigh, nudging the hem of her dress upward with his nose. "Ah, perfect." He lifted the dress and looked over his shoulder at Kendall. "No panties."

Chapter Seven

Kendall squirmed next to Ed, her own denim micro-mini skirt edging upward. She'd had enough of this cat-and-mouse teasing with the pudding. "Let me try that." She dipped her finger into the pudding and touched some to her lips first. She leaned close and kissed Ed. "Like this?"

Ed's tongue swept out to lick the pudding off Kendall's lips. "Ummm. Yes."

Now if this doesn't get you hot, I don't know what will. With the rest of the pudding, Kendall spread a line from the middle of her inner thigh up to the hem of her skirt, pushing the denim higher to expose the mound of hair over her pussy. Her finger, with the remaining pudding, slipped between her wet folds. "Like this?"

Again, Ed's tongue swept across his lips. "Ummm. Yes."

"Oh, let me." Lacey pushed past Ed and she dropped between Kendall's legs, her pretty pink tongue lapping up the banana pudding all the way to Kendall's pussy. "Oh, yes, I can see how this would get a man off. It's got me *all* excited."

Too shocked to react at first, Kendall watched as her friend licked the pudding off her skin, Lacey's mouth moving toward her clit. Her pussy creamed, her body trembling.

A hand clamped down on Lacey's shoulder. "I'll take it from here." Ed pulled Lacey away from Kendall, his eyes more stormy gray than blue, his mouth set in grim lines, the shorts he'd worn for the occasion tenting out magnificently.

Kendall hid a satisfied smile.

As Lacey moved back, she winked again at Kendall.

For the first time that evening, Kendall could actually forgive Lacey for coming between her and Ed.

"A man would be crazy not to respond to an opening like that." He lifted one of her heels from the floor and placed it on the couch, spreading her legs wide. Then he lay down between them, his tongue going directly to the pudding, lapping at her clit until every sweet drop was gone.

Pulses rippled along her folds. Kendall's back arched, her fingers lacing through his hair, drawing him closer. "Oh, yes, that's what I want."

"Here, let's try some whipped cream while we're at it." Lacey slipped her hands between Ed and Kendall and flipped the three buttons free on Kendall's shirt, peeling the edges open. Holding the can of spray whipped cream over a breast, she squirted a circle around the nipple, building it up to a point.

Sex Ed

The cool cream tightened her nipple even more.

Ed moved up Kendall's body.

"Wait, we're not done yet." Lacey reached behind her and plucked a cherry from the jar, placing it on the tip of the nipple whipped cream. "Now, enjoy your dessert."

Kendall barely heard the door open or close as Lacey left the apartment. Her attention remained riveted on Ed. He crawled up her body like a man on a mission, his eyes glazed, his body hot, his cock pressing between her legs, still constrained by the gym shorts.

He plucked the cherry from the tip of the whipped cream, then proceeded to lick every last drop of the white fluffy sweetness from her breast. "This is the best part." He took her nipple between his teeth and rolled it.

Sharp pangs of longing shot throughout Kendall's body. The sensations were great, but they weren't enough. She wanted all of him, inside her, thrusting hard and fast. Kendall reveled in his attention to her breasts, but she wanted more.

Her hands came up between them and she shoved him to arm's length. "I get the idea. But does it work both ways?"

Ed stared down at her, pausing as his eyes focused. "What?"

"Does it work both ways?"

His gaze locked on her breasts, and he shook his head. "I'm sorry. I don't know what you're talking about."

"Get off of me and let me show you."

He leaned back, allowing her to slip from beneath him. Once she made it off the couch, he collapsed onto his back, draping an arm over his face. "I'm sorry, Kendall, I shouldn't have let it go that far. I don't know what would have happened if you hadn't stopped me."

Stopped him! Kendall could have kicked herself into tomorrow. If she'd messed up her chances, she'd never forgive herself. "I have no intention of stopping you."

Ed peeked out from beneath his arm. "No?"

"No." She reached for the elastic band of his shorts and tugged them downward.

His hand captured hers before she got far. "What are you doing?"

"I told you." She tugged his hand loose and continued to pull the shorts over his hips. "I want to see if it works both ways." Before he could protest further, she yanked the shorts lower. "I've never been with a man and whipped cream at the same time. The idea intrigues me."

Ed's cock sprang free, jutting straight up. Oh yeah, she had him excited. Now if she could keep him that way until she fulfilled her own fantasy. She dipped a finger in the pudding and slathered the sweet along the length of his dick, rubbing the pudding up and down with both hands.

"Oh, baby." Ed moaned. "Do you know what you're doing?"

"Having dessert and eating it too." She grabbed the whipped cream can and sprayed a cone on the tip of his penis. Finally, she topped her creation with a bright red cherry. "Does a man like this as much as a woman?"

"It's kind of cold."

"Hmmm. Then let me clean it off." A smile played at Kendall's lips as she leaned over him, starting with the cherry. She plucked it into her mouth, chewed it quickly and swallowed, "Ummm, very nice. Anything yet?"

"Still cold, shrinking a bit."

Kendall snorted. He wasn't shrinking. He was much longer and thicker than the boys she'd played at making love with while growing up. She cupped his balls, aiming his cock for her lips then sliding it into her mouth, and an explosion of flavors burst across her tongue. Banana pudding and whipped cream…and Ed. Her tongue swirled around the hardened length, flicking against the mushroom tip.

"That's better. Much better."

Oh yeah, definitely. She released his cock, licking the whipped cream from her lips. "Would you say it's as enticing as a woman spreading sweets between her legs?"

"Oh, yes." He laced his fingers into her hair and drew her down to him, thrusting his dick into her mouth.

Kendall smiled inwardly as she sucked his cock, slipping up and down over him, enjoying the smooth slide.

Until his body tensed and he pulled free of her mouth.

"I'm not wearing panties," Kendall reminded him. She held up a foil package she'd slipped into the back pocket of her jean skirt. "I'm ready to move on to the next lesson."

Ed snatched the condom from her and tore it open with his teeth. He sat up on the couch and started to apply the contraceptive.

Kendall took the rubber from him. "I need to know how to do this properly." She slid the dome over his reddish head and down his length, her fingers slipping along, warming it as she went. God, he was huge, hard and thick.

Her pussy creamed in anticipation. She straddled his legs, placed a knee on either side of his hips, coming down over him, her channel so slick with juices he slid right in.

Ed closed his eyes as he eased into her, his face tense, his hands on her ass guiding her.

Dear, sweet Jesus, this was exactly where Kendall had hoped to go

Sex Ed

with this lesson. Heart beating wildly, she moved up and down over him. "Is this right? Or does the guy prefer to be on top?"

"Most guys don't care if they're on top, on the bottom or standing up as long as they're getting some." His eyes opened and his hands held her still, fully sheathing him. "Who is this guy you're after? Will you be doing this with him?"

Now was the time to own up to Ed that he was the one. The intensity of his stare had her balking. Tightening her thighs, Kendall rose up and slid down over him again. "Does it matter?" There, answering a question with a question would delay her having to own up to loving him. She needed to know how he felt about her before she admitted her love. In no way did she want him feeling sorry for her.

"Any other positions I should use that are particularly exciting to a man?" Kendall leaned close, flashing her breasts in his face, arching her back. Then with a great deal of restraint, she dismounted and stood in front of him. "I've never tried it, but I hear doggy-style can be quite enticing." With her skirt still hiked up over her hips, her pussy wet and warm from him, she dropped to her hands and knees on the couch beside Ed, presenting her bottom toward him.

Ed smoothed a large, rough hand over her cheeks. "I'm going to hell for this. I know it."

"No, you're not. You're helping a friend. Now is it better for the woman to be up on her hands like this or should she lean low, like this?" She dropped to her elbows, her ass jutting up, praying Ed would take her up on her blatant offer and not run screaming.

"You are so very beautiful." Ed moaned and pressed a kiss to her bottom. That one kiss was followed by another. "Connor is never going to forgive me."

Why had he mentioned her brother? She glanced over her shoulder at Ed. "What does Connor have to do with this?"

He avoided eye-contact. "Uh, he's my best friend and I'm about to...ah hell...you're his sister. I'm supposed to protect you, not fuck you."

Was that what had been holding him back? A need to protect Connor's baby sister? Kendall should have had a long talk with her brother before he'd left for the war. He needed to understand she wasn't a kid anymore, and Ed was the man she'd loved for so long she compared all men to his standard. "Ed Judson, what Connor doesn't know, won't hurt him. Besides, if it wasn't you helping me in my research..."

"It sure as hell wouldn't be Whitey." Ed scooted closer. He dipped his finger in the pudding and spread it along the crease between her butt cheeks, then licked his way along the seam, his tongue tracing the tight ring of her ass. "I'll never look at banana pudding the same."

The gentle glide of his tongue on her ass was more than she could have imagined, the sensations burning a path straight to her pussy. As her body clenched, Kendall sighed, a smile tilting the corners of her lips.

Ed might be reluctant because of his friendship to Connor, but he couldn't resist what was right there ready to be taken.

His tongue moved lower, delving into her pussy, trusting in and out. Then he was on his knees, his cock pushing into her, his hands gripping her hips.

"Yes. Oh, sweet Jesus. Yes!" Kendall called out, her fingers curling into the couch cushion as Ed rode her hard and fast, slamming into her with enough force to make skin-on-skin smacking sounds.

There was nothing gentle or tender about the way he fucked her. It was primal, hot, monkey sex and Kendall loved it, her own body tensing along with his, rising to the most incredible climax imaginable, teetering on the very edge of the ultimate release.

Ed thrust into her once more and stopped short of delivering. He held her hips for a long moment, buried inside her, then yanked out his cock, flipped her on her back and plunged into her with one final breath-stealing trust. His body froze, his dick pulsing inside her, his head flung back, eyes squeezed shut. Then he collapsed on top of her, crushing her with his weight.

Kendall didn't care that she couldn't breathe, she could die right now. She'd already gone straight to heaven in Ed's arms. Her hands rubbed along his muscled back, realizing he still wore his T-shirt. She wished he'd been naked so that her breasts would press firmly into his chest. She could easily lie here all night in Ed's arms. Hadn't she dreamed of this for years?

Ed pushed up to his elbows and stared down at Kendall. "Just who was teaching who on that lesson?"

"Why, you were teaching me, of course." Kendall smiled up at Ed and pushed a strand of hair off his forehead. It fell back as she let go. "Do I get an A for our lesson today?"

"You get an A+. You're a natural." Ed pressed a kiss to her lips.

"Thanks." Kendall pulled his head down to her and ran her tongue along the seam of his lips, tasting banana and sex. Then she pressed in, past his teeth to stroke his tongue. "You taste wonderful."

"So do you." He traced his finger along her jaw line and down her neck to the swell of her breasts. "When did you grow up?"

Kendall loved every callus on Ed's fingers. He'd earned them working hard on the Rocking G Ranch, doing a man's work. "I've been grown up, you just couldn't see anything but the little girl in ponytails I used to be."

"You're not a little girl anymore." He bent to take one nipple into his mouth, sucking on it gently, rolling the tip with his tongue.

"No, I'm not." Shivers of pleasure tickled along her skin. Kendall took a deep breath. This was the time to tell him that she was in love with him, that she wanted to be with him always. "Ed—"

A loud banging on the door made Ed's head come up.

"Who the hell is that?" Ed frowned at the door, making no move to get off of Kendall to answer it.

That had to be a good sign.

Another loud banging was followed by Lacey's voice. "Kendall, did you forget?"

Eyes narrowed, Ed stared down at Kendall. "Forget what?"

"Kendall, did you forget you had a date with Cory?" Lacey called out, her voice only slightly muffled by the solid wood door.

Kendall groaned. "I did forget." Her brows furrowed as she stared up at Ed. "I have to go."

In a fluid movement, Ed stood, reaching for his shorts. "You have a date?"

Kendall rolled off the couch, tugging her skirt down over her hips and buttoning her shirt. "I made this one a long time ago. It's a promise I have to keep."

The big cowboy pulled on his shorts, then crossed his arms over his chest. "Don't go."

Kendall's stomach fluttered. The look in Ed's eyes was everything she could have hoped for. But was she afraid of reading more than what was really there? "Cory is counting on me."

Ed's hands dropped to his sides, his fists clenching. "Cory's the dude I met earlier? The one you've had over at your place every day when I come home?"

"That 's him." Kendall leaned up on her toes and pressed a kiss to Ed's tight lips. "Thanks for the lesson. Same time tomorrow?"

His jaw tightened. "We'll see."

Kendall frowned, all joy of having made love to Ed leeching away. "Did I say something to make you mad?"

He shook his head then he grabbed her arms and stared down at her. "Don't let some jerk take advantage of you."

"What if I want him to?" Kendall teased.

Instead of laughing, Ed's frown deepened.

"Kendall?" Lacey called out.

"I'm coming," Kendall yelled. Turning back to him, she sighed. "We need to talk."

"Let's talk now."

"I can't." She turned for the door, stopping with her hand on the knob. "But we will talk." Then she left, shutting the door behind her before she could change her mind.

"I was about to give up and go without you." Lacey stood at the front door to the big old house. Her face split in a grin. "You did it, didn't you?"

Kendall sucked in a deep breath and let it out slowly. "Yes."

"And?"

A tear slipped out of the corner of her eyes.

"That good, huh?" Lacey shook her head. "Damn."

"Better. I didn't want to leave." She glanced over her shoulder at Ed's door.

"Don't do it, Kendall. He thinks you have a date. You didn't tell him the lessons were to land him, did you?"

Her throat clogged with dryness. "No, but I need to."

"Did he tell you he loves you?"

Kendall frowned. "No. But he's just getting used to the idea of making love to his best friend's little sister. I should tell him how I feel about him." Butterflies flickered in her belly. She started to turn back toward Ed's apartment.

Lacey grabbed her hand. "Not yet. You have to go through with this 'date' with Cory to see if Ed's jealous enough to come after you."

"But it's not a date and, telling Ed it is, is lying to him."

"He'll survive. And won't Plan B be worth the effort if it pushes him over the edge and makes him come to his senses?"

"What if he doesn't?" Kendall pulled free of Lacey's hand. "What if all of this was a waste of time? What if Ed doesn't love me like that?" Her shoulders slumped.

"Did you two make love?"

Kendall smiled, her eyes filling. She nodded, her throat too clogged with tears to choke out words.

"Baby, he had to love you if he'd do it with Connor's little sister."

A shoulder lifted in a shrug. "He thinks I'd go to Whitey Ross for lessons. He didn't have much of a choice."

"The man had choices. Trust me." Lacey turned Kendall toward the stairs. "Now run up and throw on a bra and panties. Going without underwear with Ed is one thing, but at the bar, you'll instill a riot at the Ugly Stick Saloon."

"It's Ladies' Night."

Lacey nodded, her eyes wide. "I know. Some of those so-called ladies are horny enough to jump a cute little thing like you, given enough provocation. Without a bra and panties, you're definitely provoking." She slapped Kendall's ass with enough oomph to send her racing up the stairs.

As soon as Cory did his dance, Kendall would head home and pick up where she and Ed had left off.

She hoped.

***

Ed paced the floor of his apartment once, twice, three times before he gave up.

Footsteps echoed through the ceiling from Kendall's apartment above him. She was probably getting ready for her date.

Anger surged through Ed. How could she go on a date after they'd made love only a few minutes ago? He spun and resumed the pacing.

Was she really in love with someone else? Were the sex lessons just that? Lessons? How could she let him do the things she did without feeling some kind of connection?

Ed sure as hell had felt a connection. Kendall Mason had rocked his world, making him see her for the first time as a fully-grown, very sexy woman. One he wanted in his bed for more than just lessons in sex lessons she'd use on another man.

Her footsteps crossed the floor above and a door opened and closed.

Damn, she was going out and he could do nothing.

Or couldn't he?

Ed raced into his bedroom, pulled on jeans over his shorts, jammed his feet into his cowboy boots and grabbed a shirt as he ran out the door. He'd follow her on her date. If Cory tried anything, damn it...well, he'd cross that bridge when he slammed into it.

Kendall's car sat in the driveway. Cory must have taken her in his topless sports car.

Ed growled. Damned sports cars didn't provide any protection in a rollover. Convertibles were too dangerous and the people who drove them tended to drive too fast. Ed would never take the woman he loved out in a convertible. No sirree.

Holy Hell. His boots skidded on the sidewalk.

Had he just thought the L-word?

Chapter Eight

Ed jumped in his truck and revved the engine, spinning gravel as he pulled out of the driveway onto the road. If he hoped to catch up with Kendall, he'd have to hurry. When he slowed for a stop sign, all he saw was Lacey's car, turning at the end of the next block. No sign of Cory's convertible.

Maybe Lacey knew where Kendall was headed. He turned where Lacey had turned and gunned the accelerator. Lacey had a heavy foot and tended to break speed limits.

Ed tried to catch her but managed to get behind a Grandma Moses, going twenty in a forty zone. Far ahead, Lacey turned west on the main road headed out of town. Ed realized she was headed for the Ugly Stick Saloon where she worked as a waitress. By the time Ed pulled into the parking lot, Lacey had rounded the back of the building and parked. He'd missed her going into the bar.

Cars and pickup trucks filled the parking lot loaded with females, all laughing, smiling and headed for the door. What was the deal? Where were the men?

Ed dropped down out of his truck, jammed his hat on his head and ran for the door, still buttoning his shirt. "Excuse me, excuse me." As he eased his way through the mob, the woman laughed, whistled at him and ran their hands over his chest and butt.

"Are you the talent?" one asked.

"I'd stuff his G-string with every bill in my wallet."

"Hell, I'd give him my credit card."

"Hey, cowboy, I got a twenty with our name on it."

Ed smiled and laughed it off, feeling like chum thrown into a shark-feeding frenzy. When he reached the door, Big Joe Sealy blocked the entrance. "Sorry, Ed, it's ladies night. No men allowed."

"What?" Ed tried to look past Joe in hope of getting Lacey's attention, but the man completely blocked his view. "I'm not staying. I just need to talk to Lacey."

"That's right, you ain't stayin'." Joe crossed his burly arms. "No men past this point. I got strict orders, only ladies are allowed in. The male talent enters through the rear entrance. If you ain't male talent, you ain't gettin' in."

The man was as loyal and as trustworthy as they come, even if he wasn't the sharpest tool in the shed. "What if I told you it was an emergency?"

"Dial 9-1-1. Now git." Joe jerked his head and let several women through.

Sex Ed

His fists clenching, Ed turned and waded through the sea of females. He got pinched twice and one stuffed a dollar into the waistband of his jeans. At this rate, he'd never catch up with Kendall.

When he'd almost cleared the line, a bleach-blonde, forty-something woman wreaking of alcohol threw her arms around him. "Are you the talent? Cause I'm callin' dibs."

He smiled down at her and untangled her arms from around his neck. "Sorry, lady. I'm taken." As soon as he made it past the crowd, he headed for the truck.

A convertible screamed into the parking lot and almost clipped him. Without slowing, it headed straight for the back of the saloon.

The pretty blond boy in the driver's seat had to be Cory. But where was Kendall? Had she come with Lacey?

Fuck. Ed rounded the side of the building and jogged to the rear. He was just in time to see Cory enter through the back door. Was that scrawny little twerp the talent? And what kind of date involved Kendall providing her own transportation? A real man came to the lady's front door and escorted her to his truck. He didn't arrange to meet her at some bar.

Shaking his head, he marched for the back entrance, ready to give Kendall and Cory a piece of his mind. As he reached for the doorknob, it jerked open.

"Oh, thank goodness. You must be the new guy. You're late." A woman with ham fists that put Big Joe Sealy's to shame, grabbed his arm and pulled him through the door. "Your costume's hanging in the changing room. It's the leather chaps and whip. If you don't have your own G-string, there's a spare on the shelf at the rear of the room. Move it, you're on in five minutes."

She gave him a hefty shove, sending him into a room crowded with pumped up, mostly naked men.

A man dressed in what might once have been a policeman's uniform hurried by. "Dude, you better hurry. The natives are restless and we're on in four minutes." As he passed, Ed noted the back of his trousers had been cut out, displaying a shocking amount of man-ass.

When Ed didn't respond, the guy looked over his shoulder. "You are Fred's fill-in, aren't you? If not, you can't be in here. It's ladies night and no men are allowed in the saloon except the talent."

Ed gulped and made his decision. "Guess that makes me the talent." He forced a smile and hurriedly added, "Are there some chaps around here? I hear that's my costume."

"On the hook over there." The cop nodded to the rear of the room.

By now, most of the men had slipped into skimpy costumes, rubbed oil on their perfectly tanned torsos and strutted to the edge of the curtain.

"Chop, chop!" The woman from the back door stepped inside and clapped her hands. She handed him a black mask. "Tonight, you're the lone ranger. Go get 'em, cowboy."

Ed stripped and grabbed a package labeled G-string. Never in all his life had he ever planned on wearing what he had always referred to as butt floss. Tonight was the exception. He packed his jewels into the triangle of material which unfortunately barely concealed half of his length. And damned if the thought of all those women out there didn't make the fit twice as bad. His cock swelled, stretching the material away from his body.

Holy Hell.

"We're on!" someone shouted.

Ed tied the chaps around his waist and the mask around his head. At least he'd be able to check on Kendall without her suspecting a thing. The music rose in a highly suggestive bump-and-grind tune. The crowd of women screamed, the cacophony drowning out the music.

His heart hammering in his chest, Ed stepped out onto a brightly lit stage, temporarily blinded by the lights pointed up at the performers.

The cop leaned over and yelled in Ed's ear, "Dance, man, dance. They tip better if you shake it in their faces."

Ed edged out onto the stage, careful to keep from turning around. His ass was cold and he didn't want to moon the women gathered for the show.

Holy Hell. What had he gotten himself into?

***

Kendall sat at the edge of the stage, Lacey next her to drinking a light beer, hootin' and hollerin' like she hadn't seen this a dozen times before.

"There he is." Kendall smiled and waved at Cory.

He danced his way over to Kendall and shook his hips, twisting and gyrating the way Kendall had taught him. Cory had natural rhythm. All Kendall had done was shown him a few moves that would get attention and hopefully land him extra tips to help him with the rent while he attended college.

Kendall was so proud of him. He had a great body, why not make enough cash in one night to pay the rent for the next two months? That way, his studies didn't have to suffer by holding down a full-time job and going to school at night.

Cory reached down his hand.

Kendall had a dollar ready to slap into his palm.

Only he didn't take the money, he pulled her up onto the stage with a quick tug.

"What are you doing?" She laughed and tried to step down.

"Rather you than one of those other horny women. Please help me with the show and save me from the masses. You're good at this." He danced around her, grinding his pelvis into her hips.

Kendall's cheeks burned. If Cory was more comfortable by dancing the first song with her, what could it hurt? She smiled and laughed, pretending to be one of the random women the men selected on occasion to fuel the crowd.

Cory twirled her around and backed her into his arms, his cock grinding against her ass, his hands sliding down her sides to her hips.

It was yet another one of the moves Kendall had taught him, and he was doing so well. Kendall should have moved off the stage and let him bring another woman up onto stage. One with money burning a hole in her pocket.

Kendall straightened, laughing. "You're on your own, Cory."

Cory jerked away and a larger pair of hands clamped around her waist, holding her in place. "What the hell?" When she twisted toward her captor, he refused to let her, his hips pumping to the rhythm of the music, his hands sliding up her waist.

Cory danced by with a shrug and a grin.

Kendall's heart raced, defensive instincts kicking in. "Let go of me."

Chaps flapped against her legs. Chaps that barely covered the massive thighs beneath them.

Kendall's heart raced and a slow burn skimmed beneath every inch of her skin. A quick glance over her shoulder did nothing to quell the rise of heat in her body. The man behind her wore a cowboy hat and a black mask. "Who are you?"

The man's mouth curved upward in a deadly sexy smile. "The Lone Ranger, ma'am. Here to rescue you," he said in a deep voice.

So deep, Kendall could have fallen into it. Her breath grew ragged as the cowboy's hands slid up from her waist to cup her breasts. Kendall leaned back into him, his tough leather and man-musk scent making her knees weak. "No, really." Her voice ragged, she swallowed hard and continued. "Who are you?"

"Ride with me into the sunset, beautiful lady, and I'll reveal all."

Her heart skipped several beats then raced to catch up. Hell, what was she thinking? She loved Ed, not this sexy cowboy who danced in strip clubs. "No. No, I can't. I have a boyfriend. I'm practically engaged."

He spun her away from him and back into his arms so that she faced him. "This Cory dude is not the man for you."

Her boobs crashed into his naked chest, forcing her breath out in a gasp. Kendall stared into the man's sky blue eyes.

He lifted his cowboy hat and winked.

"Ed?" Joy swelled in her chest as Kendall stood stock still in the middle of the dance floor. "What are you doing here?"

"Keeping you from making a mistake with pretty boy." He nodded his head toward Cory.

"By dancing naked in front of all these barracudas?" She shook her head and laughed out loud. "Really, why are you here?"

"That's just it. I couldn't let you go out on a date with Cory. He's not the right man for you."

Irritation straightened her spine. Kendall planted her fists on her hips and faced off with Ed Judson. "No? Then who is, Ed? Who is the right man for me?"

Ed opened his mouth to answer, but before any words could come out, Big Joe Sealy plucked Kendall from the stage and set her on the barroom floor. "Time's up, Kendall. Let one of the other ladies have a shot at the cowboy."

"But, Joe, I need to be up there." Kendall placed her hands on the wooden surface and tried to climb back up.

Big Joe planted a heavy hand on her shoulder. With the other hand, he helped a forty-something bleach blonde climb onto the stage where she immediately flung herself into Ed's arms.

A surge of jealousy ripped through Kendall's gut.

Ed peeled the woman's death grip from around his neck, and he spun her away from him and back.

His moves were not nearly as practiced or suggestive as the other strippers, but still fun to watch. When he turned his back to the audience, Kendall gasped and clapped a hand to her mouth.

Ed's very tight, very manly ass shone like a neon moon.

Women roared and surged toward the stage, bills clenched in their fists or hanging from their teeth. They shoved Kendall out of the way, pushing her farther and farther away from the cowboy and his gorgeous tush.

The blonde in Ed's arms pulled her top over her head and flung it out into the crowd. Wearing nothing but a black demi-bra, the woman jumped up and wrapped her legs around Ed's waist, pressing her D cups into his face. She yanked his hat off his head and waved it in the air, shouting, "Ride me, cowboy!"

Ed's eyes widened and he looked out into the crowd. When he caught a glimpse of Kendall, he mouthed the word, *help.*

Kendall crossed her arms over her chest and shook her head. "You're on your own." If Ed had hoped to stop her from seeing Cory, he

Sex Ed

deserved to be caught in his little act by all these women. Let him suffer. If he hoped to win her heart, his answers had to be faster and he had to be fully prepared to declare his love. He needed to see what a treasure he had in Kendall and that having all the women in the world was not the right answer for him.

The song faded out and a roar of applause sure to deafen every ear in the room rose to a crescendo. The men made a final pass along the edge of the stage, allowing women to stuff their G-strings with bills, then they escaped behind the curtain.

Big Joe Sealy had to untangle the blonde from Ed before he could beat a retreat.

Finally backstage, Ed sucked in a deep breath and let it out slowly.

"Not used to the meat market, are you?" The cop slapped him on the back and grinned. "Don't worry, after the first dance, you just go with the flow."

Flow, hell. Ed didn't plan on dancing another dance in front of those rabid women. All he wanted was get into his jeans and shirt, find Kendall and get her the hell out of there.

"Hey, cowboy, nice ass." A hand slapped his butt, staying there a little longer than necessary.

Ed spun, ready to defend his honor and politely tell the woman he was done playing stripper.

Lacey leaned against the wall, her lips twisted, her brows waggling. "You looked damn fine out there tonight."

"Don't get used to it."

She tipped her head, her gaze going to the flesh exposed by chaps way too small for his thick thighs. "I don't know. I think you can make a killing with that equipment.

Heat crawled across his chest and Ed covered his package with cupped hands. "Cut it out."

"So, why'd you come?"

"Would you believe I wanted to try my hand at stripping?"

Lacey shook her head. "Try again."

At just that moment, Cory entered the dressing room.

Ed straightened. "I came to talk Kendall out of dating that gigolo." His fists clenched. "Maybe I should just have a word with the man, instead of Kendall."

Lacey placed a hand in the middle of Ed's chest, stopping him before he could take a step. "Wrong."

"What do you mean wrong?" Ed heaved a ragged sigh.

"Cory's not the problem."

"Then who the hell is?" Ed raised both fists. "I'll kill him."

Lacey grinned. "You."

"Me?" His hands unclenched and jammed onto his waist.

"Yeah, big guy." Her hand fell to her side. "Why do you think Kendall was willing to let you teach her sex education lessons?"

"Because she trusts me?" Surely, that was the reason that made the most sense.

Lacey snorted and shook her head.

Ed's brows furrowed. "I couldn't let her go to Whitey Ross for lessons."

"Kendall needs lessons about sex like an alcoholic needs to learn how to drink. She gave up her virginity when she was eighteen."

His chest squeezed tight. "I'd like to punch the kid that took it."

"Why?"

"Because. She was just a kid."

"And why don't you want her to date Cory?" Lacey nodded toward the blond pretty boy. "Kendall's not a kid anymore."

"I promised Connor I'd look out for her." But damn, the girl had grown into a beautiful woman.

"What if she loves Cory?"

"I'll kill him." Blood thundered in his ears.

"Why?" Lacey looked him directly in the eye.

"Because I love her." Ed gripped Lacey's arms. "I love Kendall. Are you happy? I love my best friend's little sister."

Lacey's face split into a wide grin. "Honey, you'll have to get over that one, if you really love her and want to be with her."

Ed glanced over at Cory. "What about the pretty face over there?"

"She's been teaching him how to dance. That's all."

"To dance?" He stared from Cory back to Lacey, his head swimming with the possibility that he might have a chance with Kendall. "I thought she wanted the lessons to get a guy to notice her."

"It worked, didn't it?" Her lips spread into a wide grin. "You noticed her, didn't you?"

"You're kidding right? All that sex education bullshit was to get my attention?" Ed shook his head. He turned and walked a few steps away, oblivious to the draft on his backside, then spun and returned to Lacey. "Why didn't she just tell me?"

Lacey's cheeks reddened. "I kinda talked her into the whole Sex Ed plan."

"You?" Ed ran his hand through his hair.

"Yeah. I figured it would give her one more chance to get your attention."

"Before what?"

"Before she moved to Austin and started over."

All the air whooshed out of Ed's lungs. He had never considered Kendall might move away. If he was honest with himself, he suspected his reluctance toward building his own house had a lot to do with Kendall sharing the one he lived in. "She was right. I refused to look at her as anything other than Connor's sister."

Lacey's brows rose, a smile quirking the edges of her lips. "Yeah, but you never brought women back to your apartment."

"I couldn't." He laughed. "Bringing another woman into the same house didn't feel right."

"And you haven't married any of the women you've dated."

"Again, it just didn't feel right."

"Now that you've been with Kendall?"

Ed grinned. "She feels right." He slapped his hat on his leg. "Damn it, it feels so right I want to tell her."

Lacey frowned. "Tell her what? That it feels right?" She shook her head. "It'll take more than that to win that girl over. The big question is, do you love her?"

Ed's grin grew even wider. "Yes, ma'am. More than anything."

"Even more than disappointing your friend?"

Ed sobered. "I need to talk to Connor before I do anything."

"The sooner, the better." A smile lit Lacey's face. "You're going to marry her, aren't you?"

"Damn straight. Before she gets anymore cockamamie ideas about sex education."

Chapter Nine

Kendall pushed her way through the crowd, angling for the door to the dressing room backstage. Ed's punishment with the other women had gone on quite long enough. If Ed had come to 'rescue' her from Cory, Kendall hoped he acted because he was jealous, not just doing his brotherly-duty. Perhaps the Cory baiting had done the trick and made him realize he had a little competition, and that he'd better speak up or shut up.

Her efforts to get to the dressing room became more forceful, until she soon shoved women out of the way. What if he'd been about to declare his love when Big Joe yanked Kendall off the stage?

Ed might really be in love with her and she wanted to know now.

When she reached the dressing room, she waited until the security guard left his post for a moment to answer a question of one of the bar patrons.

Kendall ran, grabbed the door knob and jerked it open. Once inside, she slammed the door closed behind her. Another song started, and the crowd of women screamed so loud, no amount of wall insulation could muffle the cries. Several of the men had changed costumes and were headed back to the stage. One by one, the crowd of men in the dressing area thinned until Kendall finally spotted Ed on the opposite end of the room.

He had his back to her, still wearing the chaps that exposed his really fine ass in the G-string.

Kendall's steps picked up and she almost laughed out loud. She couldn't wait until she could pinch him. She had a smart-ass remark poised on her lips, ready for when he spotted her.

Ed turned to the side, his body in silhouette even more powerful and beautiful in Kendall's eyes. He smiled and laughed at someone standing in the shadows.

Then a slim pair of arms wrapped around his neck and a woman with auburn hair flung herself at him, kissing him full on the lips.

Lacey.

Kendall's feet ground to a halt and she backed behind a stage prop, her little bubble of happiness exploding deep in her chest. How could she have been so wrong? Ed looked so happy, like a man in love. In love with Lacey, not her.

Cory passed in front of her, stopped and returned. "Kendall? You're not supposed to be in here."

"It's okay, I'm leaving." Kendall spoke softly. She didn't want Ed and Lacey to find her there. If they said anything to her right then, she was likely to fall completely apart. "I just wanted to congratulate you on a great performance." She turned away from the sight of Ed and Lacey hugging and kissing, her heart so heavy she could barely breathe.

"Thanks, Kendall. I made enough in tips to pay for three months' rent on my apartment. If you hadn't taught me how to dance, I don't know how I'd have managed. Those women are crazy." He laughed and hugged her. "I better get back out there. There's more money to be made while it lasts."

"You go. I'm headed out the back door."

"Are you okay?" Cory stared into her face, a frown pulling his brows low.

"I'm fine." She waved a hand in front of her neck. "I just need air. Crowds, you know."

"Yeah, I know. Especially this one." He grinned. "Thanks again." He disappeared through the curtain, leaving Kendall to find her way out without alerting Lacey and Ed to her presence.

One of the dancers carried a large Mexican sombrero to the props shelf.

Kendall ducked behind the hat and walked with him until she could peel off and head for the rear door. Without looking back, she pushed through the door. As soon as the cool night air hit her burning cheeks, the tears fell.

Had that been Lacey's plan all along? Had she insinuated herself into the Sex Ed lessons because Ed was getting too close to Kendall and she wanted Ed for herself?

A lead weight settled in Kendall's gut. Maybe Ed had been playing her all along. Maybe he'd always loved Lacey and Kendall hadn't seen it. Had the two of them been in cahoots all along, waiting for Kendall to give up and move on?

Kendall's feet carried her through the parking lot, one slow, heavy step at a time.

A cop car cruised through, moving just as slowly.

Kendall dodged his cruiser and hit the highway, her pace increasing. The cop pulled alongside. "Lady, you need a ride home?"

Kendall kept her head averted, not one to cry in front of strangers. "No." She needed to walk out her frustrations or at least until her tears dried. Given what she'd just witnessed, that might be a very long walk.

"It's supposed to start raining," the cop said. "I don't feel right leaving you out here walking alone."

"I don't need a ride." She sniffed and scrubbed a hand across her face.

"Suit yourself." He slowed his police vehicle to a stop.

Kendall kept walking toward town. Five miles. The distance was only five miles from the saloon to the house. She could jog that in her sleep.

A fat drop of rain landed square between her eyes and dripped down over her nose. Another fell, then another, mixing with the tears. Soon the heavens opened and dumped on Kendall. She couldn't see to walk and every step landed in another dark rut filled with water. "Why?" she yelled to the sky. "Why?"

The cop car pulled up, his windshield wipers flinging even more water onto her. "Get in." Door locks clicked.

Kendall yanked open the front passenger door and got in, completely soaked and past caring. She gave the police officer her address and closed her eyes for the remainder of the short ride, determined to avoid conversation. Even if she tried, she couldn't speak past the wad of tears clogging her throat,.

As they pulled in front of the house, the cop shifted into park and turned toward her. "He's not worth it. A guy who'd let you go isn't worth the trouble." He held up his hands. "Just saying."

"Thanks for the ride." Kendall got out, closed the door and trudged up the steps to her apartment.

The cop had it right. The man wasn't worth it.

If that was the case, then why was she so broken hearted?

***

Ed dressed in the jeans and shirt he'd worn into the building and peeked around the curtain, looking for Kendall. Lacey had gone out into the crowd to find her while Ed changed.

He spotted Lacey, but no Kendall.

Lacey waved at him from across the floor and jerked her head toward the exit.

They met outside at the rear of the building. Big fat raindrops fell from the sky at random.

"Did she leave?" Ed asked.

Lacey shrugged. "I looked in the bathroom and everywhere else I could think of. She's not in the saloon."

Ed's pulse quickened. "You don't think she's in trouble, do you?"

"She rode with me." Lacey frowned.

"I'm worried something's happened."

"Let me check with Cory. Maybe he's seen her." Lacey ducked back inside the back door.

As Ed paced the parking lot, the rain let loose, dumping down on him. He headed for the door to see what was keeping Lacey and reached for the doorknob.

Sex Ed

Lacey emerged, her face pale. "Cory said Kendall was in the dressing room a few minutes ago and said she was going out the back for some air. I looked again and didn't see any sign of her anywhere."

Before Lacey finished speaking, Ed ran for his truck, his boots splashing in the puddles. "I'm headed to the house."

"I'll see you there," Lacey called out behind him.

Ed ran around to the front of the Ugly Stick Saloon and leaped into his truck, shaking the water out of his hair. Where the hell was Kendall? If she'd been in the dressing room, why hadn't she told him or Lacey that she was leaving?

All the worst-case scenarios sprang to mind. An image sprang to mind of Kendall stepping out back for a breath of air and being grabbed by some ape of a man, thrown into his car and taken into some backwoods area where he'd rape and murder her.

Anger stiffened his muscles. Ed's boot hit the accelerator hard, spitting gravel up behind him. His truck skidded sideways onto the slick highway, straightened and sped toward the house.

He couldn't let his imagination take over. Everything would be okay. A logical explanation existed for Kendall's disappearance. She probably got a ride home with someone and left a message with one of the wait staff who forgot to deliver it.

Holy Hell. Was it five miles or fifteen to his house?

His cell phone rang in his pocket and he almost had a wreck answering it. "Kendall?"

"No, it's me, Connor. Is something wrong?"

Ed wanted to shout *Yes!* But he couldn't upset his friend, not while he couldn't do anything to help. "No, nothing." He prayed.

"Why did you think I was Kendall?"

"Look, Connor, I'm in a hurry, and there's no good way to do this other than to jump in." Bracing his hands on the wheel, Ed took a deep breath and announced, "I love your sister and want to marry her."

"Holy smokes, Ed," Connor yelled into the phone. "I thought you were fixin' to give me bad news. Don't scare me like that."

Ed's foot eased up on the accelerator. "What, you're not upset or disappointed?"

"Are you kidding? About time you two got together. Kendall's been in love with you since forever."

"Why was I the last to know it?"

"Hey, I'm your friend. I wasn't going to push my kid sister at you. Besides, she had some growing up to do."

Ed's thoughts went back to banana pudding and whipped cream. "Oh, she's all grown up now."

"Yeah. Why do you think I asked you to keep an eye on her? I hoped you'd wake up to that fact."

Ed shook his head and slammed his foot on the brake. "Look, Connor, I'm driving in the rain to get to Kendall and ask her to marry me. On your next call to her, ask her what her answer is."

"Will do. And congrats."

Tossing his cell phone in the seat beside him, Ed prayed Kendall was at home and safe so that he could propose. He took all the corners too fast, hydroplaning sideways, almost clipping two stop signs. By the time he reached the house, his heart was pounding so hard, he thought it would jump right out of his chest.

Ed drove the pickup into the drive, slammed it into park and jumped out, leaving the engine running, the keys in the ignition. If Kendall wasn't home, he didn't know where he'd look, but he'd look until he found her. *Damn it, she'd better be home.*

With long strides, he took the steps two at a time. When he reached her apartment door, he banged it hard with his fists. "Kendall!" He continued banging in case she was in the shower or blow-drying her hair. She had to hear him. She had to be there.

Scared out of his wits, he backed up, ready to throw himself at the door and break it down, when the door suddenly opened.

Kendall stood there, wrapped in nothing but a towel, her eyes wide and red-rimmed, her hair dripping down around her shoulders. "Ed? Where's the fire?"

"Holy Hell." He enveloped her in his arms and hugged her so fiercely, she squeaked.

"What's wrong with you?" Kendall pushed against him.

"Is she here?" Lacey's footsteps echoed on the stairs behind Ed.

"She's here." Ed still held Kendall in his arms, even as she pushed to free herself.

"Of course, I'm here. Where else would I be?"

"In a ditch, murdered, raped, dead." Ed yanked her against his body again and held her there. "Don't ever scare me like that again."

"I'm not dead, or raped, or murdered. I just came home. Now let me go." Her hands planted firmly against his chest and she pushed so hard, Ed was forced to let go. "You left without telling anyone." Ed ran a hand through his wet hair, dragging in a deep breath. "What was I supposed to think?"

Kendall stepped away, her head averted, refusing to meet his gaze. "Ed, you're not my keeper. Whatever you promised my brother is bullshit. I'm not your responsibility."

"To hell with your brother." His hand pounded his chest. "What about me? What if I care enough to know where you are?"

"You won't have to worry about me much longer." Her chin jutted out, her bottom lip trembling. "After I graduate from college next month, I'm headed to Austin. Out of sight will be out of mind. You and Lacey can carry on without me in the way." She grabbed the edge of the door and tried to close it. "Now if you'll excuse me, I'm going to bed."

"Me and Lacey?" Ed looked at her, sure she'd lost her mind. "What do you mean, me and Lacey?"

Lacey stepped up beside Ed. " Kendall, what are you talking about?"

Kendall's eyes pooled and a dammed tear slipped out and trailed down her cheek. Hadn't she cried enough? "I thought you were my friend."

Lacey's brows drew together and she pushed past Ed, reaching out to take Kendall in her arms. "I *am* your friend."

Kendall held up her hands, backing away from Lacey. "No. How can you be when you came up with this whole Sex Ed plan? All along you wanted Ed for yourself."

Lacey's frown deepened. "Me, want Ed? No way. He's yours."

"I'm not at all into Lacey." Ed shook his head. "Where did you get an idea like that?"

"You don't have to hide it anymore." Kendall swiped at the tears streaming down her face and tipped up her chin. "I saw you two kissing in the dressing room at the Ugly Stick."

Lacey's brows rose, her eyes rounding. "You saw me kissing Ed because I was happy for him. Not because I love him. The kiss was sisterly, nothing more."

"Yeah, and I'm just a naive college girl, gullible and easily tricked. No thanks. You two can have each other." With a heavy heart, Kendall tried again to shut the door.

"Kendall, I'd just told Lacey that I love you. She was so excited that she kissed me. The kiss didn't mean anything. I love *you*." Ed pushed the door wider and made a grab for Kendall's arm.

Joy dared to spring into her heart, but she wouldn't let herself be hurt again. She dodged him and moved farther back into the apartment. "No, you just feel responsible for me because of some dumb promise you made to my brother."

"I love you. And not because of the promise I made to your brother." He followed her into the apartment, his steps slow, measured, like an animal stalking his prey. "I think I've always loved you. It took some crazy female plan to make me see it."

Kendall backed up a step further until her bottom ran into the sofa.

"I don't believe you," she whispered.

"Then let me tell you again." His hands slid up her arms and rounded to the back of her neck, tipping her head back. "I love you, Kendall Mason."

"Uh, I'll just let myself out. Maybe I'll just go turn off your truck and collect the keys." Lacey chuckled. "You two can handle things from here." The door to Kendall's apartment closed with a soft snick.

Kendall couldn't tear her gaze away from Ed's, his blue eyes burned into her, swarms of butterflies attacking her insides. "You love me?"

"Yup." He bent to brush a kiss across her lips. "I just needed a little sex education to show me how much."

"What about my brother?" Kendall leaned into Ed, her lips pressing into his.

Ed reached into his pocket and pulled out his cell phone. "Connor called me on the way to the house. He's on board and told me to plan the wedding for when he's back and can give you away proper."

"He did?" Her eyes widened and a huge swell of happiness filled her. "I love you, Ed Judson. I've loved you my entire life."

"Then why the hell did you wait so long to tell me?" He gathered her against him, his mouth slanting across hers, his tongue thrusting between her teeth.

The kiss sparked a fire inside Kendall that burned away the cold of the drenching rain and mistaken betrayal. She let go of the edge of her towel, letting it fall to the floor. "I'm ready for my next lesson," she said against his mouth.

Ed laughed out loud, scooped her up in his arms and carried her into the bedroom. "I have a feeling you could teach *me* a few things." He laid her on the bed and stripped his damp shirt from his shoulders.

"Maybe." With a wicked grin, Kendall eased open the buttons on his jeans and pushed them down over his hips. "Shall we start here?" His cock sprang free into her hands.

With slow, steady strokes, she slid her hands up and down his length, reveling in the smooth skin encasing hardened steel. He was hers. All hers.

Kendall took him into her mouth, grabbing around his hips to pull him deeper until his cock bumped against the back of her throat. His dick filled her mouth, stretching her lips.

His hands threaded into her hair as he thrust in and out, faster and faster. When his body stiffened, he pulled free and climbed on the bed with her, parting her knees.

Kendall stared up into his eyes as he drove into her body, burying his cock deep, filling her, stretching her channel in the most delicious

Sex Ed

way. Her heels dug into the sheets, pushing her up to meet him, thrust for thrust. Never in her life had she felt this complete, this loved and cherished by a man. Her body tensed, the tingling beginning at her core and spreading outward to the tips of her fingers. Kendall cried out his name as she burst over the edge. "Ed."

Ed held her hips as he plunged in one last time, his cock pulsing inside her, his fingers digging into her skin. Then he collapsed on top of her and rolled them to the side, without severing their intimate connection. "You aren't the little girl I used to know."

"Is that a bad thing?" Kendall smoothed the lock of hair off his forehead, loving that they lay naked in her bed, their bodies joined.

"Oh, it's very bad, in a very good way." He kissed her and thrust into her again.

The cell phone on Kendall's bedside table rang, vibrating so much it rattled across the wood surface.

Kendall frowned and reached to turn it off when she saw the caller id flashing *Connor Mason*. She glanced at Ed. "It's Connor."

He nodded, leaning in to nibble at her throat. "Answer."

With a smile, Kendall draped a leg over Ed's hip and poked the Talk button. "Hi, brother. How's the war?"

"Forget the war, I hear congratulations are in order. My baby sister is engaged."

Kendall frowned at the phone. "What?"

A long pause then, "Oops, did I jump the gun?"

Ed took the phone from Kendall. "I was just getting to that. Thanks, buddy." He handed back the phone.

As Kendall pressed it to her ear, Ed thrust into her.

"Will you marry me, Kendall Mason?"

"Say yes!" Connor shouted into her ear.

Kendall sucked in a deep breath and held it, the feeling of Ed hard and thick deep inside her threatening to steal the air from her lungs. "Yes," she said, all the air rushing out of her lungs at once. "Yes, Ed Judson. I'll marry you." Into the phone, she said, "Gotta go, Connor. We're celebrating our engagement."

"Hey, no babies until I can give you away at the wedding."

"I'm making no promises." Kendall clicked the disconnect button and switched off the phone. "Now where were we?" Her arms curled around Ed's neck and she drew him down for a long kiss. "Ah yes. You were about to give me the next installment of Sex Ed."

####

About the Author

Twenty years of livin' and lovin' on a South Texas ranch raising horses, cattle, goats, ostriches and emus left an indelible impression on Myla Jackson, one she likes to instill in her red-hot stories. Myla pens wildly sexy, fun adventures of all genres including historical westerns, medieval tales, romantic suspense, contemporary romance and paranormal beasties of all shapes and sexy sizes. or spending time with her family. She lives in the tree-covered hills of Northwest Arkansas with her husband of more than 20 years and her muses—the human-wanna-be canines—Chewy and Sweetpea.

To learn more about Myla Jackson and her stories visit her website at www.mylajackson.com

Other Titles by Myla Jackson

Ugly Stick Saloon Books:
Dirty Tricks: One Up On You
Dirty Tricks: Two Can Play That Game
Dirty Tricks: Three's A Charm
Dirty Tricks: Four Play
Dirty Tricks: Five-Second Seduction
Dirty Tricks: Six Degrees of Desperation
Sex Ed
Boots and Chaps
Boots and Leather
Boots and Bareback
Boots and Promises
Boots and Lace
Boots and Roses

~~~~~~~~~~~

Trouble With Harry (Tomb Raider Trouble #1)
Trouble With Will (Tomb Raider Trouble #2)
Trouble With Mitch (Tomb Raider Trouble #3)
Sex, Lies & Vampire Hunters
Honor Bound
Duty Bound
River Bound
Naked Prey
Jacq's Warlord
Shewolf
Thorn's Kiss
Fit to Be Tied

~~*~*

Cowboy Up
The Sweet Shoppe Series, Book 1
By Melissa Schroeder

Linda Wheeler's life is not going how she planned it. She left her dusty little Texas hometown years ago for the bright lights of Dallas years ago but now she is back—and not by choice. She's flat broke and without a job. Worse, she is back in that little town she never wanted to see again and having to work at the dude ranch she co owns with her high school crush, Nicodemus McCabe.

Nic had always thought of Linda as his little sister. That is until she hit eighteen. Then, she became an obsession he had to ignore. Her father had been his savior and Nic understood his place. Now that she was back, resisting her is getting more difficult by the minute.

After a trip to The Sweet Shoppe, shared erotic dreams make it even harder for both of them to resist the temptation. But will they be able to ignore their fears and take a chance on love?

Dedication

To Stephanie Vaughan, whose kindness and support are only exceeded by her ability to make me laugh when I feel like throwing in the towel. When I grow up, I want to be just like you.

The Sweet Shoppe: Cowboy Up

From the time of Arthur and Camelot, she has traveled the world, dispensing her magical sweets. Her spells allow anyone who eats the confections to fulfill their hidden fantasies with the one they love. But if the recipient doesn't believe their love is returned, then they are condemned to a life of knowing their lack of faith caused them to lose the one person they were destined to love.

Chapter One

She had arrived in hell.

Linda Wheeler blinked against the Texas sun and sighed. Only it wasn't truly hell, just her personal hell. And that was much worse than eternity spent with the Devil himself.

A drop of sweat dribbled down her back; her mouth felt as dry as sandpaper. She looked at the time and realized that showing up at the ranch at dinnertime was probably not the greatest timing, but she didn't give a damn. Life had handed her a shit sundae and she didn't give a damn what was going on. She just wanted to burrow under her old bed and pretend life wasn't so God awful.

Three days ago, she'd been happy. Somewhat happy. Okay, not that happy, but still happier than she'd ever be at the McCabe and Wheeler Dude Ranch. Living in Dallas had been a dream of hers since her teens, and she'd achieved it for the last fifteen years. Now, she was back in hell. Other people might call it West Texas. Of course, most of those people had spent their lives there and they didn't know any better. They seemed to thrive in a place filled

She ground her teeth as she turned onto the dirt road that led to the ranch house. Red Texas dust billowed out around the car, making her choke. If Charles hadn't taken off with the Honda, she would have been able to wind up the windows and turn on the A/C. And if he hadn't cleared out their bank account, sold her jewelry, and left her nothing but an empty apartment and a Dear Jane email ... He'd been nice enough to leave her his piece-of-shit car.

The ranch house came into view, and her head started to pound. It looked exactly the same as she remembered it. White with dark blue trim, the house had been the center of her world at one time. It had meant home. The wraparound porch was filled with rocking chairs. Light poured out of the windows, creating a welcome invitation to any weary traveler. She could even smell the pit barbecue in the back of the house. Six in the evening in the summer, like clockwork.

Linda's stomach roiled, and she swallowed down her panic. This was only temporary. She'd be back on the road as soon as Nic agreed to buy out her part of the ranch. She was sure he'd agree, but since Charles had cancelled her cell phone account, reaching Nic had been impossible. With the first of the month looming, and no way to pay the rent since she'd gotten fired, Linda had decided to pack up the junk pile and head to the ranch.

A multitude of pickups were parked out in front of the house. Most of them were ranch trucks. She could tell by the dents, the scratches, the later models. A few looked new. There was a minivan or two, telling her the ranch had customers.

After parking her car, she drew in a deep breath and tried her best to blink away the tears in her eyes. She would not fall apart. Amos Wheeler hadn't raised a fluffball. She'd make it through this and come out ahead. She should have indulged in the fudge she'd been craving since she'd stopped in Sullivan at the Sweet Shoppe. Licking her lips, she opened the car door and stepped out of the car. Somehow, her left foot got tangled in the seat belt, and, as she struggled, she found herself falling forward, out of the car and into the dirt. She landed with an oomph.

Sighing, she lifted herself to her hands and knees just in time to see a pair of cowboy boots come into view. Looking up, she squinted against the bright sun as she tried to discern who was standing in front of her.

"Well, if it isn't little Linda Wheeler. I think the last time I saw you was after your father's funeral two years ago."

She fell back and plopped down hard on her rear end in the dirt. Nicodemus McCabe squatted in front of her, a nasty smile curving his lips. He pushed his cowboy hat back with his thumb and looked down at her. There was nothing welcoming in his gaze. Cold, hard, and dark, the look in his eyes sent a shiver down her spine. Not in fear, but, as usual, from some sort of sick attraction she could never figure out.

"Let me see if I can remember what you said at the time. Oh, yeah. You would rather take a trip to hell and back before setting foot on this ranch again." He placed a hand beside her head on the car door and leaned forward. The scent of leather and Nic filled her senses, and her head spun. "So, Linda. How was hell?"

* * * *

Nic stared down at Linda Wheeler and wondered just what the hell she was doing at the ranch, sitting in the red dirt. He glanced at her car -- a beat-up sedan that was on its last axles -- and then back at her. She must be at the end of her rope to return to the ranch. From the looks of things, the rope had been unraveling for a while. And he hated it. As much as he thought he would enjoy her downfall, he didn't like seeing her at the bottom.

She pursed her lips, like he knew she did when she was mad. "You tell me. Since you revel in living in hell and being the gatekeeper of the inmates, I figure you know better than I."

He had to hand it to her. Her clothes looked liked she'd slept in them, her hair was a mess, and the dark smudges beneath her eyes told him she'd been losing sleep. And she could still dish it out. One tough woman. Even though she looked like she'd been put through the wringer, she smelled as if she'd just left one of those fancy-ass spas she liked to go to. All lavender and spice. When he found himself leaning closer, enjoying the scent, he pulled back and stood up.

"Whatcha doing here, Wheeler?" He couldn't help the sarcastic tone, but he did offer her a hand up.

She glanced up at his face and then his hand. Her green gaze hardened; then she grabbed hold of the opened car door and pulled herself up. The woman always had to take care of herself.

"I'm here to discuss the ranch, McCabe."

Strange. And disturbing. Linda never wanted to discuss the ranch. "Got your check last month, didn't ya?"

She frowned and crossed her arms beneath her breasts. He tried to concentrate on getting information, but it was hard with her standing there like that. Linda had never been what anyone would call top-heavy. She was more of a pear shape. But he'd bet her breasts were gorgeous. With her complexion, he was almost sure she'd have the prettiest pink nipples ... Immediately, heat shot straight to his dick. No need to be fantasizing about a woman he would never have. He shook his head and lifted his gaze to meet hers.

"No, I didn't get the check, but that's not what I want to discuss."

"Now, hold on a minute. I sent you a check last month, quarterly income."

She sighed and leaned against her car. "I'm not saying you didn't."

He studied her. Her shoulders were sagging -- her whole demeanor struck him as defeated. "You're not making sense, as usual."

She closed her eyes and rubbed her temple. "Nic, do you think we can have a chat after I get cleaned up and changed? I'm dying of thirst, I haven't eaten anything but a SNicers all day long, and all I really want to do is sink into a bubble bath."

He really wanted to push her, piss her off. If she got irritated, she might leave. Having her this close made his skin itch from the inside out. But he could tell something was wrong. They'd both lost their fathers and had little family on either side. They were almost like brother and sister.

Okay, not brother and sister. That was sick. Because she had been the subject of many a teenage fantasy while they'd been in high school.

"Tell ya what. Your father's room is always open."

Her eyes shot open. "You don't rent it out?"

He hated the warmness in her gaze, especially the way it made him feel. "Of course not. Wouldn't make any sense to rent out a master suite when these people are paying top dollar to rough it for a week."

Her lips turned down, but she didn't say anything. Nic didn't need her admiration, her hero worship. He'd had enough of that while they were growing up.

"I'll clean up and then meet you in the parlor."

He nodded curtly, but didn't say anything. The less said, the better. Linda turned to lean back into her car. The material of her skirt hiked up a few inches and stretched across her ass. When he found himself reaching to swat her, he stepped back once ... twice. Linda Wheeler was a woman with a body to adore, but a mouth and an attitude that made him want to throttle her.

When she finally pulled herself out of the car, all she held was a little white paper bag with The Sweet Shoppe written on it in gold letters. She straightened, then proceeded to walk past him.

"My bag is in the back seat."

Before she could step past him, he grabbed her arm. Again, the scent of her perfume tickled his senses. Nic forced himself not to take a deep breath. He could feel the warmth of her body through her shirt. His body's reaction was instant and annoying. More annoying was that when she narrowed her eyes and looked up at him, it aroused him more.

"Listen, Ms. Wheeler. This isn't a resort, and everyone does for themselves here. I don't take orders, and I don't take requests."

Less than gentle, he released her arm and turned on his heel, leaving her behind him. The faster she got cleaned up, the faster they could clear the air and he would be free of her. He didn't need a woman with fancy requirements screwing with his brain.

As he reached the top of the porch stairs, he almost ran headlong into Sybil Franklin. The bleached blonde had checked in Monday with her husband and had been a pain in the ass ever since he'd laid eyes on her. From what he could tell, the woman was the second wife, the trophy, and hubby either turned a blind eye to her affairs, or had no earthly idea. Tall, with a set of breasts that had probably been paid for by her husband, Sybil was the epitome of the Texas debutante. Blonde-haired -- not her original shade -- blue-eyed, and in a pair of jeans that looked to be painted on, she'd been driving the ranch hands into lust since she'd arrived. Still, her husband was a good old boy whose family had made their money in the oil fields and got out before it busted. Nic was pretty sure the old guy could handle a gun if need be.

"Seems we have a late arrival," she said, looking over his shoulder. He followed her gaze and tried not to laugh as Linda struggled to pull her suitcase out of the backseat. Curses followed each attempt to tug it out.

He turned back to Sybil. "L-- Ms. Wheeler is part-owner of the ranch and is coming to stay for a bit." And hopefully will be gone tomorrow.

Her attention shifted from Linda back to him. "Oh." Her perfectly painted lips turned down in a pouty frown he was sure would drive other men crazy. It just irritated Nic. He didn't have time for women who had agendas. "She doesn't look like someone who would know anything about a ranch."

That statement was followed by a loud curse and another oomph. He bit back a chuckle. Linda must have gotten the suitcase out of the car.

"Don't let her fancy clothes fool you. The woman knows how to ride and rope better than many of my ranch hands. She was a barrel-racing champion in high school."

He heard Linda dragging her suitcase across the rocks, cursing all the way.

"Definitely not very ladylike." Sybil frowned harder as the sound of Linda's footsteps grew closer. She apparently saw Linda as competition, but he knew there wasn't any competition involved. Because if he were going to fool around, he would never do it with a guest, and he definitely wouldn't do it with a married woman. And besides, he never could stand a fake woman.

Linda passed, without a word to either him or Sybil -- didn't even looked their way. She opened the screen door, cussing once more when her luggage got caught. One vicious yank, and the door slammed shut.

"Well, anyway ..." Sybil sighed, her breasts rising partway above the low-cut neckline of her four-hundred-dollar western shirt. "... I was wondering if I could interest you in a ride tonight."

From the way she said it, Nic knew she really wasn't talking about a horse ride. He plastered on the most genuine smile he could offer. "Sorry. With Ms. Wheeler in town, there are things we need to discuss." And thank God for that.

Her bottom lip thrust out in a genuine pout. She stepped closer, and he almost gagged when her overwhelming floral perfume reached him. He swallowed. Jesus, she must bathe in it.

"I'll let you go tonight, but I really look forward to spending more time with you."

She patted his cheek and then turned, swinging her ass as she sauntered away. Nic released a sigh. Relief poured through him. He was far from interested in a woman like that. There had been a time he would have ridden the bitch for all she was worth, not caring. Now he was too damn old to be caught with his pants down. And by a husband who might just shoot to kill.

    He turned his thoughts back to Linda as he walked to the door. She wouldn't have shown up if there wasn't something she needed, desperately. But instead of the present situation, whatever that might be, he thought of her in another situation -- naked and in his bed. The thought of her warm skin beneath his, of hearing her sigh his name, of slipping into her and having her muscles clinging to his cock, jolted him. He had to quit thinking that like. No matter how much he wanted her, she wanted something else entirely, and he'd bet it wouldn't have a thing to do with stripping him naked and jumping his bones.

The Sweet Shoppe: Cowboy Up

Chapter Two

Linda slipped out of her skirt and left it puddled on the floor, along with the rest of her clothes. Wearing only her panties, she walked into her father's bathroom and began to run a bath in the clawfoot tub. He'd been gone for two years, but she still couldn't think of this room as anything but his. Nic had left it exactly the way it had been decorated when Amos had been alive, right down to the last picture of her and her mother. Linda had been five when that was taken.

Figuring that the water was still hard as steel, she went and rummaged through her suitcase for her bubble bath. Once she found the bottle, she headed back into the bathroom and poured some beneath the running water. After the tub filled, she pulled off her panties, grabbed the bag of fudge, and then stepped into the bath. The hot water soothed her muscles, as did the musky scent of the bubble bath. With a sigh, she took out a piece of fudge, popped it in her mouth, and closed her eyes. Rich and velvety, the fudge melted on her tongue. Sinking down until the bubbles reached her chin, she tried to ignore the nagging irritation in her belly. It wasn't as if she were jealous. Okay, maybe she was, just a little bit. Probably just a knee-jerk reaction left over from their youth. Nic had always had a woman, and no time for her.

She didn't care if Nic was still a hound dog around women. Or she shouldn't. But the old feelings of resentment and ... envy ... rose as soon as she saw him talking to Miss Bleached Blonde 2005. Grabbing another piece of the fudge, she thought about the huge ring she'd seen on the woman's finger. Could be Mrs., she guessed. Nothing at the ranch ever changed. There were always horses to be taken care of, whiny guests to comfort, and Nic was always screwing someone -- usually a married someone.

She bit into the fudge, trying to will those thoughts away. The smoothness of the chocolate, the sugary sweetness, soothed her. Her muscles relaxed as her skin warmed.

Strange. She'd always loved fudge, but the quality of this was beyond anything she'd ever tasted. When she'd stopped at the little shop, she hadn't expected anything like this. But the old woman had smiled knowingly at her and led her to the fudge without Linda even telling her that was what she wanted. Linda had known she'd need something to get her through the next twenty-four hours. Coming back to the ranch brought back memories she'd rather not deal with. Memories that were better left undisturbed. The girl she'd been back then, so stupidly in love with Nicodemus McCabe that she was blinded by it, was a far cry from the woman she was today. She'd been a romantic little twerp, believing in the fairytales her father had spun. And the saddest thing was that there was never any romantic interest on Nic's part. Nothing. The man probably looked at her as a sister.

Thinking about him made her shiver. All lean muscle and leather. Even just conjuring up the image of him caused her nipples to harden. He hadn't changed a bit. She'd seen him two years ago when she had returned for her father's funeral. The grief and pain of the unexpected death had overwhelmed her, and she hadn't noticed Nic much. Before that, he seemed to be gone whenever she visited her father.

She'd known when they were teenagers he'd grow up to be beautiful. Nic had been class president, quarterback, and all-around cheerleader-dater. Linda hated cheerleaders. He'd been the gorgeous one, the one with the personality that drew both males and females to him. She'd been the odd duck out. Raised by a father who didn't know squat about feminine things, she'd rarely worn makeup or dresses, opting for her ropers and boots. It didn't allow for a lot of dates, especially when competing with the town girls. But she'd left that behind when she left for UT and never looked back. She might have still been a nerd, but she'd dated. And finally left the shadow of being the almost little sister of Nic McCabe behind her.

She shivered. Damn him for still being gorgeous. All that golden skin, that long ebony hair. His Scottish ancestors had given him a last name, but, for the most part, his Cherokee heritage dominated his physical characteristics. Tall, lean, with a long, slender nose -- broken twice that she knew of -- and those chiseled cheekbones. She sighed as her body began to heat. Arousal tugged at her belly.

Sliding her hand between her legs, she pressed against her sex. The last time she'd seen him without a shirt, she'd about expired. As she began to move her hand, she thought of him as he had looked on that day, fresh from working with the horses, his muscled chest not quite as full as it was now, but outstanding just the same. Wet with sweat, his skin had glistened in the afternoon sun. The only thought that had come to her eighteen-year-old mind was: I want. He was older by two years, and in her mind, he had to know everything there was to know about sex. She knew she couldn't have him -- but, oh, how she wanted him.

Tension curled through her, tightening her muscles as heat pooled in her groin. Just as she edged closer to her orgasm, there was a knock at the bedroom door.

"Linda, are you in there?"

She groaned. Nic. Sexual frustration and embarrassment heated her body. She'd bet her last dollar that she was getting paid back for something she'd done in another life.

The Sweet Shoppe: Cowboy Up

"Linda?"

She sighed, pulling herself out of the bath and wrapping a towel around her body. "Yeah, I'm in here."

"Are you almost ready? I have an early morning, and you've been in there a while." The impatience in his voice had her grinding her teeth. Really, he interrupted some much needed ... rest ... just so he could get back to the big-boobed blonde.

All the sexual warmth that had filled her body only moments ago disappeared. Irritation had her striding to the door and pulling it open before she could think twice. He was leaning against the wall next to the doorway, looking scruffy, tired, and hot. Really, really hot.

She shook her head, trying to push that idea away. Nic McCabe was a pain in the butt and as faithful as a tomcat.

"Listen, Nicodemus. I've had a really hard day. I was fired, I have no home, and I am now going to have to deal with you." She jabbed him in the chest to accent her opinion.

He looked down at her finger and then up at her. His lips twisted in a rueful smile as his gaze traveled down her body. It was then she realized she wore only a towel, still soaking wet. She closed her eyes in mortification as she noticed several patrons were lingering in the hallway. When she opened them, the first thing she saw was Nic grinning at her.

"Well, not that I don't appreciate the view, Ms. Wheeler, but I'll wait until you get some clothes on."

With that, he pushed away from the wall and headed toward the stairs. She stepped back into her room and slammed the door, then leaned against it. She hadn't been back a day and she had already embarrassed herself, not only in front of Nic, but also in front of his customers. Lord knew the word was probably already spreading about the owner who greeted people at the door of her room, soaking wet, wearing only a towel. And, if memory served, she knew it would be all over town tomorrow.

West Texas really was hell.

* * * *

Nic shut the office door and headed over to the small fridge in the corner. He pulled out a beer, twisted off the top, and took a long swig, then held the cold beer against his hot forehead. Damn, he'd never seen anything as inviting as Linda Wheeler standing there in nothing but a towel and bubbles.

He took another long sip. The moment she'd poked him in the chest, he'd gone rock hard. Hell, just seeing her stand there half-naked had him almost there. If he'd been dumb -- and he'd been heading that way since he'd had no blood left in his brain at that point -- he'd have snatched that towel off her. The woman tempted him to throw good sense out the window and take her to bed for a long, slow, hard fuck.

Jesus, he had to get a grip on his wayward thoughts. Damn woman was a pain in the ass, and a business partner. There was too much history between the two of them. It'd just been so long since he'd had a woman in his bed. As he wandered over to the desk and sat down, he wondered about her comments. No home? Fired? That definitely wasn't Linda's normal situation. And what happened to that boyfriend she'd been living with? He knew Chet, their lawyer, had talked to him several times on the phone.

He sighed, took another drink, and tried to calm his throbbing body. But the moment he finally seemed to grab control, Linda walked through the doorway.

She didn't say anything, just sat down and looked at his beer. Then her gaze caught his.

"Would you like a beer?"

She shook her head.

"So, what is it you wanted to talk to me about?"

She cleared her throat before she spoke. "I wanted to discuss selling my part of the ranch."

His stomach dropped about five feet. She wanted to sell out her part of the ranch? "Why?"

She licked her lips. "I ... I've run into a sort of ... cash-flow problem."

"You were fired?"

She nodded, and her gaze slid away from his. A blush crept up her cheeks. "I was fired for some missing funds."

At first, he was stunned, and then he laughed. "Yeah, right, Linda. You almost had me going there."

She pursed her lips and shot him a look that told him she wasn't joking.

"Linda, you couldn't steal. You'd chew off your right hand before you stole from someone."

Her expression softened, and she sighed. "Well, at least someone believes me. And they have no proof, but since it's questionable, they fired me."

With her shoulders slumped and a frown pulling at the corners of her mouth, it struck him again that she wasn't acting like herself. "Aren't you going to fight it?"

She shook her head. "The person I think is responsible is -- was -- my supervisor. And there's no way to prove it."

The Sweet Shoppe: Cowboy Up

He grunted at that, trying to come to terms with the fact that the woman who never backed down from a fight not only had done just that, but seemed to have lost some of her self-confidence. "And you're homeless?"

She lifted one shoulder, almost as if shrugging two shoulders would be too much effort. "That is another story entirely. One I hadn't planned on discussing and still don't. Let's just say I have lousy taste in men."

He chuckled, remembering her handful of dates in high school, and she shot him a dirty look. "Okay, so you want to sell the ranch. Problem is, I can't afford your half."

"Then I'll sell it."

Taking another long pull from the bottle, he studied her. Her hair hung in a damp ponytail down her back. Her face was pale, drawn; dark circles shadowed her eyes. "That's something I don't want, and if I don't agree, you can't sell your share."

"You'd do that, knowing that I need the money?" Her voice had deepened with her anger. Her dark green eyes now sparked with fire, and, God help him, his boner was back.

Counting to ten, he ordered his libido down and ignored the flutter of guilt curling in his gut. She was a big girl, and he wasn't giving up his livelihood because she couldn't control her spending. "Listen, you know the will. I don't have to sell. But I do have an idea." Stupid idea, but he owed her, and he owed her father for teaching him so much. "How about you help out here? Say, for six months. I should have enough money by then to buy you out."

Her eyes widened at his harsh tone, but she didn't say anything for several seconds. As if gauging her next attempt, she studied him, then said, "You want me to live here at the ranch, work for six months, and then you'll buy me out?"

It had been a spur-of-the-moment plan, but he knew he could do it. It'd be tight, but he could scrape the cash together.

"Yeah."

A flash of irritation crossed her face. He watched in awe as she pulled back from it, reining her temper in. It was an amazing feat for Linda. Her temper had been legendary when they were growing up together. Then, as if she had never been upset, her rigid posture relaxed a tad and she opened a little white bag he hadn't seen her carry in.

She pulled out a piece of fudge and bit off a piece. "There's no way for me to change your mind?"

He watched, his thoughts a jumble as she licked the fudge off her fingertips. Her tongue flitted out over each tip, and then she sucked each one. Every available brain cell went to sleep as most of his blood headed straight for his dick. Not only did he imagine her lips on him, sucking ... licking ... he could imagine the contentment on her face as she sucked him dry. Her gaze never left his as she slid her index finger into her mouth and sucked. He shifted in his seat, the chair squeaking and rough denim brushing against his cock. Biting back a curse and trying his best not to show his arousal, he lifted one eyebrow.

She smiled and offered him the bag. "I know you have a thing for ... fudge."

It hurt, but he laughed. The woman had always had a wicked and sick sense of humor. "Yeah, I do." He leaned forward, snatched the bag out of her grasp, and then pulled out the last piece of fudge. Milk chocolate, with pecans -- her favorite, and his. Before tossing it into his mouth, he asked, "So, when we were kids, did Rosarita tell you when she was making it so you could get more than me?"

She laughed, as he'd wanted her to, easing the tension -- at least for him. "Naw. She loved you, thought you could do no wrong." She shrugged. "I just hung around the kitchen when I knew she was making it."

He smiled, remembering their housekeeper, who was more mother to the two of them than employee, and popped the fudge into his mouth. The moment the chocolate hit his tongue, it melted. He groaned, and she laughed again.

"I know. Isn't it the most wonderful thing you've ever tasted? I got it when I drove through town."

As the fudge melted away, the taste of it -- luscious, rich -- gave way to something different. A tingle of heat rushed through him. Just a brush of something, as if fingers had danced across his flesh, sending his pulse racing. Swallowing, he tried to calm his already out-of-control libido, but it was impossible with Linda sitting there.

"Why don't you get a good night's sleep? We'll talk about this later."

She cocked her head to the side and licked her lips. Jesus, she was going to drive him insane. That, or he would pass out from the lack of blood in his brain.

"You look kind of strange."

Strange? If she didn't leave soon, he was going to show her strange. Like lifting her up off that chair, tearing off her clothes, and jumping her bones. But for some reason, that didn't sound as strange as it used to.

He ran his hand over his face, then through his hair. "It's been a long day. I just need some rest."

She sighed, as if completely put out, and rose from her seat. Squaring her shoulders, she looked him straight in the eye. Heat shot through him at her defiant expression. "Okay, but don't think I'm not talking to my lawyer about this."

Nodding, he watched her leave and shut the door behind her. "I'd expect no less, Ms. Wheeler." He stood and walked over to his fridge, then drew out another beer. He needed something other than the taste of fudge in his mouth and thoughts of Linda naked on his desk.

After about an hour of lying in bed and staring at the ceiling, her body still humming with arousal, Linda decided to take a sleeping pill. As exhausted as she was physically, she couldn't shut her mind down. If she wasn't worrying about what Nic was up to, she was worried about her own reaction to him. After downing the pill, she climbed back up on her father's king-sized bed. After settling, she thought about the new book she'd bought and decided against it. She didn't have the strength to get back up and rummage through her things to find it.

Within ten minutes, she was drifting away, her mind shutting down and her eyelids too heavy to hold open.

Chapter Three

Nic's hands brushed against the sides of her breasts. Linda could feel the calluses from hard work, the tenderness of his touch. He stood behind her, his bare chest against her back, his breath hot against her ear. She shivered as he skimmed his fingers over her breasts -- a light, teasing touch -- then circled her nipples. They tightened into hard pebbles. A rush of heat curled into her belly. He'd left his hair unbound. The silky strands brushed against her shoulder.

"Ahh, so you like that, do you?" The amusement in his voice didn't hide his arousal. "You always had such pretty little breasts, Linda."

She huffed, trying to sound irritated. "Little?"

He chuckled and pinched each nipple. "I like you that way. But, then, there isn't much I don't like about you."

He stepped away from her, and she started to turn around.

"No. Don't." His voice deepened, rolling over the words, making her shiver.

Slipping his fingers down her arms, he captured her hands. He tugged her forward and walked both of them to the wall. After lifting them up, he released her hands. "Now, just put them against the wall. Don't move."

She did as he ordered. He slipped her hair over her shoulders so the ends of it teased her nipples. First his lips, then his tongue, brushed against her shoulder. He inhaled deeply. "Lavender. You smell like a field of it."

As he moved back, a wash of cool night air chilled her. The next thing she felt was his lips against her skin at the base of her neck. Then, a little lower. With the softest touch, he kissed a path down her spine, his tongue flicking out over her skin. Heat rushed along her nerve endings; warm liquid filled her cunt. She trembled, not with fear but with anticipation.

His hands molded over her buttocks, squeezing, stroking her skin. Linda tried to enjoy his touch and ignore the fact that he was eye level with what she considered her worst body feature. She dropped her head forward and closed her eyes as she felt his mouth against one of her cheeks.

He hummed against her skin. "Darlin', I have to say you have one world-class ass."

"Too big." She meant to say a complete sentence, but at that moment it was impossible. Brain functions had ceased the moment he'd touched her.

Lost in his lips against her skin, his tongue leaving a wet path with the kisses, she didn't expect the slap. Shocked, she opened her eyes and stared down at him over her shoulder. He had knelt behind her, but he looked anything but the supplicant.

"What was that for?"

He swatted her again and then rubbed his hand over the area.

"I happen to like your ass. And, if I may say so, I am in a position to judge. No complaints from you." He waited for her nod, then kissed the sensitive skin he'd just smacked.

As he continued to kiss, nip, and lick, one hand slid around to her stomach, the other between her legs to her pussy. She was already dripping with arousal. Hell, just thinking about him would wet her panties, but having his hands ... his mouth ... against her skin, she was amazed she hadn't come already.

Sliding his finger along her slit, he groaned. "Spread your legs a little."

Her thighs quivered, her muscles ready to give out, but she complied, and he slipped a finger into her, his thumb rubbing against her clit.

"Goddamn, you're wet." He continued to move his finger in and out as he nipped at the roundest part of her buttocks. She should've been embarrassed. But the feel of his lips against her skin, over sensitized from his slaps, sent another blast of heat racing along her nerve endings, heating her body and making her yearn for more. She'd never been the least bit kinky, but something about Nic brought it out in her. And this interlude was tame compared to her fantasies. When he added another finger, she moaned his name.

"Yeah, that's it, baby." Excitement deepened his voice, and before she knew what he was about, he removed his hand, pressed her legs further apart, and situated himself between her and the wall.

Without a word to her, he licked her, a sound escaping from the back of his throat. Her muscles tightened as his tongue slipped between her folds, licking her, teasing her. He added a finger as he took her clit between his teeth. The pressure built, but he didn't relent. He continued, perhaps even intensified his ministrations, becoming more vocal as she neared her orgasm.

She protested as he drew his mouth away. He didn't stop moving his fingers, though, and she flexed her hips in rhythm with his thrusting.

"I want to see you come. You want it, Linda; you know you do. Come for me, do it."

Almost as if her body understood the command in his voice, heat exploded, and her body bowed and then jerked with her orgasm. Another gush of liquid poured from her cunt, and he leaned forward, lapping up her juices with relish.

Linda gasped as she woke. Sweat wet her brow, the sheets were tangled around her legs, and a hand was between her legs. She blinked, noticing the weak light that filtered through the blinds, and she figured it was just before dawn. Her body still hummed from the orgasm she'd dreamed of. As she moved her hand, she felt the wetness of her release, smelled the musky scent, and groaned. Dammit, she'd not only dreamed about the man, but she'd probably masturbated to the dream and came. She wasn't a prude -- the vibrator she'd brought with her proved that -- but she didn't need to be dreaming about Nic. It would be distracting and embarrassing if he ever found out.

She pushed the sheets away from her legs and rose from the bed, determined to get away from the memory of the dream. Her teenage fantasies were nothing compared to that. But then again, in high school she hadn't known jack shit about sex. Now that she knew, and he was in the vicinity, it'd taken less than twenty-four hours to have a wet dream about him. Sighing, she decided a shower was just what she needed to start the day. She knew she was in for a fight, but maybe if she washed away the memory of that dream, of his mouth on her, his scent, his words...

She marched into the bathroom and turned the water on cold. After she stripped out of her nightshirt, she stepped into the tub, wincing at the burst of chilly water against her heated skin.

* * * *

Dennis, the ranch's chef, made the mistake of smiling too brightly at Nic, who growled in response. All the color left the man's face as Nic brushed past him to the coffee. It was freaking early, and he didn't have to be nice. Sure, he usually liked getting up early and watching the sunrise. But those mornings, he didn't feel like hell.

He'd drunk a couple more beers after Linda had left him, then stumbled upstairs to his bed. With a hard day of work behind him, and three beers in his system, he'd immediately passed out. But he felt like he'd had no sleep. When he woke, sweat had covered his body and his dick had been in his hand. The dream. He closed his eyes as he sipped his coffee. He'd never had a dream so brilliant, so real. Hell, he could still taste her on his lips, still smell the lavender on her skin.

"What's up with you, boss?"

He opened one eye and looked at Dennis. The man wasn't smart if he didn't know to leave the boss alone when he looked like he'd been on a three-day bender. "Rough night."

The man's smile widened as he poured pancake batter into the cast-iron skillet. "I heard you spent the night drinking. Trying to get some woman off your mind."

Nic grunted in response. "I don't have Linda on my mind." Just in my dreams, coming all over my face.

Dennis stopped his actions and slanted Nic a look. "I was talking about Sybil. But I see you've had other things on your mind."

Dammit. He didn't need the staff gossiping. It was going to be bad enough over the next few months while he lived in hell. He'd always been a little attracted to Linda. They were only two years apart in age, and she'd been totally off-limits because Amos would have killed him if he'd touched the man's baby girl. But who wouldn't be attracted to the woman? She could ride a horse like a dream, and even when she'd been working with horses all day, there was always a lingering scent of lavender. Every time he smelled it, he thought of her. Maybe that dream last night would get the woman out of his system.

"Got any coffee for me?"

His dick twitched at the sound of her voice. As if it had been real, the memories of the dream flashed through his mind. The taste of her, the scent of her, teased his mind. Damn, he wouldn't be able to take it if this attraction didn't cool. Drawing in a deep breath, he turned to face her. He immediately exhaled at the sight of her.

She'd pulled her mass of curls in a ponytail, leaving nothing to frame her face. He could still detect the weariness of her trip and the stress of her situation on her face, but the dark circles were no longer as pronounced. There was more of a twinkle to her jade eyes. The rest of her was put together well. A red T-shirt molded her curves, tucked into a pair of fitted jeans. It showed off her pert, rounded breasts and her trim waist. Not to mention her fantastic ass.

"I see you're up and around early this morning, Ms. Wheeler."

A faint blush rose on her cheeks. Strange. Linda had never been a blusher, even when she'd been a teenager. She cleared her throat and avoided his gaze as she walked past him to the counter. Without a comment, she poured her coffee.

"I take it you slept well."

She fumbled with the creamer, sloshing a bit over the sides of the cup. "Y-yes. I slept just fine. Why would you ask?"

He hadn't actually asked, but he wondered at her guilty tone. Watching her mop up her mess and finish doctoring her coffee, he noted her distracted air, the fine trembling in her hand as she lifted the cup to take a sip. There was more to it than she was saying, but he knew women, and he knew this one well. Pushing her just aggravated her, and could result in a knee to the groin.

"Do you want to talk now, or later?"

She turned and gave him a strained smile. "I'd rather get this over with, if you don't mind."

His thoughts exactly. He noticed Dennis's interest and stepped closer to Linda so he could lower his voice. She took a step back and bumped into the counter. He almost laughed at the mutinous expression on her face, but there was something else he could see in her eyes that stopped him. Panic? Why would she be worried? Unless ...

He stepped closer, which was a mistake. This close, he could smell her, just as he could when he was dreaming the night before. Lavender, plus musky woman. The scent spiraled through him, heating his blood, shooting his brain cells to his dick. All the noises in the kitchen faded away. The clinking of dishes, the hurried sound of shuffling feet, the discussions, all of it disappeared as he looked down at her. She licked her lower lip and drew in a deep breath, which caused her breasts to brush against his chest. Blood rushed to his groin and his head spun.

Before he could stop them, the memories of the dream rushed back, washed over him, and he was reaching for her. He wanted to touch, taste, tease her. He needed to hear those sounds she'd made the night before, to prove he could make the dream real. But, as he touched her arms, one of the waiters dropped a tray full of glasses. The crash caused both Linda and Nic to jump apart.

He cleared his throat and looked around at the kitchen staff, who apparently hadn't noticed what had almost just happened. Thank God. He really didn't need the gossip, and Linda would never forgive him.

"If you'll meet me in my office in about ten minutes, we can go over what I want you to do to ... er ... for me."

With that, he turned and walked out of the kitchen, feeling as if he'd just escaped. And, knowing how Linda would tie him up in knots if he ever gave into his urge, he was probably right.

As he reached his office, he was disturbed to find the door open. He'd been pretty lit the night before, but he thought he remembered shutting and locking the door. When he stepped in, the sexual hum Linda had inspired turned to ice when he found Sybil Franklin in his chair. A secret smiled curved her lips as her gaze traveled from his head down to his feet.

"I thought you'd never get here, Nic."

The Sweet Shoppe: Cowboy Up

Chapter Four

Linda grabbed a piece of bread, spread it with jam, and took a huge bite. As she enjoyed the yeasty-sugary combination, she realized just how hungry she'd been. She should have eaten something other than that fudge the night before.

"Always nice to see a woman who enjoys eating."

She looked over at Dennis and smiled. He had to be at least five or six years younger than her, and years younger in world experience. She'd recognized him from his red hair and freckled face. She figured he was a Cunningham.

"I never pass up fresh-baked bread and homemade jam. And to top it off, I didn't eat much yesterday."

He frowned and cut another slice of bread. "You should take care of yourself better. Didn't Nic say you're involved with someone?"

"Was involved -- past tense." He looked embarrassed, but she placed a hand on his. "No. I'm used to everyone sharing gossip in small towns, don't worry."

He smiled, albeit shyly. "If you're going to be around for a while, I was wondering if you would like to go out for a ride sometime."

"Well ..." She didn't know what to say. It'd been so long since someone had hit on her, especially a younger someone.

"I remember watching you ride. You had such a way with horses. Used to eat my sister Beulah up something fierce. You beat her for the county title for barrel racing three years in a row." His smile widened at the comment, and she couldn't help but respond with a smile of her own before he asked, "Are you going to be here long?"

Her smile faded, and she looked to the door where Nic had disappeared. "I'm not sure, but if I am, I will definitely take you up on your offer." She drained her coffee and set the cup on the counter. "Now I have to go see a man about a ranch."

As she walked to the office, she tried to come up with all her arguments. She needed the money; she had a right to sell her portion. If she stayed more than three days on the ranch, she would go insane. And if she didn't get the hell out of here soon enough, she'd do something drastic like jump Nic's bones.

Nearing the office, she heard voices, one female, one male.

"But I thought I would surprise you." The whine in the woman's voice sounded suspiciously like the big blonde bimbo from the night before. "I don't understand why you would be angry."

There was a shuffling of papers, a few moments of silence, and then Nic spoke. "I'm not angry, but I have work to do and a meeting in a few minutes. I also have to talk to the staff about letting people into my office."

"You work so hard. If you're the owner, you should take your time off, make other people work."

Linda inched closer, her hand covering her mouth to keep the laugh from escaping. Telling Nic not to work was a crime, at least in his book. Stupid woman probably didn't realize she'd insulted him.

"It's a working ranch, Mrs. Franklin." The stiffness in his voice told Linda he was close to losing his temper.

"Oh, pooh. You can do what you want."

Deciding she'd heard enough, Linda knocked and, without waiting for an answer, opened the door. She stopped in her tracks at the sight before her. Nic was working, or looked like he was working, his desk covered with paperwork. A tinge of envy curled in her belly when she saw the woman who was with him. Draped over him was Mrs. Franklin. Her bright, two-sizes-too-small shirt looked like someone's idea of what a hooker might wear if she were to visit a ranch. Linda looked at the other woman's jeans, so tight she wondered if zipping them had caused internal organ damage. She'd pay fifty bucks to watch the woman try to get up on a horse in those.

"Linda." Relief tinged Nic's voice. "You're right on time."

She thought of his refusal to sell the ranch and decided to get back at him. "Oh, I didn't know you were busy, Nic. I can come back later." She turned to leave.

"No!" Nic jumped out of his chair, causing Ms. Tight Pants to stumble backward. If she hadn't hit the wall, she would have fallen on her ass. "No, we have a lot to discuss." He turned to the other woman. "Ms. Wheeler and I have ranch business to discuss this morning, Mrs. Franklin."

She looked at him, then toward Linda and back to him again. Her eyes narrowed, and her lips drew down in a pouty frown. "But, I thought we --"

"Sybil."

Linda jumped at the deep, masculine voice behind her. Looking back over her shoulder, she gulped when she saw the man who belonged to the voice. Several inches over six feet and at least three hundred pounds, he looked like a mountain. He glanced at her, dismissed her, and then zeroed in on his wife. "Let's go."

Without a word, Sybil followed, but she did throw one last fleeting look at Nic before she left. When the Linda shut the door, Nic exhaled.

"Damn. I wish that woman would leave me the hell alone."

She didn't say anything, just leaned against the door and raised an eyebrow.

"You don't believe me?"

"No." Although a part of her really wanted to believe. "Seems to me your MO is running as usual."

"My MO?"

"Yeah. Rich, bored wife, time on your hands, your hands on her." She shrugged. "Same thing."

He stared for a moment, an incredulous look on his face. Then his lips curved, and he laughed. "You're jealous."

"I am not." Yes, she was, but she would never admit it. Nothing would ever come of the two of them, except really good sex. Why didn't she just use him for sex? Because her heart would get involved, and he would crush it without a thought.

"Yes, you are. I can tell by the tone in your voice."

"I'm not in the mood to argue with you ... about this. I want to know what the hell you were talking about last night."

* * * *

Nic stared at Linda for a moment and tried to gather his thoughts. It was hard because the door was closed. And that just made him think about how alone they were. He could lock the door, strip her naked, and ride her hard.

One look at her pinched expression told him she would probably not agree to his idea.

"Why don't you have a seat and we can discuss this." He kept his tone light, making her be the small, petty one in the argument if she disagreed. She hesitated but then sighed and slipped into the chair.

"Tell me."

"You sure know how to sweet-talk a man, Linda." Sarcasm laced his voice. She rose to go, but he stayed her with a comment. "I need to have time to save up the money. I won't agree to selling, but I promise at the end of six months, I will have it."

"And ... where do I fit in?"

"I need an accountant."

"What?"

"I lost my accountant about a year ago. Moved to Dallas, said there was no money here. Since then, I've been trying to handle it myself."

She winced, then sighed. "Oh, Lord."

"Yeah, you can imagine. It is a mess. So, if you do that, live here, I will pay your expenses, and at the end of six months, I will buy you out."

"I could take you to court."

"You could, but it would cost you more. And in the long run, this is the best thing. For both of us."

She muttered under her breath -- something very unladylike. "I do want to talk to my lawyer, but I have a feeling you're right." She sighed and rubbed her forehead, and, for just a moment, he felt a twinge of guilt. "I don't know why you want this, but if this is the only way to get my part of the money, I'll do it."

"You'll have your money; I'll have my records back in order. Fair deal."

She sighed, shook her head, and left him with an uneasy feeling that the next six months were going to be hell.

* * * *

Three weeks later, Linda shook her head and sighed. She looked around the office Nic had set up for her -- four walls, no windows -- and wondered what time it was. Her stomach grumbled, and she realized it was probably past lunchtime and she'd missed it. Again. She stretched her back by lifting her arms above her head, and groaned as her tight muscles protested.

In the weeks since she'd taken up the job of bookkeeping for Nic, she'd realized the man had no organization. Oh, sure, he could plan a day for guests down to the last minute, but ask him where the receipt for last week's delivery of hay was, and he couldn't tell you. It'd turned into one big headache after another, trying to get the accounts caught up. Ten-hour days, seven days a week. This was worse than her last job.

And to top it all off, she'd taken over reservations. More than once, someone showed up unexpectedly because no one in this damn place wrote anything down. If they did, it was on a scrap of paper that inevitably got lost.

"You look tired."

She glanced toward the doorway and there stood Nic. Rested, clean, handsome. Looking good enough to eat. Shit. There she went again. She hadn't had any more dreams about him, but she'd not been able to push the memories of the last one out of her mind.

"After three seventy-hour weeks, I tend to get tired." So she sounded like a little kid. She didn't care. Tired, freaking hot, and hungry. It was what you got when she was in that condition.

"I was heading to town to pick up a few things. Do you want to go?"

"Do you have the key?"

He shook his head, confusion lighting his eyes. "Key?"

"For the chain here at the desk."

"Smart ass. Come on. We can even hit the Sweet Shoppe."

Nic settled the check at the feed store, remembering to pocket the

The Sweet Shoppe: Cowboy Up

receipt, and headed out the door. Squinting against the bright afternoon sun, he pulled out his sunglasses, put them on, and went in search of Linda.

He'd felt like such an ass when he realized she'd been working for days on end and had yet to leave the ranch since she'd arrived. A place she hated. He shook his head as he walked past a couple of the Ferguson boys. If Dennis hadn't volunteered to take her this afternoon, citing that she needed to get out ... Nic had nipped that in the bud, but he knew something had to be done. Especially about Dennis, who seemed to have some kind of a crush on Linda.

He chuckled when he caught sight of her through the window of the Sweet Shoppe. Knowing her love of sweets, particularly fudge, he should have known that was where he would find her. The bell jingled as he opened the door, and he pulled off his sunglasses, hanging them in his pocket by the ear piece. Linda looked back over her shoulder at him. And just for a second, just a split second, his heart skipped a beat. She'd worn a fitted T-shirt, the bright yellow color bringing out the multitude of auburn highlights in her hair. The shorts she wore hugged her generous ass and showcased her shapely legs. When his gaze reached her face again, he licked his lips, taking in the sparkle in her eyes and the smile curving her lips. He hadn't seen her this happy and relaxed since she'd arrived. The sight of her grin sent a shot of heat straight to his dick.

"Madame just made some fudge about an hour ago. And I'm not sharing." She turned back to talk to the small old woman who owned the shop. He actually didn't know her name, which was strange in a town this size. She'd just shown up one day, rented the empty store, and started selling sweets. It'd been about two months since she'd appeared, but this was his first time visiting the shop.

He moved to stand beside Linda. "I'll tell you what -- I'll buy your next bag."

She shot him a look out of the corner of her eye. "You're just doing that because you want me to share."

Smiling, he slid his arms over her shoulders and pulled her closer. Too late he realized his mistake and gritted his teeth. Her body was flushed with heat, and even with the overpowering scent of sugar in the shop, he could smell her lavender.

"Ah, you are Nicodemus wiz ze ranch." He turned his attention to the old woman and had to look down. Her head probably wouldn't reach his chest. A wealth of gray hair was twisted into a braid down her back. She was dressed in what he would call gypsy clothes, a loose peasant shirt and a full skirt. When she moved, the sound of tinkling bells could be heard. Her face was lined, but her blue eyes sparkled with humor. Her smile widened as he studied her.

"Many people tell me about you." She spoke with an accent he couldn't place, which was really odd because he was usually good with them. But it had the sound of Eastern Europe to it. "Your ranch is very profitable."

Linda snorted, and he squeezed her shoulder but then let her go. "I do well. Linda says you have some fresh fudge."

Her gaze moved from Linda to him and then back to Linda. Nic shifted his weight from foot to foot, very uncomfortable with the knowing look in her eyes. "Yes, I do. Very good, very fresh. Just for you." She whirled around, her bells tinkling, and disappeared behind a curtain.

"Did you get what you wanted at the feed shop?"

He looked down at Linda, thinking of a completely different want, like wanting to put her up on that counter and devour her, but pushed it aside. Wanting Linda was stupid; acting on it would be insane.

"Yeah, and I have the receipt." She smiled, and he thought he owned the world. A zing shot through him. Damn, he sure wished he could make her smile like that more often. He found himself leaning closer. As the smell of sweets filled his senses, he licked his lips, thinking about another treat he'd like to taste.

"I have ze fudge." The storekeeper's voice interrupted them. She handed him the bag and named the price. He winced, but paid for it nonetheless. As they left the shop, the woman stopped him with a comment. "Nicodemus." She waited for him to turn before she continued. "Make sure you are careful with zat." She smiled and waved, then disappeared behind the curtain.

The bell over the door rang, and he realized Linda had opened it. He followed her through the doorway out into the hot late-afternoon sun. The blast of heat after being in the cool shop went straight to his head. It was the only thing that could explain the lightheadedness he was feeling. Sweat gathered at the base of his neck and rolled down his spine.

"That woman is a little ... different ... for Sullivan, Texas," Linda said.

"Uh-huh." The spinning in his head got worse, and he blinked a few times. He stopped walking, dropped the bag of fudge, and fumbled for his sunglasses. Linda kept walking until she apparently noticed he'd stopped. She turned, cocked her head, and studied him, worry wrinkling her brow.

"Nic, are you all right?"

Heat spiraled through him at the sound of her voice. She touched his arm. Electric fire prickled from the place she touched him, sent a wave of lust surging through his blood. He looked down at Linda, and all he could think was that he wanted -- he wanted his mouth on hers, her breasts pressed against his chest, his cock deep in her cunt.

"Nic?" She stepped closer, and her scent flowed over him. He grabbed her by the forearms and would have attacked her right there on the street if it hadn't been for the bell ringing from the shop behind them. The moment someone opened the door, the sound broke the spell he'd been under. He released her arms and staggered back, wiping his forehead with the back of one hand. The fact that it was shaking bothered him more than the strange look on Linda's face.

He cleared his throat. "Just a ... little lightheaded. I don't think I've had enough water today."

She opened her mouth, but closed it without saying anything. He felt a little self-conscious about the way she kept looking at him. Irritated with his weird reaction, and slightly embarrassed, he reached down and grabbed the bag.

"Don't worry, nothing wrong here. Let's head back to the ranch."

She followed him to the truck and didn't say anything. But he knew she was thinking, and worrying. Linda was a worrier. He tamped down on his agitation about her viewing him like he had some kind of problem. Which he didn't. There was nothing wrong with him that a night away from the ranch wouldn't solve.

When they were finally on their way, neither of them attempted conversation. Country music filled the void of their usual banter, and he couldn't help thinking it odd. In all the time they were growing up, even through the awkward teenage years, they'd never had a problem talking. Arguing. Now, because of one weird episode, she looked at him as if he were a freak.

But it was nothing. Nothing at all that a good meal, some rest, and maybe a tumble in bed with a woman wouldn't solve. Problem was, he couldn't even think of a woman he wanted. Other than Linda.

Shit.

Chapter Five

Linda took another huge gulp of water, then rolled the cool glass against her forehead. Since they'd left the Sweet Shoppe, her head had been spinning. No, it was more than that. Since the episode with Nic, her body had been overly sensitized. Her nipples hardened at the slightest touch. All it took was for the lacy fabric of her bra to rub against them, and they beaded almost painfully.

Drawing in a deep breath, she set her glass on the coaster on her desk and tried to concentrate on work. But every time she looked down at the figures, her mind drifted to the memory of touching his arm. The jolt had shot straight to her pussy, and just that little touch had her panties wet.

This was so not good. She thought she'd gotten over the dream, but since their trip into town, memories kept surfacing, intimate memories. Not dreamlike in the least. She could remember the feel of his hair as it brushed against her shoulders, the way his mouth felt against her skin, the way his tongue slipped between her folds.

Another gush of liquid filled her cunt, and she shifted on her chair. A small ball of pressure vibrated low in her stomach, sinking down between her legs. With every move, the fabric of her panties brushed against her, further aggravating her condition. She glanced at the door. Almost everyone was in town; she could relieve her arousal without being disturbed.

She unzipped her pants and slid her hand inside. But before she could do anything, there was a sharp knock at the door, and she just had time to pull her hand out of her shorts and wheel up to the desk. Her body was hot with arousal, but more so with embarrassment. When the hell had she started acting like a cat in heat? Beneath the desk, she zipped and buttoned her pants.

Dennis, holding a dinner tray, opened the door and stepped inside. "Boss said you might be a little hungry tonight. Been at it for a while."

She cleared her throat and smiled. "Thanks, Dennis. I didn't realize just how hungry I was."

He returned her smile enthusiastically and set the tray on her desk. He'd heaped the plate with enough steak, potatoes, and corn to feed several people. Next to the plate, he'd added her fudge from this afternoon. She'd nearly forgotten about it. A wave of warmth tingled down her spine as if fingers had touched her skin. She shivered.

"Boss said you would want some tonight." Apparently he noticed her attention. "I can get you something else if you'd like."

She shook her head, but she still hadn't raised her attention from the fudge. When a few more moments of silence passed, she realized that Dennis was still standing in front of her desk.

His face was flushed, his hands in his pockets, and he looked uncomfortable. Well, he didn't know the meaning of uncomfortable. The only thing worse than almost being caught by Dennis, would be being caught by Dennis. "Was there something else you needed, Dennis?"

"Umm ..." He coughed. "I was wondering if you would be interested in going to a movie with me."

Oh, Lord. "Thank you for asking, but I just don't see getting any time off in the near future."

He chewed on his bottom lip. "I wasn't talking about tonight. I thought maybe this weekend ..." He let her assume his question, but she shook her head.

"I really need to get ahead on this, Dennis." And dating someone young enough to be her ... younger brother wasn't something she thought she wanted to do. "Nic wants me to get it done."

"Oh, the boss would let you go for the night."

"He said that?" Her voice had turned sharp. How dare the jackass get her into a situation where she would hurt Dennis's feelings?

"No. No, I just assumed ... I mean, he pretty much would let you do what you want."

She couldn't come up with a response to that. Well, the one that she did come up with included the words bull and shit.

"That's all right. I know you wouldn't normally ... ahh ... never mind."

He turned, apparently too mortified to continue.

"Dennis." She pushed the chair back and hurried around the desk. Catching him before he opened the door, she tried to ease the blow. He wouldn't look at her, and she felt like an idiot. "I would normally love to go out with you, except for two very important reasons."

That caught his attention, but she recognized suspicion in his eyes. "First, we both work together, and having done that before, I wouldn't recommend it. Second, I own this ranch and you're an employee."

He opened his mouth to argue, but she plowed ahead. "And third, I'm too old for you."

He snorted. "I should be the judge of that."

Chuckling, she kissed him on the cheek. His face flushed again. "Sweetie, you're good for my ego, but I just split with someone, so I really don't want to get involved again so soon."

Frowning, he nodded. "I can wait."

"Don't. Besides, that family who checked in this morning brought their college-age niece to watch the kids, and I saw her eyeing you."

His eyebrows rose to his hairline. "Really? The one with the short blond hair and the big --"

"Yeah, that one." Already replaced. "She's probably in the dining room right now."

He turned to leave, then surprised her by grabbing her upper arms and planting a kiss on her mouth. "Thanks, Linda."

The moment he was gone, she sighed in relief. Embarrassment and broken heart avoided, she decided to call it a night. She picked up the tray to carry to her room and almost crashed into Nic when she stepped out of her office.

"Whoa, slow down."

The plate and bowl on the tray clattered, but nothing spilled. She looked back up at Nic and frowned. "What do you want?"

"Ahhh, you missed me." He smiled down at her -- that crooked smile that never failed to make her knees weak and her nipples hard. "I just wanted to chase you out of the office."

"No need. I'm taking this to my room and then hitting the sack after a long bath."

His grin transformed, going from teasing to seductive. "Care to conserve some water?"

Flirtatious, tempting, his voice sent a rush of goosebumps up her arms. She blinked, her body responding immediately -- heat surged, her breasts swelled, and her pussy dampened. Jesus. She had to get out of there before she did something stupid. Like jump him and hump his brains out.

"Very funny, Nicodemus." She stepped around him and headed for the stairs.

"Sweet dreams, Linda." His voice floated up to her as she climbed the stairs, and she ignored her shiver in response. Nothing like a bag of fudge and a hot bath to escape her dangerous thoughts of Nic. She was sure that after a good night's sleep, she'd be right as rain.

* * * *

Nic licked the last of the fudge from his fingertips as he settled against his pillow. His back still ached from the mechanical bull riding they'd done this afternoon. He was getting too old for that shit. Besides, after his reaction to Linda this afternoon, his head had yet to clear. Every now and then, he would get a scent of lavender mixed with sugar, and he'd lose track of what he was saying or doing.

Maybe this weekend, he would take off to Midland, find himself a woman for the night. The moment he thought it, he lost all interest in the idea. He didn't know what disgusted him more -- losing interest in hooking up, or the reason for it ... Linda.

Disgusted with himself, he killed the light and rolled over to go to sleep. Although irritated, he soon found himself drifting off, his body relaxing and his eyes heavy with sleep.

Beads of water slipped down over Linda's shoulders, rolling over her breasts and dripping from her nipples. Clothed, she was a walking wet dream. Naked, wet, and aroused, she was so hot, he was amazed he didn't come just from the sight of her. Nic leaned forward, licking a drop and then taking her nipple into his mouth. The taste of her -- fresh, sweet, wet -- sank into his bones. She moaned, her hands threading through his hair.

"Nic." His name on her lips, in that husky, aroused tone, sent a jolt of lust to his dick. He felt a drop of pre-cum wet the head.

As he moved to her other breast, he cupped the first, rubbing his thumb over her nipple, enjoying the way it pebbled beneath his touch. Her uninhibited response always amazed him.

He kissed a trail up her chest, her neck, and then devoured her mouth. Her lips parted immediately, and he dove inside, his tongue tangling with hers. Spicy, sweet, and beyond tempting. Something stirred in his chest that had nothing to with arousal, or sexual need, but he pushed it aside. Right now, this was all that mattered -- the feel of her skin, the taste of her mouth.

He left her mouth to nibble on her jaw, then her earlobe. Her sigh, and the way her hands slid down his back to cup his ass, told him he was getting past all those barriers she'd constructed. Her fingers slipped over his skin, and his cock jerked against her belly.

She sighed again. "That feels really good, Nic."

He loved the way she'd said his name. It sounded like warm sex on a hot summer day. His heart hammered against his chest.

"If you think that feels good, just wait and see what I can do to you next."

Before he could slip down her body and taste that pretty little pussy, she stopped him. He looked down at her, ready to argue with her, until he saw her face. Her lips curved into a delicious, seductive smile that he felt all the way to his balls.

"Ahh, Nicodemus, you wouldn't want to keep me from making you happy -- now would you?"

The sensual playfulness in her voice shot every ounce of blood in his brain to his dick. He nodded and then swallowed -- hard. She backed him up against the tiled wall of the shower. Her hands slipped from his shoulders, down to his chest. Nic curled his toes as her fingers brushed over his nipples. But she didn't pay much attention as she apparently focused on another part of his anatomy, now standing at attention. She brushed her hands over his abdomen, and then, finally, she reached the tip of his cock.

Delicately, she grazed the top of it with the tip of her finger. It jerked in response, and a drop of cum seeped from the hole. Her gaze shot to his.

"Oh." The catch in her voice relayed her excitement. He knew if he pushed her, he could take her now. He could slide into her hot, wet pussy and pump himself dry. Before he could reach for her, she brushed her thumb over the tip of his cock again. She smiled when he drew in a deep breath.

"So ... I found something you like." Her voice was laced with amusement. Without breaking eye contact, she encircled his shaft with her hand, pumped it once, and slipped her thumb over the head. His knees almost gave way.

"Linda." He practically growled her name, but she just smiled, pumped her hand twice, and then swiped her thumb over the top again. Damn.

"Are you complaining, cowboy?"

She'd called him cowboy when they were growing up, but in a strictly derogatory way. This time, her voice purred the word, the syllables rolling off her tongue. He almost came right then.

It took him a second to realize that she was waiting for him to answer. Her hand hadn't repeated that motion, and she stood staring at him. She was naked, wet, her hair plastered against her head, and he couldn't get over the sight of her or the fact that she was there with him. She cocked her head to the side and smiled up at him, and he realized she was waiting for his answer. He nodded, not able to get the words out of his mouth.

She started working his cock in her hand again, their skin slick with the shower water, making it easy for her to work him over. Every three or four pumps, she would swipe her thumb over the tip, but the anticipation of not knowing when it would happen was almost as thrilling as the touch itself. Leaning his head back against the wall, he closed his eyes and allowed her to push him closer to the edge.

Each time her hand moved, it brushed against his belly. His muscles tensed as more blood rushed to his groin. He was moments away from spurting all over her hand, and he didn't care. He wanted to come, but before he could, she pulled her hand away.

Irritated to be so close and have her move away, he opened his eyes to argue -- but she was already sliding down to her knees in front of him. He swallowed hard as she opened her mouth and took his cock in.

Nic watched as her lips wrapped around him. Inch by inch, slowly, his cock disappeared into her mouth. When he was finally in as far as he could go, she pulled her head back, sliding her tongue along the length of him until she reached the end. Then she swiped her tongue over the tip. She continued her movements, and somewhere along the way she'd cupped his balls, squeezing them at just the right moment, prodding him along. He took her head into his hands, threading his fingers through her damp, heavy locks. His balls drew up, blood heated, and the last of it rushed to his groin. He was close, so close --

Nic jerked awake just as he came, his hand on his cock, cum spurting out and soaking his cock and hand. His heart thudded against his chest, his body throbbing as the tension eased from his muscles.

Jesus, it'd been a long time since he'd had a wet dream that intense. He could practically feel her breath on his skin, her lips on his dick ...

When his heartbeat returned to normal, he climbed out of bed and went to shower himself clean. As he turned on the water, his thoughts roamed back to the dream -- the sights, the smells, the expression on Linda's face as she took his cock between her lips ...

He looked down as his shaft went hard again. Leaning over, he turned the water completely to cold before stepping in.

Chapter Six

Linda brushed a nonexistent piece of lint off her shirt as she sat in the kitchen drinking her coffee. She couldn't get past the dream she'd had the night before. If she didn't know better, she'd have thought she'd been drugged. Dreams like these were just not ... normal for her. Oh, she had sexy dreams, but she never once woke up knowing exactly what it felt like to suck on Nic's cock. Hell, she'd swear she knew the taste of his cum.

"Up early this morning?"

His deep voice rumbled over the crowd of kitchen workers, jerking her out of her thoughts. Heat stole up her neck into her face. Dammit. She was a woman grown. Not some little teenybopper who'd been caught watching Porky's. It wasn't like she hadn't performed that act before.

She glanced up at him as he strode into the room. Nic never just walked anywhere. He walked with purpose, pride. As a girl, she'd often fantasized about him as a Comanche warrior. It all had to do with his stance, the way he carried himself. Nothing had changed, except he'd grown his hair longer, which she just loved. Today, as usual, he'd pulled his silky strands back and tied them at the base of his neck.

"Ahh, I was out like a light last night. Not used to going to sleep so early."

He poured himself a cup of coffee and then sat down next to her at the kitchen table. Dammit. She didn't need him so close. Especially with the memories of that vivid dream still fresh in her mind and him so near she could smell the fresh soap from his shower.

"Wanna ride me?"

Her breath caught in her throat and she choked. "What?"

"Wanna go for a ride with me?"

Swallowing, she calmed her heart. "Ahh, no. I need to get some stuff done in the office. Don't you have a class or something?"

"Nope. I take Wednesdays off." He sat back in his chair and studied her. His brow wrinkled as he frowned. "Come on, Linda. You haven't been up on a horse since you got here. You know you want to."

She did want to. More than she should. Not that riding was a bad thing, but wanting to go riding with Nic was ... bad. It was very bad, and very tempting. She did want to go, and maybe, if she got out of the office, she would clear her head. Too much time confined inside was probably her problem. Nic was attractive. Okay, he was a stud, but it wasn't like he usually affected her this deeply.

"Tell you what. Let me email the new web designer, and then I'll meet you outside."

"Web designer?"

"Yeah, your website sucks."

Before he could say another word, she was up and moving to the office. As soon as she finished her work, she ran upstairs, taking the steps two at a time, and was back down in less than ten minutes, changed into jeans for the ride.

The West Texas heat punched her in the face as she stepped out the door. Even though it was still early in the day, the temperature had to be close to the mid-eighties. She stopped, sucked in a breath of hot, dusty air, and let it out on a cough.

Deep, warm, masculine chuckling caught her attention. "A little hot for you, city girl?"

She turned her head and almost melted at the sight in front of her.

Nic strode toward her. She'd seen the worn straw cowboy hat on him more than once, but she'd nearly forgotten what he looked like dressed for a ride. A blue cotton T-shirt stretched over his muscular chest, emphasizing his defined pecs. Her gaze slid down his body, and her knees almost gave out. Jesus, he was wearing chaps. Even in the heat, she knew he preferred to wear them, but dammit -- did he have to do it to tempt her? There was nothing particularly sexy about them, except the fact that they accented one part of his anatomy she'd dreamed about the night before. If the memory from her dream was even halfway close to reality, she figured she'd be a lucky girl to get him into her bed.

She sighed as she walked down the steps to meet him.

"Got a hat?" His voice was abrupt and not as teasing as his last question. Knowing him to be moody at times, Linda just ignored it.

"Uh, no, I forgot. I put on some sunscreen."

He shook his head, said something about asinine city women under his breath, and brushed past her. As he did, his shoulder grazed hers, and she swallowed as a rush of heat tingled down her spine. He barely touched her, but she could already feel her nipples hardening. She was just lucky he hadn't noticed. A couple minutes later he returned, still muttering under his breath, slammed a hat down on her head, and then walked past her to the horses.

She swallowed her comments because they would have involved various places he could shove the hat, and walked to the mare he'd selected for her. Once she mounted, she relaxed immediately. It had been years since she'd ridden, but her body hadn't forgotten and immediately fell into the rhythm of riding.

Nic shot her a look over his shoulder, for what reason she didn't know. It was filled with irritation and ... arousal? No way. He wouldn't want anything to do with her. All he wanted was free accounting and then to get her out of there as quickly as possible. Still, she couldn't stop her body's reaction to the mean look. Because even an angry Nicodemus McCabe was a toe-tingling, want-to-eat-him-up-with-a-spoon, he's-so-gorgeous Nic.

* * * *

Nic scowled at Linda as she pulled alongside of him. She ignored him, as she had all morning. She'd been too much into the ride to take much notice of him anyway.

He'd forgotten how much she loved to ride. Her father had always said she'd been a natural from the time she could walk. He'd thrown her up on the horse, and with barely any instruction, she'd taken to it. Nic had never understood how she could walk away from the ranch, from the life they'd grown up in.

But, he thought moodily, she'd had bigger and better plans. He glanced at her again and thought about her seat, her posture. She was born to ride. He should've gotten her out on a horse sooner, but he'd lost track of time, and before he knew it, she'd been there almost a month.

When he'd seen her this morning, all he could think of was the dream he'd had and how much he wanted to spend time with her. Stupid, because spending time with her was dangerous. What was worse was the way she'd looked at him when she walked out of the house. Jesus, she'd looked like she wanted to lick him up one side and down the other. After the dreams from the night before, he didn't need that. He needed distance. Which, thanks to his damn mouth, he didn't get.

And watching her on the horse -- he'd forgotten how arousing it was to watch her ride. Not many women who came to the ranch had her skill. Each time he looked at her, his mind would conjure up images of Linda straddling him, riding him ...

His dick throbbed, and grimly he decided it was time to head back. Riding around with a boner was not only embarrassing, it was downright painful.

"Linda, we have to head back."

She looked over her shoulder at him and frowned. "Do we have to?"

He nodded. "Yeah, I have to get some things in town today that hadn't come in yesterday, and you need to get last month's sheet tallied."

She pouted and -- Good God, he wanted to kiss those lips. Not one woman in the world could pout like Linda and turn him on. Usually it had the opposite effect, but damn near everything she did turned him on.

With a sigh, she reined in her horse and followed him without another comment. When they reached the ranch, she dismounted and turned her mare toward the barn to go brush her down. Just what he fucking needed -- to spend more time with her while they tended the horses. He needed out of her company and fast.

Before he could offer to take care of the horse, the door to the house opened and Dennis yelled out to her.

"Linda, you have a long-distance phone call. Some guy named Charles."

She didn't say a word, just stood there, the glow from a satisfying ride quickly draining, leaving her face pale in the midday sunlight. Nic assumed this was the boyfriend.

"I guess I should take that."

"You don't have to."

She shook her head and sighed. "No, Charles would just keep calling if I didn't."

She looked like she'd rather spend another year on the ranch than talk to Charles. But he knew Linda was probably right, so he said, "Go on. I'll take care of the grooming."

Her solemn green eyes studied him for a second or two. "Are you sure?"

He nodded, and she headed to the house. With each step she took away from him, he fought the urge to call her back. He wanted the right to tell her not to talk to an asshole who'd abused her trust. But he didn't have the right. He never would.

And for the first time in his life, Nic wondered why he wanted it so damn much.

Linda rushed through the door and hurried to her office. She wanted to give Charles a piece of her mind, the jackass. Anger boiled low in her stomach. The fact that he had the nerve to call her! By the time she reached her office, though, Dennis was standing by her desk, shaking his head.

"Sorry, Linda, I think he lost reception. He was on a cell phone."

She bit back the growl threatening to choke her. She didn't want to take out her anger on Dennis. "That's okay. If I know him, he'll be calling back soon."

But after waiting ten minutes, she couldn't stand herself any longer and headed upstairs to clean up and change. She returned just fifteen minutes later, grabbed a bottle of water, and headed to her office for work.

Thirty minutes later, she was up to her eyeballs in the last month's bills and tallies and was ready to scream. Nic's filing system made the federal government look organized. She ruthlessly categorized another expenditure and then stopped for a second. The last few years on the job had been boring, to say the least. Nothing challenged her. But this, she thought, looking around at all the little pieces of paper with Nic's scribbles, was fun. She'd forgotten she liked challenges. She liked to be tested. And her ideas were already bringing in more money, as their website was going to do when it was redesigned.

Before she could figure out just what it all meant, there was a sharp knock and then the door opened. Nic glowered down at her, his frown fierce.

"So what the hell did Chuck want?"

In a split second, her anger was back. "And what the hell business is it of yours?"

He stepped into the office, shoved the door shut, and stalked to her desk. "If you run off and leaving me hanging, I won't buy your part of the ranch."

She crossed her arms beneath her breasts and gave him her meanest look. "Well, you'll still be making money, so what difference does that make?"

He didn't say anything. He tromped around her desk, grabbed her by her arms, and lifted her out of her chair. Her face was level with his. She could smell the scents of the ranch -- horses, leather, man -- all wrapped around her, and her head spun.

"I don't know."

And then he kissed her. Hard. For a second she didn't respond; she couldn't, because she was too stunned. Then a moment later, her mind and body both surrendered to the kiss.

She opened her mouth, and his tongue stole inside. He released her arms, slipped his around her waist, and pulled her against his body. His very hard body. Linda tilted her head to one side and slid her arms up, over his shoulders and then around his neck.

Pulling back from her mouth, he trailed hot, wet kisses down her neck to her collarbone. His hand stole up to her breast, and he rubbed a thumb over her nipple. It pebbled immediately. Her mind spun; her body heated. But not just from present actions. Memories of the two dreams she'd had about him intruded into her consciousness, weaving a spell that made it difficult to resist.

His hair tickled just beneath her chin, and she sighed. She reached behind his head and undid the leather strap he used to tie it back. Throwing the tie down on her desk, she gathered his long hair in her hands. It slid between her fingers, dark as midnight, silky to the touch -- she'd loved his hair forever.

He growled against her neck and then rose, his face level with hers. "Damn, that feels good." The deep satisfaction in his voice sent a rush of heat along her nerve endings. She wanted this. His cock was hard against her belly, and she knew, without a doubt in her mind, just how he would taste in her mouth. She wanted to rip off his clothes and do gloriously naughty things to him.

But before she could, the phone rang, making both of them jump apart like disobedient school children.

Her heart was beating hard against her chest. She caught her breath and picked up the phone.

"McCabe and Wheeler Ranch."

"Hey, Linda, babe -- is that you? This is Charles."

Chapter Seven

"Hello, Charles."

The name of her ex on Linda's lips irritated the living hell out of Nic. Her tone was cool, not even a bit flushed. And he was standing there with a boner you could hang a hat on.

"I've been busy."

She frowned, then noticed he was watching her, so she turned her back on him. Anger and pain twisted in his gut, in his heart. She could act like a cat in heat one second, then treat him like a dirty stable boy the next. Dammit, it wasn't right. She behaved as if nothing had happened, that she hadn't been close to letting him take her on the fucking desk.

He drew in a deep breath and pulled himself back. He should be thankful. Screwing Linda would be a class-A fuckup. They didn't need the mess of a relationship other than the one they had.

He watched her stand tall, her spine straighter than a broom handle. His gaze traveled down to her full, rounded ass, and his dick twitched. Man, he wanted her like that. He wanted her bent over her desk, naked, screaming his name. He shook his head, but the image wouldn't leave him. His hand shook as he lifted it to brush back his hair.

He had to get out of there. All he could think of was her, the way she tasted, the way she felt against him, the feel of her fingers threading through his hair.

Without another word, he turned and left her office. He licked his lips as he strode down the hall, and shit, he could still taste her. Hell, he could smell that damn lavender perfume she liked to wear. His body was hot and hard and ready to go, and she was in there talking to her ex-boyfriend, probably making plans to leave. He decided to cool his head and his body with a trip to town. Maybe by the time he got back, Linda would be packed and ready to go, and he could say good riddance to her back.

But as he slid into the cab of his pickup, he couldn't stop the burning in his chest, or the feeling that disaster loomed nearby. He pushed it aside and headed to town. He didn't need complications, didn't need prissy, hard-to-please women, and he definitely didn't need Linda.

* * * *

Linda sighed when Nic finally left her alone, and tried to ignore her body, which hadn't stopped throbbing.

"Listen, Charles, I have no reason to want you back."

There was a beat of silence. "What do you mean? You got fired; you have nowhere to live."

The Sweet Shoppe: Cowboy Up

"And I want nothing to do with you."

"Jesus, you're living on that Godforsaken ranch you despise. I would think you would be begging me to take you back."

Anger lit through her. Her dissipating arousal added to her ferocity. "Listen, Charles, I don't want you back. And for your information, I don't need you. I'm doing just fine on my own."

He sNicered. God, she hated the sound of it. And, she realized, she hated him. No, not hated, but he irritated the hell out of her. What the hell had she ever seen in him?

"Yeah, sure, Linda. You love it at the ranch. You love the smell of horses and hay. How about all those jackass clients who actually spend money to stay and work at a dude ranch?"

She thought of their customers, and for the most part, she enjoyed talking to them, learning about their lives. There had been problems, but she hadn't had to take her migraine medicine in the last week. She couldn't remember that ever happening. And she did like the smell of horses, and leather, and ... Nic.

Her head began to spin as Charles kept rattling on in her ear. Oh, gawd, she wasn't in love with him, was she? Falling in love with Nic would be a mistake. Maybe it was just the dreams. Anyone would think she was in love after something like that. But, at that instant, the dreams seemed a lifetime away, and all she could remember was the way he looked when he smiled. Or how he liked to tease. Oh, Jesus, the way he kissed. She damn near came just from kissing him.

Shit, she was in love with him.

"And, to tell you the truth, how you can be around some half-breed Neanderthal --"

"Shut the hell up, Charles." Anger turned her voice an octave lower than usual. "Nic is three times the man you'll ever be."

He snorted into the phone. "Some Indian? With a ranch? Please. You know I have more breeding in my little finger than he does in his whole body."

"I'm not talking about genes, jackass. I'm talking about character, of which you have none."

"Linda! I could have called Tina Edwards. And she would be glad --"

"Go, with my blessing, jackass." She slammed down the phone.

Sinking down on her chair, she laid her head on the desk. Dammit, what was she going to do now? She didn't want to leave, but she didn't know how Nic, who had only kissed her once, would take being told that she was in love with him.

And, for once in her life, she didn't have a plan to figure it out.

* * * *

Three weeks later, Linda still had no plan to figure it out. Other than necessary discussions, both she and Nic had avoided each other. Neither one had mentioned the kiss, but if they were within ten feet of each other, she could feel the tension between them. From the sensual look in his eyes, she could tell he could feel it, too. He didn't say anything, though.

At first, she'd been grateful. She didn't know how to sort through what she had been feeling, but now she was irritated. Did he think he could just kiss her like he wanted to take her to bed and fuck her brains out one minute, and then ignore her the next? Apparently, he did.

She noted another expenditure, entered it in the spreadsheet, and sighed. Worrying about it, being pissed about it, was getting her nowhere. She just didn't know what else to do.

There was a sharp knock on her door. It opened, and Nic's head came into view. It was as far as he'd come into her office since the kiss.

"I'm going to town. Do you need anything?"

She shook her head, but then said, "Do you mind going and getting me some fudge from the Sweet Shoppe?"

He hesitated, then nodded. A second later, he closed the door and left her alone. Again. She sighed. She'd thought since she hadn't had any more of those dreams, her feelings would fade. But, if anything, they'd deepened. Every nerve ending in her body was overly sensitive.

Pushing aside the feelings, she decided her request was just what she needed. Chocolate, good wine, and a good book. She just hoped she didn't spend all night thinking about a certain cowboy who was too damn sexy for his own good.

* * * *

Nic stepped into the Sweet Shoppe, and the smell of sugar slapped him. Damn, the place was potent. He wandered around, realizing he hadn't noticed much of the shop the day he'd been in there with Linda, three weeks earlier.

Linda. He sighed. What the hell was he going to do about her? About the feeling that, since he'd stopped talking to her except when necessary, he felt lost? It scared the hell out of him.

The sound of tinkling bells brought him out of his thoughts, and he found the owner standing behind the counter where the fudge was located.

"Ah, Nicodemus. Are you back for me or my fudge?"

Her dark eyes twinkled with speculation for a moment, then faded so fast he was convinced he'd imagined it.

"Yes. Linda would like some more of that fudge."

Her smile broadened. "Of course. And you, too. You like?"

The Sweet Shoppe: Cowboy Up

He found himself returning the smile. "Yes. I like it."

She nodded, then disappeared behind the curtain. A moment later she returned and handed him the box. "Now, you take zis to your Linda. It is special, just made."

He pulled out his billfold to pay her, but when he looked up, she was gone.

"Madame?"

Nothing. Not even the sound of bells.

Shrugging, he laid a five on the counter and then left the shop, never seeing the knowing smile creasing the old woman's face.

* * * *

Linda trudged up the stairs to her room, her back aching from an eleven-hour day in front of the computer -- but it had been worth it. Everything in the account books was up to date, the website was on its way, and she felt ... content.

She reached her room and, once inside, noticed a box with a golden ribbon on it, from the Sweet Shoppe. She hadn't seen Nic since that morning, and had thought he'd forgotten about her request. Warmth stole into her heart before she could stop it. He could be a jackass, but at least he was a considerate jackass. After pulling off her clothes, she started a bath, poured in her bubble bath, and then grabbed the box of fudge. Moments later she was up to her chest in bubbles and eating the best damn fudge she'd ever had in her life. The only thing missing was the man who'd bought it.

* * * *

Nic ate a piece of fudge as he thought about the woman driving him insane. She was a pain in the ass. She liked lists and was always telling him that he didn't know a bank statement from a horseshoe. Which was true. He should say good riddance, take out a loan, and buy her out. The truth was, he was scared to death she would leave. They hadn't talked about the discussion she'd had with her ex. Truth be told, he'd avoided her. He'd been a coward. Telling her he wanted her to stay would have shown her he wanted her there, needed her there. More than anything else, that frightened him.

What the hell was going on? Why did he have this need to see her, hear her? Okay, it had been the same when they were younger, but at this point in his life, he'd thought he'd outgrown boyhood fantasies. He pictured Linda, her curly brown hair down around her shoulders, her green eyes sparkling, her body without a stitch of clothing. His heart skipped a beat. He realized he'd begun to live for her smiles, her sarcastic mouth. These last few weeks, he'd lingered in the kitchen to hear her talk to others. Pathetic fool. Falling in love usually made a fool out of you.

Shit. Where did that thought come from? He waited for the panic to set in. But all he felt was ... warmth ... seeping into his chest, and into his heart, which had tumbled to his stomach. He didn't want her to leave, because he was in love with her. And he didn't like it one bit. He scowled. What the hell was he going to do about it?

He glanced at that last piece of fudge, then picked it up and popped it in his mouth. A rush of tingles spread throughout his body. His head spun, his heart thumped, and before he could consider the consequences, he was out of bed and out the door. It was time he did something about Linda.

Chapter Eight

After drying off, Linda slipped on her nightshirt and panties. She collapsed into bed. Her eyes were heavy, her body weary, and within moments she felt herself drifting to sleep.

His fingers slid through her hair. He had the most talented hands, Linda thought with a sigh. Never in her life had she known a man who could make her melt like fudge in July. He skimmed his hand against her jaw, her chest, then grazed her nipple with his thumb. Heat followed the path as her nipple pebbled and a gush of liquid slid to her pussy.

"Oh, Nic."

"What ya need, baby?" His voice was low, deep, and sensually teasing. Her heart jumped as the sound of it, the feel of his warm breath against her ear.

"I need you."

"Hmmm." He nipped at her earlobe, his hair sliding against her cheek and then down to her breast. "Just me. That's all you need?"

His teeth teased her lobe. She shivered, delighted. He moved away, and she opened her mouth to protest, but he was back a second later. Slowly she opened her eyes and realized ... She wasn't dreaming.

"Nic?" Her voice squeaked, much to her embarrassment. She saw the flash of white indicating he was amused.

"Ahh, don't tell me you didn't know it was me."

"No, but I was ... and you were ..." She was at a loss of what to say to explain what was happening. She did notice, though, she had lost her top somewhere along the way.

Then she noticed he was holding a chunk of fudge. "What are you doing?"

He broke it apart, and she realized it must have melted. It stretched a bit before finally breaking free. She opened her mouth to ask again, and he popped a piece into her mouth. The taste of it exploded in her mouth, sweet, rich, and hot. Oh, Lordy, so hot.

He put the other half into his mouth and then bent down. Taking her nipple between his lips, he swirled his tongue around the tip. She could feel the fudge, which had further melted in his mouth, cover her nipple. As it had in her mouth, the fudge seem to warm her skin, and it sent a flash of heat through her. Without a word, he moved to the other nipple, giving it the same treatment, and it reacted the same way. She closed her eyes as he lapped at her turgid peak, her body tensing, heating, and ripening.

His finger twirled around one nipple, then inched up to her mouth. Without opening her eyes, she took it into her mouth. Instantly, wet, hot sex was the only thing she could think of. The rich chocolate, along with the taste of him, had heat licking up her spine. His finger slid away, and she found herself trying to follow it, wanting to take another taste.

"Nic." She threaded her fingers through his hair, but he had other ideas. He pulled away and stood. Struggling to calm her heart, and her body, she pushed herself up onto her elbows and watched as he pulled off his jeans. His erection sprang free since he apparently didn't wear any underwear. She licked her lips. He groaned.

"Linda, do you have to do that?"

Her gaze shot to his, and now that her eyes had adjusted to the dark, she could see his face more clearly. He was smiling, and she returned his smile. Reaching out, she stroked a finger over his cock. Long and thick, it jutted upward from a dense tangle of dark hair. The blunt, mushroom-shaped head appeared darker, engorged.

"Do what?" She licked her lips again.

"Damn, when you look like you want to eat me up, it drives me crazy."

Her gaze shot to his, and she knew he was serious. "Really?"

He grunted, but said nothing else. Grabbing the waistband of her pants, he yanked them off her and threw them on the floor behind him. He climbed onto the bed and resumed the same position, his knees on either side of her hips.

This time, though, he held the box that contained the rest of her fudge. With a devilish smile, he scooped out a piece and bit into it, then offered the other half to her. His fingers lingered on her mouth as the fudge melted. A burst of sexual energy rolled through her body.

"Oh, my!"

"You feel it too?"

She nodded, and he pulled out another piece and repeated the gesture. Tingles spread, liquid filled her sex, and she felt his cock throbbing against her pussy.

"Nic." Even she recognized the sexual need in her voice. He threw the box on the floor beside the bed, then covered her body with his. Taking her face between his large, callused hands, he devoured her mouth. Wet, hot, his tongue tangled with hers, and the taste wasn't anything like she'd tasted before. There was need, desire -- but there was also something so unique, so much a part of Nic.

Before she'd had her fill of him, he was kissing his way down her body and settling between her legs. He growled when he pushed her legs apart.

"Damn, Linda." He bent forward and licked her. "What a pretty little pussy. And the taste ..." His voice drifted away as he pressed his mouth against her sex, his tongue sliding between her lips.

"Oh, gawd, Nic." She raised her legs up, planting her feet on the bed, pushing up, hungry for his mouth. Hot, wet, another gush filled her cunt as he tongued her clit. A ball of heat gathered in her stomach and then sank between her legs. Her head fell back, and she closed her eyes as her muscles tensed, the feelings moving faster, edging to the pinnacle. One last lick, and he sent her shooting over the edge, her body convulsing with her orgasm.

He was moving up her body, licking, nipping her skin, before she had completely recovered. Her mind was still whirling from the sensations flowing through her body when she realized he'd donned a condom. A second later, he was easing into her, her muscles clasping down hard on his cock.

"Ah, damn, Linda. You feel good, honey." He pushed until he was in to the hilt and then slowly pulled back out. She wrapped her legs around his waist as he continued his maddening rhythm. But soon, she realized his intent as her body began to heat again. Her muscles tensed, liquid rushed to her sex, and she exploded again. His mouth covered hers as her orgasm took over. She could taste herself on his lips. Nic began to pump faster, his body slick with perspiration. He broke away from the kiss, thrust once ... twice ...

"Linda." The sight of Nic in the throes of his own orgasm caught her unaware and sent her shooting over the edge again.

Moments later, he collapsed on top of her with a grunt. The scent of their lovemaking filled the air around them, and her mind wandered. He rolled over, pulling her with him, and promptly fell asleep. She should be pissed he'd just passed out, not explaining what the hell just happened. But truth be known, she didn't give a damn. She felt too good. The morning would come soon enough.

* * * *

Nic studied Linda as she slept. Why he hadn't realized that he was in love with her until last night, he had no idea. Dumb. Just plain dumb. He'd always reserved a little space in his heart for her, even when they were kids. It had taken a lot of guts to come back here and ask for money, and then take his deal. He sighed. And that was the problem.

He didn't want her thinking he was trying to get her not to sell the ranch. Knowing how her mind worked, she would suspect it in a heartbeat. He frowned. What the hell should he do?

"That isn't the look of a man who had wild, hot monkey sex three times last night."

Her amused voice brought him out of his thoughts. She offered him a sleepy smile that hit him right in the chest. Damn, he had to let her go.

She would never be happy at the ranch. She would always think he'd done this to get her to stay.

"What's wrong?"

"Nothing." He moved away from her and off the bed. Away from temptation. He wanted to climb back in and love her until she was mindless. But that wasn't going to happen. Quickly, he found his jeans, slid them on, and looked at her. Confusion darkened her eyes as she sat up and watched him.

"Don't tell me nothing, Nicodemus. There's something going on."

He sighed, knowing what he was about to do was going to make her hate him forever, but he gritted his teeth and forced the words out of his mouth.

"I decided to take out a loan and buy your part of the ranch." Before she could respond, he was out the door, his heart thudding and feeling suspiciously like it had been torn apart.

* * * *

Linda stared at the closed door, her mouth hanging open, and her heart ...

Damn. Tears filled her eyes as she tried to come to terms with what just happened. What had happened? Nic had made love to her most of the night. Sometimes tender, sometimes raunchy, the whole time with a care that told her he loved her. So, why this?

She remembered the look of fear, of pain, in his eyes as he said the words and then slipped out the door. Then the truth hit her between the eyes. The ass thought she was going to leave him. The dumb, thickheaded ass.

She gathered up the sheet, wrapped it around her body, and marched out the door. She went to his room first and, not finding him, knew he must have grabbed a shirt and headed downstairs. Not stopping to think, she found him in the lobby, surrounded by guests checking out.

"Now you listen to me, Nicodemus McCabe. Just what the hell are you thinking?" He gaped at her, his mouth opening and closing twice; then he swallowed. She ignored the interested stares of the people around them, and advanced on him. Rising up to her tiptoes, she stuck her face in his. Before she could say anything, another male voice interrupted her.

"Linda? What the hell are you doing standing in the lobby in a sheet?"

She sank to her heels and turned around. Charles Stanley Thorpe, ex-boyfriend, real, genuine asshole, stared at her as if he'd never seen her before.

"What am I doing?" He nodded. "I'm here to tell this knucklehead that I love him and that I'm not leaving him. He's stuck with me until I die. Or he dies. Which might happen soon if he doesn't stop behaving like an ass."

"This cowboy?"

She sighed. "I never realized how dense you were when we were together. Yes, this cowboy. The same one I made hot monkey love to last night. Go away, Charles."

She whirled around to Nic, ignoring the snickering from the onlookers. "And you --"

Her breath came out in a whoosh when he bent, placing one hand beneath her knees, the other beneath her back.

"If y'all will excuse us, Ms. Wheeler and I have a few things to discuss."

He took the steps two at a time and practically ran to her room. Dumping her on the bed, he didn't give her a moment to catch her breath before he was stretching out on top of her. His hair was still unbound, and it brushed her bare shoulder as he leaned closer.

"You want to repeat what you said downstairs?"

She frowned. "No." If he hadn't heard her, too bad.

He growled and kissed her, lingering over her mouth in a way that had her sighing.

"I love you, Nic."

His body shuddered, and she opened her eyes. "I love you, too, Linda."

Her heart leapt up and did a little dance. She smiled. "I knew."

Then he frowned. "Just how did you know?"

"Nic, you don't make love to a woman the way you did if all you want is a good time. How stupid do you think I am? And what was that crap about wanting me to go?"

He had the grace to blush. "I thought you wanted to go back to Charles."

She sighed. "Stupid man. Why would I want him when I have my own live cowboy?"

The smile he gave her shot straight to her heart. "Indeed. Now, Ms. Wheeler, I'm hoping you aren't going to expect me to live in sin."

She sighed as he nibbled on her earlobe. "Just make sure you bring some fudge on the honeymoon, Nicodemus, and you have a deal."

####

Out now from Melissa Schroeder and Harmless Publishing, the next exciting Harmless book.

A LITTLE HARMLESS RIDE

When this Dom falls hard, he will do anything to protect the woman he loves.

Elias St John has lived a life most people wouldn't believe. An Aussie by birth, he has found his way to the Big Island working as the right hand man to Joe Kaheaku. When his boss dies and leaves the ranch to Eli and Joe's niece Crysta Miller, Eli finds himself more than a little attracted to her.

After finding her fiancé in bed with another woman and helping her father through his illness, Crysta is ready for a new start. The offer of the ranch far away from home is perfect. The only problem she has is with Eli who constantly tells her what to do. When an argument turns into a passionate kiss, both of them get more than they were expecting.

Eli finds himself completely enthralled with Crysta as his submissive. But not everyone is as happy as Eli and Crysta. As seemingly simple accidents turn deadly, Eli realizes that someone is bent on destroying the ranch by any means possible—even murder.

» WARNING: this book contains the following: A cynical Dom, a woman ready for adventure, Hawaiian cowboys-yeah they have them, horse rides, stunning sunsets and a new island for Addicts to cherish. Remember, it's Harmless so bring on the ice water and towels.

©2013, Harmless Publishing and Melissa Schroeder

The Sweet Shoppe: Cowboy Up

Prologue

The sharp sting of the whip against his flesh jolted Eli awake. Pain surged through his body once again. He tried to swallow but found his throat too dry. He didn't know how long he'd been there...he didn't care. All he wanted to do was die.

"We can't have you falling asleep, St. John," the sultry voice whispered in his ear. He had been stupid enough to let that voice seduce him...and now he was paying for it.

He opened his eyes. Correction. He opened his right eye. The other was swollen shut. His arms were stretched above him. His wrists were shackled. He was just high enough that his feet touched the floor but he couldn't gain any traction.

Every cell, every muscle, every bone in his body hurt.

"There is too much information I want from you...Eli."

She walked in front of him and stopped. The whip she held in her hand was huge. She used it like a fucking master, as if she had been trained for it. Knowing the bitch, she had. A bullwhip, and with every flick of her wrist, she caused him more pain. Worse, he knew she was getting off on every bit of pain she caused him. Sadistic bitch.

She stepped up so their faces were only inches apart. She slipped her hand beneath his chin to raise his head so she could look at him. "Ah, Eli, does it hurt too much?"

He looked at her, then stared at that wall.

"You know, I thought you would be harder to get into my bed."

He heard the snickering. It stabbed him in the gut. After five years in SASR, he should have been known better, been more prepared for a witch like her. After the last mission though, he had wanted to forget. Just lose himself in bed and forget.

And now, he was paying for that.

"No comment?" she asked. He looked at her again and understood why he had let her get to him. She was what he liked. Dark hair, dark eyes...athletic without being too skinny. And Jesus, what an ass. But, it had all been a game to her. She wanted what was in his head.

He would die before he would give it to her.

"Tsk, tsk. I guess we need another round," she said, sick excitement filling her voice. He knew men like her in his own unit. They got off on pain, on seeing how far they could hurt someone before they could break the person they were torturing. She stepped back and flicked her wrist. The slap of the whip sent another jolt of pain coursing through his body. He was almost numb to it. He'd stopped caring the moment she had turned on him.

"Hmm, I think we need another tactic, boys. Let's get the water."

Chapter One

Eli woke stifling a scream. His heart was smacking hard against his chest as he drew in huge gulps of air. He scrubbed a hand over his face and tried his best to escape the memories of the dream. It didn't diminish the taste of bile in his mouth, or his need for a cigarette, although, he'd quit smoking five years earlier.

He opened his eyes and stared at his ceiling. The fucking nightmares were back and they were worse than before. He could blame it on all kinds of things, but he knew without a doubt why they'd returned.

Damn Joe for dying on him, the old bastard.

With a sigh, Eli slipped out of bed and headed to his bathroom. It was a long walk, he thought. His room was big enough for a family of five. Joe had insisted on it. Eli had said all he needed was a bed and a bathroom to use, but Joe wouldn't hear of it. The California king bed looked small in the middle of the room. The sitting room Eli had scoffed at now had a comfortable loveseat and a table covered with books he'd been reading.

For a guy who barely made it out of SASR and grew up in Australia's foster system, this was one damned wonderful way to end up. He turned on the cold water and splashed his face. The last bits of the nightmare dissolved, almost forgotten.

As he dried his face off, he thought of the nightmares. They'd resumed when Joe had been transferred to Queen's Medical on Oahu a few months earlier. When Joe's health had deteriorated, the dreams had intensified. Eli was pretty sure a psychologist would have a field day with it, but he didn't have time for that. The Millers were arriving today and there was a memorial service to conduct.

He turned on the shower and waited for the water to heat. He told Joe when they built the house they should have put in those heated pipes, but the man had said Eli needed time to contemplate his problems. Waiting for the shower to heat was a good way of doing that according to Joe.

The thought had Eli's lips curving—although it hurt. It was hard to think Eli would never have another conversation with Joe…that he would never get to argue about unimportant things or sit and watch the sun set over the land.

He shook himself out of his funk and decided to get on with it. He needed to keep his wits about him when dealing with Joe's relatives. He knew they weren't going to be happy—especially his brother Dave. Man wasn't going to be happy when he realized that not one inch of the Big

Island ranch was going to be his.

The other part of the family was a mystery. Joe had spent time with his niece and brother-in-law, but they had never come to the Big Island. Eli didn't have any idea how they would take an outsider owning the ranch. Of course, as far as he knew, Joe's niece hadn't stepped foot on Hawaiian soil...*ever*.

Again he shook his thoughts away and started to get ready for the day. Joe had entrusted his ranch to him, and Eli wouldn't let anything happen to it.

* * * *

Crysta Miller stared out the window of the rented car and sighed. Huge mountains shot up into the sky as green as a field of clover. The little bit of rain they had hit on the way to the ranch was now just a drizzle with the sun peeking through the clouds. Crysta thought it was perfect when she saw the rainbow. Well, perfect if Joe had been there with them.

She rubbed her hand over her chest and tried to ignore the pain. It was naïve but Crysta had always thought Joe would live forever.

"You know the Kaheaku don't live long, honey. Actually, Joe lived a pretty long life considering he was a SEAL and then worked on a ranch," her father said.

She glanced at him. For so many years it had always been just the two of them. They both knew each other well enough to guess their train of thought. When she had been a teenager, it had been disturbing but now in times like this, it was comforting.

"Stop being reasonable. I want to be sad," she said.

He chuckled. "I wished we would have made it over last year. It would have been better to see the ranch with Joe to give us a tour."

"Yeah." She looked at her father. "But, you know we couldn't come. Joe understood that you were getting treatment."

The last year and a half had been a hard one. Losing her mother at the age of five had been enough of a blow to Crysta, but when her father had been diagnosed with cancer, it had shaken her world to its very core. Logically, she knew there was a day when that would happen, but she hadn't been ready to face it last year.

Now, Joe was gone.

"Do you know anything about this St. John?" she asked.

"Not much, just that Joe had known him for awhile."

"Someone from the military he knew? I hope he takes good care of the ranch."

"You really think Joe would leave it to him?" her father asked.

"I think he should. From what Joe said, this St. John helped him build the ranch back up. I actually think he saw him as a sort of surrogate son."

She left it unsaid that neither of them wanted her other uncle to get any part of the one hundred acre ranch. He was one of the reasons Crysta's mother had left and never returned to her island home all those years ago. His prejudice against her father for being black and her for being part of him, kept her from knowing her mother's life before marriage.

"We'll see," was all her father would say.

He had been vague about his conversations with Joe the last few weeks. She'd tried to get more out of him, but Hammond Miller was a typical SEAL.

He stopped when they arrived at the gate to the ranch, which was open.

Eli stood on the front lanai of the house and watched Hammond Miller park the rental car. He had offered to pick them up at the airport, but Miller had insisted that Eli had too much on his plate to handle. He watched as Miller unfolded himself from the car and smiled. Joe had genuinely liked Miller. He had said he was a good guy, a good father and even more importantly, he had been a fine Navy officer. But, what was gaining his attention wasn't the man…but the woman with him.

The pictures Joe had of Crysta Miller hadn't done the woman justice. She was tall…like her father, her skin a softer shade of mocha than his. A wealth of curly hair was tied at the nape of her neck but a few springy tendrils had escaped. She leaned back into the car to grab her purse and Eli had to force himself to look away. The woman had a world-class ass on her.

"Eli St. John, I presume," Miller said as he approached him.

Eli pushed himself away from the post and walked down the steps. "Yes, sir."

"Please, call me Hammond, or better yet, Ham. Neither of us are in the service anymore."

So, Joe had told him he had been in SASR. Eli should have figured he'd do that.

"I'd like you to meet my daughter, Crysta."

She stepped up beside her father and Eli was jolted again. She had a face that could stop traffic. It was an old adage, but it was true. Blue eyes that curved up slightly at the edges stood out on a heart-shaped face. Her skin was so smooth his fingers itched to touch it.

"Ms. Miller," he said and dipped his hat.

She laughed. "Oh, my, what a nice greeting, but just call me Crysta. I haven't been Ms. Miller since I stopped teaching last spring."

He nodded. "I'm sure you two would like to get settled."

Ham smiled. "Yes. It's a long trip from DC to here."

"How would you know, Dad? You slept for eight hours," Crysta said as she turned to get things out of the car and stopped. His men were already pulling things out. She hurried forward and grabbed a box. "I'll take care of this."

She made the mistake of smiling at Mike, one of the younger men he'd hired recently. Mike said nothing and Eli figured it was because the kid couldn't. There probably wasn't any blood left in his brain.

Crysta seemed oblivious though. She returned to stand beside her father and smiled. "Ready when you are."

* * * *

Crysta stepped into the kitchen and sighed. Lord, it was a work of art. Long counters lined each one of the walls; there was a six-burner gas stove, and an island with a separate sink and pot rack hanging over it. Joe had always said Crysta got her love of cooking from him and the kitchen proved that.

"I take it you couldn't get rest?" Eli said. She turned and looked at him, trying her best to hide her reaction. The man was a tall drink of…well, not water. That was too bland for the delicious package of Eli St. John. He was taller than she was by a good three or four inches, had the sexy weathered look that cowboys had, and he never really smiled with those full lips of his. Add in that damned Aussie accent, and she was barely keeping her tongue in her mouth.

"What?" she asked when he kept staring at her.

"The kitchen, you approve?"

She nodded. "Love it."

She walked around and looked at the fixtures. It was pretty evident that Joe hadn't spared any expense.

"That's right. You teach this kind of stuff."

She slanted him a look then turned her attention back to stove. She'd kill to have a professional grade stovetop at home. "I taught. I resigned last spring."

There was a beat of silence. "Joe didn't tell me that."

She laughed. "I doubt all my happenings were so interesting that Joe would report them to you."

When he said nothing, she turned to face him. Nothing. No expression. Joe had said Eli had been Special Forces and apparently they were all the same. Her father, Joe and Eli were good at hiding their feelings.

"So, when is everything going on today?"

"The memorial service is in a couple of hours. We thought to do it up on the hill."

She smiled. "Oh, Joe would have liked that."

His lips curved slightly. "Yeah he would."

"More than likely he would have wanted to sit in the audience and hear all the gossip people were saying about him."

Eli nodded. "Then, we will be in the library here for the reading of the will."

She nodded and then her stomach rumbled. Her face heated. "Do you think I could rummage in your refrigerator? They fed us on the plane, but my metabolism is kind of...well, my father said he could feed an entire battle group on what I eat in a week."

"Sure."

"There's no cook that'll come in here and yell at me?"

He chuckled. "No. We have a cook for the men, out in their quarters. Joe and I did for ourselves."

She nodded and opened the fridge. It was stocked full of fruits and vegetables. She decided the best thing to have would be a salad.

"You do know there will be a meal served at the memorial, right?" Eli asked as he filled his coffee cup.

Crysta laughed. "I told you I have a high metabolism. It's probably the reason I learned to cook at an early age."

"Along with not having a mother."

She looked up at him surprised. "I guess Joe told you?"

He nodded. "Most everyone in the community knows his sister is dead."

She didn't know what community Eli was talking about, but she figured it really wasn't any of her business and let it go.

"Dad's a good cook, but as he moved up through the ranks in the Navy, he had less and less time at home. Being an only child, I learned to fend for myself."

She thought Eli would leave, but instead, he slipped into one of the chairs at the breakfast bar across the counter from her. Part of her wished he would leave her alone. She was tired and her nerves were frayed. She had too much coffee on the plane. Never before had she been this super sensitive to a man's movements-unless it was her Dom. And she hadn't had one since she'd broken off her engagement.

Still, she was sick enough that a part of her wanted him to stay. He was mysterious, which she liked. Men with deep dark secrets always intrigued her. It had been her downfall with Ted. He'd had secrets, one of which turned out to be that he was fucking his administrative assistant.

She brushed that thought away. She glanced at Eli and found him watching her. It was so...dominating the way he watched her. If he was into play, he was definitely a Dom.

Do not go there, Crysta. No playing for you.

Another reason she was interested in him was his relationship with Joe. Her uncle had admired Eli.

"Must have been a lonely upbringing."

It took her a second to remember what they had been talking about. She shrugged. "My Grandma Bessie was with us. She's the one who taught me to cook. Dad was deployed a lot, of course. After Mom died, there was talk of him leaving the Navy, but my grandmother wouldn't hear of it. She decided to stay on with us."

"Stay?"

She glanced up. "When mom got sick, she came."

"Oh." He said it as if he didn't understand. He might not. She didn't know much about Joe's foreman, but Joe had said he didn't have any extended family. To a woman who grew up with a large family—not to mention the military family for backup—it was a foreign concept.

"Would you like some salad?" she asked.

"No. I need to get out and check on a few things. You be sure to let me know if you need anything."

The way he said it made her think it was a double entendre. His expression gave nothing away and Crysta figured the jet lag was starting to get to her.

"Thanks," she said.

He picked up his cowboy hat and left without another word. The long, slow walk was so stereotypical of a cowboy, she wanted to laugh, but she didn't. He was dressed in jeans, and she couldn't help but admire the way they cupped his ass so wonderfully. Did he wear leather? God, he would be gorgeous in leather pants. She could just imagine seeing those long strong fingers wrapped around the end of a crop.

The screen door slammed, breaking her daydream. She shivered and tried to get that image out of her mind. It wouldn't be smart to get all googly-eyed over a man like that. Besides, he had been like a son to her uncle. He'd always said that St John and she would get along well. Crysta didn't know what her uncle had been talking about, but she doubted St John and she had much in common. He was quiet while Crysta well...wasn't.

With a sigh, she decided not to worry about it. She was on the Big Island for a short while to honor her uncle and spread her mother's ashes. Then, she would return to DC and sort out her life.

####

Out Now from Harmless Publishing:

The Santinis-four brothers who believe in service before self and the women who will bring them to their knees.

The Santinis: Leonardo, Book One

Leo Santini is a man who always has a plan. It is the way to live a well-ordered life. He never planned on dealing with the hardheaded physical therapist who is taking care of his friend. He definitely never planned on being so totally infatuated with her.

Maryanne Johnson doesn't have time for a romance—especially with a military man. Sure, Leo is drop dead sexy, but more than one man in a uniform had hurt her before. Unfortunately, she can't seem to resist him or his kisses. It doesn't help that the man is as sweet as he is sexy. Falling for him is easy, but she does her best to keep herself from admitting it to him.

Leo knows she wants to keep things simple but when a Santini is in love nothing will stop him from achieving his goal—even the hardheaded woman he loves.

Enjoy the entire first chapter of Leonardo's book.

Chapter One

The bright sunlight almost blinded Leo Santini the moment he walked into Jeff's hospital room.

"Dammit to hell," he muttered.

"Still a vampire, I see," Jeff said with a chuckle.

Leo squinted at him. "And you're still a sun loving freak from Florida."

As Leo approached the bed, he felt some of his anxiety dissipate. His old boot camp buddy looked better than he expected. After the report he read on Jeff's injuries, Leo hadn't been sure what to expect. Just the fact he wasn't completely medicated meant he was making strides.

"Freak? Please. You're the one who moved to Texas."

He settled in the chair beside the bed. "Please. Not like teaching at Ft Sam was my first choice. Of course, it allows me to see your sorry ass."

Leo glanced around the room. There were four beds but at the moment, only two of them were occupied.

"Smith, this is Leo Santini, an old buddy of mine who is teaching here as a medic. Leo this is Roy Smith."

"Nice to meet you, sir," he said.

"Don't call me sir, I work for a living," Leo said good-naturedly.

"I wonder what Vince would say about that."

Leo stretched out his legs as he thought about his brother who was a Marine Lt Col select.

"Last time I said it to him, he suggested I do something that was anatomically impossible."

Jeff chuckled and closed his eyes. "Santinis never mince words."

"That's definitely true. My mother is ashamed of our manners."

He looked good, almost healthy considering that an IED tried to blow him to hell and back. There were still dark circles under his eyes, but Leo understood that probably had more to do with memories than anything else. "Need me to leave?"

Jeff shook his head and opened his eyes. "I'm resting up for my physical therapy."

Smith laughed.

Jeff frowned in his direction. "That's right. Laugh it up. Me, I have to deal with her today."

"Her?" Leo asked.

"The physical therapist. Johnson. She's...scary."

"That's putting it mildly," Smith said. Leo got a better look at him and realized the soldier was much younger, probably a year or two younger than Leo's youngest brother, Gianni. His red hair and freckles along with the baby face that probably made people think he was younger than he actually was.

"Are you telling me you two are afraid of a woman?"

Jeff laughed. "Spoken like a man who has never been married. But yes, I'm afraid of her. She's tiny, but she's a terror."

"Can't you ask for someone else? It would mean just talking to her commander..."

Leo broke off when the two men started laughing again. They were so loud he doubted either of them would have heard him anyway.

"Yeah, no. That's not going to happen. First of all, she's a civilian. Most of the therapists here are. And, truthfully, I was lucky to get her. She's a battleax but she's the best from what I understand. I just wish she wasn't so mean."

He was going to ask more about the woman, but she'd obviously been eavesdropping.

"So, you brought in someone to bitch to, soldier?"

The voice was strong, southern, and—as the men had said—scary.

He turned expecting to see an older woman built like a Mac truck. Instead, he found a woman who would have been blown away from a hard wind. She was lucky if she hit five-foot-three and she was as tiny as Jeff had said. Small-boned, with long dark hair that she had up in a ponytail, she looked so…well not sweet. Her aquamarine eyes narrowed as she studied Jeff. Her scrubs had some kind of cartoon character on them, but she wasn't smiling. Instead, she settled her petite fists on her waist and frowned.

"Well, are you going to answer me, soldier? Or are you Army guys just too wussy to actually answer a little bitty woman like me."

"You didn't give me a chance," Jeff said.

"Oh, sorry. Forgot what branch of the military you're in. I will allow time for you being slow."

Irritated, Leo rose out of the chair. She looked at him, her gaze traveling the length of him. He ignored the flicker of sensual awareness as she studied him. She had to tip her head back to see his face.

"I think you need to settle down there."

She looked past him to Jeff. "Is he your bodyguard?"

"No, ma'am." Leo heard the amusement in Jeff's voice, but he ignored it.

She looked back at Leo. "I would suggest you take a seat and shut it, soldier. I'm here for Markinson not some overgrown idiot."

He stepped in front of her to stop her. That was a mistake. This close he could see the sprinkle of freckles across the bridge of her cute nose. Her skin wasn't ivory, but golden, as if she spent a lot of time in the sun. Worse, her scent teased his senses. It wasn't anything like perfume, though, just sexy, musky woman.

He shook his head and tried to keep his mind on the problem at hand. "Your attitude needs an adjustment."

She looked up at him. He expected something different than the annoyance he read in her eyes. One perfectly sculpted eyebrow rose.

"Oh, really? Listen, I have two more people to work with today and Markinson here takes the longest because he whines. A lot."

"Aw, come on, Johnson, I don't." Jeff did sound like he was whining but he wasn't about to take the nurse's side in the argument.

"Pftt. You cry more than a cheerleader with a broken fingernail."

Leo was ready to give the woman a piece of his mind but he heard Jeff chuckle. "Santini, you can cool it. Johnson is all bark and no bite."

She looked past Leo again, her attention focusing on Jeff. He could see the slight softening of her gaze. If he hadn't been watching so closely, he would have missed it.

"Don't be lying to these people here or I will make you regret it."

She had lowered her voice, but he heard the change in her tone. It hit him that she was handling Jeff the same way his mother handled him and his brothers.

When she looked back at Leo, her gaze hardened. "Are you going to move, Santini, or do I need to make you cry like a girl, too?"

He wanted to argue with her. She was mean as they said but he realized it might be part of her job. As a medic himself, he understood the position she was in. Sometimes patients needed to be pushed. He nodded and stepped aside.

"Now that the bulldog is going to let me near you I have to say I am ashamed of you. Talking about me behind my back. That's just not right, Markinson."

She motioned behind her and that's when Leo saw the orderly. Leo stepped out of the way and she pulled the curtain closed.

"You didn't have to do that," Jeff said.

"Yeah? What if some sweet little old lady walked by and got a shot of you moving and you showed her some skin. She'd pass out. Can't cause that kind of ruckus."

Leo could tell from her voice she was joking but he knew that she had done it to save his friend the embarrassment of being lifted in front of Leo. His opinion of her went up a notch.

The curtain opened quickly and he found himself face to face with her again. Well, face to chest because she was so much shorter than he was. And in that short minute, he couldn't think. She was looking up at him with those amazing eyes and his brain just stopped functioning. Her mouth opened slightly in surprise and all he could think was that he wanted a taste.

She recovered faster than he did. "Make a hole, Santini."

She barked the order like a drill sergeant. Years of being raised by a Marine and years in the military came raring up and he acted immediately. Once he did, he noticed she let out a slow breath.

"Markinson will be back in about forty five minutes if he isn't too much of a wimp today. Come on," she said and marched out the door.

"You don't have to wait around, Santini," Jeff said. "I'm not that much on company when I get back."

"Do you have any physical therapy tomorrow?"

Jeff chuckled and looked up at the orderly who answered. "No, you can avoid Maryanne tomorrow."

Then, he wheeled Jeff out the door.

"She's not as bad as she seems," Smith said.

Leo nodded, his brain still clouded with the scent of her. What the hell had that been about?

"You need anything?"

Smith smiled and shook his head. "Naw, my mamma lives just outside of San Antonio. She makes sure I have everything I need."

Leo still gave him his cell number and told him to call if there was anything he or Jeff needed. Then, he decided it was time to get back to work. As Leo walked down the hall, his mind went back to the physical therapist. It might seem silly, but he wanted to make sure that she was as good as they said she was. He owed Jeff a lot and he wanted to make sure that he was taken care of. And while his body might be attracted, he couldn't let that get in the way. Jeff was on his own since his divorce. Both his parents were gone and he had been an only child. Someone had to look out for him.

Leo knew he owed the man at least that much for saving his life.

* * * *

"I know you said he's okay, but I wanted to make sure I didn't push him too hard," Maryanne said into her cell phone as she tried to pull a basket free. The little plastic seat was stuck between two buggies. She jiggled it a few times before giving up and moving onto another one.

"He's fine, MJ," Freddy, her supervisor said. "He's tired, but you did right by him today. He needed to be pushed. He's getting a little lazy. I have a feeling someone has conflicted feelings about going back in the field."

She had seen it too many times to count these past few years—even with her own brothers. She didn't blame any of them for questioning if they wanted to go back in the field, but the truth was, she couldn't have Markinson get too lazy. He wouldn't be able to recover properly from his surgery if he didn't continue to move forward.

"Okay. Well, I'm going to pick up something for dinner here at HEB and then I am going to head home."

"You need a life, girl," Freddy said. "And a social life."

"Don't I know it, but I work for some pain in the ass at BAMC."

"I will ignore that because I love you. I know a great guy I could set you up with."

"I doubt you know a man who would be interested in me, Freddy."

"No, I promise, I have it on good authority that this one is heterosexual."

Freddy was the sweetest gay man with the worst gaydar. The last setup had been with a man who was more flamboyant than Liberace.

"No. No more setups. Call me if you have any issues with Markinson."

She clicked off the phone before Freddy could retaliate with guilt

The Sweet Shoppe: Cowboy Up

and pushed her way into the grocery store. It was already dark outside and she wanted to get home. She had stayed late to keep an eye on Markinson. Plus, she'd had a lot of paperwork to do. Before she knew it was after eight on a Friday night. Freddy was right, she thought as she looked around the produce section. She needed a life. She couldn't remember the last time she had a real date, let alone any kind of sex. Maybe that should be her mission for the summer. The mission for booty.

She chuckled to herself. She would settle for a nice night out with an attractive man. If she could find that, Maryanne was pretty sure Freddy would get off her back.

She started going through the oranges and her mind went back to Markinson. He seemed like the perfect soldier but she knew there was something holding him back. If she could figure it out, then she might be able to help him more.

Normally, the first person she would ask would be Santini, but that wasn't an option. The moment she had seen him, her body had reacted. Those wide shoulders, the buzz cut, the bigger than life presence.

She shivered.

From the time she was a teen she had a thing for military men. Military brats often went one way or another. They wanted nothing to do with the military or they were enamored with every sexy military man they could find. She wished she hadn't been in the latter category.

She was not going down that path again. Military men were not for her. Still, when he'd focused those golden brown eyes on her, she had lost all ability to think for a second or two. And that was saying a lot. Hell, she had to fight the urge to fan herself right now thinking about him. All those muscles, that bright smile, and he was tall—at least six feet.

He was in good shape thanks to his job. Markinson had told her Santini was a medic he had served with in Iraq, and that definitely showed in those massive arms. She shivered. They were the kinds of arms that made a woman feel safe.

No. No. No!

She had too many military men in her life. Her father was a marine, her brothers were all marines, and she worked daily with military men. She knew the only thing that would come out of any kind of attraction was heartbreak. It wasn't like he was going to ask her out. From his reaction to her, he probably would have some kind of background check done on her. Not that he would find anything.

She put the bag of oranges in her cart, turning she ran smack dab into a man.

"Whoa, there, Ms. Johnson."

Dammit, she knew that voice. She would probably think about it when she was…never mind thinking about that.

She tipped her head back and found Santini smiling down at her.

"Do you always run around like you're hell bent for leather?" His lips curved into a lopsided smile that had her brain shutting down. "Cat got your tongue?"

She shook her head and tried to step back. It was then that she realized he had those massive hands wrapped around her forearms. His thumbs were caressing her skin ever so slightly. This close she could smell the fresh clean scent of him. All soap and hard, sexy man.

Mother help me.

He looked down at his hands then back up at her. "Oh, sorry. Wanted to make sure you didn't fall down."

He hesitated then released her.

She studied him realizing that he hadn't changed out of his BDUs. "What are you doing here?" she asked.

"Shopping?" he said with amusement as he tipped his head toward his buggy. She eyed all the fruits and vegetables.

"That's a lot of food for one guy."

He crossed his arms over his chest and she tried to ignore the way his pecs flexed—but she failed. She swallowed—hard—and forced her attention from them to his face.

"I like to eat."

She rolled her eyes and turned to leave. She needed to get away— far away—from the temptation of Santini. If she were lucky he would leave her alone. His footsteps behind her told her she wasn't so lucky.

She stopped and he almost ran his cart into her. With a sigh she turned to face him.

"What?"

His eyes widened and she realized that she had raised her voice. A glance around the department told her she had gained the attention of the few people shopping that late at night.

Maryanne slipped around his buggy. "I thought guys like you only shopped on post."

Something that looked like guilt moved over his face before he hid it. Great, now he was coming up with a lie and they weren't even involved. What the hell was wrong with her? This is what she found attractive. The perfectly nice accountant she had dated a few months earlier never lied to her but she just lost interest, mainly because he was perfectly boring.

"I had some work, which I'm sure you did too?" he said, his smile returning.

She did not want him smiling at her. She needed him pissed at her, being mean to her, and staying away from her. When he was smiling like that it just made her want to scream. And kiss him. She really, really wanted to kiss him.

"And you decided to drive all the way over here to Universal City to shop at the HEB? Isn't there one closer to post?"

He nodded. "This one is closer to my apartment."

Oh, so not good.

"Don't tell me you live at the Live Oak Apartments."

"I sure do. Just moved in two weeks ago."

She narrowed her eyes as she studied him. Growing up as the only sister of three older brothers made her very good at detecting bullshit.

He seemed to be telling the truth, but there was that moment before that made her nervous. Worse, she wanted to believe him. Wanted to have him living near her so she could flirt with him, maybe kiss him…

Dammit.

She had no other choice than to chase him away.

"Listen, this might work with a lot of other women, but I don't like stalkers." She practically yelled it. He wore no expression on his face so she decided to get out before he could retort. Grabbing her cart, she hurried away.

Damn, she really did need to get a life.

####

About Melissa Schroeder

From an early age, Melissa loved to read. First, it was the books her mother read to her including her two favorites, *Winnie the Pooh* and the *Beatrix Potter* books. She cut her preteen teeth on *Trixie Belden* and read and reviewed *To Kill a Mockingbird* in middle school. It wasn't until she was in college that she tried to write her first stories, which were full of angst and pain, and really not that fun to read or write. After trying several different genres, she found romance in a Linda Howard book.

Since the publication of her first book in 2004, Melissa has had close to fifty romances published. She writes in genres from historical suspense to modern day erotic romance to futuristics and paranormals. Included in those releases is the bestselling Harmless series http://melissaschroeder.net/books/series/harmless.php.. In 2011, Melissa branched out into self-publishing with ***A Little Harmless Submission*** http://melissaschroeder.net/books/series/harmless.php, and the popular military spinoff, ***Infatuation: A Little Harmless Military Romance***. http://melissaschroeder.net/books/infatuation.php, Along the way she has garnered an epic nomination, a multitude of reviewer's recommended reads, over five Capa nods from TRS, three nominations for AAD Bookies and regularly tops the best seller lists on *Amazon* and *Barnes & Noble*.

Since she spent her childhood as a military brat, Melissa swore never to marry military. But, as we all know, Fate has her way with mortals. She is married to an AF major and is raising her own brats, both human and canine. She spends her days giving in to her addiction to Twitter, https://twitter.com/#!/MelSchroeder, counting down the days until her hubby retires, and cursing the military for always sticking them in a location that is filled with bugs big enough to eat her children.

You can connect with Mel all over the web:
WEBSITE http://www.melissaschroeder.net/
TWITTER http://www.twitter.com/melschroeder
FACEBOOK FAN PAGE
http://www.facebook.com/pages/melissaschroederfanpage
HARMLESS ADDICTS
https://www.facebook.com/groups/HarmlessLovers/
THE HARMLESS SERIES
https://www.facebook.com/TheHarmlessSeries
THE CURSED CLAN https://www.facebook.com/TheCursedClan
Or email her at: Contact@MelissaSchroeder.net

Other Books by Melissa Schroeder

Harmless
A Little Harmless Sex
A Little Harmless Pleasure
A Little Harmless Obsession
A Little Harmless Lie
A Little Harmless Addiction
A Little Harmless Submission
A Little Harmless Fascination
A Little Harmless Fantasy
A Little Harmless Ride
A Little Harmless Military Romance
Infatuation
Possession
Surrender
The Harmless Shorts
Prelude to a Fantasy

The Santinis
Leonardo
Marco
Gianni
Vicente

By Blood
Desire by Blood
Once Upon An Accident
The Accidental Countess
Lessons in Seduction
The Spy Who Loved Her
Leather and Lace
The Seduction of Widow McEwan
Leather and Lace—Print anthology
Texas Temptations
Conquering India
Delilah's Downfall
Hawaiian Holidays

Melissa Schroeder

Mele Kalikimaka, Baby
Sex on the Beach
Getting Lei'd
Bounty Hunters, Inc
For Love or Honor
Sinner's Delight
The Sweet Shoppe
Her Wicked Warrior
Cowboy Up
Connected Books
Seducing the Saint
Hunting Mila
Saints and Sinners—print of both books
The Hired Hand
Hands on Training
Cancer Anthology
Water—print
Stand Alone Books
Grace Under Pressure
The Last Detail
Her Mother's Killer
A Calculated Seduction
Telepathic Cravings
Coming Soon
Semper Fi Marines: Tease Me
Semper Fi Marines: Tempt Me
Semper Fi Marines: Touch Me
A Santini Christmas
Craving
Relentless
A Little Harmless Secret
Angus

~~*~*

Made in the USA
Middletown, DE
03 December 2014